The
IRVINE WELSH
Omnibus

Irvine Welsh divides his time between Amsterdam, London and Scotland. His first book, *Trainspotting*, was published in 1993 and subsequently dramatised and filmed to enormous acclaim. It was recently voted No. 10 in Waterstone's Best Books of the Century. This was followed by a collection of stories, *The Acid House* (1994) – which is being adapted for television – a second novel, *Marabou Stork Nightmares* (1995) and a trio of novellas, *Ecstasy* (1996), which was a No. 1 bestseller in the week of publication. He is currently working on a number of film and drama projects and a third novel.

BY THE SAME AUTHOR

Trainspotting (1993)
The Acid House (1994)
Marabou Stork Nightmares (1995)
Ecstasy (1996)

The
IRVINE WELSH
Omnibus

Trainspotting
The Acid House
Marabou Stork Nightmares

Jonathan Cape/Secker & Warburg
London

First published 1997

1 3 5 7 9 10 8 6 4 2

© Irvine Welsh 1993, 1994, 1995, 1997

Irvine Welsh has asserted his right under
the Copyright, Designs and Patents Act 1988
to be identified as the author of this work

Trainspotting first published in 1993
by Martin Secker & Warburg Limited

The Acid House first published in 1994
by Jonathan Cape

Marabou Stork Nightmares first published in 1995
by Jonathan Cape

This omnibus edition first published in the
United Kingdom in 1997 jointly by Jonathan Cape,
Random House (UK) Limited, 20 Vauxhall Bridge Road, London SW1V 2SA
and Martin Secker & Warburg, 81 Fulham Road, London SW3 6RB

Random House Australia (Pty) Limited
20 Alfred Street, Milsons Point, Sydney,
New South Wales 2061, Australia

Random House New Zealand Limited
18 Poland Road, Glenfield,
Auckland 10, New Zealand

Random House South Africa (Pty) Limited
Endulini, 5A Jubilee Road, Parktown 2193, South Africa

Random House UK Limited Reg. No.954009

A CIP catalogue record for this book
is available from the British Library

Papers used by Random House UK Limited are natural,
recyclable products made from wood grown in sustainable
forests. The manufacturing processes conform to the
environmental regulations of the country of origin.

ISBN 0-224-05003-6

Printed and bound in Great Britain by
Mackays of Chatham PLC

CONTENTS

TRAINSPOTTING

To Anne

Thanks to the following: Lesley Bryce, David Crystal, Margaret Fulton-Cook, Janice Galloway, Dave Harrold, Duncan McLean, Kenny McMillan, Sandy Macnair, David Millar, Robin Robertson, Julie Smith, Angela Sullivan, Dave Todd, Hamish Whyte, Kevin Williamson.

Versions of the same stories have appeared in other publications: 'The First Day of the Edinburgh Festival' in *Scream If You Want To Go Faster: New Writing Scotland 9* (ASLS), 'Traditional Sunday Breakfast' in *DOG* (Dec. 1991), 'It Goes Without Saying' in *West Coast Magazine* No. 11, 'Trainspotting at Leith Central Station' in *A Parcel of Rogues* (Clocktower Press), 'Grieving and Mourning in Port Sunshine' in *Rebel Inc.* No 1 and 'Her Man, The Elusive Mr Hunt' and 'Winter in West Granton' in *Past Tense* (Clocktower Press). The second part of 'Memories of Matty' also appeared in the aforementioned Clocktower Press publication as 'After The Burning'.

Contents

Kicking

The Skag Boys, Jean-Claude Van Damme and Mother Superior

The sweat wis lashing oafay Sick Boy; he wis trembling. Ah wis jist sitting thair, focusing oan the telly, tryin no tae notice the cunt. He wis bringing me doon. Ah tried tae keep ma attention oan the Jean-Claude Van Damme video.

As happens in such movies, they started oaf wi an obligatory dramatic opening. Then the next phase ay the picture involved building up the tension through introducing the dastardly villain and sticking the weak plot thegither. Any minute now though, auld Jean-Claude's ready tae git doon tae some serious swedgin.

— Rents. Ah've goat tae see Mother Superior, Sick Boy gasped, shaking his heid.

— Aw, ah sais. Ah wanted the radge tae jist fuck off ootay ma visage, tae go oan his ain, n jist leave us wi Jean-Claude. Oan the other hand, ah'd be gitting sick tae before long, and if that cunt went n scored, he'd haud oot oan us. They call um Sick Boy, no because he's eywis sick wi junk withdrawal, but because he's just one sick cunt.

— Let's fuckin go, he snapped desperately.

— Haud oan a second. Ah wanted tae see Jean-Claude smash up this arrogant fucker. If we went now, ah wouldnae git tae

9

watch it. Ah'd be too fucked by the time we goat back, and in any case it wid probably be a few days later. That meant ah'd git hit fir fuckin back charges fi the shoap oan a video ah hudnae even goat a deek at.

— Ah've goat tae fuckin move man! he shouts, standing up. He moves ower tae the windae and rests against it, breathing heavily, looking like a hunted animal. There's nothing in his eyes but need.

Ah switched the box oaf at the handset. — Fuckin waste. That's aw it is, a fuckin waste, ah snarled at the cunt, the fuckin irritating bastard.

He flings back his heid n raises his eyes tae the ceiling. — Ah'll gie ye the money tae git it back oot. Is that aw yir sae fuckin moosey-faced aboot? Fifty measley fuckin pence ootay Ritz!

This cunt has a wey ay makin ye feel a real petty, trivial bastard.

— That's no the fuckin point, ah sais, but withoot conviction.

— Aye. The point is ah'm really fuckin sufferin here, n ma so-called mate's draggin his feet deliberately, lovin every fuckin minute ay it! His eyes seem the size ay fitba's n look hostile, yet pleadin at the same time; poignant testimonies tae ma supposed betrayal. If ah ever live long enough tae huv a bairn, ah hope it never looks at us like Sick Boy does. The cunt is irresistible oan this form.

— Ah wisnae . . . ah protested.

— Fling yir fuckin jaykit oan well!

At the Fit ay the Walk thir wir nae taxis. They only congregated here when ye didnae need them. Supposed tae be August, but ah'm fuckin freezing ma baws oaf here. Ah'm no sick yet, but it's in the fuckin post, that's fir sure.

— Supposed tae be a rank. Supposed tae be a fuckin taxi rank. Nivir fuckin git one in the summer. Up cruising fat, rich festival cunts too fuckin lazy tae walk a hundred fuckin yards fae one poxy church hall tae another fir thir fuckin show. Taxi drivers.

Money-grabbin bastards . . . Sick Boy muttered deliriously and breathlessly tae hissel, eyes bulging and sinews in his neck straining as his heid craned up Leith Walk.

At last one came. There were a group ay young guys in shell-suits n bomber jaykits whae'd been standin thair longer than us. Ah doubt if Sick Boy even saw them. He charged straight oot intae the middle ay the Walk screaming: — TAXI!

— Hi! Whit's the fuckin score? One guy in a black, purple and aqua shell-suit wi a flat-top asks.

— Git tae fuck. We wir here first, Sick Boy sais, opening the taxi door. — Thir's another yin comin. He gestured up the Walk at an advancing black cab.

— Lucky fir youse. Smart cunts.

— Fuck off, ya plukey-faced wee hing oot. Git a fuckin ride! Sick Boy snarled as we piled intae the taxi.

— Tollcross mate, ah sais tae the driver as gob splattered against the side windae.

— Square go then smart cunt! C'moan ya crappin bastards! the shell-suit shouted. The taxi driver wisnae amused. He looked a right cunt. Maist ay them do. The stamp-peyin self-employed ur truly the lowest form ay vermin oan god's earth.

The taxi did a u-turn and sped up the Walk.

— See whit yuv done now, ya big-moothed cunt. Next time one ay us ur walkin hame oan oor Jack Jones, wi git hassle fi these wee radges. Ah wisnae chuffed at Sick Boy.

— Yir no feart ay they wee fuckin saps ur ye?

This cunt's really gittin ma fuckin goat. — Aye! Aye ah fuckin am, if ah'm oan ma tod n ah git set oan by a fuckin squad ay shell-suits! Ye think ah'm Jean-Claude Van Fuckin Damme? Fuckin doss cunt, so ye are Simon. Ah called him 'Simon' rather than 'Si' or 'Sick Boy' tae emphasise the seriousness ay what ah wis sayin.

— Ah want tae see Mother Superior n ah dinnae gie a fuck aboot any cunt or anything else. Goat that? He pokes his lips wi his forefinger, his eyes bulging oot at us. — Simone wants tae see

Mother Superior. Watch ma fuckin lips. He then turns and stares intae the back ay the taxi driver, willing the cunt tae go faster while nervously beating oot a rhythm oan his thighs.

— One ay they cunts wis a McLean. Dandy n Chancey's wee brar, ah sais.

— Wis it fuck, he sais, but he couldnae keep the anxiety oot ay his voice. — Ah ken the McLeans. Chancey's awright.

— No if ye take the pish oot ay his brar, ah sais.

He wis takin nae mair notice though. Ah stoaped harassing him, knowing thit ah wis jist wastin ma energy. His silent suffering through withdrawal now seemed so intense that thir wis nae wey that ah could add, even incrementally, tae his misery.

'Mother Superior' wis Johnny Swan; also kent as the White Swan, a dealer whae wis based in Tollcross and covered the Sighthill and Wester Hailes schemes. Ah preferred tae score fi Swanney, or his sidekick Raymie, rather than Seeker n the Muirhoose-Leith mob, if ah could. Better gear, usually. Johnny Swan hud once been a really good mate ay mines, back in the auld days. We played fitba thegither fir Porty Thistle. Now he wis a dealer. Ah remember um saying tae us once: Nae friends in this game. Jist associates.

Ah thought he wis being harsh, flippant and show-oafy, until ah got sae far in. Now ah ken precisely what the cunt meant.

Johnny wis a junky as well as a dealer. Ye hud tae go a wee bit further up the ladder before ye found a dealer whae didnae use. We called Johnny 'Mother Superior' because ay the length ay time he'd hud his habit.

Ah soon started tae feel fucking shan n aw. Bad cramps wir beginning tae hit us as we mounted the stairs tae Johnny's gaff. Ah wis dripping like a saturated sponge, every step bringing another gush fae ma pores. Sick Boy wis probably even worse, but the cunt was beginning no tae exist fir us. Ah wis only aware ay him slouching tae a halt oan the banister in front ay us, because he wis blocking ma route tae Johnny's and the skag. He wis struggling fir breath, haudin grimly oantay the railing, looking as if he wis gaunnae spew intae the stairwell.

— Awright Si? ah sais irritably, pissed off at the cunt fir haudin us up.

He waved us away, shaking his heid and screwing his eyes up. Ah sais nae mair. Whin ye feel like he did, ye dinnae want tae talk or be talked at. Ye dinnae want any fuckin fuss at aw. Ah didnae either. Sometimes ah think that people become junkies just because they subconsciously crave a wee bit ay silence.

Johnny wis bombed ootay his box whin we finally made it up the stairs. A shootin gallery wis set up.

— Ah've goat one Sick Boy, and a Rent Boy that's sick n aw! he laughed, as high as a fuckin kite. Johnny often snorted some coke wi his fix or mixed up a speedball concoction ay smack and cocaine. He reckoned that it kept um high, stoaped um fae sittin aroond starin at waws aw day. High cunts are a big fuckin drag when yir feeling like this, because thir too busy enjoying their high tae notice or gie a fuck aboot your suffering. Whereas the piss-heid in the pub wants every cunt tae git as ootay it as he is, the real junky (as opposed tae the casual user who wants a partner-in-crime) doesnae gie a fuck aboot anybody else.

Raymie and Alison wir thair. Ali wis cookin. It wis lookin promising.

Johnny waltzed over tae Alison and serenaded her. — Hey-ey good lookin, whaaat-cha got cookin . . . He turned tae Raymie, whae wis steadfastly keepin shoatie at the windae. Raymie could detect a labdick in a crowded street the wey that sharks can sense a few drops of blood in an ocean. — Pit some sounds oan Raymie. Ah'm seek ay that new Elvis Costello, bit ah cannae stoap playin the cunt. Fuckin magic man, ah'm telling ye.

— A double-ended jack plug tae the south ay Waterloo, Raymie sais. The cunt ey came oot wi irrelevant, nonsensical shite, which fucked up your brains whin ye wir sick and trying tae score fae him. It always surprised us that Raymie wis intae smack in such a big wey. Raymie wis a bit like ma mate Spud; ah'd eywis regarded them as classic acid-heids by temperament. Sick Boy hud a theory that Spud and Raymie wir the same person, although they looked fuck all like each other, purely because they never seemed tae be seen together, despite moving in the same circles.

The bad-taste bastard breaks the junky's golden rule by pitten oan 'Heroin', the version oan Lou Reed's *Rock 'n' Roll Animal*, which if anything, is even mair painful tae listen tae whin yir sick than the original version oan *The Velvet Underground and Nico*. Mind you, at least this version doesnae huv John Cale's screeching viola passage oan it. Ah couldnae huv handled that.

— Aw fuck off Raymie! Ali shouts.

— Stick in the boot, go wi the flow, shake it down baby, shake it down honey . . . cook street, spook street, we're all dead white meat . . . eat the beat . . . Raymie burst intae an impromptu rap, shakin his erse and rollin his eyes.

He then bent doon in front ay Sick Boy, whae had strategically placed hissel beside Ali, never taking his eyes oaf the contents ay the spoon she heated over a candle. Raymie pulled Sick Boy's face tae him, and kissed him hard oan the lips. Sick Boy pushed him away, trembling.

— Fuck off! Doss cunt!

Johnny n Ali laughed loudly. Ah wid huv n aw had ah no felt that each bone in ma body wis simultaneously being crushed in a vice n set aboot wi a blunt hacksaw.

Sick Boy tourniqued Ali above her elbow, obviously staking his place in the queue, and tapped up a vein oan her thin ash-white airm.

— Want me tae dae it? he asked.

She nodded.

He droaps a cotton ball intae the spoon n blaws oan it, before sucking up aboot 5 mls through the needle, intae the barrel ay the syringe. He's goat a fuckin huge blue vein tapped up, which seems tae be almost comin through Ali's airm. He pierces her flesh and injects a wee bit slowly, before sucking blood back intae the chamber. Her lips are quivering as she gazes pleadingly at him for a second or two. Sick Boy's face looks ugly, leering and reptilian, before he slams the cocktail towards her brain.

She pulls back her heid, shuts her eyes and opens her mooth, givin oot an orgasmic groan. Sick Boy's eyes are now innocent and full ay wonder, his expression like a bairn thit's come through oan Christmas morning tae a pile ay gift-wrapped presents stacked under the tree. They baith look strangely beautiful and pure in the flickering candlelight.

— That beats any meat injection . . . that beats any fuckin cock in the world . . . Ali gasps, completely serious. It unnerves us tae the extent that ah feel ma ain genitals through ma troosers tae see if they're still thair. Touchin masel like that makes us feel queasy though.

Johnny hands Sick Boy his works.

— Ye git a shot, but only if ye use this gear. Wir playin trust games the day, he smiled, but he wisnae jokin.

Sick Boy shakes his heid. — Ah dinnae share needles or syringes. Ah've goat ma ain works here.

— Now that's no very social. Rents? Raymie? Ali? Whit d'ye think ay that? Ur you tryin tae insinuate that the White Swan, the Mother Superior, has blood infected by the human immuno-deficiency virus? Ma finer feelins ur hurt. Aw ah kin say is, nae sharin, nae shootin. He gies an exaggerated smile, exposing a row ay bad teeth.

Tae me that wisnae Johnny Swan talkin. No Swanney. No fuckin way. Some malicious demon had invaded his body and poisoned his mind. This character was a million miles away fae the gentle joker ah once knew as Johnny Swan. A nice laddie, everybody sais; including ma ain Ma. Johnny Swan, so intae fitba, so easy going, that he eywis goat lumbered washin the strips eftir the fives at Meadowbank, and nivir, ivir complained.

Ah wis shitein it that ah widnae git a shot here. — Fuck sakes Johnny, listen tae yirsel. Git a fuckin grip. Wuv goat the fuckin hirays here. Ah pulled some notes ootay ma poakit.

Whether it wis through guilt, or the prospect ay cash, the auld Johnny Swan briefly reappeared.

— Dinnae git aw serious oan us. Ah'm only fuckin jokin boys. Ye think thit the White Swan wid hud oot oan his muckers? Oan yis go ma men. Yir wise men. Hygiene's important, he stated wistfully. — Ken wee Goagsie? He's goat AIDS now.

— Gen up? ah asked. Thir wis eywis rumours aboot whae wis HIV and whae wisnae. Ah usually jist ignored thum. Thing is, a few people hud been saying that aboot wee Goagsie.

— Too right. He's no goat the full AIDS likes, bit he's tested positive. Still, as ah sais tae um, it isnae the end ay the world Goagsie. Ye kin learn tae live wi the virus. Tons ay cunts dae it withoot any hassle at aw. Could be fuckin years before ye git sick, ah telt um. Any cunt withoot the virus could git run ower the morn. That's the wey ye huv tae look at it. Cannae jist cancel the gig. The show must go oan.

It's easy tae be philosophical when some other cunt's goat shite fir blood.

Anywey, Johnny even helped Sick Boy tae cook up and shoot home.

Just as Sick Boy wis aboot tae scream, he spiked the vein, drew some blood back intae the barrel, and fired the life-giving and life-taking elixir home.

Sick Boy hugged Swanney tightly, then eased off, keeping his airms aroond him. They were relaxed; like lovers in a post-coital embrace. It was now Sick Boy's turn tae serenade Johnny. — Swanney, how ah love ya, how ah love yah, my dear old Swanney . . . The adversaries ay a few minutes ago were now soul-mates.

Ah went tae take a shot. It took us ages tae find a good vein.

Ma boys don't live as close tae the surface as maist people's. When it came, ah savoured the hit. Ali wis right. Take yir best orgasm, multiply the feeling by twenty, and you're still fuckin miles off the pace. Ma dry, cracking bones are soothed and liquefied by ma beautiful heroine's tender caresses. The earth moved, and it's still moving.

Alison is tellin us that ah should go and see Kelly, who's apparently been really depressed since she hud the abortion. Although her tone's no really judgemental, she talks as if ah hud something tae dae wi Kelly's pregnancy n its subsequent termination.

— How should ah go n see her? It's goat nowt tae dae wi me, ah sais defensively.

— Yir her friend, ur ye no?

Ah'm tempted tae quote Johnny n say that we wir aw acquaintances now. It sounds good in ma heid: 'We are all acquaintances now.' It seems tae go beyond our personal junk circumstances; a brilliant metaphor for our times. Ah resist the temptation.

Instead ah content masel wi making the point that we wir aw Kelly's friends, and questioning why ah should be singled oot fir visiting duties.

— Fuck sake Mark. Ye ken she's really intae ye.

— Kelly? Away tae fuck! ah say, surprised, intrigued, and mair than a wee bit embarrassed. If this is true ah'm a blind and stupid arsehole.

— Course she is. She's telt us tons ay times. She's eywis oan aboot ye. It's Mark this, Mark that.

Hardly anybody calls us Mark. It's usually Rents, or worse, the Rent Boy. That is fuckin awful, getting called that. Ah try no tae show that it bugs us, because that only encourages cunts mair.

Sick Boy's been listening in. Ah turn tae him. — Ye reckon that's right? Kelly's goat a thing aboot us?

— Every cunt under the sun kens that she's goat the hots fir ye. It's no exactly a well-kept secret. Ah cannae understand her, mind you. She wants her fuckin heid examined.

— Thanks fir tellin us then cunt.

— If you choose tae sit in darkened rooms watchin videos aw day long, no noticing what's going on around ye, it's no up tae me tae fuckin point it oot tae ye.

— Well, she nivir sais nowt tae me, ah whinge, biscuit-ersed.

— Ye want her tae pit it oan a t-shirt? Ye dinnae ken much aboot women, do ye Mark? Alison sais. Sick Boy smirks.

Ah feel insulted by that last remark, but ah'm determined tae treat the issue lightly, in case it's a wind-up, doubtlessly orchestrated by Sick Boy. The mischief-making cunt staggers through life leaving these interpersonal booby-traps fir his mates. What fuckin pleasure the radge derives fae these activities is beyond me.

Ah score some gear fi Johnny.

— Pure as the driven snow, this shit, he tells us.

That meant thit it wisnae cut *too* much, wi anything *too* toxic.

It wis soon time fir us tae go. Johnny wis gabbin a load ay shite intae ma ear; things ah didnae want tae listen tae. Problems aboot whae hud ripped off whae, tales ay scheme vigilantes making every cunt's life a misery wi their anti-drug hysteria. He wis also babbling oan about his ain life in a maudlin sortay wey, and spouting fantasies aboot how he wis gaunnae git hissel straightened oot n take oaf tae Thailand whair the women knew how tae treat a gadge, n whair ye could live like a king if ye had a white skin n a few crisp tenners in yir poakit. He actually sais things a loat worse thin that, a loat mair cynical and exploitative. Ah telt masel, that's the evil spirit talkin again, no the White Swan. Or wis it? Who knows. Who the fuck cares.

Alison and Sick Boy hud been exchanging terse sentences, sounding like they were arranging another skag deal. Then they got up and trooped ootay the room thegither. They looked bored and passionless, but when they didnae come back, ah knew that they'd be shaggin in the bedroom. It seemed, for women, that fucking was just something that you did wi Sick Boy, like talking, or drinking tea wi other punters.

Raymie wis drawing wi crayons oan the wall. He wis in a world ay his ain, an arrangement which suited himself, and every other cunt.

Ah thought aboot what Alison hud said. Kelly hud jist hud the abortion last week. If ah went and saw her, ah'd be too squeamish tae fuck her, assuming that she'd want us tae. Surely though, there would still be something there, gunge, bits ay the thing, or even a sortay rawness? Ah wis probably being fuckin daft. Alison wis right. Ah didnae really know much aboot women. Ah didnae really know much aboot anything.

Kelly steys at the Inch, which is difficult tae git tae by bus, n ah'm now too skint fir a taxi. Mibbe ye kin git tae the Inch by bus fae here, bit ah dinnae ken which one goes. The truth ay the matter is, ah'm a bit too skaggy-bawed tae fuck n a bit too fucked tae jist talk. A number 10 comes, n ah jump oan it back tae Leith, and Jean-Claude Van Damme. Throughout the journey ah gleefully anticipate the stomping he's gaunnae gie that smart cunt.

Junk Dilemmas No. 63

Ah'm just lettin it wash all over me, or wash through me . . . clean me oot fae the inside.

This internal sea. The problem is that this beautiful ocean carries with it loads ay poisonous flotsam and jetsam . . . that poison is diluted by the sea, but once the ocean rolls out, it leaves the shite behind, inside ma body. It takes as well as gives, it washes away ma endorphins, ma pain resistance centres; they take a long time tae come back.

The wallpaper is horrific in this shite-pit ay a room. It terrorises me. Some coffin-dodger must have put it up years ago . . . appropriate, because that's what ah am, a coffin-dodger, and ma reflexes are not getting any better . . . but it's all here, all within ma sweaty grasp. Syringe, needle, spoon, candle, lighter, packet ay powder. It's all okay, it's all beautiful; but ah fear that this internal sea is gaunnae subside soon, leaving this poisonous shite washed up, stranded up in ma body.

Ah start tae cook up another shot. As ah shakily haud the spoon ower the candle, waitin for the junk tae dissolve, ah think; more short-term sea, more long-term poison. This thought though, is naewhere near sufficient tae stop us fae daein what ah huv tae dae.

The First Day of the Edinburgh Festival

Third time lucky. It wis like Sick Boy telt us: you've got tae know what it's like tae try tae come off it before ye can actually dae it. You can only learn through failure, and what ye learn is the importance ay preparation. He could be right. Anywey, this time ah've prepared. A month's rent in advance oan this big, bare room overlooking the Links. Too many bastards ken ma Montgomery Street address. Cash oan the nail! Partin wi that poppy wis the hardest bit. The easiest wis ma last shot, taken in ma left airm this morning. Ah needed something tae keep us gaun during this period ay intense preparation. Then ah wis off like a rocket roond the Kirkgate, whizzing through ma shopping list.

Ten tins ay Heinz tomato soup, eight tins ay mushroom soup (all to be consumed cold), one large tub ay vanilla ice-cream (which will melt and be drunk), two boatils ay Milk of Magnesia, one boatil ay paracetamol, one packet ay Rinstead mouth pastilles, one boatil ay multivits, five litres ay mineral water, twelve Lucozade isotonic drinks and some magazines: soft porn, *Viz, Scottish Football Today, The Punter*, etc. The most important item hus already been procured from a visit tae the parental home; ma Ma's bottle ay valium, removed from her bathroom cabinet. Ah don't feel bad about this. She never uses them now, and if she needs them her age and gender dictate that her radge GP will prescribe them like jelly tots. I lovingly tick off all the items oan ma list. It's going tae be a hard week.

Ma room is bare and uncarpeted. There's a mattress in the middle ay the flair with a sleeping-bag oan it, an electric-bar fire, and a black and white telly oan a small wooden chair. Ah've goat three brown plastic buckets, half-filled wi a mixture ay disinfectant and water for ma shite, puke and pish. Ah line up ma tins ay soup, juice and ma medicines within easy reach ay ma makeshift bed.

Ay took ma last shot in order tae git us through the horrors ay the shopping trip. Ma final score will be used tae help us sleep, and ease us oaf the skag. Ah'll try tae take it in small, measured doses. Ah need some quickly. The great decline is setting in. It starts as it generally does, with a slight nausea in the pit ay ma stomach and an irrational panic attack. As soon as ah become aware ay the sickness gripping me, it effortlessly moves from the uncomfortable tae the unbearable. A toothache starts tae spread fae ma teeth intae ma jaws and ma eye sockets, and aw through ma bones in a miserable, implacable, debilitating throb. The auld sweats arrive oan cue, and lets no forget the shivers, covering ma back like a thin layer ay autumn frost oan a car roof. It's time for action. No way can ah crash oot and face the music yet. Ah need the old 'slowburn', a soft, come-down input. The only thing ah kin move for is smack. One wee dig tae unravel those twisted limbs and send us oaf tae sleep. Then ah say goodbye tae it. Swanney's vanished, Seeker's in the nick. That leaves Raymie. Ah go tae bell the cunt fae the payphone in the hall.

Ah'm aware that as ah dial, someone has brushed past us. Ah wince fae the fleeting contact, but have no desire tae look and see whae it is. Hopefully ah'll no be here long enough tae need tae check out any ay ma new 'flatmates'. The fuckers dinnae exist fir us. Nae cunt does. Only Raymie. The money goes doon. A lassie's voice. — Hello? she sniffs. Has she goat a summer cauld or is it the skag?

— Is Raymie thair? It's Mark here. Raymie has evidently mentioned us because although ah dinnae ken her, she sure as fuck kens me. Her voice chills over. — Raymie's away, she says. — London.

— London? Fuck . . . when's he due back?

— Dinnae ken.

— He didnae leave anything fir us, did he? Chance wid be a fine thing, the cunt.

— Eh, naw . . .

Ah shakily pit the phone doon. Two choices; one: tough it oot, back in the room, two: phone that cunt Forrester and go tae Muirhoose, get fucked aboot and ripped oaf wi some crap gear. Nae contest. In twenty minutes it wis: — Muirhoose pal? tae the driver oan the 32 bus and quiveringly stickin ma forty-five pence intae the the box. Any port in a storm, and it's raging in here behind ma face.

An auld boot gies us the evil eye as ah pass her oan the wey doon the bus. No doubt ah'm fuckin boggin n look a real mess. It doesnae bother us. Nothing exists in ma life except masel and Michael Forrester and the sickening distance between us: a distance being steadily reduced by this bus.

Ah sit oan the back seat, doonstairs. The bus is nearly empty. A lassie sits across fae us, listening tae her Sony Walkman. Is she good looking? Whae fuckin cares. Even though it's supposed tae be a 'personal' stereo, ah kin hear it quite clearly. It's playing a Bowie number . . . 'Golden Years'.

> Don't let me you hear you say life's takin' you nowhere —
> Angel . . .
> Look at those skies, life's begun, nights are warm and
> the days are yu-hu-hung . . .

Ah've goat every album Bowie ever made. The fuckin lot. Tons ay fuckin bootlegs n aw. Ah dinnae gie a fuck aboot him or his music. Ah only care aboot Mike Forrester, an ugly talentless cunt whae has made no albums. Zero singles. But Mikey baby is the man of the moment. As Sick Boy once said, doubtlessly paraphrasing some other fucker: nothing exists outside the moment. (Ah think some radge oan a chocolate advert said it first.) But ah cannae even endorse these sentiments as they are at best peripheral tae the moment. The moment is me, sick, and Mikey, healer.

Some auld cunt, they're always oan the buses at this time, is fartin and shitein at the driver; firing a volley ay irrelevant questions about bus numbers, routes and times. Get the fuck oan or fuck off and die ya foostie auld cunt. Ah almost choked in silent rage at her selfish pettiness and the bus driver's pathetic indulgence of the cunt. People talk aboot youngsters and vandalism, what aboot the psychic vandalism caused by these auld bastards? When she finally gits oan the auld fucker still has the cheek tae have a gob oan her like a cat's erse.

She sits directly in front ay us. Ma eyes burrow intae the back ay her heid. Ah'm willing her tae have a brain haemorrhage or a massive cardiac arrest . . . no. Ah stoap tae think. If that happened, it would only haud us back even mair. Hers must be a slow, suffering death, tae pey her back for ma fuckin suffering. If she dies quickly, it'll gie people the chance tae fuss. They'll always take that opportunity. Cancer cells will dae nicely. Ah will a core ay bad cells tae develop and multiply in her body. Ah can feel it happening . . . but it's ma body it's happening to. Ah'm too tired tae continue. Ah've lost all hate fir the auld doll. Ah only feel total apathy. She's now ootside the moment.

Ma heid's gaun doon. It jerks up so suddenly and violently, ah feel it's gaunnae fly oaf ma shoulders ontae the lap of the testy auld boot in front ay us. Ah haud it firmly in baith hands, elbays oan ma knees. Now ah'm gaunnae miss ma stoap. No. A surge ay energy and ah get oaf at Pennywell Road, opposite the shopping centre. Ah cross over the dual carriageway and walk through the centre. Ah pass the steel-shuttered units which have never been let and cross over the car park where cars have never parked. Never since it was built. Over twenty years ago.

Forrester's maisonette flat is in a block bigger than most in Muirhouse. Maist are two stories high, but his is five, and therefore has a lift, which doesnae work. Tae conserve energy ah slide along the wall oan ma journey up the stairs.

In addition tae cramps, aches, sweats and an almost complete disintegration ay ma central nervous system, ma guts are now starting tae go. Ah feel a queasy shifting taking place, an ominous thaw in ma long period of constipation. Ah try tae pull masel together at Forrester's door. But he'll know that ah'm suffering. An ex-skag merchant always knows when someone is sick. Ah just don't want the bastard knowing how desperate ah feel. While ah would put up wi any crap, any abuse fae Forrester tae get what ah need, ah don't see the sense in advertising it tae him any mair than ah can help.

Forrester can obviously see the reflection ay ma ginger hair through the wired and dimpled glass door. He takes an age to answer. The cunt has started fuckin us aboot before ah even set foot in his hoose. He disnae greet us wi any warmth in his voice.
— Awright Rents, he sais.

— No bad Mike. He calls us 'Rents' instead ay 'Mark', ah call him 'Mike' instead ay 'Forry'. He's calling the shots awright. Is trying tae ingratiate masel tae this cunt the best policy? It's probably the only one at the moment.

— Moan in, he tersely shrugs and ah dutifully follow him.

Ah sit oan the couch, beside but a bit away fae a gross bitch with a broken leg. Her plastered limb is propped up on the coffee table and there is a repulsive swell of white flesh between the dirty plaster and her peach coloured shorts. Her tits sit on top of an oversized Guinness pot, and her brown vesty top struggles tae constrain her white flab. Her greasy, peroxide locks have an inch of insipid grey-brown at their roots. She makes no attempt tae acknowledge ma presence but lets oot a horrendous and embarrassing donkey-like laugh at some inane remark Forrester makes, which I don't catch, probably concerning my appearance. Forrester sits opposite me in a worn-out armchair, beefy-faced but thin bodied, almost bald at twenty-five. His hair loss over the last two years has been phenomenal, and ah wonder if he's goat the virus. Doubt it somehow. They say only the good die young. Normally ah would make a bitchy comment, but at this moment in time ah would rather slag ma granny aboot her colostomy bag. Mikey is, after all, my man.

In the other chair next tae Mikey is an evil-looking bastard, whose eyes are on the bloated sow, or rather the unprofessionally rolled joint she is smoking. She takes an extravagantly theatrical toke, before passing it onto the evil-looking gadge. Ah've goat fuck all against dudes with dead insect eyes set deep in keen rodent faces. They are not all bad. It's this boy's clathes that gie him away, marking him oot as wide-o extraordinaire. He's obviously been residing in one ay the Windsor group hotels; Saughton, Bar L, Perth, Peterhead, etc., and has apparently been there for some time. Dark blue flared troosers, black shoes, a mustard polo-neck wi blue bands at the collar and cuffs, and a green parka (in this fuckin weather!) draped ower the back ay the chair.

No intros are made, but that's the prerogative of my baw-faced icon, Mike Forrester. He's the man in the chair, and he certainly knows it. The bastard launches intae this spiel, talking incessantly, like a bairn trying tae stay up as late as possible. Mr Fashion, Johnny Saughton ah'll call the cunt, sais nothing, but smiles enigmatically and occasionally rolls his eyes in mock ecstasy. If ye ever saw a predator's face it wis Saughton's. The Fat Sow, god she is grotesque, hee-haws and ah force oot the odd sycophantic chuckle at times ah gauge tae be roughly appropriate.

After listening tae this shite for a while, ma pain and nausea force me tae intervene. My non-verbal signals are contemptuously ignored, so ah steam in.

— Sorry tae interrupt ye thair mate, but ah need tae be pittin ma skates oan. Ye goat the gear thair?

The reaction is over the top, even by the standards ay the crappy game Forrester is playing.

— You shut yir fuckin mouth! Fuckin radge. Ah'll fuckin tell you whin tae speak. Just shut yir fuckin erse. You dinnae like the company, you kin git tae fuck. End ay fuckin story.

— Nae offence mate . . . It's aw tame capitulation oan ma part. After all, this man is a god tae me. Ah'd walk oan ma hands and knees through broken gless fir a thousand miles tae use the cunt's shite as toothpaste and we baith know it. Ah am but a pawn in a game called 'The Marketing Of Michael Forrester As A Hard Man'. To all those who know him, it's a game based on ridiculously flawed concepts. Furthermore, it obviously aw being played fir Johnny Saughton's benefit, but what the fuck, it's Mike's gig, and ah asked tae be dealt a shite hand when ah dialled his number.

Ah take some more crass humiliation for what seems like an eternity. Ah get through it nae bother though. Ah love nothing (except junk), ah hate nothing (except forces that prevent me getting any) and ah fear nothing (except not scoring). Ah also know that a shitein cunt like Forrester would never pit us through aw this bullshit if he intended holding out on me.

It gies us some satisfaction remembering why he hates us. Mike was once infatuated wi a woman who despised him. A woman ah subsequently shagged. It hadn't meant a great deal tae either masel or the woman concerned, but it certainly bugged the fuck oot ay Mike. Now most people would put this doon tae experience, ye always want what ye cannae have and the things that ye dinnae really gie a toss aboot get handed tae ye oan a plate. That's life, so why should sex be different fae any other part ay it? Ah've hud, and brushed oaf, such reverses in the past. Every cunt has. The problem is that this shite's intent oan hoarding trivial grievances, like the fat-chopped malignant squirrel that he is. But ah still love him. Ah huv tae. He's the boy holdin.

Mikey grows bored wi his humiliation game. For a sadist, it must huv aw the interest ay sticking pins intae a plastic doll. Ah'd loved tae have given him some better sport, but ah'm too fucked tae react tae his dull-witted jibes. So he finally sais: — Goat the poppy?

Ah pull oot some crumpled notes fae ma poakits, and wi touching servility, flatten them oot oan the coffee table. Wi an air ay reverence and all due deference tae Mikey's status as The Man, ah hand them ower. Ah note for the first time that the Fat Sow has a huge arrow drawn oan her plaster in thick black marker pen, oan the inside ay her thigh, pointing tae her crotch. The letters alongside it spell out in bold capitals: INSERT COCK

HERE. Ma guts dae another quick birl, and the urge tae take the gear fae Mikey wi maximum force and get tae fuck oot ay thair is almost overwhelming. Mikey snaffles the notes and tae ma surprise, produces two white capsules, fae his poakit. Ah'd never seen the likes ay them before. They were wee hard bomb-shaped things wi a waxy coat oan them. A powerful rage gripped us, seemingly coming fae nowhere. No, not fae nowhere. Strong emotions ay this type can only be generated by junk or the possibility of its absence. — What the fuck's this shite?

— Opium. Opium suppositories, Mikey's tone has changed. It's cagey, almost apologetic. Ma outburst has shattered our sick symbiosis.

— What the fuck dae ah dae wi these? ah sais, withoot thinking, and then brek oot in a smile as it dawns oan us. It lets Mikey off the hook.

— Dae ye really want me tae tell ye? he sneers, reclaiming some ay the power he'd previously relinquished, as Saughton sniggers and Fat Sow brays. He sees that ah'm no amused, however, so he continues: — Yir no bothered aboot a hit, right? Ye want something slow, tae take away the pain, tae help ye git oaf the junk, right? Well these are perfect. Custom-fuckin-designed fir your needs. They melt through yir system, the charge builds up, then it slowly fades. That's the cunts they use in hoespitals, fir fuck sakes.

— Ye reckon these then, man?

— Listen tae the voice ay experience, he smiles, but mair at Saughton than at me. Fat Sow throws her greasy head back, exposing large, yellowing teeth.

So ah dae jist as recommended. Ah listen tae the voice ay experience. Ah excuse masel, retire tae the toilet and insert them, wi great diligence, up ma arse. It was the first time ah'd ever stuck ma finger up ma ain arsehole, and a vaguely nauseous feeling hits us. Ah look at masel in the bathroom mirror. Red hair, matted but sweaty, and a white face with loads ay disgusting spots. Two particular beauties; these ones really have tae be classified as boils. One oan the cheek, and one oan the chin. Fat Sow and I would make an excellent couple, and ah entertain a perverse vision ay us in a gondola oan the canals ay Venice. Ah return doonstairs, still sick but high fae scoring.

— It'll take time, Forrester gruffly observes, as ah swan back intae the living-room.

— You're tellin me. For aw the good they've done ah might as well huv stuck thum up ma erse. Ah get ma first smile fae Johnny Saughton for ma troubles. Ah can almost see the blood aroond his twisted mooth. Fat Sow looks at us as if ah had just ritually slaughtered her first born. That pained, incomprehensible expression ay hers makes us want tae pish ma keks wi laughter. Mike wears a very hurt I-crack-the-jokes-here look, but it's tinged wi resignation through the realisation that his power over me has gone. It ended wi the completion ay the transaction. He was now nae mair tae me than a lump ay dug shite in the shopping centre. In fact, considerably less. End ay story.

— Anywey, catch yis later folks, ah nod ower tae Saughton and Fat Sow. A smiling Saughton gies us a matey wink which seems tae sweep in the whole room. Even Fat Sow tries tae force a smile. Ah take their gestures as further evidence that the balance ay power between me and Mike has fundamentally shifted. As if tae confirm this, he follays us oot ay the flat. — Eh, ah'll see ye aroond man. Eh . . . sorry aboot aw the shite ah wis hittin ye wi back thair. That cunt Donnelly . . . he makes us dead jumpy. A fuckin heidbanger ay the first order. Ah'll tell ye the fill story later. Nae hard feelins though, eh Mark?

— Ah'll see ye later Forry, ah reply, ma voice hopefully cairryin enough promise ay threat tae cause the cunt a wee bit unease, if no real concern. Part ay me doesnae want tae burn the fucker doon though. It's a sobering thought, but ah might need him again. But that's no the way tae think. If ah keep thinkin like that, the whole fuckin exercise is pointless.

Trainspotting

By the time ah hit the bottom ay the stair ah've forgotten aw aboot ma sickness; well almost. Ah can feel it, the ache through ma body, it's just that it doesnae really bother us any mair. Ah know it's ridiculous tae con masel that the gear is making an impact already, but there's definitely some placebo effect taking place. One thing that ah'm aware ay is a great fluidity in ma guts. It feels like ah'm melting inside. Ah huvnae shat for about five or six days; now it seems tae be coming. Ah fart, and instantly follow through, feeling the wet sludge in ma pants with a quickening of ma pulse. Ah slam oan the brakes; tightening ma sphincter muscles as much as ah can. The damage has been done, however, and it's gaunnae git much worse if ah dinnae take immediate action. Ah consider going back tae Forrester's, but ah want nothing mair tae dae wi that twat for the time being. Ah remember that the bookies in the shopping centre has a toilet at the back.

Ah enter the smoke-filled shop and head straight tae the bog. What a fuckin scene; two guys stand in the doorway ay the toilet, just pishing intae the place, which has a good inch ay stagnant, spunky urine covering the flair. It's oddly reminiscent ay the foot pool at the swimming baths ah used tae go tae. The two punters shake oot their cocks in the passage and stuff them intae their flies wi as much care as ye'd take putting a dirty hanky intae yir poakit. One ay them looks at us suspiciously and bars ma path tae the toilet.

— Bog's fuckin blocked, mate. Ye'll no be able tae shite in that. He gestures tae the seatless bowl fill ay broon water, toilet paper and lumps ay floating shite.

Ah look sternly at him. — Ah've goat tae fuckin go mate.

— Yir no fuckin shootin up in thair, ur ye?

Just what ah fuckin needed. Muirhoose's Charles Bronson. Only this cunt makes Charles Bronson look like Michael J. Fox. He actually looks a bit like Elvis, like Elvis does now; a chunky, decomposing ex-Ted.

30

— Away tae fuck. Ma indignation must have been convincing, because this radge actually apologises.

— Nae offence meant, pal. Jist some ay they young cunts in the scheme huv been trying tae make this thir fucking shootin gallery. We're no intae that.

— Fuckin wide-o cunts, his mate added.

— Ah've been oan the peeve fir a couple ay days, mate. Ah'm gaun fuckin radge wi the runs here. Ah need tae shite. It looks fuckin awfay in thair, but it's either that or ma fuckin keks. Ah've nae shit oan us. Ah'm fuckin bad enough wi the bevvy, nivir mind anything else.

The cunt gies us an empathetic nod and unblocks ma way. Ah feel the pish soak intae ma trainers as ah step ower the door ridge. Ah reflect oan the ridiculousness ay saying that ah hud nae shit oan ays when ma keks are fill ay it. One piece ay good luck though, is that the lock oan the door is intact. Fuckin astounding, considering the atrocious state ay the bogs.

Ah whip oaf ma keks and sit oan the cold wet porcelain shunky. Ah empty ma guts, feeling as if everything; bowel, stomach, intestines, spleen, liver, kidneys, heart, lungs and fucking brains are aw falling through ma arsehole intae the bowl. As ah shit, flies batter oaf ma face, sending shivers through ma body. Ah grab at one, and tae ma surprise and elation, feel it buzzing in ma hand. Ah squeeze tightly enough tae immobilise it. Ah open ma mitt tae see a huge, filthy bluebottle, a big, furry currant ay a bastard.

Ah smear it against the wall opposite; tracing out an 'H' then an 'I' then a 'B' wi ma index finger, using its guts, tissue and blood as ink. Ah start oan the 'S' but ma supply grows thin. Nae problem. Ah borrow fae the 'H', which has a thick surplus, and complete the 'S'. Ah sit as far back as ah can, withoot sliding intae the shit-pit below ays, and admire ma handiwork. The vile bluebottle, which caused me a great deal of distress, has been transformed intae a work of art which gives me much pleasure tae look at. Ah am speculatively thinking about this as a positive metaphor for other things in my life, when the realisation ay what ah've done sends a paralysing jolt ay raw fear through ma body. Ah sit frozen for a moment. But only a moment.

Ah fall off the pan, ma knees splashing oantae the pishy flair. My jeans crumple tae the deck and greedily absorb the urine, but ah hardly notice. Ah roll up ma shirt sleeve and hesitate only briefly, glancing at ma scabby and occasionally weeping track marks, before plunging ma hands and forearms intae the brown water. Ah rummage fastidiously and get one ay ma bombs back straight away. Ah rub off some shite that's attached tae it. A wee bit melted, but still largely intact. Ah stick it oan toap ay the cistern. Locating the other takes several long dredges through the mess and the panhandling of the shite ay many good Muirhoose and Pilton punters. Ah gag once, but get ma white nugget ay gold, surprisingly even better preserved than the first. The feel ay water disgusts us even mair than the shite. Ma brown-stained airm reminds us ay the classic t-shirt tan. The line goes right up past ma elbow as ah hud tae go right aroond the bend.

Despite ma discomfort at the feel ay water oan ma skin, it seems appropriate tae run ma airm under the cauld tap at the sink. It's hardly the maist extensive or thorough wash ah've had, but it's aw ah can stand. Ah then wipe ma arse wi the clean part ay ma pants and chuck the shite-saturated keks intae the bowl beside the rest ay the waste.

Ah hear a knocking at the door as ah pull oan ma soaking Levis. It's the sense ay wetness oan ma legs, again, rather than the stench, which makes us feel a bit giddy. The knocking becomes a loud bang.

— C'moan ya cunt, wir fuckin burstin oot here!

— Haud yir fuckin hoarses.

Ah wis tempted tae swallay the suppositories, but ah rejected this notion almost as soon as it crossed ma mind. They were designed for anal intake, and there wis still enough ay that waxy stuff oan them tae suggest that ah'd no doubt huv a hard time keeping them doon. As ah'd shot everything oot ay ma bowels, ma boys were probably safer back thair. Home they went.

Ah goat some funny looks as ah left the bookies, no sae much fae the pish-queue gang whae piled past us wi a few derisory 'aboot-fuckin-time-n-aws' but fae one or two punters whae clocked ma wasted appearance. One radge even made some vaguely threatening remarks, but maist were too engrossed in the form cairds, or the racing oan the screen. Ah noted Elvis/Bronson was gesticulating wildly at the telly as ah left.

At the bus stop, ah realised what a sweltering hot day it had become. Ah remembered somebody sais that it wis the first day ay the Festival. Well, they certainly got the weather fir it. Ah sat oan the wall by the bus stop, letting the sun soak intae ma wet jeans. Ah saw a 32 coming, but didnae move, through apathy. The next one that came, ah got it thegither tae board the fucker and headed back tae Sunny Leith. It really is time tae clean up, ah thought, as ah mounted the stairs ay ma new flat.

In Overdrive

I do wish that ma semen-rectumed chum, the Rent Boy, would stop slavering in ma fucking ear. There's a set of VPLs (visible panty lines) on the chicky in front ay us, and all my concentration is required to ensure a thorough examination can be undertaken.

Yes! That will do me fine! I am in overdrive, over-fuckin-drive. It's one ay these days when ma hormones are shooting aroond ma body like a steelie in a pinball machine, and all these mental lights and sounds are flashing in ma heid.

And what is Rents proposing, on this beautiful afternoon of vintage cruisin weather? The cunt has the fuckin audacity tae suggest that we go back to his gaff, which reeks of alcohol, stale spunk and garbage which should have been pit oot weeks ago, tae watch videos. Draw the curtains, block out the sunlight, block out your own fucking brainwaves, and deek him sniggering like a moron wi a joint in his hand at everything that comes on the pox-box. Well, non, non, non, Monsieur Renton, Simone is not cut out to sit in darkened rooms with Leith plebs and junkies rabbiting shite aw affie. *Cause ah wis made for lovin you bay-bee, you wir made for lovin me . . .*

. . . a fat hound has waddled out in front ay the lemon wi the VPLs, blocking my view of that subliminal rear with her obese arse. She has the fuckin cheek tae wear tight leggings — totally and completely oblivious to the delicate nature of Simone's stomach!!

— There's a slim chicky! ah sarcastically observe.

— Fuck off ya sexist cunt, the Rent Boy sais.

Ah'm tempted tae ignore the bastard. Mates are a waste of fucking time. They are always ready to drag you down tae their level of social, sexual and intellectual mediocrity. I'd better dismiss the radge though, in case he thinks he's got one up on us.

— The fact that you use the term 'cunt' in the same breath as 'sexist', shows that ye display the same muddled, fucked-up thinking oan this issue as you do oan everything else.

That scoobies the cunt. Eh sais something biscuit-ersed in reply, in a pathetic attempt tae salvage the situation. Rent Boy 0, Simone 1. We both know it. *Renton, Renton, what's the score . . .*

The Bridges is hotchin wi minge. *Ooh, ooh la la, let's go dancin, ooh, ooh la la, Simon dancin . . .* There is fanny of every race, colour, creed and nationality present. Oh ya cunt, ye! It's time tae move. Two oriental types consulting a map. Simone express, that'll do nicely. Fuck Rents, he's a doss bastard, totally US.

— Can I help you? Where are you headed? ah ask. *Good old-fashioned Scoattish hoshpitality, aye, ye cannae beat it, shays the young Sean Connery, the new Bond, cause girls, this is the new bondage* . . .

— We're looking for the Royal Mile, a posh, English-colonial voice answers back in ma face. What a fucking wee pump-up-the-knickers n aw. *Simple Simon sais, put your hands on your feet* . . .

Of course, the Rent Boy is looking like a flaccid prick in a barrel-load ay fannies. Sometimes ah really think the gadge still believes that an erection is for pishing over high walls.

— Follow us. Are you going to a show? Yes, you can't beat the Festival for bringing out the mantovani.

— Yes. One of the (china) dolls hands us a piece ay paper wi *Brecht: The Caucasian Chalk Circle by Nottingham University Theatre Group* on it. Doubtless a collection of zit-encrusted, squeaky-voiced wankers playing oot a miserable pretension tae the arts before graduating to work in the power stations which give the local children leukemia or investment consultancies which shut doon factories, throwing people into poverty and despair. Still, let's git the board-treading ootay the system first. Fucking toss bags, don't you agree, Sean, ma auld fellow former milk-delivering mucker? *Yesh Shimon, I shink you may have a shtrong point thair.* Auld Sean and I have so many parallels. Both Edina lads, both ex-co-op milk boys. Ah only did the Leith run, whereas Sean, if ye listen tae any auld fucker, delivered milk tae every household in the city. Child labour laws were more lax then, I suppose. One area in which wi differ is looks. Sean is completely out-Sean in that department by Simone.

Now Rents is gibbering oan aboot *Galileo* and *Mother Courage* and *Baal* and aw that shite. The bitches seem quite impressed n aw. Why fuck me insensible! This doss cunt actually does have his uses. It's an amazing world. *Yesh Shimon, the more I shee, the less I believe.* You an me boash, Sean.

The oriental mantos depart tae the show, but they've agreed tae meet us for a drink in Deacons afterwards. Rents cannae make it. Boo-fucking-hoo. Ah'll cry masel tae sleep. He's meeting Ms Mogadon, the lovely Hazel . . . ah'll just have to amuse both chickies . . . if ah decide to show up. Ah'm a busy man. One musht put duty fursht, eh Sean? *Preshishly Shimon.*

Ah shake off Rents, he can go and kill himself with drugs. Some fucking friends I have. Spud, Second Prize, Begbie, Matty, Tommy: these punters spell L-I-M-I-T-E-D. An extremely limited company. Well, ah'm fed up to ma back teeth wi losers, no-hopers, draftpaks, schemies, junkies and the likes. I am a dynamic young man, upwardly mobile and thrusting, thrusting, thrusting . . .

. . . the socialists go on about your comrades, your class, your union, and society. Fuck all that shite. The Tories go on about your employer, your country, your family. Fuck that even mair. It's me, me, fucking ME, Simon David Williamson, NUMERO FUCKING UNO, versus the world, and it's a one-sided swedge. *It's really so fucking easy* . . . Fuck them all. *I admire your rampant individualishm, Shimon. I shee parallelsh wish myshelf ash a young man.* Glad you shed that Sean. Others have made shimilar comments.

Ugh . . . a spotty fucker in a Hearts scarf . . . yes, the cunts are at home today. Look at him; the ultimate anti-style statement. Ah'd rather see ma sister in a brothel than ma brother in a Hearts scarf n that's fuckin true . . . *ay oop, another strapping lass ahead . . . backpacker, good tan . . . mmmm . . . suck, fuck, suck, fuck* . . . we all fall down . . .

. . . where to go . . . work up a sweat in the multigym at the club, they've got a sauna and a sunbed now . . . get the muscles toned up . . . the smack heebie-jeebies are now just an unpleasant memory. The Chinky chickies, Marianne, Andrea, Ali . . . which lucky ride will ah stick it intae the night? Who's the best fuck? Why me, of course. I might even find something at the club. The dynamics are magic. Three groups; women, straight guys and gay guys. The gay guys are cruising the straight guys who are club bouncer types with huge biceps and beer guts. The straight guys are cruising the women, who are into the lithe, fit buftie boys. No bashturd actually getsh what they want. Exshept ush, eh Sean? *Preshishly Shimon.*

I hope ah don't see the buftie that cruised us the last time ah wis in. He told me in the cafeteria that he had HIV, but things were cool, it was no death sentence, he'd never felt better. What kind of a cunt tells a stranger that? It's probably bullshit.

Sleazy fuckin queen . . . that reminds us, ah must buy some flunkies . . . but there's no way you can get HIV in Edinburgh through shagging a lassie. They say that wee Goagsie got it that way, but I reckon that he's been daein a bit ay mainlining or shit-stabbing on the Q.T. If ye dinnae get it through shootin up wi the likes ay Renton, Spud, Swanney n Seeker, it's obviously no got your name on it . . . still . . . why tempt fate . . . but why not . . . at least ah know that ah'm still here, still alive, because as long as there's an opportunity tae get off wi a woman and her purse, and that's it, that is it, ah've found fuck all else, ZERO, tae fill this big, BLACK HOLE like a clenched fist in the centre ay my fucking chest . . .

Growing Up In Public

Despite the unmistakable resentment she could feel from her mother, Nina could not fathom what she had done wrong. The signals were confusing. First it was: Keep out of the way; then: Don't just stand there. A group of relatives had formed a human wall around her Auntie Alice. Nina could not actually see Alice from where she was sitting, but the fussing coos coming from across the room told her that her aunt was in there somewhere.

Her mother caught her eye. She was staring over at Nina, looking like one of the heads on a hydra. Over the there-there's and the he-was-a-good-man's Nina saw her mother mouth the word: Tea.

She tried to ignore the signal, but her mother hissed insistently, aiming her words across the room at Nina, like a fine jet: — Make more tea.

Nina threw her copy of the *NME* onto the floor. She hauled herself out of the armchair and moved over to a large dining table, picking up a tray, on which sat a teapot and an almost empty jug of milk.

Through in the kitchen, she studied her face in the mirror, focusing on a spot above her top lip. Her black hair, cut in a sloping wedge, looked greasy, although she had just washed it the night before. She rubbed her stomach, feeling bloated with fluid retention. Her period was due. It was a bummer.

Nina could not be a part of this strange festival of grief. The whole thing seemed uncool. The act of casual indifference she displayed at her Uncle Andy's death was only partly feigned. He had been her favourite relative when she was a wee lassie, and he had made her laugh, or so they all told her. And, in a sense, she could remember it. These events had happened: the joking, the tickling, the playing, the indulgent supply of ice-creams and sweeties. She could find no emotional connection though, between the her of now and the her of then, and therefore no emotional connection to Andy. To hear her relatives recount these days of infancy and childhood made her squirm with embarrassment. It seemed an essential denial of herself as she was now. Worse, it was uncool.

At least she was dressed for grief, as she was constantly reminded by everyone. She thought that her relatives were so boring. They held onto the mundane for grim life; it was a glum adhesive binding them together.

— That lassie never wears anything but black. In ma day, lassies wore nice bright colours, instead ay tryin tae look like vampires. Uncle Boab, fat, stupid Uncle Boab, had said that. The relatives had laughed. Every one of them. Stupid, petty, laughter. The nervous laughter of frightened children trying to keep on the right side of the school hardcase, rather than that of adults conveying that they had heard something funny. Nina consciously realised for the first time that laughter was about more than humour. This was about reducing tension, solidarity in face of the grim reaper. Andy's death had put that topic further up the list of items on the personal agenda of every one of them.

The kettle clicked off. Nina made another pot of tea and took it through.

— Nivir mind, Alice. Nivir mind, hen. Here's Nina wi the tea, her Auntie Avril said. Nina thought that perhaps unrealistic expectations were being invested in the PG Tips. Could they be expected to compensate for the loss of a twenty-four-year relationship?

— Terrible thing whin ye git problems wi the ticker, her Uncle Kenny stated. — Still, at least he didnae suffer. Better than the big C, rottin away in agony. Oor father went wi the ticker n aw. The curse ay the Fitzpatricks. That's your grandfather. He looked at Nina's cousin Malcolm and smiled. Although Malcolm was Kenny's nephew, he was only four years younger than his uncle, and looked older.

— Some day, aw this ticker stuff, n cancer n that, will aw be forgotten aboot, Malcolm ventured.

— Aw aye. Medical science. How's your Elsa by the way? Kenny's voice dropped.

— She's gaun in fir another op. Fallopian tube job. Apparently what they dae is . . .

Nina turned and left the room. All Malcolm seemed to want to talk about were the operations his wife had undergone to enable them to produce a child. The details made the tips of her fingers feel raw. Why did people assume that you wanted to hear that stuff? What sort of woman would go through all that just to produce a screaming brat? What sort of man would encourage her to do that? As she went to the hall, the doorbell rang. It was her Auntie Cathy and Uncle Davie. They had made good time from Leith out to Bonnyrigg.

Cathy hugged Nina. — Oh darlin. Whair is she? Whair's Alice? Nina liked her Auntie Cathy. She was the most outgoing of her aunts, and treated her like a person rather than a child.

Cathy went over and hugged Alice, her sister-in-law, then her sister Irene, Nina's mother, and her brothers Kenny and Boab, in that order. Nina thought that the order was tasteful. Davie nodded sternly at everybody.

— Christ, ye didnae waste any time getting oot here in that auld van Davie, Boab said.

— Aye. The by-pass makes a difference. Pick it up just ootside Portobellah, git off jist before Bonnyrigg, Davie explained dutifully.

The bell went again. This time it was Doctor Sim, the family GP. Sim was alert and businesslike in stance, but sombre in expression. In his bearing he attempted to convey a measure of compassion, while still maintaining a pragmatic strength in order to give the family confidence. Sim thought he wasn't doing badly.

Nina also thought so. A horde of breathless aunties fussed over him like groupies around a rock star. After a short time Bob, Kenny, Cathy, Davie and Irene accompanied Dr Sim upstairs.

Nina realised, as they began to leave the room, that her period had started. She followed them up the stairs.

— Stay oot the wey! Irene, looking back, hissed at her daughter.

— Ah'm just going tae the toilet, Nina replied, indignant.

In the lavatory she took off her clothes, starting with her black, lacy gloves. Examining the extent of the damage, she noted that the discharge had gone through her knickers but had not got into her black leggings.

— Shite, she said, as drops of thick, dark blood fell onto the bathroom carpet. She tore off a few strips of toilet paper, and held them to her in order to stem the flow. She then checked the bathroom cabinet but could find no tampons or sanitary towels. Was Alice too old for periods? Probably.

Soaking some more paper with water, she managed to get most of the stains out of the carpet.

Nina stepped tentatively into the shower. After splashing herself, she made another pad from bog-roll, and quickly dressed, leaving off her pants which she washed in the sink, wrung out, and stuffed into her jacket pocket. She squeezed the spot above her top lip, and felt much better.

Nina heard the entourage leaving the room and going downstairs. This place was the fucking dregs, she thought, and she wanted out. All she had been waiting for was an opportune moment to hit her mother for cash. She was supposed to be going into Edinburgh with Shona and Tracy to see this band at the Calton Studios. She didn't fancy going out when she was on her periods, as Shona had said that laddies can tell when you're on, they can just smell it, no matter what you do. Shona knew about laddies. She was a year younger than Nina, but had done it twice, once with Graeme Redpath, and once with a French boy she'd met at Aviemore.

Nina had not been with anyone yet, had not done it. Almost everyone she knew said it was crap. Boys were too stupid, too morose and dull, or too excitable. She enjoyed the effect she had on them, liked seeing the frozen, simpleton expressions on their faces as they watched her. When she did it, she would do it with someone who knew what they were about. Someone older, but not like Uncle Kenny, who looked at her as if he was a dog, his eyes bloody and his tongue darting slyly over his lips. She had a strange feeling that Uncle Kenny, despite his years, would be a bit like the inept boys that Shona and the rest had been with.

Despite her reservations about going to the gig, the alternative was staying in and watching television. Specifically, this meant *Bruce Forsyth's Generation Game* with her mother and her silly wee fart of a brother, who always got excited when the stuff came down the conveyor belt and recited the items quickly in his squeaky, quirky voice. Her mum wouldn't even let her smoke in the living-room. She let Dougie, her moronic man-friend smoke in the living-room. That was alright, considered to be the subject-matter of light humour rather than the cause of cancer and heart disease. Nina however, had to go upstairs for a fag and that was the pits. Her room was cold, and by the time she'd switched on the heating and it warmed up, she could have smoked a packet of twenty Marlborough. Fuck all that for a laugh. Tonight, she'd take her chances at the gig.

Leaving the bathroom, Nina looked in on Uncle Andy. The corpse lay in the bed, the covers still over it. They might have closed his mouth, she thought. It looked as if he'd expired drunkenly, belligerently, frozen by death as he was arguing about football or politics. The body was skinny and wizened, but then again, Andy always was. She remembered being tickled in the ribs by these persistent, ubiquitous, bony fingers. Perhaps Andy was always dying.

Nina decided to rake through the drawers to see if Alice had any knickers worth borrowing. Andy's socks and y-fronts were in the top section of a chest of drawers. Alice's undies were in the next one down. Nina was startled by the range of underwear Alice had. They ranged from outsized garments which Nina held against her, and which almost came down to her knees, to skimpy, lacy briefs she could never imagine her auntie wearing. One pair were made of the same material as the black lace gloves Nina had. She removed the gloves to feel the pants. Although she liked these ones, she picked a pink flowery pair, then went back into the bathroom to put them on.

When she got downstairs, she noted that alcohol had displaced tea as the gathering's principal social lubricant. Dr Sim stood, whisky in hand, talking to Uncle Kenny, Uncle Boab and Malcolm. She wondered if Malcolm would be asking him about fallopian tubes. The men were all drinking with a stoic determination, as if it was a serious duty. Despite the grief, there was no disguising the sense of relief in the air. This was Andy's third heart attack, and now that he had finally checked out, they could get on with their lives without jumping nervously whenever they heard Alice's voice on the phone.

Another cousin, Geoff, Malky's brother, had arrived. He looked at Nina with something she felt was akin to hate. It was unnerving and strange. He was a wanker though. All Nina's cousins were, the ones she knew at any rate. Her Auntie Cathy and Uncle Davie (he was from Glasgow and a Protestant), had two sons: Billy, who had just come out of the army, and Mark, who was supposed to be into drugs. They were not here, as they hardly knew Andy or any of the Bonnyrigg crowd. They would probably be at the funeral. Or perhaps not. Cathy and Davie once had a third son, also called Davie, who had died almost a year ago. He was badly mentally and physically handicapped and had lived most of his life in a hospital. Nina had only seen him once, sitting twisted in a wheelchair, mouth open and eyes vacant. She wondered how Cathy and Davie must have felt about his death. Again sad, but perhaps also relieved.

Shite. Geoff was coming over to talk to her. She had once pointed him out to Shona, who said that he looked like Marti from Wet Wet Wet. Nina hated both Marti and the Wets and, anyway, thought that Geoff was nothing like him.

— Awright, Nina?

— Aye. It's a shame aboot Uncle Andy.

— Aye, Whit kin ye say? Geoff shrugged his shoulders. He was twenty-one and Nina thought that was ancient.

— So when dae ye finish the school? he asked her.

— Next year. Ah wanted tae go now but ma Ma hassled us tae stey.

— Takin O Grades?

— Aye.

— Which yins?

— English, Maths, Arithmetic, Art, Accounts, Physics, Modern Studies.

— Gaunnae pass them?

— Aye. It's no that hard. Cept Maths.

— Then whit?

— Git a job. Or git oan a scheme.

— No gaunnae stey oan n take Highers?

— Naw.

— Ye should. You could go tae University.

— Whit fir?

Geoff had to think for a while. He had recently graduated with a degree in English Literature and was on the dole. So were most of his fellow graduates. — It's a good social life, he said.

Nina recognised that the look Geoff had been giving her was not one of hate, but of lust. He'd obviously been drinking before he had arrived and his inhibitions were lowered.

— You've really grown, Nina, he said.

— Aye, she blushed, knowing she was doing it, and hating herself for it.

— Fancy gittin oot ay here? Ah mean, can ye get intae pubs? We could go ower the road fir a drink.

Nina weighed up the offer. Even if Geoff talked student shite, it had to be better than staying here. They would be seen in the pub by somebody, this was Bonnyrigg, and somebody would talk. Shona and Tracy would find out, and would want to know who this dark, older guy was. It was too good an opportunity to miss.

Then Nina remembered the gloves. Absentmindedly, she had left them on the top of the chest of drawers in Andy's room. She excused herself from Geoff. — Aye, awright then. Ah'm jist gaun up tae the toilet.

The gloves were still on top of the chest. She picked them up and put them in a jacket pocket, but her wet pants were there so she quickly removed the gloves, and put them in the other one. She looked around at Andy. There was something different about him. He was sweating. She saw him twitch. God, she was sure she saw him twitch. She touched his hand. It was warm.

Nina ran downstairs. — It's Uncle Andy! Ah think . . . ah think . . . ye should come . . . it's like he's still thair . . .

They looked at her with incredulous expressions. Kenny was first to react, springing up the stairs three at a time, followed by Davie and Doctor Sim. Alice twitched nervously, open mouthed, but not really taking it in. — He wis a good man . . . nivir lifted his hands tae me . . . she moaned deliriously. Something inside her drove her to follow the herd upstairs.

Kenny felt his brother's sweaty brow, and his hand.

— He's burnin up! Andy's no deid! ANDY'S NO DEID!

Sim was about to examine the figure when he was pushed aside by Alice, who, having broken free of her constraints, fell upon the warm, pyjama-clad body.

— ANDY! ANDY, KIN YE HEAR ME?

Andy's head bobbed to the side, his stupid, frozen expression never changing, his body remaining limp.

Nina giggled nervously. Alice was seized and held like a

dangerous psychotic. Men and women cooed and made soothing noises at her as Dr Sim examined Andy.

— No. I'm sorry. Mr Fitzpatrick is dead. His heart has stopped, Sim said gravely. He stood back, and put his hand under the bedclothes. He then bent down and pulled a plug out of the wall. He picked up a white flex and pulled a hand switch which was attached to it, out from under the bed.

— Someone left the electric blanket on. That explains the warmth of the body and the sweating, he announced.

— Dearie me. Christ almighty, Kenny laughed. He saw Geoff's eyes blazing at him. In self-justification he said: — Andy would be pishing hissel. Ye ken whit a sense ay humour Andy had. He turned his palms outwards.

— You're a fuckin arse . . . thirs Alice here . . . Geoff stammered, enraged, before turning and bolting from the room.

— Geoff. Geoff. Wait the now, mate . . . Kenny pleaded. They heard the slamming of the front door.

Nina thought that she would piss herself. Her sides ached, as she struggled to repress the spasms of laughter which shook through her. Cathy put her arm around her.

— It's awright darlin. There ye go hen. Dinnae worry yirsel, she said, as Nina realised that she was crying like a baby. Crying with a raw power and unselfconscious abandon as the tensions ebbed from her body and she became limp in Cathy's arms. Memories, sweet childhood memories, flooded her consciousness. Memories of Andy and Alice, and the happiness and love that once lived here, in the home of her auntie and uncle.

Victory On New Year's Day

— Happy New Year, ya wee cunt! Franco wrapped his arm around Stevie's head. Stevie felt several neck muscles tear, as stiff, sober and self-conscious, he struggled to go with the flow.

He returned the greeting as heartily as he could. There followed a round of Happy-New-Years; his tentative hands crushed, his stiff back slapped, his tight and unresponsive lips kissed. All he could think of was the phone, London and Stella.

She hadn't phoned. Worse, she hadn't been in when he phoned. Not even at her mother's. Stevie had gone back to Edinburgh and left the field clear for Keith Millard. The bastard would take full advantage. They'd be together right now, just like they probably were last night. Millard was a slag. So was Stevie. So was Stella. It was a bad combination. Stella was also the most wonderful person in the world in Stevie's eyes. That fact made her less of a slag; in fact, not a slag at all.

— Loosen up fir fuck sakes! It's New fuckin Year! Franco not so much suggested, as commanded. That was his way. People would be forced to enjoy themselves if necessary.

It generally wasn't necessary. They were all frighteningly high. It was difficult for Stevie to reconcile this world with the one he'd just left. Now he was aware of them looking at him. Who were they these people? What did they want? The answer was that they were his friends, and they wanted him.

A song on the turntable drilled into his consciousness, adding to his misery.

> *I loved a lassie, a bonnie, bonnie lassie,*
> *She's as sweet as the heather in the glen,*
> *She's as sweet as the heather,*
> *The bonnie purple heather,*
> *Mary, ma Scots bluebell.*

They all joined in with gusto. — Cannae beat Harry Lauder. It New Year, likesay, Dawsie remarked.

In the joy of the faces around him, Stevie gained a measurement of his own misery. The pit of melancholy was a bottomless one, and he was descending fast, falling further away from the good times. Such times often seemed tantalisingly within reach; he could see them, going on all around him. His mind was like a cruel prison, giving his captive soul a sight of freedom, but no more.

Stevie sipped his can of Export and hoped that he could get through the night without bringing too many people down. Frank Begbie was the main problem. It was his flat, and he was determined that everyone was going to have a good time.

— Ah goat yir ticket fir the match the night, Stevie. Intae they Jambo cunts, Renton said to him.

— Naebody watchin it in the pub? Ah thoat it wis oan satellite, likesay.

Sick Boy, who'd been chatting up a small, dark-haired girl Stevie didn't know, turned to him.

— Git tae fuck Stevie. You're pickin up some bad habits doon in London, ah'm tellin ye man. I fucking detest televised football. It's like shagging wi a durex oan. Safe fuckin sex, safe fuckin fitba, safe fuckin everything. Let's all build a nice safe wee world around ourselves, he mocked, his face contorting. Stevie had forgotten the extent of Sick Boy's natural outrage.

Rents agreed with Sick Boy. That was unusual, thought Stevie. They were always slagging each other off. Generally, if one said sugar, the other said shite. — They should ban aw fitba oan the telly, and get the lazy, fat fucks oaf their erses and along tae the games.

— Yis talked us intae it, Stevie said in resigned tones.

The unity between Rents and Sick Boy didn't last.

— You kin talk aboot gittin oaf yir erse. Mister fuckin couch tattie hissel. Keep oaf the H for mair thin ten minutes and ye might make mair games this season thin ye did the last one, Sick Boy sneered.

— You've goat a fuckin nerve ya cunt . . . Rents turned tae Stevie, then flicked his thumb derisively in Sick Boy's direction. — They wir callin this cunt Boots because ay the drugs he wis cairryin.

They bickered on. Stevie would once have enjoyed this. Now it was draining him.

— Remember Stevie, ah'll be steyin wi ye fir a bit in February, Rents said to him. Stevie nodded grimly. He'd been hoping Rents had forgotten all about this, or would drop it. Rents was a mate, but he had a problem with drugs. In London, he'd be straight back on the gear again, teaming up with Tony and Nicksy. They were always sorting out addresses where they could pick up giros from. Rents never seemed to work, but always seemed to have money. The same with Sick Boy, but he treated everybody else's cash as his own, and his own in exactly the same way.

— Perty at Matty's eftir the game. His new place in Lorne Street. Be thair sharp, Frank Begbie shouted over at them.

Another party. It was almost like work to Stevie. New Year will go on and on. It'll start to fade about the 4th, when the gaps between the parties start to appear. These gaps get bigger until they become the normal week, with the parties happening at the weekend.

More first foots arrived. The small flat was heaving. Stevie had never seen Franco, the Beggar, so at ease with himself. Rab McLaughlin, or Second Prize, as they called him, hadn't even been assaulted when he'd pished up the back of Begbie's curtains. Second Prize had been incoherently drunk for weeks now. New Year was a convenient camouflage for people like him. His girlfriend, Carol, had stormed off in protest at his behaviour. Second Prize hadn't even realised that she was there in the first place.

Stevie moved into the kitchen, where it was quieter, and he

had at least a chance of hearing the phone. Like a yuppie businessman, he'd left a list of the numbers where he was likely to be at with his mother. She could pass these onto Stella, if she phoned.

Stevie had told her how he felt about her, in that ugly barn of a pub in Kentish Town, the one they never usually drank in. He laid his heart bare. Stella had said that she would have to think about what he said, that it had really freaked her out, and was too much to handle right now. She said she would phone him when he got back up to Scotland. And that was that.

They left the pub, going in separate directions. Stevie went towards the tube station to get the underground to Kings Cross, sports bag over his shoulder. He stopped, turned and watched her cross the bridge.

Her long brown curls swished wildly in the wind, as she walked away clad in her donkey jacket, short skirt, thick, black woollen tights and nine-inch Doctor Martens. He waited for her to glance back at him. She never turned around. Stevie bought a bottle of Bell's whisky at the station and had arsed the lot by the time the train rolled into Waverley.

His mood hadn't improved since then. He sat on the formica worktop, contemplating the kitchen tiles. June, Franco's girl-friend, came in and smiled at him, nervously fetching some drinks. June never spoke, and often seemed overwhelmed by such occasions. Franco spoke enough for both of them.

As June left, Nicola came in, being pursued by Spud, who trailed behind her like a faithful salivating dog.

— Hey . . . Stevie . . . Happy New Year, eh, likesay . . . Spud drawled.

— Ah've seen ye Spud. We wir up the Tron thegither, last night. Remember?

— Aw . . . right. Hang loose catboy, Spud focused, grabbing a full bottle of cider.

— Awright Stevie? How's London? Nicola asked.

God, no, thought Stevie. Nicola is so easy to talk to. I'm going to pour my heart out . . . no I'm not . . . yes I am.

Stevie started talking. Nicola listened indulgently. Spud nodded sympathetically, occasionally indicating that the whole scene was 'too fuckin heavy . . .'

He felt that he was making an arse of himself, but he couldn't stop talking. What a bore he must be to Nicola, to Spud even. But he couldn't stop. Spud eventually left, to be replaced by Kelly. Linda joined them. The football songs must be starting up in the front room.

Nicola dispensed some practical advice: — Phone her, wait fir her tae phone, or go doon n see her.

— STEVIE! 'MOAN THROUGH YA CUNT! Begbie roared. Stevie tamely allowed himself to be literally dragged back into front room. — Fuckin chatting up the mantovani in the fuckin kitchen. Yir fuckin worse thin that smarmy cunt thair, the fuckin jazz purist. He gestured over at Sick Boy, who was necking with the woman he'd been chatting up. They had previously overheard Sick Boy describe himself to her as 'basically a jazz purist'.

So wir aw off tae Dublin in the green — fuck the queen!
Whair the hel-mits glisten in the sun — fuck the huns!
And the bayonets slash, the aw-ringe sash
To the echo of the Thomson gun.

Stevie sat gloomily. The phone would never be heard above this noise.

— Shut up the now! shouted Tommy, — This is ma favourite song. The Wolfetones sang *Banna Strand*. Tommy crooned along with some of the others.

oan the lo-ho-honley Ba-nna strand.

There were a few moist eyes when the 'Tones sang *James Connolly*. — A fuckin great rebel, a fuckin great socialist and a fuckin great Hibby. James Fuckin Connolly, ya cunt, Gav said to Renton who nodded sombrely.

Some sang along, others tried to maintain conversations above the music. However, when *The Boys of the Old Brigade* came on everybody joined in. Even Sick Boy took time off his necking session.

> Oh fa-thir why are you-hoo so-ho sad
> oan this fine Ea-heas-ti-her morn

— Sing ya cunt! said Tommy, elbowing Stevie's ribs. Begbie stuck another can of beer in his hand and threw his arm around his neck.

> Whe-hen I-rish men are prow-howd ah-hand glad
> off the land where they-hey we-her born

Stevie worried about the singing. It had a desperate edge to it. It was as if by singing loudly enough, they would weld themselves into a powerful brotherhood. It was, as the song said, 'call to arms' music, and seemed to have little to do with Scotland and New Year. It was fighting music. Stevie didn't want to fight anyone. But it was also beautiful music.

Hangovers, while being pushed into the background by the drink, were also being fuelled. They were now so potentially big as to be genuinely feared. They would not stop drinking until they had to face the music, and that was when every bit of adrenalin had been burned away.

> Aw-haun be-ing just a la-had li-hike you
> I joined the I-hi-Ah-har-A — provishnil wing!

The phone rang in the passage. June got it. Then Begbie snatched it out of her hand, ushering her away. She floated back into the living-room like a ghost.

— Whae? WHAE? WHAES THAT? STEVIE? RIGHT, HAUD OAN THE NOW. HAPPY NEW YEAR DOLL, BY THE WAY

. . . Franco put the receiver down, — . . . whae ivir the fuck ye are . . . He went through to the front room. — Stevie. Some fuckin lemon oan the blower fir ye. Fuckin bools in the mooth likesay. London.

— Phoa! Ya cuntchy! Tommy laughed as Stevie sprang out off the couch. He had needed a pee for the last half-hour, but hadn't trusted his legs. Now they worked perfectly.

— Steve? She had always called him 'Steve' rather than 'Stevie'. They all did down there. — Where have you been?

— Stella . . . where have ah been . . . ah tried tae phone ye yesterday. Where are ye? What are ye daein? He almost said who are you with, but he restrained himself.

— I was at Lynne's, she told him. Of course. Her sister's. Chingford, or some equally dull and hideous place. Stevie felt a euphoric surge.

— Happy New Year! he said, relieved and brimming over.

The pips went, then more change was put into the machine. Stella was not at home. Where was she? In a pub with Millard?

— Happy New Year, Steve. I'm at Kings Cross. I'm getting on the Edinburgh train in ten minutes. Can you meet me at the station at ten forty-five?

— Fuckin hell! Yir jokin . . . fuck! There's nowhere else in the world ah'll be at ten forty-five. You've made my New Year. Stella . . . the things ah sais the other night . . . ah mean them more than ever, ye know . . .

— That's good, because I think I'm in love with you . . . all I've done is think about you.

Stevie swallowed hard. He felt tears well up in his eyes. One left its berth and rolled down his cheek.

— Steve . . . are you okay? she asked.

— Much better than that, Stella. Ah love you. No doubts, no bullshit.

— Fuck . . . the money's running out. Don't ever mess me

about, Steve, this is no fucking game . . . I'll see you at quarter to
eleven . . . I love you . . .

— I love you! I LOVE YOU! The pips went and the line died.

Stevie held the receiver tenderly, like it was something else,
some part of her. Then he put it down and went and had that
pee. He had never felt so alive. As he watched his fetid pish splash
into the pan, his brain allowed itself to be overwhelmed with
delicious thoughts. A powerful love for the world gripped him. It
was New Year. Auld Lang Syne. He loved everyone, especially
Stella, and his friends at the party. His comrades. Warm-hearted
rebels; the salt of the earth. Despite this, he even loved the
Jambos. They were good people; just supporting their team. He'd
first-foot a lot of them this year, irrespective of the result. Stevie
would enjoy taking Stella around the city to various parties. It
would be brilliant. Football divisions were a stupid and irrelevant
nonsense, acting against the interests of working-class unity,
ensuring that the bourgeoisie's hegemony went unchallenged.
Stevie had it all worked out.

He went straight into the room and put The Proclaimers'
Sunshine On Leith on the turntable. He wanted to celebrate the
fact that wherever he went, this was his home, these were his
people. After a few grumbles, it struck a chord. The catcalls at
the previous record's removal were muted at the sight of Stevie's
exuberance. He slapped Tommy, Rents and Beggar around
vigorously, sang loudly, and waltzed with Kelly, caring nothing
about people's impressions of the obviousness of his transformation.

— Nice ay ye tae join us, Gav said to him.

He was still high throughout the match, whereas for the
others it went drastically wrong. Again he became distanced
from his friends. First he couldn't share their happiness, now he
couldn't relate to their despair. Hibs were losing to Hearts. Both
teams were carving out ridiculous numbers of chances; it was
schoolboy stuff, but Hearts were putting at least some of theirs

away. Sick Boy's head was in his hands. Franco glared malevolently over towards the dancing Hearts supporters at the other end of the ground. Rents shouted for the manager's resignation. Tommy and Shaun were arguing about defensive shortcomings, trying to apportion blame for the goal. Gav cursed the referee's masonic leanings, while Dawsy was still lamenting Hibs' earlier misses. Spud (drugs) and Second Prize (alcohol) were bombed out of their boxes, still at the flat, their match tickets good for nothing except future roach material. None of this mattered for the moment, as far as Stevie was concerned. He was in love.

After the match, he left the rest of them to head to the station and meet Stella. The bulk of the Hearts support were also headed up that way. Stevie was oblivious to the heavy vibes. One guy shouted in his face. The cunts won four-one, he thought. What the fuck did they want? Blood? Obviously.

Stevie survived some unimaginative taunting on the way up to the station. Surely, he thought, they could do better than 'Hibby bastard' or 'fenian cunt'. One hero tried to trip him from behind, egged on by baying friends. He should have taken his scarf off. Who the fuck was to know? He was a London boy now, what did all this shite have to do with his life at the moment? He didn't even want to try and answer his own questions.

On the station concourse, a group marched over to him. — Hibby bastard! a youth shouted.

— You've goat it wrong boys. Ah'm a Borussia Munchengladbach man.

He felt a blow on the side of his mouth and tasted blood. Some kicks were aimed at him, as the group walked away from him.

— Happy New Year boys! Love and peace, Jambo brothers! he laughed at them, and sucked his sour, split lip.

— Cunt's a fuckin heidcase, one guy said. He thought they were going to come back for him, but they turned their attention to abusing an Asian woman and her two small children.

— Fuckin Paki slag!

— Fuck off back tae yir ain country.

They made a chorus of ape noises and gestures as they left the station.

— What charming, sensitive young men, Stevie said to the woman, who looked at him like a rabbit looks at a weasel. She saw another white youth with slurred speech, bleeding and smelling of alcohol. Above all, she saw another football scarf, like the one worn by the youths who abused her. There was no colour difference as far as she was concerned, and she was right, Stevie realised with a grim sadness. It was probably just as likely to be guys in green who hassled her. Every support had its arseholes.

The train was nearly twenty minutes late, an excellent performance by British Rail standards. Stevie wondered whether she'd be on it. Paranoia hit him. Waves of fear shuddered through his body. The stakes were high, the highest ever. He couldn't see her, couldn't even picture her in his mind's eye. Then she was almost upon him, different to how he thought of her, more real, even more beautiful. It was the smile, the look of emotion reciprocated. He ran the short distance to her and held her in his arms. They kissed for a long time. When they stopped, the platform was deserted and the train was well on its way to Dundee.

It Goes Without Saying

Ah hears the searin racket comin fae ootside the room. Sick Boy, crashed oot in the windae bay next tae us, shoots tae alertness like a dug thit's heard a whistle. Ah shudder. That noise cut right through us.

Lesley comes intae the room screaming. It's horrible. Ah wanted her tae stoap. Now. Ah couldnae handle this. Nane ay us could. No now. Ah never wanted anything mair in ma life than fir her tae stoap screamin.

— The bairn's away . . . the bairn's away . . . Dawn . . . oh my god . . . oh fuckin god, wis aboot aw ah could pick ootay the horrible sound. She collapses oantae the threadbare couch. Ma eyes stick oan a brown stain oan the wall above her. Whit the fuck was it? How did it get there?

Sick Boy wis on his feet. His eyes bulged oot like a frog's. That's what he reminded us ay, a frog. It was the wey he sort ay hops up, becomes suddenly so mobile fae a stationary position. He looks at Lesley for a few seconds, then nashes through tae the bedroom. Matty and Spud look around uncomprehendingly, but even through thir junk haze, they ken thit somethin really bad's happened. Ah kent. Christ, ah fuckin knew awright. Ah said whit ah always sais when somethin bad happens.

— Ah'm cookin up in a bit, ah tell them. Matty's eyes bore intae us. He gies us the nod. Spud stands up and moves oantae the couch, sittin a few feet fae Lesley. Her heid's in her hands. For a minute ah thought thit Spud wid touch her. Ah hoped he would. Ah'm willing um tae dae it, but he jist stares at her. Ah knew, even fae here, thit he'd be focusing oan the big mole oan her neck.

— It's ma fault . . . it's ma fault, she cries through her hands.

— Eh, Les . . . likesay, Mark's cookin up, eh . . . ye ken, likesay eh . . . Spud sais tae her. It's the first words ah kin remember hearing um say for a few days. Obviously, the cunt's spoken ower this period. He must huv, surely tae fuck.

Sick Boy comes back through. His boady's strainin, seemingly fae the neck, as if against the limits ay an invisible leash. He sounds terrible. His voice reminded us ay the demon's in the film *The Exorcist*. It shit us up.

— Fuck . . . some fuckin life, eh? Somethin like this happens, what the fuck dae ye dae? Eh?

Ah've never seen um like this before, and ah've kent the bastard practically aw my life. — What's wrong Si? What's the fuckin score?

He moves towards us. Ah thought he wis gaunnae kick us. We're best mates but we've hit each other before, in drink or rage when one ay us has wound the other up. Nowt serious, jist sort ay lashing out in anger. Mates kin dae that. No now though, no wi me startin tae feel sick. Ma bones wid huv splintered intae a million fragments had the cunt done that. He jist stood ower us. Thank fuck. Oh, thank you Sick Boy, Simon.

— The gig's fucked. It's aw fuckin fucked! he moans, in a high, desperate whine. It was like a dug that had been run ower and wis waiting fir some cunt tae pit it oot ay its misery.

Matty and Spud haul themselves up, and go through tae the bedroom. Ah follow, pushing past Sick Boy. Ah can feel death in the room before ah even see the bairn. It wis lying face doon in its cot. It, naw, she, wis cauld and deid, blue aroond the eyes. Ah didnae huv tae touch her tae ken. Just lyin thair like a discarded wee doll at the bottom ay some kid's wardrobe. That wee. So fuckin small. Wee Dawn. Fuckin shame.

— Wee Dawn . . . ah cannae believe it. Fuckin sin man . . . Matty sais, shakin his heid.

— Fuckin heavy this . . . eh, likesay em, fuck . . . Spud pits his chin oan his chest and exhales slowly.

Matty's heid's still shakin. He looks like he's gaun tae implode.

— Ah'm fuckin right ootay here, man. Ah cannae fuckin handle this.

— Fuck it Matty! Nae cunt's leavin here the now! Sick Boy shouts.

— Stay cool man. Stay cool, sais Spud, whae sounds anything but.

— We've goat fuckin gear stashed here. This street's been crawlin wi the fuckin DS for weeks now. We fuckin charge oaf now, we aw fuckin go doon. Thir's polis bastards every fuckin where ootside, sais Sick Boy, strugglin tae compose hissel. Thoughts ay polis involvement eywis concentrated the mind. On the issue of drugs, we wir classical liberals, vehemently opposed tae state intervention in any form.

— Aye, but mibbe we should git the fuck ootay here. Lesley can git the ambulance or polis once wuv tidied up and fucked off. Ah still agreed wi Matty.

— Hey . . . mibbe wuv goat tae stick wi Les, likesay. Like, mates n that. Ken? Spud ventures. That sort ay solidarity seems a bit ay a fanciful notion in the circumstances. Matty shakes his heid again. He'd just done six months in Saughton. If he wis done again, that wid be him well fucked. Ootside though, there were pigs cruising aboot. At least that's how it felt. Sick Boy's imagery had got tae me mair thin Spud's pleas tae stick thegither. Flushing aw our gear down the lavvy was just not on. Ah'd rather get sent doon.

— The way ah see it, sais Matty, is thit it's Lesley's bairn, ken? Mibbe if she'd looked eftir it right, it might not be deid. How should we git involved?

Sick Boy starts hyperventilatin.

— Hate tae say it, bit Matty's goat a point, ah sais. Ah'm startin tae hurt really badly. Ah jist want tae take a shot and fuck off.

Sick Boy's noncommittal. This is weird. Normally the

bastard's barking orders at every cunt in sight, whither they take any notice or no.

Spud sais: — We cannae, likesay, leave Les here on her puff, that's eh, ah mean like, fuck. Ken what ah mean?

Ah'm looking at Sick Boy. — Whae gied her the bairn? ah ask. Sick Boy sais nothing.

— Jimmy McGilvary, Matty sais.

— Shite it fuckin wis, Sick Boy dismissively sneers.

— Dinnae you play Mister-fuckin-innocent, Matty turns oan me.

— Eh? 'Moan tae fuck! Whit you oan aboot? ah respond, genuinely fuckin perplexed at the bastard's outburst.

— You wir thair Rents. Boab Sullivan's perty, he sais.

— Naw man, ah've never been wi Lesley. Ah'm tellin the truth, which ah realise is a mistake. In some company people will always believe the opposite ay what ye tell thum; particularly whair sex is concerned.

— How come ye wir crashed oot wi her in the mornin at Sully's perty?

— Ah wis fucked man. Ootay ma box. Ah couldnae huv goat a stiff neck wi a doorstep as a pillay. Ah cannae remember the last time ah hud a ride. Ma explanation convinces them. They ken how long ah've been using heavily and what that kin mean in the shaggin stakes.

— Like, eh . . . somebody sais it wis . . . eh, Seeker's . . . Spud suggests.

— Wisnae Seeker, Sick Boy shakes his heid. He puts a hand oan the deid bairn's cauld cheek. Tears are fillin in his eyes. Ah'm gaun tae greet n aw. There's a constricting tightness in ma chest. One mystery has been solved. Wee Dawn's dead face looks so obviously like ma mate Simon Williamson's.

Then Sick Boy pulls up his jaykit sleeve, showing the weeping sores oan his airm. — Ah'm never touchin that shite again. Ah'm fuckin clean fae now oan. He pits oan that wounded stag expression which he always uses when he wants people tae fuck or finance him. Ah almost believe him.

Matty looks at him. — C'moan Si. Dinnae jump tae the wrong fuckin conclusions. Whit happened tae the bairn's nowt tae dae wi the skag. It's no Lesley's fault either. Ah wis oot ay order saying that. She wis a good mother. She loved that bairn. It's naebody's fault. Cot death n that. Happens aw the time.

— Yeah, likesay, cot death man . . . ken what ah mean? Spud agreed.

Ah feel thit ah love thum aw. Matty, Spud, Sick Boy and Lesley. Ah want tae tell thum. Ah try, but it comes oot as: — Ah'm cookin. They look at us, fuckin scoobied. — That's me, ah shrug ma shooders, in self-justification. Ah go ben the livin-room.

This is murder. Lesley. Ah'm fuckin useless at these things. Less than useless in this condition. Of negative utility. Lesley's nivir moved. Ah feel thit ah should mibbe go and comfort her, pit my airm aroond her. But ma bones feel twisted and scraped. Ah couldnae touch anybody right now. Instead ah babble.

— Really sorry Les . . . naebody's fault though . . . cot death n that . . . wee Dawn . . . barry wee bairn . . . fuckin shame . . . fuckin sin man, ah'm tellin ye.

Lesley lifts her heid up an looks at us. Her thin, white face is like a skull wrapped in milky clingfilm; her eyes are rid raw, circled wi black rings.

— Ye cookin? Ah need a shot Mark. Ah really need a fuckin shot. C'moan Marky, cook us up a shot . . .

At last ah could be ay some practical help. There were syringes and needles lying aw ower the place. Ah tried tae remember which works wir mine. Sick Boy says that he'd never, ever share wi any cunt. That's shite. Whin yir feelin like ah am, the truth is thit ye dinnae care too much. Ah take the nearest, which at least isnae Spud's, as he's been sittin ower the other side ay the room. If Spud isnae HIV positive by now, then the Government should send a deputation ay statisticians doon tae Leith, because the laws ay probability urnae operatin properly here.

Ah produce ma spoon, lighter, and cotton balls as well as some ay this fuckin Vim or Ajax thit Seeker has the audacity to call smack. Wir joined in the room by the punters.

— Back oot ma fuckin light boys, ah snap, gesturing the cunts away wi backward sweeps ay ma hand. Ah know ah'm playing at being The Man, n part ay us hates masel, because it's horrible when some cunt does it tae you. Naebody though, could ivir be in this position and then deny the proposition thit absolute power corrupts. The gadges move a few steps back and watch in silence as ah cook. The fuckers will huv tae wait. Lesley comes first, eftir me. That goes without saying.

Junk Dilemmas No. 64

— *Mark! Mark! Answer the door! Ah ken yir in thair son! Ah ken yir in thair!*

Its ma Ma. It's been quite a while since ah've seen Ma. Ah'm lyin here jist a few feet fae the door, which leads tae a narrow hallway which leads tae another door. Behind that door is ma mother.

— *Mark! Please son, please! Answer the door! It's yir mother, Mark! Answer the door!*

It sounds like Ma's greetin. It sounded like 'doe-ho-hore'. Ah love Ma, love her too much, but in a way which is hard for us tae define, a way

*which makes it difficult, almost impossible, tae ever actually tell her. But
ah love her nonetheless. So much that ah don't want her tae have a son
like me. Ah wish ah could find her a replacement. Ah wish that because
ah don't think change is an option fir us.*

*Ah cannae go tae the door. Nae chance. Instead, ah decide tae cook
up another shot. Ma pain centres say that it's yon time already.*

Already.

Christ, life doesnae get any easier.

*This smack has too much shite in it. You can tell by the wey it's no
dissolving properly. Fuck that cunt Seeker!*

*Ah'll have tae look in oan the auld lady and the auld man sometime;
see how thir daein. Ah'll make that visit a priority; eftir ah see that cunt
Seeker, of course.*

Her Man

For fuck sake.

Wi just came oot fir a quick drink. This is pure fuckin mental.

— Did ye see that? Fuckin out of order, Tommy sais.

— Naw, fuckin leave it man. Dinnae git involved. Ye dinnae
ken the score, ah sais tae um.

Ah saw it though. Clear as day. He hit her. No a fuckin slap or
nowt like that, but a punch. It wis horrible.

Ah'm gled thit Tommy's sittin beside thum, n no me.

— Cause ah fuckin sais! That's fuckin how! The boy's shoutin at her again. Naebody bothers. A big punter at the bar wi long blond corkscrew hair n a rid coupon looks ower n smiles, then turns back tae watch the darts match. No one ay the boys playin darts turns roond.

— Is that eighty? Ah point tae Tommy's nearly empty gless.

— Aye.

Whin ah git tae the bar, thuv started again. Ah kin hear thum. So kin the barman n the corkscrew-heided cunt.

— Gaun then. Dae it again. Gaun then! She's tauntin um. Her voice is like a fuckin ghost's, shriekin n that, bit her lips dinnae seem tae be movin. Ye only ken it's her because the sound's comin fae ower thair. The fuckin pub's nearly empty tae. We could've sat anywhere. Of aw the places tae sit.

He punches her in the face. Blood spurts fae her mooth.

— Hit us again, fucking big man. Gaun then!

He does. She lets oot a scream, then starts greetin, and hauds her face in her hands. He sits, a few inches away fae her, starin at her, eyes blazing, mooth hingin open.

— Lovers' tiff, the corkscrew-heided cunt smiles, catchin ma eye. Ah smile back. Ah don't know why. Ah just seem tae feel like ah need friends. Ah'd nivir say this tae any cunt, bit ah know thit ah've goat problems wi the bevvy. Whin yir like that, yir mates tend tae keep oot yir road, unless they've goat problems wi the bevvy n aw.

Ah look ower tae the barman, an auld guy wi grey hair n a moustache. He shakes his heid n says something under his breath.

Ah take the pints back. Nivir, ivir hit a lassie, ma faither often telt us. It's the lowest scum thit dae that, son, he sais. This cunt thit's been hittin the lassie, he fits that description. He's goat greasy black hair, a thin white face n a black moustache. A wee ferret-faced fucker.

Ah dinnae want tae be here. Ah jist came oot fir a quiet drink. Only a couple, ah promised Tommy, tae git um tae come. Ah've goat the bevvyin under control. Jist pints like, nae nips. Bit this kind ay thing makes us want a wee whisky. Carol's away tae her Ma's. No comin back, she sais. Ah came fir a pint, bit ah might jist git pished yit.

Tommy's breathin heavily n lookin tense as ah sit doon.

— Fuckin tellin ye Secks . . . he sais through grinding teeth.

The lassie's eye is badly swollen and shuttin. Her jaw's swollen n aw, and her mooth is still bleedin. She's a skinny lassie n she looks like she'd snap intae pieces if he hit her again.

Still, she cairries oan.

— That's yir answer. That's eywis yir answer, she spits oot between sobs, angry n feelin sorry fir hersel at the same time.

— Shut it! Ah'm tellin ye! Shut the fuck up! He's nearly chokin wi anger.

— Whit ye gaunnae dae?

— Ya fackin . . . He seems ready tae punch her again.

— That's enough mate. Leave it. Yir oot ay order, Tommy sais tae the guy.

— It's nane ay your fuckin business! You keep oot ay this! The boy points at Tommy.

— That's enough thair. Come on now! The barman shouts. The corkscrew-heided cunt smiles and a couple ay the darts boys look ower.

— Ah'm makin it ma fuckin business. Whit you gaunnae fuckin dae aboot it? Eh? Tommy leans forward.

— Fuck sake Tommy. Cool it man. Ah half-heartedly grab his airm, thinkin ay the barman. He frees it wi a quick shake.

— You want yir mooth punched? the boy sais.

— Think ah'm gaunny jist sit here n lit ye dae it? Fuckin wide-o! Ootside then cunt. Cu-mauugghhnn! Tommy sort ay sings tauntingly.

The boy's shitein hissel. He's right tae. Tommy's quite a tidy cunt.

— Nane ay your business, he sais, no soundin sae smart.

Then the woman screams at Tommy.

— That's ma man! That's ma fackin man yir talkin tae! Tommy's too shocked tae stoap her as she leans ower an digs her nails intae his face.

Everythin happened eftir that. Tommy stood up an punched the boy in the mooth, the guy fell back oaf his seat ontae the flair. Ah wis up n straight ower tae the corkscrew-heided cunt at the bar. Ah tanned um in the jaw n grabbed a haud ay his fuckin curls, haulin his heid doon, n bootin him a couple ay times in the face.

Ah think he blocked one wi his hands, n ah doubt if the other hurt the cunt, cause ah'm wearin trainers. He swings wi his airms, brekin ma grip. Then he backs away, face beamin rid n confused. Ah thought the cunt would huv me then, he could've easily, but he jist stands thair n opens oot his hands.

— What's the fuckin score?

— It's a big joke tae you, eh? ah sais.

— Whit ye talkin aboot? The cunt seems genuinely scoobied.

— Ah'll phone the polis! Git ootay here or ah'll phone the polis! the barman sais, pickin up the receiver fir effect.

— Nae hassle in here now boys, a big, fat cunt fae the darts team sais, threateningly. He's still goat his arrays in his hand.

— It's nowt tae dae wi me mate, the corkscrew-heided cunt sais tae us.

— Mibbe ah goat it wrong likesay, ah tell um.

The woman and her man, thame thit caused the whole fuckin problem, we wir jist oot fir a quiet drink, ur skulkin oot ay the door.

— Fuckin bastards. That's ma man, she shouts tae us as they leave.

Ah feel Tommy's hand oan ma shoodir.

— C'moan Secks. Lits git ootay here, he sais.

The fat cunt fae the darts team, he's goat a rid shirt wi the pub name, a dartboard crest, and 'Stu' underneath it, he's still goat plenty tae say fir hissel.

— Dinnae come in here n cause bother, pal. This isnae your local. Ah ken your faces. Yous ur mates wi that rid-heided cunt n that Williamson laddie, the one wi the ponytail. These cunts ur fuckin drug-dealin scum. We dinnae want that fuckin trash in here.

— We dinnae deal fuckin drugs, pal, Tommy sais.

— Aye. No in this fuckin pub ye dinnae, the fat cunt goes.

— C'moan Stu. S no they boys' fault. It's that cunt Alan Venters n his burd. They're mair intae drugs thin any cunt aroond here. You ken that, this other guy wi thin fair hair sais.

— They should be daein that kind ay arguin in the hoose, no in a pub, another guy sais.

— Domestic dispute. That's whit it is. Shouldnae be botherin people thit ur jist oot fir a drink wi aw that, Fair-hair agrees.

The worse bit is gitting ootside. Ah'm shitein masel in case wi git follayed. Ah'm walkin fast, while Tommy's haudin back.

— Stall the now, he sais.

— Fuck off. Let's git ootay here.

We move doon the road. Ah look back, but nae cunt's left the pub. We see that mental couple up ahead ay us.

— Ah want a wee wurd wi that cunt, Tommy sais, ready tae start eftir thum. Ah clocks a bus comin. A 22. That'll dae us.

— Fuck it Tommy. Here's a bus. C'moan. We run tae the stoap n git oan the bus. We go upstairs tae the back, even though wir only gaun a few stoaps.

— How's ma face? Tommy asks us whin we sit doon.

— Same as usual. A fuckin mess. That burd improved it, ah tell um.

He looks at his reflection in the bus windae.

— The fuckin slag, he curses.

— The pair ay fuckin slags, ah sais.

That wis fuckin ace ay Tommy hittin the boy, likes, n no the bird, even if it wis the burd thit hit him. Ah've done loads ay things in ma time thit ah'm no proud ay, but ah've nivir hit a burd. Whit Carol sais is shite. She says thit ah used violence oan her, but ah nivir hit her. Ah jist held oantae her so thit we could talk. She sais restrainin is like hittin, it's still violence against her. Ah cannae see that. Aw ah wanted tae dae wis tae keep her thair, tae talk.

Whin ah telt this tae Rents, he sais thit Carol wis right. Eh sais she's entitled tae come n go as she wants. That's shite though. Aw ah wanted tae dae wis talk. Franco agreed wi us. It's different whin yir in a relationship, we telt Rents.

Ah felt sick n nervous oan the bus. Tommy might've felt the same, cause we nivir spoke any mair. The morn though, we'll be in some boozer wi Rents, Beggar, Spud, Sick Boy n aw thame, boasting like fuck.

Speedy Recruitment

1 — Preparation

Spud and Renton were sitting in a pub in the Royal Mile. The pub aimed at an American theme-bar effect, but not too accurately; it was a madhouse of assorted bric-à-brac.

— Fuckin weird man though, likesay, you n me gittin sent fir the same joab, ken? Spud said, slurping at his Guinness.

— Fuckin disaster fir me mate. Ah'm no wantin the fuckin joab. It'd be a fuckin nightmare. Renton shook his head.

— Yeah, ah'm likesay happy steyin oan the rock n roll the now man, ken?

— Trouble is though Spud, if ye dinnae try, if ye blow the interview oan purpose; the cunts tell the dole n these bastards stoap yir giro. Happened tae us in London. Ah'm oan ma last warnin doon thair.

— Yeah . . . me n aw man. What ye gaunnae dae, likesay?

— Well, what ye huv tae dae is tae act enthusiastic, but still fuck up the interview. As long as ye come across as keen, they cannae say fuck all. If we jist be oorselves, n be honest, thill nivir gie either ay us the fuckin joab. Problem is, if ye just sit thair n say nowt tae the cunts, thir straight oantae the dole. Thill say: That cunt jist cannae be bothered.

— It's hard for me man . . . ken? It's difficult tae git it thegither like that, likesay . . . ken? Ah git sortay likes, pure shy, ken?

— Tommy gied us some speed. What time's yir interview again?

— No till half-two, likesay.

— Well, ah'm at one. Ah'll see ye back here at two. Ah'll gie ye ma tie tae pit oan, n some speed. Buck ye up a bit, let ye sell yirsel, ken? So let's get tae work oan they appos.

They placed the application forms on the table in front of them. Renton's was already half-completed. A few entries caught Spud's eye.

— Hey . . . what's this man, likesay? George Heriots . . . you went tae Leithy man . . .

— It's a well-known fact thit ye nivir stand a fuckin chance ay gittin anything decent in this city if ye didnae go tae a posh school. Nae wey though, will they offer a George Heriots FP a porterin joab in a hotel. That's only fir us plebs; so pit doon something like that. If they see Augies or Craigy oan your form, the cunts'll offer ye the joab . . . fuck, ah'd better go. Whatever ye dae, dinnae be late. See ye back here in a bit.

2 — Process: Mr Renton (1.00 p.m.)

The trainee manager whae welcomed us wis a mucho spotty punter in a sharp suit, wi dandruff oan the shoodirs like piles ay fuckin cocaine. Ah felt like takin a rolled up fiver tae the cunt's tin flute. His biscuit-ersed face and his plukes completely ruin the image the smarmy wee shite's tryin tae achieve. Even in ma worse junk periods ah've nivir had a complexion like that, the poor wee bastard. This cunt is obviously along for the ride. The main man is the fat, stroppy-lookin gadge in the middle; tae his right thirs a coldly smiling dyke in a woman's business suit wi a thick foundation mask, who looks catalogue hideous.

This is a heavy-duty line-up for a fuckin porter's joab.

The opening gambit wis predictable. The fat cunt gies us a warm look and says: — I see from your application form that you attended George Heriots.

— Right . . . ah, those halcyon school days. It seems like a long time ago now.

Ah might huv lied on the appo, but ah huvnae at the interview. Ah did once attend George Heriots: whin ah wis an apprentice joiner at Gillsland's we did some contract work there.

— Old Fotheringham still doing his rounds?

Fuck. Select from one of two possibilities; one: he is, two: he's retired. Naw. Too risky. Keep it nebulous.

— God, you're taking me back now . . . ah laugh. The fat gadge seems tae be happy wi that. It's worrying. Ah feel that the interview is over, and that these cunts are actually going tae offer us the joab. The subsequent questions are all pleasantly asked and unchallenging. Ma hypothesis is fucked. They'd rather gie a merchant school old boy with severe brain damage a job in nuclear engineering than gie a schemie wi a Ph.D. a post as a cleaner in an abattoir. Ah've goat tae dae something here. This is terrifying. Fatso sees us as a George Heriots old boy fallen on hard times, and he wants tae help us oot. A gross miscalculation Renton, you radge.

Thank fuck for spotted dick. A fair assumption tae make, considering every other part of him seems tae be covered in zits. He gets tae nervously ask a question: — Ehm . . . ehm . . . Mr Renton . . . ehm . . . can you, ehm, explain . . . eh, your employment gaps, ehm . . .

Can you explain the gaps between your words, you doss wee cunt.

— Yes. I've had a long-standing problem with heroin addiction. I've been trying to combat this, but it has curtailed my employment activities. I feel it's important to be honest and mention this to you, as a potential future employer.

A stunning *coup de maître*. They shift nervously in their seats.

— Well, eh, thank you for being so frank with us Mr Renton . . . eh, we do have some other people to see . . . so thanks again, and we'll be in touch.

Magic. The gross git pulls down a wall of coldness and distance between us. They cannae say ah didnae try . . .

3 — Process: Mr Murphy (2.30 p.m.)

This speed is el magnifico, likesay. Ah feel sortay dynamic, ken, likesay, ah'm really lookin forward tae this interview. Rents sais: Sell yirsell Spud, n tell the truth. Let's go for it cats, let's get it on . . .

— I see from your application form that you attended George Heriots. The old Heriots FPs seem to be rather thick on the ground this afternoon.

Yeah, fat-cat.

— Actually man, ah've goat tae come clean here. Ah went tae Augie's, St. Augustine's likesay, then Craigy, eh Craigroyston, ken. Ah jist pit doon Heriots because ah thoat it wid likes, help us git the joab. Too much discrimination in this town, man, ken, likesay? As soon as suit n tie dudes see Heriots or Daniel Stewarts or Edinburgh Academy, they kinday get the hots, ken. Ah mean, would you have said, likesay, ah see you attended Craigroyston?

— Well, I was just making conversation, as I did happen to attend Heriots. The idea was to make you feel at ease. But I can certainly put your mind at rest with regards to discrimination. That's all covered in our new equal opportunities statement.

— It's cool man. Ah'm relaxed. It's jist that ah really want this job, likesay. Couldnae sleep last night though. Worried ah'd sortay blow it likesay, ken? It's jist when cats see 'Craigroyston' oan the form, they likesay think, well everybody thit went tae Craigie's a waster, right? But eh, ye ken Scott Nisbet, the fitba player likesay? He's in the Huns . . . eh Rangers first team, haudin his ain against aw they expensive international signins ay Souness's, ken? That cat wis the year below us at Craigie, man.

— Well, I can assure you Mr Murphy, we're far more interested in the qualifications you gained rather than the school you, or any other candidate, went to. It says here that you got five O Grades . . .

— Whoah. Likesay, gaunnae huv tae stoap ye thair, catboy. The O Grades wis bullshit, ken? Thought ah'd use that tae git ma fit in the door. Showin initiative, likesay. Ken? Ah really want this job, man.

— Look Mr Murphy, you were referred to us by the Department of Employment's Jobcentre. There's no need for you to lie to get your foot in the door, as you put it.

— Hey . . . whatever you say man. You're the man, the governor, the dude in the chair, so tae speak, likesay.

— Yes, well, we're not making much progress here. Why don't you just tell us why you want this job so desperately that you're prepared to lie.

— Ah need the hireys man.

— Pardon? The what?

— The poppy, likesay, eh . . . the bread, the dosh n that. Ken?

— I see. But what specifically attracts you to the leisure industry?

— Well, everybody likes tae huv a good time, a bit ay enjiymint, ken? That's leisure tae me man, likesay. Ah like tae see punters enjoy themselves, ken?

— Right. Thank you, the doll wi the makeup mask sais. Ah could sortay like, love that babe . . . — What would you see as being your main strengths? she asks us.

— Er . . . sense ay humour, likesay. Ye need that man, goatay huv it, jist goatay huv it, ken? Ah'll huv tae stoap sayin 'ken' sae much. These dudes might think ah'm a sortay pleb.

— What about weaknesses? the squeaky-voiced kitten in the suit asks. This is one spotted catboy; Rents wisnae jokin aboot the plukes. We have a real leopard cub here.

— Ah suppose man, ah'm too much ay a perfectionist, ken? It's likesay, if things go a bit dodgy, ah jist cannae be bothered, y'know? Ah git good vibes aboot this interview the day though man, ken?

— Thank you very much Mr Murphy. We'll let you know.

— Naw man, the pleasure wis mine. Best interview ah've been at, ken? ah bounds across n shakes each cat by the paw.

4 — Review

Spud met Renton back in the pub.

— How did it go Spud?

— Good catboy, good. Possibly too good, likesay. Ah think the dudes might be gaun tae offer us the job. Bad vibes. One thing though, man, ye wir right aboot this speed. Ah never seem tae like, sell masel properly in interviews. Cool times compadre, cool times.

— Let's huv a drink tae celebrate yir success. Fancy another dab at that speed?

— Wouldnae say naw man, would not say no, likes.

Relapsing

Scotland Takes Drugs In Psychic Defence

Ah couldnae mention the Barrowland gig tae Lizzy. No fuckin chance ay that man, ah kin tell ye. Ah had bought ma ticket when ah got ma Giro. That wis me pure skint. It was also her birthday. It was the ticket or a present for her. Nae contest. This was Iggy Pop. Ah thought she'd understand.

— Ye can buy fuckin tickets fir Iggy fuckin Pop but ye cannae buy me a fuckin birthday present! That wis her response. See the cross ah've goat tae fuckin bear here man? Pure madness, ma man. Dinnae git us wrong. Ye can see her point. It's ma ain fault though, like ah sais, ma ain fault. Pure naive, that's Tommy here. Auld fuck the wind. Ah lead wi ma chin aw the time. If ah wis a wee bit more, what's the word? duplicitous, ah would have said nothing aboot the tickets. Ah get too excited, and pure open ma big mooth far too wide. That's fearless Tommy Gun for ye. Pure sucker.

So ah havenae mentioned the gig since. The night before the event Lizzy tells us that she pure fancies going to the pictures to see that *The Accused*. She tells me that her that was in *Taxi Driver* is in it. Ah don't really fancy the film; too much hype and publicity. That's really besides the point though, if ye ken what ah mean, cause ah'm sitting here wi the Ig gig tickets in ma tail. So ah'm forced tae mention Barrowland and the man.

— Eh, cannae the morn. Ah've got the Iggy Pop gig at Barrowland. Me and Mitch are gaun through.

— So ye'd rather go tae a concert wi Davie fuckin Mitchell than the pictures wi me. That's pure Lizzy. The rhetorical question, the stock-in-trade weapon ay burds and psychos.

The issue's become, like, a pure referendum on our relationship. Ma instinct is tae be upfront and say 'yes', but that would probably mean bombing out Lizzy and ah'm addicted tae having sex wi her. God, ah love it. Daein it fae behind as she groans softly, her pretty head resting on the yellow silk pillow-cases in ma gaff; the ones Spud knocked for us oot ay the British Home Stores in Princes Street as a flat-warming present. Ah know ah shouldnae be disclosing aboot our life, man, but the image of her in bed is so strong that even her social coarseness and permanent sense ay outrage fail to weaken it. Ah jist pure wish that Lizzy could always be like she is in bed.

Ah try tae murmur seductive apologies, but she's so harsh and unforgiving: sweet and beautiful only in bed. The permanent viciousness of that expression will force out her beauty long before it should disappear. She calls me all the fuck-ups under the sun, then a few more for good measure. Poor old Tommy Gun. No longer the greatest fighting soldier; now the greatest shiteing soldier.

It's no Iggy's fault. Cannae really blame the boy, ken? How wis he tae know when he stuck the Barrowland doon oan his itinerary, that he'd cause punters, whae he doesnae even ken exist, aw this hassle? Pure freaky whin ye think aboot it. Still, he's just another straw on the back of the camel. Lizzy's the pure steel woman. Ah'm happy though. Even Sick Boy's jealous ay me. Being Lizzy's boyfriend does confer status, but fame costs, as they say. By the time ah leave the pub, ah am in no doubt of my lack of worth as a human being.

At home ah take a line of speed and guzzle half a bottle of Merrydown. Ah pure cannae sleep, so ah phone Rents and ask him if he fancies coming round tae watch a Chuck Norris video. Rents is off tae London the morn. He spends more time doon there than he does back here. Something tae dae wi giro-drops. The cunt's in some kind ay a syndicate wi these punters he met when he worked on the Harwich–Hook of Holland cross-channel ferry, years ago. He's gaunnae see the Ig at the Town and Country while he's in the Smoke. We toke some grass and laugh our heads off as Chuck kicks fuck out of commie antichrists by the dozen, that constipated and stoical expression never leaving his face. Straight, this is unwatchable. Stoned, it's pure unmiss-able.

The next day ah've got terrible mouth ulcers. Temps, Gav Temperley, whae's moved intae the flat, says that it serves me right. Ah'm killing myself with speed, he tells me. Temps says that I should have a job, with my qualifications. Ah tell Temps that he sounds a lot more like ma mother than any friend is entitled tae. You can see Gav's point though. He's the only one working, for the fuckin dole, and he's always getting tapped up by the rest ay us. Poor Temps. Ah think me n Rents kept him awake last night as well. Temps resents dole-moles having a good time, like all workies do. He pure resents being hit for info by Rents every day, about claim procedures.

It's tae my mother's ah go, tae tap some cash for the gig. Ah need dosh for the train fare as well as drink and drugs. Speed's my drug, it goes well with drink, and ah've always liked a drink. Tommy the pure speed freak.

My Ma gives me a lecture on the dangers of drugs, telling me what a disappointment ah've been to her, and tae my dad, who, although he doesnae say much, really worries about me. Later when he comes in from work, he says while my Ma is upstairs that she mightnae say much, but really worries about me. Frankly, he tells me, he's really disappointed in my attitude. He hopes ah'm not taking drugs, scrutinising my face as if he can tell. Funny, I know junkies, dope-heads and speed freaks, but the most fucked-up punters on drugs I know are pish-heids, like Secks. That's Rab McLaughlin, the Second Prize. He's blown the fucking lot, man.

Ah tap the cash and meet Mitch in the Hebs. Mitch is still seein that lassie Gail. It's obvious though, that he's no gittin his leg ower. Listenin tae um fir ten minutes, ye kin pure read between the lines. He's in a pure bevvying mood, so ah tap some cash off ay um. We tan four pints ay heavy then get on the train. Ah dae four cans of Export and two lines ay speed during the journey to Glasgow. We down a couple in Sammy Dow's, then get a taxi to Lynch's. After another two pints, might've been three; and another line of speed each in the bog, we sing a medley of Iggy songs and go ower tae the Saracen Head in the Gallowgate, opposite the Barrowland. We drink some cider and wine chasers, dabbing frantically at salty speed in silver foil.

All ah can see is a blurred neon sign when ah leave the pub. It is pure fucking freezing here, I kid you not my man, and we move towards the light and into the ballroom. We head straight for the bar. We have more drinks at the bar, although we can hear that Iggy's started his set. Ah rip off my torn t-shirt. Mitch lines up some Morningside speed, cocaine, on the formica-top table.

Then something changes. He says something tae us about money which ah don't catch, but ah can feel the resentment. We have a heated, slurred argument, exchanging punches, ah don't recall who strikes the first blow. We cannae really hurt each other or feel force on our fists or bodies. Too wasted. Mind you, ah step up a gear when ah sees the blood flowing fae ma nose onto my bare chest, and ower the table. Ah get Mitch's hair in a grip and ah'm trying tae smash his heid against the wall, but ma hands are so numb and heavy. Someone pulls me off, and throws us out the bar, down a passage. Ah get up, singing, following the music into the packed hall of sweating bodies, pushing and shoving ma way tae the front.

One guy headbutts me, but ah ride it, no even stopping tae

acknowledge my assailant, still pure jostling to the front. Ah'm pure jumping aroond at the front of the stage, a few feet away from The Man. They are playing 'Neon Forest'. Somebody slaps me on the back saying, — You are mental, by the way, my man. Ah sing out, a twisting, pogo-ing mass of rubber.

Iggy Pop looks right at me as he sings the line: 'America takes drugs in psychic defence'; only he changes 'America' for 'Scatlin', and defines us mair accurately in a single sentence than all the others have ever done . . .

Ah cease my St Vitus dance and stand looking him in stunned awe. His eyes are on someone else.

The Glass

The problem wi Begbie wis . . . well, thirs that many problems wi Begbie. One ay the things thit concerned us maist wis the fact thit ye couldnae really relax in his company, especially if he'd hud a bevvy. Ah always felt thit a slight shift in the cunt's perception ay ye wid be sufficient tae change yir status fae great mate intae persecuted victim. The trick wis tae indulge the radge withoot being seen tae be too much ay an obviously crawling sap.

Even so, any overt irreverence took place within strictly defined limits. These boundaries were invisible tae outsiders, but you gained an intuitive feel for them. Even then, the rules constantly changed wi the cunt's moods. Friendship wi Begbie was an ideal preparation for embarking on a relationship wi a woman. It taught ye sensitivity, an awareness ay the other person's changing needs. When ah wis wi a lassie, ah usually behaved in the same discreetly indulgent wey. For a while, anywey.

Begbie and masel hud been invited tae Gibbo's 21st. It wis an RSVP job, wi partners. Ah took Hazel, n Begbie took his burd, June. June wis up the stick, but wisnae showin. We met in a pub in Rose Street, which was Begbie's idea. Only arseholes, wankers and tourists set fit in Rose Street.

Hazel n me hud a strange relationship. We'd been seeing each other on and off now for about four years. We have a kind ay understanding, that when ah'm using, she just vanishes. The reason Hazel sticks around wi me is because she's as fucked up as me, but rather than get it sorted oot, she denies it. Wi her it's sex thit's at the root ay it rather than drugs. Hazel and I seldom have sex. This is because ah'm usually too junked tae be bothered, and in any case she's frigid. People say that there is no such thing as frigid women, only incompetent men. That's true to an extent, and ah'd be last cunt under the sun tae make any great claims fir masel in that department — ma abysmal junky track record speaks fir itself.

The thing is that Hazel wis fucked as a wee lassie by her faither. She once telt us this when she wis really oot ay it. Ah couldnae be much use, cause ah wis oot ay it as well. When ah tried tae git her tae talk aboot it later, she wisnae havin it. Every time since has been a disaster. Our sex life always has been. After k.b.ing me for ages, she'd eventually let me shag her. She'd be tensed up, gripping the mattress and gritting her teeth, while I did what I had to do. Eventually, we just stopped. It was like sleeping wi a surfboard. All the foreplay in the world couldn't make Hazel unwind. It just made her more tense, almost physically sick. Some day ah hope she finds somebody who can dae it for her. Anywey, Hazel and I had a strange pact. We used each other in a social sense, that's the only way to decribe it really, tae project this veneer of normality. It's a great cover-up for her frigidity and ma junk-induced impotence. My Ma and faither lapped Hazel up, seeing her as a potential daughter-in-law. If only they knew. Anywey, ah had called up Hazel, in order tae get her tae accompany us oan this night oot; two fuck-ups thegither.

The Beggar had been bevvyin before we met up. He looked seedy and menacing done up in a suit, the wey draftpaks do, indian ink spilling oot from under cuffs and collar onto neck and hands. Ah'm sure Beggar's tattoos move intae the light, resentful at being covered up.

— How's the fuckin Rent Boy! he rasps loudly. Appropriateness hus nivir been the cunt's strong point. — Awright doll? he sais tae Haze. — Lookin fuckin smert. See this cunt here? He points at me. — Style, he sais, enigmatically. Then he elaborates. — This is a useless bastard; but he's goat style. A man ay wit. A man ay class. A man not unlike my good self.

Begbie always constructed imaginary qualities in his friends, then shamelessly claimed them for himself.

Hazel and June, who didn't really know each other well, wisely struck up a conversation, lumbering me wi the Beggar, the General Franco. Ah realised that it hud been a long time since ah'd drank wi Begbie oan ma ain, withoot other mates tae offer occasional respite. Alone was stressful.

Tae get ma attention, Begbie smashes an elbow into ma ribs with such ferocity that it would be construed as an assault, were it not between two companions. He then starts telling us about some gratuitously violent video he's been watching. Beggar insists on acting the whole fuckin thing oot, demonstrating karate blows, throttlings, stabbings, etc., on me. His explanation ay the film lasts twice as long as the picture itself. Ah'm gaunnae huv a few bruises the morn, n ah'm no even pished yet.

We're drinking on a balcony bar, and our attention is caught by a squad of nutters entering the crowded pub below. They swagger in, noisy and intimidating.

Ah hate cunts like that. Cunts like Bebgie. Cunts that are intae baseball-batting every fucker that's different; pakis, poofs, n what huv ye. Fuckin failures in a country ay failures. It's nae good blamin it oan the English fir colonising us. Ah don't hate the English. They're just wankers. We are colonised by wankers. We can't even pick a decent, vibrant, healthy culture to be colonised by. No. We're ruled by effete arseholes. What does that make us? The lowest of the fuckin low, the scum of the earth. The most wretched, servile, miserable, pathetic trash that was ever shat intae creation. Ah don't hate the English. They just git oan wi the shite thuv goat. Ah hate the Scots.

Begbie's gaun oan aboot Julie Mathieson, whae he used tae huv the hoats fir. Julie always hated him. Ah really liked Julie, maybe that's why. She wis a really good punter. She hud a bairn whin she wis HIV, but the bairn wis all-clear, thank fuck. The hoespital sent Julie hame in an ambulance wi the bairn, wi two guys dressed in sortay radioactive-proof suits — helmets, the lot. This wis back in 1985. It had the predictable effect. The neighbours saw this, freaked, and burnt her oot the hoose. Once ye git tagged HIV, that's you fucked. Especially a lassie oan her puff. Harassment followed harassment. Eventually, she hud a nervous breakdoon and, wi her damaged immune system, wis easy prey fir the onset ay AIDS.

It wis last Christmas thit Julie died. Ah nivir made the funeral. Ah wis lyin in ma ain puke oan a mattress in Spud's gaff, too fucked tae move. It wis a shame, cause Julie n me wir good mates. Wi nivir shagged or nowt like that. Wi baith thought it wid change things too much, like it does in male/female friendships. Sex generally makes them intae real relationships, or ends them. Ye go backwards or forwards after shagging, but maintaining the status quo is difficult. Julie looked really good when she started oan smack. Maist lassies dae. It seems tae bring oot the best in them. It always seems tae gie, before it takes back, wi interest.

Begbie's epitaph tae Julie is: — Fuckin waste ay a good bit ay fanny.

Ah fight back the urge tae tell um what a fuckin waste ay a silver bullet he'd be. Ah try no tae show ma anger; it'll achieve nothing except a burst mooth fir me. Ah go doonstairs tae git another round up.

These draftpak cunts are at the bar, jostling each other, and every other fucker. Getting served is a nightmare. A mosaic shell ay scar tissue and indian ink, ah presume that there's some cunt inside it, is screaming: — DOUBLE VODDY N COKE! DOUBLE FAAHKIN VODDY N COKE THEN CUNT! at the nervous barstaff. Ah focus on the whisky bottles on the gantry, trying everything in ma power tae avoid makin eye contact wi this radge. It's like ma eyes huv a life ay thir ain, involuntarily turning tae the side. My face reddens n tingles, as if in anticipation ay a fist or a boatil. These cunts are damaged fucking goods, nutty boys of the highest order.

Ah take the drinks back, the nips first fir the women, then the pints.

Then it happens.

Aw ah did wis put a pint ay Export in front ay Begbie. He takes one fuckin gulp oot ay it; then he throws the empty gless fae his last pint straight ower the balcony, in a casual, backhand motion. It's one ay they chunky, panelled glesses wi a handle, n ah kin see it spinnin through the air oot ay the corner ay ma eye. Ah look at Begbie, whae smiles, while Hazel n June look disorientated, thir faces reflecting ma ain crippling anxiety.

The gless crashes doon oan this draftpak's heid, which splits open as he faws tae his knees. The boy's mates assume battle stances, n one ay them charges ower tae this other table n panels this innocent cunt. Another gubs some perr gadge cairryin a tray ay drinks.

Begbie's oan his feet, n racing doon the stair. He's right in the middle ay the flair.

— BOY'S BEEN FUCKIN GLESSED! NAE CUNT LEAVES HERE UNTIL AH FIND OOT WHAE FLUNG THAT FUCKIN GLESS!

He's barkin orders at innocent couples, shoutin instructions at the bar staff. Thing is, the draftpak cunts ur lappin this up.

— S awright mate. We kin handle this! Double Voddy n Coke sais.

Ah cannae hear whit Begbie sais, but it seems tae impress Double Voddy. Then the Beggar goes tae the barman: — YOU! PHONE THE FAAHKIN POLIS!

— NAW! NAW! NAE POLIS! shouts one ay the draftpak psychos. These cunts've obviously goat records the length ay yir airm. The perr cunt behind the bar's shitein hissel, no kennin whit tae dae.

Begbie stands erect, neck muscles tensed. His glare sweeps aroond the bar n up tae the balcony.

— WHAE SAW ANYTHIN? YOU CUNTS SEE ANYTHIN? he shouts at a group ay guys, Merchant school, Murrayfield type cunts, who ur crappin themselves.

— No . . . one guy wobbles out.

Ah gits doon, telling Haze n June no tae move fae the balcony bar. Begbie's like a psychopathic detective oot ay an Agatha Christie whodunit, cross-examinin every cunt. He's blowin it; it is so fuckin obvious. Ah'm doon thair, stickin a fuckin bar-towel oan the draftpak's split heid, tryin tae stem the blood. The cunt just growls at us, n ah dinnae ken whether that's um showin gratitude or ready tae stomp ma baws, but ah cairry oan.

One fat cunt fae the group ay psychos goes up tae this other group ay guys at the bar n sticks the heid oan one ay them. The place goes up. Lassies scream, guys issue threats, push each other and exchange blows as the sound ay brekin gless fills the air.

This boy's white shirt is saturated wi blood as ah push through some bodies tae git back up the stairs tae Hazel n June. Some cunt gubs us oan the side ay the face. Ah hud half-saw it fae the corner ay ma eye n moved away n time, so ah didnae git the fill force ay it. Ah turn roond and this radge's sayin: — Come ahead wide-o. Come ahead.

— Way tae fuck ya radge, ah say, shakin ma heid. This gadge's ready tae come, but his mate grabs his airm, a good thing, because ah'm no ready fir him. The cunt looks a wee bit tidy, like he could punch his weight.

— Fuckin stey ootay it, Malky. It's fuck all tae dae wi that boy, his mate sais. Ah move oan smartly. Haze n June come doon the stairs wi us. Malky, ma assailant, is panelling some other cunt now. A gap has cleared in the middle ay the flair n ah steer Haze n June through it towards the door.

— Mind the burds, pal, ah say tae these two guys whae ur aboot tae swedge, n one dives for the other one, allowing us tae slip past. Ootside the bar in the Rose Street precinct Begbie n this other cunt, it's Double Voddy, ur bootin fuck oot ay this perr bastard oan the deck. — FRAAHNK! June gies oot a blood-curdling scream. Hazel's edging away fae me, tuggin at ma hand.

— FRANCO! C'MOAN! ah shout, grabbin his airm. He stoaps tae examine his work, but brushes ma grip oaf. He turns tae look at us, and fir a minute, ah think he's gaunnae panel us. It's like he doesnae see us, doesnae recognise us. Then he goes: — Rents. Nae cunt fucks wi the YLT. Thuv goat tae fuckin learn that Rents. Thuv goat tae fuckin learn that.

— Cheers pal, sais Double Voddy, Franco's accomplice in slaughter.

Franco smiles at him, and boots the cunt in the baws. Ah felt it.

— Ah'll gie ye fackin cheers, ya cunt! he sneers, smacking Double Voddy in the face, knocking him ower. A white tooth flies like a bullet oot ay the guy's mooth, and lands a few feet away on the precinct tiles.

— Frank! What ur ye daein! June shrieks. We're pulling the cunt doon the road as polis sirens fill the air.

— That cunt, that cunt n his fuckin mates back thair, that's the cunts thit fuckin stabbed ma brar! he shouts indignantly. June looked beaten down.

That wis bullshit. Beggar's brother, Joe, was stabbed in a fight in a pub at Niddrie years ago. The fight wis ay his ain makin, and he wisnae badly hurt. In any case Franco and Joe hated each other. Still, the incident had provided Begbie wi the spurious moral ammunition he needed tae justify one ay his periodic drink and angst fuelled wars against the local populace. He'd git his one day. Nothing wis surer. Ah jist didnae want tae be aroond whin he did.

Hazel and ah fell behind Franco n June. Haze wanted tae go.
— Thirs something wrong wi him. Did ye see that guy's heid? Let's git ootay here.

Ah found masel lyin tae her, tae justify Begbie's behaviour. Fuckin horrible. Ah jist couldnae handle her outrage, n the hassle thit went wi it. It wis easy tae lie, as we all did wi Begbie in our circle. A whole Begbie mythology hud been created by oor lies tae each other n oorsels. Like us, Begbie believed that bullshit. We played a big part in making him what he was.

Myth: Begbie has a great sense ay humour.

Reality: Begbie's sense ay humour is solely activated at the misfortunes, setbacks and weaknesses ay others, usually his friends.

Myth: Begbie is a 'hard man'.

Reality: Ah would not personally rate Begbie that highly in a square-go, withoot his assortment ay stanley knives, basebaw bats, knuckledusters, beer glesses, sharpened knitting needles, etc. Masel n maist cunts are too shite-scared tae test this theory, but the impression remains. Tommy once exposed some weaknesses in Begbie, in a square-go. Gave um a good run for his money, did Tam. Mind you, Tommy's a tidy cunt, n Begbie, it has tae be said, came oot the better ay the two.

Myth: Begbie's mates like him.

Reality: They fear him.

Myth: Begbie would never waste any ay his mates.

Reality: His mates are generally too cagey tae test oot this proposition, and oan the odd occasion they huv done so, huv succeeded in disproving it.

Myth: Begbie backs up his mates.

Reality: Begbie smashes fuck oot ay innocent wee daft cunts whae accidently spill your pint or bump intae ye. Psychopaths who terrorise Begbie's mates usually dae so wi impunity, as they tend tae be closer mates ay Begbie's than the punters he hings aboot wi. He kens thum aw through approved school, prison n the casuals' networks, the freemasonaries that bams share.

Anywey, these myths gie us the basis tae rescue the night.

— Look Hazel, ah ken Franco's uptight. It's jist thit they guys pit his brar Joe oan a life-support machine. Thir a close faimlay.

Begbie is like junk, a habit. Ma first day at primary school, the teacher sais tae us: — You will sit beside Francis Begbie. It wis the same story at secondary. Ah only did well at school tae git intae an O Level class tae git away fae Begbie. Whin Begbie wis expelled n sent tae another school en route tae Polmont, ma performance declined, and ah wis pit back intae the non-certificate stream. Still, nae mair Begbie.

Then, when ah wis apprenticed as a chippy wi a Gorgie builder, ah goes along tae Telford College tae dae ma national certificate modules in joinery. Ah sat doon tae ma chips in the cafeteria, whin whae comes along but that cunt Begbie, wi a couple ay other psychos. They wir oan this specialist course in metalwork fir problem teenagers. The course seemed tae teach them tae manufacture thir ain sharp metal weapons ay destruction rather than have tae buy them fae the Army n Navy stores.

Whin ah left ma trade n went tae college fir A Levels, then oantae Aberdeen University, ah half expected tae see Beggars at the freshers ball, beating tae a pulp some four-eyed, middle-class wanker he imagined wis starin at um.

He really is a cunt ay the first order. Nae doubt about that. The big problem is, he's a mate n aw. Whit kin ye dae?

We quicken our step and follay them doon the road; a quartet of fucked-up people thegither.

A Disappointment

Ah minded ay the cunt. Fuckin sure n ah did. Ah used tae think he wis a fuckin hard cunt, back it Craigie, ken? He fuckin hung aroond wi Kev Stronach and that crowd. Fuckin bams. Dinnae git us wrong like; ah thoat the cunt wis fuckin sound. But ah mind, thir wis one time some boys asks the cunt whair he fuckin came fae. This boy goes: — Jakey! (that wis the cunt's name like), ur you fae fuckin Grantin or Roystin? The cunt goes: — Grantin is Roystin. Roystin is Grantin. The bastard went right fuckin doon in ma estimation eftir that, ken? That wis back it the fuckin school though, ken? Fuckin yonks ago now.

Anywey, the other fuckin week thair, ah wis doon the fuckin Volley wi Tommy n Secks, ken Rab, the Second Prize, likes? This cunt, this Jakey cunt, the big fuckin radge boy fae Craigie, he comes intae the pub. He nivir fuckin lits oan tae us. Ah mind ay smashin loads ay fuckin crabs tae bits wi stanes wi that cunt. Doon the fuckin harbour, ken? He nivir fuckin recognised us. Didnae fuckin ken us fae Adam . . . the cunt.

A Disappointment

Anywey, the cunt's mate, this fuckin plukey-faced wide-o, goes tae pit his fuckin money doon fir the baws it the table. Fir the pool, ken? Ah sais tae um: — That cunt's fuckin nixt mate, pointin tae this wee specky gadge. This wee cunt's goat his fuckin name up oan the board, but he wid've jist fuckin sat thair n said fuck all if ah hudnae fuckin spoke like.

Ah wis fuckin game fir a swedge. If the cunts hud've fuckin come ahead it wis nae problem like. Ah mean, you ken me, ah'm no the type ay cunt thit goes lookin fir fuckin bothir likes; but ah wis the cunt wi the fuckin pool cue in ma hand, n the plukey cunt could huv the fat end ay it in his pus if he wanted, like. Obviously, ah wis cairryin ma fuckin chib n aw. Too fuckin right. Like ah sais, ah dinnae go lookin fir fuckin bother, but if any lippy cunt wants tae start, ah'm fuckin game. So the wee specky cunt's pit his fuckin dough in, n he's rackin up n that, ken? The plukey cunt jist sits doon n sais fuck all. Ah kept ma eye oan the hard cunt, or at least he wis a fuckin hard cunt it the school, ken. The cunt nivir sais a fuckin wurd. Kept his fuckin mooth shut awright; the cunt.

Tommy sais tae us: — Hi Franco, is that boy gittin lippy? Ye ken Tam, he's no fuckin shy, that cunt. They fuckin heard um like, these cunts; but they nivir fuckin sais nowt again. The plukey cunt n the so-called hard cunt. N it wid've been two against two, cause you ken Second Prize; dinnae git us wrong, ah lap the cunt up, but he's fuckin scoobied whin it comes tae a pagger. He's pished ootay his fuckin heid n he kin hardly haud the fuckin pool cue. This is fuckin half-past eleven oan a Wednesday mornin wir talkin aboot here. So it wid've been fuckin square-gos. But they cunts sais fuck all. Ah nivir fuckin rated the plukey cunt, but ah wis fuckin disappointed in the hard cunt, or the so-called hard cunt, like. He wisnae a fuckin hard man. A fuckin shitein cunt if the truth be telt, ken. Big fuckin disappointment tae me, the cunt, ah kin tell ye.

Cock Problems

It's fuckin grotesque tryin tae find an inlet. Yesterday ah hud tae shoot intae ma cock, where the most prominent vein in ma body is. Ah dinnae want tae get intae that habit. As difficult it is tae conceive ay it at the moment, ah may yet find other uses for the organ, besides pishing.

Now the doorbell's going. Fuckin hell. That bastard shite-arsed fuck-up of a landlord: Baxter's son. Auld Baxter, god rest the diddy cunt's soul, never really bothered aboot the rent cheque. Senile auld wanker. Whenever he came roond, ah wis charm personified tae the auld cunt. Ah'd take oaf his jaykit, sit um doon, and gie um a can ay Export. We'd talk aboot the hoarses and the Hibs teams ay the fifties wi the 'Famous Five' forward line ay Smith, Johnstone, Reilly, Turnbull and Ormond. Ah knew nowt aboot hoarses and Hibs in the fifties, but as they wir auld Baxter's only talking points, ah became well-versed in both subjects. Then ah'd rifle through the auld gadge's jaykit poakits n help masel tae some cash. He eywis carried a massive wad aroond wi um. Then ah'd either pey um his ain cash, or tell the poor bastard thit ah'd already squared the cunt up.

We even used tae phone up the auld gadge if we were a bit short. Like when Spud n Sick Boy crashed here, we'd tell him a tap was leaking or windae wis broken. Sometimes we'd even break the windae oorsels, like when Sick Boy threw the auld black n white telly through it, and git the docile cunt tae come roond so's we could rifle um. Thir wis a fuckin fortune in that cunt's poakits. It goat so's thit ah wis feart no tae rip um off, in case some fucker mugged um.

Now auld Baxter has gone tae the great gig in the sky; replaced by his hospice-humoured bastard ay a son. A cunt who expects rent fir this dive.

— RENT. Somebody's shouting through the letterbox.

— Rents!

It's no the landlord. It's Tommy. What the fuck does the cunt want at this time?

— Haud oan Tommy. Jist comin.

Ah shoot intae ma knob for the second consecutive day. As the needle goes in, it looks like a horrible experiment being conducted on an ugly sea-snake. The gig is getting sicker by the minute. The rush wastes nae time in racin tae ma box. Ah git a magic high, then think ah'm gaunnae puke. Ah under-estimated how pure this shite wis, and took a wee bit too much in that shot. Ah take a deep breath and get it thegither. Ah feel as if a thin stream ay air is comin in tae ma boady fae a bullet hole in ma back. This is not an OD situation. Calm doon. Keep that auld respirator going. Easy does it. This is nice.

Ah stagger tae ma feet, n let Tommy in. *That* wisnae easy.

Tommy looks offensively fit. Majorca tan still intact; hair sun-bleached, cut short and gelled back. Gold stud and hoop in one ear; mellow sky-blue eyes. It has to be said that Tommy's a fairly handsome cunt wi a tan. It brings oot the best in him. Handsome, easy-going, intelligent, and pretty tidy in a swedge. Tommy should make you jealous, but somehow he doesnae. This is probably because Tommy doesnae have the self-confidence tae recognise n make the maist ay his qualities; nor the vanity tae be a pain in the erse aboot them tae every other cunt.

— Split up wi Lizzy, he tells us.

It's hard tae work oot whether congratulations or commiserations are in order. Lizzy is a shag extraordinaire, but has a tongue like a sailor and a castrating stare. Ah think Tommy's still tryin tae sort oot his feelins. Ah kin tell that he's deep in thought because he husnae telt us what a daft cunt ah am tae be usin, husnae even mentioned the state ah'm in.

Ah struggle tae show concern through ma self-centred smack apathy. The outside world means fuck all tae us. — Pished oaf aboot it? ah ask.

— Dinnae ken. If ah'm bein honest, ah'll miss the sex maist. That n like, jist huvin somebody, ken?

Tommy needs people a loat mair thin maist.

Ma endurin memory ay Lizzy is fae the school. Me, Begbie n Gary McVie wir lyin in the Links at the bottom ay the running track, away fae the beady eyes ay that bastard Vallance, the housemaster, a Nazi cunt ay the highest order. We took up that position so's we could see the lassies race in thir shorts n blouses, n accumulate some decent wanking material.

Lizzy pit up a game race, but finished second tae the lanky strides ay big Morag 'Jam Rag' Henderson. We wir lyin oan oor stomachs, heids propped up oan elbays n hands, watchin Lizzy struggle along wi the expression ay vicious determination which characterised everything she did. Everything? Once Tommy's over his loss, ah'll ask him about the sex. Naw ah winnae . . . aye ah will. Anywey, ah hears this heavy breathin and turns tae notice Begbie slowly swivellin his hips; starin at the lassies, gaun: — That wee Lizzy MacIntosh . . . total wee ride . . . fuckin shag the erse oafay that any day ay the week . . . the fuckin erse oan it . . . the fuckin tits oan it . . .

Then he lets his face faw doon oantae the turf. Ah wisnae as wary ay Begbie then as ah am now. He wisnae the main man in they days, jist another contender, n he wis also a bit shy ay ma brar, Billy, at the time. Tae some extent, in fact tae every extent, ah cynically lived oaf Billy's reputation, bein a closet sap. Anywey, ah pulled Begbie ower oantay his back, exposing his spunk drippin, earth-dirty knob. The cunt hud surreptitiously dug a hole in the soft turf wi his flick knife, and hud been fuckin the field. Ah wis pishin masel. Begbie wis n aw. The cunt wis lighter in they days, before he started tae believe his ain, and it must be said, oor, propaganda aboot him bein a total psychopath.

— Ya dirty cunt, Franco! Gary sais.

Begbie pits his knob away, zips up, then grabs a handfae ay spunk n earth n rubs it in Gary's face.

Ah'm nearly endin masel as Gary goes radge; standin up n bootin the sole ay Begbie's trainer. Then he storms away in the cream puff. Whin ah think aboot it, this is really a Begbie rather than a Lizzy story, though it wis her brave performance against the Jam Rag that precipitated it.

Anywey, whin Tommy copped fir Lizzy a couple ay year back, maist cunts thought: Lucky fuckin bastard. Even Sick Boy has never shagged Lizzy.

Amazingly, Tommy still husnae mentioned smack. Even wi ma works lying aw ower the place, n he can probably tell that ah'm pretty bombed. Normally Tommy's daein a bad impersonation ay ma auld lady in such circumstances; yir killin yirsel/pack it in/ye kin live yir life withoot that garbage, and other such shite.

Now he sais: — What does that stuff dae fir ye Mark? His voice is genuinely enquiring.

Ah shrug. Ah dinnae want tae talk aboot this. Thirs cunts wi degrees n diplomas at the Royal Ed n the City peyed tae go through aw this counselling shite wi us. It's done fuck-all good. Tommy's persistent though.

— Tell us Mark. Ah want tae ken.

But then, when ye think aboot it, mibbe mates, whae've stuck by ye through thick n thin, usually fuckin thin, deserve at least an attempt at an explanation, if the counsellors/thought polis get one. Ah launch intae a spiel. Ah feel surprisingly good, calm and clear, talkin aboot it.

— Ah don't really know, Tam, ah jist dinnae. It kinday makes things seem mair real tae us. Life's boring and futile. We start oaf wi high hopes, then we bottle it. We realise that we're aw gaunnae die, withoot really findin oot the big answers. We develop aw they long-winded ideas which jist interpret the reality ay oor lives in different weys, withoot really extending oor body ay worthwhile knowledge, about the big things, the real things. Basically, we live a short, disappointing life; and then we die. We fill up oor lives wi shite, things like careers and relationships tae delude oorsels that it isnae aw totally pointless. Smack's an honest drug, because it strips away these delusions. Wi smack, whin ye feel good, ye feel immortal. Whin ye feel bad, it intensifies the shite that's already thair. It's the only really honest drug. It doesnae alter yir consciousness. It just gies ye a hit and a sense ay well-being. Eftir that, ye see the misery ay the world as it is, and ye cannae anaesthetise yirsel against it.

— Shite, Tommy sais. Then: — Pure shite. He's probably right n aw. If he asked us the question last week, ah'd huv probably said something completely different. If he asks us the morn, it wid be something else again. At this point in time though, ah'll hing wi the concept that junk'll dae the business whin everything else seems boring and irrelevant.

Ma problem is, whenever ah sense the possibility, or realise the actuality ay attaining something that ah thought ah wanted, be it girlfriend, flat, job, education, money and so on, it jist seems so dull n sterile, that ah cannae value it any mair. Junk's different though. Ye cannae turn yir back oan it sae easy. It willnae let ye. Trying tae manage a junk problem is the ultimate challenge. It's also a fuckin good kick.

— It's also a fuckin good kick.

Tommy looks at us. — Gies a go. Gies a hit.

— Fuck off Tommy.

— Ye sais it's a good kick. Ah pure wantae try it.

— Ye dinnae. C'moan Tommy, take ma word fir it. This jist seems tae encourage the cunt mair.

— Ah've goat the hireys. C'moan. Cook us up a shot.

— Tommy . . . fuck sake man . . .

— Ah'm tellin ye, c'moan. Supposed tae be fuckin mates, ya cunt. Cook us up a shot. Ah kin fuckin handle it. One fuckin shot isnae gaunnae hurt us. C'moan.

Ah shrug n dae as Tommy requests. Ah gie ma works a good clean, then ah cook up a light shot and help him take it.

— This is pure fuckin brilliant Mark . . . it's a fuckin

rollercoaster ride man . . . ah'm fuckin buzzin here . . . ah'm jist pure buzzin . . .

His reaction is shitein us up. Some cunts are just so predisposed tae skag . . .

Later, when Tommy comes doon and is ready tae go, ah tell um: — Yuv done it mate. That's you goat the set now. Dope, acid, speed, E, mushies, nembies, vallies, smack, the fuckin lot. Knock it oan the heid. Make that the first n last time.

Ah said that because ah wis sure the cunt wis gaunnae ask us fir some tae take away wi him. Ah've no goat enough tae spare. Ah've *never* goat enough tae spare.

— Too fuckin right, he sais, flingin oan his jaykit.

When Tommy's gone, ah notice fir the first time thit ma cock's itchin like fuck. Ah cannae scratch it though. If ah start scratchin it, ah'll infect the bastard. Then ah've goat some real problems.

Traditional Sunday Breakfast

Oh my god, where the fuck am I. Where the fuck . . . I just don't recognise this room at all . . . think Davie, think. I can't seem to generate enough saliva to free my tongue from the roof of my mouth. What an arsehole. What a cunt . . . what a . . . never again.

OH FUCK . . . NO . . . please. No, no fuckin NO . . .

Please.

Don't let this be happening to me. Please. Surely no. Surely yes.

Yes. I woke up in a strange bed in a strange room, covered in my own mess. I had pished the bed. I had puked up in the bed. I had shat myself in the bed. My heid is fucking buzzing, and my guts are in a queasy turmoil. The bed is a mess, a total fucking mess.

I take the bottom sheet up, then remove the duvet cover and wrap them together; the pungent, toxic cocktail in the middle. It's bundled into a secure ball, with no sign of leakage. I turn the mattress over to conceal the damp patch, and go to the toilet; showering the crap off my chest, thighs and arse. I now know where I am: Gail's mother's house.

Fucking hell.

Gail's mother's. How did I get here? Who brought me here? Back in the room, I see that my clothes are neatly folded. Oh christ.

Who the fuck undressed me?

Try tracing back. It's now Sunday. Yesterday was Saturday. The semi-final at Hampden. I had got myself into some fucking state before and after the match. We've no chance, I thought, you never do at Hampden against one of the Old Firm, with the crowd and the referees firmly behind the establishment clubs. So instead of getting worked up about it, I just decided to have a good crack and make a day of it. I don't want to think about the day I made of it. I don't even remember whether or not I actually went to the game. Got on the Marksman bus at Duke Street with the Leith boys; Tommy, Rents and their mates. Fuckin heid-bangers. I remember fuck all after that pub in Rutherglen before the match; the space-cake and the speed, the acid and the dope, but most of all the drink, the bottle of vodka that I downed before we met in the pub to get onto the bus to get back into the pub . . .

Where Gail came into the picture, I'm no really sure. Fuck. So I get back into the bed, the mattress and duvet seeming cold without the sheets. A few hours later, Gail knocks at the door. Gail and I have been going out together for five weeks but have not yet had sex. Gail had said that she didn't want our relationship to start off on a physical basis, as that would be how it would principally be defined from them on in. She'd read this in *Cosmopolitan*, and wanted to test the theory. So five weeks on, I've got a pair of bollocks like watermelons. There's probably a fair bit of spunk alongside that pish, shite and puke.

— You were is some state last night David Mitchell, she said accusingly. Was she genuinely upset or playing at being upset? Difficult to tell. Then: — What happened to the covers? Genuinely upset.

— Eh, a wee accident Gail.

— Well, never mind that. Come downstairs. We're just about to have breakfast.

She left, and I wearily got dressed and tentatively crept down the stairs, wishing I was invisible. I take the bundle down with me, as I want to take it home and get it cleaned.

Gail's parents are sitting at the kitchen table. The sounds and smells of a traditional Sunday breakfast fry-up being prepared are nauseating. My guts do a quick somersault.

— Well, someone was in a state last night, Gail's Ma says, but to my relief, teasingly, and without anger.

I still flushed with embarrassment. Mr Houston, sitting at the kitchen table, tried to smooth things over for me.

— Ah well, it does ye good tae cut loose once in a while, he commented supportively.

— It would do this one good tae be tied up once in a while, Gail said, realising a minor *faux pas* as I raised ma eyebrows at her, unnoticed by her parents. A wee bit bondage would do me fine. Chance would be fine fucking thing . . .

— Eh, Mrs Houston, I point to the sheets, in a bundle at my

feet on the kitchen floor. — . . . Ah made a bit of a mess of the sheet and the duvet cover. Ah'm going tae take them home and clean them. Ah'll bring them back tomorrow.

— Aw, don't you worry about that, son. Ah'll just stick them in the washing machine. You sit down and get some breakfast.

— Naw, but, eh . . . a really bad mess. Ah feel embarrassed enough. Ah'd like tae take them home.

— Dearie dear, Mr Houston laughed.

— Now no, you sit down, son, ah'll see tae them, Mrs Houston stole across the floor towards me, and made a grab for the bundle. The kitchen was her territory, and she would not be denied. I pulled it to me, towards my chest; but Mrs Houston was as fast as fuck and deceptively strong. She got a good grip and pulled against me.

The sheets flew open and a pungent shower of skittery shite, thin alcohol sick, and vile pish splashed out across the floor. Mrs Houston stood mortified for a few seconds, then ran, heaving into the sink.

Brown flecks of runny shite stained Mr Houston's glasses, face and white shirt. It sprayed across the linoleum table and his food, like he had made a mess with watery chip-shop sauce. Gail had some on her yellow blouse.

Jesus fuck.

— God sake . . . god sake . . . Mr Houston repeated as Mrs Houston boaked and I made a pathetic effort to mop some of the mess back into the sheets.

Gail shot me a look of loathing and disgust. I can't see our relationship developing any further now. I'll never get Gail into bed. For the first time, that doesnae bother me. I just want out of here.

Junk Dilemmas No. 65

Suddenly it's cauld; very fuckin cauld. The candle's nearly melted doon. The only real light's comin fae the telly. Something black and white's on . . . but the telly's a black and white set so it was bound tae be something black and white . . . wi a colour telly, it wid be different . . . perhaps.

It's freezing, but movement only makes ye caulder; by making ye more aware that there's fuck all you can do, fuck all you can really do, tae get warm. At least if ah stey still ah can pretend to masel ah have the power tae make masel warm, by just moving aroond or switching the fire oan. The trick is tae be as still as possible. It's easier than dragging yourself across the flair tae switch that fuckin fire oan.

Somebody else is in the room wi us. It's Spud, ah think. It's hard tae tell in the dark.

— Spud . . . Spud . . .

He sais nothing.

— It's really fuckin cauld man.

Spud, if indeed it is the cunt, still says nothing. He could be deid, but probably no, because ah think his eyes are open. But that means fuck all.

Grieving and Mourning In Port Sunshine

Lenny looked at his cards, then scrutinised the expressions on his friends' faces.

— Whae's haudin? Billy, c'moan then ya cunt. Billy showed Lenny his hand.

— Two fuckin aces!

— Spawny bastard! You spawny fuckin cunt Renton. Lenny slammed his fist into his palm.

— Jist gies that fuckin loot ower here, Billy Renton said, raking up the pile of notes that lay in the centre of the floor.

— Naz. Chuck us a can ower then, Lenny asked. When the can was thrown over he missed his catch and it hit the floor. He opened it, and much of its contents gushed over Peasbo.

— Moantae fuck ya doss cunt!

— Sorry Peasbo. It's that cunt, Lenny laughed as he pointed at Naz. — Ah sais tae um tae chuck us a can ower, no tae fling it at ma fuckin heid.

Lenny rose and went to the window.

— Still nae sign ay the cunt? Naz asked. — The game's fucked withoot the big money.

— Naw. The cunt's patter's fuckin rotten, Lenny said.

— Gie the cunt a bell. Find oot whit the fuckin story is, Billy suggested.

— Aye. Right.

Lenny went into the lobby and dialled Phil Grant's number. He was upset at playing for this toytown stake. He would have been well up by now if Granty had shown up with the money.

The phone just rang.

— Nae cunt's in, or if they are, they arenae answerin the fuckin phone, he told them.

— Ah hope the fucker husnae absconded wi the fuckin loot, Peasbo laughed, but it was an uneasy laugh, the first open acknowledgement of a collective unspoken fear.

— Better no huv. Cannae stick a cunt thit rips oaf his mates, Lenny snarled.

— Whin ye think aboot it though, it's Granty's poppy. He kin spend it oan whit he likes, Jackie said.

They looked at him with bemused belligerence. Eventually Lenny spoke.

— Away ye fuckin go.

— In a wey though, the cunt won it fair n square. Ah ken what we agreed. Build up a big kitty wi the club money tae add a bit ay spice tae the caird games. Then divvi up. Ah ken aw that. Aw ah'm sayin is thit in the eyes ay the law . . . Jackie explained his position.

— It's aw oor poppy! Lenny snapped. — Granty kens the fuckin Hampden roar.

— Ah ken that. Aw ah'm sayin is thit in the eyes ay the law . . .

— Shut yir fuckin mooth ya stirrin cunt, Billy interjected, — wir no talkin aboot the eyes ay the fuckin law here. Wir talkin aboot mates. If it wis up tae the eyes ay the fuckin law you'd huv nae furniture in yir hoose ya gypo cunt.

Lenny nodded approvingly at Billy.

— Wir jumpin tae fuckin conclusions here. Might be a perfectly good reason as tae why the cunt isnae here. Mibbe he's goat held up, Naz suggested, his pock-marked face taut and tense.

— Mibbe some cunt's mugged the cunt n taken the poppy, Jackie said.

— Nae cunt wid try tae mug Granty. He's the kind ay cunt thit mugs cunts, no gits mugged fae thum. If he comes in here pullin a stunt like that, ah'll tell um whair tae fuckin go. Lenny was in a state of some anxiety. This was the club money they were talking about.

— Jist sayin thit it's daft tae be cairryin that type ay cash aroond. That's aw ah'm sayin, Jackie stated. He was a little frightened of Lenny.

Granty had not missed a Thursday night card session in six years, unless he was on holiday. He was the reliable lynchpin of the school. Lenny and Jackie had both missed periods through doing time for assault and housebreaking respectively.

The club money, the holiday money, had been a remnant of

the time they had all gone to Loret De Mar on holiday together, as teenagers. Now older, they generally went in smaller groups, or with wives or girlfriends. The strange mixing up of the card money and the club money occurred a couple of years ago when they were drunk. Peasbo, then the treasurer, jokingly threw in a wad of the club money as his stake. They played with it, for a laugh. They liked the feel of playing with all that money, got such a buzz from it, that they divvied it up and played pretend games with it. Whenever they decided that they were into serious saving, they would stop playing cards for 'real' money, and play for 'club' money. It was just like playing for monopoly money.

There were times, particularly when someone 'won' the entire pot, like Granty last week, that the bizarre and dangerous nature of their actions crossed their mind. They were mates though, and it was generally assumed that they would never do the dirty on each other. However, logic as well as loyalty underpinned this assumption. They all had ties in the area, and could never leave it for good, and not for just the £2,000 in the kitty. Leaving the area was what it would mean if one ripped off the rest. They told themselves this over and over again. The real fear was theft. The money was more secure in a bank. It had been a silly indulgence gone mad, a collective insanity.

The next morning there still no sign of Granty, and Lenny was late signing on.

— Mister Lister. You only live around the corner from this office, and you only have to sign on once every fortnight. It's hardly an excessive demand, Gavin Temperley, the clerk, told him in pompous tones.

— Ah understand the position ay your fuckin oafice, Mister Temperley. But ah'm sure thit yill take intae consideration thit ah'm a fuckin busy man wi several flourishin enterprises tae look eftir.

— Shite, Lenny. Lazy cunt thit ye are. Ah'll see ye in the Crown. Ah'm oan first lunch. Be thair it the back ay twelve.

— Aye. Ye'll need tae gie us a bung though Gav. Ah'm fuckin brassic until this rent cheque hits the mat the morn.

— Nae problem.

Lenny went down to the pub and sat at the bar with his *Daily Record* and a pint of lager. He considered lighting a cigarette, then decided against it. It was 11.04 and he'd had twelve fags already. It was always the same when he was forced to rise in the morning. He smoked far too many fags. He could cut down by staying in bed, so he generally didn't get up until 2 p.m. These Government cunts were determined, he thought, to wreck both his health and finances by forcing him up so early.

The back pages of the *Record* were full of Rangers/Celtic shite as usual. Souness spys on some fucker in the English second division, McNeill says Celts' confidence is coming back. Nothing about Hearts. No. A wee bit about Jimmy Sandison, with the same quote twice, and the short passage finishing in mid-sentence. There's also a small space on why Miller of Hibs still thinks he's the best man for the job, when they've only scored three goals in the last thirty games or something like that.

Lenny turned to page three. He preferred the scantily clad women the *Record* featured to the topless ones in the *Sun*. You had to have some imagination.

From the corner of his eye he spotted Colin Dalglish.

— Coke, he said, without looking up from his paper.

Coke pushed up a barstool alongside Lenny's. He ordered a pint of heavy. — Heard the news? Fuckin sad eh?

— Eh?

— Granty . . . ye didnae hear? . . . Coke looked straight at Lenny.

— Naw. Wha . . .

— Deid. Potted heid.

— Yir jokin! Eh? Gies a fuckin brek ya cunt . . .

— Gen up. Last night, likes.

— Whit the fuck happened . . .

— Ticker. Boom. Coke snapped his fingers. — Dodgy hert, apparently. Nae cunt kent aboot it. Perr Granty wis workin wi Pete Gilleghan, oan the side likesay. It wis jist aboot five, n Granty wis helpin Pete tidy up, ready tae shoot the craw n that likes, whin he jist hauds his chist n cowps ower. Gilly gits an ambulance, n they take the perr cunt tae the hoespital, but he dies a couple ay ooirs later. Perr Granty. Good cunt n aw. You play cairds wi the guy, eh?

— Eh . . . aye . . . one ay the nicest cunts ye could hope tae meet. That's gutted us, that hus.

A few hours later, Lenny was guttered as well as gutted. He'd tapped twenty quid off Gav Temperley for the sole purpose of getting rat-arsed. When Peasbo entered the pub late afternoon, Lenny was slurring into the ear of a sympathetic barmaid and an embarrassed and sober-looking guy in a boilersuit with a Tennent's Lager logo on it.

— . . . one ay the nicest fuckin cunts ye could hope tae meet . . .

— Awright Lenny. Ah heard the news. Peasbo grabbed one of Lenny's broad shoulders heavily. A firm grip, to ensure that *one* of his mates was still there, and to make a partial assessment of his level of drunkenness.

— Peasbo. Aye. Still cannae fuckin believe it . . . one ay the nicest cunts ye could hope tae meet n aw . . . He turned slowly back to the barmaid and refocused his gaze on her. With his thumb protruding from a clenched fist, he then pointed over his shoulder at Peasbo. — . . . this cunt'll tell ye . . . eh Peasbo? See Granty? One ay the nicest cunts any cunt could ivir hope tae meet . . . eh Peasbo? Granty? Eh?

— Aye, it's a real shock. Ah still cannae believe it man.

— That's it! One day the boy's here, now wir nivir gaunnae see the perr cunt again . . . twenty-seven year auld. The game's no straight, ah'll tell ye that for fuck all. The game's no straight . . . sure n it's fuckin no . . .

— Granty wis twenty-nine, wis eh no? Peasbo quizzed.

— Twenty-seven, twenty-nine . . . who gies a fuck? Jist a young boy. It's his burd n that wee bairn thit ah feel sorry fir . . . ye git some ay they auld cunts . . . Lenny gestured angrily over to the corner across to a group of old guys playing dominos. — . . . they've hud thair lives! Long fuckin lives! Aw they dae is moan like fuck! Granty nivir complained aboot fuck all. One ay the nicest cunts ye could hope tae meet.

He then noted three younger guys, known as Spud, Tommy and Second Prize, sitting across the other side of the pub.

— N they fuckin junky mates ay Billy's brar. They cunts, aw fuckin dyin ay AIDS. Killing thumsels. Serves the cunts right. Granty fuckin valued life. They cunts ur flingin thairs away! Lenny glowered over at them, but they were too into their own conversation to notice him.

— C'moan now Lenny. Keep the heid. Nae cunt's sayin nought against nae cunt. They boys ur awright. That's Danny Murphy. Harmless cunt. Tommy Laurence, you ken Tommy, n that guy Rab, Rab McLaughlin, used tae be a good fitba player. Man United he went doon tae. They boys ur sound. Fuck sakes, thir mates ay that mate ay yours, the boy thit works fir the dole. What's his name, Gav.

— Aye . . . but these auld cunts . . . Conceding the point, Lenny switched his attention back over to the other side of the room.

— Ah, come oan Lenny, fuck it. Harmless cunts, no botherin anybody. Down that pint, n we'll go roond fir Naz. Ah'll bell Billy n Jackie.

The mood was gloomy round at Naz's flat in Buchanan Street. They had turned away from the issue of Granty's death, onto the subject of the outstanding cash.

— The Friday before divvy day n the cunt fuckin snuffs it. One thousand n eight hundred he wis haudin. Split six weys that's three hunner each, Billy moaned.

— No much we kin dae aboot it, Jackie ventured.

— Like fuck thir isnae. That dough gits divvied every fuckin year, the fortnight before trades. Ah've booked Benidorm oan the strength ay that. Ah'm fuckin brassic without it. Sheila'll huv ma baws fir a game ay pool if ah cancel oot. Nae fuckin wey man, Naz declared.

— Too fuckin right. Ah feel sorry fir Fiona n the bairn n that, obviously. Any cunt wid. Goes withoot sayin, likes. Boatum line is, it's oor fuckin poppy, no hers. Billy said.

— It's oor ain fuckin fault. Ah knew somethin like this wid happen, Jackie shrugged.

The doorbell went. In came Lenny and Peasbo.

— S awright fir you, ya cunt. You're fuckin flush, Naz challenged.

Jackie didn't respond. He picked up a can of lager from the pile Peasbo had dumped on the floor.

— Fuckin terrible news, eh boys? Peasbo said, as Lenny morosely slurped on his can.

— One ay the nicest cunts ye could hope tae meet, Lenny said.

Naz was grateful for Lenny's intervention. He was ready to commiserate about the money, when he realised that Peasbo had been referring to Granty.

— Ah ken ye shouldnae be selfish at a time like this, but thirs the question ay the poppy tae sort oot. Divvy day's next week. Ah've goat a hoaliday tae book. Ah need they hireys, Billy said.

— Some cunt you Billy, eh? Kin we no fuckin wait until the perr cunt's still no warm before we go oan aboot aw that shite? Lenny sneered.

— Fiona might blow the fuckin lot! She'll no ken it's oor dosh if nae cunt tells her. She'll be gaun through his fuckin things, n it'll be, aye, aye, what's this? Nearly two grand. Tidy. Then she'll be oaf tae the fuckin Caribbean or somewhere while we're sittin in the fuckin Links wi a couple ay boatils ay cider fir the trades.

— Yir patter's fuckin abysmal, Billy, Lenny told him.

Peasbo looked gravely at Lenny, who could feel a betrayal coming on.

— Hate tae say it Lenny, but Billy's no far wrong. Granty didnae exactly keep Fiona in the lap ay luxury, great cunt as he wis likesay. Ah mean, dinnae git us wrong, ah'd nivir hear a word said against the cunt, but ye find two grand in yir hoose, ye spend first, n ask questions eftir. You would. Ah'm fuckin sure ah wid. Every cunt wid, if the fuckin truth be telt.

— Aw aye? Whae's askin her fir it then? Fucked if ah'm gaunnae, Lenny hissed.

— We aw will. It's aw oor poppy, Billy said.

— Right. Eftir the funeral. Oan Tuesday, Naz suggested.

— Awright, Peasbo agreed.

— Aye, Jackie shrugged.

Lenny nodded in a weary compliance. It was, he conceded, their poppy . . .

Tuesday came and went. Nobody could work up the bottle to say anything at the funeral. They all got drunk and offered more laments to Granty. The cash issue was never mentioned until late on. They met, with evil hangovers, the following afternoon, and went to Fiona's place.

Nobody answered the door.

— Probably steyin at her Ma's, Lenny said.

The woman from the flat across the landing, a grey-haired lady in a blue print dress, came out.

— Fiona left this mornin boys. Canary Islands. Left the bairn at her Ma's. She seemed to enjoy breaking the news.

— Tidy, Billy muttered.

— That's that then, Jackie said with a shrug which was a bit too smug for the liking of most of his friends. — No much we kin dae aboot it.

He was then stunned by a blow to the side of his face, delivered by Billy, which knocked him over, and sent him sprawling down the stairs. He managed to break his fall by grabbing the banister, and looked up at Billy in horror from the bend in the stair.

The rest of them were almost as shocked as Jackie by Billy's actions.

— Easy Billy. Lenny grabbed Billy's arm, but kept his gaze on his face. He was anxious and intrigued to find out the source of his outrage. — Yir ootay order. S'no Jackie's fault.

— Aw is it no? Ah kept ma fuckin gob shut, but this smart cunt's pushed us far enough. He pointed at the still prostrate figure of Jackie, whose rapidly swelling face had gained a new furtiveness.

— Whit's the fuckin score here? Naz asked.

Billy ignored him, and looked straight at Jackie. — How long's it been gaun oan Jackie?

— Whit's the cunt oan aboot? Jackie said, but his watery voice lacked assurance.

— Canary Islands ma fuckin hole. Whair ur ye meetin Fiona?

— You're fuckin tapped Billy. Ye heard whit the wifey sais, Jackie shook his head.

— Fiona's ma Sharon's fuckin sister. Ye think ah go aroond wi ma fuckin ears shut? How long ye been fuckin pokin her, Jackie?

— That wis a fuckin one oaf . . .

Billy's outrage filled the stair, and he could feel it growing, swelling, in the bre sts of the others. He stood over Jackie like a booming Old Testament god, scorning him in his judgement.

— One oaf ma hole! An whae's tae fuckin say thit Granty didnae ken? Whaes's tae say it wisnae that thit killed um? His so-called best fuckin mate, shaftin his burd!

Lenny looked at Jackie, shaking with anger. He then looked at the others, their eyes blazing. An unspoken contract was forged between them in a split-second.

Jackie's screams reverberated around the stairwell, as they booted and dragged him from landing to landing. He vainly tried to protect himself and, through his fear and pain, hoped that there would be something left of him to move out of Leith, when the ordeal was over.

Kicking Again

Inter Shitty

Oh ya cunt ye! Ma heid's fuckin nippin this mornin, ah kin fuckin tell ye. Ah make straight fir the fuckin fridge. Yes! Two boatils ay Becks. That'll dae me. Ah down the cunts in double quick time. Ah feel better right away. Huvtae fuckin watch the time, but.

She's still fuckin sleepin whin ah go back ben the bedroom. Look at her; lazy, fat cunt. Jist cause she's huvin a fuckin bairn, thinks it gies her the right tae lie aroond aw fuckin day . . . anywey, that's another fuckin story. So ah git fuckin packin . . . that cunt hud better huv washed ma fuckin jeans . . . the 501s . . . whair's they fuckin 501s? . . . thair they are. Jist as well fir her.

She's wakin up now. — Frank . . . what ur ye daein? Whair ur ye gaun? she sais tae us.

— Ah'm ootay here. Fuckin sharpish, ah sais, no lookin roond. Whair the fuck's they soacks . . . everything takes twice as fuckin long whin yir hungower n ah kin dae withoot this cunt nippin ma fuckin heid.

— Whair ur ye gaun? Whair!

— Ah telt ye, ah've goat tae fuckin nash. Me n Lexo pulled a bit ay business oaf. Ah'm sayin nae mair oan the fuckin subject, but it's best ah disappear fir a couple ay weeks. Any polis cunts come tae the door, yuv no seen us fir yonks. Ye think ah'm oan the fuckin rigs, right. Yuv no seen us, mind.

— But whair ur ye gaun Frank? Whair ur ye fuckin well gaun?

— That's fir me tae ken n you tae find oot. What ye dinnae fuckin well ken they cannae fuckin well beat oot ay ye, ah sais.

Then the fuckin boot gits up n starts fuckin screamin it us, saying thit ah cannae jist fuckin go like that. Ah punches it in the fuckin mooth, n boots it in the fuckin fanny, n the cunt faws tae the flair, moanin away. It's her fuckin fault, ah've telt the cunt thit that's what happens when any cunt talks tae us like that. That's the fuckin rules ay the game, take it or fuckin leave it.

— THE BAIRN! THE BAIRN! . . . she screams.

Ah jist goes: — THE BAIRN! THE BAIRN! back at her, likes.

— Shut yir fuckin mooth aboot the fuckin bairn! She's jist lyin thair, screamin like some fuckin tube.

It's probably no even ma fuckin bairn anyway. Besides, ah've hud bairns before, wi other lassies. Ah ken whit it's aw aboot. She thinks it's aw gaunnae be fuckin great whin the bairn comes, but she's in fir a fuckin shock. Ah kin tell ye aw aboot fuckin bairns. Pain in the fuckin erse.

Shavin gear. That's what ah fuckin need. Kent thir wis somethin.

She's still gaun oan aboot how she's aw sair n tae git the fuckin doaktir n aw that. Ah've nae fuckin time fir that shite but, ah'm fuckin late is it is thanks tae that cunt. Goat tae fuckin nash.

— FRRRAAAANNNK! she shouts as ah git ootay the fuckin door. Ah wis thinkin tae masel, it's like the fuckin advert fir Harp lager: 'Time fir a sharp exit'; that wis me awright.

It wis fuckin stowed oot doon the pub, early fuckin doors n aw. Renton, the rid-heided cunt, pots the fuckin black baw tae take the game fi Matty.

— Rab! Pit ma fuckin name up fir the pool then. Whit's every cunt fuckin wantin? Ah git up tae the bar.

Rab, the Second Prize, as we caw the cunt, he's goat a fuckin stoatir ay an eye. Some fuckin liberty-taker's been oan the cunt's case.

— Rab. Whae the fuck did this tae ye?

— Aw, a couple ay guys up Lochend, ken. Ah wis bevvied. The cunt looks at us, aw fuckin sheepish like.

— Goat names?

— Naw, but dinnae worry, ah'll git the cunts man, it's aw sorted oot.

— Be sure ye fuckin dae. D'ye ken the cunts?

— Naw, by sight, like.

— Whin me n Rents git back fae fuckin London, we'll go up tae fuckin Lochend. Dawsy goat filled in up thair a wee bit back. Thir's some questions need fuckin answering, sure n thir fuckin is.

Ah turns tae Rents: — Aw set ma man?

— Rarin tae go, Franco.

Ah racks up n slaughters the cunt, leavin the fucker two baws oaf bein grannied. — Ye might be able tae fuckin handle the likes ay Matty n Secks, bit whin Hurricane Franco gits oan the fuckin table, ye kin firget it, ya rid-heided cunt, ah tells um.

— Pool's fir arseholes man, he sais. Humpty cunt. Everything that rid-heided cunt's shite at's fir arseholes, accordin tae that cunt.

Wuv goat tae be movin, so thirs nae sense in playing any mair. Ah looks ower tae Matty n pills oot a wad. — Hi Matty! Ken whit this is? Ah waves the notes it the cunt.

— Eh . . . aye . . . he sais.

Ah points tae the bar: — Ken whit that is?

— Eh . . . aye . . . the bar. The cunt's slow. Too fuckin slow. N ah ken how.

— Ken whit this is? ah points tae ma pint.

— Eh . . . aye . . .

— Well dinnae make us fuckin spell it oot fir ye then, ya cunt. Pint ay fuckin Special n a Jack Daniels n coke then, cunt!

He comes ower, n sais tae us: — Eh Frank, ah'm a wee bit short, ken . . .

Ah ken how, awright. — Mibbe ye'll fuckin grow, ah sais. The cunt takes the hint, n hits the bar. He's fuckin usin again, that's if the cunt ivir really stoaped in the first fuckin place. Whin ah git back fae London, ah'll need tae huv another wee word in this cunt's ear. Fuckin junkies. A waste ay fuckin space. Rents's still clean though. Ye kin tell by the wey he's tannin the bevvy.

Ah'm lookin forward tae this London brek. Rents's goat his mate's flat, that Tony cunt n his burd, the shag, fir a couple ay weeks. Thair oan hoaliday somewhair. Ah ken a couple ay boys doon thair fae the jail; ah'll look the cunts up, fir auld times' sake.

That Lorraine's servin Matty. She's a fuckin wee ride. Ah goes ower tae the bar.

— Hi, Lorraine! C'mere the now. Ah pushes her hair back at the side ay her face n pits ma fingers behind her ears. Burds like that. Erogenous fuckin zones n aw that. — Ye kin tell whithir or no somebody's hud sex last night by feelin behind thir ears. The heat, ken? ah explains.

She jist laughs, n so does Matty.

— Naw, but it's fuckin scientific n aw that, ken? Some cunt's ur fuckin clueless.

— Hus Lorraine hud sex last night then? Matty asks. The wee cunt looks fuckin awfay, like death warmed up.

— That's oor secret, eh doll? ah sais tae her. Ah've goat a feelin thit she's goat the hoats fir us, cause she ey goes that fuckin quiet, shy wey whin ah fuckin talk tae her. Once ah git back fae London, ah'll fuckin move in thair, pretty fuckin sharpish n aw, ya cunt.

Fucked if ah'm gaunnae stey wi that fuckin June eftir the bairn's here. N that cunt's deid if she's made us hurt that fuckin bairn. Ivir since she's been huvin that bairn, she thinks she kin git fuckin lippy wi us. Nae cunt gits fuckin lippy wi me, bairn or nae fuckin bairn. She kens that, n she still gits fuckin smart. See if anything's happened tae that fuckin bairn . . .

— Hi Franco, Rents sais, — we'd better be movin. Wuv goat that cairry-oot tae organise, mind.

— Aye, right. What ye gittin?

— Boatil ay voddy n a few cans.

Might've guessed. Hates a fuckin voddy, that rid-heided cunt.

— Ah'm gittin a boatil ay J.D. n eight cans ay Export. Ah might git Lorraine tae fill up a couple ay draftpaks n aw.

— Thill be a couple ay draftpaks gittin well filled up oan the train gaun doon, he sais. Sometimes ah dinnae understand that cunt's sense ay humour. Me n Rents go back a long fuckin wey, but it's like the cunt's changed, n ah'm no jist takin aboot the drugs n that shite. It's like, he's goat his weys n ah've goat mines. Still a great cunt though, the rid-heided bastard.

So ah gits the draftpaks, one fill ay spesh fir me, n one fill ay lager fir that rid-heided cunt. We gits the cairry-oot n jumps a Joe Baxi up the toon n down a quick pint at that pub in the station. Ah gits crackin tae this cunt it the bar; boy fi Fife, ah kent the cunt's brar in Saughton. No a bad gadge as ah remember. Harmless cunt likes.

The London train's fuckin mobbed. This really gits ma fuckin goat, this. Ah mean, ye pey aw that fuckin dough fir a ticket, they British Rail cunts urnae fuckin shy, n then thir's nae fuckin seats! Fuck that.

Wir strugglin wi they cans n boatils. Ma cairry-oot's aboot tae burst oot the fuckin bag. It's aw they cunts wi backpacks n luggage . . . n bairns' fuckin go-carts. Shouldnae huv bairns oan a fuckin train.

— Fuckin mobbed man, Rents sais.

— The fuckin trouble is, aw they cunts thit uv booked seats. It's no sae bad bookin fae Edinburgh tae London, capital fuckin cities n that, bit it's aw they cunts thit've booked fae Berwick n aw they fuckin places. The train shouldnae stoap n aw they places; it should jist be Edinburgh tae London, end ay fuckin story. If ah hud ma fuckin wey, that wid be it, ah kin fuckin tell ye. Some cunts ur lookin at us. Ah speak ma fuckin mind, whitivir any cunt sais.

Aw they booked seats. Fuckin liberty, so it is. It should be first fuckin come, first fuckin served. Aw this bookin seats shite . . . ah'll gie the cunts bookin fuckin seats . . .

Rents sits doon beside they two burds. Fuckin tidy n aw. Good fuckin choice by the rid-heided cunt!

— These seats ur free until Darlington, he sais.

Ah grabs the reservation cairds n sticks thum in ma tail. — Thir fuckin free the whole wey doon now. Ah'll gie the cunts bookin, ah sais, smilin at one ay the burds. Too fuckin right n aw. Forty quid a fuckin ticket. No shy they British Rail cunts, ah kin fuckin tell ye. Rents jist shrugs his shoodirs. The posey cunt's goat that green basebaw cap oan. That's gaun oot the fuckin windae if the cunt fuckin faws asleep, ah kin fuckin tell ye.

Rents is tannin the voddy, n wir jist near Portybelly whin the cunt's awready made a big fuckin dent in it. Hates a voddy, that rid-heided cunt. Well, if that's the wey the cunt wants tae fuckin play it . . . ah grabs the J.D. n swigs it back.

— Here we go, here we go, here we go . . . ah sais. That cunt jist smiles. He keeps lookin ower it the burds, thir likesay American, ken. Problem wi that rid-heided cunt is thit he's no goat the gift ay the gab is far is burds go, likes, even if the cunt dis huv a certain style. No likesay me n Sick Boy. Mibbe it's wi him huvin brars instead ay sisters, he jist cannae really fuckin relate tae burds. Ye wait oan that cunt tae make the first fuckin move, ye'll be waitin a long fuckin time. Ah fuckin show the rid-heided cunt how it's done.

— No fuckin shy, they British Rail cunts, eh? ah sais, nudgin the burd next tae us.

— Pardon? it sais tae us, sortay soundin likes, 'par-dawn' ken?

— Whair's it yis come fae then?

— Sorry, I can't really understand you . . . These foreign cunts've goat trouble wi the Queen's fuckin English, ken. Ye huv tae speak louder, slower, n likesay mair posh, fir the cunts tae understand ye.

— WHERE . . . DO . . . YOU . . . COME . . . FROM?

That dis the fuckin trick. These nosey cunts in front ay us look roond. Ah stares back at the cunts. Some fucker's oan a burst mooth before the end ay this fuckin journey, ah kin see that now.

— Ehm . . . we're from Toronto, Canada.

— Tirawnto. That wis the Lone Ranger's mate, wis it no? ah sais. The burds jist look it us. Some punters dinnae fuckin understand the Scottish sense ay humour.

— Where are you from? the other burd sais. Pair ay rides n aw. That rid-heided cunt made a good fuckin move sittin here, ah kin tell ye.

— Edinburgh, Rents goes, tryin tae sound aw fuckin posh, ken. Fuckin smarmy rid-heided cunt. He's aw ready tae steam in now, aw Joe-fuckin-Cool, once Franco breks the fuckin ice.

These burds ur gaun oantay us aboot how fuckin beautiful Edinburgh is, and how lovely the fuckin castle is oan the hill ower the gairdins n aw that shite. That's aw they tourist cunts ken though, the castle n Princes Street, n the High Street. Like whin Monny's auntie came ower fae that wee village oan that Island oaf the west coast ay Ireland, wi aw her bairns.

The wifey goes up tae the council fir a hoose. The council sais tae her, whair's it ye want tae fuckin stey, like? The woman sais, ah want a hoose in Princes Street lookin oantay the castle. This wifey's fuckin scoobied likes, speaks that fuckin Gaelic is a first language; disnae even ken that much English. Perr cunt jist liked the look ay the street whin she came oaf the train, thoat the whole fuckin place wis like that. The cunts it the council jist laugh n stick the cunt n one ay they hoatline joabs in West Granton, thit nae cunt else wants. Instead ay a view ay the castle, she's goat a view ay the gasworks. That's how it fuckin works in real life, if ye urnae a rich cunt wi a big fuckin hoose n plenty poppy.

Anywey, they burds take a wee bevvy wi us, n Rents is pretty steamboats, cause ah'm feelin it n aw n ah kin drink that rid-heided cunt under the fuckin table any fuckin day ay the week. Mind you, ah wis oan the pish last night wi Lexo, eftir we pilled that joab it the jewellers it Corstorphine. That explains how ah feel that fuckin pished now. Whit ah really fancy now though, is a game ay cairds.

— Git the cairds oot Rents.

— Nivir brought any, he sais. Ah dinnae fuckin believe that cunt! Last thing ah fuckin sais tae um the other night wis: Mind the fuckin cairds.

—Ah telt ye tae mind the fuckin cairds, ya doss cunt! Whit wis the last fuckin thing ah sais tae ye the other night? Eh? Mind the fuckin cairds!

— Jist forgot, the cunt goes. Ah bet the rid-heided cunt's forgot they fuckin cairds oan purpose. It's fuckin borin withoot cairds eftir a bit.

That fuckin borin cunt starts readin a fuckin book; bad fuckin manners, then him n this Canadian burd, thir baith sortay students like, start talkin aboot aw the fuckin books thuv read. It's gettin oan ma fuckin tits. Wir supposed tae be doon here fir a fuckin laugh, no tae talk aboot fuckin books n aw that fuckin shite. See if it wis up tae me, ah'd git ivray fuckin book n pit thum on a great big fuckin pile n burn the fuckin loat. Aw books ur fir is fir smart cunts tae show oaf aboot how much shite thuv fuckin read. Ye git aw ye fuckin need tae ken ootay the paper n fae the telly. Posin cunts. Ah'll gie thum fuckin books . . .

Wi stoap it Darlington n these cunts git oan, checkin thir tickets against oor seat numbers. The train's still fuckin stowed, so they cunts ur fucked fir a seat.

— Excuse me, these are our seats. We booked them, this cunt sais, flashin a ticket in front ay us.

— I'm afraid there must be some mistake, Rents sais. The rid-heided cunt kin be quite fuckin stylish, ah huv tae gie um that; he's goat style. — There were no cards to indicate a seat reservation when we boarded the train at Edinburgh.

— But we've got the reserved tickets here, this cunt wi the John Lennon specs sais.

— Well, I can only suggest that you pursue your complaint with a member of the British Rail staff. My friend and I took these seats in good faith. I'm afraid we can't be held responsible for any errors made by British Rail. Thank you, and goodnight, he sais, startin tae laugh, the rid-heided cunt thit he is. Ah wis like too busy enjoyin the cunt's performance tae tell they cunts tae git tae fuck. Ah fuckin hate hassle, but this John Lennon cunt'll no be telt.

— We have tickets here. That's proof that these are our seats, the cunt sais. That's it.

— Hi you! ah sais. — Aye, you, lippy cunt! He turns roond. Ah stands up. — Ye heard whit the gadge sais. Oan yir fuckin bike, ya specky radge! C'moan . . . move it! ah points doon the fuckin train.

— Come on Clive, his mate sais. The cunts fuck off. Jist is fuckin well fir thaim. So ah thought that wis endy fuckin story, bit naw, these cunts come back wi this ticket gadge.

The ticket boy, ye kin see the cunt doesnae really gie a fuck, the perr cunt's jist daein his joab, starts gaun oan aboot it bein they cunts' seats, bit ah jist tells the boy straight.

— Ah'm no fuckin carin what they cunts've goat oan thir fuckin tickets, mate. Thir wis nae fuckin reservation notices oan they fuckin seats whin we fuckin sat doon in thum. Wir no fuckin movin now. That's aw thir is tae it. Ye charge enough fir yir fuckin tickets, make sure thirs a fuckin sign up the next time.

— Somebody must have taken it down, he sais. This cunt'll dae nowt.

— Mibbe they did, mibbe they didnae. That's no ma fuckin

business. Like ah sais, the seats wir free, n ah wis right fuckin in thair. End ay fuckin story.

The ticket boy jist gits intae an argument wi they cunts, eftir tellin thum thit thirs nowt he kin fuckin dae. Ah jist leave thum tae it. Thir threatenin tae complain aboot the guy, n he's gitting stroppy back.

One cunt in the seat in front's lookin roond again.

— You goat a fuckin problem mate? ah shouts ower. The cunt gits a beamer n turns roond. Shitein cunt.

Rents faws asleep. The rid-heided cunt's pished oot ay his fuckin skull. His draftpak's half-empty n maist ay the cans've been tanned. Ah takes his draftpak tae the bogs wi us, empties a bit oot, n fills it up tae the same level wi ma pish. That's what the cunt gits fir forgettin the fuckin cairds. Thir's aboot two parts lager, one part pish in it.

Ah gits back n slips it intae place. The cunt's fast asleep, so's one ay the burds. The other's goat her fuckin heid intae that book. Two rides. Dinnae ken whither ah'd rather shag the big fuckin blonde piece or the dark-heided yin the maist.

Ah wakes up that rid-heided cunt at Peterborough. — C'moan Rents. Yir fuckin strugglin wi that fuckin bevvy. A fuckin sprinter, that's aw you are. A sprinter'll nivir fuckin stand the pace wi a distance man.

— Nae problem . . . the cunt sais, takin a big fuckin swig oot ay the draftpak. He screws his face up. It's hard no tae fuckin pish masel.

— The lager's loupin. Seems tae huv gone dead flat, ken. Tastes like fuckin pish.

Ah'm daein ma best tae haud it in. — Stoap makin fuckin excuses, ya crappin cunt.

— Ah'll still drink it like, the cunt goes. Ah try tae look oot the windae, wi that daft cunt finishing the fuckin loat.

Ah'm really fuckin ootay it by the time we hit Kings Cross. They burds've fucked oaf; ah thoat we wir oantae a fuckin good thing thair n aw, n ah sortay loast Rents comin oaf the train. Ah've even goat that rid-heided cunt's bag instead ay ma ain. That cunt better huv mines. Ah dinnae even ken the fuckin address . . . but then ah clocks the rid-heided cunt talkin tae this wee cunt wi a plastic cup ootside the entrance tae the tube. Rents's goat ma fuckin bag. Lucky fir him, the cunt.

— Any change fir the boy Franco? Rents sais, n this daft-lookin wee cunt hauds oot the fuckin cup; lookin it us wi they fuckin sappy eyes.

— Git tae fuck ya gypo cunt! ah sais, knockin the cup oot ay his hand, n fuckin pishin masel it the daft cunt scramblin aroond oan the deck between cunts' legs, tae git his fuckin coins.

— Whair the fuck's this flat then? ah sais tae Rents.

— No far, Rents sais, lookin it us like ah wis fuckin . . . the wey that cunt looks it ye sometimes . . . he's gaunnae git a sair face one ay they fuckin days, mates or nae fuckin mates. Then the cunt jist turns away n ah follay um doon oantae the Victoria Line.

Na Na and Other Nazis

The Fit ay Leith Walk is really likes, mobbed oot man. It's too hot for a fair-skinned punter, likesay, ken? Some cats thrive in the heat, but the likes ay me, ken, we jist cannae handle it. Too severe a gig man.

Another total downer is being skint, likesay. Pure Joe Strummer, man. Aw ye dae is walk aroond n check people oot, ken. Every cat's dead palsy-walsy likesay, but once they suss that you're brassic lint, they sortay just drift away intae the shadows . . .

Ah clock Franco at Queen Sticky-Vicky's statue, talkin tae this big dude, a mean hombre called Lexo; a casual acquaintance, if ye catch ma drift. Funny scene, likesay, how aw the psychos seem tae ken each other, ken what ah mean, likes? Such alliances are unholy man, just unholy . . .

— Spud! Awright ya cunt! How's it gaun? The Beggar is one high catboy.

— Eh, no sae bad likesay, Franco . . . yirsel?

— Barry, he sais, turnin tae this square-shaped mountain beside um. — Ye ken Lexo, a statement likesay, no a question. Ah just sortay nods, ken, and the big hombre looks at us for a second, then turns and talks tae Franco again.

Ah can tell that those cats have, likesay, binliners tae slash open, n rubbish tae rummage through. So ah sortay sais, like: — Eh . . . goat tae nash like, catch yis later.

— Haud oan mate. How ye fixed? Franco asks us.

— Eh, basically man, ah'm totally brassic. Ah've goat thirty-two pence in ma poakit and a pound in ma account at the Abbey National. No really the kind ay investment portfolio tae cause the Charlotte Square dudes sleepless nights, likesay.

Franco slips us two tenners. Nice one, the Beggar-boy.

— Nae skag now, ya radge cunt! he gently chides us, likesay. — Gie us a bell at the weekend, or come doon fir us well.

Did ah ever say anything derogatory against ma man Franco? Well, likesay . . . he's no a bad punter. Pure jungle cat, ken, but even jungle cats sit doon n huv a wee purr tae themselves now and again, likesay, usually after they've likes, devoured somebody. Ah sortay cannae help wondering who Franco n Lexo's devoured, likesay. Frankie-baby wis doon in London wi Rents, hidin oot fae the labdicks. What had the boy been up tae? Sometimes it's better no tae ken. In fact, it's always better no tae ken, likesay.

Ah cut through Woolies, which is busy, likesay, really busy. The security dude's engrossed in chatting up this sexy catgirl on the checkout likesay, so ah pocket a set ay blank tapes . . . the pulse races, then slowly dips . . . it's a good feeling, likesay, the best . . . well maybe second best behind the smack hit and likesay comin wi a lassie. So good, that the adrenalin kick makes us want tae head up the toon, oan a choryin spree, like.

The heat, man, is . . . hot. That's the only way ye can really describe it, ken? Ah head for the shore, n sit oan a bench near the dole office. That double ten-spot feels good in ma poakit, likesay opens a few mair doors, ken? So ah sit lookin at the river. Thirs a big swan in the river, ken? Ah think aboot Johnny Swan, n gear. This swan though, is fuckin beautiful, likes. Ah wish ah'd got some bread, likesay, tae feed the punter wi.

Gav works fir the dole. Mibbe ah'll catch the cat oan his lunch brek, stand the dude a pint or two, likesay. Ah've been bought a few by him lately. Ah see Ricky Monaghan comin oot the dole. An okay gadge, ken.

— Ricky . . .

— Awright Spud. What ye up tae?

— Eh, no much gaun doon ma end catboy. Ye see the whole kit n kaboodle, likesay.

— Bad as that?

— Worse catboy, worse.

— Still oaf the collies?

— Four weeks n two days since ma last bit ay Salisbury Crag, ken? Countin every second man, countin every second. It's tick-tock, tick-tock, likesay, ken.

— Feelin better fir it?

S likesay only then thit ah realise that ah am; bored as fuck ken, but physically, likesay . . . aye. The first fortnight was an extended death trip man . . . but now, likes, ah could handle some hot sex wi a Jewish princess or a Catholic girl, complete wi white soacks, goatay be complete wi the white soacks. Ken?

— . . . Aye . . . ah do feel sortay better, likesay.

— Gaun tae Easter Road oan Setirday?

— Eh, naw . . . It's been likesay, donks, since ah went tae the fitba, ken. Mibbe ah could go though. Wi Rents . . . but Rents is in London the now . . . or Sick Boy n that. Go wi Gav, n buy um a couple ay pints . . . see the Cabs again. — . . . well, mibbe. See how it goes likesay, ken? Ye gaun?

— Naw. Ah sais last season thit ah wisnae gaun back until they goat rid ay Miller. We need a new manager.

— Yeah . . . Miller . . . we need a new cat in the manager's basket . . . Ah didnae even ken whae the manager wis, likesay, couldnae even tell ye the names ay the cats in the team, likes. Mibbe Kano . . . but ah think Kano might've moved oan. Durie! Gordon Durie!

— Durie still in the team?

Monny jist looks at us and kinday shakes his heid.

— Naw, Durie wis transferred ages ago, Spud. Eighty-six. Went tae Chelsea.

— Yeah, right man. Durie. Ah remember that cat scorin a cracker against Celtic. Or wis it Rangers? Same thing really though man, when ye think aboot it likesay . . . kinday different sides ay the same coin, ken?

He shrugs. Ah doubt ah've convinced the cat.

Ricky chums us, or it's likesay ah chums him . . . ah mean, eh, whae really kens whae's chummin whae in this cracked scene these days man? But whaever's chummin whae, it's destination Fit ay the Walk again. Life can be borin without skag. Rents is in London; Sick Boy's sniffin aroond up the toon aw the time, the famous old port just does not seem to be cool enough for that cat these days; Rab, the Second Prize likes, has just vanished and Tommy seems to have gone tae groond since he split fae that

Lizzy chick. That likesay leaves me n Franco . . . some life man, ah kin tell ye.

Ricky, Monny, Richard Monaghan, fellow Fenian freedom fighter, to be sure, to be sure, likesay fucks off, tae meet this lemon up the toon. This leaves yours truly on his Jack Jones, likesay. Ah decide tae visit Na Na in the sheltered housing gaffs at the bottom ay Easter Road, likes. Na Na hates it thair, even though she's likes, goat a barry pad. Wish ah could git one like that, ken. Dead smart, but only for aulder cats, likesay. Ye just pull a cord and an alarm goes, and this warden like, comes n sorts it aw oot fir ye, ken. That would be right up ma street man, wi Frank Zappa's daughter, that crazy chick, the Valley girl, Moon Unit Zappa as warden, likesay. A dead peachy scene that would be, ah kid you not catboy!

Na Na's pins are fucked up likes, and the quack sais that it was too radge, her strugglin up tae the toap flight ay stairs in her auld gaff at Lorne Strasse. Too right, heap big medicine man. If ye took the varicose veins oot ay Na Na's legs, likesay, thir wid be nae legs, nothin tae haud her up, ken? Ah've goat better veins in ma airms than she's goat in her scrambled eggs. She still gave the Doc some stick, likes; auld cats have been markin oot their territory, so tae speak, for likesay, donks, and git attached tae it. Sure as fuck, they arenae gaunnae gie it up withoot a scrap. Claws come oot, and fur flies, man. That's Na Na . . . Ms Mouskouri, as ah call her, ken?

There's a common-room for her block, likesay, which Na Na never uses, unless she's tryin tae cruise that Mr Bryce. The auld punter's family complained tae the Warden aboot her sexually harassing him. This Warden wifie tries tae mediate, likes, between ma Ma n Mr Bryce's daughter, but Na Na reduces the daughter tae tears by making snide remarks aboot the bad birthmark oan her face. Sortay one ay they wine stains, ken? It's likesay, thit Na Na picks oan people's weaknesses, particularly other women, and uses that against them, ken?

A series ay different locks click open, n Na Na smiles at us, n gestures us tae come in. Ah get a barry reception here, but ma Ma n sister git treated like, well, likesay, nothing. They dae everything fir Na Na n aw. But Na Na loves guys and hates lassies. She's hud, likesay, eight bairns by five different men, ken. An that's jist the ones we ken aboot.

— Hullo . . . Calum . . . Willie . . . Patrick . . . Kevin . . . Desmond . . . she lists the names ay some ay her grandchildren, still likes, missin oot mine. Doesnae bother me though, likesay, ah git called 'Spud' that often, even ma Ma calls us it, ah sometimes forget ma name tae.

— Danny.

— Danny. Danny, Danny, Danny. An ah caw Kevin Danny n aw. How could ah forget that yin, Danny Boy!

Well, likesay, how could she . . . *Danny Boy* and *Roses Ay Picardy* ur likesay the only songs she kens. Ken? She sortay sings at the toap ay her voice; a breathless, tuneless sound, wi her airms sortay raised intae the air fir effect, ken.

— George's here.

Ah look aroond the bend ay the L-shaped room n clock ma Uncle Dode, slumped in a chair, sippin a can ay Tennent's Lager.

— Dode, ah sais.

— Spud! Awright boss? How ye livin?

— Peachy catboy, peachy. Eh, yirsel likesay?

— Cannae complain. How's yir Ma?

— Er, still likesay gittin oan ma case as usual, ken?

— Hi! That's yir mother yir talkin aboot! The best friend ye'll ever huv. S'at no right Ma? he asks Na Na.

— Buckin right it is son!

'Buckin' is one ay Na Na's favourite words likesay, along wi 'pish'. Naebody says 'pish' like Na Na. She sortay drags oot the sssshhh, it's likesay, ye kin *see* the steam rising oaf the yellay jet as it hits the white porcelain, ken?

Uncle Dode gies her a big, indulgent sortay grin. Dode's

likesay half-caste, the son ay a West Indian sailor, ken, the product ay, likes, West Indian semen! Ken? Dode's auld boy pulled intae Leith long enough tae git Na Na up the kite. Then it was back tae the seven seas. Sounds a good life likes, a sailor's, likesay a burd in every port n that.

Dode's Na Na's youngest bairn.

She married ma Grandad first likes, a chancin auld cowboy fae County Wexford. The auld dude used tae sit ma Ma oan his lap n sing tae hur: Irish rebel songs, likesay. He hud hair growin oot ay his nostrils n she thought thit he wis ancient, the wey ankle-biters do, likes. The gadge could only huv been in his thirties, like. Anywey, this gadge sortay blew it likes, kinday fell fae the top-flair windae ay a tenement. He wis shaggin this other woman at the time, no Na Na likesay. Naebody could really tell whether it wis drunkenness, suicide, or likesay . . . well baith. Anywey, that yin left her wi three bairns, includin ma Ma.

Na Na's next (married) man wis a gravel-voiced dude whae hud once worked as a scaffolder, ken. The auld boy's still oan the scene in Leith. The gadge once told us in a pub that scaffoldin wis classed as a trade now, likes. Rents, whae wis a chippy at the time, told the boy that that wis a loaday shite, that it wis semi-skilled, n the boy took the cream puff, likesay. Ah still sometimes see um up the Volley, likes. He's no a bad auld punter. Lasted a year wi Na Na, but produced a bairn, wi another oan the wey, likesay.

Wee Alec, the co-op insurance man, whae'd jist been widowed, wis Na Na's next eh, victim, likesay. They said that Alec thought, ken, that the bairn Na Na wis cairyin wis his. He lasted three years, likesay, giein her another bairn, before the perr dude stormed oot, eftir likesay, catchin her shaggin another guy in the hoose.

He sortay likes, waited fir the boy in the stair, or so the story goes, likesay, wi this boatil. The guy pleaded fir mercy. Alec pit the boatil doon, sayin thit eh didnae, likes, need a weapon tae sort the likes ay that boy oot. The gadge's expression sortay changed, and he booted perr Alec aw ower the stair, draggin the perr cat intae the Walk, dazed and likesay, covered in blood, before flinging him oantae a pile ay rubbish stacked oan the kerb ootside a grocer's shoap.

Ma mother sais that Alec wis likesay, a decent wee man. He wis, ken, the only cat in Leith whae didnae ken that Na Na wis oan the game, likesay.

The last but one bairn Na Na hud wis a real mystery, likesay. That's ma Auntie Rita, whae's much nearer ma age than ma Ma's. Ah suppose ah've eywis hud the hots fir Rita, a cool chick, dead sortay sixties, ken? Naebody found oot whae Rita's faither wis, but then came Dode, whae Na Na hud whin she wis well intae her forties, ken?

When ah wis a sprog Dode eywis seemed a real spooky dude. You'd go up tae Na Na's oan a Setirday, likesay, fir yir tea, and there would be this nasty young black cat, starin at everybody, before creepin oaf, likesay roond the skirtin boards. They aw said that Dode hud this chip oan his shoodir, n ah thought so n aw, until ah began tae suss the kinday abuse the gadge wis takin, at school n in the streets n aw that. It wis naebody's business, ah kin tell ye man. Ah sortay jist laugh whin some cats say that racism's an English thing and we're aw Jock Tamson's bairns up here . . . it's likesay pure shite man, gadges talkin through their erses.

There's a strong tea-leaf tradition in ma family, likesay, ken? Aw ma uncles are oan the chorie. It wis eywis likesay, Dode, thit got the heaviest sentences for the pettiest crimes, ken. A fundamentally unsound gig man. Rents once sais, thirs nothin like a darker skin tone tae increase the vigilance ay the police n the magistrates: too right.

Anyway, me n Dode decide tae hop on doon tae the Percy for a pint. The pub's a wee bit crazy; normally the Percy's a quiet family type pub, but it's mobbed oot the day wi these Orange

cats fi the wild west, who're through here for their annual march
and rally at the Links. These cats, it has tae be said, have never
really bothered us, but ah cannae take tae them. It's aw hate,
likesay, ken. Celebratin auld battles seems, likesay, well, pretty
doss. Ken?

Ah see Rents's auld man wi his brars and nephews. Rents's
brar Billy, he's thair n aw. Rents's auld boy's a soapdodger and a
Paris Bun, but he's no really intae this sortay gig any mair. His
family fi Glesgie sure are though, and his family seems tae matter
tae Rents's papa. Rents doesnae hit it oaf wi these cats; really
sortay hates them, likesay. Doesnae like talkin aboot them.
Different story wi Billy though. He's intae aw this Orange stuff,
this sortay Jambo/Hun gig. He gies us a nod fae the bar, but ah
don't think the cat really digs us, but.

— Awright Danny! Mr R. sais.

— Eh . . . sound Davie, sound likes. Heard fi Mark?

— Naw. He must be daein awright. Only time ye hear fi that
wan is whin he's eftir somethin. He's only half jokin, and these
young nephew kittens are lookin us ower in a baaad way, so we
git a seat in a corner by the door.

Bad move . . .

Wir in the vicinity ay some unsound lookin cats. Some ur
skinheids, some urnae. Some huv Scottish, others English, or
Belfast accents. One guy's goat a Skrewdriver T-shirt oan,
another's likesay wearin an *Ulster is British* toap. They start singin a
song aboot Bobby Sands, slaggin him off, likesay. Ah dunno much
aboot politics, but Sands tae me, seemed a brave dude, likes,
whae never killed anybody. Likesay, it must take courage tae die
like that, ken?

Then one guy, the Skrewdriver dude, seems frantically tryin
tae gie us the stare, as desperately as we're tryin tae avoid eye
contact, likesay. It's no that easy whin they start singing: 'Aint no
black in the union jack'. We stay cool, but this cat won't be
denied. His claws are oot. He shouts ower at Dode.

— Oi! Wot you fucking looking at nigger!

— Fuck you, Dode sneers. It's a route the cat's travelled down before. No me though. This is fuckin, likesay, heavy.

Ah hear some Glasgow boy sayin that these guys, likesay, urnae real Orangemen, thir Nazis n that, but maist ay the Orange bastards present are lappin these cunts up, encouragin them, likesay.

They aw start singing: — You black bastard! You black bastard!

Dode gets up n goes ower tae thir table. Ah jist sees Skrewdriver's mockin, distorted face change whin he realises, at the same time as ah do, that Dode's goat a heavy gless ashtray in his hand . . . this is violence . . . this is bad news . . .

. . . he thrashes the Skrewdriver dude's heid wi it, and the boy's dome sortay splits open as he faws oaf his stool ontae the flair. Ah'm sortay shakin wi fear, raw fear man, and one guy jumps at Dode, n they've goat um doon, so ah huv tae steam in. Ah pick up a gless and chin Rid Hand Ay Ulster, whae hauds his heid, even though the gless, likesay, doesnae even brek, but some cunt punches us in the guts wi such a sharp force it feels like ah've been stabbed man . . .

— Kill that Fenyin bastard! some cunt sais, and they've goat us pinned against the waw, likes . . . ah jist starts lashin oot wi fist and boot, no feelin anything . . . n ah'm sortay likes, enjoyin masel man, because this is likesay, no like the real violence when ye see somebody like Begbie gaun radge or that, it's likesay, comic stuff . . . cause ah cannae really fight likes, but ah don't really think these dudes are great shakes either . . . it's like they aw seem tae be gettin in each other's road . . .

Ah don't really know what happened. Davie Renton, Rents's dad, n Billy, his brar, must've pulled them oafay us, cause next thing ah'm sortay standin, pullin Dode, whae looks well fucked, ootside. Ah hears Billy sayin: — Git um oot Spud. Jist git um doon the fuckin road. Now ah feel really sair, aw ower, n ah'm sortay greetin like tears ay anger n fear but maistly frustration . . .

— This is . . . likesay . . . fuck . . . this is, this is . . .

Dode's been chibbed. Ah gits um ower the road. Ah kin hear people shoutin behind us. Ah jist focus oan Na Na's door, no darin tae look back. Wir in. Ah gits Dode up the stair. He's bleedin fae his side and his airm.

Ah phones an ambulance as Na Na's cradlin his heid sayin: — Thir still buckin daein it tae ye son . . . when will they leave ye alain, ma laddie . . . since he wis it school, since he wis it the buckin school . . .

Ah'm dead fuckin angry man, but at Na Na, ken? Wi a bairn likes ay Dode, ye'd think thit Na Na wid ken how anybody thit's different, thit sortay stands oot, likesay, feels, ken? Likesay the woman wi the wine stain n that . . . but it's aw hate, hate, hate wi some punters, and whair does it git us likesay, man? Whair the fuck does it git us?

Ah chums Dode tae the hoespital. His wounds wir likesay no as bad as they looked. Ah goes intae see um lyin oan a trolley eftir thuv, likes, patched um up.

— S awright Danny. Ah've hud a loat worse n the past, and ah'll huv a hellay a loat worse in the future.

— Dinnae say that man. Dinnae say that, ken?

He looks at us like ah'll never really understand, n ah ken that he's probably right.

The First Shag In Ages

They had spent most of the day getting stoned out of their boxes. Now they are getting pished in a tacky chrome-and-neon meat market. The bar is fussy in its range of overpriced drinks, but it misses by miles the cocktail-bar sophistication it is aiming at.

People come to this place for one reason, and one reason only. However, the night is still relatively young, and the camouflage of drinking, talking and listening to music does not, at this point, seem too obvious.

The dope and drink has fuelled Spud and Renton's post-junk libidos to a rampant extent. To them, every woman in the place seems to look outstandingly sexy. Even some of the men do. They find it impossible to focus on one person who might be a potential target, as their gaze is constantly arrested by someone else. Just being here reminds the both of them how long it has been since they've had a shag.

— If ye cannae git a Joe McBride in this place, ye might as well call it a day, Sick Boy reflects, his head bobbing gently to the sounds. Sick Boy can afford detached speculation, speaking, as he generally does in such circumstances, from a position of strength. Dark circles under his eyes attest to the fact that he has just spent most of the day shagging these two American women, who are staying at the Minto Hotel. There is no chance of either Spud, Renton or Begbie making up a foursome. They are both going back with Sick Boy, and Sick Boy alone. He is merely gracing them with his presence.

— They've got excellent coke man. Ah've never had anything like it, he smiles.

— Morningside speed man, Spud remarks.

— Cocaine . . . fuckin garbage. Yuppie shite. Although he has been clean for a few weeks, Renton has the smack-head's contempt for all other drugs.

— My ladies are returning. Ah'll have to leave you gentlemen to your sordid little activities. Sick Boy shakes his head disdainfully, then scans the bar with a haughty, superior expression on his face. — The working classes at play, he derisively snorts. Spud and Renton wince.

Sexual jealousy is an in-built component in a friendship with Sick Boy.

They try to imagine all the cocaine-crazed sex games he'll be playing with the 'manto at the Minto', as he refers to the women. That is all they can do, imagine. Sick Boy never goes into any details about his sexual adventures. His discretion, however, is only observed in order to torment his less sexually prolific friends rather than as a mark of respect for the women he gets involved with. Spud and Renton realise that three-in-a-bed scenes with rich tourists and cocaine are the preserve of sexual aristocrats like Sick Boy. This shabby bar is their level.

Renton cringes as he observes Sick Boy from a distance, thinking about the bullshit that is inevitably coming out of his mouth.

At least with Sick Boy, it is to be expected. Renton and Spud are horrified to note that Begbie has bagged off. He is chatting to a woman who has quite a nice face, Spud thinks; but a fat arse, Renton bitchily observes. Some women, Renton considers with a malicious envy, are attracted to the psychopathic type. They generally pay a high price for this flaw, leading horrible lives. As an example, he smugly cites June, Begbie's girlfriend, who is currently in hospital having their child. Proud that he didn't have to go far to make his point, he takes a swig of his Becks, thinking: I rest my case.

However, Renton is going through one of his frequent self-analytical phases and this smug complacency soon evaporates. Actually, this woman's arse isn't that fat, he reasons. He notes that he is operating his self-deception mechanism again. Part of him believes that he is by far the most attractive person in the bar. The reason for this being that he can always find something hideous in the most gorgeous individual. By focusing on that isolated ugly part, he can then mentally nullify their beauty. On the other hand, his own ugly bits don't bother him, because he is used to them, and in any case, can't see them.

Anyway, he is now jealous of Frank Begbie. Surely, he considers, I can't fall any further from grace. Begbie and his new-found love are talking to Sick Boy and the American women. These women look pretty smart, or at least their tan-and-expensive-clothes packaging does. It nauseates Renton to see Begbie and Sick Boy playing the great mates, as all they generally do is to get on each other's tits. He notes the depressing haste with which the successful, in the sexual sphere as in all others, segment themselves from the failures.

— That's you n me left, Spud, he observes.

— Likesay, eh, yeah . . . it looks that way, catboy.

Renton likes it when Spud calls other people 'catboy' but he hates being referred to in that way himself. Cats make him sick.

— Ye ken, Spud, sometimes ah wish ah wis back oan the skag, Renton says, mainly, he thought, to shock Spud, to get a reaction from his hash-stoned, wasted face. As soon as it comes out, though, he realises that he actually means it.

— Hey, likesay, fuckin heavy man . . . ken? Spud forces some air out from between tightened lips.

It dawns on Renton that the speed they'd done in the toilet, which he'd denounced as shite, is now taking effect. The problem with being off smack, Renton decides, is that they are stupid, irresponsible fuckers, taking anything that they can get their hands on. At least with smack, there is no room for all the other crap.

He has an urge to talk. The speed is a good lap ahead of the dope and alcohol in his system.

— Thing is though, Spud, whin yir intae skag, that's it. That's aw yuv goat tae worry aboot. Ken Billy, ma brar, likes? He's jist signed up tae go back intae the fuckin army. He's gaun tae fuckin

Belfast, the stupid cunt. Ah always knew that the fucker wis tapped. Fuckin imperialist lackey. Ken whit the daft cunt turned roond n sais tae us? He goes: Ah cannae fuckin stick civvy street. Bein in the army, it's like bein a junky. The only difference is thit ye dinnae git shot at sae often bein a junky. Besides, it's usually you that does the shootin.

— That, eh, likesay, seems a bit eh, fucked up like man. Ken?

— Naw but, listen the now. You jist think aboot it. In the army they dae everything fir they daft cunts. Feed thum, gie the cunts cheap bevvy in scabby camp clubs tae keep thum fae gaun intae toon n lowerin the fuckin tone, upsettin the locals n that. Whin they git intae civvy street, thuv goat tae dae it aw fir thumsells.

— Yeah, but likesay, it's different though, cause . . . Spud tries to cut in, but Renton is in full flight. A bottle in the face is the only thing that could shut him up at this point; even then only for a few seconds.

— Uh, uh . . . wait a minute, mate. Hear us oot. Listen tae whit ah've goat tae say here . . . what the fuck wis ah sayin . . . aye! Right. Whin yir oan junk, aw ye worry aboot is scorin. Oaf the gear, ye worry aboot loads ay things. Nae money, cannae git pished. Goat money, drinkin too much. Cannae git a burd, nae chance ay a ride. Git a burd, too much hassle, cannae breathe withoot her gittin oan yir case. Either that, or ye blow it, and feel aw guilty. Ye worry aboot bills, food, bailiffs, these Jambo Nazi scum beatin us, aw the things that ye couldnae gie a fuck aboot whin yuv goat a real junk habit. Yuv just goat one thing tae worry aboot. The simplicity ay it aw. Ken whit ah mean? Renton stops to give his jaws another grind.

— Yeah, but it's a fuckin miserable life, likesay, man. It's nae life at aw, ken? Likesay whin yir sick man . . . that is the fuckin lowest ay the low . . . the grindin bones . . . the poison man, the pure poison . . . Dinnae tell us ye want aw that again, cause that's likesay, fuckin bullshit. The response packs a bit of venom, especially by Spud's gentle, laid-back standards. Renton notes he's obviously touched a nerve.

— Aye. Ah'm talkin a loaday shite. It's the Lou Reed.

Spud gives Renton the kind of smile that would make old wifies in the street want to adopt him like a stray cat.

They clock Sick Boy preparing to leave with Annabel and Louise, the two Americans. He'd spent his obligatory half hour boosting Beggar's ego. That is, Renton decides, the sole function of any mate of Begbie's. He reflects on the insanity of being a friend of a person he obviously dislikes. It was custom and practice. Begbie, like junk, was a habit. He was also a dangerous one. Statistically speaking, he reflects, you're more likely to be killed by a member of your own family or a close friend, than by anyone else. Some tubes surround themselves with psycho mates imagining that this makes them strong, less likely to get hurt by our cruel world, when obviously the reverse is true.

On his way out the door with the American women, Sick Boy turns back, raising one eyebrow at Renton, Roger Moore style, as he vacates the bar. A speed-induced flash of paranoia hit Renton. He wonders if perhaps Sick Boy's success with women is based on his ability to raise the one eyebrow. Renton knows how difficult it is. He'd spent many an evening practising the skill in front of the mirror, but both brows kept elevating simultaneously.

The amount of drink consumed and the passage of time conspired to concentrate the mind. With an hour to go before closing time, somebody you wouldn't think about getting off with becomes acceptable. With half an hour left, they are positively desirable.

Renton's wandering eyes now keep stopping at this slim girl with straight, longish brown hair, slightly turned up at the edges. She has a good tan and delicate features tastefully picked out by makeup. She wears a brown top with white trousers. Renton feels the blood leave his stomach when the woman puts her hands in her pockets, displaying visible panty lines. That is the moment for him.

The woman and her friend are being chatted up by a guy with a round, puffy face, and an open-neck shirt which strains at his bloated guts. Renton, who has a cheerfully undisguised prejudice against overweight people, takes the opportunity to indulge it.

— Spud: deek the fat radge. Gluttonous bastard. Ah dinnae go fir aw that shite aboot it bein a glandular or metabolic thing. Ye dinnae see any fat bastards on tv footage fi Ethiopia. Dae they no huv glands ower thair? Stroll on. Spud just responds to his outburst with a stoned smile.

Renton thinks the girl has taste, because she cold-shoulders the fat guy. He likes the way she does it. Assertively and with dignity, not making a real arse out of him, but letting him know in no uncertain terms that she isn't interested. The guy smiles, extends his palms and cocks his head to the side, accompanied by a volley of derisive laughter from his mates. This incident makes Renton even more determined to talk to the woman.

Renton gestures to Spud to move over with him. Hating to make the first move, he is delighted when Spud starts talking to her mate, because Spud never normally takes the initiative in that way. The speed's obviously helping, however, even though he is somewhat distraught to hear that Spud is rabbiting on about Frank Zappa.

Renton tries an approach he considers is relaxed but interested, sincere but light.

— Sorry tae butt intae yir conversation. Ah jist wanted tae tell ye that ah admired yir excellent taste in kicking that fat bastard intae touch just now. Ah thought that ye might be an interesting person tae talk tae. If you tell us tae go the way of the fat bastard, ah won't be upset though. Ah'm Mark, by the by.

The woman smiles at him in a slightly confused and condescending way, but Renton feels that it at least beats 'fuck off' by a good few furlongs. As they talk, Renton begins to get self-conscious about his looks. The speed kick is running down a little. He worries that his hair looks daft, dyed black, as his orange freckles, the curse of the red-headed bastard, are prominent. He used to think that he looked like the Ziggy Stardust era Bowie. A few years ago, though, a woman told him that he was a dead ringer for Alec McLeish, the Aberdeen and Scotland footballer. Since then the tag had stuck. When Alec McLeish hangs up his boots, Renton has resolved to travel up to Aberdeen for his testimonial as a token of gratitude. He remembers an occasion where Sick Boy shook his head sadly, and asked how some cunt who looked like Alec McLeish could ever hope to be attractive to women.

So Renton has dyed his hair black and spiked it in an attempt to shed the McLeish image. Now he worries that any woman he gets off with will laugh her head off when he removes his clothes and she is confronted with ginger pubes. He has also dyed his eyebrows, and thought about dyeing his pubic hair. Stupidly, he had asked his mother for her advice.

— Dinnae be sae fuckin silly, Mark, she told him, nippy with the hormonal imbalance caused by the change in life.

The woman is called Dianne. Renton thinks that he thinks she is beautiful. Qualification is necessary, as his past experiences have taught him never to quite trust his judgement when there are chemicals racing around in his body and brain. The conversation turns to music. Dianne informs Renton that she likes the Simple Minds and they have their first mild argument. Renton does not like the Simple Minds.

— The Simple Minds huv been pure shite since they jumped on the committed, passion-rock bandwagon of U2. Ah've never trusted them since they left their pomp-rock roots and started aw this patently insincere political-wi-a-very-small-p stuff. Ah loved the early stuff, but ever since *New Gold Dream* thuv been garbage. Aw this Mandela stuff is embarrassing puke, he rants.

Dianne tells him that she believes that they are genuine in

their support of Mandela and the movement towards a multi-racial South Africa.

Renton shakes his head briskly, wanting to be cool, but hopelessly wound up by the amphetamine and her contention. — Ah've goat auld NME's gaun back tae 1979, well ah did huv but ah flung thum oot a few years back, and ah can recall interviews when Kerr slags off the political commitment by other bands, n sais that the Minds are just intae the music, man.

— People can change, Dianne counters.

Renton is a little bit taken aback by the purity and simplicity of this statement. It makes him admire her even more. He just shrugs his shoulders and concedes the point, although his mind is racing with the notion that Kerr has always been one step behind his guru, Peter Gabriel and that since Live Aid, it's become fashionable for rock stars to want to be seen as nice guys. However, he keeps this to himself and resolves to try to be less dogmatic about his views on music in the future. In the larger scheme of things, he's thinking, it doesn't matter a fuck.

After a while, Dianne and her pal go to the bogs to discuss and assess Renton and Spud. Dianne can't make her mind up about Renton. She thinks he's a bit of an arsehole, but the place is full of them and he seems a bit different. Not different enough to go overboard about though. But it was getting late . . .

Spud turns and says something to Renton, who can't hear him above a song by The Farm, which, Renton considers, like all their songs, is only listenable if you're E'd out of your box, and if you're E'd out of your box it would be a waste listening to The Farm, you'd be better off at some rave freaking out to heavy techno-sounds. Even if he could have heard Spud, his brain is now too fucked to respond, taking a well-earned rest from holding itself together to talk to Dianne.

Renton then starts talking personal shite to a guy from Liverpool who's up on holiday, just because the guy's accent and bearing remind of his mate Davo. After a while, he realises that the guy is nothing like Davo and that he was wrong to disclose to him such intimacies. He tries to get back to the bar, then loses Spud, and realises that he's well and truly out of it. Dianne becomes just a memory, a vague feeling of intent behind his drug stupor.

He goes outside to get some air and sees Dianne about to enter a taxi on her own. He wonders with a jealous anguish if this means that Spud's bagged off with her mate? The possibility of being the only one not to bag off horrifies him, and sheer desperation propels him unselfconsciously towards her.

— Dianne. Mind if ah share yir Joe Baxi?

Dianne looks doubtful. — Ah go to Forrester Park.

— Barry. Ah'm headed in that direction masel, Renton lied, then told himself: Well, ah am now.

They talked in the taxi. Dianne had had an argument wi Lisa, her pal, and decided to go home. Lisa was, as far as she knew, still bopping on the dancefloor with Spud and some other cretin, playing them off against each other. Renton's dough was on the other cretin.

Dianne's face took on a cartoon sour look as she told Renton what a horrible person Lisa was, cataloguing her misdemeanours, which to him seemed petty enough, with a venom he found slightly disturbing. He was appropriately crawling, agreeing that Lisa was all the selfish pricks under the sun. He changed the subject, as it was bringing her down, and that was no good to him. He told her jocular stories about Spud and Begbie, sanitising them tastefully. Renton never mentioned Sick Boy, because women liked Sick Boy and he had an urge to keep the women he met as far away from Sick Boy as possible, even conversationally.

When she was lighter-hearted he asked her if she minded if he kissed her. She shrugged, leaving him to determine whether this indicated indifference or an inability to make up her mind. Still, he reasoned, indifference is preferable to outright rejection.

They necked for a bit. He found the smell of her perfume

arousing. She thought that he was too skinny and bony, but he kissed well.

When they came up for air, Renton confessed that he didn't live near Forrester Park, he only said that so that he could spend more time with her. In spite of herself, Dianne felt flattered.

— Do you want to come up for a cup of coffee? she asked.

— That would be great. Renton tried to sound casually pleased rather than rapturous.

— Only a coffee mind, Dianne added, in such a way that Renton struggled to determine what sense she was defining terms in. She spoke slyly enough to put sex on the agenda for negotiation, but at the same time assertively enough to mean exactly what she said. He just nodded like a confused village idiot.

— We'll have to be really quiet. There's people asleep, Dianne said. This seemed less promising, Renton thought, envisaging a baby in the flat, with a sitter. He realised that he'd never done it with anybody that had had a baby before. The thought made him feel a bit strange.

While he could sense people in the flat, he couldn't pick up that distinctive smell of pish, puke and powder that babies have.

He went to speak. — Dia . . .

— Ssh! They're asleep, Dianne cut him off. — Don't wake them, or there'll be trouble.

— Whae's asleep? he whispered nervously.

— Ssh!

This was disconcerting for Renton. His mind raced through past horrors experienced first hand and from the accounts of others. He mentally flipped through a grim database which contained everything from vegan flatmates to psychotic pimps.

Dianne took him through to a bedroom and sat him down on a single bed. Then she vanished, returning a few minutes later with two mugs of coffee. He noted that his was sugared, which he usually hated, but he wasn't tasting much.

— Are we going to bed? she whispered with a strangely casual intensity, raising her eyebrows.

— Eh . . . that would be nice . . . he said, almost spluttering out some coffee. His pulse raced and he felt nervous, awkward and virginal, worrying about the potential effects of the drug and alcohol cocktail on his erection.

— We'll really have to be quiet, she said. He nodded.

He quickly pulled off his jumper and t-shirt, then his trainers, socks and jeans. Self-conscious of his ginger pubes, he got into the bed before sliding his underpants off.

Renton was relieved to get hard as he watched Dianne undress. Unlike him, she took her time, and seemed completely unselfconscious. He thought that her body looked great. He couldn't help a football mantra of 'here we go' playing repeatedly in his head.

— Ah want to go on top of you, Dianne said, throwing back the covers, exposing Renton's ginger pubes. Fortunately, she didn't seem to notice. Renton was pleased with his cock. It seemed so much bigger than usual. This was probably because, he realised, he'd become accustomed to not seeing it erect. Dianne was less impressed. She'd seen worse, that was about it.

They began touching each other. Dianne was enjoying the foreplay. Renton's enthusiasm for this was a pleasant change from most of the guys she'd been with, but she felt his fingers go to her vagina and she stiffened and pushed his hand away.

— I'm well lubricated enough, she told him. This made Renton feel a bit numb, it seemed so cold and mechanistic. He even thought at one stage that his erection had started to subside, but no, she was lowering herself onto it, and it was, miracle of miracles, holding firm.

He groaned softly as she enclosed him. They started moving slowly together, penetrating deeper. He felt her tongue in his mouth and his hands were lightly feeling her arse. It seemed, it had been, so long; he thought that he was going to come straight away. Dianne sensed his extreme excitement. Not another useless prick, please no, she thought to herself.

Renton stopped feeling her and tried to imagine that he was shagging Margaret Thatcher, Paul Daniels, Wallace Mercer, Jimmy Savile and other turn-offs, in order to bring himself off the boil.

Dianne took the opportunity, and rode herself into a climax, Renton lying there like a dildo on a large skateboard. It was only the image of Dianne biting into her forefinger, in an attempt to stifle the strange squeaks she made as she came, her other hand on his chest, that caused Renton to get there himself. Even the thought of rimming Wallace Mercer's arse couldn't have stopped him by that time. When he started to come, he thought that he'd never stop. His cock spurted like a water pistol in the hands of a persistently mischievous child. Abstinence had made the sperm-count go through the roof.

It had been close enough to a simultaneous climax for him to have described it in such a way, had he been one to kiss-and-tell. He realised the reason he'd never do this was because you always get more stud credibility from the enigmatic shrug and smile, than from divulging graphic details for the entertainment of radges. That was something he'd learned from Sick Boy. Even his anti-sexism was therefore overlayed with sexist self-interest. Men are pathetic cunts, he thought to himself.

As Dianne dismounted him, Renton was drifting off into a blissful sleep, resolving to wake in the night and have more sex. He would be more relaxed, but also more active, and would show her what he could do, now that he had broken this bad run. He compared himself to a striker who had just come through a lean spell in front of goal, and now couldn't wait for the next match.

He was therefore cut to the bone when Dianne said: — You have to go.

Before he could argue, she was out of the bed. She pulled on her pants to catch his thick spunk as it started to leave her and trickle down the insides of her thighs. For the first time he began to think about unprotected penetrative sex and the HIV risk. He'd taken the test, after he'd last shared, so he was clear. He worried about her, however; thinking that anyone who would sleep with him would sleep with anybody. Her intention to banish him had already shattered his fragile sexual ego, turning him from cool stud back into trembling inadequate in a depressingly short time. He thought that it would just be his luck to get HIV from one shag after sharing needles, although never the large communal syringes favoured in the galleries, over a period of years.

— But kin ah no stey here? He heard his voice sound puny and biscuit-ersed, in tones that Sick Boy would mock mercilessly, had he been present. Dianne looked straight at him and shook her head. — No. You can stay on the couch. If you're quiet. If you see anybody, this never happened. Put something on.

Once again, self-conscious of his incongruously ginger pubic hair, he was happy to oblige.

Dianne led Renton through to the couch in the front room. She left him shivering in his underpants before she returned with a sleeping-bag and his clothes.

— Sorry about this, she whispered, kissing him. They necked for a bit and he started to get hard again. When he tried to put his hand inside her dressing gown she stopped him.

— Ah have to go, she said firmly.

Dianne departed, leaving Renton feeling empty and confused. He got onto the couch, pulled the sleeping-bag around him and zipped up. He lay awake in the dark, trying to define the contents of the room.

Renton imagined Dianne's flatmates to be dour bastards who disapproved of her bringing someone back. Perhaps, he decided, she didn't want them to think that she would pick up a strange guy, bring him back and just fuck him like that. He bolstered his ego by telling himself that it was his sparkling wit and his unique, if flawed, beauty, which had swept her resistance away. He almost believed himself.

Eventually he fell into a fitful sleep, characterised by some strange dreams. While he was prone to such weird dreams, these disturbed him as they were particularly vivid and surprisingly easy to recall. He was chained to a wall in a white room lit by blue neon, watching Yoko Ono and Gordon Hunter, the Hibs defender, munching on the flesh and bones of human bodies which lay dismembered on a series of large formica-topped tables. They were both hurling horrendous insults at him, their mouths dripping with blood as they tore at strips of flesh and chewed heartily between curses. Renton knew that he was next on the tables. He tried to do a bit of crawling to 'Geebsie' Hunter, telling him that he was a big fan of his, but the Easter Road defender lived up to his uncompromising tag and just laughed in his face. It was a great relief when the dream changed and Renton found himself naked, covered in runny shite and eating a plate of egg, tomato and fried bread with a fully clothed Sick Boy by the Water of Leith. Then he dreamt that he was being seduced by a beautiful woman who was wearing only a two-piece swimsuit made out of Alcan foil. The woman was in fact a man, and they were fucking each other slowly through different holes in their bodies which oozed a substance resembling shaving foam.

He woke to the sound of cutlery clinking and the smell of bacon frying. He caught a glance of the back of a woman, not Dianne, disappearing into a small kitchen which was just off the living room. Then he felt a spasm of fear as he heard a man's voice. The last thing Renton wanted to hear, hungover, in a strange place, wearing only his keks, was a male voice. He played at being asleep.

Surreptitiously, under his eyelids, he noted a guy about his height, maybe smaller, edging into the kitchen. Although they spoke in low voices, he could still hear them.

— So Dianne's brought another friend back, the man said. Renton didn't like the slightly mocking intonation on the term 'friend'.

— Mmm. But shush. Don't you start being unpleasant, and jumping to the wrong conclusions again.

He heard them coming back into the front room, then leaving it. Quickly, he pulled on his t-shirt and jumper. Then he unzipped the bag and threw his legs off the couch and jumped into his jeans, almost in one movement. Folding the sleeping-bag neatly, he stuck the settee's displaced cushions back where they belonged. His socks and trainers were smelly as he put them on. He hoped, but in a futility that was obvious to him, that nobody else had noticed.

Renton was too nervy to feel badly wasted. He was aware of the hangover though; it lurked in the shadows of his psyche like an infinitely patient mugger, just biding its time before coming out to stomp him.

— Hello. The woman who wasn't Dianne came back in.

She was pretty with nice big eyes and a fine, pointed jawline. He thought he recognised her face from somewhere.

— Hiya. Ah'm Mark, by the way, he said. She declined to introduce herself. Instead, she sought more information about him.

— So you're a friend of Dianne's? Her tone was slightly aggressive. Renton decided to play safe and tell a lie which wouldn't sound too blatant, and therefore could be delivered with some conviction. The problem was that he had developed the junky's skill of lying with conviction and could now lie more convincingly than he told the truth. He faltered, thinking that you can always take the junk out of the punter before you can the junky.

— Well, she's more a friend of a friend. You know Lisa?

She nodded. Renton continued, warming to his lies, finding the comforting rhythm of deceit.

— Well, this is actually a wee bit embarrassing. It wis ma birthday yesterday, and ah must confess ah got pretty drunk. Ah managed tae lose ma flat keys and ma flatmate's in Greece oan holiday. That wis me snookered. I could have just went home and forced the door, but the state ah wis in, ah just couldnae think straight. Ah would probably have got arrested for breaking intae ma own flat! Fortunately, ah met Dianne, who was kind enough to let me sleep on the couch. You're her flatmate, right?

— Oh . . . well, in a way, she laughed strangely, as he struggled to find out the score. Something was not right.

The man came and joined them. He nodded curtly at Renton, who smiled weakly back.

— This is Mark, the woman told him.

— Awright, the guy said, noncommittally.

Renton thought that they looked about his age, perhaps a bit older, but he was hopeless with ages. Dianne was obviously a bit younger that the lot of them. Perhaps, he allowed himself to speculate, they had some perverse parental feelings for her. He had noted that with older people. They often try to control younger, more popular and vivacious people; usually due to the fact that they are jealous of the qualities the younger people have and they lack. These inadequacies are disguised with a benign, protective attitude. He could sense this in them, and felt a growing hostility towards them.

Then Renton was hit by a wave of shock which threatened to knock him incoherent. A girl came into the room. As he watched her, a coldness came over him. She was the double of Dianne, but this girl looked barely secondary school age.

It took him a few seconds to realise that it was Dianne. Renton instantly knew why women, when referring to the removal of their makeup, often say that they are 'taking their faces off'. Dianne seemed about ten years old. She saw the shock on his face.

He looked at the other couple. Their attitude to Dianne was

parental, precisely because they *were* her parents. Even through his anxiety, Renton still felt such a fool for not seeing it sooner. Dianne was so much like her mother.

They sat down to breakfast with a bemused Renton being gently cross-examined by Dianne's parents.

— So what is it you do, Mark? the mother asked him.

What he did, at least work-wise, was nothing. He was in a syndicate which operated a giro fraud system, and he claimed benefit at five different addresses, one each in Edinburgh, Livingston and Glasgow, and two in London, at Shepherd's Bush and Hackney. Defrauding the Government in such a way always made Renton feel virtuous, and it was difficult to remain discreet about his achievements. He knew he had to though, as sanctimonious, self-righteous, nosey bastards were everywhere, just waiting to tip off the authorities. Renton felt that he deserved this money, as the management skills employed to maintain such a state of affairs were fairly extensive, especially for someone struggling to control a heroin habit. He had to sign on in different parts of the country, liaise with others in the syndicate at the giro-drop addresses, hitch down at short notice to interviews in London on a phone tip-off from Tony, Caroline or Nicksy. His Shepherd's Bush giro was in doubt now, because he had declined the exciting career opportunity to work in the Burger King in Notting Hill Gate.

— Ah'm a curator at the museums section of the District Council's Recreation Department. Ah work wi the social history collection, based mainly at the People's Story in the High Street, Renton lied, delving into his portfolio of bogus employment identities.

They looked impressed, if slightly baffled, which was just the reaction he'd hoped for. Encouraged, he attempted to score further Brownie points by projecting himself as the modest type who didn't take himself seriously, and self-deprecatingly added:

— Ah rake around in people's rubbish for things that've been discarded, and present them as authentic historical artefacts ay working people's everyday lives. The ah make sure that they dinnae fall apart when they're oan exhibition.

— Ye need brains fir that, the father said, addressing Renton, but looking at Dianne. Renton couldn't make eye-contact with the daughter. He was aware that such avoidance was more likely to arouse suspicion than anything else, but he just couldn't look at her.

— Ah wouldnae say that, Renton shrugged.

— No, but qualifications though.

— Aye, well, ah've goat a degree in history fae Aberdeen University. This in fact, was almost true. He'd got into Aberdeen University, and found the course easy, but was forced to leave mid-way through the first year after blowing his grant money on drugs and prostitutes. It seemed to him that he thus became the first ever student in the history of Aberdeen University to fuck a non-student. He reflected that you were better making history than studying it.

— Education's important. That's what we're always telling this one here, said the father, again taking the opportunity to make a point to Dianne. Renton didn't like his attitude, and liked himself even less for this tacit collusion with it. He felt like a pervert uncle of Dianne's.

It was just as he was consciously thinking: Please let her be sitting her Highers, that Dianne's mother smashed that prospect of damage limitation.

— Dianne's sitting her O Grade History next year, she smiled, — and French, English, Art, Maths and Arithmetic, she continued proudly.

Renton cringed inside for the umpteenth time.

— Mark's not interested in that, Dianne said, trying to sound superior and mature, patronising to her parents, the way kids deprived of power who become the 'subject' of a conversation do. The way, Renton shakily reflected, that *he* did often enough, when his auld man and auld doll got started. The problem was Dianne just sounded so surly, so like a child, she achieved the opposite effect of the one she was aiming for.

Renton's mind was working overtime. *Stoat the baw, they call it. Ye kin git put away fir it. Too right ye kin, wi the key flung away. Branded a sex criminal; git ma face split open in Saughton oan a daily basis. Sex Criminal. Child Rapist. Nonce. Short-eyes.* He could hear the psycho lags now, cunts, he reflected, like Begbie: — Ah heard thit the wee lassie wis jist six. — They telt me it wis rape. — Could've been your bairn or mine. Fuck me, he thought, shuddering.

The bacon he was eating disgusted him. He'd been a vegetarian for years. This was nothing to do with politics or morality; he just hated the taste of meat. He said nothing though, so keen was he to keep in the good books of Dianne's parents. He drew the line at touching the sausage, however, as he reckoned that these things were loaded with poison. Thinking of all the junk he had done, he sardonically reflected to himself: You have to watch what you put into your body. He wondered whether Dianne would like it, and started sniggering uncontrollably, through nerves, at his own hideous *double entendre*.

Feebly, he attempted to cover up by shaking his head and telling a tale, or rather, re-telling it. — God, what an idiot ah am. Ah wis in some state last night. I'm not really used to alcohol. Still, I suppose you're only twenty-two once in a lifetime.

Dianne's parents looked as unconvinced as Renton by the last remark. He was twenty-five going on forty. Nonetheless, they listened politely. — Ah lost ma jacket and keys, like ah wis saying. Thank god for Dianne, and you folks. It's really hospitable of you to let me stay the night and to make such a nice breakfast for me this morning. Ah feel really bad about not finishing this sausage. It's just that ah'm so full. Ah'm no used tae big breakfasts.

— Too thin, that's your trouble, the mother said.

— That's what comes ay living in flats. East is east, west is west, but home is best, the father said. There was a nervous silence at this moronic comment. Embarrassed, he added: — That's what they say anyway. He then took the opportunity to change the subject. — How are ye going tae get into the flat?

Such people really scared the fuck out off Renton. They looked to him as if they hadn't done anything illegal in their lives. No wonder Dianne was like the way she was, picking up strange guys in bars. This couple looked so obscenely wholesome to him. The father had slightly thinning hair, there were faint crow's feet at the mother's eyes, but he realised that any onlooker would put them in the same age bracket as him, only describing them as healthier.

— Ah'll jist huv tae force the door. It's only oan a Yale. Silly really. Ah've been meaning tae get a mortice for ages. Good thing ah didnae now. There's an entry-phone in the stair, but the people next door will let me in.

— Ah could help you out there. I'm a joiner. Where do you live? the father asked. Renton was a little fazed, but happy that they had bought his bullshit.

— It's no problem. Ah was a chippy masel before ah went tae the Uni. Thanks for the offer though. This again, was true. It felt strange telling the truth, he'd got so comfortable with deception. It made him feel real, and consequently vulnerable.

— Ah wis an apprentice at Gillsland's in Gorgie, he added, prompted by the father's raised eyebrows.

— Ah ken Ralphy Gillsland. Miserable sod, the father snorted, his voice more natural now. They had established a point of contact.

— One ay the reasons ah'm no longer in the trade.

Renton went cold as he felt Dianne's leg rubbing against his under the table. He swallowed hard on his tea.

— Well, ah must be making a move. Thanks again.

— Hold on, ah'll just get ready and chum you intae town. Dianne was up and out of the room before he could protest.

Renton made half-hearted attempts to help tidy up, before the father ushered him onto the couch and the mother busied herself in the kitchen. His heart sank, expecting the ah'm-wide-fir-your-game-cunt line when they were alone. Not a bit of it though. They talked aboot Ralphy Gillsland and his brother Colin, who, Renton found himself pleased tae hear, had committed suicide, and other guys they both knew from jobs.

They talked football, and the father turned out to be be a Hearts fan. Renton followed Hibs, who hadn't enjoyed their best season against their local rivals; they hadn't enjoyed their best season against anybody, and the father wasted no time in reminding him of it.

— The Hibbies didnae do too well against us, did they?

Renton smiled, glad for the first time, for reasons other than sexual ones, to have shagged this man's daughter. It was amazing, he decided, how things like sex and Hibs, which were nothing to him when he was on smack, suddenly became all-important. He speculated that his drug problems might be related to Hibs poor performances over the eighties.

Dianne was ready. With less makeup on than last night, she looked about sixteen, two years older than she was. As they hit the streets, Renton felt relieved to be leaving the house, but a little embarrassed in case anyone he knew saw them. He had a few acquaintances in the area, mainly users and dealers. They would, he thought, think that he'd gone in for pimping if they came across him now.

They took the train from South Gyle into Haymarket. Dianne held Renton's hand on the journey, and talked incessantly. She was relieved to be liberated from the inhibiting influence of her parents. She wanted to check Renton out in more detail. He could be a source of blow.

Renton thought about last night and wondered chillingly what

Dianne had done, and with whom, to gain such sexual experience, such confidence. He felt fifty-five instead of twenty-five, and he was sure that people were looking at them.

Renton looked scruffy, sweaty and bleary in last night's clothes. Dianne was wearing black leggings, the type so thin that they almost looked like tights, with a white mini-skirt over them. Either of the garments, Renton considered, would have sufficed on its own. One guy was looking at her in Haymarket Station as she waited for Renton to buy a *Scotsman* and a *Daily Record*. He noticed this and, strangely enraged, he found himself aggressively staring the guy down. Perhaps, he thought, it was self-loathing projected.

They went into a record shop on Dalry Road, and thumbed through some album sleeves. Renton was now pretty jumpy, as his hangover was growing at a rapid rate. Dianne kept handing him record sleeves for examination, announcing that this one was 'brilliant' and that one 'superb'. He thought that most of them were crap, but was too nervy to argue.

— Awright Rents! How's ma man? A hand hit his shoulder. He felt his skeleton and central nervous system briefly rip out of his skin, like wire through plasticine, then jump back in. He turned to see Deek Swan, Johnny Swan's brother.

— No bad Deek. How ye livin? he responded with an affected casualness which belied his racing heartbeat.

— No sae bad boss, no sae bad. Deek noted that Renton had company, and gave him a knowing leer. — Ah've goat tae nash likes. See ye aroond. Tell Sick Boy tae gie us a bell if ye see um. The bastard owes us twenty fuckin bar.

— You n me both mate.

— His patter's pure abysmal. Anywey, see ye Mark, he said turning to Dianne. — See ye doll. Yir man here's too rude tae introduce us. Must be love. Watch this punter. They smiled uneasily at this first external definition of them, as Deek departed.

Renton realised that he had to be alone. His hangover was growing brutal, and he just couldn't handle this.

— Eh, look Dianne . . . ah've goat tae nash. Meetin some mates doon in Leith. The fitba n that.

Dianne raised her eyes in knowing, weary acknowledgement, accompanying this gesture with what Renton thought were some strange clucking noises. She was annoyed that he was going before she could ask him about hash.

— What's your address? She produced a pen and a piece of paper from her bag. — No the Forrester Park one, she added, smiling. Renton wrote down his real address in Montgomery Street, simply because he was too out of it to think up a false one.

As she departed, he felt a powerful twinge of self-loathing. He was unsure as to whether it came from having had sex with her, or the knowledge that he couldn't possibly again.

However, that evening he heard the bell go. He was skint so he was staying in this Saturday night, watching *Braddock: Missing in Action 3* on video. He opened the door and Dianne stood before him. Made-up, she was restored in his eyes to the same state of desirability as the previous evening.

— Moan in, he said, wondering how easily he'd be able to adjust to a prison regime.

Dianne thought she could smell hash. She really hoped so.

Strolling Through The Meadows

The pubs, likesay, dead busy, full ay loco-locals and festival types, having a wee snort before heading off tae the next show. Some ay they shows look okay . . . a bit heavy oan the hirays though, likesay.

Begbie's pished his jeans . . .

— Pished yir keks, Franco? Rents asks him, pointing at a wet patch oan the faded blue denim.

— Like fuck ah huv! It's jist fuckin water. Washin ma fuckin hands. No thit you'd fuckin ken aboot that, ya rid-heided cunt. This cunt's allergic tae water, especially if ye mix it wi fuckin soap.

Sick Boy's scannin the bar for women . . . chick crazy that kid. It's like he gets bored in the company of punters eftir a while. Mibbe that's why Sick Boy's good wi women; like mibbe cause he has tae be. Yeah, that could be it. Matty's talkin quietly tae hissel, shakin his heid. Thirs likesay somethin wrong wi Matty . . . no jist smack. It's Matty's mind, it's like a bad depression, likes.

Renton and Begbie are arguing. Rents hud better watch what he's daein, likesay. That Begbie, man, it's likesay . . . that's a fuckin jungle cat. We're just ordinary funky feline types. Domestic cats, likesay.

— They cunts've goat the fuckin poppy. You're the cunt thits eywis fuckin gaun oan aboot killin the rich n aw that anarchy shite. Now ye want tae fuckin shite oot! Begbie sneers at Rents, and it's, likes, very ugly n aw; they dark eyebrows oan toap ay they darker eyes, that thick black hair, slightly longer than a skinheid.

— S no a question ay shitein oot Franco. Ah'm jist no intae it. Wir huvin a barry crack here. Wuv goat the speed n the E. Let's jist enjoy oorsels, mibbe go tae a rave club, instead ay wanderin aboot the fuckin Meadows aw night. Thuv goat a big fuckin theatre tent thair, n a fuckin fun fair up. It'll be crawlin wi polis. It's too much fuckin hassle man.

— Ah'm no gaun tae any fuckin rave clubs. You sais yirsel thit thir fir fuckin bairns.

— Aye, but that wis before ah went tae yin.

— Well ah'm no fuckin gaun tae yin. So let's fuckin pub crawl well, n git some cunt in the fuckin bogs.

— Nah. Ah cannae be ersed.

— Fuckin shitein cunt! Yir still fuckin shitein yir keks aboot the other weekend in the Bull and Bush.

— Naw ah'm no. It wis jist unnecessary, that's aw. The whole fuckin thing.

Begbie looked at Rents, and likes, really tensed up in his seat. He's straining forward, n ah thoat the dude wis gaunnae gub the Rent Boy, likesay, ken.

— Eh? Eh! Ah'll fuckin unnecessary ye, ya radge cunt!

— C'moan Franco. Take it easy man, Sick Boy says.

Begbie seems tae realise that he's ower the top, likesay, even fir him. Keep these claws in catboy. Show the world some soft pads. This is a bad cat, a big, bad panther.

— We fill in some fuckin Sherman Tank. Whaes he tae you? The smart cunt deserved ivraything he goat! Besides, ah didnae see you fucking lookin the other wey whin we wir in the fuckin snug at the Barley divvyin up the fuckin loot.

— The guy ended up unconscious in the hoespital, he loast a loat ay fuckin blood. It wis in the *News* . . .

— The cunt's awright now though! It fuckin sais! Nae fuckin herm done tae nae cunt. N even if thir wis, so fuck? Some fuckin rich American cunt whae shouldnae even fuckin be here in the first place. Whae gies a fuck aboot that cunt? N you ya cunt, you've chibbed some cunt before; Eck Wilson, at the school, so dinnae you fuckin start gaun aw fuckin squeamish.

That sortay shuts Rents up cause he likesay hates talkin aboot that, but it sortay happened, ken? That wis jist lashin oot at some cat that wis scratchin ye like, no likesay plannin tae dae some radge ower. Beggars likesay cannae see the difference but. It wis bad though, really sick likesay . . . the Yank, the boy likes, jist wouldnae hand ower the wallet, even when Begbie pulled the chib, likesay . . . the last words ah heard the dude say wis: You won't use that.

Begbie went fucking crazy, goat that carried away likesay, wi the bladework, ken, we nearly forgoat the wallet likes. Ah goat intae the guy's poakits and fished it oot while Begbie wis bootin um in the face. Blood wis flowin intae the latrine, mixin wi the pish. Ugly, ugly, ugly man, likesay, ken? Ah still shake thinkin aboot it. Ah lie in bed n likes, shudder. Everytime ah see a punter, likesay, whae looks like our catboy, Richard Hauser of Des Moines, Iowa, USA, ah freeze. Whenever ah hear a Yank voice in the toon, ah jump. Violence is fuckin ugly man. The Beggar, dear old Franco, he raped us likesay, raped us aw that night, sort ay shafted us up oor erses n peyed us oaf, like we wir hoors man, ken likes? Bad cat Beggar. A wild, wild cat.

— Whae's comin? Spud? Begbie's talkin tae us. He's bitin his bottom lip.

— Eh, likesay . . . eh . . . violence n that . . . isnae really ma sortay gig . . . ah'll jist stey n git bombed . . . likesay, ken?

— Another shitein cunt, he turns away fae me . . . no disappointed, like he sort ay expects nothin fae us in this kinday gig likesay . . . which is mibbe good n mibbe no sae good, but who really kens the score aboot anything these days, likesay?

Sick Boy says somethin aboot bein a lover, no a fighter, and Begbie's aboot tae say somethin, whin Matty goes: — Ah'm game.

This diverts Begbie's attention fae Sick Boy. The Beggar Boy then starts tae praise Matty, likes, n calls us aw the shitein cunts under the sun; but it's like tae me thit Matty's the shitein cunt, likesay, because he's the groover that goes along wi everything Franco sais . . . ah've never really liked Matty . . . one fucked up punter. Mates take the pish oot ay each other likes, bit whin Matty slags ye, it's likesay, ye kin feel mair thin that, ye kin feel . . . likesay . . . hate, ken? Jist bein happy. That's the crime whin Matty's aboot. He cannae bear tae see a gadge happy, likesay.

Ah realise that ah never see Matty oan his ain, likesay. It's likesay sometimes jist me n Rents . . . or jist me n Tommy . . . or jist me n Rab . . . or jist me n Sick Boy . . . or even jist me and Generalissimo Franco . . . but never jist me n Matty. That sortay sais something, likesay.

These bad cats leave the basket tae stalk their prey, and the atmosphere is like . . . brilliant. Sick Boy brings oot some E. White doves, ah think. It's mental gear. Most Ecstasy hasnae any MDMA in it, it's just likesay, ken, part speed, part acid in its effects . . . but the gear ah've hud is always jist likesay good speed, ken? This gear is pure freaky though, pure Zappaesque man . . . that's the word, Zappaesque . . . ah'm thinkin aboot Frank Zappa wi Joe's Garage n yellow snow n Jewish princesses n Catholic girls n ah think that it wid be really great tae huv a woman . . . tae love likesay . . . no shaggin likes, well no jist shaggin . . . but tae love, cause ah sortay feel like lovin everybody, but no sortay wi sex . . . jist huvin somebody tae love . . . but likesay Rents' goat that Hazel n Sick Boy . . . well, Sick Boy's goat tons ay burds . . . but these catpersons don't seem any happier than moi . . .

— The other man's grass is always greener, the sun shines brighter on the other side . . . ah'm fuckin singing likesay, ah never sing . . . ah've goat some gear n ah'm singing . . . ah'm thinkin aboot Frank Zappa's daughter, Moon, likesay . . . she'd dae us fine . . . hingin oot wi her auld man . . . in the recording studio . . . jist tae see likesay the creative process, ken, the creative process . . .

— This is fuckin mad . . . goat tae move or ah'll git gouchy . . . Sick Boy's goat his hands in his heid.

Renton's shirt's unbuttoned n he's sortay tweakin his nipples, likesay . . .

— Spud . . . look at ma nipples . . . they feel fuckin weird man . . . nae cunt's goat nipples like mine . . .

Ah'm talkin tae him aboot love, n Rents says that love doesnae exist, it's like religion, n likesay the state wants ye tae believe in that kinday crap so's they kin control ye, n fuck yir heid up . . . some cats cannae enjoy thirsels withoot bringing in politics, ken . . . but he doesnae bring us doon . . . because, it's likesay he doesnae believe it hissel . . . because . . . because wi laugh at everything in sight . . . the mad guy at the bar wi the burst blood-vessels in his coupon . . . the snobby English Festival-type lemon whae looks like somebody's just farted under her nose . . .

Sick Boy sais: — Let's hit the Meadows n take the fuckin pish ootay Begbie n Matty . . . straight, boring, draftpak, schemie cunts!

— Ris-kay catboy, ris-kay . . . he's pure radge, likesay . . . ah sais.

— Let's do it for the fans, Rents sais. Him n Sick Boy picked this up fae a Hibs programme advertising the Isle Of Man pre-season soccer tournament. It's got Hibs top cat Alex Miller looking really stoned in the picture, wi the caption that sais, likesay, 'Let's Do It For The Fans'. Whenever thir's drugs aroond . . . that's what they say.

We float ootay the pub n cross over tae the Meadows. We start tae sing, likesay Sinatra, in exaggerated American Noo Yawk voices:

> Yoo en I, were justa like-a kapil aff taahts
> strollin acrass the Meadows
> pickin up laahts aff farget-me-naahts.

Thir's likesay two lassies comin doon the path towards us . . . we ken them . . . it's likesay that wee Roseanna n Jill . . . two pure honey cats, fae that posh school, is it Gillespie's or Mary Erskine's? . . . they hing aboot the Southern likesay, for the sounds, the drugs, the experiences . . .

. . . Sick Boy outstretches his airms and sortay grabs wee Jill in a bear hug, n Rents likesay does the same wi Roseanna . . . ah'm left jist looking at the clouds likesay, Mr Spare Prick at a hoors convention.

Thir neckin away thegither. This is cruel man, cruel. Rents breks away first, but keeps his airm roond Roseanna. It's a sortay joke wi Rents likesay . . . mind you . . . that wee bird Rents goat off wi at Donovan's she wisnae that auld. What wis her name, Dianne? Bad cat, Rents. Sick Boy, well Sick Boy's likesay bundled wee Jill against a tree.

— How ye daein doll? Whit ye up tae? he asks her.

— Goin to the Southern, she sais, a bit stoned . . . a little stoned princess, Jewish? No a blemish oan her face . . . wow, those chicks try tae act cool, but thir a bit nervous ay Rents n Sick Boy. They'll let those superstar wasted junkies dae anything wi them, likes. Real cool chicks would slap their pusses, likesay, and jist watch the bastards crumble intae a heap. These lassies are playin at it . . . gaun through an upset-yir-posh-Ma-n-Dad phase . . . no thit Rents wid take advantage ay this, mind you, ah suppose he awready has, but Sick Boy's a different matter. His hands are inside that wee Jill's jeans . . .

— Ah know about you girls, that's whair yis hide the drugs . . .

— Simon! I've not got anything! Simon! Siiimoon! . . .

Sensin a freak oot, he sortay lets the lassie go. Every cat laughs nervously, tryin tae aw pretend it wis a big game likesay, then they go.

— Mibbe see you dolls the night! Sick Boy shouts after them.

— Yeah . . . down the Southern, Jill shouts, walking backwards.

Sick Boy sortay likes, slaps his thigh. — Should've taken they wee rides back tae the gaff n banged thum senseless. Wee slags wir fuckin gantin oan it. It wis like he sais this tae hissel rather than me n Rents.

Rents starts shoutin and pointin.

— Si! There's a fuckin squirrel at yir feet! Kill the cunt!

Sick Boy's nearest tae it, n tries tae entice it tae him, but it scampers a bit away, movin really weird, archin its whole boady likesay. Magic wee silvery grey thing . . . ken?

Rents picks up a stane and flings it at the squirrel. Ah feel likes, sick, ma hert misses a beat as it whizzes past the wee gadge. He goes tae pick up another, laughin like a maniac, but ah stoap um.

— Leave it man. Squirrel's botherin nae cunt likesay! Ah hate it the wey Mark's intae hurtin animals . . . it's wrong man. Ye cannae love yirsel if ye want tae hurt things like that . . . ah mean . . . what hope is thir? The squirrel's likes fuckin lovely. He's daein his ain thing. He's free. That's mibbe what Rents cannae stand. The squirrel's free, man.

Rents is still laughin as ah haud oantay um. Two posh lookin wifies, gie us the eye as they pass us. They look likesay, disgusted. Rents gits a glint in his eye.

— GIT A HAUD AY THE CUNT! he shouts at Sick Boy, but makin sure that the wifies kin hear um. — WRAP IT IN CELLOPHANE SO'S IT DISNAE SPLIT WHIN YE FUCK IT!

The squirrel's dancin away fae Sick Boy, but the wifies turn roond and look really repelled by us, like we wir shite, ken? Ah'm laughin now n aw, bit still haudin oantay Rents.

— Whae's that foostie-minged fucker starin at? Fuckin tea-room hag! Rents says, loud enough fir the wifies tae hear.

They turn and increase thir pace. Sick Boy shouts: — FUCK OFF GOBI DESERT FANNY! Then he turns tae us n sais, — Ah dinnae ken what these auld hounds are cruisin us for. Naebody's gaunnae fuck them, even doon here at this time. Ah'd rather stick it between a couple ay B&Q sandin blocks.

— Fahk aff! You'd shag the crack ay dawn if it hud hairs oan it, Rents said.

Ah think he felt bad aboot this as soon as he said it, likesay, cause Dawn wis a wee bairn thit died, Lesley's bairn, it died ay that cot death n that, likesay, n everybody sortay kens it wis likesay Sick Boy thit gied her the bairn . . .

Aw Sick Boy sais though, is: — Fuck off spunk-gullet. You're the city dog pound man here. Every burd ah've fucked, and there has been plen-tee, has been worth fucking.

Ah remember this burd fae Stenhoose, thit Sick Boy once took hame whin he wis pished . . . couldnae really likesay say she wis anything special . . . ah suppose every cat's got thir sortay achilles heel, ken.

— Eh, remember that Stenhoose chick, eh, what's-her-name?

— Dinnae *you* start talkin! *You* couldnae git a fuckin ride in a brothel wi yir cock sandwiched between American Express n Access cairds.

We start slaggin each other, then wir walkin fir a bit, bit ah start thinkin ay wee Dawn, the bairn, n that squirrel, like free n botherin naebody . . . n they wid jist kill it, like that ken, n fir what? It makes us feel really sick, n sad, n angry . . .

Ah'm gittin away fae they people. Ah turn n walk away. Rents comes eftir us. — C'moan Spud . . . fuck sakes man, what is it?

— Youse wir gaunnae kill that squirrel.

— S only a fuckin squirrel, Spud. Thir vermin . . . he sais. He pits his airm roond ma shoodirs.

— It's mibbe nae mair vermin thin you or me, likesay . . . whae's tae say what's vermin . . . they posh wifies think people like us ur vermin, likesay, does that make it right thit they should kill us, ah goes.

— Sorry, Danny . . . s only a squirrel. Sorry mate. Ah ken how ye feel aboot animals. Ah jist, like . . . ye ken whit ah mean Danny, it's like . . . fuck, ah mean, ah'm fucked up, Danny. Ah dinnae ken. Begbie n that . . . the gear. Ah dinnae ken what ah'm daein wi ma life . . . it's aw jist a mess, Danny. Ah dinnae ken whit the fuckin score is. Sorry man.

Rents husnae called us 'Danny' for ages, now he cannae stoap callin us it. He looks really upset, likesay.

— Hey . . . hang loose catboy . . . it's jist likesay animals n that, likes . . . dinnae worry aboot that shit . . . ah wis jist thinkin ay innocent wee things, like Dawn the bairn, ken . . . ye shouldnae hurt things, likes . . .

He likesay, grabs a haud ay us n hugs us. — Yir one ay the best, man. Remember that.That's no drink n drugs talkin, that's me talkin. It's jist thit ye git called aw the poofs under the sun if ye tell other guys how ye feel aboot them if yir no wrecked . . . Ah slaps his back, n it's likesay ah want tae tell him the same, but it would sound, likesay, ah wis jist sayin it cause he sais it tae me first. Ah sais it anywey though.

We hear Sick Boy's voice at oor backs. — You two fuckin buftie-boys. Either go intae they trees n fuck each other, or come n help us find Beggars n Matty.

Wi break oor embrace n laugh. Wi both ken that likesay Sick Boy, for aw the cat's desire tae rip open every binliner in toon, is one ay the best n aw.

Blowing It

Courting Disaster

The magistrate's expression seems tae oscillate between pity n loathing, as he looks doon at me n Spud in the dock.

— You stole the books from Waterstone's bookshop, with the intention of selling them, he states. Sell fuckin books. Ma fuckin erse.

— No, ah sais.

— Aye, Spud sais, at the same time. We turn aroond n look at each other. Aw the time we spent gittin oor story straight n it takes the doss cunt two minutes tae blow it.

The magistrate lets oot a sharp exhalation. It isnae a brilliant job the cunt's goat, whin ye think aboot it. It must git pretty tiresome dealin wi radges aw day. Still, ah bet the poppy's fuckin good, n naebody's asking the cunt tae dae it. He should try tae be a wee bit mair professional, a bit mair pragmatic, rather than showin his annoyance so much.

— Mr Renton, you did not intend to sell the books?

— Naw. Eh, no, your honour. They were for reading.

— So you read Kierkegaard. Tell us about him, Mr Renton, the patronising cunt sais.

— I'm interested in his concepts of subjectivity and truth, and particularly his ideas concerning choice; the notion that genuine

171

choice is made out of doubt and uncertainty, and without recourse to the experience or advice of others. It could be argued, with some justification, that it's primarily a bourgeois, existential philosophy and would therefore seek to undermine collective societal wisdom. However, it's also a liberating philosophy, because when such societal wisdom is negated, the basis for social control over the individual becomes weakened and . . . but I'm rabbiting a bit here. Ah cut myself short. They hate a smart cunt. It's easy to talk yourself into a bigger fine, or fuck sake, a higher sentence. Think deference Renton, think deference.

The magistrate snorts derisively. As an educated man ah'm sure he kens far mair aboot the great philosophers than a pleb like me. Yiv goat tae huv fuckin brains tae be a fuckin judge. S no iviry cunt thit kin dae that fuckin joab. Ah can almost hear Begbie sayin that tae Sick Boy in the public gallery.

— And you, Mr Murphy, you intended to sell the books, like you sell everything else that you steal, in order to finance your heroin habit?

— That's spot on man . . . eh . . . ye goat it, likesay, Spud nodded, his thoughtful expression sliding into confusion.

— You, Mister Murphy, are an habitual thief. Spud shakes his shoodirs as if tae say, its no ma fault. — The reports state that you are still addicted to heroin. You are also addicted to the act of theft, Mr Murphy. People have to work hard to produce the goods you repeatedly steal. Others have to work hard to earn the money to purchase them. Repeated attempts to get you to cease these petty, but persistent crimes, have so far proved fruitless. I am therefore going to give you a custodial sentence of ten months.

— Thanks . . . eh, ah mean . . . nae hassle, likesay . . .

The cunt turns tae me. Fuck sakes.

— You, Mr Renton, are a different matter. The reports say that you are also a heroin addict; but have been trying to control your drug problem. You claim that your behaviour is related to depression experienced due to withdrawal from the drug. I am prepared to accept this. I am also prepared to accept your claim that you intended to push Mr Rhodes away, in order to stop him from assaulting you, rather than to cause him to fall over. I am therefore going to suspend a sentence of six months on the condition that you continue to seek appropriate treatment for this addiction. Social services will monitor your progress. While I can accept that you had the cannabis in your possession for your own use, I cannot condone the use of an illegal drug; even though you claim you take it in order to combat the depression you suffer from as the result of heroin withdrawal. For the possession of this controlled drug, you will be fined one hundred pounds. I suggest that you find other ways to fight depression in the future. Should you, like your friend Daniel Murphy, fail to take the opportunity presented to you and appear before this court again, I shall have no hesitation in recommending a custodial sentence. Do I make myself clear?

Clear as a bell, you fuckin docile cunt. I love you, shite-for-brains.

— Thank you, your honour. I'm only too well aware of the disappointment I've been to my family and friends and that I am now wasting valuable court time. However, one of the key elements in rehabilitation is the ability to recognise that the problem exists. I have been attending the clinic regularly, and am undergoing maintenance therapy having been prescribed methadone and temazepan. I'm no longer indulging in self-deception. With god's help, I'll beat this disease. Thank you again.

The magistrate looks closely at us tae see if thirs any sign ay mockery oan ma face. No chance it'll show. Ah'm used tae keepin deadpan whin windin up Begbie. Deadpan's better than dead. Convinced it's no bullshit, the doss cunt dismisses the session. Ah walk tae freedom; perr auld Spud gits taken doon.

A polisman gestures tae him tae move.

— Sorry mate, ah sais, feelin cuntish.

— Nae hassle man . . . I'll git oaf the skag, and Saughton's barry fir hash. It'll be a piece ay pish likesay . . . he sais, as he's escorted away by a po-faced labdick.

In the hall ootside the courtroom, ma Ma comes up tae us n hugs us. She looks worn oot, wi black circles under her eyes.

— Aw laddie, laddie, whit ah'm ah gaunnae dae wi ye? she sais.

— Silly bastard. That shite'll kill ye. Ma brother Billy shakes his heid.

Ah wis gaunnae say something tae the cunt. Nae fucker asked him tae come here, and his crass observations are equally unwelcome. However, Frank Begbie came ower as ah wis aboot tae speak.

— Rents! Nice one ma man! Some fuckin result, eh? Shame aboot Spud, but it's better thin we fuckin expected. He'll no dae ten months. Be oot in fuckin six, wi good behaviour. Less, even.

Sick Boy, looking like an advertising executive, pits his airm aroond ma Ma, and gies us a reptilian smile.

— This calls fir a fuckin celebration. Deacon's? Franco suggests. Like junkies, we file out after him. Nobody hus the motivation tae dae anything else, and pish wins by default.

— If you knew what you've done tae me n yir faither . . . ma Ma looked at us, deadly serious.

— Stupid fucker, Billy sneered, — nickin books oot ay shoaps. This cunt wis gettin ma fuckin goat.

— Ah've been nickin books oot ay fuckin shoaps fir the last six years. Ah've goat four grand's worth ay books at Ma's n in ma flat. Ye think ah boat any ay thaim? That's a four-grand profit oan nickin books, doss cunt.

— Aw Mark, ye didnae, no aw they books . . . Ma looked heartbroken.

— But that's me finished now, Ma. Ah eywis sais thit the first time ah goat caught; that wis it over. Yir snookered eftir that.

Time tae hang up yir boots. Finito. Endy story. Ah was serious aboot this. Ma must've thought so tae, cause she changes tack.

— And watch your language. You as well, she turned tae Billy.

— Ah dunno whair yis got that fae, cause yis nivir heard it in ma hoose.

Billy raises his eyebrows dubiously at me, and ah'm gieing him the same gesture back, a rare display ay sibling unity between us.

Everybody gits a bit pished quickly. Ma embarrasses Billy n me, by talkin aboot her periods. Jist because she wis forty-seven n still goat periods, she hud tae make sure everybody kent aboot it.

— Ah wis flooded. Tampons ur useless wi me. Like tryin tae stoap a burst water main wi an *Evening News*, she laughed loudly, throwing her heid back in that sickening, sluttish too-many-Carlsberg-Specials-at-the-Leith-Dockers-Club gesture ah knew so well. Ah realise that Ma's been drinkin this morning. Probably mixin it wi the vallies.

— Awright Ma, ah sais.

— Dinnae tell us yir auld mother's embarrassing ye? She grabs ma thin cheek in between her thumb n forefinger. — Ah'm jist gled thit thuv no taken ma wee bairn away. He hates bein called that. Ye'll always be ma wee bairns, the two ay yis. Remember whin ah used tae sing ye yir favourite song, whin ye wir a wee thing in yir pushchair?

Ah clamped ma teeth tightly thegither, as ah felt ma throat go dry and the blood drain fae ma face. Surely tae fuck, naw.

— Momma's little baby loves shortnin shortnin, momma's little baby loves shortnin bread . . . she sang tunelessly. Sick Boy gleefully joined in. Ah wished that ah hud gone doon instead ay that lucky cunt Spud.

— Wid momma's little baby like another pint? Begbie asked.

— Aye, yis might bloody sing as well. Ye might bloody sing, ya fuckin bastards! Spud's Ma had come intae the pub.

— Really sorry aboot Danny, Mrs Murphy . . . ah began.

— Sorry! Ah'll gie yis sorry! If it wisnae for you n this crowd ay bloody rubbish, ma Danny widnae be in the fuckin jail right now!

— Come oan now Colleen hen. Ah ken yir upset, but that's no fair. Ma stood up.

— Ah'll tell ye bloody fair! It wis this yin! She pointed venomously at me. — This yin goat ma Danny oantae that stuff. Bloody standin up thair, fill ay his fancy talk in the court. This yin thair, and that bloody pair. Sick Boy and Beggars were included, tae ma relief, in her anger.

Sick Boy said nothing, but raised himself slowly in the chair with an I've-never-been-so-insulted-in-all-my-life expression, followed by a sad, patronising shake of his head.

— That's fuckin oot ay order! Begbie snapped ferociously. There were no sacred cows for that cunt, not even auld ones fae Leith whose laddies had jist been sent tae jail. — Ah nivir touch that shite, and ah've telt Rents n Spu . . . Mark n Danny thit thir radges daein it! Sick . . . Simon's been clean fir fuckin months. Begbie stood up, fuelled by his own indignation. He thrashed at his own chest with his fist, as if to stop himself from striking Mrs Murphy, and screamed in her face: — AH WIS THE FACKIN CUNT TRYIN TAE GIT UM OAF IT!

Mrs Murphy turned away and ran oot ay the pub. The expression oan her face got tae us; it wis one ay total defeat. No only hud she loast her son tae prison, she'd hud her image ay him compromised. Ah felt fir the woman, and resented Franco.

— Aye, she's the billy ay the washhoose, that yin, Ma commented, but adding wistfully, — ah kin feel fir her though. Her laddie gaun tae jail. She looked at me, shaking her head. — For aw the hassle, ye wouldnae be withoot them. How's your wee yin, Frank? She turned to Begbie.

I cringed to think about how easily people like ma Ma were taken in by punters like Franco.

— Barry, Mrs Renton. Gittin some some fuckin size.

— Call us Cathy. Ah'll Mrs Renton yis! Yis make us feel ancient!

— Ye are, ah commented. She ignored us completely, and naebody else laughed, no even Billy. Indeed, Begbie and Sick Boy looked at us like disapproving uncles do tae a cheeky brat whae it isnae their place tae chastise. Ah'm now relegated tae the same status as Begbie's bairn.

— Wee laddie, is it Frank? Ma asks her fellow parent.

— Aye, too right. Ah sais tae Ju, ah sais, if it's a lassie it's gaun right back.

Ah could just see 'Ju' now, wi that grey, porridge-coloured skin, greasy hair and thin body with the sagging flesh still hanging off it, her face frozen neutral, deathly; unable tae smile or frown. The valium taking the edge off her nerves as the bairn lets rip with another volley of shudder-inducing screams. She'll love that child, as much as Franco'll be indifferent tae the perr wee cunt. It'll be a smothering, indulgent, unquestioning, forgiving love, which will ensure that the kid turns oot tae be jist like its daddy. That kid's name wis doon fir H.M. Prison Saughton when it was still in June's womb, as sure as the foetus of a rich bastard is Eton-bound. While this process is going on, daddy Franco will be whair he is now: the boozer.

— Ah'll be an auld grandma masel soon! God, ye widnae believe it. Ma Ma looked at Billy with awe and pride. He simpered proudly. Since he'd got his lemon, Sharon, up the stick, he was my Ma and faither's golden boy. Forgotten is the fact thit that cunt's brought the labdicks tae the hoose mair times thin ah hud ivir done; at least ah hud the decency no tae shite oan ma ain doorstep. This now means fuck all. Just because he's signed up fir the fuckin army again, six bastard years this time, and bairned some slag. Ma Ma n faither ought tae be askin the cunt what the fuck he's daein wi his life. But naw. It's aw proud smiles.

— If it's a lassie Billy, git her tae take it back, Begbie repeated, slurring this time. The bevvy wis getting to him. Another cunt whae's been oan the pish since fuck knows when.

— That's the spirit Franco, Sick Boy slapped Begbie on the back, tryin tae encourage the radge, tae gie him mair rope so that he'll come oot with another crass Begbie classic or two. We collect aw his stupidest, most sexist and violent quotes tae use whin impersonating him whin he's no aroond. We kin make oorsels almost ill wi convulsive laughter. The game hus an edge: thinking aboot how he'd respond if he found oot. Sick Boy hus even started makin faces behind his back. One day, either one ay us or the baith ay us'll go too far, and be marked by fist, bottle or subjected tae 'the discipline ay the basebaw bat'. (One ay Begbie's choice quotes.)

We taxied doon tae Leith. Begbie hud began grumbling aboot 'toon prices' and hud started tae pursue a totally irrational advocacy ay Leith as an entertainment centre. Billy agreed, wantin tae get closer tae hame, reasoning that his pregnant burd wid be mair easily appeased if the placatory phone call came fi a local pub.

Sick Boy would huv heartily denounced Leith, hud ah no done so first. The cunt therefore took great delight in phoning the taxi. We goat intae a pub at the Fit ay the Walk, one thit ah've nivir liked, but one thit we always seemed tae git stuck in. Fat Malcolm, behind the bar, goat us a double voddy oan the house.

— Heard ye goat a result. Well done that man.

Ah shrugged. A couple ay auldish guys wir treatin Begbie like he wis a Hollywood star; listening indulgently tae one ay his stories that wisnae particularly funny, and this they'd probably heard many times before anyway.

Sick Boy bought a roond ay drinks, makin a total meal ay it, ostentatiously waving his money aboot.

— BILLY! LAGER? MRS RENTON . . . EH CATHY! WHAT'S THAT? GIN N BITTER LEMON? he shouted back at the corner table fae the bar.

Ah realised thit Begbie, now involved in a conspiratorial tale wi an ugly, box-heided wanker, the type who ye avoid like the plague, hud slipped Sick Boy the dough tae git the bevvy up.

Billy wis arguing wi Sharon oan the phone.

— Ma fuckin brar gits oaf fi gittin sent doon! Nickin books, assaultin a member ay the shoap's staff, possession ay drugs. The spawny cunt gits a result. Even ma Ma's here! Ah'm entitled tae celebrate, fuck sake . . .

He must have been desperate if he wis reduced tae playin the brotherly love caird.

—Thair's Planet Ay The Apes, Sick Boy whispered tae us, noddin ower at a guy whae drank in the pub. He looked like an extra fi that film. As always, he wis pished n tryin tae find company. Unfortunately, his eye caught mine, n he came ower tae us.

— Interested in hoarses? he asks.

— Naw.

— Interested in fitba? he slurs.

— Naw.

— Rugby? he's soundin desperate now.

— Naw, ah sais. Whether he wis oan the make or jist wanted company wis difficult tae determine. Ah don't think the cunt knew hissel. He hud lost interest in me anywey, n turned tae Sick Boy.

— Interested in hoarses?

— Naw. Ah hate fitba n rugby n aw. Films ah like though. Especially yon *Planet Ay The Apes*? Ivir seen that yin? Ah lap that up.

— Aye! Ah remember that yin! *Planet Ay The Apes*. Charlton Fuckin Heston. Roddy Mc . . . what's the boy's name? Wee cunt. Ye ken whae ah'm talkin aboot. He kens whae ah'm talkin aboot! Planet Ay The Apes turns tae us.

— McDowall.

— That's the cunt! He says triumphantly. He turns tae Sick Boy again. — Whair's yir wee burd the day?

— Eh? Whae's that? Sick Boy asks, totally scoobied.

— That wee blonde piece, the one ye wir in here wi the other night.

— Aw, aye, her.

— Tidy wee bit ay fanny . . . if ye dinnae mind us sayin, likesay. Nae offence likes, pal.

— Naw, nae problem mate. Yours fir fifty bar, n that's nae joke. Sick Boy's voice droaps.

— You serious?

— Aye. Nae kinky stuff, jist a straight hump. Cost ye fifty bar.

Ah couldnae believe ma ears. Sick Boy wisnae jokin. He wis gaun tae try tae set up Planet Ay The Apes wi wee Maria Anderson, this junky he'd been fucking on and oaf for a few months. The cunt wanted tae pimp her oot. Ah felt sickened at what he'd come tae, what we'd aw come tae, and started tae envy Spud again.

Ah pull um aside. — Whit's the fuckin score?

— The score is ah'm looking eftir numero uno. Whit's your fuckin problem? When did you go intae social work?

— This is fuckin different. Ah dinnae ken whit the fuck's gaun oan wi you mate, ah really dinnae.

— So you're Mister fuckin Squeaky Clean now, eh?

— Naw, bit ah dinnae fuck ower any cunt else.

— Git ootay ma face. Tell us it wisnae you thit turned Tommy oantae Seeker n that crowd. His eyes wir crystal clear and treacherous, untainted by conscience or compassion. He turned away n moved back ower tae Planet Ay The Apes.

Ah wis gaunny say thit Tommy hud a choice; wee Maria disnae. Aw that would huv done wis precipitate an argument aboot whair choice began and ended. How many shots does it take before the concept ay choice becomes obsolete? Wish tae fuck ah knew. Wish tae fuck ah knew anything.

As if oan cue, Tommy came intae the pub; follayed by Second Prize, whae wis guttered. Tommy's started using. He nivir used before. It's probably our fault; probably ma fault. Speed wis eywis Tommy's drug. Lizzy's kicked um intae touch. He's awfay quiet, awfay subdued. Second Prize isnae.

— The Rent Boy knocks it oaf! Hey! Ya fuckin cunt thit ye are! he shouts, crushin ma hand.

A chorus ay 'there's only one Mark Renton' echoes throughout the pub. Auld, toothless Willie Shane is giein it laldy. So's Beggars's grandfaither, a nice auld cunt wi one leg. Beggars and two ay his psychotic friends whae ah dinnae even ken ur singing, so's Sick Boy n Billy, even ma Ma.

Tommy slaps us oan the back. — Nice one ma man, he sais. Then: — Goat any smack?

Ah tell um tae forget it, leave it alane while he still can. He tells us, aw the cocky cunt like, thit he can handle it. Seems tae me ah've heard that line before. Ah've spun it masel, n probably ah'll dae so again.

Ah'm surrounded by the cunts thit ur closest tae us; but ah've nivir felt so alone. Nivir in ma puff.

Planet Ay The Apes hus insinuated hissel intae the company. The thought ay that cunt shaggin wee Maria Anderson is not aesthetically appealing. The thought ay that cunt shaggin anybody isnae aesthetically appealing. If he tries tae talk tae ma Ma, ah'll gless the fucker's primate pus.

Andy Logan comes intae the pub. He's an exuberant cunt who reeks ay petty crime and prison. Ah met Loags a couple ay years ago when we were baith workin as park attendants at a council golf course, and pocklin loads ay cash. It wis the ticket checker in the park patrol van whae pit us oantae the scam. Lucrative times; ah nivir used tae touch ma wages. Ah like Loags, bit oor friendship nivir developed. Aw he could talk aboot wir these times.

Everybody wis at it, the reminiscing game. Each conversation began wi 'mind the time whin . . .' and we were talkin aboot perr auld Spud now.

Flocksy came intae the boozer and gestured us ower tae the bar. He asked us fir skag. Ah'm oan the programme. It's mad. It wis ironic thit ah git nicked fir stealin books whin ah'm tryin tae git sorted oot. Its this methadone though, it's a fuckin killer. Gies us the heebie-jeebies. Ah hud it bad in the bookshoap whin that baw-faced cunt hud tae try tae play the hero.

Ah tell Flocksy ah'm oan the maintenance, n he jist fucks off without sayin another word.

Billy clocked us talkin tae um n follays the cunt ootside, but ah bombs ower n pulls his airm.

— Ah'm gaunnae brek that fuckin trash up . . . he hisses through his teeth.

— Leave um, he's awright. Flocksy's headin doon the road, oblivious tae aw this, oblivious tae everything except the procurement ay smack.

— Fuckin trash. Ye deserve eveything ye fuckin git hingin aboot wi that scum.

He goes back in n sits doon, bit only because he sees Sharon n June comin doon the road.

When Begbie clocks June in the pub, he glowers accusingly at her.

— Whair's the bairn?

— He's at ma sisters, June sais timidly.

Begbie's belligerent eyes, open mouth and frozen face turn away from her, trying to absorb this information and decide whether he feels good, bad or indifferent about it. Eventually he turns tae Tommy and affectionately tells him that he's some cunt.

What huv ah goat here? Billy's fuckin nosey, reactionary bastard's outrage. Sharon lookin at us like ah've goat two heids. Ma, drunk and sluttish, Sick Boy . . . the cunt. Spud in the jail. Matty in the hospital, and nae cunt's been tae see um, nae cunt even talks aboot um, it's like he never existed. Begbie . . . fuck sakes, glowing, while June looks like a pile ay crumpled bones in that hideous shell-suit, an unflattering garment at the best ay times, but highlighting her jagged shapelessness.

Ah go tae the bog and when ah finish ma pish ah ken ah cannae go back in thair tae face that shite. Ah sneak out through the side door. It's still fourteen hours n fifteen minutes until ah kin git ma new fix. The state-sponsored addiction: substitute methadone for smack, the sickly jellies, three a day, for the hit. Ah've no known many junkies oan that programme whae didnae take aw three jellies at once and go oot scorin. The morn's mornin, that's how long ah've goat tae wait till. Ah decide ah cannae wait that long. Ah'm off tae Johnny Swan's for ONE hit, just ONE FUCKIN HIT tae get us ower this long, hard, day.

Junk Dilemmas No. 66

It's a challenge tae move: but it shouldnae be. Ah can move. It has been done before. By definition, we, humans, likes, are matter in motion. Why move anyway, when you have everything you need right here. Ah'll soon huv tae move though. Ah'll move when ah'm sick enough; ah know that through experience as well. Ah jist cannae conceive ay ever being that sick that ah'll want tae move. This frightens me, because ah'll need tae move soon.

Surely ah'll be able tae dae it; surely tae fuck.

Deid Dugs

Ah . . . the enemy ish in shite, as the old Bond would have said, and what a fuckin sight the cunt looks as well. Skinheid haircut, green bomber-jaykit, nine-inch DMs. A stereotypical twat; and there's the woof-woof trailing loyally behind. Pit Bull, shit bull, bullshit terrier . . . a fuckin set ay jaws on four legs. Aw, it's pishing by a tree. *Here boy, here boy.*

The sport ay living over a park. Ah fix the beast in ma telescopic sights; it could just be my imagination, but they seem tae be a wee bitty out these days, veering tae the right. Still, Simone is a good enough marksman tae compensate for this malfunction in his trusted technology, this old .22 air rifle. Ah swing ower tae the skinheid, targeting his face. Ah then travel up and doon his body, up and doon, up and doon . . . *take it easy baby* . . . *take it one more time* . . . nobody has ever given the bastard this much attention, this much care, this much . . . yes, love, in his puff. It's a great feeling, knowing that you have the power to inflict such pain, fae yir ain front room. *Call me the unsheen ashashin Mish Moneypenny.*

It's the Pit Bull ah'm eftir though; ah want tae get him tae turn on his master, tae sever the touching man-beast relationship along with his owner's testicles. I hope the shit-bull's got mair bollocks than that stupid Rottweiler ah shot the other day. Ah blasted the big cunt in the side ay the face, and did the pathetic bastard turn on his glakit master in the shell-suit? Did he heckers laik, as Vera and Ivy oot ay *Coronation Street* would say. The cunt just started whimpering.

They call me the Sick Boy, the scourge of the schemie, the blooterer of the brain-dead. This one's for you Fido, or Rocky, or Rambo, or Tyson or whatever the fuck your shite-brained, fuck-wit of an owner has dubbed you. This is fir aw the bairns you've slaughtered, faces you've disfigured and shite you've deposited in our streets. Above all though, it's for the shite you've done in the parks, shite which always finds its way onto Simone's body whenever he puts in a sliding tackle in his midfield role for Abbeyhill Athletic in the Lothian Sunday Amateurs' League.

They're now alongside each other, man and beast. Ah squeeze the trigger and take a step back.

Brilliant! The dug yelps and leaps at the skinhead, attaching its jaws ontae the cunt's airm. *Good shooting Shimon.* Why shank you Sean.

— SHANE! SHANE! YA CUNT! AH'LL FUCKIN KILL YE! SHAAYYNNE! the boy's screamin, and bootin at the dug, but his Docs are nae use against this monster. It has just clamped him, and these things do not let go; the only attraction ay huvin them for doss cunts is their ferocity. The boy is really gaun mental, first strugglin, then tryin tae stey still, because it's too sair tae struggle; alternatively threatening then pleading with this fucking compassionless killing machine. An auld cunt comes ower tae try tae help, but backs oaf as the dug swivels his eyes roond and growls through its nose, as if to say: You're next cunt.

Ah'm doon the stair at high speed, aluminium baseball bat in ma hand. This is what ah've been waitin for, this is what it's all about. Man the hunter. Ma mooth's dry wi anticipation; the Sick Boy is on safari. *A little problem for you to short out, Shimon.* I think I can handle that, Sean.

— HELP US! HELP US! the skinhead squeals. He's younger than ah thought.

— S awright mate. Stay cool, ah tell um. Have no fear, Simone's here.

Ah stealthily creep up behind the dug; ah don't want the fucker tae break its grip and go for me, even though there is very little chance ay that. Blood is oozing fae the guy's airm and the dug's mooth, saturating the side ay the boy's jaykit. The guy thinks ah'm gaunnae batter the dug's nut wi the bat, but that would be like sending Renton or Spud tae sexually satisfy Laura McEwan.

Instead ah gently lift the dug's collar up and stick the bat's handle under it. Ah twist, and twist . . . *Twist and shout* . . . Still the cunt hauds oan. This skinheid's falling tae his knees, nearly ready tae black oot wi the pain. Ah just keep twisting, and ah can feel the thick muscles in the dug's neck beginning tae yield, tae relax. Ah keep twisting. *Let's twist again, like wi did last suhmah.*

The dug lets oot a series ay hideous gasps through its nose and muffled jaws, as ah throttle the cunt tae death. Even in its death throes, and after, when it's as still as a sack ay tatties, it keeps its grip. Ah take the bat fae its collar, tae help us lever its jaws open, freeing the gadge's airm. By this time the polis have arrived, and ah've wrapped the boy's airm wi the rest ay his jaykit.

The skinhead is singing ma praises tae the polis n the ambulanceman. He's upset at Shane, he still cannae understand what turned this loving pet whae 'wouldnae hurt a fly', the cunt actually said that, mouthed that hideous cliché, intae a deranged monster. *Theshe beashts can turn at any time.*

As they led him into the ambulance, the young cop shook his heid. — Fuckin stupid works. These things are just killers. It's a big ego-trip for these daft cunts tae own them, but they always go berserk sooner or later.

The aulder polisman is gently interrogative aboot ma need tae huv a baseball bat, and ah tell him it's for home security, as there have been a lot of break-ins in the area. Not that Simone, I explain, would ever dream of talking the law into his own hands, but, well, it just gives one a certain peace of mind. Ah wonder if anybody this side of the Atlantic has ever bought a baseball bat with playing baseball in mind.

— Ah can understand that, the auld cop says. I'll bet you can, you dippet cunt. *The offishers of the law are rather shilly, eh Sean? Not particularly impreshiff, Shimon.*

The guys are telling me that I'm a brave gadge, and that they will be recommending a commendation. *Why shank you offisher, but it'sh nothing really.*

The Sick Boy is going round tae Marianne's the night for some sick fun. Doggy style must certainly be on the menu, if only as a tribute to Shane.

I am as high as a kite and horny as a field of stags. It's been a fucking beautiful day.

Searching for the Inner Man

Ah've never been incarcerated for junk. However, loads ay cunts have had stabs at rehabilitating me. Rehabilitation is shite; sometimes ah think ah'd rather be banged up. Rehabilitation means the surrender ay the self.

Ah've been referred tae a variety of counsellors, wi backgrounds ranging fae pure psychiatry through clinical psychology to social work. Doctor Forbes, the psychiatrist, used non-directive counselling techniques, basing his approach largely on Freudian psychoanalysis. This involved getting us tae talk aboot ma past life and focus oan unresolved conflicts, the assumption presumably bein that the indentification and resolution ay such conflicts will remove the anger which fuels ma self-destructive behaviour, that behaviour manifesting itself in ma use ay hard drugs.

A typical exchange:

Dr Forbes: You mentioned your brother, the one with the, eh, disability. The one that died. Can we talk about him?

	(pause)
Me:	Why?
	(pause)
Dr Forbes:	You're reluctant to talk about your brother?
Me:	Naw. It's just that ah dinnae see the relevance ay that tae me bein oan smack.

Dr Forbes: It seems that you started using heavily around the time of your brother's death.

Me: A loat happened aroond that time. Ah'm no really sure how relevant it is tae isolate ma brar's death. Ah went up tae Aberdeen at the time; the Uni. Ah hated it. Then ah started oan the cross-channel ferries, tae Holland. Access tae aw the collies ye could hope fir.

(pause)

Dr Forbes: I'd like to go back to Aberdeen. You say you hated Aberdeen?

Me: Aye.

Dr Forbes: What was it about Aberdeen you hated?

Me: The University. The staff, the students and aw that. Ah thought they were aw boring middle-class cunts.

Dr Forbes: I see. You were unable to form relationships with people there.

Me: No sae much unable, as unwilling, although ah suppose it means the same, for your purposes (noncommittal shrug fae Dr Forbes) . . . ah hudnae any interest in any fucker thair.

(pause)

Ah mean ah didnae really see the point. Ah knew ah wisnae gaunnae stey fir long. If ah wanted a blether, ah'd go tae the pub. If ah wanted a ride ah'd go tae a prostitute.

Dr Forbes: You spent time with prostitutes?

Me:	Aye.
Dr Forbes:	Was this because you lacked confidence in your ability to form social and sexual attachments with women at the University? (pause)
Me:	Naw, ah did meet a couple ay lassies.
Dr Forbes:	What happened?
Me:	Ah wis only interested in sex, rather than a relationship. Ah didnae really huv the motivation tae disguise that fact. Ah saw these women purely as a means ay satisfying ma sexual urges. Ah decided it wis mair honest tae go tae a prostitute instead, rather than play a game ay deception. Ah wis quite a moral fucker in these days. So ah blew ma grant money oan prostitutes, and nicked food and books. That's what started the thievin. It wisnae really the junk, though that obviously didnae help.
Dr Forbes:	Mmmm. Can we go back to your brother, the one with the handicap. How did you feel about him?
Me:	No really sure . . . look, the guy wis jist ootay it. He wisnae thair. Totally paralysed. Aw he'd dae wis tae sit in that chair wi his heid turned tae the side. Aw he could dae wis blink n swallow. Sometimes he made wee noises . . . he wis like an object, rather than a person. (pause) Ah suppose ah resented um whin ah wis younger. Ah mean, ma Ma would just take um oot in this pram. This big, outsized thing in a fuckin pram, likes. It made me n ma big brar, Billy, the laughin stock wi the other kids. Wid git: 'Your brother's a spastic' or 'Your brother's a zombie' and aw that sortay shite. Jist bairns, ah ken, but it

doesnae seem like that at the time. Because ah wis tall n awkward as a wee laddie, ah started tae believe thit thir wis something wrong wi me n aw, that ah wis somehow like Davie . . .

(long pause)

Dr Forbes: So you felt a resentment towards your brother.

Me: Aye, as a bairn, a wee laddie, like. Then he went intae the hoespital. Ah suppose it wis, likes, problem solved, ken. Sortay ootay sight, ootay mind. Ah visited um a few times, but thir didnae seem tae be any point. Nae interaction, ken? Ah jist saw it as a cruel twist ay life. Perr Davie goat dealt the shitest possible hand. Fuckin sad, but ye cannae greet aboot it fir the rest ay yir puff. He wis in the best place fir um, gittin well looked eftir. Whin he died, ah felt guilty aboot resentin um, guilty aboot mibbe no huvin made a bit mair ay an effort. What kin ye dae though?

(pause)

Dr Forbes: Have you talked about these feelings before?

Me: Naw . . . well, mibbe mentioned it tae ma Ma n faither . . . . . .

That was how it used tae go. A loat ay issues brought up; some trivial, some heavy, some dull, some interesting. Sometimes ah telt the truth, sometimes ah lied. When ah lied, ah sometimes said the things that ah thought he'd like tae hear, n sometimes said something which ah thought would wind him up, or confuse him.

Fucked if ah could see the connection between any ay that and me takin smack, but.

Ah did learn a few things though, based oan Forbes's disclosures and ma ain researches into psychoanalysis and how ma behaviour should be interpreted. Ah have an unresolved relationship wi ma deid brother, Davie, as ah huv been unable tae work oot or express ma feelings about his catatonic life and subsequent death. Ah have oedipal feelings towards ma mother and an attendant unresolved jealousy towards ma faither. Ma junk behaviour is anal in concept, attention-seeking, yes, but instead of withholding the faeces tae rebel against parental authority, ah'm pittin smack intae ma body tae claim power over it vis-à-vis society in general. Radge, eh?

Aw this might or might no be true. Ah've pondered ower a loat ay it, and ah'm willin tae explore it; ah don't feel defensive aboot any ay it. However, ah feel that it's at best peripheral tae the issue ay ma addiction. Certainly, talking about it extensively has done fuck all good. Ah think Forbes is as scoobied as ah am.

Molly Greaves, the clinical psychologist, tended to look at ma behaviour and ways of modifying it, rather than determining its causes. It seemed like Forbes had done his bit, now it was time tae get us sorted oot. That wis when ah started oan the reduction programme, which simply didnae work, then the methadone treatment, which made us worse.

Tom Curzon, the counsellor fae the drugs agency, a guy wi a social work rather than medical background, was intae Rogerian client-centred counselling. Ah went tae the Central Library and read Carl Rogers's *On Becoming A Person*. Ah thought that the book wis shite, but ah huv tae admit that Tom seemed tae get us closer tae what ah believe the truth might be. Ah despised masel and the world because ah failed tae face up tae ma ain, and life's, limitations.

The acceptance ay self-defeating limitations seemed then tae constitute mental health, or non-deviant behaviour.

Success and failure simply mean the satisfaction and frustration ay desire. Desire can either be predominantly intrinsic, based oan oor individual drives, or extrinsic, primarily stimulated by advertising, or societal role models as presented through the media and popular culture. Tom feels that ma concept ay success and failure only operates on an individual rather than an individual and societal level. Due tae this failure tae recognise societal reward, success (and failure) can only ever be fleeting experiences for me, as that experience cannae be sustained by the socially-supported condoning of wealth, power, status, etc., nor, in the case ay failure, by stigma or reproach. So, according tae Tom, it's nae good tellin us that ah've done well in ma exams, or got a good job, or got off wi a nice burd; that kind ay acclaim means nowt tae us. Of course, ah enjoy these things at the time, or for themselves, but their value cannae be sustained because there's nae recognition ay the society which values them. What Tom's trying tae say, ah suppose, is that ah dinnae gie a fuck. Why?

So it goes back tae ma alienation from society. The problem is that Tom refuses tae accept ma view that society cannae be changed tae make it significantly better, or that ah cannae change tae accommodate it. Such a state ay affairs induces depression on ma part, aw the anger gets turned in. That's what depression is, they say. However, depression also results in demotivation. A void grows within ye. Junk fills the void, and also helps us tae satisfy ma need tae destroy masel, the anger turned in bit again.

So basically ah agree wi Tom here. Whair we depart is that he refuses tae see this picture in its total bleakness. He believes that ah'm suffering fae low self-esteem, and that ah'm refusing tae acknowledge that by projecting the blame oantae society. He feels that ma means ay emasculating the rewards and praise (and conversely condemnation) available tae me by society is not a rejection ay these values per se, but an indication that ah dinnae feel good enough (or bad enough) aboot masel tae accept them. Rather than come oot and say: Ah don't think ah have these qualities (or ah think ah'm better than that), Ah say: It's a loaday fuckin shite anyway.

Hazel said tae us, jist before she telt us that she didnae wantae see us again, whin ah started using for the umpteenth time: — You just want tae fuck up on drugs so that everyone'll think how deep and fucking complex you are. It's pathetic, and fucking boring.

In a sense ah prefer Hazel's view. Thir is an element ay ego in it. Hazel understands ego needs. She's a windae dresser in a department store, but describes hersel as a 'consumer display artist' or something like that. Why should ah reject the world, see masel as better than it? Because ah do, that's why. Because ah fuckin am, and that's that.

The upshot ay this attitude is that ah was sent tae this therapy/ counselling shite. Ah didnae want aw this. It wis this or the jail. Ah'm startin tae think that Spud goat the soft option. This shite muddies the waters for us; confuses rather than clarifies issues. Basically, aw ah ask is that cunts mind their ain business and ah'll dae the same. Why is it that because ye use hard drugs every cunt feels that they have a right tae dissect and analyse ye?

Once ye accept that they huv that right, ye'll join them in the search fir this holy grail, this thing that makes ye tick. Ye'll then defer tae them, allowin yersel tae be conned intae believin any biscuit-ersed theory ay behaviour they choose tae attach tae ye. Then yir theirs, no yir ain; the dependency shifts from the drug to them.

Society invents a spurious convoluted logic tae absorb and change people whae's behaviour is outside its mainstream. Suppose that ah ken aw the pros and cons, know that ah'm gaunnae huv a short life, am ay sound mind etcetera, etcetera, but still want tae use smack? They won't let ye dae it. They won't let ye dae it, because it's seen as a sign ay thir ain failure. The fact that ye jist simply choose tae reject whit they huv tae offer. Choose us. Choose life. Choose mortgage payments; choose washing machines; choose cars; choose sitting oan a couch watching mind-numbing and spirit-crushing game shows, stuffing fuckin junk food intae yir mooth. Choose rotting away, pishing and shiteing yersel in a home, a total fuckin embarrassment tae the selfish, fucked-up brats ye've produced. Choose life.

Well, ah choose no tae choose life. If the cunts cannae handle that, it's thair fuckin problem. As Harry Lauder sais, ah jist intend tae keep right on to the end of the road . . .

House Arrest

This bed is familiar, or rather, the wall opposite it is. Paddy Stanton looks doon at us wi his seventies sideboards. Iggy Pop sits smashing a pile ay records wi a claw hammer. Ma auld bedroom, in the parental home. Ma heid struggles tae piece thegither how ah've goat here. Ah can remember Johnny Swan's place, then feeling like ah wis gaunnae die. Then it comes back; Swanney n Alison takin us doon the stairs, gittin us intae a taxi n bombin up tae the Infirmary.

Funny thing wis, jist before this, ah remembered boastin thit ah'd niver OD'd in ma puff. Thir's a first time fir everything. It wis Swanney's fault. His gear's normally cut tae fuck, so ye always bung that wee bit mair intae the cooking spoon tae compensate. Then whit does the cunt dae? He hits ye wi some pure shit. Literally takes yir breath away. Daft cunt that he is, Swanney must've gave thum ma Ma's address. So eftir a few days in the hoespital gittin ma breathin stabilised, here ah am.

Here ah am in the junky's limbo; too sick tae sleep, too tired tae stay awake. A twilight zone ay the senses where nothing's real

194

except the crushing, omnipresent misery n pain in your mind n body. Ah notice with a start that ma Ma's actually sitting on my bed, looking silently at me.

As soon as ah'm aware ay this, she could be sitting oan ma chest for the level ay crushing discomfort ah feel.

She puts her hand oantae ma sweaty brow. Her touch feels horrible, creepy, violating.

— Yir oan fire laddie, she sais softly, shaking her heid, concern etched oantay her face.

Ah raise a hand above the covers tae brush hers aside. Misinterpreting ma gesture, she grabs ma hand in both ay hers and squeezes tightly, cripplingly. Ah want tae scream.

— Ah'll help ye son. Ah'll help ye fight this disease. Ye'll stay here wi me n yir faither until yir better. Wir gaunnae beat this son, wir gaunnae beat it!

Her eyes have an intense, glazed look about them and her voice has a crusading zeal.

Shoo'nuff momma, shoo'nuff.

— Ye'll git through it though son. Doctor Mathews sais that it's jist really like a bad flu, this withdrawal, she tell us.

When wis the last time auld Mathews hud cauld turkey? Ah'd like tae lock that dangerous auld radge in a padded cell fir a fortnight, and gie um a couple ay injections ay diamorphine a day, then leave the cunt for a few days. He'd be beggin us fir it eftir that. Ah'd jist shake ma heid and say: Take it easy mate. What's the fuckin problem? It's jist like a bad flu.

— Did he gie us temazepan? ah ask.

— Naw! Ah telt um, nane ay that rubbish. Ye wir worse comin oaf that thin ye wir wi heroin. Cramps, sickness, diarrhoea . . . ye wir in a hell ay a state. Nae mair drugs.

— Mibbe ah could go back tae the clinic, Ma, ah hopefully suggest.

— Naw! Nae clinics. Nae methadone. That made ye worse, son, ye said so yirsel. Ye lied tae us, son. Tae yir ain mother n faither! Ye took that methadone n still went oot scorin. Fae now oan son it's a clean brek. Yir stayin here whair ah kin keep an eye oan ye. Ah've loast one laddie already, ah'm no losin another yin! Tears welled up in her eyes.

Poor Ma, still blaming hersel fir that fucked-up gene that caused ma brother Davie tae be born a cabbage. Her guilt, eftir struggling wi him fir years, at pittin him in the hoespital. Her devastation at his death last year. Ma kens whit everybody thinks ay her, the neighbours n that. They see her as flighty and brazen, because ay her blonde hair-dye, clathes too young fir her, and her liberal consumption ay Carlsberg Specials. They think thit her n ma faither used Davie's profound handicap tae git oot ay the Fort n git this nice Housing Association flat by the river, then cynically dumped the poor cunt in the residential care.

Fuck the facts, these trivial things, they petty jealousies become part ay the mythology in a place like Leith, a place fill ay nosey cunts who willnae mind their ain business. A place ay dispossessed white trash in a trash country fill ay dispossessed white trash. Some say that the Irish are the trash ay Europe. That's shite. It's the Scots. The Irish hud the bottle tae win thir country back, or at least maist ay it. Ah remember gettin wound up when Nicksy's brar, down in London, described the Scots as 'porridge wogs'. Now ah realise that the only thing offensive about that statement was its racism against black people. Otherwise it's spot-on. Anybody will tell you; the Scots make good soldiers. Like ma brar, Billy.

They suspect the auld man here as well. His Glasgow accent, the fact thit since being made redundant fi Parson's he's punted gear in the markets at Ingliston n East Fortune instead ay sittin in Strathie's Bar moanin his fuckin box oaf aboot everything.

They mean well, and they mean well tae me, but there's nae way under the sun that they can appreciate what ah feel, what ah need.

Protect me from those who wish tae help us.

— Ma . . . ah appreciate whit yir tryin tae dae, but ah need jist one score, tae ease masel oaf it. Jist the one, likes, ah plead.

— Forget it son. Ma auld man hus come intae the room withoot us hearin um. The auld girl nivir even gits a chance tae speak. — Your tea's oot. You'd better shape up pal, ah'm tellin ye.

He looks stony-faced, his chin jutting forward, his airms by his sides, as if in readiness tae huv a square go wi us.

— Aye . . . . right, ah mumble miserably, fae under the duvet. Ma pits a protective hand oan ma shoodir. We've both regressed.

— Mucked up everythin, he accuses, then reads oot the charges: — Apprenticeship. University. That nice wee lassie ye wir seein. Aw the chances ye hud Mark, n ye blew them.

He disnae need tae say aboot how he nivir hud they chances growin up in Govan n leavin school at fifteen n takin an apprenticeship. That's implicit. When ye think aboot it though, it isnae that much different fae growin up in Leith n leaving school at sixteen n takin an apprenticeship. Especially as he nivir grew up in an era ay mass unemployment. Still, ah'm in nae shape tae argue, n even if ah wis, it's pointless wi Weedjies. Ah've never met one Weedjie whae didnae think that they are the only genuinely suffering proletarians in Scotland, Western Europe, the World. Weedjie experience ay hardship is the only relevant experience ay it. Ah try another suggestion.

— Eh, mibbe ah'll go back doon tae London. Git a joab likes. Ah'm almost delirious. Ah imagine that Matty's in the room. — Matty . . . Ah think ah said it. The fuckin pain's starting tae.

— Yir in cloud cuckoo land son. Yir gaun naewhair. If ye shite, ah wahnt tae know aboot it.

There wisnae much chance ay that. The rock ah hud compacting in ma bowels would huv tae be surgically removed. Ah'd huv tae start forcin doon the Milk ay Magnesia solution and keep at it fir days tae git a result thair.

Whin the auld man shot the craw, ah managed tae cajole ma Ma intae giein us a couple ay her valium. She wis oan them fir six months after Davie died. The thing is, because she kicked them, she now regards hersel as an expert oan drug rehabilitation. This is smack, fir fuck's sake, mother dear.

I am tae be under house arrest.

The morning wisnae pleasant, but it wis a picnic compared tae the eftirnin. The auld man came back fae his fact-finding mission. Libraries, health-board establishments and social-work offices had been visited. Research hud been undertaken, advice hud been sought, leaflets procured.

He wanted tae take us tae git tested fir HIV. Ah don't want tae go through aw that shite again.

Ah git up fir ma tea, frail, bent and brittle as ah struggle doon the stairs. Every move makes ma blood soar tae ma throbbing heid. At one stage ah thought that it wid just burst open, like a balloon, sending blood, skull fragments and grey matter splattering oantae Ma's cream woodchip.

The auld girl sticks us in the comfy chair by the fire in front ay the telly, and puts a tray oan ma lap. Ah'm convulsing inside anyway, but the mince looks revolting.

— Ah've telt ye ah dinnae eat meat Ma, ah sais.

— Ye eywis liked yir mince n tatties. That's whair ye've gone wrong son, no eating the right things. Ye need meat.

Now there is apparently a causal link between heroin addiction and vegetarianism.

— It's good steak mince. Ye'll eat it, ma faither says. This is fuckin ridiculous.

Ah thought there and then about making for the door, even though ah'm wearing a tracksuit and slippers. As if reading ma mind, the auld man produces a set ay keys.

— The door stays locked. Ah'm fittin a lock oan yir room as well.

— This is fuckin fascism, ah sais, wi feelin.

— Dinnae gies yir crap. Ye kin cry it whit ye like; if that's whit it takes, that's whit you'll get. An mind yir language in the hoose.

Ma bursts intae a passionate rant: — Me n yir faither son, s no as if we wanted this. S no likesay that at aw. It's because we love ye son, yir aw wuv goat, you n Billy. Faither's hand faws oan toap ay hers.

Ah cannae eat ma food. The auld man isnae prepared tae go tae the extent ay force-feeding us, so he's forced tae accept the fact that good steak mince is going tae waste. No really tae waste, as he hus mine. Instead ah sip oan some cauld Heinz tomatay soup, which is aw ah kin take whin ah'm sick. Ah seemed tae leave ma body fir a while, watching a game show oan the box. Ah could hear ma auld man talking tae ma auld girl, bit ah couldnae take ma eyes fae the ugly-looking game-show host and turn ma heid tae face ma parents. Faither's voice seems almost tae be comin fae the set.

— . . . said here that Scotland's goat eight per cent o the UK population but sixteen per cent o the UK HIV cases . . . *What's the scores, Miss Ford? . . .* Embra's goat eight per cent o the Scottish population but ower sixty per cent o the Scottish HIV infection, by far the highest rate in Britain . . . *Daphne and John have scored eleven points, but Lucy and Chris, have fifteen! . . .* they say thit they discovered this blood-testin punters in Muirhoose fir summit else, hepatitis or that, n discovered the scale o the problem . . . *oooh . . . oooh . . . well, tough luck to the very sporting losers, give 'em a hand then, give 'em a hand . . .* the scumbags thit did this tae the boey, if ah git thir names, ah'll git a squad thegither n sort them oot masel, obviously the polis arenae interested, lettin thum deal that shite oan the streets . . . *won't be going away empty handed . . .* even if he is HIV it's no an automatic death sentence. That's aw ah'm saying Cathy, it's no an automatic death sentence . . . *Tom and Sylvia Heath of Leek in Staffordshire . . .* he sais he's no been sharin needles, but he's been proved a liar in the past . . . *it says here Sylvia darling, that you met Tom when he was looking under your bonnet, oooh . . .* wir jist sayin 'if' now Cathy . . . *he was fixing your car which had gone in for a service, oh, I see . . .* hopefully he hud mair sense . . . *first game's called 'Shoot To Kill' . . .* but it isnae an automatic death sentence . . . *and who better to show us the ropes than my old mate, from the Royal Archery Society of Great Britain, the one and only Len Holmes! . . .* that's aw ah'm sayin Cathy . . .

Ah started tae feel a crippling nausea and the room began tae spin. Ah fell oot ay the chair n puked tomatay soup aw ower the fireside rug. Ah don't remember getting pit tae bed. *There goes my first love woo-hoo . . .*

Ma body was being twisted and crushed. It wis like ah hud collapsed in the street and a skip hud been lowered oan top ay us, n a squad ay vicious workies wir loading it up wi heavy building materials, while at the same time sticking sharp rods underneath to skewer ma body. *With the guy I used to . . .*

What's the fuckin time? Ah wonder what the fuck 7:28. *I can't forget her . . .*

Hazel

My heart is breaking woo-hoo when I see her . . .

Ah throw back the weighty duvet and look at Paddy Stanton. Paddy. Whit am ah gaunny dae? Gordon Durie. Juke Box. What's the fuckin score here? Why did ye leave us Juke Box, ya cunt? Iggy . . . you've been thair. Help us man. HELP ME.

What did you say aboot it aw?

YOU'RE NO FUCKIN HELP YA CUNT . . . NO FUCKIN HELP AT AW . . .

Blood flows oantae the pillow. Ah've bitten ma tongue. Severely severed by the looks ay it. Every cell in ma body wants tae leave it, every cell is sick hurting marinated in pure fuckin poison

cancer

death

sick sick sick

death death death

AIDS AIDS fuck yis aw FUCKIN CUNTS FUCK YIS AW
SELF-INFLICTED PEOPLE WI CANCER – NAE CHOICE
FIR THAIM   DESERVING
AIN FAULT   AUTOMATIC DEATH SENTENCE
THROWIN AWAY YIR LIFE   DOESNAE NEED TAE BE
AN AUTOMATIC DEATH SENTENCE   DESTROY
REHABILITATE
FASCISM
NICE WIFE
NICE BAIRNS
NICE HOOSE
NICE JOAB
NICE
NICE TA SEE YA, TA SEE YA. . . .
NICE NICE NICE   BRAIN DISORDER
                                    DEMENTIA
HERPES THRUSH PNUEMONIA
WHOLE LIFE AHEAD AY YE MEET A NICE LASSIE N
SETTLE DOON . . .

She's still ma first lurve

BROAT IT OAN YIRSEL.

Sleep.

More terrors. Am ah asleep or awake? Who fuckin knows or
cares? No me. The pain's still here. Ah know one thing. If ah
move, ah'll swallow ma tongue. Nice bit ay tongue. That's what
ah cannae wait for ma Ma giein us, just like in the old days.
Tongue salad. Poison your children.
    Ye'll eat that tongue. That's a nice, tasty bit ay tongue thair
son.

YE'LL EAT THAT TONGUE.

If ah don't move, ma tongue will slide down ma gullet anyway. Ah can feel it moving. Ah sit up, consumed by a blind panic, and retch, but thir's nowt comin up. Ma heart's thrashing in my chest, and sweat's lashing from my emaciated frame.

Is this sllllleeeeeeeeepppppppp.

Oh fuck. Thir's somethin in this room wi me it is comin oot the fuckin ceiling above the bed.

It's a baby. Wee Dawn, crawlin along the ceilin. Greetin. But it's lookin doon it us now.

— You let me fuckin diieeeeee, it sais. It's no Dawn. No the wee bairn.

Naw, ah mean, this is fuckin crazy.

The bairn has sharp, vampire teeth wi blood drippin fae them. It's covered in a sick yellow-green slime. It's eyes are the eyes ay every psychopath ah've ever met.

— Yefuckinkilledme litmefuckindie junkedupootyirfuckin-heids watchinthefuckinwaws ya fuckindopeyjunkycunt ah'llfuck-inripyefuckinopen n feedoanyirfuckinmiserablesickgreyjunky-flesh startinwiyirjunkycockcauseahdiedafuckinvirginahllnivirgit-afuckinridenivirgittaewearfuckinmakeupncoolclathesnivirgittae-beanythin causeyoufuckinjunkycuntsnivircheckedus yisletusfuck-indiefuckinsuffocatetaefuckindeath yiskenwhitthatfeelslikeyacunts causeahvegoatafuckinsoulnahkinstillknowfuckinpainnyousecunts youseselfishfuckinjunkycuntswiyirfuckinskagtookitawawayfius soahmgaunnychewyourfuckindiseasedprickoafWANTAFUCK-INBLOWJOBWANTAFUCKINBLOWJOBWANTAFAAAAA-AAAACKIN

It springs fae the ceilin doon oan top ay us. Ma fingers rip and tear at the soft, plasticine flesh and messy gunge but the ugly shrill voice is still screa.nin n mockin n ah jerk n jolt n feel like the bed's sprung vertical n ah'm fawin through the fuckin flair . . .

Is this ssslllleeeeeeeeepppppp.

There goes ma first lurve.

Then ah'm back in the bed, still haudin the bairn, softly cradlin it. Wee Dawn. Fuckin shame.

It's jist ma pillay. There's blood oan ma pillay. Mibbe it wis fae ma tongue; mibbe wee Dawn hus been here.

Thir must be less tae life than this.

More pain, then more sleep/pain.

When ah re-assemble intae consciousness ah'm aware that a period ay time has passed. How much ah don't know. The clock sais: 2:21.

Sick Boy is sitting in the chair looking at us. He has an expression ay mild concern overlaid wi a benign and patronising contempt. As he sips his cup ay tea and munches oan a chocolate digestive, ah realise that ma Ma and faither are also in the room.

What's the fuckin score?

The fuckin score is

— Simon's here, Ma announces, confirming that ah'm no hallucinating unless the mirage has audio as well as visual content. Like Dawn. Each dawn I die.

Ah smile at him. Dawn's dad. – Awright Si.

The bastard is charm itself. Jocular and matey banter about fitba wi ma Hun auld man, coming ower like the concerned GP family friend wi ma auld girl.

— It's a mug's game, Mrs Renton. Ah'm no tryin tae say thit ah'm blameless masel, far from it, but there comes a point whin ye jist huv tae turn yir back on that nonsense and say no.

Just say no. It's easy. Choose Life. Skin Kay-uh boi Eroin.

My parents find it impossible to believe that 'Young Simon' (who's four months aulder than me, and ah never git called 'Young Mark') could possibly have anything to do wi drugs, beyond the odd youthful experimental flirtation. Young Simon is identified with conspicuous success in their eyes. There's Young Simon's girlfriends, Young Simon's smart clathes, Young Simon's suntan, Young Simon's flat up the toon. Even Young Simon's jaunts to London are seen as more colourful chapters in the trendy, swashbuckling adventures of Leith Bannanay Flats's lovable cavalier, while my trips south invariably have a seedy and unsavoury association in their eyes. Young Simon can do no wrong though. They see the cunt as some sort ay *Oor Wullie* for the video generation.

Does Dawn intrude intae Sick Boy's dreams? No.

Although they have never came out and said it, ma Ma n faither suspect that ma drug problems ur due tae ma association wi 'the laddie Murphy'. This is because Spud is a lazy, scruffy bastard, who's naturally spaced out and seems as if he's oan drugs, even when he's clean. Spud is incapable ay upsettin a spurned lover wi a bad hangover. On the other hand Begbie, total fuckin crazy psycho Beggars, is held up as an archetypal model of manhood Ecosse. Yes, there may be poor bastards picking bits ay beer glass oot ay thir faces when Franco goes oan the rampage, but the laddie works hard and plays hard etcetera, etcetera.

After being treated like a simple cunt for an hour or so by all present, ma parents leave the room, convinced that Sick Boy is truly drug-free and not intending to slip their off-spring any H, more's the fuckin pity.

— Like auld times up here, eh? he sais, looking around at ma posters.

— Hing oan, ah'll bring oot the Subbuteo and the dirty books. We used to wank off tae porno mags as wee laddies. Stud thit he is these days, Sick Boy hates tae be reminded ay his fledging sexual development. Typically, he changes the subject.

— You've goat a right lam oan, he sais. What the fuck does the cunt expect in the circumstances?

— Too fuckin right ah huv. Ah'm fuckin sick here, Si. Yiv goat tae score us some smack.

— Nae chance. Ah'm steyin clean Mark. If ah start hingin roond losers like Spud, Swanney n that, ah'm back tae usin again in nae time at aw. No way José, he blaws through pursed lips n shakes his heid.

— Thanks mate. Yir aw fuckin heart.

— Stoap fah-kin whingein. Ah ken how bad it is. Ah went through this a few times n aw remember. Yiv been oaf it a couple ay days now. Yir nearly through the fuckin worst. Ah ken it's sair, bit if ye start shootin now, that's the gig fucked. Keep takin the vallies. Ah'll score ye some hash fir the weekend.

— Hash? Hash! You're a fuckin comedian. Might as well try tae combat third world famine wi a packet ay frozen peas.

— Naw, but listen tae us man. Once the pain goes away, that's whin the real fuckin battle starts. Depression. Boredom. Ah'm tellin ye man, ye'll feel so fuckin low ye'll want tae fuckin top yirsell. Ye need something tae keep ye gaun. Ah started bevvyin like fuck eftir ah came oaf the gear. Ah wis creamin a boatil ay tequila a day at one stage. Second Prize wis embarrassed in ma company! Ah'm oaf the bevvy now, n seein a few birds.

Eh handed us a picture. It showed Sick Boy wi this gorgeous looking lassie.

— Fabienne. French likes. Ower oan hoaliday. That wis taken up the Scott Monument. Ah'm gaun ower tae her bit in Paris next month. Then it's oaf tae Corsica. Hur folks've goat a wee place thair. Fuckin subliminal scene man. Hearin a woman speak in French when yir shaggin her is such a big turn oan.

— Aye, but whit's she saying? Ah bet it's somethin like: Your deek eez so how you say, tynee, 'ave you starteed yet . . . Ah bet that's whit she speaks in French fir.

He gave us that patient, patronising have-you-quite-finished smile.

— Oan that particular subject, ah wis talkin tae Laura McEwan last week. She indicated tae me that you had problems in that self-same area. Told us ye couldnae raise a smile the last time she ended up wi ye.

Ah raise a smile, and shrug. Ah thought ah'd got away with that disaster.

— Says thit ye couldnae satisfy yersel, nivir mind any cunt else, wi that fuckin thimble yuv goat the nerve tae call a penis.

Thir isnae much ah kin say tae Sick Boy on the subject ay cock size. His is bigger, no doubt about it. Whin we wir younger we used tae git pictures taken ay oor knobs in the passport photo booth at Waverley Station. Then we'd stick the photaes doon behind the glass panels in the auld grey bus shelters fir people tae look at. Wi used tae call thum oor public art exhibitions. Conscious ay the fact thit Sick Boy wis bigger, ah'd put ma dick as far up tae the camera lens as ah could. Unfortunately, the cunt soon tippled us n started daein the same.

Oan the particular subject ay ma disaster wi Laura McEwan thir wis even less tae say. Laura's a nutter. Intimidating at the best ay times. Ah've goat mair scar tissue oan ma boady fi one night wi her, than ah ever goat fi needles. Ah'd made aw the excuses ah could aboot that event. It's so depressing that people willnae let they things go. Sick Boy's determined tae let every fucker ken what a crap shag ah am.

— Awright, ah admit, that wis a pish-poor performance. But ah wis bevvied n stoned, n it wis her thit dragged me intae the bedroom, no the other wey roond. What the fuck did she expect?

He sniggered at me. The bastard always gave ye the impression he hud even mair choice slaggin material that he wis haudin back for another occasion.

— Well mate, jist think whit yir missin. Ah wis sniffin aroond in the gairdins the other day. Schoolies everywhere. Ye light up a joint and thir like flies aroond a crap. The manto's hoachin. Thir's foreign fanny aw ower the place, some ay them gaggin oan it. Ah've even seen a few wee honeys in Leith, fir fuck sakes. And speakin ay wee honeys, Mickey Weir wis fuckin brilliant at Easter Road oan Saturday. Aw the boys wir askin whair yiv been. Mind, thir's Iggy Pop and The Pogues gigs comin up shortly. It's aboot fuckin time that you goat yirsel thegither n started livin yir fuckin life. Ye cannae hide away in darkened rooms fir the rest ay yir puff.

Ah wisnae really interested in the cunt's shite.

— Ah really need jist one wee fix Si, tae ease us oaf the gear. Even a swallay ay methadone . . .

— If yir a good boy, ye might git a bit ay watered doon Tartan Special. Yir Ma wis sayin thit she might take ye tae the Dockers' Club oan Friday night; if yir oan yir best behaviour.

When the patronising cunt left, ah missed him. He nearly took us oot ay masel. It *wis* like auld times, but in a sense, that only served tae remind us ay how much things hud changed. Something hud happened. Junk hud happened. Whether ah lived wi it, died wi it, or lived withoot it, ah knew that things could never be the same again. Ah huv tae git oot ay Leith, oot ay Scotland. For good. Right away, no jist doon tae London fir six months. The limitations and ugliness ay this place hud been exposed tae us and ah could never see it in the same light again.

Ower the next few days, the pain abated slightly. Ah even started tae dae some cooking. Every cunt under the sun thinks thit thir Ma's the best cook in the world. Ah thought so tae, until ah went tae live oan ma ain. Ah realised then thit ma Ma's a shite cook. So ah've started tae make the tea. The auld man sneers at 'rabbit food' but ah think he secretly enjoys ma chillis, curries and casseroles. The auld girl seems vaguely resentful at ma encroachment intae whit she sees us her territory, the kitchen, and bleats aboot the need fir meat in a diet; but ah think she enjoys the scran n aw.

However, the pain is being replaced by an ugly, stark, black depression. Ah've never known such a sense ay complete and utter hopelessness, punctuated only by bouts ay raw anxiety. It immobilises me to the extent that ah'm sittin in the chair hating a tv programme, yet ah feel something terrible will happen if ah try tae switch ower. Ah sit burstin fir a pish, but too feart tae go up tae the bog in case thir's something lurking on the stairs. Sick Boy hud warned us aboot this, and ah'd experienced it in the past masel; but nae amount ay pre-warning or previous experience can fully prepare ye fir it. It makes the worse alcohol hangover seem like an idyllic wet dream.

My heart is breaking woo-hoo. The flick of a switch. Thank god for the remote control handset. You can move into different worlds at the press of a button. When I see her holding The replacement of worn-out sports equipment the guy sais something about a glaring lack of comprehensive detailed input and output measures which can be aggregated to enable the benefits to be evaluated and validated, at an area level, in terms of their effectiveness and efficiency, and this is something which the taxpayer, who after all will have to foot the bill will

— Coffee Mark? Ye wantin a coffee? Ma asks.

Ah can't respond. Yes please. No thanks. Ah do n ah dinnae. Say nothing. Let Ma decide whether or not I should have a coffee. Devolve or delegate that level of power, or decision making, to her. Power devolved is power retained.

— Ah goat a nice wee dress fir Angela's wee yin, Ma sais, holding up what could indeed only be described as a nice wee dress. Ma doesn't seem to realise that ah don't know who Angela is, let alone the child who will be the intended recipient of this nice wee dress. Ah just nod and smile. Ma's life and mines shot off on different tangents years ago. The point of contact is strong but obscure. Ah could say: Ah bought a nice wee bit ay skag oafay Seeker's mate, the buck-tooth cunt whaes name escapes me. That's it: Ma buys dresses fir people ah don't know, ah buy skag fae people she disnae know.

Faither's growing a moustache. With his close-cropped hair he will look like a liberated homosexual, a clone. Freddie Mercury. He disnae understand the culture. Ah explain it tae him and he's dismissive.

The next day, however, the moustache is gone. Faither now

'cannae be bothered' growing it. Claire Grogan's singing 'Don't Talk To Me About Love' on Radio Forth and Ma's making lentil soup in the kitchen. I've been singing Joy Division's 'She's Lost Control' in my head all day. Ian Curtis. Matty. I think of them intertwined in some way; but the only thing they have in common is a death wish.

That's aw that's worth mentioning aboot that day.

By the weekend, it isnae quite sae bad. Si hud goat us some blaw, but it wis standard Edinburgh hash, which is generally shite. Ah make some space-cake oot ay it, and that improves it. Ah even git a bit trippy in ma room in the eftirnoon. Ah still didnae feel up tae gaun oot though, especially tae the fuckin Dockers' Club n wi ma Ma n faither, bit ah resolved tae make the effort fir thair sakes, as they needed a brek. Ma n faither seldom missed a Saturday night at the club.

Ah stroll self-consciously doon Great Junction Street, the auld man nivir takin his eyes oaf us in case ah try tae dae a runner. Ah run intae Mally at the Fit ay the Walk, n we crack away fir a bit. The auld man intervenes, ushering us along, n lookin at Mally as if he wanted tae brek this evil pusher's legs. Poor Mally, whae widnae even touch a joint. Lloyd Beattie, whae used tae be a good mate ay oors years ago, before every cunt found oot he'd been shaggin his ain sister, gied us a meek nod.

In the club, people huv big smiles for the auld man n auld lady and strained ones fir me. Ah wis conscious ay some whispers n nods, followed by silences as we took a table. Faither slaps us oan the back n winks n Ma gies us a heart-wrenchingly tender and smotheringly indulgent smile. Nae doubt aboot it, thir no bad auld cunts. Ah love the fuck oot ay the bastards, if the truth be telt.

Ah think aboot how they must feel aboot me huvin turned oot the wey ah huv. Fuckin shame. Still, ah'm here. Perr Lesley's nivir gaunnae see wee Dawn grow up. Les and Sick fuck n Lesley, they say she's in the Southern General in Glesgie now, oan life-support. Paracetamol joab. She went through tae Glesgie tae git away fae the smack scene in Muirhoose n ended up movin intae Possil wi Skreel n Garbo. There's nae escape fir some fuckers. Hara-kiri wis Les's best option.

Swanney wis his customary sensitive self: — Fuckin Weedjies git aw the best gear these days. Thair oan that pure pharmaceutical shite while we're reduced tae crushin up any fuckin jack n jills wi kin git oor hands oan. Good gear's wasted oan these cunts, maist ay thum dinnae even inject. Smokin and snortin skag, a fuckin waste, he hissed contemptuously. — N that fuckin Lesley: she should be turnin the White Swan oantae that gear. Does she punt any ay it ma wey? Naw. She just sits feelin sorry fir hersel aboot her bairn. Shame n that, ken, dinnae git us wrong. Thing is, thir's opportunities n aw. Freedom fae the responsibility ay bein a single parent n that. Ye'd think she'd lap up the chance tae spread her wings.

Freedom fae responsibility. That sounds good. Ah'd like freedom fae the responsibility ay sittin in this fuckin club.

Jocky Linton comes ower tae join us. Jocky's pus is shaped like an egg oan its side. He's goat thick black hair flecked wi silver. He wears a blue shirt which is short-sleeved and exposes his tattoos. Oan one airm he's goat 'Jocky & Elaine — True Love Will Never Die' and 'Scotland' wi a Lion Rampant oan the other. Unfortunately, true love did bite the dust and Elaine shot the craw a long time ago. Jocky's now livin wi Margaret whae obviously hates the tattoo, but everytime he goes tae git another one pit ower it, he bottles oot, makin excuses aboot the fear ay HIV wi the needles. It's obviously shite, a feeble cop-oot because he still huds a candle fir Elaine. The thing ah remember maist aboot Jocky is his singing at pairties. He used tae sing George Harrison's *My Sweet Lord*, that wis his perty-piece. Jocky niver quite mastered the lyrics tae it though. He only kent the title and 'ah really want tae see you Lord' and the rest wis da-da-da-da-da-da-da.

— Day-vie. Cah-thy. Loo-kin-gor-jis-the-night-doll. Din-nae-you-be-tur-nin-yer-back-Ren-tin-or-ah'll-be-ruh-nin-ah-way-wi-her! Gles-kay-kee-lay-thit-ye-ur. Jocky spat out his syllables Kalashnikov style.

The auld girl tries tae look coy, her expression makin us feel a bit queasy inside. Ah jist hide behind a pint ay lager and fir once in ma puff am gled tae observe the total silence that the club bingo game imposes. Ma customary irritation at huvin ma every word policed by morons is now a replaced by a feeling ay sheer bliss.

Ah should have hud a house, bit ah didnae want tae speak, tae draw any attention tae masel whatsoever. It seemed though that fate — n Jocky — wir determined no tae respect ma desire fir anonymity. The cunt notices ma caird.

— HOUSE! That's-you-Mark. He's-goat-hoose. OWER-HERE! Wis-nae-eve-in-gaunn-ae-shout-oot. Cu-moan-son. Git-a-fu-kin-grip-ay-yir-sel.

Ah smile benignly at Jocky, all the time wishing a prompt and violent death oan the nosey cunt.

The lager is like the contents ay a bunged-up latrine, shot through wi CO_2. Eftir one gulp, a violent, wretching, spasm seizes us. Faither slaps ma back. Ah cannae touch ma pint eftir this, but Jocky n the auld man are flinging them back steadily. Margaret comes in, and before very long, she and the auld girl are makin good progress oan the vodka n tonics n the Carlsberg Specials. The band strikes up, which ah at first welcome as a respite fae talkin.

Ma Ma n faither git up tae dance tae 'Sultans Of Swing'.

— Ah like that Dire Straits, Margaret observes. — They appeal tae young ones, but aw ages like them.

Ah'm almost tempted tae vigorously refute this cretinous statement. However, ah content masel wi talking fitba wi Jocky.

— Rox-burgh wants shoot-in. That's-the-worst-Scot-lind-squad-ah've-ivir-seen, Jocky states, jaw jutting forward.

— S no really his fault. Ye kin only pish wi the cock yiv goat. Whae else is thir?

— Aye, right-e-nuff . . . but-ah'd-like-tae-see-John-Raw-birt-sin-git-un-ext-ten-did-run. Des-erves-it. Scot-lind's-maist-kin-sist-tint-strik-ir.

We continue our ritualistic argument, me trying tae find even a semblance ay passion which would breathe life intae it, and failing miserably.

Ah note that Jocky n Margaret hud been briefed tae ensure thit ah didnae try tae slip away. They aw took shifts tae mind us, the four ay them nivir up dancin at the same time. Jocky n ma Ma tae 'The Wanderer', Margaret n ma faither tae 'Jolene', Ma n faither again tae 'Rollin Down The River', Margaret n Jocky tae 'Save The Last Dance For Me'.

As the fat singer launches intae 'Song Sung Blue', the auld lady pulls us oantae the danceflair like ah wis a rag doll. Sweat spills oot ay us under the lights as Ma struts her stuff n ah self-consciously twitch. The humiliation intensifies as ah realise that the cunts ur daein a Neil Diamond medley. Ah huv tae go through 'Forever In Blue Jeans', 'Love On The Rocks' and 'Beautiful Noise'. By the time 'Sweet Caroline' comes oan, ah'm ready tae collapse. The auld lady forces us tae ape the rest ay the radges in the place by waving ma hands in the air as they sing:

— HAAANDS . . . TOUCHING HAANDS . . . REACHING OUUUT . . . TOUCHING YOOOU . . . TOUCH-ING MEEE . . .

Ah glance back at the table, n Jocky is in his element, a Leith Al Jolson.

Eftir this ordeal, thirs another tae follow. The auld man slips us a tenner and tells us tae git a round in. Social-skills development and confidence-building training are obviously on the agenda tonight. Ah take the tray up tae the bar n join the queue. Ah look over tae the door, feeling the crisp note in my hand. A few grains worth. Ah could be at Seeker's or Johnny Swan's, the Mother Superior's, in half an hour; shootin ma wey oot ay this nightmare. Then ah clock the auld man standing by the doorway, looking us ower like he wis a bouncer n ah wis a potential troublemaker. Only his role was tae stoap us fae leavin, rather than tae fling us oot.

This is a perverse gig.

Ah turn back intae the queue n ah see this lassie Tricia McKinlay whae ah'd been at school wi. Ah'd rather no talk tae anybody, but ah cannae ignore her now, as her smile is expanding in recognition.

— Awright Tricia?

— Aw, hiya Mark. Long time no see. How ye daein?

— No sae bad. Yirsel?

— Ye see it aw. This is Gerry. Gerry, this is Mark, he wis in ma class at school. Seems a long time ago now, eh?

She introduces me to a surly, sweaty gorilla who grunts in ma direction. Ah nod.

— Aye. Certainly does.

— Still see Simon? Aw the manto ask eftir Sick Boy. It makes us ill.

— Aye. He wis up at the hoose the day. He's away tae Paris soon. Then Corsica.

Tricia smiles and the gorilla looks on in disapproval. The guy has a face that just disapproves ay the world in general and looks ready for a square go wi it. Ah'm sure he's one ay the Sutherlands. Tricia could definitely huv done better for herself. Loads ay punters at school used tae fancy her. Ah used tae hing aroond her in the hope that people would think ah wis gaun oot wi her, in the hope that ah *would* be, by a sortay osmosis. Ah once started tae believe ma ain propaganda, and goat a healthy slap in the pus when ah tried tae put my hand up her jersey when we were up the disused railway line. Sick Boy fucked her though, the cunt.

— He eywis goat aroond did oor Simon, she sais wi a wistful smile.

Daddy Simone.

— Sure did. Stoat the baw, pimpin, drug-dealin, extortin money fae people. That's oor Simon. The bitterness in ma voice surprised us. Sick Boy wis ma best mate, well, Sick Boy n Spud . . . n maybe Tommy. Why am ah giein the cunt such a bad press? Is it solely because ay his neglect ay parental duties, or indeed his lack of acknowledgement ay parental status? It's more likely because I envy the cunt. He doesnae care. Because he doesnae care, he cannae be hurt. Never.

Whatever the reason, it freaks Tricia.

— Eh . . . well, right, eh, see ye Mark.

They leave quicky, Tricia cairryin the tray ay drinks and the Sutherland gorilla (or ah think he wis a Sutherland) lookin back at us, his knuckles nearly scrapin the varnish oan the dance flair.

It wis oot ay order bad-mouthin Sick Boy like that. Ah jist hate it whin the cunt gits oaf scot-free and ah'm painted as the big villain ay the piece. Ah suppose that's jist ma perception ay things. Sick Boy hus his anxieties, his personal pain. He also probably hus mair enemies thin me. He undoubtedly does. Still, what the fuck.

Ah take the drinks tae the table.

— Awright son? Ma asks us.

— Brand new Ma, brand new, ah sais, tryin tae sound like Jimmy Cagney n failin pathetically; like ah dae wi maist things. Still, failure, success, what is it? Whae gies a fuck. We aw live, then we die, in quite a short space ay time n aw. That's it; end ay fuckin story.

Bang to Rites

It's a beautiful day. That seems to mean

Concentrate. On the job at hand. Ma first burial. Somebody sais: — C'moan Mark, a gentle voice. Ah step forward and grab a length of the cord.

Ah help ma faither n ma uncles, Charlie n Dougie, tae lower the remains ay ma brother intae the groond. The army's pit up the hireys fir this do. Leave it to us, the softly-spoken Army Welfare Officer told Ma. Leave it to us.

Yes, this is the first burial ah've been at. Usually it's cremations these days. Ah wonder what's in the boax. No much ay Billy, that's fir sure. Ah look ower at ma Ma n Sharon, Billy's burd, who are being comforted by an assortment ay aunties. Lenny, Peasbo n Naz, Billy's mates, ur here, along wi some ay his squaddie pals.

Billy Boy, Billy Boy. Hello, hello, we are the. It's nothing tae dae wi

Ah keep thinking ay that auld Walker Brothers number, the one Midge Ure covered: *There's no regrets, no tears goodbye, I don't want you back* etcetera, etcetera.

Ah cannae feel remorse, only anger and contempt. Ah seethed when ah saw that fuckin Union Jack oan his coffin, n watched that smarmy, wimpy cunt ay an officer, obviously oot ay his depth here, tryin tae talk tae ma Ma. Worse still, these Glasgow cunts, the auld boy's side, are through here en masse. They're fill ay shite aboot how he died in the service ay his country n aw that servile Hun crap. Billy was a silly cunt, pure and simple. No a hero, no a martyr, jist a daft cunt.

A fit ay giggles hits us, threatening tae completely overwhelm us. Ah nearly cowped ower laughing hysterically, when ma faither's brar, Charlie, grabbed us by the airm. He looked hostile, but that cunt always does. Effie, his wife, pulls the fucker away sayin, — The boey's upset. It's jist his wey Chick. The boey's upset.

Get a fuckin wash ya soapdodgin Weedjie cunts.

Billy Boy. That's what these cunts called him as a laddie. It wis: Awright Billy Boey? Wi me, skulking behind the couch, it wis a grudging: Aye son.

Billy Boy, Billy Boy. Ah remember you sitting oan toap ay us. Me helplessly pinned tae the flair. Windpipe constricted tae the width ay a straw. Praying, as the oxygen drained fae ma lungs and brain, that Ma would return fae Presto's before you crushed the life oot ay ma skinny body. The smell ay pish fae your genitals, a damp patch on your short troosers. Was it really that exciting, Billy Boy? Ah hope so. Ah cannae really grudge ye it now. You always had a problem that way; those inappropriate discharges of faeces and urine that used tae drive Ma tae distraction. Who's the best team, you'd ask us, crushing, digging or twisting harder. No respite for me until ah sais: Hearts. Even after we'd fucked yous seven-nil on New Year's Day at Tynecastle, you still made me say Hearts. Ah suppose ah should have been flattered that an utterance from me carried more weight than the actual result.

Ma beloved brother was on Her Majesty's Service, on patrol near their base at Crossmaglen in Ireland, the part under British rule. They had left their vehicle to examine this road block, when POW! ZAP! BANG! ZOWIE!, and they were no more. Just three weeks before the end ay this tour of duty.

He died a hero they sais. Ah remember that song: 'Billy Don't Be A Hero'. In fact, he died a spare prick in a uniform, walking along a country road wi a rifle in his hand. He died an ignorant victim ay imperialism, understanding fuck all about the myriad circumstances which led tae his death. That wis the biggest crime, he understood fuck all about it. Aw he hud tae guide um through this great adventure in Ireland, which led tae his death, wis a few vaguely formed sectarian sentiments. The cunt died as he lived: completely fuckin scoobied.

His death wis good fir me. He made the *News at Ten*. In Warholian terms, the cunt had a posthumous fifteen minutes ay fame. People offered us sympathy, n although it wis misguided, it wis nice tae accept anywey. Ye dinnae want tae disappoint folk.

Some ruling class cunt, a junior minister or something, says in his Oxbridge voice how Billy wis a brave young man. He wis exactly the kind ay cunt they'd huv branded as a cowardly thug if he wis in civvy street rather than on Her Majesty's Service. This fucking walking abortion says that his killers will be ruthlessly hunted down. So they fuckin should. Aw the wey tae the fuckin Houses ay Parliament.

Savour small victories against this white-trash tool of the rich that's no no no

Billy being tormented by the Sutherland Brothers and entourage, who certainly made him quiver ha fuckin ha as they danced around him singing: YOUR BROTHER'S A SPASTIC, one of the great Leith street hits of the seventies, generally performed when the legs got too tired to sustain the twenty-two-a-side game ay fitba. Were they talking about Davie, or perhaps even me? Didnae matter. They didnae see me looking doon fae the bridge. Billy, your head stayed bowed. Impotence. How does it feel Billy Boy? Not good. I know because

It's weird by the graveside. Spud's here somewhere, clean, jist oot ay Saughton. Tommy n aw. It's crazy, Spud lookin healthy, n Tommy lookin like death warmed up. Complete role reversal. Davie Mitchell, a good mate ay Tommy's, a guy whae ah once worked wi oan site as an apprentice chippy way back, hus shown up. Davie caught HIV fae this lassie. Brave ay the cunt tae come. That's fuckin real bravery. Begbie, just when ah could make use ay the cunt's evil presence and capacity tae cause chaos, is oan hoaliday in Benidorm. Ah could do with his immoral support vis-à-vis my Weedjie relations. Sick Boy's still in France, livin oot his fantasies.

Billy Boy. Ah remember sharing that room. How the fuck ah did it for aw they years beats

The sun has a power. You can understand why people worship it. It's there, we know the sun, we can see it, and we need it.

You had first call on the room Billy. Fifteen months ma senior. Might is right. You'd bring gaunt-faced, vicious-eyed, gum-chewing lassies back to fuck, or at least heavy pet. They'd look at me with android contempt as you banished me, whoever was with me, and my Subbuteo into the lobby. Ah particularly recall the needless crunching of one Liverpool and two Sheffield Wednesday players under your heel. Unnecessary, but then total domination requires its symbolism, eh no Billy Boy?

Ma cousin Nina looks intensely shaftable. She's goat long, dark hair, and is wearing an ankle-length, black coat. Seems tae be a bit ay a Goth. Noting some ay Willie's squaddy pals and ma Weedjie uncles gettin oan well, ah find masel whistling 'The Foggy Dew'. One squaddy wi big, protruding front teeth, cottons oan and looks at us in surprise n then anger, so ah blaws the cunt a kiss. He stares at me for a bit, then looks away, shit up. Good. Wabbit season.

Billy Boy, ah wis your other spastic brother, the one who'd never had a ride, as you'd tell your mate Lenny. Lenny'd laugh and laugh until he'd almost have an asthma attack. It wisnae particularly Billy no you stupid, fuckin cunt

Ah give Nina a broad wink and she smiles, embarrassed. Ma faither's been clocking this and he steams ower tae me.

— Wahn fuckin bit ay crap oot ay you n that's us finished. Right?

His eyes were tired, sunk deep intae thir sockets. Thir wis a sad and unsettling vulnerability aboot him ah'd nivir seen before. Ah wanted tae say so much tae the man, but ah resented him fir allowing this circus tae take place.

— See ye up the hoose, faither. Ah'm gaun tae see Ma.

An overhead conversation in the kitchen, fuck-knows when.

Faither goes: — Thir's something wrong wi that laddie Cathy. Sittin in aw the time. It's no natural. Ah mean, look at Billy.

Ma sais back: — The laddie's jist different Davie, that's aw.

Different fae Billy. Not a Billy Boy. You won't know him by his noise, but by his silence. When he comes for you, he won't come screaming, announcing his intentions, but he'll come. Hello, hello. Goodbye.

Ah git a lift fae Tommy, Spud n Mitch. They urnae fir comin in. They depart quickly. Ah see ma auld lady, delirious, bein helped oot ay the taxi by her sister Irene, and sister-in-law Alice. The Weedjie aunties are clucking around in the background, ah can hear these horrible accents; bad enough oan a man, fuckin revolting oan a woman. These hatchet-faced auld boots dinnae look comfortable. Obviously, thir mair in their niche at the funeral ay an elderly relative whin thir's goodies up fir grabs.

Ma grabs the airm ay Sharon, Billy's burd, whae's goat a big bun in her oven. Why the fuck dae people ey grab each other's airms at funerals?

— He wid'uv made an honest wimmin ay ye hen. You wir eywis the one fir him. The wey she sais it, it was like she was trying tae convince herself as much as Sharon. Perr Ma. Two years ago, she hud three sons, now she's only got one, whae's a junky. The game's no straight.

— Dae ye think the army'll huv anything fir me? ah heard Sharon asking ma Auntie Effie, as we got intae the hoose. — Ah'm cairryin his bairn . . . it's Billy's bairn . . . she pleads.

— Dae ye think the moon's made oot ay green fuckin knob cheese? ah remark.

Fortunately, everyone seems too loast in thumsels tae pick it up.

Like Billy. He started to ignore me when I became invisible.

Billy, ma contempt for you jist grew over the years. It displaced the fear, jist sortay squeezed it oot, like pus fae a pluke. Of course, there's the blade. A great leveller, very good at negating physical assets; as Eck Wilson found oot tae his cost in second year. You loved us for that, once you got ower yir shock. Respected and loved me as a brother fir the first time. Ah despised you mair than ever.

You knew that your strength became superfluous once ah'd discovered the blade. You knew that, ya crappin bastard. The blade and the bomb. Just like the Naw. No the fuckin bomb. No

Ma embarrassment and discomfort grows. People fill their glasses and say what a great cunt Billy wis. Ah cannae really think ay anything good tae say aboot him, so ah shut up. Unfortunately, one ay his squaddy mates, the rabbit-toothed punter ah blew a kiss at, sidles up tae me. — You wir his brother, he sais, choppers hingin oot tae dry.

Ah might've guessed. Another Weedjie Orange bigot. Nae wonder he's hit it oaf wi faither's side. It put us oan the spot. Every cunt's eyes focus oan us. Dwat that pesky wabbit.

— Indeed I was, as you say, his brother, ah jocularly agree. Ah can feel the resentment mounting up against us. Ah huv tae play tae the crowd.

The best way ah knew tae strike a chord without compromising too much tae the sickening hypocrisy, perversely peddled as decency, which fills the room, is tae stick tae the clichés. People love them at this time, because they become real, and actually mean something.

— Billy n me nivir agreed oan that much . . .

— Ah well, vive le difference . . . said Kenny, an uncle oan ma Ma's side, tryin tae be helpful.

— . . . but one thing we hud in common wis thit we both liked a good bevvy and a good crack. If he can see us now, he'll be laughin his heid oaf at us sittin here aw moosey faced. He'd be sayin, enjoy yirsels, fir god sake! Ah've goat friends n family here. We've no seen each other fir ages.

An exchange of cards:

To Billy

Merry Christmas and a Happy New Year

(except between 3.00 and 4.40
on New Year's Day)

From Mark.

Mark

Merry Christmas and a Happy New Year

Billy

HMFC OK

To Billy,

Happy Birthday

From Mark

Then Billy and Sharon are

```
Mark

Happy Birthday

From Billy and Sharon
```

In Sharon's handwriting, which is like

The Weedjie white trash that were ma faither's family, came through for the Orange walk every July, and occasionally when Rangers were at Easter Road or Tynecastle. Ah wished the cunts would stay in Drumchapel. They receive my touching little tribute tae Billy well enough though, and all nod solemnly. All except Charlie, whae saw through ma mood.

— It's all a fuckin gemme tae you, int it son?

— If you must know, yes.

— Ah feel sorry for you. He shook his heid.

— Naw ye dinnae, ah tell him. He walks away, still shakin his heid.

More McEwan's Export and whisky follows. Auntie Effie starts tae sing, a nasal, country-style whine. Ah move ower tae Nina.

— You've really blossomed intae a wee honey, ken that? ah drunkenly slaver. She looks at me as if she's heard it aw before. Ah wis gaunnae suggest that we sneak away ower tae Fox's, or back tae ma flat at Montgomery Street. Is it against the law tae shag yir cousin? Probably. Thuv goat laws for stoapin ye daein everything else.

— Shame aboot Billy, she sais. Ah kin tell she thinks ah'm a total wanker. Of course, she's completely right. Ah thought that every cunt over twenty was a toss an no worth speakin tae, until ah hit twenty. The mair ah see, the mair ah think ah wis right. After that it's aw ugly compromise, aw timid surrender, progressively until death.

Unfortunately, Charlie, or Chick-chicy-chic-chicky-chicky, has clocked the solicitous nature ay my conversation, and moves in to protect Nina's virtue. No that she needs the assistance ay a fat soapdodger.

The bastard gestures me aside. When ah ignore him, he takes ma airm. He's pretty bevvied. His whisper is hard, an ah can smell the whisky oan his breath.

— Listen son, if you don't get oan yir fuckin bike, ah'm gaunnae tan your jaw. If it wisnae fir yir faither thair, ah've done it a long time ago. Ah don't like you son. Ah never huv. Yir brother wis ten times the man you'll ever be, ya fuckin junky. If you knew the misery yuv caused yir Ma n Da . . .

— You can speak frankly, ah cut in, anger throbbing in my chest but nonetheless contained by a delicious glee that comes fae knowing that ah've upset the cunt. Stay cool. It's the only way tae fuck a self-righteous bastard over.

— Oh ah'll speak frankly aw right, Mr University smart cunt. Ah'll knock ye through that fuckin waw. His chunky, indian-inked fist was just a few inches fae ma face. Ma grip tensed oan the whisky gless ah wis haudin. Ah wisnae gaunnae let the cunt touch us wi they fuckin hands. If he moved he wis gittin this gless.

Ah pushed his raised hand aside.

— If ye did gie us a kickin, ye'd be daein me a favour. Ah'd jist huv a wank aboot it later on. We University drop-oot smart cunt junkies are kinky that wey. Cause that's aw you're worth, ya fuckin trash. Yir also takin a wee bit for granted. Ye want tae go ootside, just say the fuckin word.

Ah gestured at the door. The room seemed tae shrink tae the size ay Billy's coffin, and be populated only by masel n Chick. But thir wir others. People wir looking roond at us now.

The cunt pushed us gently in the chest.

— Wuv hud wahn funeral in the family the day, wir no wahntin another.

Ma Uncle Kenny came ower and pulled us away.

— Ignore these orange bastards. C'moan Mark, look at yir Ma. It wid fuckin kill hur if ye got involved here, it Billy's funeral. Remember whair ye are, fir fuck sakes.

Kenny wis aw right, well a bit ay a fuckin erse if the truth be telt, but fir aw thir faults, ah'd rather huv an ayesur thin a soapdodger. Ah come fae some stock, right enough. Ayesur papish bastards oan ma Ma's side, soapdodging orange cunts oan ma faither's.

Ah gulped at the whisky, enjoying the burning sour taste ay it in ma throat n chest, wincing as it hit ma queasy stomach. Ah went through tae the toilet.

Sharon, Billy's burd, wis comin oot. Ah barred her wey. Sharon n me huv mibbe spoken about half-a-dozen sentences tae each other. She wis drunk n dazed, her face flushed and bloated wi alcohol n pregnancy.

— Hud oan the now Sharon. You n me need tae huv a wee blether, likes. It's pretty confidential in here. Ah usher her intae the toilet n loak the door behind us.

Ah start tae feel her up, while rabbitin a load ay shite aboot how we huv tae stick thegither at a time like this. Ah'm feelin her lump, n gaun oan aboot how much responsibility ah felt taewards ma unborn niece or nephew. We start kissin, and ah move ma hand doon, feelin the visible panty lines through the cotton material ay her maternity dress. Ah wis soon fingerin her fanny, and she hud goat ma prick oot ay ma troosers. Ah wis still bullshittin, tellin her that ah'd always admired her as a person and a woman, which she disnae really need tae hear because she's gaun doon oan us, bit it's somehow comfortin tae say. She takes ma semi intae her mooth n ah firm up quickly. There's no doubt aboot it, she gies a good blow-job. Ah think aboot her daein this wi ma brar, n wondered what hud happened tae his prick in the explosion.

If only Billy could see us now, ah'm thinkin, but in a surprisingly reverential way. Ah wondered if he could, n hoped so. It wis the first good thoughts aboot him ah'd hud. Ah withdraw jist before comin, and guide Sharon intae the doggy position. Ah hike up hur dress and pulled her panties down. Her heavy belly sags towards the flair. Ah try tae put it intae her arsehole first but it's too tight and it hurts ma knob end tae force it.

— No that wey, no that wey, she's saying, so ah stopped ma rummage for some cream, and scoop ma fingers intae hur fanny. She has a powerful ivy smell. Then again, ma cock also smells pretty foul and flecks of knob cheese are visible oan the helmet. Ah've never really been too much intae personal hygiene; probably the soapdodger in us, or the junky.

Ah concur wi Sharon's wishes n fuck her in the fanny. It's a wee bit like throwin the proverbial sausage up a close, but ah find ma stroke n she tightens up. Ah think aboot how close she is tae poppin and how far up ah am, an ah can see masel stickin it in the foetus's mooth. Some concept, a shag and a blow-job simultaneously. It torments us. They say that a shag is good for an unborn child, they get the circulation of blood, or some shite. The least ah kin dae is take an interest in the bairn's welfare.

A knock oan the door, follayed by Effie's nasal voice.

— Whit yis daein in thair?

— S awright, Sharon's bein sick. Too much bevvy in her condition, ah groaned.

— Ur you seein tae her son?

— Aye . . . ah'm seein tae her . . . ah panted as Sharon's groans grew louder.

— Awright well.

Ah blurt oot ma muck n pull oot. Ah gently push hur prostrate, helping her turn ower, and scoop hur huge milky tits oot ay her dress. Ah smuggle intae them like a bairn. She starts strokin ma heid. Ah feel wonderful, so at peace.

— That wis fuckin barry, ah gasp contentedly.

— Will we keep seein each other now? she sais. — Eh? Thir's a desperate, pleading edge tae her voice. What a fuckin radge.

Ah sat up n kissed her face, which wis like a swollen, overipe piece of fruit. Ah didnae want tae git heavy here. The truth wis, Sharon repulsed me now. This radge thinks that wi one fuck she can substitute one brar fir the other. Thing is, she's probably no far wrong.

— We huv tae git up Sharon, git cleaned likes, ken. They widnae understand if they caught us. They don't know anything. Ah know that yir a good lassie, Sharon, but they dinnae understand fuck all.

— Ah ken you're a nice laddie, she said supportively, but without a great deal of conviction. She was certainly far too good for Billy, then again Myra Hindley or Margaret Thatcher were far too good for Billy. She was caught in this git-a-man, git-a-bairn, git-a-hoose shite that lassies git drummed intae them, and hud nae real chance ay defining hersel ootside ay they mashed-tattie-fir-brains terms ay reference.

Thir wis another knock at the door.

— If yis dinnae open that door, ah'm gaunny knock it doon. It wis Charlie's son, Cammy. A fucking young polisman who looked like the Scottish Cup; big jug ears, nae chin, slender neck. The cunt obviously thought thit ah wis shootin up. Well, ah wis, but no in the sense he imagined.

— Ah'm awright . . . we'll be oot in a minute. Sharon wipes hersel n tugs up her pants and re-arranges things. Ah'm fascinated at the speed wi which she moves for a heavily pregnant lassie. Ah couldnae believe ah'd jist shagged her. Ah'd feel bad aboot it the morn, but, as Sick Boy's prone tae sayin, the morn takes care ay itsel. Thir isnae an embarrassment in the world that cannae be erased by a bit ay blether and a few bevvies.

Ah open the door.

— Take it easy, Dixon ay Dock Green. No seen a lady up the kite before? His glaikit, open-moothed expression inspired ma instant contempt.

Ah didnae like the vibes, so ah took Sharon back tae ma flat. We jist talked. She telt us a loat ay things thit ah wanted tae hear, things ma Ma n faither never knew, and would hate tae ken. How Billy wis a cunt tae her. How he battered her oan occasions, humiliated her, n generally treated her like an exceptionally foul piece ay shite.

— Whit did ye stey wi um fir?

— He wis ma felly. Ye eywis think it'll be different, thit ye kin change thum, thit ye kin make a difference.

Ah understood that. But it's wrong. The only fuckers thit ever made a difference tae Billy wir the Provos, and they were cunts as well. Ah've no illusions about them as freedom fighters. The bastards made ma brother intae a pile ay catfood. But they only pulled the switch. His death wis conceived by these orange cunts, comin through every July wi thir sashes and flutes, fillin Billy's stupid heid wi nonsense about crown and country n aw that shite. They'll go hame chuffed fae the day. They can tell aw thir mates aboot how one ay the family died, murdered by the IRA, while defending Ulster. It'll fuel thir pointless anger, git thum bought drinks in pubs, and establish thir doss-bastard credibility wi other sectarian arseholes.

Ah dinnae want any cunt fuckin aboot wi ma brar. Those were the words Billy Boy spoke to Pops Graham and Dougie Hood as they came into the pub hassling me, determined that ah had tae pey for ma drugs. Billy's statement. Oh yes. Delivered wi such clarity and assurance, that it went beyond a threat. Ma irritants just looked at each other and skulked off oot ay the pub. Ah sniggered. So did Spud. We were high, and cared aboot fuck all. Billy Boy sneered at us, something like: You're a fuckin erse, and joined a couple ay his mates, whae looked disappointed that Pops and Dougie had fucked off, depriving them of an excuse fir a swedge. Ah still giggled. Thanks guys, it's been

Billy Boy told me that ah wis ruining ma life wi that shite. He told me this on numerous occasions. It's been real

Fuck. Fuck. Fuck. What's it aw aboot. Aw Billy. Aw fuck sakes. Ah didnae

Sharon was right. It's hard tae change people.

Every cause needs its martyrs though. So now ah'm wishing thit she wid fuck off so ah kin git tae ma stash, cook up a shot and git a hit, in the cause ay oblivion.

Junk Dilemmas No. 67

Deprivation's relative. There are bairns starvin tae death, dying every second like flies. The fact that this is happening in another place, doesnae negate that fundamental truth. In the time it takes us tae crush up these pills, cook them and inject them, thousands ay bairns in other countries, and mibbe a few in this yin, will be deid. In the time it takes us tae dae this, thousands ay rich bastards will be thousands ay pounds richer, as investments ripen.

Crushin pills up: what a fuckin doss-heid. Ah should really leave the jack n jills tae the stomach. Brain and vein are too fragile tae carry that stuff direct.

Like Dennis Ross.

Dennis hud a great hit fae that whisky he injected intae hissel. Then

his eyes started rollin, blood flooded fae his nostrils, n that wis Denny. Once ye see the blood fae yir nose hit the flair at that rate . . . the gig's over. Junky machismo . . . naw. Junky need.

Ah'm feart awright, shitein ma keks, but the me that's shitein it is a different me tae the one that's crushin up the pills. The me that's crushin up the pills sais that death cannae be worse than daein nowt tae arrest this consistent decline. That me eywis wins the arguments.

Thir's nivir any real dilemmas wi junk. They only come when ye run oot.

Exile

London Crawling

No go. Whair the fuck are the cunts? Ma ain bastard fault. Should've phoned tae tell them ah wis comin doon. Well, the surprise is mine. Nae fucker's in. The black door has a coldness, a stern, deathly front which seems tae say tae us thit they've been gone a long time, and willnae be back fir a longer yin, if ever. Ah deek though the letter boax, bit ah cannae see if thir's any envelopes at the bottom ay the door.

Ah boot the door in frustration. The woman across the landing, a mumpy hoor as ah remember, opens her door and pokes hur heid oot. She stares at us as if tae ask us a question. Ah ignore her.

— They ain't in. Ain't been in for a couple of days, she tells us, looking suspiciously at ma sports bag as if thir wis explosives contained in it.

— Nice one, ah gruffly mumble, turnin ma heid ceilingwards in exasperation, hoping that this show ay desperation will encourage the woman tae say something like: I know you. You used to stay there. You must be exhausted travelling all the way down from Scotland. Come in, have a nice cup ay tea, and wait for your friends.

Whit she does say is: — Naah . . . ain't seem em for at least two days.

233

Cunt. Fuck. Bastard. Shite.

They could be anywhere. They could be naewhaire. They could be back at anytime. They might never be back.

Ah walk doon Hammersmith Broadway, London seeming strange and alien, after only a three-month absence, as familiar places do when you've been away. It's as if everything is a copy of what you knew before, similar, yet somehow lacking in its usual qualities, a bit like the wey things are in a dream. They say you have to live in a place to know it, but you have to come fresh tae it tae really see it. Ah remember walkin along Princes Street wi Spud, we both hate walkin along that hideous street, deadened by tourists and shoppers, the twin curses ay modern capitalism. Ah looked up at the castle and thought, it's just another building tae us. It registers in oor heids just like the British Home Stores or Virgin Records. We were heading tae these places oan a shoplifting spree. But when ye come back oot ay Waverley Station eftir bein away fir a bit, ye think: Hi, this isnae bad.

Everything in the street today seems soft focus. It's probably lack of sleep and lack of drugs.

The pub sign is a new one, but its message is old. The Britannia. Rule Britannia. Ah've never felt British, because ah'm not. It's ugly and artificial. Ah've never really felt Scottish either, though. Scotland the brave, ma arse; Scotland the shitein cunt. We'd throttle the life oot ay each other fir the privilege ay rimmin some English aristocrat's piles. Ah've never felt a fuckin thing aboot countries, other than total disgust. They should abolish the fuckin lot ay them. Kill every fuckin parasite politician that ever stood up and mouthed lies and fascist platitudes in a suit and a smarmy smile.

The board tells us thit there is a gay skinheads night oan in the back bar. Cults and subcultures segment and cross-matrix in a place like this. Ye can be freer here, no because it's London, but because it isnae Leith. Wir all slags on holiday.

In the public bar, ah scan for a familiar face. The layout and decor of the place has radically changed, for the worse. What was once a good, grotty local where you could fling beer over your mates and get sucked off in the women's or men's toilets is now a frighteningly sanitised hole. A few locals wi hard, bemused faces and cheap clathes, cling tae a corner ay the bar like shipwrecked survivors tae driftwood as yuppies guffaw loudly. Still at work, always in the office, but wi alcohol instead ay phones. This place is now geared up tae supplying all-day meals to workers ay the offices that continue to encroach into the Borough. Davo and Suzy widnae drink in a soulless toilet like this.

One ay the barmen, though, looks vaguely familiar.

— Does Paul Davis still drink in here? ah ask him.

— You wot Jock, the coloured geezer that plays for the Arsenal? he laughs.

— Naw, this is a big scouser. Dark, spiked hair, nose like a fuckin ski slope. Ye couldnae miss this guy.

— Roight . . . yeah, oi know the geezer. Davo. Angs around wiff that bird, little gel, short, black hair. Nah, ain't seen that crowd in ere for ages. Don't even know if they're still on the manor.

Ah drink a pint ay fizzy pish, and crack wi the guy aboot his new customers.

— Fing is Jock, most orf them geezers ain't even genuine yuppies, he disdainfully gestures over to a crowd of suits in the corner. — Mostly fucking shiny-arsed clerks or commission-based insurance salesmen that get a handful orf fucking roice each week in wages. It's orl fucking image, innit. These cahnts are all up to their fucking eyes in debt. Strutting around the fucking city in expensive suits pretendin that they're on fifty K a year. Most orf them aint even got a five-figure salary, ave they.

Thir wis a lot in what the guy said, bitter as the cunt wis. Thir wis certainly mair dosh kickin aboot down here thin up the road, but one thing the cunts doon here hud swallayed, wis the idea thit aw ye hud tae dae wis tae look the part, n it wid aw come your way, which wis fuckin shite. Ah've known scheme junkies in Edinburgh wi a healthier asset-tae-debt ratio thin some two-waged, heavily-mortgaged couples doon here. It'll hit the fan one day. Thir are sackloads ay repossession orders in the post.

Ah go back up tae the flat. Still nae sign ay the cunts.

The woman across the wey comes back oot. — You won't find em in. Her voice is smug and gloating. What a cunt ay the first order this old slag is. A black cat meanders past her, out ontae the landing.

— Choatah! Choatah! C'mere you bleedin little . . . She picks the cat up and holds it protectively to her bosom like a baby, staring at us bitterly as if ah somehow intended tae herm the bag ay shite.

Ah fuckin hate cats, nearly as much as ah hate dugs. Ah advocate the banning ay the use ay animals as pets and the extermination ay aw dugs, except a few, which could be exhibited in a zoo. That's one ay the few things that me n Sick Boy consistently agree aboot.

Cunts. Whair the fuck ur they?

Ah go back doon tae the pub n huv another couple ay pints. It's fuckin soul destroying, what the bastards have done tae this place. The nights we used tae huv in here. It's like the past hus been eradicated along wi the auld fittings.

Withoot thinking consciously, ah've left the pub, n ah'm walking back the wey ah came, towards Victoria. Ah stoap oaf at a pay-phone, pull oot some loose change n ma battered address book. Time tae look fir alternative digs. Could be dodgy. Ah've fucked up wi Stevie or Stella, no way I'd be welcome back there. Andreas is back in Greece, Caroline is oan hoaliday in Spain, Tony, stupid fuckin doss cunt Tony, is wi Sick Boy, whae's ower fae France, back up in fuckin Edinburgh. Ah forgot tae git the cunt's keys, n the bastard forgot tae remind us.

Charlene Hill. She's Brixton. First choice. Might even git a ride, if ah play ma cairds right. Could certainly dae wi one . . .

that's whit being straight, well straightish, does tae ye . . .
torture.

— Hello? Another woman's voice.

— Hi. Can I speak to Charlene?

— Charlene . . . she don't live ere anymore. Don't know
where she is now, Stockwell, I fink . . . ain't got an address . . .
old on . . . MICK! MICK! YOU GOT CHARLENE'S
ADDRESS? . . . . CHARLEEENE . . . . Na. Sorry. Ain't got it.

No ma fuckin day. Hus tae be Nicksy.

— No. No. No Brian Nixon. Gone. Gone; an Asian voice.

— Goat an address fir um mate?

— No. Gone. Gone. No Brian Nixon.

— Whair's he steyin likesay but?

— What? What? I cannot understand you . . .

— Where-is-my-friend-Bri-an-Nicks-on-stay-ing?

— No Brian Nixon. No drugs. Go. Go. The cunt slams the
phone doon oan us.

It's gettin late, and this city has shut me oot. An alko wi a
Glasgow accent taps twenty pence fi us.

— Yir a fuckin good boey, ah'll tell ye that son . . . he groans.

— You're orlroight Jock, ah tell um, in ma best Cockney.
Other Scots in London ur a pain in the erse. Particularly
Weedjies, whae irritate us at the best ay times wi thir nosey cunt
patter, which they pretend is friendliness. The last thing ah want
right now is tae be stuck wi a fuckin soapdodger in tow.

Ah think aboot gittin the 38 or 55 up tae Hackney, and callin
oan Mel at Dalston. If Mel's no in, and the cunt's no oan the
phone, then ma boats ur well n truly burned.

Instead ah find masel peyin tae git intae the all-night cinema
in Victoria. It shows porno movies throughout the night, until
five a.m. It's a crash pad for every low-life under the sun. Winos,
junkies, vagrants, sex-fiends, psychos, they all converge here at
night. Ah pledged tae masel thit ah'd nivir spend a night here
again, eftir the last time.

A few years back ah wis in here wi Nicksy n some boy goat stabbed. The polis came n jist lifted every cunt they could git thir hands oan includin us. We hud a quart ay hash oan us n hud tae eat the lot. We couldnae even fuckin speak by the time they goat roond tae interviewin us doon the station. They kept us in the cells overnight. Next day they took us roond tae Bow Street magistrates court, it's right next tae the nick, and fined every cunt whae wis too incoherent tae give evidence wi a breach ay the peace. Nicksy n me goat stung fir thirty bar each; whin it wis thirty bar.

Here ah am again though. If anything, the place has gone downhill since ma last visit. Aw the films are pornographic, except fir one excruciatingly violent documentary, where various animals tear each other apart in exotic locations. Its graphic nature takes it a million miles fae David Attenborough's jobs.

— Ya black bastards! Fuckin black bastards! roars a Scots voice as a group ay natives hurl spears intae the side ay a big bison-like creature.

A racist Scottish animal lover. Odds-on he's a Hun.

— Dirty fucking jungle-bunnies, a sycophantic Cockney voice adds.

Whit a fuckin place tae be. Ah try tae git intae the films tae take ma mind oaf the screaming and heavy breathing gaun oan around us.

The best film is a German one overdubbed wi American English. The plot is no great shakes. It concerns this young lassie in a Bavarian costume who gets fucked in a variety of ways and locations by almost every male and a few ay the females oan the farm. The set pieces are quite imaginative though, and ah'm gettin intae it. These images are obviously the nearest most cunts in this dive ever come tae sex, although having said that, ye can tell by the sounds that some men and women and men and men are fucking. Ah find ah've goat a hard-on, and ah'm even tempted tae have a wank, but the next film crushes ma erection.

It's a British one, inevitably. It's set in a London office during the party season and is imaginatively entitled: *The Office Party*. It stars Mike Baldwin, or the actor Johnny Briggs, whae plays the cunt in *Coronation Street*. It's like a Carry-On film wi less humour and mair sex. Mike eventually gets fucked, but he disnae deserve tae, lookin like an irritating wee sleazebag fir maist ay the film.

Ah keep driftin oaf intae a delirious sleep, and waking with a start, ma head jerking back like it's gaunnae snap oaf ma shoodirs.

Out ay the corner ay ma eye, ah see a guy movin seats tae sit next tae us. He puts his hand oan ma thigh. Ah pull his hand oaf.

— Git tae fuck. You wantin yir heid n hands tae play wi, ya cunt?

— Sorry. Sorry, he sais in a European accent. He's an auld cunt n aw. He sounds really pathetic, n he's goat a wizened wee face. Ah actually start feelin sorry fir um.

— Ah'm no a buftie pal, ah tell um. He looks confused. — No homosexual, ah point at masel, feeling vaguely ridiculous. What a fuckin daft thing tae say.

— Sorry. Sorry.

This sortay gits us thinkin. How the fuck dae ah ken ah'm no a homosexual if ah've nivir been wi another guy? Ah mean, really fir sure? Ah've always hud a notion tae go aw the wey wi another guy, tae see what it wis like. Ah mean, yuv goat tae try everything once. Huvin said that, ah'd huvtae be in the drivin seat. Ah couldnae handle some cunt's knob up *ma* erse. One time ah picked up this gorgeous young queen in the London Apprentice. Ah took um back tae the auld gaff in Poplar. Tony n Caroline came in n caught us giein the boy a gam. It wis a total embarrassment. Giein a guy whae wis wearin a condom a blow-job. It wis like sucking a plastic dildo. Ah wis bored tae fuck, bit the boy hud sucked me oaf first so ah felt ah hud tae reciprocate.

It wis a good blow-job he gave, technically speaking. However, ah hud kept gaun soft n collapsing wi laughter at the expression oan his face. He looked like this lassie ah used tae fancy ages ago, so wi a bit ay imagination and concentration ah managed, tae ma surprise, tae shoot ma load intae the rubber.

Ah took a real slaggin fae Tony fir this episode, but Caroline thought that it wis cool, n confessed tae us this she wis as jealous as fuck. She thought the guy wis a honey.

Anywey, ah widnae mind gaun aw the wey wi a gadge, if it felt right. Jist fir the experience. Problem is, ah only really fancy birds. Guys jist dinnae look sexy. It's aw aboot aesthetics, fuck all tae dae wi morality.

The auld cunt disnae exactly look like he'd be high oan the list ay candidates tae lose yir homosexual virginity tae. He tells us though, thit he's goat a place up in Stoke Newington n asks us if ah'd like tae crash the night. Well, Stokie's no far fae Mel's bit at Dalston, so ah thoat: Fuck it.

The auld cunt's Italian, n he's called Gi, short fir Giovanni, ah'd imagine. He tells us that he's workin in a restaurant and that he's goat a wife n bairns back in Italy. Ah git a feelin thit this disnae quite ring true. One ay the great things aboot bein intae junk is thit ye come across loads ay liars. Ye develop a certain expertise in that area yirsel, and a keen nose for the bullshit.

Wi git a night bus up tae Stokie fi Victoria. Thirs loads ay young punters oan the bus; stoned, pished, gaun tae perties, comin fae perties. Ah wished tae fuck that ah wis in one ay they squads instead ay wi this auld cunt. Still.

Gi's basement flat is somewhair oafay Church Street. Ah'm loast eftir that, but ah ken thit wir no as far in as Newington Green. It's extremely fuckin dingy inside. Thir's an auld sideboard, a chest ay drawers and a big, brass bed in the middle ay this musty smelling room, which has a kitchen and toilet off it.

Given ma previous vibe aboot this cunt, ah'm surprised tae see pictures ay a woman n bairns aw ower the place.

— Yir family mate?

— Yes, this is my family. Soon they will be joining me.

This still didnae sound plausible tae me. Perhaps ah've become that used tae lies, thit the truth sounds indecently false. But still.

— Must miss thum.

— Yes. Oh yes, he goes, then he sais — Lie down on the bed my friend. You can sleep. I like you. You can stay for a while.

Ah gie the wee cunt a hard stare. He's nae physical threat, so ah thought, fuck it, ah'm knackered, n ah climbed oantae the bed. Ah hud a flicker ay doubt as ah remembered Dennis Nilsen. Ah bet thir wis some cunts whae thought thit he wis nae physical threat; before he throttled thum, decapitated thum n biled thir heids in a big pan. Nilsen used tae work in the same Jobcentre in Cricklewood as this guy fae Greenock ah knew. The Greenock guy told me that one Christmas Nilsen brought in a curry he'd made fir the staff ay the centre. Mibbe bullshit, but ye nivir know. Anywey, ah'm so fucked that ah shut ma eyes, succumbing tae ma tiredness. Ah tensed slightly when ah felt him gittin oantae the bed beside us, but ah soon relaxed because he made nae move tae touch us n we wir both fully clathed. Ah felt masel driftin oaf intae a sick, disorientated sleep.

Ah woke up, wi nae idea ay how long ah'd been asleep; ma mooth dried oot and a strange wet sensation oan ma face. Ah touched the side ay ma cheek. Egg-white strands of thick, sticky fluid trailed from ma hand. Ah turned n saw the auld cunt lyin beside us, now naked, spunk drippin fae ehs small, fat cock.

— Ya dirty auld cunt! . . . wankin ower us in ma fuckin sleep . . . ya fuckin mingin auld bastard! Ah felt like a dirty hanky, just used, just nothing. A rage gripped us n ah smacked the wee cunt in the mooth n pulled um oaf the bed. He looked like a repulsive, fat gnome wi his bloated stomach n roond heid. Ah booted um a few times as he cowered oan the deck, then ah stoaped as ah realised he wis sobbin.

— Fuck sake. Dirty wee cunt. Fuckin . . . Ah paced up and

doon the room. His greetin wis disturbing. Ah pulled a dressing-gown oaf one ay the brass knobs oan the edge ay the bed n draped it roond his ugly nakedness.

— Maria. Antonio, he sobs. Ah realise thit ah've goat ma airm aroond the wee bastard n ah'm comforting him.

— S awright mate. S awright. Sorry. Didnae mean tae hurt ye, it's jist likesay, nae cunts wanked ower us before.

That wis certainly true.

— You are kind . . . what can I do? Maria. My Maria . . . He wis howling. His mooth dominated his face, a huge black hole in the twilight. He smelt ay stale drink, sweat n spunk.

— Look, c'moan we'll go doon tae a cafe. Huv a wee blether. Ah'll git ye some breakfast. Oan me. Thir's a good place doon Ridley Road, by the market, ken? It'll be open by now.

My suggestion wis as much motivated by self-interest as altruism. It took us nearer tae Mel's place at Dalston, and ah wanted oot ay this depressing basement room.

He goat dressed n we left. We padded the hoof doon Stokie High Street n Kingsland Road, doon tae the market. The cafe wis surprisingly busy, but we goat a table. Ah hud a cheese n tomatay bagel n the auld cunt hus this horrible black boiled meat, the stuff that the Jewish punters up at Stamford Hill seem tae be intae.

The cunt starts gabbin aboot Italy. He wis married tae this Maria woman fir years. The family found oot thit him n Antonio, Maria's younger brother, wir fucking each other. Ah shouldnae really put it like that, mair like thit they wir lovers. Ah think he loved the guy, but he loved Maria n aw. Ah thought ah wis bad wi drugs, but the mess some cunts make ay thir lives wi love. It disnae bear thinkin aboot.

Anywey, thir wis two other brothers, macho, Catholic n according tae Gi, involved wi the Neopolitan Camorra. These cunts couldnae handle this. They goat a haud ay Gi, ootside the family restaurant. They kicked ten types ay shite oot ay the perr wee cunt. Antonio goat the same treatment later oan.

Antonio topped hissel eftir that. It means a loat in that culture, Gi telt us, tae be disgraced in that wey. Ah'm thinkin, it means a loat in any fuckin culture. Gi then tells us thit Antonio flung hissel in front ay a train. Ah thought, mibbe it does mean mair in that culture eftir aw. Gi fled tae England, whair he's been working in various Italian restaurants; living in seedy gaffs, drinking too much, exploiting or being exploited by the young guys and auld wifies he picks up. It sounds a pretty miserable life.

Ma spirits soared whin we goat doon the road tae Mel's and ah heard reggae music blastin intae the street and saw the lights oan. The fag-end ay what must huv been a considerable party wis still gaun.

It wis good tae git amongst auld faces. They wir aw thair, aw the cunts, Davo, Suzy, Nicksy (bombed oot ay his boax), n Charlene. Bodies wir crashed oot aw ower the place. Two lassies wir dancin wi each other, n Char wis dancin wi this guy. Paul n Nicksy wir smokin; opium, no hash. Maist English junkies ah know smoke horse rather than shoot it up. Needles seem tae be mair ay a Scottish, Edinburgh, thing. Ah take a toke fae the cunts anywey.

— Farking great tuh see yah again, me old sahn! Nicksy slaps us oan the back. Clockin Gi, he whispers, — Oose the old cahnt then, eh? Ah'd brought the wee bastard along. Ah didnae huv the heart tae leave the cunt eftir listening tae aw his tales ay woe.

— Sound mate. Great tae see ye. This is Gi. Good mate ay mines. Steys up in Stokie. Ah slaps auld Gi oan the back. The perr wee fucker wears an expression like ye'd see oan a rabbit at the bars ay its cage asking fir a bit ay lettuce.

Ah go fir a wander, leavin Gi talking tae Paul n Nicksy aboot Napoli, Liverpool and West Ham, the international male language ay fitba. Sometimes ah lap up that talk, other times its pointless tediousness depresses the fuck oot ay us.

In the kitchen, two guys are arguin aboot the poll tax. One

boy's sussed oot, the other's a fuckin spineless Labour/Tory Party servile wankboy.

— You're a fuckin arsehole oan two counts. One, if ye think the Labour Party's goat a fuckin chance ay ever gettin in again this century, two, if ye think it would make a blind bit ay fuckin difference if they ever did, ah jist butt in and tell the cunt. He stands thair open-moothed, while the other guy smiles.

— That's joost wot oi was troi-ing to tell the bastid, he sais in a Brummie accent.

Ah split, leaving the servile cunt still bemused. Ah go intae in a bedroom whair this guy's licking oot this lassie, aboot three feet away fae whair some junkies are usin. Ah look at the junkies. Fuck me, thir usin works, shootin up n that. So much fir ma theories.

— You want a photograph mate? this skinny wee Goth wide-o whae's cookin asks.

— You want a fuckin burst mooth, cunt? Ah answer his question wi a question. He looks away n keeps cookin. Ah stare at the toap ay his heid fir a bit. Content that the cunt's shat his load, ah loosen up. Whenever ah go doon south, ah seem tae huv that kind ay attitude. It goes eftir a couple ay days. Ah think ah ken why ah huv it, but it wid take too long tae explain, n sound too pathetic. As ah leave the room, ah hear the lassie groanin oan the bed n the guy sayin, — Wot a fucking sweet cunt you got gel . . .

Ah stagger through the door, wi that soft, slow voice resonating in ma ear: — Wot a fucking sweet cunt you got gel . . . and it starkly makes explicit to me just what ah've been looking around for.

Ah'm no exactly spoiled fir choice here. The scene's pish-poor in the potential bag-off stakes. At this time ay the morning, the most desirable women huv either bagged off or fucked off. Charlene's copped, so's the woman that Sick Boy shagged oan her 21st birthday. Even the lassie wi the eyes like Marty Feldman and the hair like pubes, is spoken for.

Story ay ma fuckin life. Arrive too early, git too pished or stoned oot ay boredom n blow it, or git thair too fuckin late.

Wee Gi's standing by the fireplace, sipping a can ay lager. He looks frightened and bemused. Ah think tae masel, ah might end up whappin it up the wee cunt's choc-box yit.

The thought depresses the fuck oot ay us. Still, we are all slags oan hoaliday.

Bad Blood

I first meet Alan Venters through the 'HIV and Positive' self-help group, although he wasn't part of that group for long. Venters didn't look after himself very well, and soon developed one of the many opportunistic infections we're prone to. I always find the term 'opportunistic infection' amusing. In our culture, it seems to invoke some admirable quality. I think of the 'opportunism' of the entrepreneur who spots a gap in the market, or that of the striker in the penalty box. Tricky buggers, those opportunistic infections.

The members of the group were in a roughly similar medical condition. We were all anti-body positive, but still largely asymptomatic. Paranoia was never far from the surface at our meetings; everybody seemed to be furtively checking out everyone else's lymph glands for signs of swelling. It was disconcerting to feel people's eyes stray to the side of your face during conversation.

This type of behaviour added further to the sense of unreality which hung over me at the time. I really couldn't conceive of what had happened to me. The test results at first just seemed unbelievable, so incongruous with the healthy way I felt and looked. Part of me remained convinced that there had to be a mistake, in spite of taking the test three times. My self-delusion should have been shattered when Donna refused to see me, but it was always hanging on in the background with a grim resolution. We always seem to believe what we want to believe.

I stopped going to the group meetings after they put Alan Venters in the hospice. It just depressed me and, anyway, I wanted to spend my time visiting him. Tom, my key worker and one of the group counsellors, reluctantly accepted my decision.

— Look Dave, I think that you seeing Alan in hospital is really great; for him. I'm more concerned about you at the moment, though. You're in great health, and the purpose of the group is to encourage us to make the most of things. We don't stop living just because we're HIV positive . . .

Poor Tom. His first *faux pas* of the day. — Is that the royal 'we' Tom? When you're HIV positive, tell me aw about it.

Tom's healthy, pink cheeks flushed. He couldn't help it. Years of intensive interpersonal skills practice had taught him to hide the nervy visual and verbal giveaways. No shifty eye contact or quavering voice from him in the face of embarrassment. Not old Tom. Unfortunately, Tom cannae do a thing about the glowing red smears which rush up the side of his face on such occasions.

— I'm sorry, Tom apologised assertively. He had the right to make mistakes. He always said that people had that right. Try telling that to my damaged immune system.

— I'm just concerned that you're choosing to spend your time with Alan. Watching him wasting away won't be good for you and, besides, Alan was hardly the most positive member of the group.

— He was certainly the most HIV positive member.

Tom chose to ignore my remark. He had a right not to respond to the negative behaviour of others. We all had such a right, he told us. I liked Tom; he ploughed a lonely furrow, always trying to be positive. I thought that my job, which involved watching slumbering bodies being opened up by the cruel scalpel of Howison, was depressing and alienating. It's a veritable picnic however, compared to watching souls being wrenched apart. That was what Tom had to put up with at the group meetings.

Most members of 'HIV and Positive' were intravenous drug-users. They picked up HIV from the shooting galleries which flourished in the city in the mid-eighties, after the Bread Street surgical suppliers was shut down. That stopped the flow of fresh needles and syringes. After that, it was large communal syringes and share and share alike. I've got a mate called Tommy who started using smack through hanging around with these guys in Leith. One of them I know, a guy called Mark Renton, whom I worked with way back in my chippy days. It's ironic that Mark has been shooting smack for years, and is, so far as I know, still not infected with HIV, while I've never touched the stuff in my life. There were, however, enough smack-heads present in the group to make you realise that he could be the exception, rather than the rule.

Group meetings were generally tense affairs. The junkies resented the two homosexuals in the group. They believed that HIV originally spread into the city's drug-using community through an exploitative buftie landlord, who fucked his sick junky tenants for the rent. Myself and two women, one the non-drug-using partner of a junk addict, resented everyone as we were neither homosexual nor junkies. At first I, like everyone else, believed that I had been 'innocently' infected. It was all too easy to blame the smack-heads or the buftie-boys at that time. However, I had seen the posters and read the leaflets. I remember in the punk era, the Sex Pistols saying that 'no one is innocent'. Too true. What also has to be said though, is that some are more guilty than others. This brings me back to Venters.

I gave him a chance; a chance to show repentance. This was a sight more than the bastard deserved. At a group session, I told the first of several lies, the trail of which would lead to my grip on the soul of Alan Venters.

I told the group that I had had unprotected, penetrative sex with people, knowing full well that I was HIV positive, and that I now regretted it. The room went deathly silent.

People shifted nervously in their seats. Then a woman called Linda began to cry, shaking her head. Tom asked her if she wanted to leave the meeting. She said no, she would wait and hear what people had to say, venomously addressing her reply in my direction. I was largely oblivious to her anger though; I never took my eyes off Venters. He had that characteristic, perpetually bored expression on his face. I was sure a faint smile briefly played across his lips.

— That was a very brave thing to say, Davie. I'm sure it took a lot of courage, Tom said solemnly.

Not really you doss prick, it was a fucking lie. I shrugged.

— I'm sure a terrific burden of guilt has been lifted from you, Tom continued, raising his brows, inviting me to come in. I accepted the opportunity this time.

— Yes, Tom. Just to be able to share it with you all. It's terrible . . . I don't expect people to forgive . . .

The other woman in the group, Marjory, directed a sneering insult towards me, which I didn't quite catch, while Linda continued crying. No reaction was forthcoming from the cunt who sat in the chair opposite me. His selfishness and lack of morality sickened me. I wanted to take him apart with my bare hands, there and then. I fought to control me senses, savouring the richness of my plan to destroy him. The disease could have his body; that was its victory, whatever malignant force it was. Mine would be a greater one, a more crushing one. I wanted his spirit. I planned to carve mortal wounds into his supposedly everlasting soul. Ay-men.

Tom looked around the circle: — Does anyone empathise with Davie? How do people feel about this?

After a bout of silence, during which my eyes stayed trained on the impassive figure of Venters, Wee Goagsie, a junky in the group, started to croak nervously. Then he blurted out, in a terrible rant, what I'd been waiting for from Venters.

— Ah'm gled Davie sais that . . . ah did the same . . . ah did the fuckin same . . . an innocent lassie that nivir did a fuckin thing tae naebody . . . ah jist hated the world . . . ah mean . . . ah thought, how the fuck should ah care? What huv ah goat fae life . . . ah'm twenty-three an ah've hud nothin, no even a fuckin joab . . . why should ah care . . . whin ah telt the lassie, she jist freaked . . . he sobbed like a child. Then he looked up at us and produced, through his tears, the most beautiful smile I have ever seen on anyone in my life. — . . . but it wis awright. She took the test. Three times ower six months. Nuthin. Shi wisnae infected . . .

Marjory, who in the same circumstances *was* infected, hissed at us. Then it happened. That cunt Venters rolled his eyes and smiled at me. That did it. That was the moment. The anger was still there, but it was fused with a great calmness, a powerful clarity. I smiled back at him, feeling like a semi-submerged crocodile eyeing a soft, furry animal drinking at the river's edge.

— Naw . . . wee Goagsie whined piteously at Marjory, — it wisnae like that . . . waitin fir her test results wis worse thin waiting fir ma ain . . . yis dinnae understand . . . ah didnae . . . ah mean ah dinnae . . . it's no like . . .

Tom came to the aid of the quivering, inarticulate mass he had become.

— Let's not forget the tremendous anger, resentment and bitterness that you all felt when you learned that you were antibody positive.

This was the cue for one of our customary, on-going series of arguments to shunt into full gear. Tom saw it as 'dealing with our anger' by 'confronting reality'. The process was supposed to be therapeutic, and indeed it seemed to be for many of the group, but I found it exhausting and depressing. Perhaps this was because, at the time, my personal agenda was different.

Throughout this debate on personal responsibility, Venters, as was typical on such occasions, made his customary helpful and enlightening contribution. — Shite, he exclaimed, whenever someone made a point with passion. Tom would ask him, as he always did, why he felt that way.

— Jist do, Venters replied with a shrug. Tom asked if he could explain why.

— It's jist one person's view against the other's.

Tom responded by asking Alan what his view was. Alan either said: Ah'm no bothered, or: Ah dinnae gie a fuck. I forget his exact words.

Tom then asked him why he was here. Venters said: — Ah'll go then. He left, and the atmosphere instantly improved. It was as if someone who had done a vile and odious fart had somehow sucked it back up their arsehole.

He came back though, as he always did, sporting that sneering, gloating expression. It was as if Venters believed that he alone was immortal. He enjoyed watching others trying to be positive, then deflating them. Never blatantly enough to get kicked out of the group, but enough to significantly lower its morale. The disease which racked his body was a sweetheart compared to the more obscure one that possessed his sick mind.

Ironically, Venters saw me as a kindred spirit, unaware that my sole purpose of attending the meetings was to scrutinise him. I never spoke in the group, and perfected a cynical look whenever anyone else did. Such behaviour provided the basis on which I was able to pal up with Alan Venters.

It had been easy to befriend this guy. Nobody else wanted to know him; I simply became his friend by default. We started drinking together; him recklessly, me carefully. I began to learn about his life, accumulating knowledge steadily, thoroughly and systematically. I had done a degree in Chemistry at Strathclyde University, but I never approached my studies of that subject with anything like the rigour or enthusiasm with which I approached the study of Venters.

Venters had got HIV infection, like most people in Edinburgh, through the sharing of needles while taking heroin. Ironically, prior to being diagnosed HIV positive, he had kicked the junk, but was now a hopeless pisshead. The way he drank indiscriminately, occasionally stuffing a pub roll or toastie into his face during a marathon drinking bout, meant that his weakened frame was easy prey to all sorts of potentially killer infections. During his period of socialising with me, I confidently prophesied that he would last no time.

That was how it turned out; a number of infections were soon coursing through his body. This made no difference to him. Venters carried on behaving as he had always done. He started to attend the hospice, or the unit, as they called it; first as an outpatient, then with a berth of his very own.

It always seemed to be raining when I made that journey to the hospice; a wet, freezing, persistent rain, with winds that cut through your layers of clothing like an X-ray. Chills equal colds and colds can equal death, but this meant little to me at the time. Now, of course, I look after myself. Then, however, I had an all-consuming mission: there was work to be done.

The hospice building is not unattractive. They have faced over the grey blocks with some nice yellow brickwork. There is no yellow brick approach road to the place, however.

Every visit to Alan Venters brought my last one, and my final revenge, closer to hand. The point soon came when there was no time left to try and illicit heartfelt apologies from him. At one stage I thought that I wanted repentance from Venters more than revenge for myself. If I got it, I would have died with a belief in the fundamental goodness of the human spirit.

The shrivelled vessel of skin and bone which contained the life-force of Venters seemed to be an inadequate home for a spirit of any sorts, let alone one in which to invest your hopes for humanity. However, a weakened, decaying body was supposed to bring the spirit closer to the surface, and make it more apparent to we mortals. That was what Gillian from the hospital where I worked told me. Gillian is very religious, and it suits her to believe that. We all see what we want to see.

What did I really want? Perhaps it was always revenge, rather than repentance. Venters could have babbled for forgiveness like a greetin-faced bairn. It might not have been enough to stop me from doing what I planned to do.

This internal discoursing; it's a by-product of all that counselling I got from Tom. He emphasised basic truths: you are not dying yet, you have to live your life until you are. Underpinning them was the belief that the grim reality of impending death can be talked away by trying to invest in the present reality of life. I didn't believe that at the time, but now I do. By definition, you have to live until you die. Better to make that life as complete and enjoyable an experience as possible, in case death is shite, which I suspect it will be.

The nurse at the hospital looked a bit like Gail, a woman I'd once gone out with, pretty disastrously, as it happens. She wore the same cool expression on her face. In her case she had good reason, as I recognised it as one of professional concern. In Gail's case, such detachment was, I feel, inappropriate. This nurse looked at me in that strained, serious and patronising way.

— Alan's very weak. Please don't stay too long.

— I understand, I smiled, benign and sombre. As she was playing the caring professional, I thought that I had better play the concerned friend. I seemed to be playing the part quite well.

— He's very fortunate to have such a good friend, she said,

obviously perplexed that such a bastard abomination could have *any* friends. I grunted something noncommittal and moved into the small room. Alan looked terrible. I was worried sick; gravely concerned that this bastard might not last the week, that he might escape from the terrible destiny I'd carved out for him. The timing had to be right.

It had given me great pleasure, at the start, to witness Venters's great physical agony. I will never let myself get into a state like that when I get sick; fuck that. I'll leave that engine running in the lock-up garage. Venters, shite that he is, did not have the guts to leave the gig of his own accord. He'd hang on till the grim end, if only to maximise the inconvenience to everyone.

— Awright Al? I asked him. A silly question really. Convention always imposes its lunacy on us at such inappropriate times.

— No bad . . . he wheezed.

Are you quite sure, Alan, dear boy? Nothing wrong? You look a bit peaky. Probably just a touch of this little bug that's doing the rounds. Straight to bed with a couple of disprins and you'll be as right as rain tomorrow.

— Any pain? I ask hopefully.

— Naw . . . they goat drugs . . . jist ma breathin . . . I held his hand and felt a twinge of amusement as his pathetic, bony fingers squeezed tightly. I thought I was going to laugh in his skeletal face as his tired eyes kept shutting.

Alas poor Alan, I knew him Nurse. He was a wanker, an infinite pest. I watched, stifling smirks, as he groped for breath.

— S awright mate. Ah'm here, I said.

— You're a good guy, Davie . . . he spluttered. — . . . pity we nivir knew each other before this . . . He opened his eyes and shut them again.

— It was a fuckin pity awright you trash-faced little cunt . . . I hissed at his closed eyes.

— What? . . . what was that . . . he was delirious with fatigue and drugs.

Lazy cunt. Spends too long in that scratcher. Should get off his hole for a wee bit of exercise. A quick jog around the park. Fifty press-ups. Two dozen squat thrusts.

— I said, it's a shame we had to meet under such circumstances.

He groaned contentedly and fell into a sleep. I extracted his scrawny fingers from my hand.

Unpleasant dreams, cunt.

The nurse came in to check on my man. — Most anti-social. Hardly the way to treat a guest, I smiled, looking down on the slumbering near-corpse that was Venters. She forced a nervous laugh, probably thinking it's the black humour of the homosexual or the junky, or the haemophiliac or whatever she imagines me to be. I don't give a toss about her perception of me. I see myself as the avenging angel.

Killing this shitebag would only do him a big favour. That was the problem, but one which I managed to resolve. How do you hurt a man who's going to die soon, knows it, and doesnae give a toss? Talking, but more crucially, listening to Venters, I found out how. *You hurt them through the living, through the people they care for.*

The song says that 'everybody loves somebody sometime', but Venters seemed to defy that generalisation. The man just did not like people, and they more than reciprocated. With other men Venters saw himself in an adversarial role. Past acquaintances were described with bitterness: 'a rip-off merchant', or derision: 'a fuckin sap'. The description employed depended on who had abused, exploited or manipulated whom, on the particular occasion in question.

Women fell into two indistinct categories. They either had 'a fanny like a fish supper', or 'a fanny like a burst couch'. Venters evidently saw little in a woman beyond 'the furry hole', as he called it. Even some disparaging remarks about their tits or arses would have represented a considerable broadening of vision. I got despondent. How could this bastard ever love anybody? I gave it time, however, and patience reaped its reward.

Despicable shite though he was, Venters did care for one person. There was no mistaking the change in his conversational tone when he employed the phrase: 'the wee felly'. I discreetly pumped him for information about the five-year-old son he had by this woman in Wester Hailes, a 'cow' who would not let him see the child, named Kevin. Part of me loved this woman already.

The child showed me how Venters could be hurt. In contrast to his normal bearing, he was stricken with pain and incoherent with sentiment when he talked about how he'd never see *his* son grow up, about how much he loved 'the wee felly'. That was why Venters did not fear death. He actually believed that he would live on, in some sense or other, through his son.

It hadn't been difficult to insinuate myself into the life of Frances, Venters's ex-girlfriend. She hated Venters with a vitriol which endeared her to me even though I wasn't attracted to her in any other way.

After checking her out, I cruised her accidentally-on-purpose at a trashy disco, where I played the role of charming and attentive suitor. Of course, money was no object. She was soon well into it, obviously having never been treated decently by a man in her life, and she wasn't used to cash, living on the breadline with a kid to bring up.

The worst part was when it came to sex. I insisted, of course, on wearing a condom. She had, prior to us getting to that stage, told me about Venters. I nobly said that I trusted her and would be prepared to make love without a condom, but I wanted to remove the element of uncertainty from her mind, and I had to be honest, I had been with a few different people. Given her past experience with Venters, such doubts were bound to be present. When she started to cry, I thought I had blown it. Her tears were due to gratitude however.

— You're a really nice person, Davie, dae ye ken that? she said. If she knew what I was going to do, she wouldn't have held such a lofty opinion. It made me feel bad, but whenever I thought of Venters, the feeling evaporated. I would go through with it alright.

I timed my courtship of Frances to coincide with Venter's decline into serious illness and his attendant incapacity in the hospice. A number of illnesses were in the frame to finish Venters, the leader of the field being pneumonia. Venters, in common with a lot of HIV-infected punters who take the junk route, escaped the horrible skin cancers more prevalent amongst gays. The main rival to his pneumonia was the prolific thrush which went into his throat and stomach. Thrush was not the first thing to want to choke the living shit out of the bastard, but it could be the last unless I moved quickly. His decline was very rapid, at one stage too rapid for my liking. I thought that the cunt would cash in his chips before I could execute my plan.

My opportunity came, in the event, at exactly the right time; in the end it was probably fifty-fifty luck and planning. Venters was struggling, no more than a wrinkled parcel of skin and bone. The doctor had said: any day now.

I had got Frances to trust me with the babysitting. I encouraged her to get out with her friends. She was planning to go out for a curry on the Saturday night, leaving me alone in her flat with the kid. I would take the opportunity presented to me. On the Wednesday before the big day, I decided to visit my parents. I had thought about telling them of my medical condition, and knew it would probably be my last visit.

My parents' home was a flat in Oxgangs. The place had always seemed so modern to me when I was a kid. Now it looked strange, a shantytown relic of a bygone era. The auld girl answered the door. For a second she looked tentative. Then she realised it was me and not my younger brother, and therefore the purse could be kept in mothballs. She welcomed me, her enthusiasm generated by relief. — Hu-low stranger, she sang, ushering me in with haste.

I noted the reason for the hurry, *Coronation Street* was on. Mike Baldwin had apparently reached a point where he had to confront live-in-lover Alma Sedgewick and tell her that he was really into rich widow Jackie Ingram. Mike couldn't help it. He was a prisoner of love, a force external to him, which compelled him to behave the way he did. I could, as Tom would have put it, empathise. I was a prisoner of hate, a force which was an equally demanding taskmaster. I sat down on the couch.

— Hello stranger, ma old man repeated, not looking at me from behind his *Evening News*. — What have you been up tae then? he asked wearily.

— Nuthin' much.

Nothing really pater. Oh, did I mention I'm antibody positive? It's very fashionable now, you know. One simply must have a damaged immune system these days.

— Two million Chinkies. Two million ay the buggers. That's whit we're gaunnae huv ower here whin Hong Kong goes back tae China. He let out a long exhalation of breath. — Two million Wee Willie Winkies, he mused.

I said nothing, refusing to rise to the bait. Ever since I'd gone to university, jacking in what my parents habitually described as 'a good trade', the auld man had cast himself as hard-nosed reactionary to my student revolutionary. At first it had been a joke, but with the passing years I grew out of my role as he began to embrace his more firmly.

— You're a fascist. It's all to do with inadequate penis size, I told him cheerfully. *Coronation Street*'s vice-like grip on my Ma's psyche was broken briefly as she turned to us with a knowing smirk.

— Dinnae talk bloody nonsense. Ah've proved *ma* manhood son, he belligerently replied, digging at the fact I'd managed to reach the age of twenty-five without obtaining a wife or producing children. For a second I even thought that he was going to pull out his cock to try and prove me wrong. Instead he shrugged off my remark and returned to his chosen theme. —— How'd you like two million Chinkies in your street? I thought of the term 'Chinky' and visualised loads of aluminium cartons of half-eaten food lying in my road. It was an easy image to call to mind, as it was a scene I observed every Sunday morning.

—— It sometimes seems like I already huv, I thought out loud.

—— There ye are then, he said, as if I'd conceded a point. —— Another two million ur oan thir way. How'd ye like that?

—— Presumably the whole two million won't move into Caledonian Place. I mean, conditions are cramped enough in the Dalry ghetto as it is.

—— Laugh if ye like. Whit aboot joabs? Two million on the dole already. Hooses? Aw they perr buggers livin in cardboard city. God, was he nipping my heid. Thankfully, the mighty Ma, guardian of the soap box, intervened.

—— Shut up, will yis! Ah'm tryin tae watch the telly!

Sorry mater. I know that it's a trifle self-indulgent of me, your HIV offspring, to crave your attention when Mike Baldwin is making an important choice which will determine his future. Which grotesque auld hing-oot will the shrivelled post-menopausal slag want tae shaft? Stay tuned.

I decide not to mention my HIV. My parents don't have very progressive views on such things. Or maybe they do. Who knows? At any rate, it just did not feel right. Tom always tells us to keep in tune with our feelings. My feelings were that my parents married at eighteen and had produced four screaming brats by the time they were my age. They think I'm 'queer' already. Bringing AIDS into the picture will only serve to confirm this suspicion.

Instead I drank a can of Export and quietly talked fitba with the auld man. He hasn't been to a game since 1970. Colour television had gone for his legs. Twenty years later, satellite came along and fucked them up completely. Nonetheless, he still regarded himself as an expert on the game. The opinions of others were worthless. In any event, it was a waste of time attempting to venture them. As with politics, he'd eventually come around to the opposite viewpoint from the one he'd previously advocated and express it just as stridently. All you needed to do was put up no hard front for him to argue against and he'd gradually talk himself around to your way of thinking.

I sat for a while, nodding intently. Then I made some banal excuse and left.

I returned home and checked my toolbox. A former chippie's collection of various sharp implements. On Saturday, I took it round to Frances's flat in Wester Hailes. I had a few odd jobs to do. One of them she knew nothing about.

Fran had been looking forward to the meal out with her pals. She talked incessantly as she got ready. I tried to respond beyond a series of low groans which sounded like 'aye' and 'right', but my mind was spinning with thoughts of what I had to do. I sat hunched and tense on the bed, frequently rising to the window to peer out, as she put her 'face' on.

After what seemed like a lifetime, I heard the sound of a motor rolling into the deserted, shabby car park. I sprang to the window, cheerfully announcing: — Taxi's here!

Frances left me in custody of her sleeping child.

The whole operation went smoothly enough. Afterwards I felt terrible. Was I any better than Venters? Wee Kevin. We had some good times together. I'd taken him to the shows at the Meadows festival, to Kirkcaldy for a League Cup tie, and to the Museum of Childhood. While it doesn't seem a great deal, it's a sight more than his auld boy ever did for the poor wee bastard. Frances said as much to me.

Bad as I felt then, it was only a foretaste of the horror that hit me when I developed the photographs. As the prints formed into clarity, I shook with fear and remorse. I put them on the dryer and made myself a coffee, which I used to wash down two valium. Then I took the prints and went to the hospice to visit Venters.

Physically, there was not a great deal left of him. I feared the worst when I looked into his glazed eyes. Some people with AIDS had been developing pre-senile dementia. The disease could have his body. If it had also taken his mind, it would deprive me of my revenge.

Thankfully, Venters soon registered my presence, his initial lack of response probably a side-effect of the medication he was on. His eyes soon fixed me in their gaze, acquiring the sneaky, furtive look I associated with him. I could feel his contempt for me oozing through his sickly smile. He thought he'd found a sappy cunt to indulge him until the end. I sat with him, holding his hand. I felt like snapping off his scrawny fingers and sticking them into his orifices. I blamed him for what I had to do to Kevin, as well as all the other issues.

— You're a good guy Davie. Pity we didnae meet in different circumstances, he wheezed, repeating that well-worn phrase he used on all my visits. I tightened my grasp on his hand. He looked at me uncomprehendingly. Good. The bastard could still feel physical pain. It wasn't going to be that kind of pain which would hurt him, but it was a nice extra. I spoke in clear, measured tones.

— I told you I got infected through shooting up, Al. Well, I lied. I lied tae ye aboot tons ay things.

— What's aw this, Davie?

— Just listen for a minute, Al. Ah got infected through this bird ah'd been seein. She didnae ken thit she wis HIV. She goat infected by a piece ay shite that she met one night in a pub. She was a bit pished and a bit naive, this wee bird. Ken? This cunt sais that he had a wee bit ay dope back at his gaff. So she went wi the cunt. Back tae his flat. The bastard raped her. Ye ken whit he did, Al?

— Davie . . . whit is this . . .

— Ah'll fuckin tell ye. Threatened her wi a fuckin blade. Tied her doon. Fucked her fanny, fucked her arse, made her go doon oan him. The lassie wis terrified, as well as being hurt. Does this sound familiar then cunt?

— Ah dinnae . . . ah dinnae ken whit the fuck yir oan aboot Davie . . .

— Di-nnae fah-kin start. You remember Donna. You remember the Southern Bar.

— Ah wis fucked up man . . . — you remember whit you sais . . .

— That wis lies. Bullshit. *Ah* couldnae huv goat a fuckin root oan if ah knew ah hud that shite in *ma* come. Ah couldnae huv raised a fuckin smile.

— Wee Goagsie . . . mind ay him?

— Shut yir fuckin mooth. Wee Goagsie took his fuckin chance. You sat thair like it wis a fuckin pantomime whin you hud yours, I rasped, watching drops of my gob disseminate into the film of sweat which covered his shrunken coupon. I composed myself, continuing my story.

— The lassie went through a heavy time. She was strong-willed though. It would huv fucked up a lot ay women, but Donna tried tae shrug it off. Why let one spunk-gobbed cunt ruin your life? Easier said than done, but she did it. What she didnae ken wis thit the scumbag in question wis HIV positive. Then she meets this other guy. They hit it off. He likes her, but he kens that she's goat problems wi men and sex. Nae fuckin wonder, eh? I wanted to strangle the perverse force which passed for life out of the cunt's body. Not yet, I told myself. Not yet, you doss fucker. I drew a heavy breath, and continued my tale, reliving the horror of it.

— They worked it oot, this lassie and the other guy. Things were barry for a bit. Then she discovered that the rapist fuckbag was HIV. Then she discovered that she was. But what was worse for this person, a *real* person, a fuckin *moral* person, was when she found out that her new felly was. All because of *you*, the rapist cunt. *Ah* wis the new felly. *Me.* Big fuckin sap here, I pointed to myself.

— Davie . . . ah'm sorry man . . . — whit kin ah say? Yiv been a good mate . . . it's that disease . . . it's a fuckin horrible disease, Davie. It kills the innocent, Davie . . . it kills the innocent . . .

— It's too late fir that shite now. Ye hud yir chance at the time. Like Wee Goagsie.

He laughed in my face. It was a deep, wheezing sound.

— So what are ye . . . what are ye gaunnae dae aboot it? . . . Kill me? Go ahead . . . ye'd be daein us a favour . . . ah dinnae gie a fuck. His wizened death mask seemed to become animated, to fill with a strange, ugly energy. This was not a human being. Obviously, it suited me to believe that, made it easier to do what I had to do, but in cold light of day I believe it still. It was time to play my cards. I calmly produced the photographs from my inside pocket.

— It's not so much what ah'm gaunnae dae aboot it, mair what ah already have done aboot it, I smiled, drinking the expression of perplexed fear which etched onto his face.

— Whit's this . . . whit dae ye mean? I felt wonderful. Shock waves tripped over him, his scrawny head oscillating as his mind grappled with his greatest fears. He looked at the photographs in terror, unable to make them out, wondering what dreadful secrets they held.

— Think of the worst possible thing I could do to make you pissed off, Al. Then multiply it by one thousand . . . and you're not even fuckin close. I shook my head mournfully.

I showed him a photograph of myself and Frances. We were posing confidently, casually displaying the arrogance of lovers in their first flush.

— What the fuck, he spluttered, trying pathetically to pull his scrawny frame up in the bed. I thrust my hand to his chest and effortlessly pushed him back home. I did this slowly, savouring my power, and his impotence in that one gorgeous motion.

— Relax, Al, relax. Unwind. Loosen up a little. Take it easy. Remember what the doctors and nurses say. You need your rest. I flipped the first photo over, exposing the next picture to him. — That wis Kevin thit took the last picture. Takes a good photae fir a wee laddie, eh? There he is, the wee felly. The next photograph showed Kevin, dressed in a Scotland football strip, on my shoulders.

— What have you fuckin done . . . It was a sound, rather than a voice. It seemed to come from an unspecific part of his decaying body rather than his mouth. The unearthliness of it stung me, but I made the effort to continue sounding nonchalant.

— Basically this. I produced the third photo. It showed Kevin, bound to a kitchen chair. His head hung heavily to one side, and his eyes were closed. Had Venters looked at the detail, he may have noticed a bluish tint to his son's eyelids and lips, and the almost clownish whiteness of his complexion. It's almost certain that all Venters noticed were the dark wounds on his head, chest, and knees, and the blood which oozed from them, covering his body, at first making it hard to note that he was naked.

The blood was everywhere. It covered the lino in a dark puddle underneath Kevin's chair. Some of it shot outwards across the kitchen floor in squirted trails. An assortment of power tools, including a Bosch drill and a Black and Decker sander, in addition to various sharpened knives and screwdrivers, were laid out at the feet of the upright body.

— Naw . . . naw . . . Kevin . . . for god's sake naw . . . he done nuthin . . . he hurt naebody . . . naw . . . he moaned on, an ugly, whingey sound devoid of hope or humanity. I gripped his thin hair crudely, and wrenched his head up from the pillow. I observed in perverse fascination as the bony skull seemed to sink to the bottom of the loose skin. I thrust the picture in his face.

— I thought that young Kev should be just like Daddy. So when I got bored fucking your old girlfriend, I decided I'd give wee Kev one up his . . . eh . . . tradesman's entrance. I thought, if HIV's good enough for Daddy it's good enough for his brat.

— Kevin . . . Kevin . . . he groaned on.

— Unfortunately, his arsehole was a bit too tight for me, so I had to extend it a little with the masonry drill. Sadly, I got a wee bit carried away and started making holes all over the place. It's just that he reminded me so much of you, Al. I'd love to say it was painless, but I cannae. At least it was relatively quick. Quicker than rotting away in a bed. It took him about twenty minutes to die. Twenty screaming, miserable minutes. Poor Kev. As you sais, Al, it's a disease which kills the innocent.

Tears rolled down his cheeks. He kept saying 'no' over and over again in low, choking sobs. His head jerked in my grip. Worried that the nurse would come, I pulled out one of the pillows from behind him.

— The last word wee Kevin sais wis 'Daddy'. That wis yir bairn's last words, Al. Sorry pal. Daddy's away. That wis whit ah telt him. Daddy's away. I looked straight into his eyes, all pupils, just a black void of fear and total defeat.

I pushed his head back down, and put the pillow over his face stifling the sickening moans. I held it firmly down and pressed my head on it, half-gasping, half-singing the paraphrased words of an old Boney M song: 'Daddy, Daddy Cool, Daddy, Daddy Cool . . . you been a fuckin fool, bye bye Daddy Cool . . .'

I merrily sang until Venter's feeble resistance subsided.

Keeping the pillow firmly over his face, I pulled a *Penthouse* magazine off his locker. The bastard would have been too weak to even turn the pages, let alone raise a wank. However, his homophobia was so strong that he'd probably kept it on prominent display to make some absurd statement about his sexuality. Rotting away, and his greatest concern is that nobody thinks he's a buftie. I set the magazine on the pillow and thumbed through it in a leisurely manner before taking Venters's pulse. Nothing. He'd checked out. More importantly, he'd done it in a state of tortured, agonised, misery.

Taking the pillow off the corpse, I pulled its ugly frail head forward, then let it fall back. For a few moments I contemplated what I saw before me. The eyes were open, as was the mouth. It looked stupid, a sick caricature of a human being. I suppose that's what corpses are. Mind you, Venters always was.

My searing scorn quickly gave way to a surge of sadness. I couldn't quite determine why that should have happened. I looked away from the body. After sitting for another couple of minutes, I went to tell the nurse that Venters had left the stadium.

I attended Venters's funeral at Seafield Crematorium with Frances. It was an emotional time for her, and I felt obliged to lend support. It was never an event destined to break any attendance records. His mother and sister showed up, as did Tom, with a couple of punters from 'HIV and Positive'.

The minister could find little decent to say about Venters and, to his credit, he didn't bullshit. It was a short and sweet performance. Alan had made many mistakes in his life, he said. Nobody was contradicting him. Alan would, like all of us, be judged by God, who would grant him salvation. It is an interesting notion, but I feel that the gaffer in the sky has a fair bit of graft ahead of him if that bastard's checked in up there. If he has, I think I'll take my chances in the other place, thank you very much.

Outside, I checked out the wreaths. Venters only had one. 'Alan. Love Mum and Sylvia.' To my knowledge they had never visited him in the hospice. Very wise of them. Some people are easier to love when you don't have to be around them. I pumped the hands of Tom and the others, then took Fran and Kev for some de luxe ice-cream at Lucas in Musselburgh.

Obviously, I had deceived Venters about the things I did to

Kevin. Unlike him, I'm not a fuckin animal. I'm far from proud about what I *did* do. I took great risks with the bairn's well being. Working in a hospital operating theatre, I know all about the crucial role of the anaesthetist. They're the punters that keep you alive, not sadistic fuck-pigs like Howison. After the jab puts you under, you're kept unconscious by the anaesthetic and put onto a life-support system. All your vital signs are monitored in highly controlled conditions. They take care.

Chloroform is much more of a blunt instrument, and very dangerous. I still shudder when I think of the risk I took with the wee man. Thankfully, Kevin woke up, with only a sore head and some bad dreams as a remnant of his trip to the kitchen.

The joke shop and Humbrol enamel paints provided the wounds. I worked wonders with Fran's makeup and talc for Kev's death mask. My greatest coup, though, was the three plastic pint bags of blood I took from the fridge in the path lab at the hospital. I got paranoid when that fucker Howison gave me the evil eye as I walked down the corridor past him. He always does though. I think it's because I once addressed him as 'Doctor' instead of 'Mister'. He's a funny cunt. Most surgeons are. You'd have to be to do that job. Like Tom's job, I suppose.

Putting Kevin under turned out to be easy. The biggest problem I had was setting up and dismantling the entire scene inside half an hour. The most difficult part involved cleaning him up before getting him back to bed. I had to use turps as well as water. I spent the rest of the night cleaning up the kitchen before Frances got back. It was worth the effort however. The pictures looked authentic. Authentic enough to fuck up Venters.

Since I helped Al on his way to the great gig in the sky, life has been pretty good. Frances and I have gone our separate ways. We were never really compatible. She only really saw me as a babysitter and a wallet. For me, obviously, the relationship became largely superfluous after Venters's death. I miss Kev more. It makes me wish that I had a kid. Now that'll never be.

One thing that Fran did say was that I had revived her faith in men after Venters. Ironically, it seems as if I found my role in life — cleaning up that prick's emotional garbage.

My health, touch wood, has been good. I'm still asymptomatic. I fear colds and get obsessive from time to time, but I take care of myself. Apart from the odd can of beer, I never bevvy. I watch what I eat, and have a daily programme of light exercises. I get regular blood checks and pay attention to my T4 count. It's still way over the crucial 800 mark; in fact it's not gone down at all.

I'm now back with Donna, who inadvertently acted as the conduit for HIV between me and Venters. We found something that we probably wouldn't have got from each other in different circumstances. Or maybe we would. Anyway, we don't analyse it, not having the luxury of time. However, I must give old Tom at the group his due. He said that I'd have to work through my anger, and he was right. I took the quick route though, by sending Venters to oblivion. Now all I get is a bit of guilt, but I can handle that.

I eventually told my parents about my being HIV positive. My Ma just cried and held me. The auld man said nothing. The colour had drained from his face as he sat and watched *A Question of Sport*. When he was pressed by his wailing wife to speak, he just said: — Well, there's nothin tae say. He kept repeating that sentence. He never looked me in the eye.

That night, back at my flat, I heard the buzzer go. Assuming it to be Donna, who had been out, I opened the stair and house doors. A few minutes later, my auld man stood in the doorway with tears in his eyes. It was the first time he'd ever been to my flat. He moved over to me and held me in a crushing grip, sobbing, and repeating: — Ma laddie. It felt a world or two better than: 'Well, there's nothin tae say.'

I cried loudly and unselfconsciously. As with Donna, so with my family. We have found an intimacy which may have otherwise eluded us. I wish I hadn't waited so long to become a human being. Better late than never though, believe you me.

There's some kids playing out in the back, the strip of grass luminated an electric green by the brilliant sunlight. The sky is a delicious clear blue. Life is beautiful. I'm going to enjoy it, and I'm going to have a long life. I'll be what the medical staff call a long-term survivor. I just *know* that I will.

There Is A Light That Never Goes Out

They emerge from the stairdoor into the darkness of the deserted street. Some of them move in a jerky, manic way; exuberant and noisy. Others cruise along silently, like ghosts; hurting inside, yet fearful of the imminence of even greater pain and discomfort.

Their destination is a pub which seems to prop up a crumbling tenement set on a side-street between Easter Road and Leith Walk. This street has missed out on the stone-cleaning process its neighbours have enjoyed and the building is the sooty-black colour of a forty-a-day man's lungs. The night is so dark that it is difficult to establish the outline of the tenement against the sky. It can only be defined through an isolated light glaring from a top-floor window, or the luminous street-lamp jutting out from its side.

The pub's façade is painted a thick, glossy dark blue and its sign is the early 1970s design favoured by its brewing chain when the paradigm was that every bar had to have a standard look and play down any individual character it might have. Like the tenement above and around it, the pub has enjoyed nothing other than the most superficial maintenance for almost twenty years.

It is 5.06 a.m. and the hostelry's yellow lights are on, a haven in the dark, wet and lifeless streets. It had been, Spud reflects, a few days since he'd seen the light. They were like vampires, living a largely nocturnal existence, completely out of synchronisation with most of the other people who inhabited the tenements and lived by a rota of sleep and work. It was good to be different.

Despite the fact that its doors have only been open for a few minutes, the pub is busy. Inside, there is a long formica-topped bar with several pumps and fonts. Battered tables in the same formica style stand shakily on dirty lino. Behind the bar towers an incongruously grandiose finely-carved wooden gantry. Sickly yellow light from the shadeless bulbs bounces harshly off the nicotine-stained walls.

The pub contains *bona fide* shift workers from the brewery and the hospital, and this is as it should be, given the avowed purpose of the early licence. There is also a smattering, however, of the more desperate: those who are there because they need to be.

The group entering the pub are also driven by need. The need for more alcohol to maintain the high, or to regain it, and fight off the onset of grim, depressive hangovers. They are also drawn by a greater need, the need to belong to each other, to hold on to whatever force has fused them together during the last few days of partying.

Their entry to the pub is observed by an indeterminately old drunkard who is propped up against the bar. The man's face has been destroyed by the consumption of cheap spirits and over-exposure to the frozen wind blasting cruelly from the North Sea. It seems as if every blood vessel in it has ruptured under the skin, leaving it resembling the undercooked square sausages served up in the local cafes. His eyes are a contrasting cool blue, although the whites of them are the identical colour of the pub walls. His face strains in vague recognition as the noisy group move up to the bar. One of the young men, perhaps more than one, he sardonically thinks, is his son. He had been responsible for bringing quite a few of them into the world at one time, when a certain type of woman found him attractive. That was before the drink had destroyed his appearance and distorted the output of his cruel, sharp tongue to an incomprehensible growl. He looks at the young man in question and considers saying something, before deciding that he has nothing to say to him. He never had. The young man doesn't even see him, his attention focused on getting in the drinks. The old drunkard sees that the young man enjoys his company and his drink. He remembers when he himself was in that position. The enjoyment and the company faded away, but the drink didn't. In fact, it expanded to fill the gap left by their departure.

The last thing Spud wants is another pint. Prior to their departure he had examined his face in the bathroom mirror back in Dawsy's flat. It was pale, yet marked with blotches, with heavy, hooded eyelids attempting to draw the shutters on reality. This face was topped by sticking-up tufts of sandy hair. It might be an idea, he considers, to have a tomato juice for his aching guts, or a fresh orange and lemonade to combat his dehydration, before drinking alcohol again.

The hopelessness of the situation is confirmed when he mildly accepts the pint of lager Frank Begbie, first to the bar, had got up.

— Cheers, Franco.

— Guinness fir me Franco, Renton requests. He has just returned from London. He feels as good to be back as he did to get away in the first place.

— The Guinness is shite in here, Gav Temperley tells him.

— Still though.

Dawsy is raising his eyebrows and singing at the barmaid.

— *Yeah, yeah, yeah, you're a beautiful lover.*

They'd had a crappest song competition, and Dawsy hadn't stopped singing his winning entry.

— Shut the fuck up, Dawsy. Alison nudges him in the ribs. — Ye want tae git us flung oot?

The barmaid is ignoring him anyway. He turns to sing at Renton instead. Renton just smiles wearily. He considers that the trouble with Dawsy is, that if you encourage him, he'll tear the arse out of a situation. It was mildly amusing a couple of days ago, and in any case, he feels, it had not been as funny as his own version of Rupert Holmes's 'Escape (The Pina Colada Song)'.

— *Ah kin remember the night that we met down in Rio . . .* that Guinness is fuckin loupin. Yir mad gittin Guinness in here, Mark.

— Telt um, Gav says, triumphantly.

— Aw the same but, Renton replies, a lazy grin still on his face. He feels drunk. He feels Kelly's hand inside his shirt, tweaking his nipple. She'd been doing that to him all night, telling him that she really liked flat, hairless chests. It feels good having his nipples touched. By Kelly, it feels better than good.

— Vodka n tonic, she says to Begbie, who gestures to her from the bar. — Gin n lemonade for Ali. She's jist away tae the bog.

Spud and Gav continue talking at the bar while the rest grab some seats in the corner.

— How's June? Kelly asks Franco Begbie, referring to his girlfriend, suspected to be pregnant again after having just recently given birth to a child.

— Who? Franco shrugs aggressively. End of conversation.

Renton looks up at the early morning programme on the television.

— That Anne Diamond.

— Eh? Kelly looks at him.

— Ah'd fuckin shag it, Begbie says.

Alison and Kelly raise their eyebrows and look to the ceiling.

— Naw but, her bairn hud that cot death. Same as Lesley's bairn. Wee Dawn.

— That wis a real shame, Kelly says.

— Good thing really bit. Wee lassie would've died ay fuckin AIDS if it hudnae died ay cot death. Easier fuckin death fir a bairn, Begbie states.

— Lesley did not have HIV! Dawn was a perfectly healthy baby! Alison hisses at him, enraged. Despite being upset himself, Renton cannot not help noting that Alison always speaks posh when she is angry. He feels a vague surge of guilt at being so trivial. Begbie is grinning.

— Whae's tae say though? Dawsy says sycophantically. Renton looks at him with a hard, challenging stare, which he'd never dare do with Begbie. Aggression displaced to where it will not be reciprocated.

—

— Aw ah'm sayin is, nae cunt really kens, Dawsy shrugs tamely.

At the bar, Spud and Gav are slurring a conversation together.

— Reckon Rents'll shag Kelly? Gav asks.

— Dunno. She's finished wi that Des dude, likesay, n Rents isnae seein Hazel now. Free agents n that likesay, ken.

— That cunt Des. Ah hate that wanker.

— . . . dunno the cat, likesay . . . ken.

— Ye fuckin do! He's your fuckin cousin, Spud. Des! Des Feeney!

— . . . right man . . . *that* Des. Still dinnae really ken the boy. Only likesay run intae the gadge a couple ay times since we wir ankle-biters, ken? It's heavy though, Hazel bein at the perty wi that other guy, likes, n Rents wi Kelly, ken . . . heavy.

— That Hazel's a torn-faced cow anyway. Ah've nivir seen that lassie wi a smile oan her face. Nae wonder, mind you, gaun oot wi Rents. Cannie be much fun hingin aroond wi some cunt thit's eywis bombed ootay his box.

— Yeah, likesay . . . it's too heavy . . . Spud briefly wonders whether or not Gav is having an indirect dig at him, by going on about people who are always bombed, before deciding that it's an innocent remark. Gav was alright.

Spud's muddled brain turns to sex. Everyone seemed to bag off at the party, everyone except him. He really fancies a ride. His problem is that he is too shy when straight or sober, and too incoherent when stoned or drunk, to make an impression on women. He currently has a thing about Nicola Hanlon, whom he thinks looks a bit like Kylie Minogue.

A few months ago, Nicola had been talking to him as they walked from a party at Sighthill to one at Wester Hailes. They had been having a good crack, becoming detached from the rest of the group. She had been very responsive, and Spud had chatted freely, high on speed. In fact, she seemed to be hanging on his every word. Spud wanted to never get to that party, wishing that they could just go on walking and talking. They went down into the underpass and Spud thought that he should try to put his arm around Nicola. Then a passage from a Smiths' song, one he'd always liked called: 'There Is A Light That Never Goes Out', came into his head:

> and in the darkened underpass
> I thought Oh God my chance has come at last
> but then a strange fear gripped me
> and I just couldn't ask

Morrissey's sad voice summed up his feelings. He didn't put his arm around Nicola, and his attempts to chat her up were half-arsed after that. Instead, he jacked up in a bedroom with Rents and Matty, enjoying blissful freedom from the anxiety of wondering whether or not he'd get off with her.

When sex did happen for Spud, it was generally when he was possessed by a more forceful will. Even then, disaster never seemed to be too far away. One evening, Laura McEwan, a girl with an awesome sexual reputation, grabbed a hold of him in a Grassmarket pub, and took him home.

— Ah want you to take my arse virginity, she had told him.

— Eh? Spud could not believe it.

— Fuck me in the arse. Ah've never done it that way before.

— Eh yeah, that sounds . . . barry, eh likesay, eh right . . .

Spud felt like the chosen one. He knew that Sick Boy, Renton, and Matty had all been with Laura, who tended to attach herself to a company, fuck every guy in it, and then move on. The thing was, they had never done what he was about to do.

However, Laura wanted to do some things with Spud first. She bound his wrists, then his ankles together with sellotape.

— I'm daein this because ah don't want you to hurt me. Dae ye understand? We do it from the side. The minute ah start tae feel pain it's fuckin over. Right? Because nobody hurts me. No fuckin guy ever hurts me. Ye understand me? She spoke harshly and bitterly.

— Yeah . . . sound likesay, sound . . . Spud said. He didn't want to hurt anyone. He was shocked at the imputation.

Laura stood back and admired her handiwork.

— Fuck me, that's beautiful, she said, rubbing her crotch as a naked Spud lay trussed up on the bed. Spud felt vulnerable, and strangely coy. He'd never been tied up before, and never been told that he was beautiful. Laura then took Spud's long, thin cock into her mouth and started to suck him off.

She stopped, with an expertise part intuitive, part learned, just before an ecstatic Spud was about to come. Then she left the room. Spud started to get paranoid about the bondage. Everyone said Laura was a nutter. She'd been shagging everyone in sight since she'd got her long-term partner, a guy called Roy, committed to a psychiatric hospital, fed up with his impotence, incontinence and depression. But mostly the former.

— He never fucked me properly for ages, Laura had told Spud, as if that was justification for getting him banged up in the nuthouse. However, Spud reasoned, her cruelty and ruthlessness was part of her attraction. Sick Boy referred to her as the 'Sex Goddess'.

She came back into the bedroom, and looked at him, bound and at her mercy.

— Ah want you to dae us in the arse now. First though, ah'm gaunnae Vaseline your dick heavily, so that it doesnae hurt me when you put it in. My muscles'll be tight, cause this is new tae me, but I'll try tae relax. She toked hard on a joint.

Laura was not being strictly accurate. She couldn't find any Vaseline in the bathroom cabinet. She did, however, find some other stuff she could use as a lubricant. It was sticky and gooey. She applied it liberally to Spud's dick. It was Vick.

It burned into him, and Spud screamed in excruciating agony. He writhed fitfully against his bonds, feeling like the tip of his penis had been guillotined off.

— Fuck. Sorry Spud, Laura said, open-mouthed.

She helped him off the bed, and assisted him into the toilet. He hopped along, tears of pain blinding him. She filled the sink with water, and then left the room to search for knife to cut the binding on his ankles and wrists.

Balancing precariously, Spud put his cock into the water. It stung even more violently, the shock making him recoil. As he fell back, his head crashed against the toilet bowl and split open above his eye. When Laura came back, Spud was unconscious, and thick, dark blood was oozing onto the lino.

Laura called the ambulance, and Spud woke up in hospital with six stitches above his eye, heavily concussed.

He never did get to fuck her in the arsehole. The rumour was that a frustrated Laura phoned up Sick Boy shortly after this, who came and stood in for his friend.

Soon after this disaster, Spud turned his attention to Nicola Hanlon.

— Eh, surprised wee Nicky wisnae it the perty, likesay . . . wee Nicky, ken, likesay? he told Gav.

— Aye. She's a dirty wee hoor. Takes it aw weys, Gav said casually.

— Aye?

Noting, and savouring, the ill-disguised trepidation and concern on Spud's face, Gav continues, gleeful inside, but talking in a stiff, brisk, businesslike manner. — Aw aye. Ah've poked it a few times. No a bad wee ride, likes. Sick Boy's been thair. Rents n aw. Ah think Tommy tae. He wis certainly sniffin roond it fir a bit.

— Aye? . . . eh, right . . . Spud feels deflated, and optimistic at the same time. He'll have to try to stay straighter, he resolves, thinking that he seems to miss everything that is going on under his nose.

Over at the table, Begbie indicates that he is in need of more solid nourishment: — Ah'm fuckin Lee Marvin. Lit's git some scran, then hit a decent fuckin boozer. He looks bitterly around the cavernous, nicotine-stained bar, like an arrogant aristocrat finding himself in reduced circumstances. In fact, he has just seen the old drunkard at the bar.

It is still dark when they leave the pub, and go to a cafe in Portland Street.

— Fill breakfasts aw roond, Begbie enthusiastically looks at the others.

They all nod approvingly, except Renton.

— Naw. Ah'm no wantin meat, he says.

— Ah'll huv your fuckin bacon n sausage n fuckin black puddin then, Begbie suggests.

— Aye, sure, Renton says sarcastically.

— Ah'll fuckin swap ye ma fuckin egg n beans n tomatay then ya cunt!

— Awright, begins Renton, then he turns to the waitress. — Dae ye use vegetable oil whin ye fry, or fat?

— Naw, fat, the waitress says, looking at him as if he is an imbecile.

— Moantae fuck, Rents. Makes nae difference, Gav says.

— S up tae Mark what he eats, Kelly says supportively. Alison nods. Renton feels like a smug pimp.

— Fuckin well spoilin it fir ivray cunt, Rents, Begbie growls.

— How am ah spoilin it? Cheese salad roll, he turns to the waitress.

— We aw fuckin agreed. Fill fuckin breakfasts aw roond, Begbie states.

Renton cannot believe this. He wants to tell Begbie to fuck off. Instead he fights the instinct and slowly shakes his head. — Ah dinnae eat meat, Franco.

— Fuckin vegetarianism. Fuckin loaday shite. Ye need meat. A fuckin junky fuckin worryin aboot what he pits in his boady! That's a fuckin laugh!

— Jist dinnae like meat, Renton says, feelin silly as they all snigger.

— Dinnae fuckin tell us ye hate killin fuckin animals. Remember they fuckin dugs n cats we used tae fuckin shoot wi the air rifles! N the fuckin pigeons we used tae set oan fire. Used tae fuckin tape bangers — fireworks likes — tae white mice, this cunt.

— No bothered aboot killin animals. Jist dinnae like eatin thum, Renton shrugs, embarrassed that his adolescent cruelties have been exposed to Kelly.

— Fuckin cruel bastards. Dinnae ken how anybody could shoot a dug, Alison sneers, shaking her head.

— Well, ah dinnae ken now anybody could kill and eat a pig, Renton points to the bacon and sausage on her plate.

— S no the same.

Spud looks around: — It's eh, likesay . . . Rents is daein the right thing, but it's kinday the wrong reasons. We'll nivir likesay, learn tae love oorsels, until we kin look eftir weaker things, likesay animals n that . . . but it's good thit Rents is vegetarian . . . likesay, if ye kin keep it up . . . likesay . . .

Begbie vibrates his body in a floppy way and gives the peace sign to Spud. The others laugh. Renton, appreciative at Spud's attempt to back him up, cuts in to deflect the slagging away from his ally.

— Keepin it up's nae problem. Ah jist hate meat. It makes us puke. Endy story.

— Well, ah still fuckin say yir fuckin spoilin it fir ivray cunt else.

— How?

— Cause ah fuckin sais, that's fuckin how! Begbie hisses, pointing to himself.

Renton shrugs again. There was little sense in arguing further.

They hurry the meal down, all except Kelly, who plays with her food, oblivious to the ravenous stares of the others. Eventually, she scrapes some bits and pieces onto Franco and Gav's empty plates.

They are asked to leave after chanting: — *Oooh to, ooh to be, oooh to be a Hibby!* when a nervous and uncomfortable looking guy in a Hearts shell-top walks in for a takeaway. This sets off a medley of football and crap pop songs. The woman at the counter threatens to phone the police, but they vacate the premises with good grace.

They stop off at another pub. Renton and Kelly stay for one drink, then slope off together. Gav, Dawsy, Begbie, Spud and Alison continue drinking heavily. Dawsy, who has been teetering for some time, passes out. Begbie gets in tow with a couple of psychos that he knows at the bar, and Gav has a proprietory arm around Alison.

Spud hears T'Pau's 'China In Your Hand' starting, and immediately realises that Begbie is up at the juke-box. He always seemed to put on either that one, Berlin's 'Take My Breath Away', the Human League's 'Don't You Want Me' or a Rod Stewart song.

When Gav staggers off to the toilet, Alison turns to Spud. — Spu . . . Danny. Let's get ootay here. Ah want tae go hame.

— Eh . . . aye . . . likesay.

— Ah dinnae want tae go hame oan ma ain Danny. Come wi us.

— Eh, yeah . . . hame, right . . . eh . . . right.

They slink out of the smoke-filled bar as surreptitiously as their wasted bodies allow.

— Come hame an stey wi us fir a while Danny. Nae drugs or anything. Ah dinnae want tae be oan ma ain just now, Danny. Ken what ah'm sayin? Alison looks at him tensely, tearfully, as they lurch along the street.

Spud nods. He thinks he knows what she is saying, because he doesn't want to be alone either. He can never be sure though, never, ever quite sure.

Feeling Free

Alison's getting really terrible. Ah'm sitting here wi her in this cafe, tryin tae make sense ay the rubbish that she's talkin. She's bad-mouthing Mark, which is fair enough, but it's starting tae get oan ma wick. I know that she means well, but what about her and Simon, who just comes along and uses her when he's got naebody else tae fuck? She isnae exactly in the best position tae talk.

— Dinnae get me wrong, Kelly. Ah like Mark. It's jist that he's goat a load ay problems. He isnae what you need right now.

Ali's being protective because ah got fucked about wi Des, and the abortion and aw that. It's such a pain in the arse though. She should hear herself. Tryin tae kick heroin, n she feels she's in a position tae tell everybody else how tae live thir lives.

— Aw aye, n Simon's what you need?

— Ah'm no sayin that Kelly. That's nothing tae dae wi it. Simon's at least tryin tae keep off the smack, Mark doesnae gie a toss.

— Mark isnae a junky, he jist uses sometimes.

— Aye sure. What fuckin planet are you oan Kelly? That's how that Hazel lassie tore up his caird. He cannae leave the gear alane. You're even talkin like a junky yirsel. Keep thinkin like that, n you'll be oan it as well, soon enough.

Ah'm no gaunnae argue wi her. It's time for her appointment at the Housing Department anyway.

Ali's doon tae see aboot her rent arrears. She's pretty mad, like, screwed-up and tense; but the guy behind the desk's awright. Ali explains that she's oaf the gear n she's been for a few job interviews. It goes quite well. She gits given a set amount tae pay back each week.

Ah kin tell thit Ali's still uptight though, because ay the wey she reacts when these guys, workies, whistle at us ootside the GPO.

— Awright doll? one shouts.

Ali, crazy fuckin cow that she is, turns oan the guy.

— Have you goat a girlfriend? Ah doubt it, because yir a fat, ugly prick. Why no just go intae the toilet wi a dirty book and have sex wi the only person crazy enough tae touch ye — yirsel.

The guy looks at her wi real hate, but he was lookin like that anywey. It's only like, now he's got a reason tae hate her, rather than just because she's a woman.

The guy's mates are gaun: — Whoooaah! Whoooaah!, sortay egging this guy on, n he's jist standin thair shakin wi anger. One ay the workies is danglin like an ape fi the scaffoldin. That's what thir like, low primates. Too mad!

— Fuck off ya boot! he snarls.

Ali stands her ground though. This is embarrassing, but sortay fun n aw, cause a few people have stopped tae check out the hassle. Two other women, like student types wi backpacks, are standing alongside us. It makes me feel, like really good. Crazy!

Ali, god, that woman is mental, sais: — So ah wis a doll a minute ago whin ye wir hasslin us. Now that ah tell ye tae fuck off, ah'm a boot. Well, you are still a fat, ugly prick, son, and ye always will be.

— And so say all of us, one ay the backpacker women sais, in an Australian accent.

— Fuckin dykes! another guy shouts. That gets right on ma tits, getting called a dyke, just because ah object tae being hassled by revolting, ignorant radges.

— If aw guys wir as repulsive as you, ah'd be fuckin proud tae be a lesbian, son! ah shouts back. Did ah really say that? Too mad!

— You guys have obviously got a problem. Why don't you just go and fuck each other? the other Aussie says.

Quite a crowd's gathered and two auld wifies are listening in.

— That's terrible. Lassies talkin like that tae the laddies, one sais.

— It's no terrible at aw. Thir bloody pests. It's good tae see young lassies stickin up for thirsels. Wish it happened in ma day.

— The language though, Hilda, the language. The first wifie puckers her lips and shudders.

— Aye, well what aboot *their* language? ah sais tae her.

The guys are looking embarrassed, really shit up by the crowd that's developed. It's sortay like, feeding off itself. Crazy! Then this foreman, playin at being fuckin Rambo, comes along.

— Can't you control these animals? one ay the Aussie women sais. — Haven't they got any work to do instead of harassing people?

— Back inside yous! the foreman snaps, gesturing the guys away. We sortay let oot a cheer. It wis brilliant. Crazy!

Me n Ali went back over the road tae the Cafe Rio wi the Aussies and the two wifies came along as well. The 'Aussies' actually turned out tae be New Zealand lassies, who *were* lesbians, but that's got fuck all tae dae wi anything. They were jist travelling around the world together. That's too mad! Ah'd love tae gie that a go. Me n Ali; that would be crazy. Imagine coming tae Scotland in November, but. That is too fundamentally mad. We all just blethered for ages about everything in sight, and even Ali didnae seem so screwed up aboot things.

Eftir a bit we decided tae go back tae ma place for a smoke ay hash and some more tea. We tried tae get the wifies tae come, but they had tae go hame and get their men's teas on, despite us telling them to let the bastards get their ain food.

One was really tempted: — Ah wish ah wis your age again hen, ah'd dae it aw different, ah kin tell ye.

Ah'm feelin brilliant, really likes, free. We all are. Magic! Ali, Veronica and Jane (the New Zealanders) and masel got really stoned back at ma place. We slagged off men, agreeing that they are stupid, inadequate and inferior creatures. Ah've never felt so close tae other women before, and I really did wish I was gay. Sometimes I think that all men are good for is the odd shag. Other than that, they can be a real fuckin pain. Mibbe that's crazy, but it's true when you think aboot it. Our problem is, we don't think aboot it that often and jist accept the bullshit these pricks dish oot tae us.

The door goes, and it's Mark. Ah cannae help smirkin in his face. He comes in looking completely bewildered as we fall aboot laughing at him, stoned oota oor boxes. Mibbe it's the dope, but he just looks so strange; *men* just look so strange, these funny, flat bodies and weird heads. It's like Jane said, they're freaky looking things that cairry their reproductive organs on the ootside ay their bodies. Pure radge!

— Awright doll! Ali shouts, in a mock workie's voice.

— Get 'em off! Veronica laughs.

— Ah've fuckin shagged it. No a bad fuckin ride as ah remember. Bit oan the fuckin smaw side likes! ah sais, pointing at him, impersonating Franco's voice. Frank Begbie, every woman's dream, I don't think, has been getting well slagged by me and Ali.

He takes it well though, poor Mark, ah'll say that for him. Just shakes his heid n laughs.

— Ah've obviously called at an inconvenient time. Ah'll gie ye a bell the morn, he sais tae me.

— Aw . . . perr Mark . . . wir just havin a woman's crack . . . ye ken the score . . . Ali sais, guiltily. Ah laugh oot loud at what she said.

— Which woman's crack are we havin? ah sais. We're all fallin about laughing wildly. Ali n me maybe should've been born men, wi see sex in everything. Especially when wir stoned.

— It's awright. See yis, he turns n leaves, giein me a wink.

— I suppose some of them are okay, Jane sais, eftir we've composed oorselves.

— Aye, when they're in the fucking minority thir okay, ah sais, wondering where the edge in ma voice had come fae, then no wantin tae wonder too much.

The Elusive Mr Hunt

Kelly is working behind the bar at a punter's pub in the South Side. She is kept busy, as it is a popular shop. It is particularly mobbed out this Saturday afternoon when Renton, Spud and Gav call in for a drink.

Sick Boy, positioned at the phone in another pub over the road, calls the bar.

— Be wi ye in a minute Mark, Kelly says, as Renton goes up to get the drinks in. She picks up the ringing phone. — Rutherford's Bar, she sings.

— Hi, says Sick Boy, disguising his voice, Malcolm Rifkind merchant-school style. — Is there a Mark Hunt in the bar?

— Thir's a Mark Renton, Kelly tells him. Sick Boy thinks for a second that he's been rumbled. However, he carries on.

— No, it's Mark Hunt I'm looking for, the plummy voice stresses.

— MARK HUNT! Kelly shouts across the bar. The drinkers, who are almost exclusively male, look around at her; faces breaking into smiles. — ANYBODY SEEN MARK HUNT? Some guys at the bar collapse into loud laughter.

— Naw, but ah'd like tae! one says.

Kelly still doesn't catch on. With a puzzled expression at the reaction she is getting, she says: — This guy on the phone wis after Mark Hunt . . . then her voice tails off, her eyes widen and she puts her hand to her mouth, understanding at last.

— He's no the only one, Renton smiles, as Sick Boy comes into the pub.

They practically have to hold each other up, as they are so overwhelmed with laughter.

Kelly throws the half-empty contents of a water jug at them, but they scarcely notice. While it's all a laugh to them, she feels humiliated. She feels bad about feeling bad, about not being able to take a joke.

Until she realises that it's not the joke that bothers her, but the men in the bar's reaction to it. Behind the bar, she feels like a caged animal in a zoo who has done something amusing. She watches their faces, distorted into a red, gaping, gloating commonality. The joke is on the woman again, she thinks, the silly wee lassie behind the bar.

Renton looks at her and sees her pain and anger. It cuts him up. It confuses him. Kelly has a great sense of humour. What's wrong with her? The knee-jerk thought: *Wrong time of the month* is forming in his head when he looks about and picks up the intonations of the laughter around the bar. It's not funny laughter.

This is lynch mob laughter.

How was ah tae know, he thinks. How the fuck was ah tae know?

Home

Easy Money for the Professionals

It wis a piece ay pish, a total piece ay pish, but likesay, Begbie's so fuckin uncool man; ah'm tellin ye, likes.

— Say fuckin nowt tae nae cunt, mind. Nowt tae nae fucker, he sais tae us.

— Eh, likesay, readin ye loud n clear man, likesay, crystal clear. Chill oot Franco man, chill oot. We cracked the gig likesay, ken.

— Aye, but fuckin nowt tae nae cunt. No even fuckin Rents n that. Mind.

There's nae reasoning wi some cats. You say 'reason', they mew 'treason'. Ken?

— N nae fuckin drugs. Keep the fuckin dough back fir a bit, he adds. Now the cat is tellin us how tae spend the brass, likesay.

This is a tacky scene, likes. We've goat a couple ay grand apiece, eftir wuv peyed oaf the young guy, likesay, and this cat's fur's still standin oan end. The Beggar-boy is one feline whae willnae jist curl up in a nice warm basket n purrrrrrr . . .

We down another pint, then call a Joe Baxi. These sports bags wir cairryin man, they should have SWAG oan the side ay thum, instead ay ADIDAS and HEAD, likesay. Two fuckin grand, likes. Phoah! *Don't you-ho be te-heh-heh-rified, it's just a token of my extreme* . . . as the other Franco, one Mister Zappa, would say.

The taxi takes us tae Begbie's. June's in, and she's got the Begbie ankle-biter up, oan her lap.

— Bairn woke, she sais tae Franco, likesay she's explainin. Franco looks at her like he wants tae kill them baith.

— Fuck sakes. C'moan Spud, the fuckin bedroom. Cannae even git a bit ay fuckin peace in yir ain fuckin hoose! He gestures tae the door, like.

— What's aw this? June asks.

— Dinnae fuckin ask. Jist you fuckin see tae yir fuckin bairn! Begbie snaps. The wey he sais it, it's likesay, it's no his bairn n aw, ken? Ah suppose in a wey he's right, likesay; Franco's no what ye'd really sortay call the parental type, ken . . . eh, what sortay type is Franco?

It wis beautiful though man. Nae violence, nae hassle, ken. A set ay dummy keys, n we jist likesay, walked in. This wis the false panel in the flair tile behind the counter, under the till, and thair wis that big, canvas bag full ay that lovely poppy. Peachy! Aw they beautiful notes and coins. Ma passport tae better times man, ma passport tae better times.

The doorbell rings. Me n Franco are a bit shit up in case it's the labdicks, but it turns oot tae be the wee gadge, up fir his cut. Just as well, likesay, cause Franco n me's goat coins n notes aw ower the bed; divvyin up likesay, ken?

— Yis git it? the wee dude sais, eyes then wide in disbelief at the sight ay the goodies oan the bed.

— Sit fuckin doon! You shut yir fuckin pus aboot this, right? Franco growls. The wee guy's shiters, likesay.

Ah wanted tae tell Franco tae go easy on the kiddo, ken? That's likesay, the kitten that turned us oantay this bread. The wee guy told us the story, even slipped us the keys tae copy, likesay. Even though ah say nowt likes, the Begbie cat can still read ma face.

— This wee cunt'll be straight back doon the fuckin school throwin his fuckin poppy aboot tae impress his fuckin mates, n aw the wee burds.

— Naw ah'll no, the wee guy says.

— Shut the fuck up! Begbie sneers. The guy shites it again. Begbie turns tae us. — Fuckin sure ah'd be, if it wis me.

He stands up n throws three darts intae this board oan the waw, wi real force, real violence, man. The wee guy's lookin worried.

— Thir's one fuckin thing worse thin a grassin cunt, he sais, takin the darts ootay the board n flingin thum back intae it wi the same evil force. — N that's a fuckin lippy cunt. The cunt thit shoots his fuckin mooth oaf eywis does mair fuckin damage thin the grass. That's the cunts thit fuckin feed the grass. The grass feeds the fuckin polis. Then wir aw fucked.

Eh flings a dart straight at the wee guy's face. Ah jump, n the wee boy screams, n starts greetin hysterically, shakin, like he's huvin a fit, likesay.

Ah see thit Begbie's jist flung the plastic flight, huvin slyly screwed oaf the metal spike n barrel before flingin it. The wee guy's still greetin, likesay, wi shock n that.

— The fuckin flight, ya daft wee cunt! A wee bit ay fuckin plastic! Franco laughs scornfully and counts oot a load ay notes, but maistly jist the coins, fir the wee man. — Polis stoap ye, ye won it fae the shows at Porty, or in a fuckin arcade. Breathe a fuckin word ay this tae any cunt, n ye better fuckin hope thit the polis git a haud ay ye n send ye tae fuckin Polmont before ah fuckin catch up wi ye, ye hear us?

— Aye . . the wee boy's still tremblin, likesay.

— Now fuck off, back tae yir fuckin Setirday joab at the DIY. Remember, if ah fuckin hear ay you flashin that fuckin poppy aroond, ah'll be right fuckin doon tae your bit before ye ken whit's fuckin hit ye.

The wee guy takes his dough n leaves. Perr wee cunt goat

nuthin really, aboot a couple ay hundred quid fae nears enough five grand, likesay. Still, bags ay loot for a cat that age, if ye catch ma drift. Mind you, ah still say thit Franco's been a bit hard oan the nipper.

— Hey man, that kids's made us a couple ay grand each man . . . eh, jist sortay saying Franco, likesay, mibbe ye wir a bit hard oan the gadge, likesay, ken?

— Ah dinnae fuckin want that wee cunt boastin, or flashin a fuckin wad aroond. Daein anythin wi wee cunts like that, it's the riskiest fuckin business gaun. Thuv nae fuckin discretion, ken? That's how ah like tae go screwin fuckin shoaps n hooses wi you Spud. Yir a true fuckin professional, like masel, n ye nivir say nowt tae nae cunt. Ah respect that fuckin professionalism, Spud. Whin ye goat true professionals oan a joab, it's nae fuckin problem, ya cunt.

— Yeah . . . right man, likesay, ah sais. What else *kin* ye say, likesay, ken? True professionals. Sounds awright tae me; sounds peachy.

A Present

Ah decided that ah couldnae handle steyin at ma auld girl's; too much ay a heid-nip. So Gav's pittin us up fir the duration ay Matty's funeral. The train journey up wis uneventful; jist the wey ah wanted it. Some Fall tapes oan the Walkman, four cans ay lager n ma H.P. Lovecraft book. Nazi cunt, auld H.P., but he kin spin a good yarn. Ah set ma coupon intae the do-not-disturb-or-else-cunt mode every time a smiling jackass apologetically squeezes into the seat opposite me. It's an enjoyable journey, and therefore a short one.

Gav's new gaff is in McDonald Road; ah decide tae pad the hoof. Whin ah git doon tae his place, he isnae in a happy frame ay mind. Ah'm jist aboot tae git a bit para; likes ah've mibbe imposed masel, when he indicates the source ay his misery.

— Telling ye Rents, see that cunt Second Prize, he sais, shakin his heid bitterly n pointing tae an empty front room, — ah gave um the cash tae dae this place up; a bit ay plasterin and paintin. Ah'm away doon the B&Q, he sais tae us this mornin. No seen the cunt since.

Ma instinct wis tae tell Gav thit he wis crazy tae commission Second Prize tae dae the joab in the first place; n totally fuckin doolally giein the cunt the poppy up front. Ah suspect, however, that's no whit he wants tae hear right now, n ah am his guest. Instead, ah dump ma bag n the spare room n take um doon tae the pub.

Ah want tae hear aboot Matty; what happened tae the cunt. Ah wis obviously shocked by the news, though it hus tae be said, far fae surprised.

— Matty nivir knew he wis HIV, Gav said. — He probably hud been fir some time.

— Wis it pneumonia or cancer, likes? ah ask.

— Naw, eh toxoplasmosis. A stroke, ken.

— Eh? Ah'm scoobied here.

— Fuckin sad. Could only uv happened tae Matty, Gav shook his heid. — He wanted tae see his wee lassie, that wee Lisa, Shirley's bairn, ken? Shirley widnae let um near the hoose. Nae wonder, the state ay um at the time. Anywey, ken wee Nicola Hanlon?

— Aye, wee Nicky, aye.

— Her cat hud kittens, so Matty gits one oafay her. The idea is thit the cunt's gaunnae take it tae Shirley's tae gie it tae the bairn ken? So he takes it oot tae Wester Hailes, tae gie it tae wee Lisa; a present fir her, ken?

Ah cannae really see the connection between the kitten n Matty huvin a stroke, but this sounds a typical Matty tale. Ah shake me heid. — That sums Matty up. Git a wee cat as a gesture, then leave it fir some other fucker tae look eftir. Ah bet ye Shirley gave um the short shrift.

— Exactly, the clueless cunt, Gav smiles, nodding grimly. — She says: Ah'm no wantin a cat tae look eftir, take it away, git tae fuck. So thair's Matty stuck wi this kitten. Ye kin imagine whit happened. The thing wis neglected; the litter tray swimmin in pish; shite aw ower the hoose. Matty's jist lyin aroond, fucked ootay his eyeballs oan smack or downers; or jist depressed, ye ken the wey he goat. As ah sais, he didnae ken he wis HIV. He didnae ken thit ye could git that toxoplasmosis fae cat shit.

— Ah didnae ken either, ah sais. — Whit the fuck is it?

— Aw, it's fuckin horrible, man. It's likesay brain abscesses, ken?

Ah shivered, n felt a crushin weight oan ma chist, thinkin ay perr Matty. Ah hud an abscess oan ma knob once. Imagine huvin one oan yir fuckin brain, inside, yir fuckin heid bein full ay pus. Fuck sakes. Matty. Fuckin hell. — So whit happened?

— He starts gittin heidaches, so he jist uses mair; tae blot oot the pain, ken? Then he hus, like a stroke. A boy ay twinty-five; a fuckin stroke, it's no real. Ah didnae recognise the cunt eftir it. Nearly walked past um in the street; this is doon the Walk, ken? He looked fuckin ancient. He wis aw bent tae one side, hobblin like a cripple, wi his face aw twisted. He wis only like that fir aboot three weeks; then he hud a second stroke n died. He died in the hoose. The perr bastard hud been thair fir ages before the neighbours complained aboot the kitten's miaows n the stench thit wis comin fae the place. The polis broke the door doon.

Matty wis lyin deid, face doon in a pool ay dried vomit. The kitten wis fine.

Ah thoat aboot the squat Matty n me shared in Shepherd's Bush; that wis him at his happiest. He loved the whole punk thing. They loved him doon thair. He shagged every burd in that squat, includin that lassie fae Manchester thit ah'd been tryin tae git oaf wi fir donks, the spawny wee cunt. It aw started tae go wrong fir the perr bastard whin we came back up here. It nivir stoaped gaun wrong eftir that. Perr Matty.

— Fuck sake, Gav muttered, — that cunt Perfume James. That's aw we fuckin need.

Ah looked up n saw the open, smilin face ay Perfume James comin taewards us. He hud his case n aw.

— Awright James?

— No bad boys, no bad. Whair ye been hidin yersel Mark?

— London, ah goes. Perfume James wis a pain in the erse; he wis eywis tryin tae punt perfume tae ye.

— Romantically involved these days, Mark?

— Naw, ah took great pleasure in informin him.

Perfume James frowned and puckered his lips: — Gav, how's your good lady?

— Awright, Gav mumbles.

— If ah'm no mistaken, the last time ah saw ye doon here wi yir good lady, she wis wearin Nina Ricci, yeah?

— Ah'm no wantin any perfume, Gav states with a cold finality.

Perfume James twists his heid tae the side n extends his palms. — Your loss. Ah kin tell ye though, thir's nae better way tae impress a lassie thin perfume. Flooirs are too temporary n ye kin firget chocolates in these figure-conscious times. Still, nae skin oafey ma nose, Perfume James smiles, opening his case anywey, as if the very sight ay these boatils ay pish'll make us change oor minds. — Ah've done well the day though, ah cannae complain. Your mate, Second Prize, as a matter ay fact. Ah ran intae um in the Shrub an hour or so ago. He wis quite bevvied. He sais: Geez some ay that perfume, ah'm away doon tae Carol's. Ah've treated her like shite, it's time tae spoil ur a bit. Boat a fuckin stack, so he did.

Gav's chin visibly droaps. He clenches his fists n shakes his heid in angry resignation. Perfume James bounds over tae the lounge in search ay another victim.

Ah flings back ma pint. — Let's see if wi kin find Second Prize; before the cunt drinks every bit ay yir money away. Much did ye gie um?

— Two hundred sobs, Gav sais.

— Doss cunt, ah sais, sniggerin. Ah couldnae help it, it wis jist nerves.

— Ah want ma fuckin heid looked at, Gav concedes, but he cannae force a smile. Ah suppose, whin all's said n done, thir isnae a fuckin loat tae smile aboot.

Memories of Matty

1

— Awright Nelly? Long fuckin time no see, ya cunt thit ye are, Franco smiled at Nelly, who looked incongruous in a suit, with a tattooed snake coiling up his neck and a palm-treed desert island with the sea lapping up drilled onto his forehead.

— Pity it hus tae be under they circumstances likes, Nelly replied soberly. Renton, who was talking to Spud, Alison and Stevie, allowed himself a smile, upon hearing the first funeral cliché of the day.

Taking up the cue, Spud said: — Perr Matty. Fuckin bad news, likesay, ken.

— That's it for me. Ah'm steyin clean, Alison said, shuddering, despite having her arms wrapped around herself.

— Wir aw gaunnae be wiped oot if we dinnae git it thegither. That's as sure as fuck, Renton acknowledged. — You taken the test yit Spud? he asked.

— Hey . . . come oan man, this isnae the time tae be talkin aboot that . . . Matty's funeral, likesay.

— When is the time? Renton asked.

— Ye really should, Danny, ye really should, Alison implored.

— Mibbe yir better no tae ken. Ah mean, likesay, whit sortay life did Matty huv whin he kent he wis HIV?

— That wis Matty. Whit sortay life did he huv *before* he kent he wis HIV? Alison said. Spud and Renton nodded acquiescence at this point.

Inside the small chapel attached to the crematorium, the minister gave a short spiel about Matty. He had a lot of burnings to fit in that morning and couldn't afford to fuck about. A few quick comments, a couple of hymns, one or two prayers and a click of a switch to send the corpse down into the incinerator. Just a few more of these, and that was his shift finished.

— To those of us gathered here today, Matthew Connell filled a number of different roles in our lives. Matthew was a son, a brother, a father and a friend. Matthew's last days in his young life were bleak, suffering ones. Yet, we must remember the real Matthew, the loving young man who had a great lust for life. A keen musician, Matthew loved to entertain friends with his guitar-playing . . .

Renton could not make eye contact with Spud, standing next

to him in the pew, as nervous laughter gripped him. Matty was the shitest guitarest he'd known, and could only play the Doors' 'Roadhouse Blues' and a few Clash and Status Quo numbers with any sort of proficiency. He tried hard to do the riff from 'Clash City Rockers', but could never quite master it. Nonetheless, Matty loved that Fender Strat. It was the last thing he sold, holding onto it after the amplifier had been flogged off in order to fill his veins with shite. Perr Matty, Renton thought. How well did any of us really know him? How well can anybody really know anybody else?

Stevie was wishing he was four hundred miles away, in his Holloway flat with Stella. It was the first time they'd been apart since they moved in together. He was ill at ease. Try as he might, he could not sustain the image of Matty in his head. Matty kept turning into Stella.

Spud thought that it must be really crap to live in Australia. The heat, the insects, and all these dull suburban places that you see on *Neighbours* and *Home and Away*. It seemed like there were no real pubs in Australia, and that the place was like a warm version of Baberton Mains, Buckstone or East Craigs. It just seemed so boring, so shite. He wondered what it was like in the older parts of Melbourne and Sydney and whether they had tenements there, like in Edinburgh, or Glasgow or even New York, and if so, why they never showed them on the telly. He also wondered why he thought of Australia in connection with Matty. Probably because whenever they called round, he was lying junked on his mattress, watching an Aussie soap opera.

Alison remembered the time when she had sex with Matty. That was ages ago now, before she was using. She would have been eighteen. She tried to remember Matty's cock, the dimensions of it, but couldn't visualise it. Matty's body came to mind though. It was lean and firm, though not particularly muscular. He had skinny good looks and busy, penetrating eyes, which gave away the restlessness of his character. What she remembered most however was what Matty said to her as they got into bed that time. He told her: — I'm gaunnae fuck you like you've never been fucked in your life. He was right. She'd never been fucked that badly, either before or since. Matty came in seconds, depositing his load into her and rolling off her, gasping breathlessly.

She made no attempt to hide her displeasure. — That was fuckin rubbish, she told him, getting out of the bed, all anxious and tense, charged up but unsatisfied, wanting to scream in frustration. She pulled her clothes on. He said nothing and never moved, but she was sure that she saw tears spill from his eyes as she left. This image stuck with her as she looked at the wooden box, and she wished she'd been a bit kinder.

Franco Begbie felt angry and confused. Any injury to a friend he took as a personal insult. He prided himself on looking after his mates. The death of one of them confronted him with his own impotence. Franco resolved this problem by turning his anger on Matty. He remembered the time that Matty shat it off Gypo and Mikey Forrester in Lothian Road, and he had to have both the cunts on his puff. Not that it presented him with any difficulty. It was the principle of the thing though. You had to back up your mates. He'd made Matty pay for his cowardice: physically, with beatings, and socially, with heaps of humiliating slaggings. Now he realised, he'd not made the cunt pay enough.

Mrs Connell was thinking about Matty as a wee laddie. All boys were dirty, but Matty had been particularly bad. Hard on shoes, reducing clothes to threadbare status in no time at all. She was therefore not concerned when he grew into punk as he grew into adolescence. It seemed merely to be making a virtue out of necessity. Matty had always been a punk. One particular incident came to her mind. As a child, he had accompanied her to get her false teeth fitted. She felt self-conscious on the bus home. Matty insisted upon telling everyone on the bus that his Ma had false teeth put in. He was a particularly loving child. You lose them, she thought. After they get to seven, they're no longer yours. Then, just when you adjust, it happens again at fourteen. Something happens. Then when you put heroin into it, they're no longer their own. Less Matty, more heroin.

She sobbed softly and rhythmically, the valium measuring out her grief in sickening little breezes, attempting to dissipate the raging hurricane of raw angst and misery within her, which it simultaneously struggled to keep under wraps.

Anthony, Matty's younger brother, was thinking about revenge. Revenge on all the scumbags who'd brought his brother down. He knew them, some of them had the fucking gall to be here today. Murphy, Renton and Williamson. These pathetic arseholes, who breezed around like they shat ice-cream cones, like they knew something nobody else did, when all they were was junky trash. Them, and the more sinister figures behind them. His brother, his fucking weak, stupid brother, had got in tow with that scum.

Anthony's mind cast back to the occasion that Derek Sutherland had beaten him up badly at the disused railway yard. Matty found out, and went to have Deek Sutherland, who was the same age as Anthony, and two years younger than himself. Anthony remembered his eager anticipation of Deek Sutherland's complete humiliation at the hands of his brother. In the event, it was Anthony who was again humiliated, this time by proxy. It was almost as intense as the one he'd received from Deek Sutherland himself, as he watched his old adversary almost casually overwhelm and kick the shite out of his brother. Matty had let him down there. He had let everybody down since.

Wee Lisa Connell felt sad that her Daddy was in that box, but he would have wings like an angel and go up to heaven. Her Nana had cried when Lisa had suggested that might happen. It was like he was sleeping in that box. Her Nana said that the box went away, to heaven. Lisa thought that angels grew wings and flew to heaven. It mildly concerned her that he would not be able to fly, unless they let him out of the box. Still, they probably knew what they were doing. Heaven sounded good. She would go there some day, and see her dad. When he had come to see her in Wester Hailes he usually wasn't well so she wasn't allowed to talk to him. It would be good to go to heaven, to play with him, like they used to when she was really wee. He'd be well again in heaven. Heaven would be different from Wester Hailes.

Shirley held her daughter's hand tightly, and tousled her curls. Lisa seemed to be the only evidence that Matty's life was not a futile one. Yet, looking at the child, few could argue that it was not substantial evidence. Matty, though, had been a father in name only. The minister had irritated Shirley by describing him as such. She was the father, as well as the mother. Matty had provided the sperm, came around and played with Lisa a few times, before the junk had really got to him. That was his sole contribution.

There had always been a weakness about him, an inability to face his responsibilities, and also to face the force of his emotions. Most junkies she had met were closet romantics. Matty was. Shirely had loved that in him, loved it when he was open, tender, loving and full of life. It never lasted. Even before smack, a harshness and bitterness would descend upon him. He used to write her love poems. They were beautiful, not in a literary sense perhaps, but in the marvellous purity of the wonderful emotions they conveyed to her. Once, he read and then set fire to a particularly lovely verse he'd written to her. Through her tears, she asked him why he'd done that, as the flames seemed so symbolic. It was the most hurtful thing Shirley had experienced in her life.

He turned around and surveyed the squalor of the flat. — Look at this. Ye shouldnae huv dreams livin like this. Yir jist connin yirsel, torturin yirsel.

His eyes were black and inpenetrable. His infectious cynicism and despair took away Shirley's hope for a better life. It had once threatened to crush that very life out of her, before she bravely said: No more.

2

— Keep it down, please gentlemen, the harassed-looking barman pleaded with the hard core of heavy drinkers the group of mourners had whittled down to. Hours of stoical drinking and wistful nostalgia had finally given way to song. They felt great singing. The tension flowed from them. The barman was ignored.

> *Shame on ye, Seamus O'Brien,*
> *All the young girls in Dublin are cryin,*
> *They're tired o' your cheatin and lyin,*
> *So shame on ye, Seamus O'Brien!*

— PLEASE! Will you be quiet! he shouted. The small hotel on the posh side of Leith Links was not used to this sort of behaviour, especially on a weekday.

— What the fuck's that cunt fuckin sayin? Entitled tae gie the fuckin mate a fuckin send oaf! Begbie cast a predatory eye over the barman.

— Hi Franco. Renton grabbed Begbie's shoulder, realising the danger, and trying to move him quickly into a less aggressive frame of mind. — Mind yon time when you, me n Matty went doon tae Aintree fir the National?

— Aye! Ah fuckin minday that! Ah fuckin telt that cunt thit's oan the fuckin telly tae goan fuck hissel. Whit wis the cunt's name?

— Keith Chegwin. Cheggers.

— That's the cunt. Cheggers.

— The guy oan the telly likes? *Cheggers Plays Pop?* Mind that? Gav asked.

— The very same cunt, Renton said, as Franco smirked

indulgently at him, encouraging him to continue the story. —
Wi wir at the National, right? This cunt Cheggers is daein
interviews fir City Radio Liverpool, jist blethering shite tae
punters in the crowd, ken? Well, he comes ower tae us, n we
didnae wantae talk tae the cunt, but ye ken Matty, he's thinkin,
this is fuckin stardom, n he's gaun oan aboot how great it is tae be
here in Liverpool, Keith, n wir having a whale ay a time, n aw
that shite. Then this doss cunt, this Cheggers fucker, or whativir
ye call the cunt, thrusts the microphone in front ay Franco.
Renton gestured towards Begbie. — This cunt goes: Away n fuck
yirsel ya radge cunt! Cheggers wis fuckin crimson. They've goat
that three-second delay oan the so-called live radio, tae edit that
sortay thing oot.

As they laughed, Begbie justified his actions.

— Wir fuckin doon thair fir the fuckin racin, no tae talk tae
some fuckin doss cunt oan the fuckin radio. His expression was
that of a man-of-affairs, bored with being hassled by the media
for interviews.

Franco could always find something to be enraged about,
however.

— Fuckin Sick Boy should've been here. Matty wis his fuckin
mate, he announced.

— Eh, he's in France but . . . wi that burd, likesay. Probably
couldnae cut it man, ken . . . ah mean . . . France, likesay, Spud
drunkenly observed.

— Makes nae fuckin difference. Rents n Stevie came up fae
London for this. If Rents n Stevie kin come up fae fuckin London,
Sick Boy kin come up fae fuckin France.

Spud's senses were dangerously dulled with the alcohol.
Stupidly, he kept the argument going. — Yeah, but, eh . . .
France is further away . . . wir talkin aboot the south ay France
here, likesay. Ken?

Begbie looked incredulously at Spud. Obviously the message
had not got across. He spoke slower, higher and with a snarl

twisting his cruel mouth into a strange shape below his blazing eyes.

— IF RENTS N STEVIE KIN COME UP FI FUCKIN LONDON, SICK BOY KIN COME UP FAE FUCKIN FRANCE!

— Yeah . . . right enough. Should've made the effort. Mate's funeral likesay, ken. Spud thought that the Conservative Party in Scotland could do with a few Begbies. It's not what the message is, the problem is just communication. Begbie is good at getting the message across.

Stevie was badly feeling the session. He was out of practice for this type of thing. Franco whipped an arm around him and another one around Renton.

— It's fuckin great tae see yous cunts again. The fuckin baith ay yis. Stevie, ah want ye tae fuckin look eftir this cunt doon in London, he turned to Renton. — If you go the same fuckin wey as Matty, ah'll fuckin sort you right oot ya cunt. Listen tae fuckin Franco talkin here.

— If ah go the same wey as Matty, th'ill be nowt left ay us tae sort oot.

— Dinnae you fuckin believe it. Ah'll dig yir fuckin boady up n boot it up n doon Leith fuckin Walk. Git us?

— Nice tae ken thit ye care Frank.

— Course ah fuckin care. Ye back up yir mates. S'at fuckin right Nelly?

— Eh? Nelly turned around slowly, drunk.

— Ah'm jist fuckin tellin this cunt here, ye back up yir fuckin mates.

— Too fuckin right ye do.

Spud and Alison were talking. Renton slipped away from Franco to join them. Franco was holding Stevie up, displaying him like a trophy to Nelly telling him what a great cunt he was.

Spud turned to Renton: — Jist sayin tae Ali, this is heavy shite, aw this, likesay, man. Ah've been tae too many funerals fir a gadge ma age, likesay. Wonder whae's next?

Renton shrugged. — At least we'll be prepared, whaeivir the fuck it is. If they gave oot qualifications in bereavement, ah'd be a fuckin Ph.D. by now.

They filed out into the cold night at closing time, heading for Begbie's place with a carry-out. They'd already spent twelve hours drinking and pontificating about Matty's life and his motivations. In truth, the more reflective of them realised, all their insights pooled and processed, did little to illuminate the cruel puzzle of it all.

They were no wiser now than at the start.

Straight Dilemmas No. 1

— C'mon, have a bit of this, it's alright, she sais, holding the joint towards me. How the fuck did ah get here? Ah should've gaun hame n got changed, then watched telly or went down The Princess Diana. It's Mick's fault, him and his quick-one-after-work.

Now ah'm oot ay place here, still in ma suit n tie, sitting in this comfortable flat amidst denim and t-shirt punters who think they're bigger wasters than they are. Weekend zanies are such a drag.

— Leave 'im alone Paula, sais the woman ah met in the pub. She's really trying tae get intae ma keks, with that frantically obvious desperation ye tend tae find in such London scenes. She'll probably succeed, despite the fact that whenever ah go to the bathroom and try tae think of what she looks like, ah can't conjure up even an approximate image. These types are irritating twats; plastic bastards. All you can do is fuck them, take from them, and then go. They even give you the impression that they'd be disappointed if you did anything else. Ah'm soundin like Sick Boy now, but his attitude does have its place, which is here and now.

— Nah, come on Mister Suit en Tie. I'll bet you ain't had nuffink like this in your life.

Ah sip at ma vodka and study this lassie. She has a good tan, and well-groomed hair, but this only seems to highlight rather than obscure a slightly wizened, unhealthy look. I spy with my little eye: another doss fucker in search of street cred. The cemeteries are full ay them.

Ah take the joint, sniff it, and hand it back. — Grass, with some opium in it, right? ah ask. It actually smells like good gear.

— Yeah . . . she sais, a wee bit fazed out.

Ah look again at the joint burning away in her hand. Ah try tae feel something. Anything. What ah'm really looking for is the demon, the bad bastard, the radge inside ay me who shuts down ma brain, who propels hand to joint and joint to lips and sucks and sucks like a vacuum cleaner. He's no coming oot tae play. Maybe he doesnae live here any mair. All that's left is the nine-to-five arsehole.

— Ah think ah'll pass on your kind offer. Call me a wanker if ye will, but ah've always been a wee bit nervous around drugs. Ah know a few people who've been intae them, and run intae difficulties.

She looks intently at me, seeming to suss that it's what I'm not saying that's important. She obviously feels a bit of a tit, and gets up and leaves us.

— You're mad, you are, the woman ah met in the pub, what

the fuck did she say her name was again, laughs too loudly. Ah miss Kelly, who's now back in Scotland. Kelly had a nice laugh.

The truth ay the matter is, the drugs thing just seems such a bore now; even though ah'm actually much more boring now than ah was when ah wis oan the skag. The thing is, this sort ay boredom's new tae us, and therefore no quite as tedious as it appears tae be. Ah'll just run wi it for a wee bit. For a wee bit.

Eating Out

Oh god, you can tell; it's just going tae be one ay these nights. Ah prefer it when it's busy, but when it's deid like this, time drags. No chance ay tips either. Shite!

There's hardly anybody in the bar. Andy's sitting looking bored, reading the *Evening News*. Graham's in the kitchen, preparing food that he hopes will be eaten. Ah'm leaning against the bar, feeling really tired. I've got an essay tae hand in the morn, for the philosophy class. It's on morality: whether it's relative or absolute, and in which circumstances, etcetera, etcetera. It depresses me tae think aboot it. Once ah finish this shift ah'll be up all night writing it up. It's too mad.

Ah don't miss London, but ah do miss Mark . . . a wee bit. Well, maybe a bit more than jist a wee bit, but no as much as ah thought. He said if ah wanted tae go tae University, ah could dae it in London jist as easy as back hame. When ah told him it wisnae easy living on a grant anywhere, but in London, it was impossible, jist arithmetically impossible, he said that he was making good money, and that we'd manage awright. When ah told him that ah didnae want tae be kept, like he's the big pimp and ah'm the cerebal whore, he said it wouldnae be like that. Anyway, ah came back, he steyed, and ah don't think either ay us really regrets it. Mark can be affectionate, but he doesnae seem tae really need people. Ah lived with him for six months, and ah still don't think ah really know him. Sometimes ah feel that ah was looking for too much, and that there's a lot less tae him than meets the eye.

Four guys come intae the resturant, obviously drunk. Crazy. One looks vaguely familiar. Ah think ah might have seen him at the University.

— What can I get you? Andy asks them.

— A couple of bottles of your best piss . . . and a table for four . . . he slurs. Ah can tell by their accents, dress and bearing that they are middle to upper-middle-class English. The city's full of such white-settler types, says she, who's just back from London! You used to get Geordies and Scousers and Brummies and Cockneys at the Uni, now it's a playground for failed Oxbridge home-counties types, with a few Edinburgh merchant-school punters representing Scotland.

Ah smile at them. Ah must stop having these preconceived notions, and learn to treat people as people. It's Mark's influence, his prejudices are infectious, the crazy prick. They sit down.

One sais: — What do you call a good-looking girl in Scotland?

Another snaps: — A tourist! They speak very loudly. Cheeky cunts.

One then sais, gesturing in ma direction: — I don't know though. I wouldn't kick that out of bed.

You prick. You fucking doss prick.

Ah'm seething inwardly, trying tae pretend ah didnae hear that remark. Ah cannae afford tae lose this job. Ah need the money. No cash; no Uni, no degree. Ah want that degree. Ah really fuckin want it more than anything.

As they study the menu, one ay the guys, a dark-haired skinny wanker wi a long fringe, smiles lecherously at us. — Orlroit dahlin? he sais, in a put-on Cockney accent. It's a vogue thing for the rich tae dae on occasion, I understand. God, ah want tae tell this creep tae fuck off. Ah dinnae need this shite . . . aye ah do.

— Give us a smile then, girlie! a fatter guys sais, in a booming, officious voice. The voice ay arrogant, ignorant wealth unchallenged, untainted by sensitivity or intellect. Ah try tae smile in a condescending wey, but ma face muscles are frozen. Thank fuck as well.

Taking the order is a nightmare. They are engrossed in conversations aboot careers; commodity broking, public relations and company law seeming tae be the most popular, in between casually patronising and trying tae humiliate me. The skinny creep actually asks me what time ah finish, and ah ignore him, as the rest make whooping noises and dae a drum roll on the table. Ah complete the order, feeling shattered and debased, and depart tae the kitchen.

Ah'm really shaking wi rage, wondering how long ah can control this, wishing that Louise or Marisa were on tonight, another woman tae talk tae.

— Can't ye get these fuckin arseholes oot ay here? ah snap at Graham.

— It's business. The customer's always right, even if he's a fuckin knob-end.

Ah remember Mark telling me aboot the time he worked at the Horse Of The Year Show at Wembley, doing catering wi Sick Boy, one summer years ago. He always said that waiters have power; never mess wi a waiter. He's right, of course. It's now time tae use that power.

Ah'm smack-bang in the middle ay a heavy period, and ah'm feeling that scraped out, drained way. Ah go tae the toilet and change tampons, wrapping the used one, which is saturated wi discharge, intae some toilet paper.

A couple ay these rich, imperialist bastards have ordered soup; our trendy tomato and orange. As Graham's busy preparing the main courses, ah take the bloodied tampon and lower it, like a tea-bag, intae the first bowl ay soup. Ah then squeeze its manky contents oot wi a fork. A couple ay strands ay black, uteral lining float in the soup, before being dissolved wi a healthy stir.

Ah deliver the two paté starters and two soups tae the table, making sure that the skinny, gelled fuck-up has got the spiked one. One ay the party, a guy wi a brown beard and phenomenally ugly, protruding teeth, is telling the table, again very loudly, aboot how terrible Hawaii is.

— Too bloody hot. Not that I mind the heat, it's just that it's not like the rich, baking heat of Southern California. This place is so bloody humid, you just sweat like a pig all the time. One is also continually harassed by peasant scum trying to sell you all their ridiculous trinkets.

— More wine! the fat, fair-heided prick petulantly booms at us.

Ah go back tae the lavvy and fill a saucepan with ma urine. Cystitis is a problem for me, particularly during ma periods. Ma pish has that stagnant, cloudy look, which suggests a urinary-tract infection.

Ah dilute the carafe ay wine with ma pish; it looks a bit cloudy, but they're so smashed they winnae notice. Ah pour a quarter ay the wine intae the sink, topping up the carafe with ma pish de resistance.

Ah pour some more ay ma pish ontae the fish. It's the same colour and consistency as the sauces which marinate it. Crazy!

These pricks eat and drink everything withoot even noticing.

It's hard tae shite ontae a piece of newspaper in the toilet; the bog is small, and it's difficult tae squat. Graham's also shouting aboot something. Ah manage a small runny turd, which ah take through and mix up wi some cream intae the liquidiser, and merge the resultant mess wi the chocolate sauce, heating away in a pan. Ah pour it ower the profiteroles. It looks good enough tae eat. Too radge!

Ah feel charged wi a great power, actually enjoying their insults. It's a lot easier tae keep smiling now. The fat bastard has drawn the short straw though; his ice-cream is laced wi ground up traces of rat poison. Ah hope Graham doesnae get intae trouble. I hope they dinnae close the restaurant doon.

In my essay, ah now think that ah'd be forced tae put that, in some circumstances, morality is relative. That's if ah was being honest with masel. This is not Dr Lamont's view though, so ah may stick wi absolutes in order tae curry favour and get high marks.

It's all too mad.

Trainspotting at Leith Central Station

The toon seems sinister and alien as ah pad it doon fae the Waverley. Two guys are screaming at each other under the archway in Calton Road, by the Post Office depot. Either that, or the cunts are screaming at me. What a place and time for a kicking. Is there ever a good one, though? Ah quicken ma pace — which isnae easy wi this heavy holdall — and get oantae Leith

Street. What the fuck's it aw aboot? Wide cunts. Ah'll fuckin . . .

Ah'll fuckin keep moving. Sharpish. By the time ah get tae the Playhouse, the noise fae the two arseholes has been replaced by the appreciative chattering ay groups ay middle-class cunts as they troop oot ay the opera: *Carmen*. Some of them are making for the restaurants at the top ay the Walk, where reservations have been made. Ah stroll on. It's downhill all the way.

Ah pass ma auld Montgomery Street gaff, then the former junk zone of Albert Street, now sandblasted and tarted up. A polis car frantically lets rip on the siren as it hurtles doon the Walk. Three guys stagger oot ay a pub and intae a Chinky. One ay the cunts is willing us tae make eye-contact. Any flimsy pretext tae fill some fucker in, some wide-os will grasp it wi baith hands. It's the auld discreet increase of pace again.

In terms ay probability, the further ye go doon the Walk at this time ay night, the mair likely ye are tae git a burst mooth. Perversely, ah feel safer the further doon ah git. It's Leith. Ah suppose that means hame.

Ah hear gagging sounds and look doon this alley which leads tae a builder's yard. Ah witness Second Prize boakin up a load ay bile. Ah discreetly wait fir um tae pull umsel thegither, before talkin tae um.

— Rab. Ye awright man?

He turns roond and wobbles oan the spot, tryin tae focus oan us, when aw his heavy eyelids want tae dae is crash doon, like the steel shutters ay a late-night Asian shoap ower the road.

Second Prize sais something which sounds a bit like: — Hey Rents, sound as a fuckin pound . . . ya cunt . . . Then his face sortay changes and he sais: — . . . fuckin cunt . . . ah'll fuckin have you ya cunt . . . He lurches forward and swings at us. Even wi ma holdall, a kin still step back fast enough and the nondy cunt crashes intae the wall, then staggers backwards, fawin oan his erse.

Ah help um up and he's talkin a loaday shite which ah cannae make oot, but he's at least mair passive now.

As soon as ah put ma airm aroond um tae help um along the road, the radge collapses like a pack ay cairds, wi that learned helplessness that chronic drunks have, as he completely surrenders hissel tae us. Ah huv tae droap ma travel bag tae support the fucker, tae stop him fawin and taking another second prize fae the pavement. This is useless.

A taxi cruises up the Walk and ah flag it doon and stick Second Prize in the back ay it. The cabbie doesnae look too pleased, but ah gie him a fiver and say: — Let um oot doon the Bowtow, pal. Hawthornvale. He'll find his wey hame fae thair. It's the festive period, eftir aw. Cunts like Second Prize jist blend in at this time ay the year.

Ah wis tempted tae git intae the taxi wi Secks, and jump oaf at ma Ma's, but Tommy Younger's looked too tempting. Begbie's in, haudin court wi a few wide-os, one ay whom looks familiar.

— Rents! How ye fuckin daein, ya cunt! This you jist up fi London?

— Aye, ah shook his hand and he pilled us tae him, slappin us hard oan the back. — Jist dumped Second Prize in a Joe Baxi, ah said.

— That cunt. Ah telt um tae fuck oaf. Second fuckin bookable offence ay the night. Cunt's a fuckin liability. That's worse thin a fuckin junky, yon. If it hudnae been Christmas n that, ah'd huv fuckin tanned the cunt masel. That's me n him fuckin finished. Endy fuckin story.

Begbie introduces us tae the cunts in his company. What Second Prize did tae git flung oot ay that crowd, ah didnae even want tae ken. One ay the cunts wis that guy Donnelly, the Saughton Kid, a radge whae Mikey Forrester used tae erselick. Seems the cunt tired ay Forrester one day and gave um a sound stomping. Hoespitalisation joab. Couldnae huv happened tae a nicer guy.

Begbie pulls us aside n droaps his voice.

— Ye ken thit Tommy's fuckin sick?

— Aye. Ah'd heard.

— Go n fuckin see the cunt whin yir up.

— Aye. Ah plan tae dae that.

— Too fuckin right. You ay aw fuckin people should. Ah'm no fuckin blamin you Rents, ah sais that tae fuckin Second Prize; ah'm no fuckin blamin Rents fir Tommy. It's every cunt's ain fuckin life. Ah fuckin telt that tae Second Prize.

Begbie then goes oan tae tell us what a great cunt ah am, looking fir us tae reciprocate, which ah dutifully do.

Ah act as a prop fir Begbie's customary ego-boosting fir a while, playing the straight man and telling the company some classic Begbie stories, which portray the cunt as hardman and stud extraordinaire. It always seems more authentic coming fae somebody else. The pair ay us then leave the pub thegither and head doon the Walk. Ah jist want tae git ma heid doon at ma Ma's, but The Beggar insists that ah come back tae his bit fir a bevvy.

Strutting doon the Walk wi Begbie makes us feel like a predator, rather than a victim, and ah start looking fir cunts tae gie the eye tae, until ah realise what a pathetic arsehole ah'm being.

We go fir a pish in the auld Central Station at the Fit ay the Walk, now a barren, desolate hangar, which is soon tae be demolished and replaced by a supermarket and swimming centre. Somehow, that makes us sad, even though ah wis eywis too young tae mind ay trains ever being there.

— Some size ay a station this wis. Git a train tae anywhair fae here, at one time, or so they sais, ah sais, watchin ma steaming pish splash oantae the cauld stane.

— If it still hud fuckin trains, ah'd be oan one oot ay this fuckin dive, Begbie said. It wis uncharacteristic for him tae talk aboot Leith in that way. He tended tae romanticise the place.

An auld drunkard, whom Begbie had been looking at, lurched up tae us, wine boatil in his hand. Loads ay them used this place tae bevvy and crash in.

— What yis up tae lads? Trainspottin, eh? He sais, laughing uncontrollably at his ain fuckin wit.

— Aye. That's right, Begbie sais. Then under his breath: — Fuckin auld cunt.

— Ah well, ah'll leave yis tae it. Keep up the trainspottin mind! He staggered oaf, his rasping, drunkard's cackles filling the desolate barn. Ah noticed that Begbie seemed strangely subdued and uncomfortable. He wis turned away fae us.

It wis only then ah realised thit the auld wino wis Begbie's faither.

We were silent on our journey towards Begbie's until we came upon a guy in Duke Street. Begbie hit him in the face, and he fell. The gadge briefly looked up before trying to pull himself intae a foetal position. Aw Begbie said wis 'wide cunt' as he put the boot intae the prostrate body a couple ay times. The expression the guy had when he looked up at Begbie was mair one ay resignation than fear. The boy understood everything.

Ah didnae even feel like tryin tae intervene, even in a token wey. Eventually Begbie turned tae me and nodded in the direction we were headed. We left the guy slumped on the pavement as we continued our walk in silence, neither ay us looking back once.

A Leg-Over Situation

It wis the first time ah'd seen Johnny since his amputation. Ah didnae ken what state ah'd find the cunt in. The last time ah'd seen um he'd been covered in abscesses n still talkin shite aboot gaun tae Bangkok.

Tae me surprise, the cunt wis exuberant for somebody thit hud recently loast a leg. — Rents! Ma man! How ye diddlin?

— No bad Johnny. Look, ah'm really sorry aboot the leg, man.

He laughed at ma concern. — Promising fitba career up the creek. Still, it nivir stoaped Gary Mackay, did it?

Ah jist smiled.

— The White Swan winnae be in dock fir long. Once ah git the hing ay that fuckin crutch, ah'll be back oan the streets. This is one bird's wings that cannae be clipped. Thill take ma legs bit nivir they wings. He wrapped an airm roond his shoodir tae pat tae whair his wings would huv been if the cunt hud any. Ah think he believes thit he does. — *En this bord you kenot chay-ay-ay-ay-aynge . . .* , he sang. Ah wondered whit the cunt wis oan.

As if readin ma mind he sais: — Ye goatay try that cyclozine. Shite oan its ain, but see whin ye mix it wi the methadone; phoah ya cunt! Best fuckin high ah've hud in ma puff. That includes that Colombian shit we hud back in eighty-four. Ah ken yir clean they days, but see if ye try nowt else, try that cocktail.

— Reckon it, aye?

— It's the fuckin best. You ken the Mother Superior, Rents. Ah believe in the free market whin it comes tae drugs. Ah've goat tae gie the NHS its due though. Since ah hud this pin oaf n went oan the maintenance therapy ah've started tae believe thit the state kin compete wi private enterprise in oor industry, n produce a satisfyin product at low cost tae the consumer. The methadone n cyclozine combined; ah'm tellin ya man, fuck me. Ah jist go doon, git ma jellies fi the clinic, then look up some ay the boys thit git the cyclozine oan script. They gie it tae the perr cunts wi cancer, fi AIDS, likes. A wee swap, n every cunt's chuffed tae fuckin bits.

Johnny ran oot ay veins and started shooting intae his arteries. It only took a few ay they shots tae gie um gangrine. Then the leg hud tae go. He catches us looking at the bandaged stump; ah cannae stoap masel.

— Ah ken whit yir thinkin, ya cunt. Well, they nivir took the White Swan's middle leg!

— Ah wisnae, ah protest, but he's pullin his dick oot ay the toap ay his boxer shorts.

— No thit it's much fuckin use tae us, he laughs.

Ah note that his knob's covered in dry scabs, which indicates that it's healin up. — Seems tae be dryin oot though Johnny, they abscesses likes.

— Aye. Ah've been tryin tae stick tae the methadone n cyclozine n stoap the injectin. Ah thoat whin ah saw the stump thit it wis an opportunity, another access point, but the hoespital cunt sais: Forget it. Stick a needle in thair n that's you well fucked. The maintenance therapy's no too bad though. The White Swan's strategy is tae git mobile, git clean n then start dealin properly, jist fir profit rather thin use. He pulls oot the waistband oan his shorts n scoops his scabby gear back in.

— Ye want tae gie it a fuckin bye, man, ah suggest. The cunt doesnae hear a word ah'm sayin.

— Naah, the aim's tae git a fuckin bankroll thegither, then it's oaf tae Bangkok.

His leg might have gone, but his Thailand escape fantasy's still intact.

— Mind you, he sais, — ah dinnae want tae wait until ah git tae Thailand before ah git a fuckin ride. That's whit this reduced dosage shite does fir ye. Ah hud some root oan us the other day thair whin the nurse came roond tae dae the dressin. An auld boot n aw, n thair's me sittin wi a bairn's airm wi an aypil oan the end ay it.

— Once ye git yirsel mobile Johnny, ah venture encouragingly.

— Like fuck. Whae wants tae shag a one-legged cunt? Ah'll huv tae pey fir it; a big come-doon fir the White Swan. Still, yir better peyin fir it wi burds. Keep the fuckin relationship oan a strictly business footin. He sounded bitter. — Ye still knobbin Kelly?

— Naw, she's back up here. Ah didnae like the wey he said that, n ah didnae like the wey ah responded.

— That cunt Alison came roond the other day, he sais, revealing the source ay his spite. Ali n Kelly ur best mates.

— Aw aye?

— Tae see the fuckin freak show, he nods at his bandaged stump.

— C'moan Johnny, Ali widnae huv that attitude.

He laughs again, reaching for a decaffeinated Diet Coke, ripping the ring back and taking a sip. — Thir's yin in the fridge, he offers, pointing tae the kitchen. Ah nod in the negative.

— Aye, she wis roond the other day. Well, a few weeks ago now, ah suppose. Ah goes, whit aboot a gam, doll? Fir auld time's sake, likes. Ah mean, it wis the least she could dae fir the Mother Superior, the White Swan, whae fuckin saw her awright plenty times. The cauld-hearted bitch k.b.d us, he shook his heid in disgust. — Ah nivir legged that wee hoor, ye ken? Nivir in ma puff. Even whin she wis gantin oan it. She'd uv let us fuck her aw weys fir a fix it one time.

— Right enough, ah conceded. It wis true, or wis it? Thir wis always a wee bit ay silent antagonism between masel n Ali. Dinnae really ken why. Whatever the reason, it makes it easier fir us tae believe the worst aboot her.

— The White Swan wid nivir take advantage ay a damsel in distress though, he smiles.

— Aye, sure, ah sais, totally unconvinced.

— Too right ah widnae, he stridently contends. — Ah didnae, did ah? The proof ay the puddin's in the fuckin eatin.

— Aye, only because ye hud skag in yir baws.

— Uh, uh, uh, he goes, touchin his chist wi the can ay coke. — The White Swan disnae fuck ower his mates. Golden rule number one. No fir smack, no fir nowt. Nivir question the integrity ay the White Swan oan that issue, Rents. Ah wisnae skaggy-bawed aw the time. Ah could've hud her cunt oan toast if ah hud've wanted it. Even whin ah wis skaggy-bawed; ah could've pimped her oot. Easy fuckin meat. Ah could've hud the bitch doon Easter Road in a short skirt n nae keks; gave her a jab tae keep her quiet, n stuck her oan the flair ay the pish-hoose behind the shed. Could've hud the whole fuckin home support oan a line-up, wi the White Swan standin ootside chargin a fiver a skull. Even wi a flunky thrown in, the margins wid be astro-fuckin-nomical. Then doon tae Tyney the next week, let aw they infected Jambo bastards go in eftir the boys hud hud thir fill.

Incredibly, Johnny's still HIV negative, in spite ay bein involved in settin up mair shootin galleries than Mr Cadona. He has a bizarre theory that only Jambos get HIV and Hibbies are immune. — Ah'd uv been set up. Retirement joab. A few weeks ay that n ah could've been in Thailand, a posse ay oriental buttocks parked oan ma coupon. Didnae dae it though; cause ye cannae fuck ower yir mates.

— It's tough bein a man ay principles, Johnny, ah smile. Ah'm wantin tae leave. Ah couldnae handle a round ay Johnny's fantasised oriental adventures.

— Fuckin right it is. Ma problem wis ah forgot the wrong yins. Nae sympathy in business, n wir aw acquaintances whin it comes tae the law ay the dragon. Bit naw, soft-herted bastard that the White Swan is, he lets friendship come intae it. N how does that selfish wee hing-oot repay us? Ah asks her fir a wee blow-job, that's aw. She wis gaunny gie us it n aw, oot ay sympathy fir the leg, ken. Ah hud even goat her tae git mair ay the make-up n lipstick oan, heavy duty likes, ken? So ah whips it oot. She takes one look it the weepin sores n boatils oot. Ah sais, dinnae worry, saliva's a natural antiseptic.

— That's whit they say right enough, ah acknowledge. It's gettin oan.

— Aye. N ah'll tell ye somethin else Rents, we hud the right idea back in sivinty-sivin. Aw that gobbin wi did. Drown the whole fuckin world in saliva.

— Pity we aw dried up, ah sais, risin tae make a move.

— Aye, too right, Johnny Swan says, quieter now.

It's time ah wisnae here.

Winter In West Granton

Tommy looks well. It's terrifying. He's gaunny die. Sometime between the next few weeks and next fifteen years, Tommy will be no more. The chances are that ah'll be exactly the same. The difference is, we ken this wi Tommy.

— Awright Tommy, ah sais. He looks so well.

— Aye, he sais. Tommy's sitting in a battered armchair. The air smells ay damp, and rubbish that should have been pit oot ages ago.

— How ye feelin?

— No bad.

— Want tae talk aboot it? Ah huv tae ask.

— No really, he sais, like he does.

Ah sit down awkwardly, in an identical chair. It feels hard, and has springs coming through. Many years ago, this wis some rich cunt's chair. It's hud at least a couple ay decades in poor homes though. Now it's winded up wi Tommy.

Now ah see that Tommy doesnae look so well. Thir's something missin, some part ay him; as if he's an incomplete jigsaw puzzle. It's mair thin shock or depression. It's like a bit ay Tommy's awready died, n ah'm mourin fir it. Ah realise now thit death is usually a process, rather than an event. People generally die by degrees, incrementally. They rot away slowly in homes and hoespitals, or places like this.

Tommy cannae get oot ay West Granton. He's blown things wi his Ma. This is one ay the varicose-vein flats, called so because of the plastered cracks all over its facing. Tommy got it through the council's hotline. Fifteen thousand people on the waiting list and naebody wanted this one. It's a prison. It's no really the council's fault; the Government made them sell off all the good hooses, leaving the dross for the likes ay Tommy. It makes perfect sense politically. There's nae votes for the Government doon here, so why bother daein anything fir people whae urnae gaunnae support ye? Morally, it's another thing. What's morality goat tae dae wi politics, but? It's aw aboot poppy.

— How's London? he asks.

— No bad Tommy. Really jist the same as up here, ken.

— Aye, ah bet, he sais, sarcastically.

PLAGUER wis painted on the heavy plywood-enforced door in big, black letters. Also HIVER and JUNKY. Draftpak kids will harass anybody. Naebody's said anything tae Tommy's face yet. Tommy's a tidy bastard, he believes in what Begbie caws the discipline ay the baseball bat. He's also goat hard mates, like Beggars, and no-sae-hard mates, like me. In spite ay this, Tommy will become mair vulnerable tae persecution. His friends will decline in their numbers as his needs increase. The inverse, or perverse, mathematics ay life.

— You took the test, he sais.

— Aye.

— Clear?

— Aye.

Tommy looks at us. It's like he's angry and pleading, baith at the same time.

— You used mair thin me. And ye shared works. Sick Boy's, Keezbo's, Raymie's, Spud's, Swanney's . . . ye used Matty's fir fuck sake. Tell us ye nivir used Matty's works!

— Ah nivir shared, Tommy. Every cunt sais that, but ah nivir shared, no in the galleries, anyway, ah telt um. Funny, ah'd forgotten aw aboot Keezbo. He'd been inside now fir a couple ay year. Been meanin tae go and visit the cunt fir donks. Ah ken thit ah'll nivir git roond tae it though.

— Bullshit! Cunt! You fuckin shared! Tommy leans forward. He's startin tae greet. Ah remember thinking that if he did, ah might n aw. Aw ah feel though, is an ugly, choking anger.

— Ah nivir shared, ah shake me heid.

He sits back and smiles tae himself; no even looking at us as he talks reflectively, now without any bitterness.

— Funny how it aw works oot, eh? It wis you n Spud n Sick Boy n Swanney n that, thit goat us intae the H. Ah used tae sit n huv a bevvy wi Second Prize n Franco an laugh at yis, call yis aw the daft cunts under the sun. Then ah split fae Lizzy, mind? Went tae your bit. Ah asked ye fir a hit. Ah thoat, fuck it, ah'll try anythin once. Been tryin it once ivir since.

Ah remember that. Christ, it wis only a few months ago. Some poor bastards are just so much more predisposed tae addiction wi certain drugs than others. Like Second Prize wi pish. Tommy took tae the skag wi a vengeance. Nae cunt kin really control it, but ah've known some fuckers, like myself, tae accommodate it. Ah've kicked a few times now. Kicking and using again is like gaun tae prison. Everytime ye go to jail, the probability ay ye ever becoming free fae that kind ay life decreases. It's the same every time ye go back tae smack. Ye decrease yir chances ay ever bein able tae dae withoot it. Wis it me thit encouraged Tommy tae take that first shot, jist by having the gear thair? Possibly. Probably. How guilty did that make us? Guilty enough.

— Ah'm really sorry, Tommy.

— Ah dinnae ken whit tae fuckin dae, Mark. Whit ah'm ah gaunnae dae?

Ah just sit there, heid slightly bowed. Ah wanted tae tell Tommy: Git oan wi yir life. It's aw ye can dae. Look eftir yirsel. Ye might no git bad. Look at Davie Mitchell. Davie's one ay Tommy's best mates. He's HIV and he's nivir used skag in his puff. Davie's okay though. He leads a normal life, well as normal a life as any cunt ah ken leads.

But ah know that Tommy cannae afford tae heat this gaff. He isnae Davie Mitchell, never mind Derek Jarman. Tommy cannae put hissel in a bubble, live in the warm, eat good fresh food, keep his mind stimulated wi new challenges. He willnae live five, or ten, or fifteen years before he's crushed by pneumonia or cancer.

Tommy will not survive winter in West Granton.

— Ah'm sorry mate. Ah'm really sorry, ah just repeat.

— Goat any gear? he asks, raising his heid and looking straight at me.

— Ah'm clean now Tommy. Whin ah tell him, he doesnae even sneer.

— Sub us then mate. Ah'm expectin a rent cheque.

Ah dig intae ma poakits and produce two crumpled fivers. Ah'm thinkin aboot Matty's funeral. It's odds on Tommy's next and there's fuck all anybody kin dae aboot it. Especially me.

He takes the money. Oor eyes meet, and something flashes between us. It's something ah cannae define, but it's something really good. It's thair jist fir a second; then it's gone.

A Scottish Soldier

Johnny Swan examines his close-shaven head in the bathroom mirror. His long, filthy hair had been shorn off a few weeks back. Now he had to get rid of this growth on his chin. Shaving was a drag when you only had one leg, and Johnny still hadn't quite got his balance sorted out. However, after a few scares, he managed what is a passable attempt. He was determined that he'd never go back into that wheelchair again, that was for sure.

— Back oan the mooch, he says to himself, as he studies his face in the mirror. Johnny looked clean. It was not a nice feeling and the process had caused him a great deal of discomfort; but people expect standards from an old soldier. He starts whistling the tune *A Scottish Soldier*; indulging himself further he gives his reflection a stiff, regimental salute.

The bandage on his stump gives Johnny some cause for concern. It looks filthy. Mrs Harvey, the community nurse, is coming today to change it, doubtless with a few accompanying choice words on personal hygiene.

He examines his remaining leg. It was never the best of the two. That knee was dodgy; the remnant of a footballing incident many moons ago. It'll get dodgier still as the sole bearer of his weight. Johnny thinks that he should've injected into the artery in this leg; let this one have been the cunt that went gangrenous and got hacked off by the surgeon. The curse of being right-sided, he reflects.

Outside in the cold streets, he swings and lurches towards the Waverley Station. Each step is a cruel one. The pain doesn't come from the extremity of his stump, but seems to be all over his body; however, the two methadone jellies and the barbiturates he has swallowed take the edge off it. Johnny sets up his pitch at the Market Street exit. His large piece of cardboard reads, in black letters:

FALKLANDS VETERAN — I LOST MY LEG FOR MY COUNTRY. PLEASE HELP.

A junky called Silver, Johnny doesn't know his real name, approaches him in freeze-frame movements.

— Any skag Swanney? he asks.

— Nothin happenin mate. Raymie's oan fir Setirday, or so ah hear.

— Setirday's nae good, Silver wheezes. — Thir's a fuckin ape oan ma back wants feedin.

— The White Swan here's a businessman Silver, Johnny points at himself. — If he hud merchandise tae punt, he'd dae jist that.

Silver looks downcast. A filthy, black overcoat hangs loosely on his grey, emaciated flesh. — Blootered oaf aw ma methy script, he states, neither looking for sympathy nor expecting it. Then a slight glint comes into his dead eyes. — Hey Swanney, dae ye make any poppy oot ay that?

— As one door shuts, another opens, Johnny smiles, his teeth a rotting mass in his mouth. — Ah make mair hireys daein this thin ah do oan the punt. Now if yill excuse us Silver, ah've goat a fuckin livin tae earn here. An upright soldier like masel cannae be seen talkin tae junkies. See ye aroond.

Silver barely registers his comments, let alone takes offence. — Ah'll jist head doon tae the clinic then. Some cunt might sell us a jelly.

— Au revoir, Johnny shouts at his back.

He does steady business. Some people furtively drop coins into his hat. Others, resentful at the intrusion of misery into their lives, turn away or resolutely look ahead. Women give more than men; young people more than their elders; people who appear to be of the most modest means seem more generous than the affluent looking.

A fiver lands in the hat. — God bless ye sir, Johnny acknowledges.

— Not at all, a middle-aged man says, — we owe you lads. It must be terrible to suffer that loss so young.

— Ah've nae regrets. Ye cannae allow yersel tae be bitter, pal. That's ma philosophy anyway. Ah love ma country; ah'd dae it aw again. Besides, ah regard masel is one ay the lucky yins; ah came back. Ah loast some good mates in that swedge at Goose Green, ah kin tell ye. Johnny let his eyes take on a glazed, faraway look; he almost believed himself. He turned back to the man. — Still, meetin people like yirsel, whae remember, whae care; that makes it aw worthwhile.

— Good luck, the man says softly, before turning and mounting the steps up to Market Street.

— Fackin radge cunt, Johnny mutters to himself, shaking his bowed head, as spasms of light laughter ripple up his sides.

He makes £26.78 after a couple of hours. It's not bad going and it's easy work. Johnny's good at waiting; even British Rail on a bad day couldn't fuck up his junky karma. However, withdrawal gives advance notice of its cruel intentions with an icy burn which causes his pulse to kick up a gear and his pores to excrete a rich, toxic sweat. He is about to pack up and leave when a thin, frail woman approaches him.

— Wir ye a Royal Scot son? Ma Brian wis a Royal Scot, Brian Laidlaw.

— Eh, Marines, missis. Johnny shrugs.

— Brian nivir came back, god love um. Twinty-one he wis. Ma laddie. A fine laddie n aw. The woman's eyes are welling up with tears. Her voice lowers to a concentrated hiss, which is all the more pitiful for its impotence. — Ye know son, ah'll hate that Thatcher till ma dyin day. Thir isnae a day goes by whin ah dinnae curse her.

She takes out her purse and, producing a twenty-pound note, crushes it into Johnny's hand. — Here son, here. It's aw ah've goat, bit ah want you tae huv it. She breaks into a sob and almost staggers away from him; it was like she'd been stabbed.

— God bless ye, Johnny Swan shouts after her. — God bless the Royal Jocks. Then he thrashes his hands together at the prospect of adding some cyclozine to the methadone he already has. Psycho-methy cocktail: his ticket to better times, that wee private heaven the uninitiated pour scorn on, but they could never conceive of its bliss. Albo has a stack of cyclozine, prescribed for his cancer. Johnny will visit his sick friend this afternoon. Albo needs Johnny's jellies as much as Johnny needs his psychos. A mutual coincidence of wants. Yes, god bless the Royal Jocks, and god bless the NHS.

Exit

Station to Station

It is a foul and dreich night. Filthy clouds hang overhead; waiting to spew their dark load on the shuffling citizens below, for the umpteenth time since the break of dawn. The bus station concourse is like a Social Security office turned inside out and doused with oil. A lot of young people living on big dreams and small budgets stand sombrely in line at the London rank. The only cheaper way down is by thumb.

The bus has come from Aberdeen with a stop at Dundee. Begbie stoically checks the seat reservation tickets, then fixes a malevolent glare at the people already on the bus. Turning away, he looks back at the Adidas holdall at his feet.

Renton, out of Begbie's earshot, turns to Spud and nods towards their uptight friend. — The cunt's jist hopin some fucker's grabbed oor seats; gie um an excuse tae cause hassle.

Spud smiles, and raises his eyebrows. Looking at him, Renton reflects, you'd never guess how high the stakes are. This is the big one, no doubt about it. He'd needed that shot, to keep his nerves straight. It had been his first one in months.

Begbie turns around, his nerves jangling, and shoots them an angry grimace, almost as if he can sense their irreverence. — Whair the fuck's Sick Boy?

— Eh, ah'm scoobied, likesay, Spud shrugs.

— He'll be here, Renton says, nodding at the Adidas bag. — That's twenty percent ay his gear yir haudin.

This shot off an attack of paranoia — Keep yir fuckin voice doon ya fuckin radge! Begbie hisses at Renton. He looks around, staring at the other passengers, feeling a desperate need for one, just one, to make eye-contact, to give him a target to unleash the fury within him which threatens to overwhelm him, and fuck the consequences.

No. He had to stay in control. There was too much at stake. There was everything at stake.

There is nobody looking at Begbie though. Those who are not oblivious to him, can feel the vibes he is giving out. They employ that special talent people have: pretending nutters are invisible. Even his companions won't meet his gaze. Renton has pulled his green baseball cap down over his eyes. Spud, wearing a Republic of Ireland football strip, is eyeing a backpacker who has blonde hair, and has just removed her pack to give him a view of her tight-arsed jeans. Second Prize, who stands a bit apart from the others, is just drinking steadily; protective of the sizeable carry-out which sits at his feet in two white plastic bags.

Over the concourse, behind the pillbox which calls itself a pub, Sick Boy is talking to a girl named Molly. She is a prostitute and is HIV positive. She sometimes hangs around the station at night, looking for punters. Molly had been in love with Sick Boy since he necked with her in a seedy disco-bar in Leith a few weeks ago. Sick Boy had made a drunken point about HIV transmission and to illustrate it had spent most of the night french-kissing her. Later, he had a bad attack of nerves and brushed his teeth half-a-dozen times before turning in for a sleepless, anxiety-filled night.

Sick Boy has been peeking out at his friends from behind the pub. He'd keep the bastards waiting. He wants to make sure that no labdicks pounce before they get on the bus. If that happens, these cunts can go down alone.

— Sub us a ten-spot doll, he asks Molly, not forgetting that he has a three-and-a-half grand stake in the contents of the Adidas bag. These are assets, however. This is cash-flow, which is always a problem.

— Here ye are. The unquestioning way Molly goes for her purse almost touches Sick Boy. Then, with some bitterness, he notes the health of her wad, and curses inwardly for not making it twenty.

— Cheers babes . . . well, ah'd better leave ye tae yir punters. The Smoke beckons. He tousles her curly hair and kisses her; this time though, a derisory brush on the cheek.

— Phone us whin ye git back Simon, she shouts after him, watching his lean but sturdy body bounce away from her. He turns around.

— You jist try stoapin us babes, you jist try stoapin us. Look eftir yirsel how. He winks at her and flashes an open, heart-warming smile before turning away.

— Fucked-up wee hoor, he mutters under his breath, his face freezing in a contemptuous scowl. Molly was an amateur, nowhere near cynical enough for the game she was in. A total victim, he thinks, with an odd mixture of compassion and scorn. He turns the corner and bounds over to the others, head swishing from side to side, trying to detect the presence of the police.

He is not amused at what he sees as they prepare to board the bus. Begbie curses him for his lateness. You always had to watch that radge, but with the stakes as high as they were, that meant he'd be even more uptight than usual. He remembered the bizarre contingency plans of violence that Begbie had hatched at the impromptu party they'd had last night. His temper could send them all to prison for life. Second Prize was in an advanced state of inebriation; to be expected. On the other hand, what loose-mouthed drunkard's talk had the cunt been coming out with, prior to being here? If he can't remember where he is, how the fuck can he be expected to remember what he says? This is such a fuckin dodgy scam, he reflects, allowing a shiver of anxiety to convulse through him.

What chews Sick Boy up the most, however, is the state of Spud and Renton. They were obviously smacked out of their eyeballs. It was just like these bastards to fuck up. Renton, who has now been clean for ages, since long before he packed in his London job and came back up, could not resist that uncut Colombian brown Seeker had supplied them with. It was the real thing, he had argued, a once-in-a-lifetime hit for an Edinburgh junky used to cheap Pakistani heroin. Spud, as always, had gone along for the ride.

That was Spud. His effortless ability to transform the most innocent of pastimes into criminality always amazed Sick Boy. Even in his Ma's womb, you would have had to define Spud less as a foetus, more as a set of dormant drug and personality problems. He'd probably draw the polis onto them through knocking a salt-cellar out of the Little Chef. Forget Begbie, he bitterly reflects, if one cunt is going to mess up the gig, it'll be Spud.

Sick Boy looks harshly at Second Prize; this nickname resulting from his drink-fuelled fantasy that he could fight, and the attendant disastrous results. Second Prize's sport had not been boxing, but football. He was a Scotland schoolboy international star of remarkable ability, who went south to Manchester United at the age of sixteen. By then, he already had an embryonic drink problem. One of soccer's unsung miracles was how Second Prize had managed to wring two years from the club before being kicked back to Scotland. The conventional wisdom was that Second Prize had wasted a great talent. Sick Boy understood the harsher truth, however. Second Prize was a mass of despair; in terms of his life as a whole, footballing ability was a frivolous deviation rather than alcoholism a cruel curse.

They file onto the bus, Renton and Spud moving in the smack-head's freeze-frame manner. They are as disorientated by the sequence of events as they are by the junk. There they were, pulling off the big one, and heading for a break in Paris. All they had to do was to convert the smack into hard cash, which had all been set up by Andreas in London. Sick Boy, though, had greeted them like a sinkful of dirty dishes. He was obviously in a bad mood and Sick Boy believed that the nasty things in life should be shared.

As he climbs onto the bus, Sick Boy hears a voice call his name.

— Simon.

— No that hoor again, he curses under his breath, before noting a younger girl. He shouts: — Git ma seat Franco, ah'll just be a minute.

Taking his seat, Bebgie feels hatred, fused with more than a twinge of jealousy, as he watches a young girl in a blue cagoul hold hands with Sick Boy.

— That cunt n his fuckin aboot wi fanny'll fuck us aw up! he snarls at Renton, who looks bemused.

Begbie tries to define the girl's shape through the cagoul. He'd admired her before. He fantasises what he'd like to do with her. He notes her face is even prettier when understated without make-up. It is hard to focus on Sick Boy, but Begbie sees his mouth turned down and his eyes opened wide in contrived sincerity. Begbie gets more and more anxious until he is ready to just get up and drag Sick Boy onto the bus. As he goes to haul himself out off the seat, he sees Sick Boy is coming back onto the vehicle, staring balefully out of the windows.

They are sitting at the back of the bus, beside the chemical toilet which already smells of spilled pish. Second Prize has cornered the back seat for himself and his carry-out. Spud and Renton sit in front of him, with Begbie and Sick Boy ahead of them.

— That wis Tam McGregor's wee lassie, Sick Boy, eh? Renton's face grins idiotically at him through the gap between the seat's headrests.

— Aye.

— He still fuckin hasslin ye? Begbie asks.

— The cunt's goat a lam oan because ah've been pokin his wee slut ay a daughter. Meanwhile, he's playing stoat-the-baw wi every wee hairy that drinks in his shitey club. Fuckin hypocrite.

— Pulled ye up ootside the fuckin Fiddlers, ah heard. They fuckin telt us ye shat yir fuckin load, Begbie mocks.

— Like fuck ah did! Whae telt ye that? The cunt says tae us: if you lay a finger oan her . . . Ah jist goes: Lay a finger oan her? Ah've been pimpin it oot fir fuckin months, ya cunt!

Renton smirks softly at this, and Second Prize, who didn't really hear it, laughs loudly. He is not, as yet, pickled enough to feel completely comfortable forgoing the bare bones of social contact. Spud says nothing, but grimaces as the vice-like grip of junk withdrawal squeezes harder on his brittle bones.

Begbie is unconvinced that Sick Boy would have the bottle to stand up to McGregor.

— Shite. You wouldnae fuckin mess wi that cunt.

— Fuck off. Jimmy Busby wis wi us. That cunt McGregor shites it fae the Buzz-Bomb. He's shit-scared ay aw the Cashies. The last thing he wants is a squad ay the Family swedgin in his club.

— Jimmy Busby . . . he's no a fuckin hard cunt. A fuckin shitein cunt. Ah stoated that radge in the Dean. You minday that time, Rents, eh? Rents! Mind the time ah panelled that Busby cunt? Begbie glances over the seat for support but Renton is starting to feel like Spud. A shudder twists through his body and a grim nausea hits him. He can only nod unconvincingly, rather than provide the elaboration Begbie is looking for.

— That wis years ago. Ye widnae dae it now, Sick Boy contended.

— Whae fuckin widnae! Eh? Think ah fuckin widnae? Ya fuckin radge! Begbie challenges aggressively.

— It's aw a loaday shite anyway, Sick Boy meekly counters, using one of his classic tactics. If you can't win the fine detail of the argument, then rubbish its context.

— That cunt kens no tae fuckin mess, Begbie says, in a low growl. Sick Boy does not respond, knowing that this was a warning by proxy, directed at him, through the absent Busby. He realises that he's been pushing his luck.

Spud Murphy's face is smeared against the glass window. He sits in silent misery, lashing sweat and feeling like his bones are grinding against each other. Sick Boy turns to Begbie, seizing the opportunity to make a common cause.

— These cunts, Franco, he nods backwards, — sais they wid stey clean. Lyin bastards. Fuck us aw up. His tone is a mixture of disgust and self-pity, as if he is resigned to the fact that his lot in life is to have all his moves sabotaged by the weak fools he was unfortunate enough to have to call his friends.

Nonetheless, Sick Boy fails to strike an empathetic chord with Begbie, who dislikes his attitude even more than he disapproves of Renton and Spud's behaviour.

— Stoap fuckin moanin. You've fuckin been thair often enough.

— No fir ages. These nondy cunts never grow up.

— So ye'll no be wantin any fuckin speed then? Begbie teased, dabbing at some salty granules in silver foil.

Sick Boy really wants some Billy Whizz, to cut down the hideous travelling time. He is fucked if he going to plead with Begbie however. He sits staring ahead, gently shaking his head and muttering under his breath, a wrenching anxiety in his guts forcing his mind to flip through unresolved grievance after unresolved grievance. He then springs up and goes to grab a can of McEwan's Export from Second Prize's pile.

— Ah telt ye thit ye should've goat yir ain cairry-oot! Second

Prize's face resembled that of an ugly bird whose eggs are under threat from a stalking predator.

— One can then, ya tight cunt! Fuck sakes! Sick Boy slaps his forehead with his palm in exasperation. Second Prize reluctantly hands a can over, which, in the event, Sick Boy cannot drink. He has not eaten for a while and the fluid feels heavy and sickly in his raw guts.

Behind him, Renton's slide into the misery of withdrawal continues apace. He knows he has to act. This means holding out on Spud. However, there was no sympathy in business, and much less in this particular one than in any other. Turning to his partner he says: — Man, ah've goat a fuckin bad rock in ma erse. Ah've goat tae spend a bit ay time in the bog.

Spud shoots to life for a second. — Yir no haudin, ur ye?

— Away tae fuck, Renton convincingly snaps. Spud turns and melts miserably back into the window.

Renton goes into the toilet and secures the door. He wipes the pish off the rim of the aluminium pan. It is not hygiene that concerns him, merely the avoidance of a wet sensation on his creeping skin.

On the tiny sink he places his cooking spoon, syringe, needle and cotton balls. Producing a small packet of browny-white powder from his pocket, he tips the contents diligently into his prized piece of cutlery. Sucking 5 mls of water into the syringe and squirting it slowly into the spoon, Renton takes care to avoid flushing away the grains. His trembling hand firms up with the concentration only junk preparation can facilitate. Passing the flame from the Benidorm plastic lighter under the spoon, he stirs at the stubborn dregs with the needle tip until he has produced an injectable solution.

The bus lurches violently, but he moves with it; his junky's vestibular sense tuned in, like radar, to every bump and bend on the A1. Not a precious drop is spilled as he lowers the cotton ball onto the cooking spoon.

Sticking the needle into the ball, he sucks the rusty liquid into the chamber. He pulls off his belt, cursing as the studs catch in the tabs of his jeans. He violently jerks it free, feeling as if his insides are folding in on themselves. Tightening the belt around his arm just below a puny bicep, he clamps yellowing teeth onto the leather to hold it fast. The sinew in his neck strains as he maintains the position; teasing up through patient, probing taps, a reluctant healthy vein.

A brief flicker of hesitancy glows in the corner of his mind, only to be snuffed cruelly by a twisting spasm which convulses his sick body. He zeros in, watching the tender flesh give way to the penetrating steel. He pushes the plunger part of the way home, for a split-second, before sucking back to fill the chamber with blood. He then releases the tension in the belt and flushes everything into his vein. He raises his head, and savours the hit. He sits for a period which could be minutes or hours, before standing up and looking at himself in the mirror.

— You're fuckin gorgeous, he observes, kissing the reflection; feeling the cold glass against his hot lips. He turns and puts his cheek on the glass, then licks at it with his tongue. Then he stands back and adjusts his features into a forced mask of misery. Spud's eyes would be on him as soon as he opened the door. He must contrive to act sick, which is not going to be easy.

Second Prize has drunk off a crippling hangover and is having what would have been described a second wind, had his constant state of inebriation and withdrawal not rendered such a term superfluous. Begbie, realising that they are well on their way and have not been intercepted by the Lothian and Borders Constabulary, the labdicks, is more relaxed. Victory was in sight. Spud takes a troubled junky sleep. Renton feels a little more animated. Even Sick Boy senses that things are going well, and unwinds.

The fragile unity is shattered when Sick Boy and Renton have an argument about the merits of the pre and post Velvet

Underground achievements of Lou Reed. Sick Boy is uncharacteristically tongue-tied under an onslaught from Renton.

— Naw, naw . . . he weakly shakes his head and turns away, devoid of inspiration to counter Renton's arguments. Renton had stolen the cloak of indignation that Sick Boy likes to wear on such occasions.

Savouring his adversary's capitulation, Renton pulls his head back sharply and smugly; folding his arms in a gesture of triumphant belligerence, the way he'd once seen Mussolini do in an old newsreel.

Sick Boy contents himself with checking out the other passengers. There are two auld wifies in front of him, who have been intermittently looking around with disapproving expressions and making clucking references to 'the language'. They have, he notes, the auld wifie smell of pish and sweat, partially obscured by layers of stale talcum.

Opposite him sits an overweight couple in shell-suits. Shell-suited bastards are another breed apart, he caustically thinks. They should be fuckin exterminated. It surprised Sick Boy that the Beggar did not have a shell-suit in his wardrobe. Once they coined in the dough, he thinks he'll treat the bastard to one, just for the crack. Additionally, he resolves to present Begbie with an American Pit-Bull pup. Even if Begbie neglected it, it wouldn't go hungry with the bairn in the house.

There was one rose amongst thorns on the bus, however. Sick Boy's eyes cease their critical scrutiny of his fellow passengers when they focus on the streaked-blonde backpacker. She sits all by herself, in front of the shell-suited couple.

Renton feels full of mischief and pulls out the Benidorm lighter and starts burning Sick Boy's ponytail. Hair crackles, and yet another unpleasant smell mingles with the rest at the back of the bus. Sick Boy, realising what is happening, springs round in his seat. — Fuck off! he snarls, thrashing at Renton's now raised wrists. — Immature cunts! he hisses as the laughter of Begbie,

Second Prize and Renton mocks him, ricocheting around the bus.

Renton's intervention though, gives Sick Boy the excuse he scarcely needs to leave them and join the backpacker. He pulls off his *Italians Do It Better* t-shirt, exposing a wiry, tanned torso. Sick Boy's mother is Italian, but he wears the t-shirt less to show pride in his origins, as to wind up the others at his pretension. He pulls down his bag and rummages through its contents. There is a *Mandela Day* shirt, which was politically sound and rock enough, but too mainstream, too sloganistic. Worse, it was dated. He felt that Mandela would prove to be just another tedious old cunt once everyone got used to him being out of the jail. He only gave *Hibernian F.C.* — *European Campaigners* a cursory glance before rejecting it out of hand. The Sandinistas were also passé now. He settled for a Fall t-shirt which at least had the virtue of being white and would show off his Corsican tan to its best effect. Pulling it on, he moved over and slid into the seat beside the woman.

— Excuse me. Sorry, I'm going to have to join you. My travelling companions' behaviour is a touch immature for my taste.

Renton observes, with a mixture of admiration and distaste, the metamorphosis of Sick Boy from waster into this woman's ideal man. Voice modulation and accent subtly change. An interested, earnest expression comes over his face as he fires seductively interrogative questions at his new companion. Renton winces as he hears Sick Boy say: — Yeah, I'm more of a jazz purist myself.

— Sick Boy's cracked it, he observes, turning to Begbie.

— Ah'm fuckin pleased fir the cunt, Begbie says bitterly. — At least it fuckin keeps the moosey-faced cunt away fae us. Fuckin nondy cunt's done fuck all but fuckin moan since we saw um . . . the cunt.

— Every cunt's a wee bit tense, Franco. Thir's a loat at stake.

We did aw that speed the other night thair. Everybody's bound tae be a wee bit para.

— Dinnae keep fuckin stickin up fir that cunt. Needs a fuckin lesson in manners that fuckin wide-o. Might soon be fuckin well gittin yin n aw. Disnae fuckin cost nowt tae huv manners.

Renton, realising that the discussion cannot be fruitfully advanced, settles down into his seat, letting the gear massage him; unravel the knots, and smooth out the creases. It was quality stuff alright.

Begbie's bitterness towards Sick Boy is not so much fuelled by jealousy but resentment at his departure; he is missing sitting beside someone. He now has a big speed kick on. His mind flashes with insight after insight, which Begbie thinks are just too good not to share. He needs someone to talk at. Renton notes the danger signs. Behind him, Second Prize is snoring loudly. Begbie would get little from him.

Renton pulls the baseball cap down over his eyes, while simultaneously nudging Spud awake.

— Ye sleepin Rents? Begbie asks.

— Mmmmm . . . Renton murmurs.

— Spud?

— What? says Spud irritably.

It was a mistake. Begbie turns in the seat; resting on his knees, he overhangs Spud and starts to repeat an oft-told story.

— . . . so ah'm oan toap ay it, ken, cowpin it likes, gaun fuckin radge n it's fuckin screamin likes n ah thinks fuck me, this dirty cow's right fuckin intae it, likes but it pushes us oaf, ken n she's bleedin ootay her fanny ken, like it's fuckin rag week, n ah'm aboot tae say, that disnae bother me, specially no wi a fuckin root oan like ah hud, ah'm fuckin tellin ye. Anywey, it turns oot thit the cunt's huvin a fuckin miscarriage thair n then.

— Yeah.

— Aye, n ah'll fuckin tell ye something else n aw; did ah tell ye aboot the time whin me n Shaun picked up they two fuckin hounds in the Oblomov?

— Yeah . . . Spud moans weakly, his face feeling like a cathode-ray tube which is imploding in slow motion.

The coach swings into the service station. While it provides Spud with some much-needed respite, Second Prize is not happy. Sleep had only just taken him, but the harsh lights of the bus are switched on, cruelly ripping him from his comforting oblivion. He wakes disorientated, in an alcoholic stupor; bemused eyes unable to focus, ringing ears assaulted by a cacophony of indistinguishable voices, flapping dried-up mouth unable to shut. He instinctively reaches for a purple can of Tennent's Super Lager, letting the sickly drink act as surrogate saliva.

They slouch across the motorway's fly-over bridge, persecuted by the cold, as well as the tiredness and drugs in their bodies. The exception is Sick Boy, who waltzes confidently ahead of them with the backpacker.

In the garish Trust House Forte cafeteria, Begbie grabs Sick Boy by an arm and extracts him from the queue.

— Dinnae you fuckin rip oaf that burd. Wir no wantin the fuckin polis swarmin aw ower us for a few hundred quid ay some fuckin student's holiday poppy. No whin wuv goat eighteen fuckin grand's worth ay skag oan us.

— Ye think ah'm fuckin daft? Sick Boy snaps, outraged, but at the same time confessing to himself that Begbie has provided him with a timely reminder. He had been necking with the woman, but his bulging chameleon eyes were always frantically scanning; trying to work out where her money was stashed. The visit to the cafe had been his opportunity. Begbie was right however, this was no time for a move like that. You couldn't always trust your instincts, Sick Boy reflected.

He tears himself away from Begbie with an injured pout, and rejoins his new girlfriend in the queue.

Sick Boy starts to lose interest in the woman after this. He is finding it hard to maintain an acceptable level of concentration on her excited tales of going to Spain for eight months, before taking up a place on a law degree course at Southampton University. He gets the address of the hotel in London she is staying at, noting with some distaste that it seems to be a cheap Kings Cross job, rather than a more salubrious place in the West End, which he'd enjoy hanging out in for a day or two. He was supremely confident that he'd get a shag out of this woman once they got the business with Andreas settled.

The bus eventually starts to roll through north London's brickwork suburbs. Sick Boy looks out nostalgically as they pass the Swiss Cottage, wondering whether a woman he knew still worked behind the bar. Doubtlessly not, he reasons. Six months is a quite a while behind the bar of a London pub. Even so early in the morning, the bus is reduced to a crawl as it reaches central London, and it takes a depressingly long time to wind down to Victoria Bus station.

They disembark like pieces of broken crockery being poured out of a packing case. A debate develops about whether they should go down to the railway station and get a Victoria Line tube up to Finsbury Park, or jump a taxi. They decide that a taxi is a better bet than messing about through London with a load of smack.

They squeeze into the Hackney cab, telling the talkative driver that they are down for the Pogues gig, which will take place in a tent in Finsbury Park. It provided ideal cover, as they all planned to go to the concert, combining pleasure with business, before heading to Paris for a break. The cab almost backtracks the way the bus had come in, prior to stopping at Andreas's hotel, which overlooks the park.

Andreas, who came from a London-Greek family, had inherited the hotel on the death of his father. Under the old man, the hotel had predominantly housed emergency homeless families. Local councils had the responsibility to find short-stay accommodation for people in such circumstances, and as the Finsbury Park district was sliced up between three London Boroughs, Hackney, Harringey and Islington, business had been good. On taking over the hotel, however, Andreas saw that it could be even more lucrative as a knocking-shop for London businessmen. While he never really hit the top end of the market he aimed at, he provided a safe haven for a small number of prostitutes. Mid-ranking city punters admired his discretion and the cleanliness and safety of his establishment.

Sick Boy and Andreas had got to know each other through going out with the same woman, who had been mesmerised by the both of them. They hit it off instantly, and worked a few scams together, mainly petty insurance fiddles and bank-card frauds. On taking over the hotel, Andreas had started to distance himself from Sick Boy, deciding that he was now in a bigger league. However, Sick Boy had approached him about a batch of quality heroin he had got a hold of. Andreas was cursed with a dangerous fantasy, and a timeless one: namely that he could hang around with villains to boost his ego, without paying an attendant price. The price Andreas paid was getting Pete Gilbert together with the Edinburgh consortium.

Gilbert was a professional who had worked in drug-dealing for a long time. He'd buy and sell anything. For him, it was strictly business, and he refused to differentiate it from any other entrepreneurial activity. State intervention in the form of police and courts merely constituted another business risk. It was however, a risk worth taking, considering the supernormal profits. A classic middle-man, Gilbert was, by nature of his contacts and his venture capital, able to procure drugs, hold them, cut them and sell them to smaller distributors.

Straight away, Gilbert clocks the Scottish guys as small-time wasters who have stumbled on a big deal. He is impressed however, by the quality of their gear. He offers them £15,000, prepared to go as high as £17,000. They want £20,000, prepared to go as low as £18,000. The deal is clinched at £16,000. Gilbert will make £60,000 minimum once the gear is cut and distributed.

He finds it tiresome negotiating with a bunch of fucked-up losers from the wrong side of the border. He'd rather be dealing with the person who sold it to them. If their supplier was desperate enough to punt such good gear to this squad of fuck-ups, then he didn't really understand the business. Gilbert could have turned him onto some real money.

More than tiresome, it was dangerous. Despite their assurances to the contrary, it would be impossible, he decided, for this bunch of wasted Jocks to *ever* be discreet. It was more than possible that the D.S. had stuck a tail on them. For that reason, he has two experienced punters outside in the car with their eyes peeled. Despite his reservations, he cultivated his new business associates. Anyone desperate enough to punt them this gear once, could be daft enough to do it again.

The deal concluded, Spud and Second Prize hit Soho to celebrate. They are typical new boys in town, attracted to that famous square mile like kids to a toy shop. Sick Boy and Begbie go to shoot what proves to be a competitive game of pool in the Sir George Robey with two Irish guys they team up with. London old stagers, they are contemptuous of their friends' fascination for Soho.

— Aw thill git thair is plastic polisman's hats, union jacks, Carnaby Street signs and overpriced pints ay pish, Sick Boy scoffed.

— They'd git a cheaper fuckin ride back it yir mate's hotel, what the fuck d'ye call um, the Greek cunt?

— Andreas. But that's the last thing these cunts want, says Sick Boy, racking up the balls, — and that fucker Rents. That's the umpteenth time he's tried tae kick. Doss cunt chucked in a good joab n barry flat doon here n aw. Ah think me n him'll go oor separate weys eftir this.

— It's a good joab he's fuckin back thair though. Some cunt's goat tae watch the fuckin loot. Ah widnae trust Second Prize or Spud tae look eftir it.

— Aye, Sick Boy says, wondering how he can ditch Begbie and get off in search of women's company. He wonders who he will call up, or whether he'll check out the backpacker. Whatever he decided, he'd move soon.

Back at Andreas's place, Renton is sick, but not quite as sick as he'd led them to believe. He looks out onto the back garden and sees Andreas cavorting with Sarah, his girlfriend.

He looks back at the Adidas bag, stuffed full of cash, the first time Begbie has let it out of his sight. He turfs its contents out onto the bed. Renton has never seen so much money. Almost without thinking, he empties the contents of Begbie's Head bag; putting them into the empty Adidas bag. Then stuffs the cash into the Head bag, and puts his own clothes in, on top of the money.

Briefly, he glimpses out of the window. Andreas has his hand inside Sarah's purple bikini pants and she is laughing and shrieking: — Dahnt Endreas . . . dahnt . . . Gripping the Head bag firmly, Renton turns and stealthily scuttles out of the room, down the stairs and along the hallway. He looks back briefly before striding out the door. If he bumped into Begbie now, he was finished. As soon as he lets that thought form consciously in his head, he almost collapses with fear. There is nobody in the street, however. He crosses the road.

He hears chanting noises and freezes. A group of young guys in Celtic football tops, obviously down for the Pogues gig in the afternoon, are staggering towards him, out of their heads on alcohol. He walks tensely past them, although they ignore him; and to his relief, he sees a 253 bus coming. He jumps on, and away from Finsbury Park.

Renton is on automatic pilot as he alights in Hackney to get a bus to Liverpool Street. Nonetheless, he feels paranoid and self-conscious with the bag full of money. Every person looks like a potential mugger or bag-snatcher to him. Whenever he sees a black leather jacket similar to Begbie's, his blood turns to ice. He even considers going back when he is on the bus to Liverpool Street, but he sticks his hand in the bag and feels the bundles of notes. At his destination, he walks into an Abbey National branch and adds £9,000 in cash to the £27.32 already in his account. The cashier does not even blink. This is the City, after all.

Feeling better with only £7,000 on him, Renton goes down to Liverpool Street station and buys a return ticket to Amsterdam, only intending to go one way. He watches the county of Essex transmute from concrete and brick into lush green as they rumble out towards Harwich. He has an hour's wait at Parkston Quay, before the boat sails to the Hook of Holland. This is no problem. Junkies are good at waiting. A few years back, he worked on this ferry, as a steward. He hopes that nobody recognises him from those days.

Renton's paranoia subsides on the boat, but it is replaced by his first real feelings of guilt. He thinks about Sick Boy, and all the things they went through together. They had shared some good times, some awful times, but they had shared them. Sick Boy would recoup the cash; he was a born exploiter. It was the betrayal. He could see Sick Boy's more-hurt-than-angry expression already. However, they had been drifting apart for years now. Their mutual antagonism, once a joke, a performance for the benefit of others, had slowly become, through being ritualised in that way, a mundane reality. It was better this way, Renton thought. In a way, Sick Boy would understand, even have a grudging admiration for his actions. His main anger would be directed at himself for not having had the bottle to do it first.

It didn't take much effort to rationalise that he had done Second Prize a favour. He felt pity when he thought of Second Prize using his criminal injuries compensation board cash to front his stake. However, Second Prize was so busy destroying himself, he'd scarcely notice anyone giving him a hand. You would be as well giving him a bottle of paraquat to drink, as three grand to spend. It would be a quicker and ultimately more painless way of killing him. Some, he considered, would argue that it was Second Prize's choice, but did not the nature of his disease destroy his capacity to make a meaningful choice? He smirks at the irony of him, a junky who has just ripped off his best mates, pontificating in such a manner. But was he a junky? True, he had just used again, but the gaps between his using were growing. However, he couldn't really answer this question now. Only time could do that.

Renton's real guilt was centred around Spud. He loved Spud. Spud had never hurt anybody, with the exception perhaps of a bit of mental distress caused by his tendency to liberate the contents of people's pockets, purses and homes. People got too het up about things though. They invested too much emotion in objects. Spud could not be held responsible for society's materialism and commodity fetishism. Nothing had gone right for Spud. The world had shat on him, and now his mate had joined it. If there was one person whom Renton would try to compensate, it was Spud.

That left Begbie. He could find no sympathy for that fucker. A psycho who used sharpened knitting needles when he went to sort some poor cunt out. Less chance of hitting the rib cage than with a knife, he'd boast. Renton recalled the time when Begbie had glassed Roy Sneddon, in The Vine, for fuck all. Nothing other than the guy had an irritating voice and Begbie was hungover. It was ugly, sickening and pointless. Even uglier than the act itself, was the way that they all, including Renton, had colluded with it, even to the extent of creating fictitious scenarios to justify it. It was just another way of building Begbie's status as somebody not to mess with, and their own indirectly, through their association with him. He saw it for the extreme moral cowardice it was. Alongside this, his crime in ripping off Begbie was almost virtuous.

Ironically, it was Begbie who was the key. Ripping off your mates was the highest offence in his book, and he would demand the severest penalty. Renton had used Begbie, used him to burn his boats completely and utterly. It was Begbie who ensured he could never return. He had done what he wanted to do. He could now never go back to Leith, to Edinburgh, even to Scotland, ever again. There, he could not be anything other than he was. Now, free from them all, for good, he could be what he wanted to be. He'd stand or fall alone. This thought both terrified and excited him as he contemplated life in Amsterdam.

THE ACID HOUSE

For my parents, Peter and Jean Welsh,
for all their love and support

Some stories in this collection have appeared in the following magazines and anthologies: 'Disnae Matter' in *Rebel Inc.*, 'Where the Debris Meets the Sea' in *Pig Squealing: New Writing Scotland 10*, 'Sport For All' in *The Ghost of Liberace: New Writing Scotland. 11.* 'The Sexual Disaster Quartet' appeared in *Folk*, published by Clocktower Press.

Thank you to the editors: Janice Galloway, A. L. Kennedy, Duncan McLean, Hamish Whyte and Kevin Williamson.

Thanks also to the following whose inspiration, ideas, encouragement, and cruel slaggings have influenced this collection:

Lesley Bryce, Colin Campbell, Jim Carrol, Max Davis, Debbie Donovan, Gary Dunn, Jimmy Easton, James Ferguson, Tam Ferguson, Adeline Finlay, Minna Fry, Janet Hay, Davie Inglis, Mark Kennedy, Stan Kieltyka, Miles Leitch, John McCartney, Helen McCartney, Willie McDermott, Kenny McMillan, James McMilla Sandy Macnair, Andrew Miller, Robin Robertson, Stuart Russell, Rosie Savin, Colin Shearer, John Shearer, Bobby Shipton, George Shipton, Susan Smith, Angela Sullivan, Dave Todd and Kevin Williamson (again).

Special thanks to that soul-brother of the new salons of psychic insurrection, Paul Reekie, for permission to use his poem.

Extra-special thanks to Anne, for the lot.

Rave on.

When Caesar's mushroom is in season
It is the reversal of the mushroom season
As Caesar's mushroom comes in March
The mushroom season is in September
Six months earlier
One half year
Equinoctal
Autumnal to vernal

Do you hope for more
Than a better balance
Between fear and desire
It'll only be the straying
That finds the path direct
Neither in the woods nor in the field
No robes, like Caesar's, trimmed with purple
Rather an entire street trimmed with purple
And every door in it
Wrapped in a different sort of christmas paper

The September mushrooms of midnight
Show the rhythms of vision
Can't move for tripping over them
Wipe your tapes
Wipe your tapes with lightning.

PAUL REEKIE
'When Caesar's Mushroom is in Season . . .'

CONTENTS

THE SHOOTER

— Lovely casserole, Marge, I remarked in between frantic
mouthfuls. It really was good.

— Glad ya like it, she replied, her face screwing up in an
indulgent smile behind her glasses. Marge was a good-looking
woman, no doubt about it.

I was enjoying myself, but Lisa was pushing the food around
her plate, her bottom lip curling outwards and downwards.

— Doncha like it, Lisa? Marge quizzed.

The child said nothing, merely shook her head, her
expression unaltered.

Gary's eyes burned in his face. Little Lisa was spot-on keeping
her gaze firmly on the plate.

— Oi! You'll bleedin well eat that, my gel! he snapped ferociously. Lisa buckled as if his words had a physical impact.

— Leave er, Gary. If she don wan it, she don need ta eat it,
Marge reasoned. Gary's gaze left the child. Seizing the opportunity, Lisa sprang from the table and left the room.

— Where do you think . . . Gary began.

— Oh leave er be, Marge snorted.

Gary looked at her and gestured manicaliy with his fork. — I
says one fing, you say another. No wonder I don't get no fuckin
respect in my own bleedin house!

Marge shrugged sheepishly. Gary had a temper and he'd been
really uptight since he got out. He turned to me, pleading for
understanding. — You see how it is, Jock? Every fucking time!
Treated like I'm bleedin invisible! My own fucking house. My

own bleedin kid! My own bleedin missus for Christ sakes, he moaned, pointing derisively at Marge.

— Take it easy, Gal, I said, — Marge's done us proud wi this spread. Great bit of scran, Marge. It isnae Lisa's fault that she doesnae like it, ye know how weans are. Different taste buds fae us n aw that. Marge smiled approvingly; Gary just shrugged and scowled into space. We ate the rest of the meal, punctuating our scoffing with stiff ritualised conversations; the Arsenal's chances for next season's championship were discussed, the merits of the new Co-op store in Dalston indoor centre were compared to that of the existing Sainsbury's over the road, the likely parentage and sexual orientation of the new manager who'd taken over Murphy's was ascertained, and the pros and cons of re-opening London Fields local railway station, shut down years ago due to fire damage, was passionlessly debated.

Eventually Gary sat back and belched, then stretched and stood up. — Nice bit of tucker, gel, he said appeasingly. Then he turned to me: — You fit?

— Aye, I replied, rising.

Gary answered the query on Marge's quizzical face. — Me n Jock ere, we got a bit of business to talk about, ain't we.

Marge's face set into a tense snarl. — You ain't thievin again are ya?

— I told ya I wasn't, didn't I? Gary aggressively replied. Her twisted mouth and narrowed eyes met his stare. — You promised me! YOU FUCKING PROMISED! All those fucking things you said . . .

— I ain't thieving! Jock! he appealed. Marge fixed her large pleading eyes on me. Was she begging me to tell her the truth or to tell her what she wanted to hear? Gary's promises. The number of times made, the number of times broken. Irrespective of what I said to her at that point, she'd be let down again: by Gary, or by some other guy. For some people there's no escaping certain types of disappointment.

— Naw, this is legit. Straight up, I smiled.

My bullshit was authentic enough to give Gary confidence.

Taking on an expression of injured innocence he said: — There. You got it straight from the horse's maff, gel.

Gary went upstairs to take a slash. Marge shook her head and dropped her voice. — He worries me, Jock. He's been so uptight lately.

— He worries aboot you n the wean, Marge. That's Gal; he's a worrier. It's in his nature.

We're all fuckin worriers.

— You ready or wot? Gary poked his head round the door.

We departed for the Tanners. I made for the back room, and Gary followed me with two pints of best. He set them down slowly on the polished table, with great concentration. He looked at the pints and said softly, shaking his head: — The problem ain't Whitworth.

— He's a fuckin problem tae me. Two fuckin grands' worth of a problem.

— You ain't gettin my drift, Jock. Ain't him that's the problem, innit. It's you, his extended digit rigidly pointed at me, — and me, he said, drumming his finger heavily on his chest. — The fucking donkeys here. We can forget that dough, Jock.

— Like fuck . . .

— Whitworth's gonna bullshit us, stonewall us, ignore us, until we just shut up abaht it, like two good little boys, he smiled grimly, his voice carrying a cold, implacable resonance. — He don't take us seriously, Jock.

— So what're ye saying, Gal?

— Either we forget it, or we make him take us seriously.

I let his words play around inside my head, checking and double-checking their implication, an implication in reality I had instantly recognised.

— So what dae we dae?

Gary took in a deep breath. It was strange that he was now so calm and reasoned, compared to his uptight state over the meal. — We teach the slag to take us seriously. Teach him a fucking lesson. Teach him a little bit of respect, innit.

How he proposed we did that, Gary made crystal clear. We

would get tooled up and take a drive to Whitworth's flat in Haggerston. Then we would knock seven types of shite out of him on his doorstep and issue a deadline for the repayment of the money owed to us.

I pondered this strategy. Certainly, there was no chance of resolving this matter legally. Moral and emotional pressure had failed to prove fruitful, and, Gary was right, had actually compromised our credibility. It was our money, and Whitworth had been given every opportunity to repay us. But I was scared. We were about to open an ugly Pandora's box and I felt that events were spinning out of my control. I had visions of the Scrubs, or worse, concrete slippers and a dip in the Thames, or some variation on the cliché, amounting in reality to much the same thing. Whitworth himself would be no problem, he was all flash; mouthy, but not a man of violence. The issue was: how well was he connected? We'd soon find out. I had to go along with this. Either way I couldn't win. If I didn't go ahead I'd lose credibility with Gary, and I needed him more than he needed me. More importantly, someone would have my money and I'd be left skint and consumed with self-hatred for having capitulated so tamely.

— Let's sort the cunt out, I said.

— That's my man, Gary slapped my back. — Alway's knew you had the bottle, Jock. All you fucking Jocks, all fucking crazy! We'll show that cunt Whitworth just who he's fucking abaht wiff here.

— When? I asked, feeling a bit nauseous with exciteı.ent and anxiety.

Gary shrugged and raised an eyebrow. — Ain't no time like the present.

— You mean right now? I gasped. It was broad daylight.

— Tonight. I'll call for you at eight with a motor.

— Eight, I agreed weakly. I had been feeling big vibes of anxiety about Gary's unstable behaviour lately. — Listen Gal, there isnae anything other than money between you and Tony Whitworth, is there?

— The money's enough in my circumstances, Jock. More than enough, innit, he said, throwing back his pint and rising. — I'm orf home. You should go too. You don't wanna be knocking back too much of the Jonathan Ross, he pointed at my glass. — We got a job to do.

I watched him lumber away purposefully, pausing only to wave at old Gerry O'Hagan at the bar.

I left shortly after, taking Gal's advice about the sauce consumption. I went up to the sports store in Dalston and purchased a baseball bat. I thought about buying a ski mask, but that would be too obvious, so I went to the Army and Navy and got a balaclava. I sat in my gaff, unable for a while to look at the purchases. Then I picked up the bat and began swinging it through the air. I pulled the mattress off my bed and stuck it against the wall. I thrashed at it with the bat, checking swing, stance and balance. The anxiety flowed from me as I swiped, lunged and snarled like a maniac.

It was not long in returning. It had gone eight and I thought that Gary may have had a bout of sanity and called the whole thing off, perhaps after Marge tippled that something was up and got on his case. At 8.11 on the digital clock radio I heard the car horn blast truculently outside. I didn't even go to the window. I just picked up the balaclava and the bat and went downstairs. My grip on the weapon now felt weak and insipid.

I climbed into the passenger seat. — I see you're prepared, Gary smiled. Even after he'd spoken, his face remained frozen in that strange smile, like a bizarre Halloween mask.

— What've you got? I feared that he'd produce a knife.

My heart stopped when, from under the seat, he pulled out a sawn-off shotgun.

— No way, man. No fuckin way. I moved to get out of the car. His hand fell on my arm.

— Relax! Ain't fucking loaded, is it? You know me, Jock, for fuck sakes. Shooters ain't my fucking scene, never have been. Credit me wiff a little bit bleedin sense, innit.

— You're telling me that gun is empty?

— Course it's bleedin empty, innit. You think I'm fucking daft? Do it this way, we don't need no violence. No aggravation, nobody gets hurt. A geezer inside told me; people change when you point a gun at them. The way I see it is: we want our money. We ain't bothered about hurting the cunt; we just want the dough. If you get carried away wiff that bat, you might make im into a bleedin cabbage. Then we got no money and a berth in the bleedin Scrubs. We terrorise him, we show him this – he waved the shooter, which now seemed like a pathetic toy, — and he's shiting pound notes at us.

I had to concede that it sounded so much simpler Gary's way. Scaring Whitworth was preferable to doing him over. Smash the cunt up and he'd possibly get a team together for revenge. If you scared the shit out of him with a shooter, the chances were that he'd know not to fuck with you. We knew the gun wasn't loaded, Whitworth didn't. Who would take the risk?

Whitworth's flat was on the ground floor of a 1960s systems-built maisonette block in a small council estate off the Queensbridge Road. It was dark, though not pitch black, as we parked the car a few yards from his front door. I debated whether or not to put on the balaclava, then decided against it. Gary had no mask, and besides, we wanted Tony Whitworth to see who was pointing the gun. Instead I concealed the bat under my long coat as we stepped out the car.

— Ring the fucking bell, Gary urged.

I pressed the buzzer.

A hall light clicked on, shining through the gap at the top of the door. Gary stuck his hand inside his coat. The door opened ⊲ and a boy of about eight years old, wearing an Arsenal tracksuit, stood warily before us.

— Tony in? Gary asked.

I hadn't bargained for this. I'd made Whitworth into a cartoon figure, a mouthy ponce-spiv stereotype, in order to justify what we were going to do to him. I'd never imagined him as a real person, with kids, people who depended on him, probably even loved him. I tried to make a signal to Gary that this was not the time or place, but the young boy had vanished back into the house and was almost simultaneously replaced in the doorway by Whitworth. He wore a white t-shirt and jeans, and a beaming smile across his face.

— The lads, he grinned expansively. — Glad to see ya! I've got somefink for ya, if . . . he stopped in mid-sentence as his eyes grew bigger and the colour drained from him completely. The side of his face seemed to crinkle up as if he was having some kind of stroke.

Gary had whipped out the shooter and was pointing it straight at him.

— Oh no, please to god, I've got what you want, Gal, that's what I was trying to say . . . Jock . . .

— Gal, I started, but he ignored me.

— We got what you want cunt! he snapped at Whitworth, as he squeezed the trigger.

There was a shuddering bang and Whitworth seemed to vanish into the house. For an instant, it was like some kind of theatrical illusion, as if he was never there. In that split-second I thought I'd been the victim of an orchestrated wind-up between Gal and Tony Whitworth. I even started laughing. Then I looked into the lobby. Tony Whitworth's convulsing body lay there. What was once his face was now a broken, crushed mass of blood and grey matter.

I remember nothing after that until I was in the car and we were driving along the Balls Pond Road. Then I remember getting out, into another motor and heading back towards Stoke Newington. Gary started laughing and ranting like he was on speed. — Did you see the cunt's fucking head?

I felt like I was on heroin.

— Did ya? he asked, then he grabbed my wrist. — Jock, I'm really fucking sorry, mate, sorry to have got you involved. I couldn't have done it on my own though. I had to do it Jock, I had to waste the cunt. When I was in the Scrubs, you know, I heard all abaht him. He was round ours all the time, hanging around Marge, flashing his fucking wad abaht. Marge broke down, Jock, told me the whole fucking story. Course I don't blame her, Jock, it ain't that, it was my fault getting banged up. I should've been around; any woman skint with her old man banged up is gonna be tempted by some flash git with dough fussing over er. The cunt beasted little Lisa though, Jock. Made her go down on him, you know what I'm saying here, Jock? Yeah? You'd've done the same, Jock, don't fucking tell me otherwise cause you're a liar; if it was your bleedin kid, you'd've done the same. You n me, we're the same, Jock, we look after each other, we look after our own. I'll make the money up to you one day, Jock, I bleedin well swear I will, believe you me, mate, I'll sort it all out. Couldn't have done nuffink else, Jock, it just festered away inside of me. I tried to ignore it. That's why I wanted to work with Whitworth, suss out the slag's MO, see if I could find a way to get him back. I thought abaht hurting one of his kids, like an eye for an eye an all that bleeding cobblers. I couldn't have done anything like that though, Jock, not to a little kiddie, that would make me no better than that fucking beast, that fucking nonce slag . . .

— Yeah . . .

— Sorry to drag you into this mess, Jock, but as soon as you got word of this fucking scam with Whitworth, you wouldn't fucking leave it. Had to be involved, you did. Gis a stake, Gal, you kept saying; mates n all that. You was like my bleedin shadow, you was. I tried to send out the fucking vibes, but no, you didn't pick them up. Had to cut you in for a piece of the action, didn't I? That was how you needed to have it, Jock; mates, partners.

We went back to my place. My lonely flat, even lonelier with two people in it. I sat on the couch, Gary sat in the chair opposite. I put the radio on. Despite the fact that she'd taken her stuff and gone months ago, there was still traces of her here; a glove, a scarf, a poster she'd bought stuck up on the wall, these Russian dolls we'd got from Covent Garden. The presence of such articles always loomed large in times of stress. Now they

were overpowering. Gary and I sat drinking neat vodka and
waiting for the bulletins.

After a bit Gary got up to take a piss. When he returned, he
came back with the gun. He then sat back down in the chair
opposite me. He ran his fingers along the narrow barrel. When
he spoke his voice seemed strange; far away and disembodied.

— Did ya see his face, Jock?

— It wisnae fuckin funny, Gal, ya fuckin stupid cunt! I hissed,
anger finally spilling through my sick fear.

— Yeah, but his face, Jock. That fucking smarmy nonce face.
It's true, Jock, people change when you pull a gun on them.

He's looking right at me. Now he's pointing the shooter at
me.

— Gal . . . dinnae fuck about man . . . dinnae . . .

I can't breathe, I feel my bones shaking; from the soles of my
feet upwards, shaking my whole body in a jarring, sickening
rhythm.

— Yeah, he says, — people change when you pull a gun on
them.

The weapon is still pointed at me. He reloaded it when he
took that slash. I know it.

— I heard that you were seeing quite a bit of my missus when
I was inside, mate, he says softly, caressingly.

I try to say something, try to reason, try to plead, but my
voice is dry in my throat as his finger tenses on the trigger.

EUROTRASH

I was anti-everything and everyone. I didn't want people around me. This aversion was not some big crippling anxiety; merely a mature recognition of my own psychological vulnerability and my lack of suitability as a companion. Thoughts jostled for space in my crowded brain as I struggled to give them some order which might serve to motivate my listless life.

For others Amsterdam was a place of magic. A bright summer; young people enjoying the attractions of a city that epitomised personal freedom. For me it was but a dull, blurred series of shadows. I was repelled by the harsh sunlight, seldom venturing out until it got dark. During the day I watched English and Dutch language programmes on the television and smoked a lot of marijuana. Rab was a less than enthusiastic host. Without any sense of his own ridiculousness he informed me that here in Amsterdam he was known as 'Robbie'.

Rab/Robbie's revulsion for me seemed to blaze behind his face, sucking the oxygen from the air in the small front room on which I had made up a couch-bed. I'd note his cheek muscles twitch in repressed anger as he'd come in, dirty, grimy and tired from a hard, physical job, to find me mellow in front of the box, the ubiquitous spliff in my hand.

I was a burden. I had been here for only a fortnight and clean for three weeks. My physical symptoms had abated. If you can stay clean for a month you've got a chance. However, I felt it was time I looked for a place of my own. My friendship with Rab (now, of course, re-invented as Robbie) could not survive the one-sided, exploitative basis I had re-modelled it on. The worse thing was: I didn't really care.

One evening, about a fortnight into my stay, it seemed he'd had enough. — When ye gaunny start lookin for a job, man? he asked, with obviously forced nonchalance.

— I am, mate. I hud a wee shuftie aroond yesterday, trying tae check a few things out, y'know? The lie of the land, I said with contrived sincerity. We went on like this; forced civility, with a subtext of mutual antagonism.

I took tram number 17 from Rab/Robbie's depressing little scheme in the western sector into the city centre. Nothing happens in places like the one we stayed in, Slotter Vaart they call it; breeze-block and concrete everywhere; one bar, one supermarket, one Chinese restaurant. It could've been any-where. You need a city centre to give you a sense of place. I could've been back in Wester Hailes, or on Kingsmead, back in one of those places I came here to get away from. Only I hadn't got away. One dustbin for the poor outside of *action strasser* is much the same as any other, regardless of the city it serves.

In my frame of mind, I hated being approached by people. Amsterdam is the wrong place to be in such circumstances. No sooner had I alighted in The Damrak than I was hassled. I'd made the mistake of looking around to get my bearings. — French? American? English? an Arabic-looking guy asked.

— Fuck off, I hissed.

Even as I walked away from him into the English bookshop I could hear his voice reeling of a list of drugs. — Hashish, heroin, cocaine, ecstasy . . .

During what was meant to be a relaxing browse, I found myself staging an internal debate as to whether or not I would shoplift a book; deciding against it, I left before the urge became unbearable. Feeling pleased with myself, I crossed over Dam Square into the red-light district. A cool twilight had descended on the city. I strolled, enjoying the fall of darkness. On a side-street off a canal, near where the whores sit in the windows, a man approached me at a threatening pace. I decided quickly that

I would put my hands around his neck and choke him to death if he attempted to make any contact with me at all. I focused on his Adam's apple with murderous intent, my face twisting into a sneer as his cold, insect eyes slowly filled with apprehension. — Time . . . do you have the time? he asked fearfully.

I curtly nodded negative, striding satisfyingly past him as he arched his body to avoid being brushed onto the pavement. In Warmoesstraat it was not so easy. A group of youths were fighting a series of running battles; Ajax and Salzburg fans. The UEFA Cup. Yes. I could not handle the movement and the screaming. It was the noise and motion I was averse to more than the threat of violence. I took the line of least resistance, and slipped down a side-street into a brown bar.

It was a quiet, tranquil haven. Apart from a dark-skinned man with yellow teeth (I had never seen teeth so yellow), who was wired up to the pinball machine, the only other occupants of the place were the barman and a woman who sat on a stool at the bar. They were sharing a bottle of tequila and their laughter and intimate behaviour indicated that their relationship went beyond that of publican-customer.

The barman was setting the woman up with tequila shots. They were a little drunk, displaying a saccharine flirtatiousness. It took the man a while to register my presence at the bar. Indeed, the woman had to draw his attention to me. His response was to give her an embarrassed shrug, though it was obvious that he couldn't care less about me. Indeed, I sensed that I was an inconvenience.

In certain states of mind I would have been offended by this negligence and would definitely have spoken up. In other states of mind I would have done a lot more. At this point in time, however, I was happy to be ignored; it confirmed that I was as effectively invisible as I intended to be. I didn't care.

I ordered a Heineken. The woman seemed intent on drawing me into their conversation. I was just as intent on avoiding contact. I had nothing to say to these people.

— So where do you come from with an accent like that? she

laughed, her X-ray gaze sweeping over me. When her eyes met mine I saw a type of person who, despite their apparent camaraderie, has an instinctive drive towards manipulative schemes. Perhaps I was looking at my reflection.

I smiled. — Scotland.

— Yeah? Where about? Glasgow? Edinburgh?

— All over really, I replied, bland and blasé. Did it really matter which indistinct shite-arsed towns and schemes I was dragged through, growing up in that dull and dire little country?

She laughed, however, and looked thoughtful, as if I'd said something really profound. — All over, she mused. — Just like me. All over. She introduced herself as Chrissie. Her boyfriend, or he who, given his indulgence of her, intended to be her boyfriend, was called Richard.

From behind the bar, Richard stole injured glances at me, before I turned to face him, having clocked this in a bar mirror. He responded with a ducking motion of his head, followed by a 'Hi' in a dislocated hiss, and a furtive grope of a ratty beard which grew out of a pock-marked face but merely seemed to accentuate rather than conceal the lunar landscape it sprang from.

Chrissie talked in a rambling, expansive way, making observations about the world and citing mundane examples from her own experience to back them up.

It's a habit of mine to look at people's bare arms. Chrissie's were covered in healed track marks; the kind where ugly scar tissues is always left. Even more evident were the slash marks; judging by depth and position, the self-hating, response-to-frustration type rather than the serious suicide-bid variety. Her face was open and animated but her eyes had that watery, diminished aspect common to the traumatised. I read her as a grubby map of all the places you didn't want to go to: addiction, mental breakdown, drug psychosis, sexual exploitation. In Chrissie I saw someone who'd felt bad about herself and the world and had tried to shoot and fuck herself into better times without realising that she was only compounding the problem. I was no stranger to at least some of the places Chrissie had been. She looked as if she was very ill-equipped for these visits, however, and that she tended to stick around a bit too long.

At the moment her problems seemed to be drink and Richard. My first thought was that she was welcome to both. I found Chrissie pretty repulsive. Her body was layered with hard fat around her gut, thighs and hips. I saw a beaten woman whose only resistance to the attentions of middle-age was to wear clothes too youthful, tight and revealing for her meaty figure.

Her doughy face twisted flirtatiously at me. I was vaguely nauseated at this woman; gone to seed, yet unselfconsciously attempting to display a sexual magnetism she no longer possessed, and seemingly unaware of the grotesque vaudevillian caricature which had supplanted it.

It was then, parodoxically, that a horrible impulse struck me, which appeared to have its origins in an unspecific area behind my genitals: this person who repulsed me, this woman, would become my lover.

Why should this be? Perhaps it was my natural perversity; perhaps Chrissie was that strange arena where repulsion and attraction meet. Maybe I admired her stubborn refusal to acknowledge the remorseless shrinking of her possibilities. She acted as if new, exciting, enriching experiences were just around the corner, in spite of all the evidence to the contrary. I felt a gratuitous urge, as I often do with such people, to shake her and scream the truth in her face: *You're a useless, ugly piece of meat. Your life has been desperate and abominable so far, and it's only going to get worse. Stop fucking kidding yourself.*

A conflicting mass of emotions, I was actively despising someone while simultaneously planning their seduction. It was only later that I acknowledged, with some horror and shame, that these feelings didn't really conflict at all. At that stage, though, I was unsure as to whether Chrissie was flirting with me or merely trying to tease the seedy Richard. Perhaps she wasn't sure herself.

— We're going to the beach tomorrow. You must come, she said.

— That would be great, I smiled lavishly, as the colour drained from Richard's face.

— I may have to work . . . he stammered nervously.

— Well, if you won't drive us, we'll just go alone! she simpered in a little-girl manner, a tactic commonly used by whores, which she almost certainly once was, when she still had the looks to make it pay.

I was definitely pushing at an open door.

We drank and talked until the increasingly nervous Richard shut the bar and then we went to a cafe for some blow. The date was formalised; tomorrow I was forsaking my nocturnal life for a day of seaside frolics with Chrissie and Richard.

Richard was very uptight the following day when he drove us down to the beach. I derived pleasure from watching his knuckles go white on the steering wheel as Chrissie, arched around from the front passenger sat, indulged in some frivolous and mildly flirtatious banter with me. Every bad joke or dull anecdote which spilled lazily from my lips was greeted with frenetic peals of laughter from Chrissie, as Richard suffered in tense silence. I could feel his hatred for me growing in increments, constricting him, impairing his breathing, muddying his thought processes. I felt like a nasty child jacking up the volume on the handset of the television control for the purpose of annoying an adult.

He inadvertently gained some measure of revenge, sticking on a Carpenters tape. I writhed in discomfort as he and Chrissie sung along. — Such a terrible loss, Karen Carpenter, she said solemnly. Richard nodded in sombre agreement. — Sad, isn't it, Euan? Chrissie asked, wanting to include me in their strange little festival of grief for this dead pop star.

I smiled in a good-natured, carefree way. — I couldn't give a toss. There's people all over the world who haven't got enough to eat. Why should I give a fuck about some over-privileged fucked-up Yank who's too screwed up to lift a forkful of scran into her gub?

There was a stunned silence. Eventually Chrissie wailed, — You've a very nasty, cynical mind, Euan! Richard whole-heartedly agreed, unable to conceal his glee that I'd upset her. He even started singing along to 'Top of the World'. After this, he and Chrissie began conversing in Dutch and laughing.

I was unperturbed at this temporary exclusion. In fact I was enjoying their reaction. Richard simply did not understand the type of person Chrissie was. I sensed that she was attracted to ugliness and cynicism because she saw herself as an agent of change. I was a challenge to her. Richard's servile indulgence would amuse her from time to time; it was, however, just a holiday retreat, not a permanent home, ultimately bland and boring. In trying to be what he thought she wanted, he had given her nothing to change; denied her the satisfaction of making a real impact in their relationship. In the meantime, she would string this fool along, as he indulged her boundless vanity.

We lay on the beach. We threw a ball at each other. It was like a caricature of what people should do at the seaside. I grew uncomfortable with the scene and the heat and lay down in the shade. Richard ran around in his cut-offs; tanned and athletic, despite a slightly distended stomach. Chrissie looked embarrass-ingly flabby.

When she went to get ice-cream, leaving Richard and I alone for the first time, I felt a little bit nervous.

— She's great, isn't she, he enthused.

I reluctantly smiled.

— Chrissie has come through a lot.

— Yes, I acknowledged. That I had already deduced.

— I feel differently about her than I've done about anyone else. I've known her a long time. Sometimes I think she needs to be protected from herself.

— That's a wee bit too conceptual for me, Richard.

— You know what I mean. You keep your arms covered up.

I felt my bottom lip curl in knee-jerk petulance. It was the childlike, dishonest response of someone who isn't really hurt but is pretending to be so in order to justify future aggression towards, or elicit retraction from, the other party. It was second nature to me. I was pleased that he felt he had my measure; with a delusion of power over me he'd get cocky and therefore careless. I'd pick my moment and tear out his heart. It was hardly a difficult target, lying right there on the sleeve of his blouse. This whole thing was as much about me and Richard as it was about me and Chrissie; in a sense she was only the battleground on which our duel was being fought. Our natural antipathy on first meeting had incubated in the hothouse of our continuing contact. In an astonishingly short time it had blossomed into fully-fledged hatred.

Richard was unrepentant about his indiscreet comment. Far from it, he followed up his attack, attempting to construct in me an appropriate figure for his hatred. — We Dutch, we went to South Africa. You British oppressed us. You put us into concentration camps. It was you people who invented the concentration camp, not the Nazis. You taught them that, like you taught them genocide. You were far more effective at that with the Maoris in New Zealand than Hitler was with the Jews. I'm not condoning what the Boers are doing in South Africa. No way. Never. But you British put the hatred in their hearts, made them harsh. Oppression breeds oppression, not resolution.

I felt a surge of anger rise in me. I was almost tempted to go into a spiel about how I was Scottish, not British, and that the Scots were the last oppressed colony of the British Empire. I don't really believe it, though; the Scots oppress themselves by their obsession with the English which breeds the negatives of hatred, fear, servility, contempt and dependency. Besides, I would not be drawn into an argument with this moronic queen.

— I don't profess to know a great deal about politics, Richard. I do find your analysis a tad subjective, however. I stood up, smiling at Chrissie who had returned with cartons of Häagen-Dazs topped with *slagroom*.

— You know what you are, Euan? Do you? she teased. Chrissie had obviously been exploring some theme while she was getting the ices. Now she'd inflict her observations on us. I shrugged. — Look at him, Mister Cool. Been there, done it all. You're just like Richard and me. Bumming around. Where was it you said you wanted to head for later on?

— Ibiza, I told her, or Rimini.

— For the rave scene, the ecstasy, she prompted.

— It's a good scene to get into, I nodded. — Safer than junk.

— Well that's as maybe, she said petulantly. — You're just Eurotrash, Euan. We all are. This is where all the scum gets washed up. The Port of Amsterdam. A dustbin for the Eurotrash.

— I smiled and opened another Heineken from Richard's cold basket. — I'll drink to that. To Eurotrash! I toasted.

Chrissie enthusiastically bashed my bottle with hers. Richard reluctantly joined in.

While Richard was obviously Dutch, I found Chrissie's accent hard to place. She occasionally had a Liverpool affectation to what generally seemed to be a hybrid of middle-class English and French, although I was sure it was all a pose. But there was no way I was going to ask her where she was from just so that she could say: all over.

When we got back to the 'Dam that night, I could see that Richard feared the worst. At the bar he tried to ply us with drink in what was obviously a desperate attempt to render what was about to happen null and void. His face was set into a beaten expression. I was going home with Chrissie; it couldn't have been more obvious had she taken out an advertisement in the newspaper.

— I'm shattered, she yawned. — The sea air. Will you see me home, Euan?

— Why don't you wait until I finish my shift? Richard desperately pleaded.

— Oh Richard, I'm completely exhausted. Don't worry about me. Euan doesn't mind taking me to the station, do you?

— Where do you stay? Richard interjected, addressing me, trying to gain some control over events.

I flipped up my palm in a halting gesture, and turned back to Chrissie. — The very least I could do after yourself and Richard giving me such a good time today. Besides, I really need to get my head down too, I continued, in a low, oily voice, allowing a dripping, languid smile to mould my face.

Chrissie pecked Richard on the cheek. — Phone you tomorrow baby, she said, scrutinising him in the manner of an indulgent mother with a sulking toddler.

— Goodnight, Richard, I smiled as we made to leave. I held the door open for Chrissie and as she exited I looked back at the tortured fool behind the bar, winked and raised my eyebrows: — Sweet dreams.

We walked through the red-light district, by the Voorburg and Achterburg canals, enjoying the air and the bustle. — Richard is incredibly possessive. It's such a drag, Chrissie mused.

— No doubt his heart's in the right place, I said.

We walked in silence towards Centraal Station where Chrissie would pick up the tram to where she stayed, just past the Ajax Stadium. I decided that the time was ripe to declare my intentions. I turned to her and said. — Chrissie, I'd like to spend the night with you.

She turned to me with her eyes half shut and her jaw jutting out. — I thought you might, she smugly replied. There was an incredible arrogance about her.

A dealer, positioned on a bridge over the Achterburg canal, caught us in his gaze. Displaying a keen sense of timing and market awareness he hissed, — Ecstasy for the sex. Chrissie raised an eyebrow and made to stall, but I steered her on. People say that Es are good for shagging, but I find that I only want to dance and hug on them. Besides, it had been so long that my gonads felt like space hoppers. The last thing I needed was an aphrodisiac. I didn't fancy Chrissie. I needed a fuck; it was as simple as that. Junk tends to impose a sexual moratorium and the post-smack sexual awakening nags at you uncompromisingly; an itch that just has to be scratched. I was sick of sitting wanking in Rab/Robbie's front room, the stale musty smell of my spunk mixing with the hashish fumes.

Chrissie shared an apartment with a tense, pretty girl called Margriet who bit her nails, chewed her lower lip and spoke in fast Dutch and slow English. We all talked for a bit, then Chrissie and I went through to the bed in her pastel-coloured room.

I began kissing and touching her, with Richard never far from my thoughts. I didn't want foreplay, I didn't want to *make love*, not to this woman. I wanted to fuck her. Now. The only reason I was feeling her up was for Richard; thinking that if I took my time and made a good job of this, it would give me a greater hold over her and therefore the opportunity to cause him much more discomfort.

— Fuck me . . . she murmured. I pulled up the duvet and winced involuntarily as I caught a glimpse of her vagina. It looked ugly; red and scarred. She was slightly embarrassed and sheepishly explained: — A girlfriend and I were playing some games . . . with beer bottles. It was just one of those things that got a bit out of hand. I'm so sore down there . . . she rubbed her crotch, — do it in my bottom, Euan, I like it that way. I've got the jelly here. She stretched over to the bedside locker, and fumbled in a drawer, pulling a jar of KY out. She began greasing my erect cock. — You don't mind putting it in my bum, do you? Let's love like animals, Euan . . . that's what we are, the Eurotrash, remember? She spun round and started to apply the jelly to her arse, beginning with the cleft between her buttocks, then working it right into her arsehole. When she'd finished I put my finger in to check for shite. Anal I don't mind, but I can't handle shite. It was clean though, and certainly prettier than her cunt. It would be a better fuck than that floppy, scarred mess. Dyke games. Fuck that. With Margriet? Surely not! Putting aesthetics aside, I had castration anxiety, visualising her fanny still being full of broken glass. I'd settle for her arse.

She'd obviously done this before, many times, there was so much give as I entered her arsehole. I grabbed her heavy buttocks in both hands as her repulsive body arched out in front of me. Thinking of Richard, I whispered at her, — I think you need to be protected from yourself. I thrust urgently and got a shock as I caught a glimpse of my face in a wall mirror, twisted, sneering, ugly. Rubbing her injured cunt ferociously, Chrissie came, her fat folds wobbling from side to side as I shunted my load into her rectum.

After the sex, I felt really revolted by her. It was an effort just to lie beside her. Nausea almost overwhelmed me. I tried to turn away from her at one point, but she wrapped her large flabby arms around me and pulled me to her breast. I lay there sweating coldly, full of tense self-loathing, crushed against her tits, which were surprisingly small for her build.

Over the weeks Chrissie and I continued to fuck, always in the same way. Richard's bitterness towards me increased in direct correlation to these sexual activities, for although I had agreed with Chrissie not to disclose our relationship to him, it was more or less an open secret. In any other circumstances I would have demanded clarification of the role of this sweetie-wife in our scene. However, I was already planning to extract myself from my relationship with Chrissie. To do this, I reasoned, it would be better if I kept Chrissie and Richard close. The strange thing about them was that they seemed to have no wider network of close friends; only casual acquaintances like Cyrus, the guy who played pinball in Richard's bar. With this in mind, the last thing I wanted to do was to alienate them from each other. If that happened, I'd never be shot of Chrissie without causing the unstable bitch a great deal of pain. Whatever her faults, she didn't need any more of that.

I didn't deceive Chrissie; this isn't merely a retrospective attempt at self-justification for what was to happen. I can say this with confidence as I clearly recall a conversation that we had in a coffee shop in Utrechtesstraat. Chrissie was being very presumptuous and starting to make plans about me moving in with her. This was glaringly inappropriate. I said overtly what I had been telling her covertly with my behaviour towards her, had she cared to take note of it.

— Don't expect anything from me, Chrissie. I can't give. It's nothing to do with you. It's me. I can't get involved. I can never be what you want me to be. I can be your friend. We can fuck. But don't ask me to give. I can't.

— Somebody must have hurt you really badly, she said shaking her head as she blew hashish smoke across the table. She was trying to convert her obvious hurt into feelings of pity for me, and she was failing miserably.

I remember that conversation in the coffee shop because it had the opposite effect to the one I'd wanted. She became even more intense towards me; I was now more of a challenge.

So that was the truth, but perhaps not the whole truth. I couldn't give *with Chrissie*. You can never put feelings where they're not. But things were changing for me. I was feeling physically and mentally stronger, more prepared to open myself up, ready to cast aside this impregnable cloak of bitterness. I just needed the right person to do it with.

I landed a job as a reception-clerk-cum-porter-cum-dogsbody in a small hotel in The Damrak. The hours were long and unsocial and I would sit watching television or reading at the reception, gently ssshhing the young drunk and stoned guests who flopped in at all hours. During the day I started to attend Dutch language classes.

To the relief of Rab/Robbie, I moved out of his place to a room in a beautiful apartment in a particularly narrow canal house in the Jordaan. The house was new; it had been totally rebuilt due to subsidence of the previous building into the weak, sandy Amsterdam soil, but it was built in the same traditional style of its neighbours. It was surprisingly affordable.

After I moved out, Rab/Robbie seemed more like his old self. He was more friendly and sociable towards me, he wanted me to go out drinking and smoking with him; to meet all the friends he'd vigilantly kept away from me, lest they might be corrupted by this junky. They were typical sixties time-warp Amsterdam types, who smoked a lot of hash and were shit-scared of what they called 'hard drugs'. Although I didn't have much time for them, it was good to get back onto an even footing with Rab/Robbie. One Saturday afternoon we were stoned in the Floyd cafe and we felt comfortable enough to put our cards on the table.

— It's good to see you settled, man, he said. — You were in a bad way when you came here.

— It was really good of you to put us up, Rab . . . Robbie, but you weren't the friendliest of hosts, it has to be said. You had some coupon on ye when you walked in at night.

He smiled. — I take your point, man. I suppose I made ye even more uptight than ye were. It just freaked me a bit, y'know? Workin like fuck aw day and ye come in and there's this wasted cunt whae's trying tae git oaf smack . . . ah mean I was thinkin, likes, what have I taken oan here, man?

— Aye, I suppose I did impose myself, and I was a bit of a leech.

— Naw, you wirnae really that bad, man, he conceded, all mellow. — Ah was far too uptight, likes. It's just, you know, man, I'm the sort of punter who needs my own personal space, y'know?

— I can understand that, man. I said, then, swallowing a lump of spacecake, smirked. — I dig the cosmic vibes you're sending out here, man.

Rab/Robbie smiled and toked hard on a spliff. The pollem was very mellow. — You know, man, ye really caught me out acting the arsehole. All that Robbie shit. Call me what you always called me, back in Scotland. Back up Tollcross. Rab. That's who ah am. That's who ah'll always be. Rab Doran. Tollcross Rebels. T.C.R. Some fuckin times back there, eh man?

They were pretty desperate times really, but home always looks better when you're away from it, and even more so through a haze of hash. I colluded in his fantasies and we reminisced over more joints before hitting some bars and getting rat-arsed on alcohol. .

Despite the rediscovery of our friendship, I spent very little time with Rab, due mainly to the shifts I was working. During the day, if I wasn't taking my language classes, I'd be swotting up, or getting my head down before my shift at the hotel. One of the people who lived in the flat was a woman named Valerie. She helped me with my Dutch, which was coming along in leaps and bounds. My phrasebook French, Spanish and German were also improving rapidly due to the number of tourists I was coming into contact with in the hotel. Valerie became a good friend to me; more importantly, she had a friend called Anna, with whom I fell in love.

It was a beautiful time for me. My cynicism evaporated and life started to seem like an adventure of limitless possibilities. Needless to say, I stopped seeing Chrissie and Richard and seldom went near the red-light district. They seemed a remnant of a seedier, more sordid time that I felt I had left behind. I didn't want or need to smear that gel on my cock and bury it in Chrissie's flabby arse anymore. I had a beautiful young girlfriend to make love to and that was what I did most of the day before staggering onto my late shift, strung out on sex.

Life was nothing short of idyllic for the rest of that summer. This state of affairs changed one day; a warm, clear day when Anna and I found ourselves on Dam Square. I tensed as I saw Chrissie coming towards us. She was wearing dark glasses and looked even more bloated than ever. She was cloyingly pleasant and insisted we went to Richard's bar in Warmoesstraat for a drink. Though edgy, I felt that a greater scene would have been caused by cold-shouldering her.

Richard was delighted I had a girlfriend that wasn't Chrissie. I had never seen him so open towards me. I felt a vague shame about my torturing of him. He talked of his home town of Utrecht.

— Who famous comes from Utrecht? I gently chided him.

— Oh, lots of people.

— Aye? Name one?

— Let me see, eh, Gerald Vanenberg.

— The PSV guy?

— Yes.

Chrissie looked at us in a hostile manner. — Who the fuck is Gerald Vanenburg? she snapped, then turned to Anna and looked at her with raised eyebrows as if Richard and I had said something ridiculous.

— A famous international footballer, Richard bleated. Trying to reduce the tension he added. — He used to go out with my sister.

— I bet you wish he used to go out with you, Chrissie said bitterly. There was an embarrassed silence before Richard set us up with more tequila slammers.

Chrissie had been making a fuss of Anna. She was stroking her bare arms, telling her that she was so slim and beautiful. Anna was probably embarrassed but was handling it well. I resented that fat dyke touching up my girlfriend. She became more hostile towards me as the drinks flowed, asking me how I was getting on, what I was up to. A challenging tone had entered her voice.

— Only we don't see him so much these days, do we, Richard?

— Leave it, Chrissie . . . Richard said uneasily.

Chrissie stroked Anna's peach cheek. Anna smiled back awkwardly.

— Does he fuck you like he fucks me? In your pretty little bottom? she asked.

I felt as if the flesh had been stripped from my bones. Anna's face contorted in discomfort, as she turned towards me.

— I think we'd better go, I said.

Chrissie threw a glass of beer over me and began verbally abusing me. Richard held her from behind the bar, otherwise she'd have struck me. — TAKE YOUR FUCKING LITTLE SLUT AND GO! A REAL WOMAN'S TOO MUCH FOR YOU, YOU FUCKING JUNKY VERMIN! HAVE YOU SHOWN HER YOUR ARMS YET?

— Chrissie . . . I said weakly.

— FUCK OFF! JUST FUCK OFF! BANG YOUR SILLY

LITTLE GIRL YOU FUCKING PAEDOPHILE! I'M A
REAL WOMAN, A REAL FUCKING WOMAN . . .

I ushered Anna out of the bar. Cyrus flashed his yellow teeth
at me and shrugged his broad shoulders. I looked back to see
Richard comforting Chrissie. — I'm a real woman, not a silly
little girl.

— You're a beautiful woman, Chrissie. The most beautiful, I
heard Richard say soothingly.

In a sense, it was a blessing. Anna and I went for a drink and I
told her the whole story of Chrissie and Richard, leaving
nothing out. I told her how fucked up and bitter I was, and
how, while I'd promised her nothing, I'd treated Chrissie fairly
shabbily. Anna understood, and we put the episode behind us.
As a result of that conversation I felt even better and more
uninhibited, my last little problem in Amsterdam seemingly
resolved.

It was strange, but as Chrissie was such a fuck-up, I half
thought of her a few days later when they said that the body of a
woman had been fished out of Oosterdok, by Centraal Station. I
quickly forgot about it, however. I was enjoying life, or trying
to, although circumstances were working against us. Anna had
just started college, studying fashion design, and with my shifts
at the hotel we were like ships in the night, so I was thinking of
chucking it and getting another job. I'd saved up quite a healthy
wad of guilders.

I was pondering this one afternoon, when I heard someone
banging at the door. It was Richard, and as I opened up he spat
in my face. I was too shocked to be angry. — Fucking murderer!
he sneered.

— What . . . I knew, but couldn't comprehend. A thousand
impulses flowed through my body, fusing me into immobility.

— Chrissie's dead.

— Oosterdok . . . it was Chrissie . . .

— Yes, it was Chrissie. I suppose you'll be happy now.

— NAW MAN . . . NAW! I protested.

— Liar! Fucking hypocrite! You treated her like shit. You and others like you. You were no good for her. Used her like an old rag then discarded her. Took advantage of her weakness, of her need to give. People like you always do.

— Naw! It wasn't like that, I pleaded, knowing full well it was exactly like that.

He stood and looked at me for a while. It was like he was looking beyond me, seeing something that wasn't apparent from my vantage point. I broke a silence which probably lasted only seconds, but seemed like minutes. — I want to go to the funeral, Richard.

— He smiled cruelly at me. — In Jersey? You won't go there.

— The Channel Islands . . . I said, hesitantly. I didn't know Chrissie was from there. — I will go, I told him. I was determined to go. I felt culpable enough. I had to go.

Richard examined me contemptuously, then started talking in a low, terse voice. — St Helier, Jersey. The home of Robert Le Marchand, Chrissie's father. It's next Tuesday. Her sister was here, making arrangements to take the body back.

— I want to go. Are you?

He scoffed at me. — No. She's dead. I wanted to help her when she was alive. He turned and walked away. I watched his back recede into nothingness, then went into the flat, shaking uncontrollably.

I had to get to St Helier by Tuesday. I'd find details of the Le Marchands' whereabouts when I got there. Anna wanted to come. I said I'd be a poor travelling companion, but she insisted. Accompanied by her, and a sense of guilt which seemed to seep into the body of the rented car, I drove along the highways of Europe, through Holland, Belgium and France to the small port of St Malo. I started thinking, about Chrissie, yes, but about other things, which I would generally never concern myself with. I started to think about the politics of European integration, whether it was a good or bad thing. I tried to marry up the politicians' vision with the paradox I saw in the miles of these ugly highways of Europe; absurd incompatibilities with an inexorable shared destiny. The politicians' vision seemed just another money-making scam or another crass power-trip. We ate up these dull roads before reaching St Malo. After checking into a cheap hotel Anna and I got roaring drunk. The next morning we boarded the ferry to Jersey.

We arrived Monday afternoon and found another hotel. There were no funeral notices in the *Jersey Evening Post*. I got a phonebook and looked up Le Marchand. There were six, but only one R. A man's voice came down the receiver.

— Hello.

— Hello. Could I speak to Mister Robert Le Marchand?

— Speaking.

— I'm really sorry to bother you at this time. We're friends of Chrissie's, over from Holland for the funeral. We understand that it's tomorrow. Would it be alright if we attended?

— From Holland? he repeated wearily.

— Yes. We're at Gardener's Hotel.

— Well, you have come a long way, he stated. His posh, bland, English accent grated. — The funeral's at ten. St Thomas's chapel, just around the corner from your hotel as a matter of fact.

— Thanks, I said, as the line clicked dead. *As a matter of fact . . .* It seemed as if everything was simply a matter of fact to Mr Le Marchand.

I felt totally drained. No doubt the man's coldness and hostility were due to assumptions made about Chrissie's friends in Amsterdam and the nature of her death; her body was full of barbituates when it was fished out of the dock, bloated further by the water.

At the funeral, I introduced myself to her mother and father. Her mother was a small, wizened woman, diminished even further by this tragedy into a brittle near-nothingness. Her father looked like a man who had a great deal of guilt to shed. I could detect his sense of failure and horror and it made me feel less guilty about my small, but decisive role in Chrissie's demise.

— I won't be a hypocrite, he said. — We didn't always like each other, but Christopher was my son, and I loved him.

I felt a lump in my chest. There was a buzzing in my ears and the air seemed to grow thin. I could not pick out any sound. I managed to nod, and excused myself, moving away from the cluster of mourners gathered around the graveside.

I stood shaking in confusion, past events cascading through my mind. Anna put her arm tightly around me, and the congregation must have thought I was grief-stricken. A woman approached us. She was a younger, slimmer, prettier version of Chrissie . . . Chris . . .

— You know, don't you?

I stood gaping into space.

—· Please don't say anything to Mum and Dad. Didn't Richard tell you?

I nodded blankly.

— It would kill Mum and Dad. They don't know about his change . . . I took the body home. I had them cut his hair and dress him in a suit. I bribed them to say nothing . . . it would only cause hurt. He wasn't a woman. He was my brother, you see? He was a man. That's how he was born, that's how he was buried. Anything else would only cause hurt to the people who are left to pick up the pieces. Don't you see that? she pleaded. — Chris was confused. A mess. A mess in here, she pointed to her head. — God I tried, we all tried. Mum and Dad could handle the drugs, even the homosexuality. It was all experiments with Christopher. Trying to find himself . . . you know how they are. She looked at me with an embarrassed contempt, — I mean that sort of person. She started to sob.

She was consumed with grief and anger. In such circumstances she needed the benefit of the doubt, though what were they covering up? What was the problem? What was wrong with reality? As an ex-junky I knew the answer to that. Often plenty was wrong with reality. Whose reality was it, anyway?

— It's okay, I said. She nodded appreciatively before joining the rest of her family. We didn't stick around. There was a ferry to catch.

When we got back to Amsterdam, I sought out Richard. He

was apologetic at having dropped me in it. — I misjudged you. Chris was confused. It was little to do with you. It was nasty to let you go without knowing the truth.

— Naw, I deserved it. Shite of the year, that was me, I said sadly.

Over some beers he told me Chrissie's story. The breakdowns, the decision to radically re-order her life and gender; spending a substantial inheritance on the treatment. She started off on a treatment of female hormones, both oestrogen and progesterone. These developed her breasts, softened her skin and reduced her bodily hair. Her muscular strength was diminished and the distribution of her subcutaneous fat was altered in a female direction. She had electrolysis to remove facial hair. This was followed by throat surgery on her voicebox, which resulted in the removal of the Adam's apple and a softening of the voice, when complemented by a course of speech therapy.

She went around like this for three years, before the most radical surgery, which was undertaken in four stages. These were penectomy, castration, plastic reconstruction and vaginoplasty, the formation of an artificial vagina, constructed by creating a cavity between the prostrate and the rectum. The vagina was formed from skin grafts from the thigh and lined with penile, and/or scrotal skin, which, Richard explained, made orgasmic sensation possible. The shape of the vagina was maintained by her wearing a mould for several weeks after the operation.

In Chrissie's case, the operations caused her great distress, and she therefore relied heavily on painkilling drugs which, given her history, was probably not the best thing. That, Richard reckoned, was the real key to her demise. He saw her walking out of his bar towards Dam Square. She bought some barbs, took them, was seen out of her box in a couple of bars before she wandered along by the canal. It could have been suicide or an accident, or perhaps that grey area in between.

Christopher and Richard had been lovers. He spoke affectionately of Christopher, glad now to be able to refer to him as Chris. He talked of all his obsessions, ambitions and dreams; all *their* obsessions, ambitions and dreams. They often got close to finding their niche; in Paris, Laguna Beach, Ibiza and Hamburg; they got close, but never quite close enough. Not Eurotrash, just people trying to get by.

STOKE NEWINGTON BLUES

I took my last shot in the toilet on the ferry, then made my way to the deck. It was amazing; spray in my face as squawking gulls chased the boat; a prolonged rush surging through my body. All hands on deck. I grip the rail and vomit acrid bile into the North Sea. A woman gives me a concerned glance. I respond with a smile of acknowledgement. — Struggling to find my sea legs, I shout, before retiring to the lounge to order a black coffee which I've no intention of drinking.

The crossing is okay. I'm mellow. I sit in silence, no doubt a blank corpse to all the other passengers, but engaged in a meaningful inner dialogue with myself. I replay recent history, casting myself in a virtuous role, justifying the minor atrocities I've inflicted on others as offering them important insight and knowledge.

I start to hurt on the boat train: Harwich — Colchester — Marks Tey — Kelvedon — Chelmsford — Shenfield THIS TRAIN SHOULD NOT STOP AT FUCKIN SHEN-FIELD — Romford EVERY INCH OF TRACK I WILL THIS TRAIN ON (What about Manningtree, where the fuck's Manningtree got to in all this?) TO LONDON Liverpool Street. The tube goes everywhere except Hackney. Too marshy. I alight at Bethnal Green and jump on the 253 to Lower Clapton Road. I shuffle down Homerton Road and into the Kingsmead Estate. I hope that Donovan is still squatting on the second floor. I hope that he isn't grudging about the Stockwell incident, water under the bridge by now, surely. I push past some harsh-faced domestic-pet-killing children who are aerosoling stylishly illegible slogans on the wall. So passé, so ghetto.

— Watch it! Fucking junky!

Should I fuck these children before, or after I kill them?

I do nothing of the kind. It's yon time.

Don's still there. That fortified door. Now I only have to worry about whether or not he's in, and if he is, whether or not he'll let me in. I rap heavily.

— Who is it? Angie's voice. Don and Ange. I'm not surprised; I always thought they'd end up getting it on.

— Open up, Ange, for fuck's sake. It's me, Euan.

A series of locks click open and Ange looks at me, her sharp features more prominent than ever, defined and sculpted by skag. She bades me enter and secures the door.

— Don aroond?

— Nah, gone out, ain't he.

— Any skag?

Her mouth turns downwards and her dark eyes hold me like those of a cat that's cornered a mouse. She contemplates a lie then, noting my desperation, decides against it.

— How was the 'Dam? She's toying with me, the fuckin cow.

— Ah need a shot, Ange.

She produces some gear and helps me cook up and take a shot. A rush shoots through me, followed by a rising tide of nausea. All hands on deck. I throw up on a *Daily Mirror*. Paul Gascoigne is on the front, winking and giving the thumbs up in traction and plaster cast. This paper is eight months old.

Ange prepares a shot for herself, using my works. I'm not too happy about this but I can't really say much. I look at her cold, fish eyes, cut into that crystalline flesh. You could lacerate yourself badly on her nose, cheekbones and jawline.

She sits beside me, but looks straight ahead instead of turning to face me. She starts to talk incessantly about her life in a slow, even monotone. I feel like a junky priest. She tells me that she was raped by a squad of guys and has felt so bad about it she's had a habit since then. I get a feeling of déjà vu here. I'm sure she's told me this before.

— It hurts, Euan. It fucking hurts inside. The gear's the only thing that takes the pain away. There's nuffink I can do about it. I'm dead inside. You won't be able to understand. No man can understand. They killed a part of me, Euan. The best part. Wot you see here's a fucking ghost. It don't matter much wot happens to a fucking ghost. She taps up a wire, jabs home and convulses appreciatively as the gear pumps into her circuit.

At least the rush shuts her up. There was something unsettling about her talking in that disembodied way. I look at the *Mirror*. Several flies are feasting on Gazza.

— The rapist punters. Get a squad the gither, get the cunts, I venture.

She turns towards me, shakes her head slowly, then turns back. — No, it don't work like that. Nobody is more connected than these guys. They're still doing it to women. One of them pulls at a club, brings the woman back. The rest are waiting and they just use her like a fucking hanky for as long as they want.

I suppose to get close to understanding how it feels you have to think of about a dozen guys giving it Clapham Junction up your arsehole.

— That's the last, she murmurs in wistful content. — I hope Don brings some back.

— You n me both, doll, you n me both.

It could have been hours or minutes, but Donovan did show.

— What the fuck are you doing here man? He set his hands on his hips and thrust out his neck at me.

— Good tae see you n aw, mate.

It looked as if Don's skin tone had been diluted by the smack. Michael Jackson probably paid millions to get the same effect Don has from junk. He was like a Jubilee that the ice had been sucked out of. Come to think of it, Ange had been more pink in the past. It seemed that if you took enough junk you would lose all racial characteristics completely. Junk really did make every other feature of a person irrelevant.

— You holdin? His accent changed from a high-pitched effeminate North London whine to a rich, heavy Jamaican dread.

— Like fuck. Ah'm here tae score.

Don turned to Ange. You could tell he hadn't scored and was about to hit the roof at her for giving the last to me. Just as he started to speak, there was a bang at the door and although it held firm, after another couple of thrashes the frame split from the wall and the whole thing tumbled inwards. Two guys stood in the doorway with sledgehammers. They looked so mental I was almost relieved when a group of pigs stormed in and swarmed all over us. I watched the expression of disappointment on the face of one seasoned DS fucker. He knew that had we been holding it would have been a race to the lavvy to flush the gear away, but none of us had moved. Nobody was holding. They ritually turned the place over. One cop picked up my works and looked sneeringly at me. I raised my eyebrows and smiled lazily at him. — Let's get this rubbish down the fucking station, he shouted. We were bundled out of the flat, down the stairs and into a meatwagon. There was a loud crash as a bottle hit the top of the van. It stopped and a couple of cops got out, but couldn't be bothered giving chase to the kids who probably threw it from the balcony. They crushed us between their bulk, muttering the occasionally dark threat.

I looked at Don sat opposite. The car whizzed past the Lower Clapton Road cop shop, then past Dalston station. We were going to Stoke Newington. A name station. The name on my mind and almost certainly on Don's was Earl Barratt.

At the station they asked me to turn out my pockets. I did, but dropped a set of keys on the floor. I bent to pick them up and my scarf trailed on the ground. A cop stood on it, just pinning me there helpless, bent double, unable to lift my head up.

— Get up! another one snapped.

— You're standing on my scarf.

— Get your fucking sick junky arse up ere!

— I cannae fuckin move, yir standin oan ma scarf!

— I'll give you fucking scarves, you Jock cunt. He booted or punched me in the side and I toppled over onto the floor, collapsing like a deckchair. It was more from the shock rather than the force of the blow.

— Get up! Get fucking up!

I staggered to my feet, blood soaring to my head, and was pushed into an interview room. My brain felt hazy as they barked some questions at me. I manage to mumble some weak replies before they threw me in the drunk tank. It was a large white-tiled room with perimeter benches and an assortment of foam and vinyl mattresses on the floor. The place was full of piss-heads, petty criminals and cannabis dealers. I recognised a couple of black guys from the Line, at Sandringham Road. I tried not to make eye contact. The dealers up there hate smack-heads. They get hassled by the racists pigs for skag when all they deal in is blow.

Fortunately their attention is diverted from me as two heavily-built white guys, one with a strong Irish accent, begin booting fuck out of a one-eared transvestite. When they feel they've done enough they start pissing on his prostrate figure.

I seem to be there for an age; getting sicker and sicker and more and more desperate. Then Don gets flung in, sick and hurting. The polis who bundles him into the tank can see that the one-eared boy on the deck has been well fucked over, but he just shakes his head contemptuously and bolts the door. Don sits beside me on the bench, his face in his hands. At first I notice blood on his hands, but then I see that it is coming from his nose and mouth which are quite badly swollen. He'd obviously slipped on something and fallen down a flight of stairs. This tended to happen in Stokie police station to black punters. Like Earl Barratt. Don is shivering. I decide to speak.

— Tell ye, man, ah'm a wee bitty disappointed wi the criminal justice system of this country, at least as locally administered here in Stokie.

He turned towards me, showing the full extent of his kicking. It was quite healthy. — I ain't coming out of here man, he trembled, his eyes wide with fear. He was serious. — You heard about Barratt. This place is known for it. I'm the wrong fucking colour, especially for a guy with a habit. I ain't comin out alive.

I was about to try and calm him, but it seemed that he wasn't far off the mark. Three black guys came over to us. They'd been watching and listening.

— Hey brother, you hang around with this trash, you get what comes around to you, one guy scoffed. We were on a kicking. The guys started on about skag and dealers, working themselves up to unleash their fury on us. The kicking the whites had given the one-eared transvestite had obviously whetted their appetite.

It was cops to the rescue. As they grabbed us and crudely pushed us along, I thought about the frying pan and the fire. We were taken back into separate interview rooms. There were no chairs in the room so I sat on a table. I was made to wait for a long time.

I sprang up as two pigs came in and joined me. They brought in some chairs. A silver-haired but still fresh-faced pig told me to sit down. — Who gave you the stuff? C'mon, Jock. Euan, isn't it? You ain't a dealer. Who's knocking this gear out? he asked, his eyes filled with lazy tired compassion. He looked like a sound guy.

THEY'VE GOT FUCK ALL ON ME.

Another cop, stocky, bull-like and dark-haired with a kind of pudding-basin haircut snapped, — His fucking nigger friend. Old jungle-juice boy through there, innit, Jock? Well, you had better speak up, my son, cause we got the world's first black canary chirping away twenty to the dozen next door, and you would not, believe me, not like the song he is singing.

They kept this up for a while, but they couldn't get to the place in my head I'd crawled into.

Then one of them pulled out a bag of white powder. It looked good gear.

— Little kiddies over in the school been using this gear. Who's been giving it to em, Euan? Silver Dream boy asks.

THEY'VE GOT FUCK ALL ON ME.

— Ah jist use now and again. Ah've no goat enough for masel, nivir mind any cunt else.

— I can see we'll have to get a fucking interpreter in ere. Any cunt on duty tonight speak Jock? the black-haired cunt asks. Silver Dream Machine ignores him. He carries on. — That's the thing about you fucking scumbags. You all fucking use, don't you? Nobody sells it. It just grows on fucking trees, dunnit?

— Naw, fields, I said, regretting it instantly.

— What did you fucking say? he rose, knuckles white on the table.

— Poppy fields. Opium. Grows in fields, I mumbled.

His hand goes around my neck and he squeezes. He keeps squeezing. It's like I'm watching some other cunt being choked to death. Both my hands grab his arm, but I can't break his grip. Silver does. — Leave it, George. That's enough. Get your breath back, son. My head pounds remorselessly and I feel as if my lungs will never fill up to full capacity again.

— We know the score, son; we've prepared a statement for you to sign. Now I don't want you signing something you're not happy about. Take your time. Look at it. Read it. Digest it. As I said, take your time. Anything you want to change, we can change, he cooed soothingly.

The dark guy dropped the hostility from his tone. — Give us the wog, son, and you can walk right out of here with this. The best pharmaceutical gear, eh Fred? He waved the skag tantalisingly in front of me.

— So they tell me, George. C'mon, Euan, make it easy on yourself. You seem a decent enough sort, underneath it all. You're in way over your head here, sunshine.

— Jocks, Englishmen, don't matter none, does it? We're all white men. Do time for some bleeding Congo? Wise up, Jock. One more fucking shit-skin gets banged up, wot's he to you, eh? Ain't exactly a shortage of em, is there?

The Met. The cunts with the white shirts. They did over Drew, down from Monktonhall to Orgreave for the '84 strike.

Now they wanted Donovan. Wrong skin colour. They're fitting up the daft cunt as Mister Big. This statement reads like Agatha Christie. Don and I have crossed swords but he's alright. In fact he's more of a brother than I've ever had. But what was he saying about me? Solidarity, or was he talking me down the river? This fucking statement reads like Agatha Christie. What about Ange? She's probably blabbed to every cunt to save her skin. I'm starting to hurt, really bad. If I sign up, get the skag, I can fix myself up. Tell the story of how they got the confession to the papers. THEY'VE GOT FUCK ALL ON ME. Hurt. Poison Don. TOUGH IT OOT hurt skag GIVE ME THE FUCKIN PEN they'll pit Don away, pit him away fir fuck all Agatha fuckin Christie GIVE ME THE FUCKIN PEN.

— Give me the pen.

— Knew you'd see sense, Jock.

I stuck the packet of powder, my thirty pieces of silver, in my tail. They ripped up the charge sheet.

I was free to go. When I got to the reception, Ange was sitting there. I knew that she'd sold out as well. She looked at me bitterly.

— Right, you two, a desk cop said. — On your way, and keep out of trouble. The two cops who'd interrogated me were standing behind him. I was glad to leave. Ange was so eager she walked into the plate-glass door just as the cop told us to watch out for it. There was a sickening smack as the glass and her head connected. She seemed to reel back on the balls of her feet, vibrating, like a cartoon character. I laughed through nerves, joining the guffaws of the cops.

— Stupid fucking slag, the dark cop sneered.

Ange was in some distress when I got her out into the air. Tears were streaming down her face. An egg was forming on her forehead. — You fucking grassed him up, didn't ya? DIDN'T YA? Her eyeliner was running. She looked like Alice Cooper.

It was a lame performance though. — You didnae, then?

Her silence spoke volumes, then she wearily conceded.

— Yeah, well, had to for the time being, didn't we? Mean to say, I just had to get out. I had it really bad in there.

— Ken what ye mean, I agreed. — We'll git it sorted oot later. See a lawyer. Tell the cunt we made the statements under duress. Don'll walk oot laughin. Even git compensation. Aye, git sorted, then clean up, straighten oot n see a lawyer. A spell in remand'll dae Don good in the long run. Git him cleaned up. He'll fucking thank us fir it!

I knew, even as I spoke, that it was all pie in the sky. I'd vanish; leave Don to whatever fate befell him. It just made me feel better to go through this scenario.

— Yeah, get him cleaned up, Ange agreed.

Outside the station there was a group of demonstrators. It seemed like they had been on an all-night vigil. They were protesting about the treatment of young blacks by the local Old Bill, and particularly about Earl Barratt, a guy who went into the Stokie nick one night and came back out stiffed in a placky bag. Slippy fuckers, those stairs.

I recognised a guy from the black press, *The Voice*, and made up to him. — Listen, mate, they've got a black guy in there. They've really done him over. They forced us tae sign statements.

— What's his name? the guy asked, a posh English-African voice.

— Donovan Prescott.

— The guy from the Kingsmead? The smack head?

I stood looking at him as his face hardened.

— He didn't do nothing wrong, Ange pleaded.

I pointed at him, projecting my anger at myself out towards him. — Fuckin publish and be damned, ya cunt! Doesnae matter what he is, he's goat as much right as any other fucker!

— What's your name, mon, a sidekick asked.

— What's that tae dae wi anything?

— Come down the office. Get your picture taken, the African guy smiled. He knew there was no way. I'd say nothing to nae cunt; the polis would make it open season on me.

— Dae what yis fuckin like, I said, turning away.

A large woman came up to me and started shouting: — They holdin good Christian boys in there. Leroy Ducane and Orit Campbell. Boys that never done no wrong. That's the boys we're talking about here, not some dirty drug devil.

A tall rasta with John Lennon specs waved a placard threateningly in my face. It read:

ANDS OFF DE BLACK YUTE

I turned to Ange and slid, trembling, away from the scene, a few jeers and threats ringing in my ears. I thought we were being followed for a bit. We walked off in silence and didn't speak until Dalston Kingsland Station. Paranoia City.

— Where you off ta? Ange asked.

— Ah'm gittin the overland, the North London line tae this mate Albie's in Kentish Town. Ah'm gaunny git sorted wi this pig gear, then it's down to the Bush. Civilised there, ye ken? I've fuckin had it wi Hackney, it's worse than back up the road. Too fuckin parochial. Too many self-righteous nosey cunts. Isolated, that's its problem. Nae tube. No enough social contact wi the rest ay the Smoke. A fuckin urban backwater.

I was ranting. Sick and ranting.

— I gotta come with ya. The flat's fucked. It'll be torched by now. The pigs wouldn't bother to secure the door.

I didn't want Ange in tow; she had the bad luck virus really bad. Bad luck is usually transmitted by close proximity to habitual sufferers. There was little I could do or say, however, as the train pulled up and we boarded it, sitting opposite each other in crushed, sick silence.

As the train started I stole a glance at her. I hope she didn't expect me to sleep with her. I'm not into sex right now. Maybe Albie would, if she wanted it. It was a disturbing thought, but only because all thought on matters external to me was disturbing. I'd soon be free from it all though; free from its niggling persistence, I thought, fingering the packet in my trouser pocket.

VAT '96

Fiona had been hassling Valerie to get us to come for a meal at her and Keith's for an indecently long period of time. We'd let things slide, the way people do, but eventually we got embarrassed making excuses and it seemed less hassle to actually set a date and go round to their place one evening.

We found Fiona in high spirits. She'd gained a promotion in her job which was in corporate insurance, selling policies to big businesses. Selling policies at that level was ninety percent public relations, which, in turn, as any candid PR person will tell you, is ninety-five percent hospitality and five percent information. The problem with Fiona was, like many career-minded people, she couldn't switch off her occupational role and could therefore be a crushing bore.

— Come in! Wonderful to see you! Gosh! Gorgeous outfit, Val! Where did you get it? Crawford, you're putting on the beef. It suits you though. Has he been doing weights, Val? *Have* you been doing weights, Crawford? You're looking great, both of you! I'm going to get some drinks. Vodka and tonic for you, Val, sit down, sit down, I want to hear all your adventures, everything, gosh, have I got some things to tell you . . . I suppose you want a Jack Daniels, Crawford?

— Eh, a can of beer would do fine.

— Oh, beer. Oh. Sorry. Gosh. We're all out of beer. Oh God. Crawford and his beer!

After making a fuss, she ticked me off for the cardinal sin of asking for a beer. I settled for a Jack Daniels, which Fiona had got in *especially* for me.

— Oh Val, gosh, I must tell you about this amazing guy I met . . . Fiona began, before noticing our surprise and discomfort.

We didn't really have to say: Where's Keith? as our eyes must have done the talking for us.

— Gosh, I don't quite know how to put this. Some rather bad news on the Keithy-weithy-woo's front, I'm afraid. She crossed the spacious room and lifted the cover from a glass tank which stood against the wall. She clicked on a light at the side of the tank and said, — Wakey, wakey, Valerie and Crawford are here!

At first I thought it was a fish tank, that Keith had just shot the craw, and that Fiona, devastated, had transferred her emotional energy onto pets in the form of some tropical fish. With the benefit of retrospect, it was always an unlikely notion.

Then I noted that the tank had a head inside it. A human head, disembodied, decapitated. Moreover, the head seemed alive. I moved closer. The eyes in the head were moving. The hair was spread around it, Medusa-like, made weightless by the watery, yellow fluid it was immersed in. Various pipes, tubes and wires were going into the head, mainly at the neck, but also at other points. Under the tank was a control console, with various dials, switches and lights.

— Keith . . . I stammered.

The head winked at me.

— Don't expect much in the way of conversation, Fiona said. She looked down at the tank, — Poor darling. He can't speak. No lungs, you see. She kissed the tank, then fussed at the smudge of lipstick she'd left.

— What happened to him? Valerie took one step forward and two steps back.

— This machine keeps him alive. Wonderful, isn't it? It cost us four hundred and thirty-two thousand pounds. She mouthed the figure with a slow, conspirital deliberation and feigned shock. — I know, I know, she continued, — you're wondering how we can afford it.

— Actually, I said icily, — we were wondering what happened to Keith.

— Oh gosh yes, so sorry! It must be a hell of a shock to you. Keith was tearing down the M25 towards Guildford when the Porsche left the road. Tyre blow-out. Apparently, the car bounced across a couple of lanes, over the crush-barrier and straight into the on-coming traffic. So there's a head-on with this huge artic; the Porsche was a complete write-off, as you'd expect. Keith was almost finished; well in a sense he was. Poor Keithyweithy-woo's. She looked down at the tank, appearing slightly strained and sad for the first time.

— The health-care company man said to me: In a sense, your husband is dead. His body has been smashed to pieces. Most of his major organs are useless. However, his head and brain are still intact. We have a new machine which has been developed in Germany and pioneered in the States. We'd like your consent to give Keith treatment. It's very costly, but we can do a deal on the life insurance because he's technically dead. It's a difficult question, the health-care man said, and we'll leave the ethics of it to the philosophers. After all, that's why we pay our taxes to have them sit and deliberate in their ivory towers. That was what he said. I rather liked that. Anyway, he told me that their legal people still had a few i's to dot and t's to cross, but they were confident of, as he put it, getting a result. Do we have your consent, he asked me. Well, gosh, what could I say?

I looked at Val, then down at Keith. There wasn't much to say. Perhaps some day, with the advances in medical science, they'd find a body with a useless damaged head and be able to do a transplant. There's no shortage of them; I was thinking of various politicians. I assumed that finding a healthy body to attach the head to was the reason for this sordid and bizarre exercise. I didn't really want to know.

We sat down to the meal. Fiona might have said the evening was a success, like a work-based task or a project which had to be completed. There were one or two minor blunders, like when I refused a glass of wine.

— I'm driving, Fiona. I'd better screw the nut . . . I looked at what was left of Keith in the tank and mouthed an apology. His eyes flickered.

While Fiona was darting around, in and out of the kitchen, Valerie bade her to sit down and relax. She almost told her she was running around like a headless chicken, but managed to change it to blue-arsed fly.

However, the evening was not too excruciating and the meal was edible. We made small talk for the rest of the night. As we got ready to go I meekly and self-consciously gave Keith the thumbs up sign. He winked again.

Valerie whispered to Fiona in the hallway, — One thing you didn't tell us, who's this super new man?

— Oh gosh . . . it's so strange how things work out. He's the chap from the health-care company who suggested the treatment for Keith. Gosh, Val, he's such a ram. The other day he just grabbed me, threw me down on the couch and had me right there and then . . . She put her hand to her mouth and looked at me. — Oh gosh! I'm not embarrassing you, Crawford, am I?

— Yes, I lied, unconvincingly.

— Good! she said cheerfully, then swept us back into the room. — One last thing I need your advice on: do you think that Keithy-kins would look better on the other side of the room, next to the CD unit?

Val gazed nervously at me.

— Yes, I began, noting that the couch was presently positioned directly opposite Keith's tank, — I think he definitely would.

A SOFT TOUCH

It wis good fir a while wi Katriona, but she did wrong by me. And that's no jist something ye can forget; no jist like that. She came in the other day, intae the pub, while ah was oan the bandit likes. It was the first time ah'd seen her in yonks.

— Still playing the bandit, John, she sais, in that radge, nasal sortay voice she's goat.

Ah wis gaunny say something like, naw, ah'm fuckin well swimming at the Commie Pool, but ah jist goes: — Aye, looks like it.

— No goat the money to get ays a drink, John? she asked ays. Katriona looked bloated: mair bloated than ever. Maybe she wis pregnant again. She liked being up the stick, liked the fuss people made. Bairns she had nae time fir but she liked being up the stick. Thing wis, every time she wis, people made less ay a thing about it than they did the time before. It goat boring; besides, people kent what she wis like.

— You in the family wey again, ah asked, concentrating oan getting a nudge oan the bandit. A set ay grapes. That'll dae me.

Gamble.

Collect.

Hit collect.

Tokens. Eywis fuckin tokens. Ah thought Colin sais tae ays that the new machine peyed cash.

— Is it that obvious, Johnny? she goes, lifting up her checked blouse and pulling her leggings ower a mound ay gut. Ah thought ay her tits and arse then. Ah didnae look at them likes, didnae stare or nowt like that; ah jist thought ay them. Katriona had a great pair ay tits and a nice big arse. That's what ah like in a bird. Tits and arse.

— Ah'm oan the table, ah sais, moving past her, ower tae the pool. The boy fae Crawford's bakeries had beat Bri Ramage. Must be a no bad player. Ah goat the baws oot and racked up. The boy fae Crawford's seemed awright.

— How's Chantel? Katriona goes.

— Awright, ah sais. She should go doon tae ma Ma's and see the bairn. No that she'd be welcome thair mind you. It's her bairn though, and that must count fir something. Mind you, ah should go n aw. It's ma bairn n aw, but ah love that bairn. Everybody kens that. A mother though, a mother that abandons her bairn, that's no bothered aboot her bairn; that's no a mother, no a real mother. No tae me. That's a fucking slag, a slut, that's what that is. A common person as ma Ma says.

Ah wonder whae's bairn she's cairrying now. Probably Larry's. Ah hope so. It would serve the cunts right; the baith ay them. It's the bairn ah feels sorry for but. She'll leave that bairn like she left Chantel; like she left the two other bairns she's hud. Two other bairns ah nivir even kent aboot until ah saw them at oor weddin reception.

Aye, ma Ma wis right aboot her. She's common, Ma said. And no jist because she wis a Doyle. It wis her drinking; no like a lassie, Ma thought. Mind you, ah liked that. At first ah liked it, until ah got peyed oaf and the hirey's wir short. That wis me toiling. Then the bairn came. That wis when her drinking goat tae be a total pain; a total fuckin pain in the erse.

She eywis laughed at ays behind ma back. Ah'd catch sight ay her twisted smile when she thought ah wisnae looking. This wis usually when she wis wi her sisters. The three ay them would laugh when ah played the bandit or the pool. Ah'd feel them looking at me. After a while, they stopped kidding that they wirnae daein it.

Ah nivir coped well wi the bairn; ah mean as a really wee bairn like. It seemed to take everything over; aw that noise fae that wee size. So ah suppose ah went oot a lot eftir the bairn came. Maybe a bit ay it wis my fault; ah'm no saying otherwise. There wis things gaun oan wi her though. Like the time ah gied her that money.

She wis skint so ah gies her twenty notes and sais: You go oot doll, enjoy yirself. Go oot wi yir mates. Ah mind that night fine well because she goes n gits made up like a tart. Make-up, tons ay it, and that dress she wore. Ah asked her where she wis gaun dressed like that. She just stood thair, smiling at me. Where, ah sais. You wanted ays tae go out, so ah'm fuckin well gaun oot, she telt ays. Where but? ah asked. Ah mean, ah wis entitled tae ken. She just ignored ays but, ignored ays and left, laughing in ma face like a fuckin hyena.

When she came back she wis covered in love bites. Ah checked her purse when she wis oan the toilet daein a long, drunken pish. Forty quid she had in it. Ah gave her twenty quid and she came back wi forty fuckin bar in her purse. Ah wis fuckin demented. Ah goes, whit's this, eh? She just laughed at ays. Ah wanted tae check her fanny; tae see if ah could tell that she'd been shagged. She started screaming and saying that if ah touched her, her brothers would be roond. They're radge, the Doyles, every fucker in the scheme kens that. Ah'm radge, if the truth be telt, ever getting involved wi a Doyle. Yir a soft touch son, ma Ma once said. These people, they see that in ye. They ken yir a worker, they ken yir easy meat fir thum.

Funny thing was, a Doyle can dae what they like, but ah thought that if ah goat in wi the Doyles then ah could dae what ah liked. And ah could fir a bit. Nae cunt messed wi ays, ah wis well in. Then the tapping started; the bumming ay fags, drinks, cash. Then they had ays, or that cunt Alec Doyle, he had ays looking eftir stuff fir um. Drugs. No hash or nowt like that; wir talking aboot smack here.

Ah could've gone doon. Done time; fuckin years ah could have done. Fuckin years for the Doyles and thir hoor ay a sister. Anywey, ah never messed wi the Doyles. Never ever. So ah didnae touch Katriona that night and we slept in different rooms; me oan the couch, likes.

It wis jist eftir that ah started knocking aroond wi Larry upstairs. His wife had just left um and he wis lonely. For me it wis, likesay, insurance: Larry wis a nutter, one ay the few guys living in the scheme even the Doyles gied a bit ay respect tae.

Ah wis working oan the Employment Training. Painting. Ah wis daein the painting in the Sheltered Hooses fir the auld folks, like. Ah wis oot maist ay the time. Thing is when ah came back in ah'd either find Larry in oor place or her up at his. Half-fuckin-bevvied aw the time; the baith ay thum. Ah kent he wis shagging her. Then she started tae stey up thair some nights. Then she jist moved upstairs wi him aw the gither; leaving me doonstairs wi the bairn. That meant ah hud tae pack in the painting; fir the bairn's sake, like, ken?

When ah took the bairn doon tae ma Ma's or tae the shops in the go-cart, ah'd sometimes see the two ay thum at the windae. They'd be laughing at ays. One day ah gits back tae the hoose and it's been broken intae; the telly and video are away. Ah kent whae had taken thum, but thir wis nothing ah could dae. No against Larry and the Doyles.

Their noise kept me and the bairn awake. Her ain bairn. The noise ay them shagging, arguing, partying.

Then one time thir wis a knock at the door. It wis Larry. He jist pushed past ays intae the flat, blethering away in that excited, quick wey he goes on. Alright mate, he sais. Listen, ah need a wee favour. Fuckin electric cunts have only gone and cut ays off, eh.

He goes ower tae ma front windae and opens it and pulls in this plug that's swingin doon fae his front room above. He takes it and plugs it intae one ay ma sockets. That's me sorted oot, he smiles at ays. Eh, ah goes. He tells ays that he's got an extension cable wi a block upstairs but he jist needs access tae a power point. Ah tell him that he's ootay order, it's ma electric he's using and ah goes ower tae switch it oaf. He goes: See if you ivir touch that fuckin plug or that switch, you're fuckin deid, Johnny! Ah'm fuckin telling ye! He means it n aw.

Larry then starts telling ays that he still regards me and him as mates, in spite ay everything. He sais tae ays that we'll go halfers oan the bills, which ah knew then wouldnae happen. Ah sais that his bills would be higher than mine because ah've no got anything left in the hoose that uses electricity. Ah wis thinking aboot ma video and telly which ah kent he had up the stair. He goes: What's that supposed tae mean then, Johnny? Ah just goes: Nowt. He says: It better fuckin no mean nowt. Ah sais nowt eftir that because Larry's crazy; a total radge.

Then his face changed and he sortay broke intae this smile. He nodded up at the ceiling: No bad ride, eh John? Sorry tae huv tae move in thair, mate. One ay these things though, eh? Ah jist nodded. Gies a barry gam though, he sais. I felt like shite. Ma electricity. Ma woman.

Ever fucked it up the erse? he asked. Ah jist shrugged. He crosses one ay his airms ower the other one. Ah've started giein it the message that wey, he said, jist cause ah dinnae want it up the stick. Bairn daft, that cunt. Once ye git a cunt up the stick, they think thuv goat thir hand in yir poakit fir the rest ay yir puff. Yir dough's no yir ain. Isnae ma fuckin scene, ah kin tell ye. Ah'll keep ma money. Tell ye one thing, Johnny, he laughed, ah hope you've no goat AIDS or nowt like that, cause if ye huv ye'd've gied it tae me by now. Ah never use a rubber when ah shaft her up the stairs thair. No way. Ah'd rather have a fuckin wank man.

Naw, ah've no goat nowt like that, ah telt him, wishing for the first time in ma life that ah did.

Just as well, ya dirty wee cunt, Larry laughed.

Then he stretched intae the playpen and patted Chantel on the heid. Ah started tae feel sick. If he tried tae touch that bairn again, ah'd've stabbed the cunt; disnae matter whae he is. Ah jist wouldnae care. It's awright, he goes, ah'm no gaunny take yir bairn away. She wants it mind, and ah suppose that a bairn belongs wi its Ma. Thing is, John, like ah sais, ah'm no intae huving a bairn aroond the house. So yuv goat me to thank fir still huvin the bairn, think aboot it like that. He went aw upset and angry and pointed tae hisel. Think aboot it that wey before ye start making accusations aboot other people. Then he goes cheery again; this cunt can jist change like that, and sais: See that draw for the quarter-finals? The winners ay St Johnstone v. Kilmarnock. At Easter Road, likes, he smiles at ays, then twists his face aroond the room. Fuckin pit this, he sais, before turning tae go. Just as he's at the front door he stops and turns tae me. One other thing, John, if ye want a poke at it again, he points at the ceiling, jist gies a shout. A tenner tae you. Gen up, likes.

Ah mind ay aw that, cause just after it ah took the bairn tae ma Ma's. That wis that; Ma goat ontae the Social Work; goat things sorted oot. They went and saw her; she didnae want tae ken. Ah goat a kicking fir that, fae Alec and Mikey Doyle. Ah goat another yin, a bad yin, fae Larry and Mikey Doyle when ma electric wis cut oaf. They grabbed ays in the stair and dragged ays through the back. They goat ays doon and started kicking ays. Ah wis worried cause ah hud a bit ay money ah'd won fae the bandit. Ah wis shitein it in case they'd go through ma poakits. Fifteen quid ah hud taken the bandit fir. They just booted intae ays but. Booted ays and she wis screamin: KICK THE CUNT! KILL THE CUNT! OOR FUCKIN ELEC-TRIC! IT WIS OOR FUCKIN ELECTRICITY! HE'S GOAT MA FUCKIN BAIRN! HIS FUCKIN AULD HOOR AY A MOTHER'S GOAT MA FUCKIN BAIRN! GO BACK TAE YIR FUCKIN MA! LICK YIR MA'S FUCKIN PISS-FLAPS YA CUNT!

Thank fuck they left ays withoot checking ma poakits. Ah thoat; well, that's seekened they cunts' pusses anywey, as ah staggered tae ma Ma's tae git cleaned up. Ma nose wis broken and ah hud two cracked ribs. Ah hud tae go tae the A and E at the Infirmary. Ma sais that ah should nivir huv goat involved wi Katriona Doyle. That's easy tae say now but, ah telt her, but see if ah hudnae, jist sayin like, jist supposin ah hudnae; we would nivir huv hud Chantel, like. Yuv goat tae think aboot it that wey. Aye, right enough, ma Ma said, she's a wee princess.

The thing wis thit some cunt in the stair hud called the polis. Ah wis thinking that it could mean criminal injuries compensation money fir me. Ah gied them a false description ay two guys thit looked nowt like Larry n Mikey. But then the polis talked like they thought ah wis the criminal, that ah wis the cunt in the wrong. Me, wi a face like a piece ay bad fruit, two cracked ribs and a broken nose.

Her and Larry moved away fae upstairs eftir that and ah just thought: good riddance tae bad rubbish. Ah think the council evicted them fir arrears; rehoosed them in another scheme. The bairn wis better oaf at ma Ma's and ah goat a job, a proper job, no just oan some training scheme. It wis in a supermarket; stackin shelves and checking stock levels, that kind ay thing. No a bad wee number: bags ay overtime. The money wisnae brilliant but it kept ays oot ay the pub, ken wi the long hours, like.

Things are gaun awright. Ah've been shaggin one or two burds lately. There's this lassie fae the supermarket, she's mairried, but she's no wi the guy. She's awright, a clean lassie, like. Then there's the wee burds fae roond the scheme, some ay them are jist at the school. A couple ay thum come up at dinnertime if ah'm oan backshift. Once ye git tae ken one, yir well in. They aw come roond; just fir somewhere tae muck aboot cause thirs nowt fir thum tae dae. Ye might git a feel or a gam. Like ah sais, one or two, especially that wee Wendy, thir game fir a poke. Nae wey dae ah want tae git involved again aw heavy like but.

As fir her, well, this is the first ah've seen ay her fir ages.

— How's Larry? ah ask, gaun doon tae connect wi a partially covered stripe. One guy's squinting his eye and saying that's no oan. The Crawford's bakery boy goes: — Hi you! Admiral Fuckin Nelson thair! Let the boy play his ain game. Nae coaching fae the touchline!

— Oh him, she goes as the cue clips the stripe and heads towards the boatum cushion. — He's gaun back inside. Ah'm back at ma Ma's.

Ah jist looked at her.

— He found oot that ah wis pregnant and he jist fucked off, she sais. — He's been steying wi some fucking slut, she goes. Ah felt like saying, ah fuckin well ken that, ah'm staring her in the fuckin face.

But ah says nowt.

Then her voice goes aw that high, funny way, like it eywis goes when she wants something. — Why don't we go oot fir a drink the night, Johnny? Up the toon likes? We wir good, Johnny, good the gither you n me. Everybody said, mind? Mind we used tae go tae the Bull and Bush up Lothian Road, Johnny?

— Ah suppose so, ah sais. Thing wis, ah supposed ah still loved her; ah suppose ah never really stoaped. Ah liked gaun up the Bull and Bush. Ah wis always a bit lucky oan the bandit up there. It's probably a new one now though; but still.

THE LAST RESORT
ON THE ADRIATIC

I never supposed for the love of me that it would all be so vivid;
it makes what I plan to do feel just right. I mean, I almost expect
to see Joan on the boat, to just sort of run into her on deck, in
the dining-room, or the bar, or even the casino. When I get to
thinking about her in that way, my heart races and I feel giddy
and generally have to retire to the cabin. When I turn the key I
even think that I might find her there, perhaps in bed, reading.
It's ridiculous I know, the whole thing, just blessed ridiculous.

I've been on this liner now for two weeks; two lonely weeks.
The sight of people having fun can be so hurtful, so offensive,
when you feel like I do. All I do is wander around the ship; as if
I'm looking for something. That and the weights, of course.
Surely I don't expect to see Joan here; surely not? I can't settle. I
can't lie on the deck with Harold Robbins or Dick Francis or
Desmond Bagley. I can't sit at the bar and get drunk. I can't
engage in any of these trivial conversations which take place
concerning the weather or the itinerary. I've walked out of two
movies in the cinema. *Dead Again*, with that British chap playing the American detective. Terrible film. There was another
one with that American fellow, the white-haired chap who used
to be funny but isn't anymore. Perhaps that's just me: a lot of
thing aren't funny anymore.

I go to my cabin and prepare my sports bag for another
excursion to the gym. The only blessed place I've any interest in
going to.

— You must be the fittest man on this ship, the instructor says to me. I just smile. I don't want to make conversation with this fellow. Funny fellow, if you know what I mean. Nothing against them myself, live and let live and all that, but I don't want to talk to anyone right now, let alone some blessed nancy boy.

— Never out of this place, he persists, giving a quick nod to a fat, puffing red-faced man on an exercise bike, — are you Mister Banks?

— Excellent facilities, I reply curtly, surveying the free weights and picking up two hand dumb-bells.

Thankfully the instructor chappie has noticed an overweight lady in a scarlet leotard attempting to do sit-ups. — No no no Mrs Coxton! Not like that! You're putting too much of a strain on your back. Sit further up and bend those knees. Forty-five degrees. Lovely. And one . . . and two . . .

I take a couple of weights from the dumb-bell and surreptitiously stick them into my sports bag. I go through the motions, but I don't need exercise. I'm fit enough. Joan always said that I had a good body; wiry, she used to say. That's what a lifetime in the building trade, combined with sober habits does for you. I have to concede that there is a bit of a paunch, as I've let myself go since Joan. Seemed no point. I drink more now than I've ever done, since the retirement. Well, I was never one for the golf.

Back in my cabin I lie down and drift off into that realm between thought and sleep, thinking of Joan. She was such a wonderful and decent woman, all you could hope for in a wife and mother.

Why Joan? Why, my darling, why? These could have been the best years of our life. Paul's at university, Sally's living in the nurses' home. They finally left the nest, Joan. We would have had it all to ourselves. The way they coped though, Joan, they were a credit to you, both of them. A credit to us. Me? Well I died with you, Joanie. I'm just a blessed ghost.

I'm not asleep. I'm awake and talking to myself and crying. Ten years after Joan.

At dinner I'm alone at the table with Marianne Howells. The Kennedys, Nick and Patsy, a very nice outgoing young couple, have not shown up for the meal. It's a deliberate ploy. Patsy Kennedy has a conspiratorial eye. Marianne and I are alone for the first time on the cruise. Marianne: unmarried, here to get away from her own bereavement, the recent death of her widowed mother.

— So I'm to have you all to myself, Jim, she said, in a manner far too jocular and self-deprecating to be flirtatious. There is no doubt, though, that Marianne is a fine-looking woman. Someone ought to have married a woman like that. A waste. No, that's a dreadful way to think. Old chauvinistic Jim Banks at it again. Perhaps that's the way Marianne wanted it, perhaps she got the best from life that way. Perhaps if Joanie and I hadn't . . . No. The seafood, the seafood.

— Yes, I smile, — this seafood salad is excellent. Still, if you can't get good seafood at sea, where can you get it, eh?

Marianne grins and we small-talk for a bit. Then she says, — It's a tragedy about Yugoslavia.

I'm wondering whether she means because we can't land there because of the troubles, or because of the misery the troubles have inflicted on people. I decide to plump for the compassionate interpretation. Marianne seems a caring sort. — Yes, terrible suffering. Dubrovnik was one of the highlights of the trip when I was here with Joan.

— Oh yes, your wife . . . what happened to her, if you don't mind me asking?

— Eh, an accident. If it's all the same to you, I'd rather not talk about it, I said, shoving a forkful of that lettuce into my mouth. I'm sure it's a garnish rather than there to be eaten, something to do with where it's positioned on the plate. I was never one for etiquette. Joanie, you'd have kept me right.

— I'm really sorry, Jim, she says.

I smile. The accident. On this boat, on this cruise. An accident? No.

She'd been down for a while. Depressed. The change in life,

or who can say what? I don't know why. That's the most horrible thing about it, I don't know why. I thought that the cruise would do her the world of good. It even seemed to, for a while. Just as we got towards the end of the Adriatic, on the way back into the Med, she took the pills and just slipped off the side of the boat into the night. Into the sea. I woke up alone; I've been alone ever since. It was my fault, Joan, the whole blessed thing. If I'd tried to understand how you felt. If I hadn't booked this bloody cruise. That's stupid old bloody idiot Jim Banks. Take the easy way out. I should have sat you down and talked, talked, and talked again. We could have sorted it all out, Joan.

I feel a hand on mine. Marianne's. There's tears in my eyes, like I'm some damned funny fella.

— I've upset you, Jim. I'm really so sorry.

— No, not at all, I smile.

— I really understand, you know I do. Mother . . . she was so difficult, she says. Now she's starting the waterworks. What a blessed pair we are. — I did all I could. I had my chances to make a different life for myself. I didn't really know what I wanted. A woman always has to choose, Jim, choose between marriage and children and a career. Always at some point. I don't know. Mother was always there, always needing. She won by default. The career girl became the old maid, you see.

She seemed so hurt and upset. My hand stiffened on hers. The way she looks at the floor and her head suddenly rises as her eyes meet mine: it reminds me of Joan.

— Don't sell yourself short, I tell her. — You're an exceptionally brave lady and a very beautiful one.

She smiles, more composed now, — You're a real gent, Jim Banks, and you say the nicest things.

All I can do is smile back.

I was enjoying being with Marianne. It had been a long time since I'd been like this with a woman. Since I'd had that intimacy. We talked all night. No subjects were taboo and I was able to talk about Joan without seeming maudlin and bringing the company down, as would have happened had the Kennedys been present. People don't want to listen to all that on holiday. However, Marianne, with her bereavement, could relate to it.

I talked and I talked, nonsense mostly, but to me beautiful, painful memories. I'd never talked like this to anyone before. — I remember on the boat with Joanie. I got into a terrible situation. There were some Dutch folk, lovely people, at the table next to us. We shared a table with a rather stand-offish French chap and a lovely Italian girl. Real film-star looks. Strangely, the French chap wasn't interested. I think he may have been, well, that way, if you know what I mean. Anyway, this was a proper old League of Nations. The thing was that we had this elderly couple from Worcester who did not like Germans one bit, thinking back to the war years and all that stuff. Well, I feel that those things are best left in the past. So old Jim Banks here decided to play the peacemaker . . .

God, how I rabbitted on. My inhibitions seemed to dissolve with every sip of the wine, and we were soon on the second bottle, Marianne nodding conspiratorially at me as I ordered it. After the meal we proceeded to the bar where we had a few more drinks.

— I've really enjoyed myself tonight, Jim. I just wanted to tell you that, she said, smiling.

— It's been one of the best nights I've had . . . in years, I told her. I was almost going to say, since Joanie. It has though. This wonderful lady has made me feel blessed human again. She really is a fine person.

She held my hand as we sat looking into each other's eyes for a few seconds.

I cleared my throat with a sip of scotch. — One of the great things about getting older, Marianne, is that the impending presence of the grim reaper concentrates the mind somewhat. I'm very attracted to you Marianne, and please don't be offended by this, but I'd like to spend the night with you.

— I'm not offended, Jim. I think that would be marvellous, she glowed.

This made me a little coy. — Might be somewhat less than marvellous. I'm a little bit out of practice for this sort of thing.

— They say it's a little like swimming or riding a bike, she simpered, a little drunk.

Well, if that was the case, Old Jim Banks was about to get back in the saddle after a gap of ten years. We went to her room.

Despite the alcohol, I had no problem in getting an erection. Marianne pulled off her dress to expose a body that would have done justice to some women many decades, never mind years, younger. We embraced for a little while, before slipping under the duvet and making love, first slowly and tenderly, then with increasing passion. I was lost in it. Her nails scored the flesh on my back and I was screaming, — By God Joanie, by God . . .

She froze like a stiff corpse underneath me, and punched the mattress in frustration as tears bubbled up from her eyes. I moved off her. — I'm sorry, I half moaned, half sobbed.

She sat up and shrugged, staring into space. She spoke in a dulled, metallic tone, but without bitterness, as if conducting a cool and dispassionate epitaph. — I find a man I care about and when he makes love to me he's imagining I'm somebody else.

— It wasn't like that, Marianne . . .

She started sobbing; I put my arm around her. Well, Jim Banks, I thought, you've got yourself into another right blessed muddle-up here, haven't you?

— I'm sorry, she said.

I started to pull my clothes on. — I'd better go, I said. I walked towards the door, then turned back. — You're a wonderful woman, Marianne. I hope you find someone who can give you what you deserve. Old Banksie here, I pointed sadly at myself, — I'm just kidding myself. I'm a one-woman man. I exited, leaving her with her tears. I now had my business to attend to. There was to be no reprieve after all. I knew it was for the best; I knew it now more than ever. The kids, Paul and Sally, were strong enough. They'd understand.

Back at my cabin I left Marianne a note. I'd left letters for the kids in the ship's mail with a videotaped recording, explaining what I intended to do. The note to Marianne didn't say much. I just told her that I was here for a specific purpose; I was sorry we'd got so involved. I had to fulfil my destiny, that was how I saw it.

According to the maps I consulted we were in the Adriatic now, no doubt about it. I tied the length of cord through the holes in the middle of the weights, and slung it over my shoulder. It was difficult to get the stretchy tracksuit bottoms over the weights and the rest of my clothes on. I fought into my waterproofs, barely able to walk by the time I left my cabin.

I slipped along the empty deck, struggling to remain erect. The sea was calm and the night balmy. A couple of lovers enjoying the moonlight looked suspiciously at me as I shuffled past them to my spot on the starboard side. Ten years, almost to the day, Joan, when you slipped out and away from me, away from the pain and hurt. I lift one leg, with an almighty effort, over the barrier. I'll just get my blessed breath back, take one last long look at the purple sky, then allow my weight to shift and I'll spill from this rail into the Adriatic.

SEXUAL DISASTER QUARTET

A GOOD SON

He was a good son, and like all good sons, he really loved his mother. In fact, he completely worshipped the woman.

Yet he couldn't make love to her; not with his father sitting there, watching them.

He got out of bed and threw a dressing-gown around his self-conscious nakedness. As he passed his father on his way out of the room, he heard the old man say: Aye Oedipus, yir a complex fucker right enough.

THE CRUEL BASTARD AND THE SELFISH FUCKER
GET IT ON

She was a cruel bastard; he was a selfish fucker. They literally bumped into each other one night in a Grassmarket pub. They were vaguely acquainted from somewhere neither could remember. Or at least that was what they told themselves and each other.

She was highly insulting, but he didn't mind as he was indifferent to everything except the eighty shilling he was tipping down his throat. They decided to go back to her place for a shag. He didn't have a place of his own; as his parents did everything for him, he saw little point in getting one.

Sitting up in bed, she watched him undressing. Her face hardened in a contemptuous scowl as he removed his purple boxer-shorts. — Who dae ye expect tae satisfy wi that? she asked.

— Masel, he said, getting into bed beside her.

After the event, she bitterly disparaged his performance with a vitriol which would have torn the fragile sexual ego of most men to shreds. He scarcely heard a word she said. His final thoughts as he drifted into a drunken sleep were concerned with breakfast. He hoped she had plenty of provisions in and that she made a good fry-up.

Within a few weeks they were living together. People say it seems to be working out.

LOTS OF LAUGHTER AND SEX

You said, when we embarked on this great adventure together, that lots of laughter was essential in a relationship.

I agreed.

You also made the point that a great deal of sex was of equal importance.

Again, I agreed. Wholeheartedly.

In fact I remember your exact words: laughter and sex are the barometers of a relationship. This was the statement you made, if I remember correctly.

Don't get me wrong. I couldn't agree more. But no at the same time, ya fuckin cow.

ROBERT K. LAIRD: A SEXUAL HISTORY

Rab's nivir hud a ride in ehs puff; perr wee cunt. Disnae seem too bothered, mind you.

SNUFF

The television screen flickered luminously in the darkness as the credits at the end of the movie came up. Not long to go now, Ian Smith noted, as he reached across to his dog-eared copy of *Halliwell's Film Guide*. With a yellow fluorescent pen, he highlighted the boldly-typed entry: *Goodfellas*. In small capital letters he wrote in the margin:

8. BRILLIANT, ANOTHER MESMERISING PERFORMANCE FROM DE NIRO. SCORSESE THE UNDISPUTED MASTER OF HIS GENRE.

He then removed the video cassette and inserted another, *Mad Max Beyond Thunderdome*. Fast-forwarding it past the trailers, he scrutinised the grimly serious face of the Radio One disc jockey who described the certification of the film. Finding the appropriate entry in this most up-to-date but already well-worn copy of *Halliwell's*, Smith was tempted to highlight it now, prior to viewing the film. He resisted this impulse, reasoning that you had to actually watch the movie first. There were so many things that could happen to stop you. You could be disturbed by the phone or a knock at the door. The video could malfunction and chew up the tape. You could be struck down by a massive cardiac arrest. Such happenings were, he considered, equally unlikely for him, nonetheless he held to his superstition.

They called him the Video Kid in the office where he worked, but only behind his back. He had no real friends and had the sort of personality which defied familiarity. It was not that he was unpleasant or aggressive, far from it. Ian Smith, the

Video Kid, was just extremely self-contained. Although he had worked with the Council's Planning Department for four years, most of his colleagues knew little about him. He did not social-ise with them, and the extent of his self-disclosure was extremely limited. As Smith was not interested in his workma-tes, they reciprocated, not being concerned enough about this unobtrusive person to detect a hint of enigma in his silence.

Every evening, Smith rented between two and four video-tapes at the shop he passed on the way home from work. The actual number rented depended on what was on television, and as a subscriber to satellite he had a lot of options. Additionally, he enjoyed membership of several specialist video clubs, which catered for old, rare, foreign, arthouse and pornographic films which were unobtainable from the shops but listed in *Halliwell's*. His dinner-break was usually spent making up a schedule of forthcoming viewings, which, once compiled, was never devi-ated from.

While Ian Smith occasionally watched a few soaps and a bit of football on Sky Sport, this was usually just filling in time if there was nothing satisfactory on offer on Sky's Movie Channel, in the video shop, or arriving through the post. He always kept the most recent *Halliwell's Film Guide*, religiously crossing off every film he had seen with a yellow highlighter pen, also giving it his own rating on an advancing scale of 0–10. Additionally, he kept a notebook to list any offerings too new to find their way into the 'bible'. Every time a new edition of *Halliwell's* came out, Smith would have to transfer the highlighted ticks across to the new text and throw the old one away. He often felt compelled to spend his lunch hours on this mundane undertaking. There were now very few films left unhighlighted.

As a broader concept, beyond the daily routine of work, viewing and sleep; time became insignificant for Smith. The weeks and months which flew by could not be delineated by changes or events in his life. He had almost complete control over the narrow process he imposed upon his existence.

Sometimes, however, Smith would become disengaged from

the film and he would be forced to contemplate this life of his. This happened during *Mad Max Beyond Thunderdome*. The film was a disappointment. The first two Max efforts were a couple of low-budget cult classics. The sequel was an attempt to give Max the Hollywood treatment. It struggled to hold Smith's attention, the span of which always decreased as the night wore on. But it had to be watched; it was another mark-off in his book and there were not many left now. Tonight he was tired. Though anything but a reflective person, when Smith was tired, thoughts he normally repressed could spill into the realm of conscious cerebral activity.

His wife had left him almost a year ago. Smith sat in his armchair, trying to allow himself to feel the loss, the pain, yet somehow he couldn't. He could feel nothing, only a vague uncomfortable guilt at having no feelings. He thought of her face, of having sex with her, and he aroused himself and managed to come through minimal masturbation, but he could feel nothing else beyond the resultant reduction in tension. His wife seemed not to exist beyond a transient image in his mind, indistinguishable from the ones he relieved himself to in the more pornographic films he rented. He had never achieved climax as easily when he had actually been with her.

Ian Smith forced his attention back to the film. Something in his mind always seemed to shut down a line of thought before it could cause him discomfort; a form of psychic quality control.

Smith did not like to talk about his hobby at work; after all, he did not really like to talk. One day in the office, however, Mike Flynn caught him compulsively highlighting his *Halliwell's*, and made a comment which Smith didn't quite catch, but he did pick up the derisive laughter from his colleagues. Stirred, he found himself, somewhat to his surprise, rabbitting uncharacteristically, almost uncontrollably, about his passion and the extent of it.

— You must like videos, Yvonne Lumsden said, raising her eyebrows suggestively.

— Always liked films, Smith shrugged.

— Tell me, Ian, Mike asked him, — what will you do when you've seen all the films listed? What happens after you've marked off the lot?

These words hit Smith hard in the chest. He couldn't think straight. His heart pounded.

What happens after you've marked off the lot?

Julie had left him because she found him boring. She went to hitchhike around Europe with a promiscuous friend whom Smith mildly resented as a contributory factor in the break-up of his marriage. The only consolation was Julie's praise for his sexual prowess. While he had always found it difficult to come with someone, she had climax after climax, often in spite of herself. Afterwards, Julie would feel inadequate, worrying at her inability to give her husband that ultimate pleasure. Insecurity defeated rationality and forced her to look inwards; she did not consider the simple truth that the man she had married was an aberration in terms of male sexuality. — Wasn't it good for you? she'd ask him.

— Great, Smith would reply, trying, and invariably failing, to project passion through his indifference. Then he'd say: — Well, it's time for lights out.

Julie hated the words 'lights out' more than any other ones which came from his lips. They made her almost physically sick. Smith would click off the bedside lamp and fall into an instant deep sleep. She would wonder why she stuck with him. The answer lay within her throbbing sex and her exhausted body; he was hung like a horse and he could fuck all night.

That wasn't enough though. One day Julie casually walked into the sitting-room where Smith was preparing to view a video, and said: — Ian, I'm leaving you. We're incompatible. I don't mean sexually, the problem isn't in bed. In fact you've given me more orgasms than any of the other . . . I mean what I'm trying to say is, you're good in bed, but useless everywhere else. There's no excitement in our lives, we never talk . . . I mean . . . oh, what's the use? I mean to say, you couldn't change, even if you wanted to.

Smith calmly replied: — Are you sure you've thought this one out? It's a big step to take.

All the while, the prospect of being able to install that satellite dish his wife had resisted gnawed excitingly at the back of his mind.

He waited until a decent period had passed, then, convinced that she was not returning, had the dish fitted.

Smith's social life had not exactly been hectic prior to Julie's departure and the purchase of the satellite dish. After these events, however, the minimal and token social ties he had with the outside world were severed. Apart from going to work he became a recluse. He stopped visiting his parents on Sundays. They were relieved, weary at attempting to force conversation, jumpy in the embarrassed silences to which Smith seemed oblivious. His infrequent visits to the local pub also ceased. His brother Pete and his best friend Dave Carter (or at any rate the best man at his wedding) didn't really notice his absence. One local said: — Never see what's his name in here these days.

— Aye, said Dave. — Don't know what he's up to.

— Pimping, protection racketeering, contract killings, probably, Pete laughed sardonically.

In the tenement block where Smith lived, the Marshal children would be screaming, fraying their distraught and isolated mother's nerves further. Peter and Melody Syme would be screwing with all the passion of a couple just back from honeymoon. Old Mrs McArthur would be making tea or fussing over her orange and white cat. Jimmy Quinn next door would have some mates round and they would be smoking hash. Ian Smith would be watching videos.

At work, one particular newspaper story was bothering people. A six-year-old girl named Amanda Heatley had been snatched from the pavement into a car a few yards from her school.

— What sort of animal does that? Mike Flynn asked, in a state of indignant rage. — If ah could git ma hands oan the bastard . . . he let his voice tail off menacingly.

— He obviously needs help, Yvonne Lumsden said.

— Ah'd gie um help. A bullet through his skull.

They argued from their polarised positions, one focusing on the fate of the kidnapped girl, the other on the motivations of the kidnapper. At an impasse, they turned to an uncomfortable looking Smith in appeal.

— What do you think, Ian? Yvonne asked.

— Dunno. Just hope they find the kid unharmed.

Yvonne thought that Ian Smith's tone indicated that he didn't hold out much hope of that.

It was shortly after this discussion that Smith decided to ask Yvonne out. She said no. He was neither surprised nor disappointed. In fact, he only asked her out because he felt that it was something he should do, rather than something he wanted to. An invitation to a cousin's wedding had come through the post. Smith felt that he should attend with a partner. As usual, he went home to a weekend of videos. He resolved that he would decline the invitation, and cite illness as an excuse. There was a bug doing the rounds.

That Saturday evening, his brother Pete came up to see him. Smith heard the bell but chose to ignore it. He could not be bothered freezing the action on *Point Break* as it was at a key scene where undercover FBI agent Keanu Reeves was about to be befriended by surfer Patrick Swayze and they were going to join forces against some formidable-looking adversaries. The next evening, the bell went again. Smith ignored it, immersed as he was in *Blue Velvet*.

A note dropped through the door, which was not discovered by Smith until Monday morning, when he was ready to leave for work. It told him that his mother had had a stroke and was seriously ill. He phoned Pete up.

— How's Mum? he asked, guilty at not being able to instil more concern into his tone.

— She died last night, Pete's flat, hollow voice told him.

— Aw . . . right . . . Smith said, then put down the phone. He didn't know what else to say.

In the year since he got satellite television, Ian Smith had gained three stones in weight, just by sitting in the armchair and munching biscuits, chocolate bars, ice-creams, fish suppers, pizzas, Chinese takeaways, and convenience snacks from the microwave. He had even started to take the odd day off work on the sick so that he could watch videos in the morning and afternoon. However, on the morning he learned of his mother's death, he went into work.

There was a soft ache in his chest at the funeral; a contrast to the shell-shocked grief of his brother and the disbelieving hysteria displayed by his older sister. Smith's pain was at its most acute when he thought of the love she'd given him as a child. However, images from films kept interspersing with those memories, anaesthetising the pain. Try as he might, Smith was unable to sustain these reflections to an extent that their poignancy might hurt him. As soon as the opportunity presented itself, he sloped off from the funeral and headed home via two video rental shops, his chest pounding and mouth salivating in anticipation of being able to tick off another couple of entries from *Halliwell's*. He was getting closer.

Over the days that followed, he took advantage of his bereavement by using the special leave to watch more videos. He hardly slept, staying up all night and most of the day. On occasion, he took amphetamine, scored from his neighbour Jimmy Quinn, in order to keep him awake. His mind was not at its customary ease, however; images of Julie seemed to be sandwiched between his every conscious thought. He never thought of his mother; it was as if she had never existed. Eventually he came to inhabit a zone which embraced conscious thought, dreams and the passive viewing of the television screen, but where the boundaries between these states could not be easily discerned.

It became too much, even for Ian Smith. Barring work, his only forays outside his flat had been quick visits to the video shops and the supermarket. One evening he switched off the video and went for a walk by the Water of Leith, unsettled and unable to concentrate on his evening's viewing. A row of cherry blossoms by the landscaped bank of the stagnant river gave off a pleasing aroma. Smith strolled along as the twilight began to give way to darkness. His steps disturbed a group of youths in hooded tops who dropped their voices and sneaked furtive then brazenly threatening looks at him. Smith, blind to them in his thoughts, strode on. He passed the wheezing alcoholics on the benches, whose dislocated growls snapped at demons remembered or imagined; the empty cans of superlager; the broken glass; the used condoms and the dog shite. A hundred yards away an old stone bridge arched darkly across the still, rancid waters.

Someone stood on the bridge. Smith increased his stride, observing her figure as it came into focus. Approaching her, he stood for a moment watching her smoke a cigarette. Her sallow face buckled inwards as she inhaled powerfully. It gave him the strange impression that the tobacco was the consumer and she was the depreciating product: with every puff she was being used up. On reflection, he considered, that impression was spot on.

— Ye lookin fir a date? she asked him, without any charm in her voice.

— Eh, aye, ah suppose, Smith shrugged. He really didn't know.

Her eyes travelled down his body and she quickly coughed out a short list of terms and conditions. Smith nodded in the same vague acquiescence. They walked silently back to his flat, taking a narrow road bounded by disused warehouses on one side and a large stone wall on the other. A car trundled slowly over the cobblestones, pulling up at the solitary figure of another woman, who, after a short conversation, disappeared into it.

At Smith's flat they went straight to the bedroom and undressed. The stale stench of her breath did not stop him from kissing her. She never brushed her teeth because she hated men kissing her. They could do anything except that. Kissing was the only thing which prevented her from forgetting what she was doing, which made her confront its hideous reality. Smith, however, had no intention of kissing her.

He mounted her thin body, at first uncomfortable on her jagged bonyness. Her expression was frozen; her eyes clouded by opiates or apathy. Smith saw his own countenance reflected in hers. He forced himself through her dryness in short jabs, the both of them gritting their teeth in pain and concentrating until her juices began to flow. Smith found a rhythm and pumped mechanically, all the time wondering why he was doing this. She moved with him, bored and grudging. The minutes passed; Smith implacably maintained his activity. After a certain length of time had elapsed, Smith knew he would never come. His penis seemed to grow harder but at the same time experience a growing numbness. Expressions of shock, then denial, then disbelief came over the woman as a demanding ache in her body forced her reluctant mind into step with it, joining it in the chase for the climax.

After she came, fighting to maintain her silence, he stopped, still hard and erect. He withdrew, and made his way to his jacket pocket where he extracted some notes and paid her. She felt confused, and vulnerable; a failure in the only thing she had ever been able to do successfully. She got dressed and left full of shame, unable to make eye contact.

— Cheers then, Smith said, as she exited into the stair.

— Prick. Fuckin prick, she hissed back at him.

As far as he was concerned there was nothing more to say.

A few days after this incident, a far more significant event took place. Smith came into the office whistling. This constituted an extrovert performance by his normal standards of behaviour and was picked up on by his workmates.

— You're looking pleased with yourself, Ian, Mike Flynn observed.

— Just bought a new video camera, Smith stated, then added, with unbecoming smugness, — state of the art.

— Christ, there'll be nae stopping ye now, Ian eh? Hollywood here we come! Tell you what, we'll get Yvonne here to star in a porno movie. You direct, I'll produce.

Yvonne Lumsden looked bitterly at them. She had recently rejected clumsy, drunken advances from Mike on a night out, and was concerned that they might be colluding against her, nasty in rejection, reverting to adolescence, like some men tended to do.

Mike turned to Smith and said: — No, we'd better keep Yvonne out of it. We want it to be a box-office success, after all. She threw a pencil eraser at him, which bounced off his forehead, causing him more alarm than he let on. Alistair, the thin, anaemic supervisor looked over with a tetchy expression designed to register his disapproval of this horseplay. He liked things to be what he constantly referred to as 'ordered'.

— Alistair can be the leading man, Mike whispered, but Smith's expression had returned to its normal state: a study in detachment.

That evening Smith took the bus home as it was raining heavily. Scanning the evening paper he noted that eighteen-year-old Paul McCallum was in the Royal Infirmary intensive-care unit, fighting for his life after being the victim of an apparently motiveless attack in the city centre yesterday evening. I hope the boy makes it, Smith thought. He reflected that human life has to be sacred, it has to be the most important thing in the world. There was still no news of Amanda Heatley, the kidnapped child. Smith went to his flat, tried out the camera, then watched another video.

The video is hard to get into. Smith's mind wanders. He tries to make himself feel hurt, forces himself to think about Julie. Did he love her? He thinks so. He can't be sure, because whenever that rising feeling in his chest starts, something seems to just shut it off.

The next day Smith notes that there is nothing about the guy Paul McCallum in the paper. He doesn't know whether this is good or bad. What is no news? He opens *Halliwell's* and trembles with excitement. The book has been completed. Every film listed has been viewed and reviewed. The words that Mike Flynn had spoken at the office came back to haunt him: *What do you do when you've marked off the lot?* The highlighter pen cruises over the title: *Three Men and a Little Lady*. He briefly thinks of Amanda Heatley. One man and a little lady. Real life was often less sentimental than Hollywood. Then something hits Smith. He realises that out of all the entries, this one, the last one, is the only one he has ever ranked zero. He writes in the margin:

0. SICKENING YANK SCHMALTZ, A SEQUEL EVEN MORE NAUSEATING THAN THE ORIGINAL.

Then he wonders: surely there must have been a worse film than that. He checks the entry on the Marty Robbins produced, directed, written, starred-in and soundtracked effort *El Paso*, but no, that got one point. He checks out some of the British films, because if the British know how to do one thing, it is how to make terrible films, but even *Sammy and Rosie Get Laid* scored two points. It's time, he decides. He stands up and puts another videotape in the machine. He stares at the screen.

The video Smith is watching shows a man climbing a set of stepladders with diligence, but at the same time looking straight into the camera. His eyes are full of fear, staring out at Smith. Smith feels and mirrors his fear and gazes straight back at the screen. Still staring out, the man reaches for a rope tied like a noose, which is secured to decorative but sturdy, parallel pine beams which run across the ceiling. He puts the noose round his neck, tightens it and kicks away the stepladders. Smith feels himself being pulled into the air and experiences a disorientation as the room swings and jerks and he feels a weight crashing around his neck, choking him. He spins around in the air and catches a glimpse of the figure on the screen; kicking, swinging, dying. Smith tries to scream CUT! but he cannot make a sound. He thinks that human life is important, always sacred. He thinks this, but his arms cannot reach up to the beams to take his weight nor can they free the tightening band from around his neck. He asphyxiates; his head hangs to one side and piss streams down the inside of his leg.

The camera is positioned above the TV screen; its cold, mechanical eye dispassionately observing everything. The apparatus is set up on RECORD. It keeps running as the body hangs limp, turning gently towards a complete stillness. Then the tape runs out without saying THE END, but that is what it is.

A BLOCKAGE IN THE SYSTEM

Knoxie wis hoverin in the doorway; ehs face set in that kind ay expression thit cries out fir our attention, whin eh kens thit every cunt'll ignore um until eh speaks. Then will git some bullshit about how eh'd telt Manderson tae stick ehs fuckin joab up ehs erse whin the truth is thit the cunt's shat ehs fuckin keks again.

— That cunt Manderson, eh wheezed.

— Trouble at mill? ah asked, no lookin up fae ma cairds. This wis a shite hand. Ah turned tae gie ma foreman ma undivided attention, as a conscientious employee. A null n void declaration by Knoxie here wid suit ays doon tae a fuckin tee, the shite ah'm hudin.

— Wuv goat tae jildy. Thir's fuckin chaos doon at the flats.

— Hud oan the now, Lozy sais nervously. Obviously this wide-o's goat the maist tae lose.

Pickin up ehs anxiety, Calum flings ehs hand in. Ah follay suit.

— Duty calls, Calum laughs.

— Fuck sakes, ah'm oan a fuckin straight run here, ya cunts! Lozy whinges.

— Tough titty then, cuntybaws. Yir peyed good money by the council, that's the fuckin poll-tax peyer tae you, tae dae a joab ay work, no tae sit oan yir erse playing fuckin cairds aw day, Calum smirked.

— That's right, Knoxie said. — It's a pure bastard ay a joab n aw, boys. Thir's a blockage doon at Anstruther Court again. An auld boy oan the first flair goes through tae ehs lavvy fir a wash n shave. Aw they cunts oan the flairs above uv been shitein oot thir weekend curry n lager this mornin; one ay they near simultaneous flushin joabs. Aw the shite faws doon, n remember wir talking twinty storeys it Anstruther Court, hits the fuckin blockage n comes back up it the first available space. Yis ken whair that wis.

Wi collectively screwed up oor eyes and sucked in smoky air through puckered lips.

— Aw the shite came ootay the auld boy's pan wi such force thit it hit the fuckin roof. We've goatay sort this oot.

Lozy wisnae too chuffed. — Sounds like it's the drains ootside the flats tae me. Mair like a joab fir the Region, no us.

— Dinnae gies that shite! Call yirsels tradesmen? Tell ye one thing, if we dinnae fuckin shape up, will aw be doon the fuckin road. Ye ken how much money the DLO's losin?

— Ah bit that's no the point, Knoxie. We're oan the council now, no workin fir a private contractor. Thir's a nae redundancy policy.

— Wir under fuckin compulsory competitive tendrin. If we cannae git oor act the gither wir fucked. Simple as that. That's the governmint, that's the fuckin law. It disnae matter a fuck whit some fuckin toss in the Labour Party thit gits ehsel voted oantay the council sais. Wi dinnae dae the business, wi dinnae win contracts. Wi dinnae win contracts, thir's nae Direct Labour Organisation. Endy fuckin story.

— Naw it's no endy story, Lozy continued, — because the union boy wis sayin . . .

— That's jist some cunt thit gits made rep because nae other fucker wants the job. These cunts talk through thir fuckin erses. C'moan! Lit's move it.

Ah jist shrugged, — Well, as one anarchist plumber sais tae the other: smash the cistern.

We jumped intae the van. Knoxie's been deid nippy since eh came back fae that Supervision Part Two course up the City Chambers. They seemed tae fuck the cunt's heid up thair. Eftir Part One, eh wis aw sweetness n light tae us. Wisnae Knoxie.

Made us right fuckin suspicious. Ah goat a deek ay the notes they gave the cunt. Went oan aboot the motivation ay staff in an action-centred leadership framework. Sais thit it's no the supervisor's joab tae dae the work, it's the supervisor's joab tae make sure thit the work gits done. It sais thit the supervisor gits the joab done by meetin the individual and group needs ay the team. So we pilled Knoxie up aboot this. Calum sais thit eh needed tae score some Es fir this rave eh wis gaun tae; Lozy sais thit eh needed tae spend some time in a massage parlour. As a group wi needed an all-day bevvy session in the *Blue Blazer*. Could Knoxie arrange aw that? The cunt wisnae chuffed. Eh sais that wisnae whit it wis aboot n thit wi shouldnae be lookin it ehs notes unless wid been oan the course.

Anywey, it didnae last. It wis soon back tae the same auld Knoxie. So we wir quite lookin forward tae gittin the cunt oot the road fir a couple ay days, whin they pit um oantay Part Two. Ah dinnae ken whit they did tae the fucker this time bit; whitivir it wis it made um even mair ay a Nazi. Now the the radge jist willnae listen tae reason. N Lozy's right. The blockage is bound tae be in the fuckin drain. We've no goat the tools tae go doon thair, even it if wis oor joab.

Doon at the flats it's really fuckin boggin. Thir's a polisman standin aroond like a spare prick. This housin officer boy n this social worker lassie uv goat the perr auld cunt oan the couch wi some forms, tryin tae git um sorted oot. The environmental health boys ur doon here n aw. Thir wis nae wey ah wis gaun intae that bathroom.

Calum goes tae ays, — Wir talkin aboot an ootside joab here. Defo.

Knoxie overheard n goat aw fuckin stroppy. — Eh? eh goes.

— Likesay, jist sayin thit the blockage'll be doon in the drains, ken, no the stink pipe. Probably the bend, likes.

— That would seem logical, ah sais in ma Spock-oot-ay-*Star Trek* voice.

— Nae cunt kens that fir sure until we gie it a go, Knoxie contended.

Ah wisnae fir gaun intae that bog tae check it oot. — Ye ken whit happens, Knoxie. Burds pit thir fanny pads doon the pan, they aw clog up at the bend, ken?

— It's these cunts thit flush they fuckin disposable nappies away, that's the cunts thit git oan ma fuckin tits, Lozy shook ehs heid. — That's whit does the real fuckin damage, no the jamrags.

— Ah'm no arguin wi yous cunts. Git they fuckin rods oot the van n doon that fuckin pan.

— Thir's nae point, ah goes. — Fill in an MRN 2 n lit they drainage cunts fae the Region sort it oot. Thill huv tae in the long run, wir jist wastin oor time here.

— Dinnae you tell me ma fuckin joab, son! Right! Knoxie isnae pleased. The cunt's bein too nippy here. Eh's no backin doon. Well, ah'm no either.

— Waste ay fuckin time, ah repeated.

— Aw aye, n whit else wid ye be daein? Sittin in the fuckin howf playin cairds!

— That's no the fuckin point, Lozy sais, — it's no oor fuckin joab. MRN 2 up tae the Region. That's whit's needed.

This social worker lassie turns roond n gies us a stroppy look. Ah jist smiles bit she looked away aw fuckin nippy likes. Disnae cost nowt tae be social. A social worker thit cannae be fuckin social; that's nae good tae nae cunt, thon. Like a lifeguard thit cannae fuckin swim. Shouldnae be daein that kinday joab.

— Yous cunts, jist fuck off. Ah'll dae it masel. Gaun, jist fuck off, Knoxie sais.

We jist looked it each other. Every cunt wis scoobied, so we jist turned n went doon the stair. We jist thought: if that's whit the cunt wants . . .

— Dis that mean wuv goat oor cairds? Calum asked.

Lozy jist fuckin laughed in the cunt's face, — The only cairds ye git at the DLO come in packs ay fifty-two. We're jist obeyin orders n ye eywis follay the last yin. Go, the cunt sais, so wir gaun. Eh shrugged.

— Whin ye think ay it though, ah sais, — Knoxie didnae

learn much fae that fuckin course. They sais thit it's the super-visor's joab tae make sure thit the work gits done, no tae dae it ehsel. There's the cunt up thair graftin oan ehs puff while we're aw oot here.

— Fancy a pint? Lozy asks. — Whitsons?

Calum raises a hopeful eyebrow.

— Why no, ah goes, — if yir gaunny git hung fir stealin a sheep ye might as well shag it n aw.

We walked across the forecourt. Thir wis a pungent, shitey smell and Lozy's face crinkled up aw that satisfied wey n eh nods doon tae a river ay stagnant water thit wis bubblin tae the surface fae aroond the rim ay a rusty iron drain-cover.

Calum turned back taewards the flats and raised baith airms in the air. Eh gave a double V-sign. — Game set and match, ya masonic bastard.

Lozy goes: — The union boy'll chew ehs fuckin nuts oaf if eh tries tae take this yin tae a disciplinary.

— Widnae git that far, ah sais, — we gave oor professional opinion. Whit's it the gadge thit took us fir the ONC at Telford College sais? The maist important skill in any trade is accurate problem diagnosis. Ah goat a fuckin distinction, ah pointed at masel.

Lozy raised ehs eyebrows, the cheeky cunt.

— Eh did, Calum backs ays up.

— Aye, n that cunt Knoxie chose tae disregard oor pro-fessional advice.

— Waste ay council resources, Lozy agreed. — Manderson'll nivir back that cunt up.

We swagger through the centre towards the pub. That pint's gaunny taste sweet, right enough.

WAYNE FOSTER

Two Sparryheids sit at a table in a public house talking shite about the football. The Sparryheids are almost indistinguishable from each other with their soft brown feathery heads, open, tense, belligerent beaks and slimy liquorice eyes. The only thing that sets them apart is that one Sparryheid has a trail of black gunge weeping from the corner of his left eye, the result perhaps of some injury or infection.

— Some trouble the day at the match, eh?

— Aye, casual infiltrators. Shouldnae huv been thair, no at that end.

— Ah heard it wisnae casuals, but. Ah heard it wis a couple ay boys thit wir in each other's company, arguing about Wayne Foster. One cunt goes: Git that fuckin English cunt oaf the park. The other boy sais: Gie the cunt a chance. So the first boy sais something back and one things leads tae another, one boy panels the other. Next thing ye ken, yuv goat a big fuckin swedge oan yir hands.

— Naw, says one Sparryheid, with an unconvinced shake of his beak, — it'll be they fuckin casuals. No interested in the fitba, these cunts.

— Naw naw. This wis aboot Wayne Foster. That's what ah heard.

— Casuals, the unconvinced Sparryheid shakes his beak again. A few brown feathers float to the lino floor, — that's who it'd be. Fuckin troublemakers.

— Naw, explains his friend, now slightly exasperated, — no this the day. Ah agree wi ye aboot the casuals, but wir talkin

440

aboot *this the day.* This wis two boys thit kent each other. They started swedgin, then every other cunt jumps in. Frustration, ken. Frustration wi the way things are gaun. Ken?

— Awright, mibbe, n wir jist sayin mibbe, it wis they boys n Foster, Wayne Foster – who's awright by the way; at least ye always git one hundred and ten percent fae Foster – mibbe it wis Foster this time thit started it, but it's usually they casuals . . . that's aw ah'm sayin.

— Aye, bit no this time. This the day wis definitely this Foster thing. Ah heard two boys spraffin aboot it.

— Admittedly Foster husnae goat that much skill. Fast as fuck though, man.

— Foster . . .

— Another thing aboot Foster, wi goat that cunt for fuck all. Derek fuckin Ferguson; three quarters ay a million fir that! A fuckin prima donna!

— Naw, that's a fitba player, man.

— Foster. That's the boy. See if they aw hud Foster's commitment . . .

— Awright, awright. If ye could combine Foster's commitment wi Ferguson's class . . .

— Aye, nods the other Sparryheid, — ah'll gie ye that.

— Foster's commitment n speed wi Ferguson's class n vision.

— Foster.

— Right. Foster, ya cunt.

— Aye. Wayne Foster. Right enough, the Sparryheid considers, before turning to his mate: — Another pint?

— Aye.

One Sparryheid goes up to the bar but the barman refuses him service as he, the barman, has sectarian leanings which make him averse to Sparryheided cunts. Additionally this barman has enjoyed the benefits of a classical education which makes him feel superior to most people, particularly Sparryheids, who he hates to wait on. There is another reason. *She* is in the bar. Worse still: *She* is in the bar with *Her.* The Sparryheid's keen vision is focused on these two women, who sit in the corner of the bar, deep in conversation. If *She* went home with a Sparryheid it would be the end for the Classical Scholar; as for *Her*, well she could do what she wanted.

— Bit how no? asks the Sparryheid at the bar, how's it wir no gittin served? His beak is open at ninety degrees and his huge black eyes radiate anxiety.

The barman is no ornothologist. The classics are his field, but even he can sense the Sparryheid's discomfort. However, he shakes his head slowly, refusing to make eye contact with the Sparryheid. Instead, he makes a grim, intense ritual of washing a glass.

The Sparryheid at the bar goes back over to the table. — Wir no gettin served! he announces to his friend.

— Eh! Whit for no?

The Sparryheids move over to the other end of the bar to make an appeal to Ernie, the other duty barman. The Classical Scholar was head duty barman, and even if Ernie had the power to overide his decision, he would be reluctant to do so as he also enjoyed seeing Sparryheids distressed. — It's no up tae me, boys, he shrugged at the bemused beaks and went back to his conversation with two guys at the bar.

The Classical Scholar looks over at the two women in the corner. In particular he looks at *She*; even more particularly he is unable to take his eyes off her glossy lips. He recalls that blow-job at New Year; that had been something else. There was always a tension in his mind and body; this was part and parcel of being a classical scholar in a world where the classics were undervalued. His depth and breadth of knowledge went unrecognised. He was forced to pull pints for Sparryheids. This caused depression, anxiety, tension. That blow-job at New Year; that had sucked all the tension out of his tightly-strung body, taken all the poisonous thoughts out of his head. He'd lain there for a bit, on the bed outside the coats; just lain there in a daze. When he recovered she'd left the room. He went through to find her but when he approached her she was cold and off-hand.

— Please keep away from me, she had said to him. — I'm not

interested in you. This is New Year. I'm a bit pissed. Understand, that was a one-off, okay?

All he could do was respond with a bemused nod, stagger through to the kitchen and get drunk.

Now *She* was in the bar with *Her*, a woman he'd gone home with previously; a woman he'd fucked. He didn't like *Her*, but the thought that he'd been with both of them made him feel good. Two women under thirty in the bar and he'd shagged both of them. Well, shagged one and got a blow-job from the other one. A technicality, surely. He replayed it: two women under thirty in the bar and he'd come with his prick inside a different orifice with each one. That sounded even better. But it didn't feel better for long because *She* was looking over at him and laughing; they both were. *She* held her hands up at the level of her chest, protruding index fingers a few inches apart. The other woman, *Her*, nodded negatively as they stole another glance at the Classical Scholar, then *She* put her fingers closer together until there was hardly any space between them and *Her* head bobbed approvingly, before they both collapsed into heaps of laughter.

The Classical Scholar was far too sensitive a man to be treated in this manner. He went into the small room at the back of the bar and picked up an old hard yellow piece of soap from the dirty sink. He chewed a chunk off the cake and after wincing at the sickening taste, swallowed hard. It burned all the way down to his stomach in a slow, poisonous trail. He slammed a fist into his palm, curled his toes and began humming a soft mantra: — Slags slags slags slags slags . . .

Getting control of himself, he emerged to find one of the Sparryheids standing before him at the bar.

— How's it wir no gittin served, mate? Whit huv wi done? Wir no steamin or nowt like that. Jist in fir a quiet drink, ken. Jist spraffin aboot the match, ken? Wayne Foster n that.

The best thing to do was not to even talk to Sparryheids. It was important to remember the golden rules of barwork as they related to Sparryheids.

1. **ACT DECISIVELY.**
2. **REMAIN IMPLACABLY IN CONTROL OF THAT INITIAL DECISION, IRRESPECTIVE OF WHETHER THAT DECISION IS JUST OR NOT.**
3. **NEVER ATTEMPT TO EXPLAIN TO THE SPARRYHEID THE REASON(S) FOR YOUR DECISION. BY JUSTIFYING OR RATIONALISING YOU MERELY COMPROMISE YOUR AUTHORITY.**

Those were the rules of the game. Always.

He shook his head negatively at the Sparryheids. They uttered some curses and left.

A few minutes later *She* stood up. Ernie, positioned at the other end of the bar moved over to serve her, but went back to chatting to a couple of customers as he realised she was heading for the Classical Scholar.

— Craig, she said to him, — I liked the way you handed those weird beaky guys with the feathered faces. They were giving us the creeps. When do you finish tonight?

— Eh, half an hour.

— Good, I want you to come back with me and my friend Rosalyn. You know Rosalyn don't you . . . ha ha ha of course you do.

— Okay.

— Understand, Craig, we won't fuck you, you'll get nothing off us. You're quite a sexy man but you take yourself far too seriously. We want to show you something about yourself. Right? She smiled and moved back over to where her friend was sitting.

The Classical Scholar wondered what they wanted him for. He would go, though. It could be enlightening. It didn't matter whether you were a Sparryheid, or even a Classical Scholar; there were always lessons to be learned in life.

WHERE THE DEBRIS MEETS
THE SEA

The house in Santa Monica sat tastefully back from Palisades Beach Road, the town's bustling ocean boulevard. This was the top end of the town, its opulence serving as the height to aspire to for the yuppie dwellers of the condominiums further down the Pacific coast. It was a two-floored Spanish-style dwelling, partly obscured from the road by a huge stone wall and a range of indigenous American and imported trees. A few yards inside the wall, an electrified security fence ran around the perimeter of the property. Inside the gate at the entrance to the grounds, a portable cabin was discreetly tucked, and outside it sat a burly guard with mirror-lens shades.

Wealth was certainly the overall impression given by the property. Unlike nearby Beverly Hills, however, the concept of wealth here seemed more utilitarian, rather than concerned with status. The impression was that wealth was here to be consumed, rather than flaunted ostentatiously for the purpose of inducing respect, awe or envy.

The pool at the back of the house had been drained; this was not a home that was occupied all the year round. Inside, the house was expensively furnished, yet in a stark, practical style.

Four women relaxed in a large room which led, through patio doors, to the dry pool. They were at ease, lounging around silently. The only sounds came from the television, which one of them was watching, and the soft hissing of the air-conditioning which pumped cool, dry air into the house.

A pile of glossy magazines lay on a large black coffee table. They bore such titles as *Wide-o, Scheme Scene* and *Bevvy*

Merchants. Madonna flicked idly through the magazine called *Radge*, coming to an abrupt halt as her eyes feasted on the pallid figure of Deek Prentice, resplendent in a purple, aqua and black shell-suit.

'Phoah! Ah'd shag the erse oafay that anywey,' she lustily exclaimed, breaking the silence, and thrusting the picture under Kylie Minogue's nose.

Kylie inspected the image clinically, 'Hmm . . . ah dunno . . . No bad erse oan it like, bit ah'm no really intae flat-toaps. Still, ah widnae kick it oot ay bed, likesay, ken?'

'Whae's that?' Victoria Principal asked, filing her nails as she reclined on the couch.

'Deek Prentice fi Gilmerton. Used tae be in the casuals, bit eh's no intae that anymair,' Madonna said, popping a piece of chewing-gum into her mouth.

Victoria was enthusiastic. 'Total fuckin ride. Ah bet eh's hung like a hoarse. Like that photae ah goat ay Tam McKenzie, ken fi the Young Leith Team, original seventies line-up. Fuckin welt oan it, man, ah'm telling ye. Phoah, ya cunt ye! Even through the shell-suit, ye kin see ehs tackle bulgin oot. Ah thoat, fuck me, ah'd gie ma eye teeth tae get ma gums aroond that.'

'Ye'd probably huv tae, if ehzis big is ye say!' smirked Kylie. They all laughed loudly, except Kim Basinger, who sat curled up in a chair watching the television.

'Wishful thinkin gits ye naewhaire,' she mused. Kim was studying the sensual image of Dode Chalmers; bold shaved head, Castlemaine XXXX t-shirt and Levis. Although Rocky, his faithful American pit-bull terrier was not visible on the screen, Kim noted that his leather and chain leash was bound around Dode's strong, tattooed arm. The eroticism of the image was intense. She wished that she'd videotaped this programme.

The camera swung over to Rocky, whom Dode described to the interviewer as: 'My one faithful friend in life. We have an uncanny telepathy which goes beyond the archetypal man-beast relationship . . . in a real sense Rocky is an extension of myself.'

Kim found this a bit pretentious. Certainly, there was little doubt that Rocky was an integral part of the Dode Chalmers legend. They went everywhere together. Kim cynically wondered, however, just how much of this was a dubious gimmick, manufactured, perhaps, by public relations people.

'Fuck . . .' gasped Kylie, open mouthed, '. . . what ah'd gie tae be in that dug's position now. Wearin a collar, chained tae Dode's airm. That wid dae me fine.'

'Some fuckin chance,' Kim laughed, more derisively than she'd intended.

Madonna looked across at her. 'Awright then, smart cunt. Dinnae you be sae fuckin smug,' she said challengingly.

'Aye Kim, dinnae tell ays ye widnae git intae his keks if ye hud the chance,' Victoria sneered.

'That's whit ah sais, bit. Ah'm no gaunny git the chance, so whit good's it talkin aboot it, likesay? Ah'm here in Southern California n Dode's ower in fuckin Leith.'

They fell into a silence, and watched Dode being interviewed on *The Jimmy McGilvary Show.* Kim thought that McGilvary was a pain in the arse, who seemed to feel that he was as big a star as his guests. He was asking Dode about his love-life.

'In all honesty, I don't have time for heavy relationships at the moment. Right now I'm only interested in all the overtime I can get. After all, one has to remember that trades fortnight isn't that far away,' Dode explained, slightly flushed, his thin mouth almost curling in a smile.

'Ah'd cowp it,' Kylie licked her bottom lip.

'In a fuckin minute,' Victoria nodded severely, eyes widened.

Madonna was more interested in Deek Prentice. She turned her attention back to the article and continued reading. She was hoping to read something about Deek's split from the casuals. The full story had not come out about that one, and it would be interesting to hear Deek's side of things.

there is hope for us all yet, as Deek is keeping an open mind on romance since his much publicised split with sexy cinema usherette,

*Sandra Riley. It's obviously an issue where Deek is keen to set the
record straight.*

'I suppose, in a way, we loved each other too much. There's
certainly no hard feelings or bitterness on either side. In fact, I was
talking to Sandra on the phone only the other night, so we're still
the best of friends. Our respective careers made it difficult to see as
much of each other as we would have liked. Obviously cinema isn't
a nine-to-five thing, and furniture removals can take me all over the
country, with overnight stays. We got used to not being together,
and sort of drifted apart. Unfortunately, it's the nature of the
business we're in. Relationships are difficult to sustain.'

*Deek's social life is another area where he feels that he has had more
than his share of unwelcome publicity. While he makes no secret of
an enjoyment of the high life, he feels that 'certain parties' have
somewhat exaggerated things.*

'So I enjoy the odd game of pool with Dode Chalmers and Cha
Telfer. All I can say is: guilty as charged. Yes, I'm in the habit of
visiting places like the Spey Lounge, Swanneys and the Clan
Tavern; and I enjoy a few pints of lager. However, the public only
see the glamorous side. It's not as if I'm swilling away every
night. Most evenings I'm home, watching Coronation Street and
EastEnders. Just to illustrate how the press get hold of nonsense, a
report appeared in a Sunday newspaper, which shall be nameless,
stating that I was involved in an altercation at a stag night in Fox's
Bar. It's not a boozer I use, and in any case I was working overtime
that night! If I was in the pub as often as certain gossip columnists
claim, I'd hardly be able to hold down my driving job with
Northern Removals. With three million people unemployed, I've
certainly no intention of resting on my laurels.'

*Deek's boss, the experienced supervisor Rab Logan, agrees. Rab
probably knows Deek better than anyone in the business, and Deek
unreservedly credits the dour Leither with saving his career. Rab
told us: 'Deek came to us with a reputation for being, should we
say, somewhat difficult. He's very much an individual, rather than*

*a team man, and tended to go off to the pub whenever it took his
fancy. Obviously, with a flit to complete, this lack of application
caused some bad feeling with the rest of the team. We crossed swords
for the first and last time, and since then, Deek's been a joy to work
with. I can't speak highly enough of him.'*

*Deek is only too willing to acknowledge his debt to the removal
Svengali.*

   *'I owe it all to Rab. He took me aside and told me that I had
what it took to make it in the removals game. The choice was mine.
At the time I was arrogant, and nobody could tell me anything.
However, I remember that exceptionally grim and lonely journey
home on the number six bus that day Rab told me a few home
truths. He has a habit of stating the transparently obvious, when
you're so close to it, you can't see the woods for the trees. After a
dressing-down from Rab Logan, one tends to shape up. The lesson
I learned from Rab that day was an important one. In a sense, the
removal business is like any other. The bottom line is, you're only as
good as your last flit.'*

   What Deek eventually wants however, is the opportunity to

'Thir's nought tae stoap us gaun tae Leith, fir a hoaliday n
that,' Victoria suggested, tearing Madonna's attention from the
magazine.

   'Hoaliday . . . hoaliday . . .' Madonna sang.

   'Aye! We could go tae the *Clan*,' Kylie enthused. 'Imagine the
cock in thair. Comin oot the fuckin waws.' She screwed up her
eyes, puckered her lips and blew hard, shaking her head from
side to side.

   'Ye'd nivir git served in thair,' Kim sniffed.

   'Ken your problem, Kim? Ye nivir think fuckin positively
enough. We've goat the poppy. Dinnae you sit thair n tell ays
ye've no goat the hireys,' Madonna remonstrated.

   'Ah nivir sais that. It's no jist aboot poppy . . .'

   'Well then. We could go tae Leith. Huv a fuckin barry time.

Hoaliday ay a lifetime,' Madonna told her, then continued her singing. 'It wid be, it wid be so nice, hoaliday . . .'

Victoria and Kylie nodded enthusiastically in agreement. Kim looked unconvinced.

'You cunts crack ays up.' She shook her head. 'No fuckin real.'

'Whit's wrong wi your fuckin pus, ya stroppy cunt?' Madonna mouthed belligerently, sitting up in the chair. 'Ye git oan ma fuckin tits, Kim, so ye do.'

'We'll nivir go tae fuckin Leith!' Kim said, in a tone of scornful dismissal. 'Yous ur fuckin dreamin.'

'We might go one time!' said Kylie, with just a hint of desperation in her voice. The others nodded in agreement.

But in their heart of hearts, they knew that Kim was right.

GRANNY'S OLD JUNK

The warden, Mrs French I think they call her, is looking me up and down. It's fairly obvious that she doesn't like what she sees; her gaze has a steely ice to it; it's definitely a negative evaluation I'm getting here.

— So, she says, hands on hips, eyes flitting suspiciously in that glistening yellow-brown foundation mask topped by a brittle head of brown hair, — you're Mrs Abercrombie's grandson?

— Aye, I acknowledge. I shouldn't resent Mrs French. She's only doing her job. Were she less than vigilant in keeping her eye on the auld doll, complaints from the family would ensue. I also have to acknowledge that I am less than presentable; lank, greasy black hair, a scrawny growth sprouting from a deathly white face broken up by a few red and yellow spots. My overcoat has seen better days and I can't remember when I changed into these jeans, sweatshirt, t-shirt, trainers, socks and boxershorts.

— Well, I suppose you'd better come in, Mrs French said, reluctantly shifting her sizeable bulk. I squeezed past, still brushing against her. Mrs French was like an oil tanker, it took a while for her to actually change direction. — She's on the second floor. You don't come to see her very often, do you? she said with an accusatory pout.

No. This is the first time I've been to see the auld doll since she moved into this Sheltered Housing scheme. That must be over five years ago now. Very few families are close nowadays. People move around, live in different parts of the country, lead different lives. It's pointless lamenting something as inevitable as

451

the decline of the extended family network; in a way it's a good thing because it gives people like Mrs French jobs.

— Ah don't stay local, I mumble, making my way down the corridor, feeling a twinge of self-hate for justifying myself to the warden.

The corridors have a rank, fetid smell of pish and stale bodies. Most people here seem in such an advanced state of infirmity it merely confirms my intuitive feeling that such places are just ante-chambers to death. It follows from this that my actions won't alter the auld doll's quality of life: she'll scarcely notice that the money's gone. Some of it would probably be mine anyway, when she finally snuffs it; so what the fuck's the point of waiting until it's no good to me? The auld doll could hang on for donkey's years as a cabbage. It would be utterly perverse, self-defeating nonsense not to rip her off now, to allow oneself to be constrained by some stupid, irrelevant set of taboos which pass as morality. I need what's in her tin.

It's been in the family for so long: Gran's shortbread tin. Just sitting there under her bed, crammed full of bundles of notes. I remember, as a sprog, her opening it up on our birthdays and peeling off a few notes from what seemed to be a fortune, the absence of which made no impact on the wad.

Her life savings. Savings for what? Savings for us, that's what, the daft auld cunt: too feeble, too inadequate to enjoy or even use her wealth. Well I shall just have my share now, Granny, thank you very much.

I rap on the door. Abercrombie, with a red tartan background. My back chills and my joints feel stiff and aching. I haven't got long.

She opens the door. She looks so small, like a wizened puppet, like Zelda out of *Terrahawks*.

— Gran, I smile.

— Graham! she says, her face expanding warmly. — God, ah cannae believe it! Come in! Come in!

She sits me down, babbling excitedly, hobbling back and

forth from her small adjoining kitchen as she slowly and cum-
bersomely prepares tea.

— Ah keep askin yir mother how ye nivir come tae see me.
Ye always used tae come oan Saturday for yir dinner, mind? For
yir mince, remember, Graham? she says.

— Aye, the mince, Gran.

— At the auld place, mind? she said wistfully.

— Ah remember it well, Gran, I nodded. It was a vermin-
infested hovel unfit for human habitation. I hated that grotty
tenement: those stairs, the top floor surprise surfuckingprise,
with the backs of my legs already fucked from the sickening
ritual of walking up and down Leith Walk and Junction Street;
her standing oblivious to our pain and discomfort as she prattled
on a load of irrelevant, mundane shite with every other auld
hound that crossed our path; big brother Alan taking his exasperation out on me by punching me or booting me or twisting
my airm when she wisnae looking, and if she was she didnae
bother. Mickey Weir gets more protection from Syme at Ibrox
than I ever did from that auld cunt. Then, after all that, the
fuckin stairs. God, I detested those fuckin stairs!

She comes in and looks at me sadly, and shakes her head with
her chin on her chest. — Your mother was saying that yuv been
gettin intae trouble. Wi these drugs n things. Ah sais, no oor
Graham, surely no.

— People exaggerate, Gran, I said as a spasm of pain shot
through my bones, and a delirious shivering tremor triggered off
an excretion of stale perspiration from my pores. Fuck fuck
fuck.

She re-emerges from the kitchen, popping out like a crumpled jack-in-the box. — Ah thoat so. Ah sais tae oor Joyce: No
oor Graham, he's goat mair sense thin that.

— Ma goes oan a bit. Ah enjoy masel, Gran, ah'm no sayin
otherwise, bit ah dinnae touch drugs, eh. Ye dinnae need drugs
tae enjoy yirself.

— That's whit ah sais tae yir mother. The laddie's an Abercrombie, ah telt her, works hard and plays hard.

My name was Millar, not Abercrombie, that's the auld lady's
side. This auld hound seemed to believe that being referred to as
an Abercrombie is the highest possible accolade one can aspire
to; though perhaps, if you want to demonstrate expertise in
alcoholism and theft, this may very well be the case.

— Aye, some crowd the Abercrombies, eh Gran?

— That's right, son. Ma Eddie — yir grandfaither — he wis
the same. Worked hard n played hard, n a finer man nivir
walked the earth. He nivir kept us short, she smiled proudly.

Short.

I have my works in my inside pocket. Needle, spoon, cotton
balls, lighter. All I need is a few grains of smack, then just add
water and it's all better. My passport's in that tin.

— Whair's the lavvy, Gran?

Despite the small size of the flat, she insisted on escorting
me to the bog, as if I'd get lost on the way. She fussed, clucked
and farted as if we were preparing to go on safari. I tried
a quick slash, but couldn't pee, so I stealthily tiptoed into the
bedroom.

I lifted up the bedclothes that hung to the floor. The large old
shortbread tin with the view of Holyrood Palace sat in full
magnificent view under the bed. It was ridiculous, an act of
absolute criminal stupidity to have that just lying around in this
day and age. I was more convinced than ever that I had to rip
her off. If I didn't somebody else would. Surely she'd want me to
have the money, rather than some stranger? If I didn't take the
cash, I'd be worried sick about it. Anyway, I was planning to get
clean soon; maybe get a job or go to college or something. The
auld hound would get it back right enough. No problem.

Prising open the lid of the fucker was proving extremely
difficult. My hands were trembling and I couldn't get any purchase on it. I was starting to make headway when I heard her
voice behind me.

— So! That's whit this is aw aboot! She was standing right
over me. I thought I'd have heard the clumsy auld boot sneaking

up on me, but she was like a fuckin ghost. — Yir mother wis
right. Yir a thief! Feeding yir habit, yir drugs habit, is that it?

— Naw Gran, it's jist . . .

— Dinnae lie, son. Dinnae lie. A thief, a thief thit steals fae
his ain is bad, but a liar's even worse. Ye dinnae ken whair ye
stand wi a liar. Get away fae that bloody tin! she snapped so
suddenly that I was taken aback, but I sat where I was.

— I need something, right?

— Yill find nae money in thair, she said, but I could tell by
the anxiety in her voice that she was lying. I prised, and it
transpired that she wasn't. On top of a pile of old photos lay
some whitish-brown powder in a plastic bag. I'd never seen so
much gear.

— What the fuckin hell's this . . .

— Git away fae thair! Git away! Fuckin thief! Her bony,
spindly leg lashed out and caught me in the side of the face. It
didn't hurt but it shocked me. Her swearing shocked me even
more.

— Ya fuckin auld . . . I sprang to my feet, holding the bag in
the air, beyond her outstretched hands. — Better call the
warden, Gran. She'll be interested in this.

She pouted bitterly and sat down on the bed. — You got
works? she asked.

— Aye, I said.

— Cook up a shot then, make yourself useful.

I started to do as she said. — How Gran? How? I asked,
relieved and bemused.

— Eddie, the Merchant Navy. He came back wi a habit. We
had contacts. The docks. The money wis good, son. Thing is,
ah kept feedin it, now ah huv tae sell tae the young ones tae keep
gaun. The money aw goes upfront. She shook her head, looking
hard at me. — Thir's a couple ay young yins ah git tae run
messages fir me, but that fat nosey yin doonstairs, the warden,
she's gittin suspicious.

I took up her cue. Talk about falling on your feet. — Gran,
maybe we kin work the gither on this.

The animal hostility on her small, pinched face dissolved into a scheming grin. — Yir an Abercrombie right enough, she told me.

— Aye, right enough, I acknowledged with a queasy defeatism.

THE HOUSE OF JOHN DEAF

John Deaf's hoose wis weird. Ah mean, thir wis eywis some scruffy hooses in the scheme, bit nowt like John Deaf's. Fir a start, John Deaf's hoose hud fuck all in it; nae furniture or nowt like that. Nowt oan the flair, no even any lino. Jist they cauld black tiles thit ivray hoose hud, fir the underflair heatin thit nae cunt could afford tae switch oan.

Aw thit wis in John Deaf's hoose wis one chair thit ehs Grandfaither sat oan, ben the livin-room. Thir wis a boax wi a telly oan toap ay it. The auld cunt jist used tae sit thair watchin the telly aw day n night. Thir wis eywis loads ay boatils n cans it ehs feet. The auld radge must've slept in that chair, cause thir wis jist one mattress in the hoose, n that wis in John Deaf's room. Thir wis nae beds or nowt like that.

The only thing thit wis in the hoose wis the white mice. Loads ay thum, crawlin aboot ivraywhair. John Deaf really liked white mice. Eh boat thum ootay Dofo's Pet Shoap, took thum back tae the hoose n jist lit thum go. Eh wis it Dofo's ivray Setirday. Whin they tippled tae what the cunt wis aboot, they knocked um back. Aw he'd dae though, wis jist gie one ay us the money tae go in n git um the mice.

So the mice ran aroond free. They jist multiplied, scurryin aroond the place, aw ower they black tiles. Sometimes eh'd hurt thum. Some ay thum goat crushed tae death, n thir wis one thit eh hud kicked thit hud baith ay its back legs broken. It used tae drag itsel acroass the flair wi its front legs. Wi used tae git a fuckin laugh at it. That yin though, that wis John Deaf's favourite. Ye could stomp any ay the wee cunts, bit eh widnae lit ye touch that yin.

Wi didnae call John Deaf John Deaf cause the cunt wis deef n dumb. Eh wis, bit that wisnae the main reason. It wis cause thir wis a John Hyslop n a Johnny Paterson n soas no tae git thum mixed up. That wis the main reason. Aw John Deaf could say wis ehs name, n thit eh wis deef. Whin eh moved intae the scheme, intae Rab's block, ye'd go up n say tae um: Whit's yir name, mate? n eh'd say: John. Then ye'd say somethin else bit eh'd jist touch ehs ear n go: Deaf.

So John Deaf it wis.

Ivray cunt kent um is John Deaf. The guy thit took us fir the fitba it Sporting Pilton used tae say: Ah want John Deaf tae play oot wide oan the wing. Ah want yis tae feed John Deaf. Remember, feed John Deaf, eh'd say tae us. Naebody could run like John Deaf. Eh wis really strong n aw. Eh'd go fuckin radge if some cunt did a sneaky tackle fae behind oan um, bit that wis the only wey ye could stoap John Deaf. The cunt's strength n speed wirnae real, believe you me.

John Deaf nivir went tae school. They didnae ken eh existed. Course, John Deaf wid huv went tae one ay they special schools, fir the deef, likesay that big posh yin it Haymarket, bit eh didnae go tae any school at aw. Ivray time one ay us wis skivin, we'd meet up wi John Deaf, sure as fuck.

Wi aw used tae hing aroond in John Deaf's hoose. It wis really mingin likesay, bit that nivir bothered ye sae much in they days. It wis like oor base, oor HQ. Ehs auld grandfaither nivir hassled naebday, jist sat thair watchin the telly n drinkin ehs cans ay beer. He wis deef n aw.

Once whin wi wir in John Deaf's hoose, jist fartin aboot likes; wi couldnae find John Deaf or ma sister. Wi went up the stairs n heard noises comin fae the the big press whair the water tank wis. Whin wi opened the door wi saw that cunt John fuckin Deaf n ma sister. Thir fuckin neckin n John Deaf's goat ehs willy oot n eh's goat ehs hand up hur skirt.

Now she gits called a slag n that makes me look a right fuckin

cunt, nae two weys aboot it. So ah pills hur away n pushes hur
doon the stairs, tellin hur tae git tae fuck. She wis shitin ursel n
so she fuckin shoulduv been, cause there wis me thinkin: see if
the auld man kent aboot it . . . Bit anywey ah punches John Deaf
in the mooth n wi starts swedgin which wis a bad fuckin move
oan ma part because ay John Deaf's strength, n eh gits oan toap
ay ays n ehs knockin fuck oot ay ays, batterin ma heid oaf they
black tiles. Ah suppose it wis then thit ah tippled tae how auld
John Deaf wis. It wisnae sae much the size ay ehs willy, because
it wis still oot, wi this cunt oan toap ay ays, or the baws wi hairs
oan thum. It wis mair the bumfluff oan ehs face, n ehs strength.
In spite ay ehs wee height, it came tae ays thit John Deaf wisnae
the same age as the rest ay us. Eh wis mibbe sixteen; mibbe even
mair. Whin ah realised this, that's whin ah really shat ma keks.
Ah'm greetin ma eyes oot, ah wis only aboot eleven likes, n
ivray cunt's sayin: Eh's hud enough. Leave um.

Bit John Deaf's deef, right?

Anywey, it wis some fuckin doin ah goat. It only stoaped
whin some cunt drags John Deaf oafay ays tae git um tae go
doonstairs. Ah think it wis Cammy, bit ah'm no really sure.
Anywey, whaeivir it wis, eh starts pillin John Deaf doon the stair.
John Deaf didnae resist, ah suppose eh could tell fae the boy's
face thit somethin wis wrong.

Ah staggers tae ma feet, ma sister tryin tae help ays up. Ah
pushes hur ootay the road. Dirty cow deserved tae be shopped
tae the auld man. Ah wis thinkin, mibbe ah will, mibbe ah
willnae, cause ah thoat thit ma Ma n Dad wid'uv went radge.

Whin ah gits doonstairs, thir aw crowded aroond the grandfaither's chair. Thir's a big pool ay pish under it. The auld gadge's
heid's twisted tae the side, ehs eyes ur shut, bit ehs mooth's open.
White mice ur walkin aroond the edge ay the puddle ay pish.
One wis in it, the cunt wi the broken back legs, draggin ehsel
through it. Making sure thit John Deaf wisnae noticin, ah
brought ma heel doon hard oan the wee cunt. Ah kent John
Deaf liked that moose, n that wid help tae pey the cunt back fir
the doin eh'd gied ays. Whin ah looked doon, the moose wis

still alive, bit sortay split open. Its spilled guts wir trailin in the pish; bit it wis still dragging its boady forward.

Ah didnae ken whithir or no the auld cunt in the chair wis deid, bit eh wisnae far oaf it. Ah wis really sair, especially ma heid, bit ah wis happy, because ah kent thit they'd take John Deaf away cause ay the auld cunt bein deid, or half-deid.

They did n aw. John Deaf nivir came back tae the scheme. Thir wis loads ay stories gaun aboot: like the auld gadge wisnae really John Deaf's grandfaither n they baith slept oan that one mattress, if ye git ma meanin. Ah widnae pit it past thum, that's aw ah'm sayin oan the subject. It's jist talk bit, n the only two people thit really ken whit went oan in that hoose cannae tell any cunt aboot it.

Ah nivir sais nowt tae ma Ma n faither aboot ma sister n John Deaf. She kent tae watch ur mooth aroond ays bit, n no gie ays any lip. They soon worked oot thit somethin wis wrong though, n whin they asked ur aboot it, she started greetin. Thing wis, ah wis the cunt thit goat the fuckin blame! Me! The auld man sais thit ah wis a blackmailer, n ah blackmailer wis the lowest ay the low, specially wi faimly n that. Eh telt ays this story aboot how this poof eh kent in the army wis blackmailed n the perr wee cunt kilt ehsel. So ah gits leathered n she gits aw this sympathy oafay thum. Fuckin ootay order man, ah'm tellin ye.

Ah wis gled whin they took that John Deaf away. Ah hated the radge. Ah've nivir been the same since that doin eh gied ays, ah kin tell ye.

ACROSS THE HALL

15/2
COLLINGWOOD

it's not being kept in the picture
that i resent the most. he sees me
as a glorified typist; never tells
me anything. not that i want to be
a secretary forever, but i saw this
as a stepping stone to something a
little more interesting. i'm
planning to go to college and take
the institute of marketing
diploma exams, that's if i get day
release; which is a big if, working
for him. and that's if i even get the
chance to ask him for day release
in the first place. he's so sexist and
patronising as well, if you know
what i mean. not like you mister
gillespie . . . sorry frank, of
course. am i embarrassing you
frank? you see it's not that i'm a
big feminist or anything like that,
well i am, but i don't believe in
that brand of feminism that says
it's only men that are power-
crazed warmongers, i mean look

15/8
GILLESPIE

that's important to me. it's him
getting it, after all the experience
in the firm i've gained over the
years. and let's be upfront about
it, it's not only me that's saying it,
most of my colleagues feel the
same; he simply isn't up to the
job. it's not the money i'm
worried about, it's just that good
numbers like that are hard to
come by nowadays. mind you,
i'm not really that upset about it. a
fair day's work for a fair day's pay:
that's my philosophy; and with
the sweeties they pay at that
bloody place, it means that they
get the bare minimum out of old
frank gillespie here. i wouldn't
give you the bare minimum
though stephanie, but then
you're special. i don't mean to be
crude stephanie, i'm not a coarse
person, but when my passions are
aroused i say what i feel. i want

at thatcher in the falklands, it's you to know that i'm a sensitive just that i don't want you to think guy and i don't go in for all that i'm on some big dykey castrating caveman stuff, i see a woman as a men trip here because it's not that person first and foremost. if i'm at all. i really know how to please attracted to someone i'll just a man frank, and how to get a come right out and say it. i may man to please me so why don't not put a lot into my work these you show me what you've got days, but when it comes to frank, why don't you give it to me relationships, especially the baby, why don't you frank? i bet physical side of things, i've never it's a big one, yes! you can always been found wanting. i know you tell in a man, it's something about want it stephanie. is this what the way he carries himself . . . yes you want? i think you want it it is big, and it feels good in my really badly. what about it then? is hand, throbbing away like that, this enough for you? I could tell but it would feel even better that you wanted it, right from inside me . . . frank . . . now the very start, as much as i did . . . frank . . . OHHH god, your skin's so smooth . . . YESSS! that feels so you're so beautiful . . . i want to wonderful, magnificent, fuck you, stephanie . . . let's you really . . . let's just do it baby . . . OHHH it keep doing it like feels so wonderful, oh god this is this . . . getting there beautiful, OH SHIT . . . i'm already . . . this is FUCKING BEAUTIFUL . . . so . . . OH . . . OH . . . OH . . . OH . . . OH . . . OH . . . OH . . .

Stephanie lay on the bed naked, enjoying the sense of brief contentment. It was fleeting; she knew her heart would hollow and she'd soon feel tense and debased again, her self-esteem starting to crumble at the edges like a faulty dam. She unplugged the vibrator, which was wet with her come, then pulled herself off the bed and went through to the bathroom.

Frank looked at the deflating plastic doll, its latex vagina filled with his semen. It seemed to be dissolving simultaneously with his erection. His genitals looked like an ugly, embarrassing growth; alien, external to his self. The doll now just looked like what it was: a sheet of plastic spilling from a grotesque mannequin head.

Later that evening, Stephanie passed Frank in the hallway. She was going out to see an arthouse movie and she was going alone. He was returning from the Chinese takeaway with some food. They blushed in mutual recognition, then he smiled meekly at her, and she timidly returned the compliment. He cleared his throat to speak. — It's raining outside, he lisped self-consciously.

— Is it? Stephanie replied shakily.

— Quite heavy, Frank mumbled.

They stood facing each other for an excruciating few seconds, both lost for words. Then they smiled in tense synchronicity before Frank retreated to his room and Stephanie marched down the hall. Out of sight of each other, both stiffened as if trying to stop the spasm, that pulse of pain, self-loathing and embarrassment.

LISA'S MUM
MEETS THE QUEEN MUM

I was so excited when we met the Queen Mum; oh, it was marvellous. It was a shame about my little girl Lisa's presentation to her. That bit went horribly wrong. It was my little girl Lisa, her fault. Didn't understand, you see. I've always told Lisa to tell the truth: truth at all times, madam, I tell her. Well, you never really know what to tell them these days, do you?

The Queen Mum was coming to Ilford to open Lisa's new infant school. The local MP was going to be there too. We was ever so thrilled when Lisa was picked to present the Queen Mum with the bouquet of flowers. I had Lisa practising her curtseying all the time. Anybody who came in I'd say: show Mummy your curtsey, Lisa, the one you're going to do for the Queen's mummy . . .

Cause she really is lovely, the Queen Mum, ain't she? Really, really, really, really, lovely. We was ever so excited. My mum was going back to the time when she met the Queen Mum at the Festival of Britain. She's really lovely, marvellous for her age; the Queen Mum that is, not my mum. Mind you, my mum's a treasure, I don't know what I would've done without her, after Derek left me. Yeah, I wouldn't swap my mum for all the Queen Mums in the world, really.

Anyway, Mrs Kent, that's Lisa's headmistress, said to me that Lisa would be lovely presenting the Queen Mum with the bouquet. My friend Angela went a bit funny with me, because her little girl, Sinead, wasn't picked. I suppose that I'd have been the same if it had been the other way around and Sinead had got picked instead of Lisa. It was the Queen Mum after all. It don't happen every day, does it?

Well she looked really lovely, the Queen Mum, really really lovely; a lovely hat she had on. I was ever so proud of Lisa, I just wanted to tell the whole world; that's my little gel Lisa! Lisa West, Golfe Road Infants, Ilford actually . . .

So Lisa hands over the bouquet, but she didn't curtsey nice, not nice n proper like we'd practised. The Queen Mum takes the bouquet and bends down to give Lisa a little kiss but Lisa turns away with her little face all screwed up and runs over to me.

That old lady's got bad breath and smells of wee, Lisa said to me. This was in front of all the other mums and Mrs Kent and Mrs Fry n all. Mrs Fry was ever so upset.

You're a naughty little girl, Lisa! Mummy's ever so cross, I told her.

I'm sure I saw my friend Angela sniggering out of the side her mouth, the rotten cow.

Well, she was smiling on the other side of her face when Mrs Kent took *me* over to the Queen Mum and introduced me as Lisa's mum! The Queen Mum was lovely. Nice to meet you again, Mister Chamberlain, she said to me. Poor thing must get a bit confused, all these people she meets. They work ever so hard, you've got to give them that. Not like some I could mention, Derek, Lisa's dad, being a case in point. Not that I'm going into that little story just now, thank you very much.

Another thing was that Lisa had managed to get a stain down the front of her dress. I hoped the Queen Mum didn't notice. Just wait till I get you home, madam, I thought. Ooh, I was ever so cross. Really, really cross.

THE TWO PHILOSOPHERS

It was damn hot for Glasgow, Lou Ornstein thought, as he pulled his sweating body into the Byres Road hostelry. Gus McGlone was already at the bar, chatting to a young woman.

— Gus, how goes it? Ornstein asked, slapping his friend on the shoulder.

— Ah Lou. Very well indeed. And yourself?

— Great, Ornstein said, noting that McGlone's attention was still very much centred on the young woman.

The woman whispered something to McGlone, then flashed Ornstein a searing smile which was all teeth and eyes. It cut through him. — Professor Ornstein, she began in the Scotch tearoom accent he found so attractive, — at the risk of sounding sycophantic I just wanted to say that your paper on the rational construction of magic was just superb.

— Why thank you. I shall accept that as a scholarly, rather than sycophantic view, Ornstein smiled. He thought that was quite a self-conscious response, but hell, he was an academic.

— I find your central hypothesis interesting . . . the young woman continued, as Ornstein felt a small pellet of resentment crystallise in his breast. This day was about drinking beer, not conducting an involuntary seminar with one of Gus's naive students. Oblivious to his growing unease, the woman continued, — . . . tell me, if you don't mind, how do you distinguish between what you call 'unknown science' and what we generally refer to as magic?

I do goddamn mind, thought Ornstein. Pretty young women were all the same; completely goddamned self-obsessed. He had

had to earn the right to be self-obsessed, to slog his guts out in libraries for years and brown-nose the right people, generally assholes who you wouldn't piss upon if they were on fire. Along comes some some nineteen-year-old undergrad destined for at best a lower second honours, who thinks that her opinion counts, that she's important, just because she has a sweet face and a god-given ass. The horrible thing, the worst goddamn thing about it, thought Ornstein, was that she was absolutely right.

— He can't, McGlone smugly remarked.

This intervention by his old adversary was enough to set Ornstein off. Accepting his pint of eighty shilling, he began, — Don't listen to this old Popperian cynic. These guys are just anti-social science, which means anti-science, and each generation of them get increasingly goddamn juvenile in their analysis. My contention is a fairly standard materialist proposition: so-called unexplained phenomena are merely scientific blind-spots. We have to accept the inherently logical concept of further knowledge outside of the human range of what we consciously, and even sub-consciously know. Human history illustrates this; our forefathers would have described the sun, or the internal combustion engine as magic, when they are nothing of the kind. Magic, like ghosts and all that stuff, it's just hocus-pocus bullshit for the ignorant, while unknown science is a phenomena that we may or may not be able to observe but cannot yet explain. That does not mean that it is inexplicable; merely that it cannot be explained with due reference to our current body of knowledge. That body of knowledge is constantly expanding; some day we will be able to explain unknown science.

— Don't get him started, Fiona, McGlone smiled, — he'll go on all night.

— Not if you don't beat me to it. Indoctrinating your students with Popperian orthodoxies.

— Indoctrination's what the other side do, Lou. We educate, McGlone smiled. The two philosophers laughed at that one, an old quip from their student days. Fiona, the young student, excused herself. She had a lecture to attend.

The two philosophers watched her leave the pub.

— One of my brightest undergrads, McGlone smirked.

— Terrific ass, Ornstein nodded.

They adjourned to a conspiratorial corner of the pub. Lou took a mouthful of beer. — It's great to see you again, Gus. But listen buddy, we gotta enter into a pact. As much as I enjoy coming through to Glasgow to see you, I get a little pissed at us going through the same argument. No matter how much we say we ain't gonna do it, we always go back to the Popper-Kuhn debate.

McGlone gave a sombre nod. — It's a pain in the arse. It's made our careers, but it seems to overshadow our friendship. You were just in the door and we were at it again. It's always the same. We talk about Mary, Philippa, the kids, then we go back to work, slag off a few people. As the bevvy takes effect, it's back to Popper-Kuhn. Problem is, Lou, we're philosophers. Debate and argument are as natural to us as breathing is to others.

This was indeed the case. They had argued with each other over the years; in bars, at conferences and in print in philosophical journals. They had started off as undergraduate students of philosophy at Cambridge University, developing a bond of friendship, based on drinking and womanising; the former usually conducted with more success than the latter.

Both men swam against the ideological tide of their country's culture. The Scot Gus McGlone was a supporter of the Conservative Party. He regarded himself as a classical liberal, a descendant of Hume and Ferguson, though he found the classical economists, even Adam Smith, and his latter disciples with philosophical bents like Hayek and Friedman, a little bland. His real hero was Karl Popper, whom he had studied under as a post-graduate student in London. As a follower of Popper's, he was antagonistic to what he saw as the deterministic theories of

Marxism and Freudianism and what he considered to be the attendant dogma of their disciples.

The American Lou Ornstein, a Chicago-born Jew, was a convinced rationalist, who believed in Marxist dialectical materialism. His interest was science and scientific ideas. He was greatly influenced by the philosopher Thomas Kuhn's concept that the rightness of pure science does not necessarily prevail. If ideas went against the current paradigm, they would be rejected by vested interests. Such ideas, while perhaps scientific 'truths', rarely become recognised as such until the pressure for change becomes unbearable. This, Ornstein felt, was in tune with his political belief in the need for revolutionary social change.

Ornstein and McGlone had had parallel careers, working together in London and then in Edinburgh and Glasgow respectively. McGlone had advanced to a professorial chair about eight months before Ornstein. This irked the American, who considered his friend's elevation had been the result of the political fashionability of his ideas under the Thatcher paradigm. Ornstein contented himself with noting he had a greater publication track record.

The natural political antagonism of the two men was centred around a famous debate between Kuhn and Popper. Popper, who had established himself as a great philosopher by attacking the approaches of the intellectual nineteenth-century giants Sigmund Freud and Karl Marx, and what he saw as the partisanship associated with their ideologies, was less than temperate when he himself had his views of scientific progression attacked by Thomas Kuhn, in his seminal work, *The Logic Of Scientific Discovery.*

Yet one thing was agreed on by both Ornstein and McGlone: the argument, which was their bread and butter, always spilled over from the professional into the personal. They tried all sorts of ways to break this pattern, but nothing could prevent this energy-sapping subject from re-emerging. On a couple of occasions, the friends, exasperated and drunk, had almost come to blows.

— I wish we could find some way to keep it to the journals and conferences and out of our shitfaced sessions, Lou mused.

— Yeah, but how? We've tried everything. I've tried using your arguments, you've tried using mine; we've agreed to say nothing but it inevitably resurfaces. What can we do?

— I think I know a way out of this cul-de-sac, Gus, Lou gave a coy look.

— What are you suggesting?

— Independent arbitration.

— Come on, Lou. No philosopher, no member of our peers could satisfy us as to their independence of mind. They would have formed a prior view on the issue.

— I'm not suggesting a peer. I'm suggesting we find someone in the street, or better still, a pub, and advance our propositions, and let them decide which is the superior argument.

— Ridiculous!

— Hold on, Gus, hear me out. I'm not suggesting for one minute that we let go of our academic standpoints on the basis of one informed opinion. That would be ludicrous.

— What are you suggesting?

— I'm suggesting that we have to split the professional from the personal. Let's remove the argument from our social context by letting another party judge the relative merits of our propositions from that social, pub point of view. It will prove nothing academically, but at least it will let us see whose argument is the most user-friendly for the average man in the street.

— Mmmm . . . I suppose that way we can accept that our various arguments have strengths and weaknesses with the lay person . . .

— Exactly. What we are doing is subjecting those ideas to the real world where they are not discussed, the world of our drinking. What we are agreeing to is giving the victor's ideas sovereignty in the pub context.

— This is nonsense, Lou, but it's interesting nonsense and good sport. I accept your challenge, not because it will validate anything, but because it will hold the loser to shutting up about the scientific logic debate.

They shook hands firmly. Ornstein then took McGlone onto the underground at Hillhead station. — Too many student and intelligentsia types around here, Gus. The last thing I wanna do is get into some discussion with some squeaky undergrad fuck. We need a better laboratory for this little experiment.

Gus McGlone was somewhat uneasy when they alighted at Govan. Despite the Glasgow wide-boy persona he cultivated, he was in fact from Newton Mearns and had led quite a closeted life. It was easy to con the impressionable bourgeois who filled the University staff-rooms that he was the genuine article. In somewhere like Govan, it was another matter.

Lou strode purposefully down the street. There was a feel to the place, a mixture of the traditional and the new, and the huge gap sites reminded him of the Jewish-Irish neighbourhood he'd grown up in on Chicago's North Side. Gus McGlone sauntered behind him, trying to affect a casualness he didn't feel. Ornstein stopped an old woman in the street.

— Pardon me, ma'am, can you tell us where the nearest pub is?

The small woman dropped her shopping bag, turned around and pointed across the road. — Yir right here, son.

— Brechin's Bar! Excellent, Lou enthused.

— It's Breekins Bar, not Bretchins, Gus corrected Lou.

— As in Brechin City, right? Brechin City two, Forfar one, yeah?

— Yeah.

— So the guys that drink in here must root for Brechin City.

— I think not, Gus said, as two men in blue scarves exited from the bar. There was a big game on today at Ibrox; Rangers versus Celtic. Even McGlone, who had little interest in football, knew that.

They went in. The formica-topped island bar was busy, with some groups of men watching TV, others playing dominoes. There were only two women in the place. One was a barmaid of indeterminate middle age, the other a slavering old drunkard. A group of young men in blue scarves were singing a song about something that their father wore, which Lou couldn't quite make out. — Is that a Scottish football song? he asked Gus.

— Something like that, Gus remarked uneasily as he procured two pints. They found a seat beside two old guys who were playing dominoes.

— Awright boeys? one of the old men smiled.

— Yeah, sure thing, buddy, Ornstein nodded.

— You're no fae roond here, the old guy laughed, and they struck up a conversation.

One of the old domino players was particularly talkative, and seemed to have a view on everything. The two philosophers gave each other a sly nod: this was their man. They started to spell out their respective arguments.

The two old guys considered the points. — It's like the boey here sais, one opined, — thir's mair tae this world thin we know about.

— S'only names bit, the other one said. — Magic, science, whit the fuck's the difference? S'only names we gie thum!

The debate raged on, and became increasingly passionate as more drink was consumed. The two philosophers felt a little drunk, and grew very antagonistic towards each other. They had scarcely realised that the argument had attracted several spectators, young men decked in blue, red and white, who had surrounded their table.

However, the atmosphere began to get tense as the younger men got more drunk and charged up with the prospect of the football match. One bloated youth in a blue football strip intervened in the discussion. He carried a distinct air of menace which unnerved the philosophers. — See yous cunts? Yous come doon here fill ah aw yir shite, treat ma da's auld mate, auld Tommy thair, like a fuckin monkey.

— The boey's awright, the boey's awright, auld Tommy

said, but he was speaking to himself, in a soft drunken mantra.

— It wasn't like that, McGlone said shakily.

— You! Shut it! The fat youth sneered. — Yous come doon here wi yir silly wee arguments, n yis still canny agree. Thir's only wahn way tae settle this argument: yous two in a squerr go ootside.

— Ridiculous, McGlone said, worried at the changing vibes.

Ornstein shrugged. He realised that part of him had wanted to punch McGlone's smug face for ages. There had been a girl, at Magdalen College. McGlone had known how he felt about her but he still . . . goddamn his ass . . .

The fat youth took Ornstein's shrug as a signal of acquiescence. — Squerr goes it is then!

— But . . . McGlone was pulled to his feet. He and Ornstein were taken to an empty carpark at the back of a shopping centre. The youths in blue formed a ring around the two philosophers.

McGlone was about to speak, to appeal for rational and civilised behaviour, but to his shock saw the Professor of Metaphysics from the University of Edinburgh bearing down on him. Ornstein struck the first blow, a solid jab to McGlone's chin. — Come on, asshole! he snarled, taking up a boxing stance.

McGlone felt a surge of rage and swung at his friend, and soon the two philosophers were tearing into each other, urged on by the swelling ranks of the Ibrox enclosure mob.

Ornstein gained the upper hand quickly. The telling blow was a powerful punch to the classical liberal's stomach, causing him to double over. Ornstein then hit the Glasgow professor on the side of the jaw. Gus McGlone staggered back from the blow, losing his footing. His head hit the paving-stones with a hollow crack so jarring you felt that outright death would be preferable to the messy range of possibilities which lay just to this side of it. The Chicago materialist, urged on by the crowd, put the boot into the prostrate classical liberal.

Lou Ornstein stood back and examined the gasping, bloodied

figure of McGlone. Far from feeling shame, Ornstein had never felt better. He was basking so thoroughly in his triumph, it took him a while to recognise the dispersal of the crowd and the appearance of a police van. As Gus McGlone rose unsteadily to his feet and tried to get his bearings, he was unceremoniously bundled into a meatwagon.

The two philosophers were locked up in separate cells.

The duty sergeant was going through his routine of asking each brawling set of prisoners who the Billy and who the Tim was. If the handshake is right he will let the Billy go and slap the Tim around a bit. That way everybody's happy. The Billy gets to feel superior and delude himself that being a non-churchgoing 'protestant' is somehow important; the Tim gets to feel persecuted and indulge his paranoia about masonic conspiracies; the sergeant gets to slap the Tim around.

— Whit fit ye kick wi, mate? Duty Sergeant Fotheringham asked McGlone.

— I don't kick with any. I am Professor Angus McGlone, John Pulanzo Professor of Moral Philosophy at the University of Glasgow.

Fotheringham shook his head. Another bampot turfed out the nuthouse under this community care bullshit. — Aye, of course ye are son, he said encouragingly, — n ye know who ah am?

— No . . . McGlone said unsteadily.

— Ah'm David Attenborough. N ah'm used tae dealin wi fuckin animals. Animals like you that terrorise the public . . .

— You stupid bloody fool. You don't know who I am! I could get you into serious trouble. I sit on several government committees and I number . . . McGlone never got to finish the sentence. He was silenced by another digging blow to his stomach and taken to the cells where he was detained before being charged with breach of the peace.

Lou Ornstein, who was on his best behaviour with the police, and whose story was believed due to his accent, emerged from the station without being charged. He made his way to the underground. He had never known that he could fight, and had learned something about himself.

A small youth came up to him. — Ah saw you fightin this eftirnin, big man. Ye were magic, so ye wir.

— No, Ornstein replied, — I was unknown science.

DISNAE MATTER

Ah wis it that Disneyland in Florida, ken. Took hur n the bairn. Wi me gittin peyed oaf fi Ferranti's, ah thoat it's either dae somethin wi the dough or pish it doon the bog it the Willie Muir. Ah saw whit happened tae a loat ay other cunts; livin like kings fir a while: taxis ivraywhair, chinkies ivray night, cairry-oots, ye ken the score. N whit dae they huv tae show fir it? Scottish Fuckin Fitba Association, that's what, ya cunt.

Now ah wisnae that keen oan Disneyland, bit ah thoat: fir the bairn's sake, ken? Wish ah hudnae bothered. It wis shite. Big fuckin queues tae git oan aw the rides. That's awright if ye like that sortay thing, but it's no ma fuckin scene. The beer ower thair's pish n aw. They go oan aboot aw thir beer, thir Budweiser n aw that; its like drinkin fuckin cauld water. One thing ah did like aboot the States though is the scran. Loadsay it, beyond yir wildest dreams, n the service n aw. Ah mind in one place ah sais tae hur: Fill yir fuckin boots while ye kin, hen, cause whin wi git back hame will be livin oafay McCain's oven chips till fuck knows when.

Anywey, it this fuckin Disneyland shite, this daft cunt in a bear suit jumps oot in front ay us, ken? Wavin ehs airms aboot n that. The bairn starts fuckin screamin, gied ur a real fright, ken? So ah fuckin panels the cunt, punches the fuckin wide-o in the mooth, or whair ah thought ehs mooth wis, under that suit, ken? Too fuckin right! Disneyland or nae fuckin Disneyland, disnae gie the cunt the excuse tae jump oot in front ay the bairn, ken.

Thing is, these polis cunts, fuckin guns n aw ya cunt, nae

fuckin joke, ah'm tellin ye, they sais tae ays: Whit's the fucking score here, mate, bit likesay American, ken? So ah goes, noddin ower tae this bear cunt: Cunt jumped oot in front ay the bairn. Well ootay fuckin order. The polis cunt jist says somethin aboot the boy mibbe bein a bit too keen it ehs joab, ken. The other yin sais somethin like: Mibbe the wee lassie's frightened ay bears, ken?

So then this radge in a yellay jaykit comes along. Ah tipples right away thit eh's that bear cunt's gaffer, likesay. Eh apologises tae ays, then turns tae the bear cunt n sais: Wir gaunny huv tae lit ye go mate. They wir jist gaunny, likes, gie the boy ehs fucking cairds like that. This is nae good tae us, eh tells the boy. This perr cunt in the bear suit, eh's goat the head oaf now, likes; the cunt's nearly greetin, gaun oan aboot needin the joab tae pey ehs wey through college. So ah gits a hud ay this radge in the yellay jaykit n sais: Hi mate, yir ootay order here. Thir's nae need tae gie the boy ehs cairds. It's aw sorted oot.

Mean tae say, ah banged the cunt awright, bit ah didnae want the boy tae lose ehs joab, ken. Ah ken whit it's fuckin like. It's aw a great laugh whin they chuck that redundancy poppy it ye, bit that disnae last firivir, ken. Aw they doss cunts thit blow the dough oan nowt. Thuv goat mates they nivir kent they hud — till the fuckin hireys run oot. Anywey, this supervisor radge goes: S'up tae you mate. You're happy, cunt keeps ehs joab. Then eh turns tae the boy n sais: Yir fuckin lucky, ah'm tellin ye. If it wisnae fir the boy here, ken, ye'd be pickin up yir cairds, but this is aw American, likesay, ye ken how aw they doss cunts talk, oan the telly n that.

The cunt ah gubbed, this bear cunt goes: Really sorry, mate, ma fault, ken. So ah jist sais: Sound by me. The polis n the supervisor boy fucked off n the bear cunt turns n sais: Thanks a lot, buddy. Have a nice day. Ah thoat fir a minute, ah'll fucking gie ye nice day, ya cunt, jumpin oot in front ay the fuckin bairn. Bit ah jist left it, ken, nae hassle tae nae cunt. Boy's entitled tae keep ehs joab; that wis ma good deed fir the day. Ah jist goes: Aye, you n aw, mate.

THE GRANTON STAR CAUSE

It hit Boab Coyle hard, right in the centre of his chest. He stood at the bar, open-mouthed, as his mate Kev Hyslop explained the position to him.

— Sorry, Boab, but we aw agree. We cannae guarantee ye a game. Wuv goat Tambo n wee Grant now. This team's gaun places.

— Gaun places!? Gaun places!? Churches League Division Three! It's a kick aboot, ya pretentious cunt. A fuckin kick aboot!

Kev did not like Boab's stroppy response. Surely the Granton Star cause was bigger than any one individual's ego. After all, in an open vote, he had been the one entrusted with the captain's armband for the season. The Star were challenging for promotion to Division Two of the Edinburgh Churches League. Additionally, they were only three games away from a cup-final appearance at City Park – with nets – in the Tom Logan Memorial Trophy. The stakes were high, and Kev wanted to be the man who skippered the Star to cup glory in their own backyard. He knew, though, that part of his responsibilities involved making unpopular decisions. Friendships had to be put on the back burner.

— Yir bound tae be disappointed mate . . .

— Disappointed!? Too fuckin right ah'm disappointed. Which cunt washes the strips nearly every week? Eh? Boab pleaded, pointing to himself.

— C'moan Boab, huv another pint . . .

— Stick yir fuckin pint up yir erse! Some mates yous, eh?

Well fuck yis! Boab stormed out of the pub as Kev turned to the rest of the boys and shrugged.

Before returning home, Boab went for a few unenjoyable pints of lager on his own in two other pubs. He brimmed with resentment when he thought of Tambo, who had had his eye on Boab's number 10 jersey ever since the posing cunt had got involved with the Star at the start of the season. Orange-juice drinking bastard. It had been a mistake to fill the side with wankers like that. It was, after all, just a kick about; a laugh with the mates. *Fresh orange n lemonade. Fresh orange n lemonade.* Tambo's nasal tones grated mercilessly in his head.

In the pubs Boab visited, he failed to recognise anybody. This was unusual. Additionally, auld drunkards who normally plagued him, looking for company, or to cadge a pint, avoided him like he was a leper.

Boab's mother was hoovering when her son returned home. As soon as she heard him at the door, however, she switched the machine off. Doreen Coyle looked conspiratorially at her husband, Boab senior, who shifted his considerable bulk in his chair and cast the *Evening News* onto the coffee table.

— Ah want a wee word, son, Boab senior said.

— Eh? Boab was somewhat alarmed by the challenging and confrontational tone of his father's voice.

But before Boab senior could speak, Doreen started to rant nervously.

— S'no likesay wir tryin tae git rid ay ye, son. S'no likesay that at aw.

Boab stood there, a sense of foreboding cutting through his bemusement.

— That's enough, Doreen, Boab's father said, with a hint of irritation. — Thing is, son, it's time ye wir ootay this hoose. Yir twenty-three now, which is far too auld fir a laddie tae be steyin wi his ma n faither. A mean, ah wis away tae sea wi the Merchant Navy at seventeen. It's jist no natural, son, d'ye understand?

Boab said nothing. He couldn't think straight. His father continued.

— Dinnae want yir mates tae think thit yir some kinday queer felly, now dae ye? Anywey, yir ma n me's no gittin any younger. Wir ent'rin a funny phase in oor lives, son. Some might say . . . Boab Coyle looked at his wife, — . . . a dangerous phase. Yir ma n me son, we need time tae sort oot oor lives. Tae git it the gither, if ye ken whit ah mean. You've goat a lassie, wee Evelyn. You ken the score! Boab senior winked at his son, examing his face for a sign of understanding. Although none was apparent, he carried on. — Yir problem is, son, yir huvin yir cake n eatin it. N whae suffers? Ah'll tell ye whae. Muggins here, Boab senior pointed to himself. — Yir ma n me. Now ah ken it's no that easy tae find somewhair tae stey these days, especially whin yuv hud everybody else, like muggins here, runnin aroond eftir ye. Bit we'll no say nowt aboot that. Thing is, me n yir ma, wir prepared tae gie ye two weeks' grace. Jist as long as ye make sure that yir ootay here within a fortnight.

Somewhat stunned, Boab could only say, — Aye . . . right . . .

— Dinnae think thit wir tryin tae git rid ay ye, son. It's jist thit yir faither n me think thit it wid be mutually advantageous, tae baith parties, likesay, if ye found yir ain place.

— That's it, Doe, Boab's faither sang triumphantly. — Mutually advantageous tae baith parties. Ah like that. Any brains you n oor Cathy've got, son, they definitely come fae yir ma thair, nivir mind muggins here.

Boab looked at his parents. They seemed somehow different. He had always regarded his auld man as a fat, wheezing, chronic asthmatic, and his auld girl as a blobby woman in a tracksuit. Physically they looked the same, but he could, for the first time, detect an unsettling edge of sexuality about them which he'd previously been oblivious to. He saw them for what they were: sleazy, lecherous bastards. He now realised that the look they gave him when he took Evelyn upstairs for sex, was not of embarrassment or resentment, but one of anticipation. Far from concerning themselves with what he was doing, it gave them the chance to do their own thing.

Evelyn. Once he talked to her things would be better. Ev always understood. Ideas of formal engagement and marriage, so long pooh-poohed by Boab, now fluttered through his mind. He'd been daft not to see the possibilities in it before. Their own place. He could watch videos all evening. A ride every night. He'd get another club; fuck the Star! Evelyn could wash the strips. Suddenly buoyant again, he went out, down to the call-box at the shops. He already felt like an intruder in his parents' home.

Evelyn picked up the phone. Boab's spirits rose further at the prospect of company. The prospect of understanding. The prospect of sex.

— Ev? Boab. Awright?

— Aye.

— Fancy comin ower?

— . . .

— Eh? Ev? Fancy comin ower, likesay?

— Naw.

— How no? Something wasn't right. A shuddering anxiety shot through Boab.

— Jist dinnae.

— But how no? Ah've hud a bad day, Ev. Ah need tae talk tae ye.

— Aye. Well, talk tae yir mates well.

— Dinnae be like that, Ev! Ah sais ah've hud a hard day! Whit is it? Whit's wrong?

— You n me. That's whit's wrong.

— Eh?

— Wir finished. Finito. Kaput. Endy story. Goodnight Vienna.

— Whit've ah done, Ev? Whit've ah done? Boab could not believe his ears.

— You ken.

— Ev . . .

481

— It's no whit yuv done, it's whit yuv no done!

— But Ev . . .

— Me n you Boab. Ah want a guy whae kin dae things fir ays. Somebody whae kin really make love tae a woman. No some fat bastard whae sits oan ehs erse talkin aboot fitba n drinkin pints ay lager wi his mates. A real man, Boab. A sexy man. Ah'm twinty Boab. Twinty years auld. Ah'm no gaun tae tie masel doon tae a slob!

— Whit's goat intae you? Eh? Evelyn? Yuv nivir complained before. You n me. Ye wir jist a daft wee lassie before ye met me. Nivir knew whit a ride wis, fir fuck sake . . .

— Aye! Well that's aw changed! Cos ah've met somebody, Boab Coyle! Mair ay a fuckin man thin you'll ivir be!

— . . . Eh? . . . Eh? . . . WHAE? . . . WHAE IS THE CUUUHHNNT!

— That's fir me tae ken n you tae find oot!

— Ev . . . how could ye dae this tae ays . . . you n me, Ev . . . it wis eywis you n me . . . engagement n that . . .

— Sorry, Boab. Bit ah've been wi you since ah wis sixteen. Ah might huv kent nowt aboot love then, bit ah sure as fuck ken a bit mair now!

— YA FAAHKIN SLAG! . . . YA HORRIBLE FUCKIN HING-OOT! . . .

Evelyn slammed the receiver down.

— Ev . . . Ev . . . Ah love ye . . . Boab spoke those words for the first time, down a dead telephone line.

— SLAAHT! FAAHKIN SLAAAHHT! He smashed the receiver around in the box. His segged brogues booted out two glass panels and he tried to wrench the phone from its mounting.

Boab was unaware that a police squad-car had pulled up outside the phone-box.

Down at the local police station, the arresting officer, PC Brian Cochrane, was typing up Boab's statement when Duty Sergeant Morrison appeared. Boab sat in depressed silence at the foot of the desk while Cochrane typed with two fingers.

— Evening, sarge, PC Cochrane said.

The sergeant mumbled something which may or may not have been 'Brian', not pausing to look around. He put a sausage roll into the microwave. When he opened the cupboard above the oven, Morrison was angered to note that there was no tomato sauce. He despised snacks without ketchup. Upset, he turned to PC Cochrane.

— Thir's nae fuckin ketchup, Brian. Whae's turn wis it tae git the provisions?

— Eh . . . sorry sarge . . . slipped up, the constable said, embarrassed. — Eh . . . busy night, sarge, likes.

Morrison shook his head sadly and let out a long exhalation of breath.

— So what've we goat the night, Brian?

— Well, there's the rapist, the guy who stabbed the boy at the shopping centre and this comedian here, he pointed at Boab.

— Right . . . ah've already been doon n hud a word wi the rapist. Seems a nice enough young felly. Telt ays the daft wee hoor wis askin fir it. S'the wey ay the world, Brian. The guy who knifed the boy . . . well, silly bugger, but boys will be boys. What aboot this tube-stake?

— Caught him smashin up a phone-box.

Sergeant Morrison clenched his teeth shut. Trying to contain a surge of anger which threatened to overwhelm him, he spoke slowly and deliberately: — Get this cowboy doon tae the cells. Ah want a wee word wi this cunt.

Somebody else wanting a wee word. Boab was beginning to feel that these 'wee words' were never to his advantage.

Sergeant Morrison was a British Telecom shareholder. If one thing made him more angry than snacks without tomato ketchup, it was seeing the capital assets of BT, which made up part of his investment, depreciated by wanton vandalism.

Down in the cells, Morrison pummelled Boab's stomach, ribs and testicles. As Boab lay lying groaning on the cold, tiled floor, the sergeant smiled down at him.

— Ye ken, it jist goes tae show ye the effectiveness ay they privatisation policies. Ah would nivir huv reacted like that if ye hud smashed up a phone-box when they were nationalised. Ah know it's jist the same really; vandalism meant increased taxes for me then, while now it means lower dividends. Thing is, ah feel like ah've goat mair ay a stake now, son. So ah don't want any lumpen-proletarian malcontents threatening ma investment.

Boab lay moaning miserably, ravaged by sickening aches and oppressed by mental torment and anguish.

Sergeant Morrison prided himself on being a fair man. Like the rest of the punters detained in the cells, Boab was given his cup of stewed tea and jam roll for breakfast. He couldn't touch it. They had put butter and jam on together. He couldn't touch the piece but was charged with breach of the peace, as well as criminal damage.

Although it was 6.15 a.m. when he was released, he felt too fragile to go home. Instead, he decided to go straight to his work after stopping off at a cafe for a scrambled-egg roll and a cup of coffee. He found a likely place and ordered up.

After his nourishment, Boab went to settle the bill.

— One pound, sixty-five pence. The cafe owner was a large, fat, greasy man, badly pock-marked.

— Eh? Bit steep, Boab counted out his money. He hadn't really thought about how much money he had, even though the police had taken it all from him, with his keys and shoelaces, and he'd had to sign for them in the morning.

He had one pound, thirty-eight pence. He counted out the money. The cafe proprietor looked at Boab's unshaven, bleary appearance. He was trying to run a respectable establishment, not a haven for dossers. He came from behind the counter and jostled Boab out of the door.

— Fuckin wise cunt . . . wide-o . . . ye kin see the prices . . . ah'll fuckin steep ye, ya cunt . . .

Out in the cold, blue morning street, the fat man punched Boab on the jaw. More through fatigue and disorientation than the power of the blow, Boab fell backwards, cracking his head off the pavement.

He lay there for a while, and began weeping, cursing God, Kev, Tambo, Evelyn, his parents, the police and the cafe owner.

Despite being physically and mentally shattered, Boab put in a lot of graft that morning, to try and forget his worries and make the day pass quickly. Normally, he did very little lifting, reasoning that as he was the driver, it wasn't really his job. Today, however, he had his sleeves rolled up. The first flit his crew worked on saw them take the possessions of some rich bastards from a big posh house in Cramond to a big posh house in the Grange. The other boys in the team, Benny, Drew and Zippo, were far less talkative than usual. Normally Boab would have been suspicious of the silence. Now, feeling dreadful, he welcomed the respite it offered.

They got back to the Canonmills depot at 12.30 for dinner. Boab was surprised to be summoned into the office of Mike Rafferty, the gaffer.

— Sit doon, Boab. I'll come straight to the point, mate, Rafferty said, doing anything but. — Standards, he said enigmatically, and pointed to the Hauliers and Removals Association plaque on the wall, bearing a logo which decorated each one of his fleet of lorries. — Counts for nothing now. It's all about price these days, Boab. And all these cowboys, who have fewer overheads and lower costs, they're trimming us, Boab.

— Whit ur ye tryin tae say?

— We've goat tae cut costs, Boab. Where can ah cut costs? This place? He looked out of the glass and wooden box of an office and across the floor of the warehouse. — We're tied doon tae a five-year lease here. No. It has to be capital and labour costs. It's aw doon tae market positioning, Boab. We have to find our niche in the market. That niche is as a quality firm specialising in local moves for the As, Bs and Cs.

— So ah'm sacked? Boab asked, with an air of resignation.

Rafferty looked Boab in the eye. He had recently been on a training course entitled: 'Positively Managing The Redundancy Scenario.'

— Your post is being made redundant, Boab. It's important

to remember that it's not the person we make redundant, it's the post. We've overstretched ourselves, Boab. Got geared up for continental removals. Tried, and I have to say failed, to compete with the big boys. Got a wee bit too carried away by 1992, the single market and all that. I'm going to have to let the big lorry go. We also need to lose a driver's job. This isnae easy, Boab, but it has tae be last one in, first one out. Now ah'll put it around in the trade that I know of a reliable driver who's looking for something, and obviously, ah'll give you an excellent reference.

— Obviously, said Boab, with sarcastic bitterness.

Boab left at lunchtime and went for a pint and a toastie down the local pub. He didn't bother to go back. As he sat and drank alone, a stranger approached him, sitting down next to him, even though plenty free seats were available. The man looked in his fifties, not particularly tall, yet with a definite presence. His white hair and white beard reminded Boab of a folk singer, the guy from the Corries, or maybe the boy in the Dubliners.

— Yuv fucked this one up, ya daft cunt, the man said to him, raising a pint of eighty shilling to his lips.

— Eh? What? Boab was suprised again.

— You. Boab Coyle. Nae hoose, nae joab, nae burd, nae mates, polis record, sair face, aw in the space ay a few ooirs. Nice one, he winked and toasted Boab with his pint. This angered, but intrigued Boab.

— How the fuck dae you ken? Whae the fuckin hell ur you?

The man shook his head, — It's ma fuckin business tae ken. Ah'm God.

— Way tae fuck ya auld radge! Boab laughed loudly, throwing his head back.

— Fuckin hell. Another wise cunt, said the man tiredly. He then trudged out a spiel with the bored, urbane air of someone who had been through all this more times than they cared to remember.

— Robert Anthony Coyle, born on Friday the 23rd of July, 1968, to Robert McNamara Coyle and Doreen Sharp. Younger brother of Cathleen Siobhain Shaw, who is married to James

Allan Shaw. They live at 21 Parkglen Cresent in Gilmerton and they have a child, also called James. You have a sickle-shaped birthmark on your inner thigh. You attended Granton Primary School and Ainslie Park Secondary, where you obtained two SCE O Grades, in Woodwork and Technical Drawing. Until recently, you worked in furniture removals, lived at hame, hud a bird called Evelyn, whom you couldn't sexually satisfy, and played football for Granton Star, like you made love, employing little effort and even less skill.

Boab sat totally deflated. There seemed to be an almost translucent aura around this man. He spoke with certainty and conviction. Boab almost believed him. He didn't know what to believe anymore.

— If you're God, what ur ye daein wastin yir time oan me?

— Good question, Boab. Good question.

— Ah mean, thir's bairns starvin, likesay, oan telly n that. If ye wir that good, ye could sort aw that oot, instead ay sitting here bevvyin wi the likes ay me.

God looked Boab in the eye. He seemed upset.

— Jist hud oan a minute, pal. Lit's git one thing straight. Every fuckin time ah come doon here, some wide-o pills ays up aboot what ah should n shouldnae be fuckin daein. Either that or ah huv tae enter intae some philosophical fuckin discourse wi some wee undergraduate twat aboot the nature ay masel, the extent ay ma omnipotence n aw that shite. Ah'm gittin a wee bit fed up wi aw this self-justification; it's no for yous cunts tae criticise me. Ah made yous cunts in ma ain image. Yous git oan wi it; yous fuckin well sort it oot. That cunt Nietzsche wis wide ay the mark whin he sais ah wis deid. Ah'm no deid; ah jist dinnae gie a fuck. It's no fir me tae sort every cunt's problems oot. Nae other cunt gies a fuck so how should ah? Eh?

Boab found God's whingeing pathetic. — You fuckin toss. If ah hud your powers . . .

— If you hud ma powers ye'd dae what ye dae right now: sweet fuck all. You've goat the power tae cut doon oan the pints ay lager, aye?

— Aye, bit . . .

— Nae buts aboot it. You've goat the power tae git fit and make a mair positive contribution tae the Granton Star cause. You hud the power tae pey mair attention tae that wee burd ay yours. She wis tidy. Ye could've done a loat better there, Boab.

— Mibbe ah could, mibbe ah couldnae. Whit's it tae you?

— Ye hud the power tae git oot fae under yir ma n dad's feet, so's they could huv a decent cowp in peace. Bit naw. No selfish cunt Coyle. Jist sits thair watchin *Coronation Street* n *Brookside* while they perr cunts ur gaun up the waws wi frustration.

— S 'nane ay your business.

— Everything's ma business. Ye hud the power tae fight back against the fat cunt fi the cafe. Ye jist lit the cunt panel ye, fir a few fuckin pence. That wis ootay order, bit ye lit the cunt git away wi it.

— Ah wis in a state ay shock . . .

— And that cunt Rafferty. Ye didnae even tell the cunt tae stick his fuckin joab up his erse.

— So what! So fuckin what!

— So ye hud they powers, ye jist couldnae be bothered usin thum. That's why ah'm interested in ye Boab. You're jist like me. A lazy, apathetic, slovenly cunt. Now ah hate bein like this, n bein immortal, ah cannae punish masel. Ah kin punish you though, mate. That's whit ah intend tae dae.

— But ah could . . .

— Shut it cunt! Ah've fuckin hud it up tae ma eyebaws wi aw this repentence shite. Vengeance is mine, n ah intend tae take it, oan ma ain lazy n selfish nature, through the species ah created, through thir representative. That's you.

God stood up. Although he was almost shaking with anger, Boab saw that this was not easy for him. He could still be talked out of doing whatever he was going to do. — Ye look jist like ah always imagined . . . Boab said sycophantically.

— That's cause ye've nae imagination, ya daft cunt. Ye see ays n hear ays as ye imagine ays. Now you're fuckin claimed, radge.

— Bit ah'm no the worst . . . Boab pleaded. — . . . Whit

aboot the murderers, the serial killers, dictators, torturers, politicians . . . the cunt's thit shut factories doon tae preserve thir profit levels . . . aw they greedy rich bastards . . . what aboot thaim? Eh?

— Might git round tae they cunts, might no. That's ma fuckin business. You've hud it cunt! Yir a piece ay slime, Coyle. An insect. That's it! An insect . . . God said, inspired. — . . . ah'm gaunny make ye look like the dirty, lazy pest thit ye are!

God looked Boab in the eye again. A force of invisible energy seemed to leave his body and travel a few feet across the table, penetrating Boab through to his bones. The force pinned him back in his chair, but it was over in a second, and all Boab was left with was a racing heartbeat and a sweating brow, genitals and armpits. The whole performance seemed to take it out of God. He stood up shakily in his chair and looked at Boab. — Ah'm away tae ma fuckin kip, he wheezed, turning and leaving the pub.

Boab sat there, mind racing, feverishly trying to rationalise what had happened to him. Kevin came into the pub for a quick pint a few minutes after this. He noted Boab, but was reluctant to approach him, after Boab's outburst in the pub the day before.

When Kevin eventually did come over, Boab told him that he had just met God, who was going to turn him into an insect.

— You dinnae half talk some shite, Boab, he told his distraught friend, before leaving him.

That evening, Kevin was at home alone, eating a fish supper. His girlfriend was on a night out with some friends. A large bluebottle landed on the edge of his plate. It just sat there, looking at him. Something told him not to swat it.

The bluebottle then flew into a blob of tomato sauce on the edge of the plate, and soared up to the wall before Kev could react. To his astonishment, it began to trace out KEV against the white woodchip paper. It had to make a second journey to the sauce to finish what it had started. Kev shuddered. This was crazy, but there it was; his name, spelt by an insect . . .

— Boab? Is that really you? Fuckin hell! Eh, buzz twice fir aye, once fir naw.

Two buzzes.

— Did eh, what's his name, did God dae this?

Two buzzes.

— Whit the fuck ur ye gaunny dae?

Frantic buzzing.

— Sorry Boab . . . kin ah git ye anything? Scran, likesay?

They shared the fish supper. Kev had the lion's share, Boab sat near the edge of the plate licking at a little bit of fish, grease and sauce.

Boab stayed with Kev Hyslop for a few days. He was encouraged to lie low, in case Julie, Kev's girlfriend, discovered him. Kev threw the fly-spray away. He bought a pot of ink and some notepaper. He'd pour some ink into a saucer, and let Boab trace out some laborious messages on the paper. One, particulary, was written in anxiety: CUNT OF A SPIDER IN BATHROOM. Kev flushed the spider down the toilet. Whenever he came in from work, Kev was concerned that something might have happened to Boab. He could not relax until he heard that familiar buzz.

From his location behind the bedroom curtains, Boab plotted revenge. He'd all but absolved Kev for dropping him from the Star, on account of his kindness. However, he was determined to get back at his parents, Evelyn, Rafferty, and the others.

It wasn't all bad being a bluebottle. The power of flight was something he'd have hated to have missed; there had been few greater pleasures than soaring around outside. He also gained a taste for excrement, its rich, sour moistness tantalising his long insect tongue. The other bluebottles who crowded onto the hot shite were not so bad. Boab was attracted to some of them. He learned to appreciate the beauty of the insect body; the sexy, huge, brown eyes, the glistening external skeleton, the appealing mosaic of blue and green, the rough, coarse hairs and the shimmering wings which refracted the sun's golden light.

One day, he flew over by Evelyn's, and caught sight of her

leaving the house. He followed her, to her new boyfriend's place. The guy was Tambo, who'd displaced Boab in the Granton Star line-up. He found himself buzzing involuntarily. After watching them fuck like rabbits in every conceivable position, he flew down into the cat's litter tray, checking first that the creature was asleep in its basket.

He munched at a skittery turd not properly buried in the gravel. He then flew into the kitchen, and puked the shite into a curry that Tambo had made. He made several journeys.

The next day Tambo and Evelyn were violently ill with food-poisoning. Observing them feverish and sick gave Boab a sense of power. This encouraged him to fly over to his old workplace. When he got there, he lifted some smaller granules of blue rat-poison from a matchbox on the floor, and inserted them into Rafferty's cheese salad sandwich.

Rafferty was very sick the next day, having to go to casualty and get his stomach pumped. The doctor reckoned he'd been given rat-poison. In addition to feeling terrible physically, Rafferty was also devastated with paranoia. Like most bosses, who are regarded with at best contempt and at worst hated by all their subordinates, except the most cringing sycophants, he imagined himself to be popular and respected. He wondered: Who could have done this to me?

Boab's next journey was to his parents' home. This was one journey he wished he hadn't made. He took up a position high on the wall, and tears condensed in his massive brown eyes as he surveyed the scene below him.

His father was clad in a black nylon body-stocking with a hole at the crotch. His arms were outstretched with his hands on the mantelpiece and his legs spread. Boab senior's flab rippled in his clinging costume. Boab's mother was naked, apart from a belt which was fastened so tightly around her body it cut sharply into her wobbling flesh, making her look like a pillow tied in the middle with a piece of string. Attached to the belt was a massive latex dildo, most of which was in Boab senior's anus. Most, but still not enough for Boab senior.

— Keep pushin Doe . . . keep pushin . . . ah kin take mair . . . ah *need* mair . . .

— Wir nearly at the hilt already . . . yir an awfay man, Boab Coyle . . . Doreen grunted and sweated, pushing further, smearing more KY jelly around Boab senior's flabby arse and onto the still-visible part of the shaft.

— The questionin, Doe . . . gies the questionin . . .

— Tell ays whae it is! Tell ays ya fuckin philandering bastard! Doreen screeched, as Boab the bluebottle shuddered on the wall.

— Ah'll nivir talk . . . Boab senior's wheezing tones concerned Doreen.

— Ye awright, Boab? Mind yir asthma n that . . .

— Aye . . . aye . . . keep up the questionin, Doreen . . . the crocodile clips, GIT THE CROC CLIPS DOE! Boab senior filled his cheeks with air.

Doreen took the first clip from the mantlepiece and attached it to one of Boab senior's nipples. She did the same with the other one. The third clip was a larger one, and she snapped it harshly onto his wizened scrotum. Turned on by his screams, she pushed the dildo in further.

— Tell ays, Boab! WHAE HUV YE BEEN SEEIN?

—AAAGGHHH . . .' Boab senior screamed, then whispered, — . . . Dolly Parton.

— Whae? Ah cannae hear ye, Doreen said, menacingly.

— DOLLY PARTON!

— That fuckin slut . . . ah knew it . . . whae else?:

— Anna Ford . . . n that Madonna . . . bit jist the once . . .

— SCUMBAG! BASTARD! YA DIRTY FUCKIN PRICK! . . . Ye ken whit this means!

— No the shite, Doe . . . ah cannae eat yir shite . . .

— Ah'm gaunny shite in your mooth, Boab Coyle! It's whit wi baith want! Dinnae deny it!

— Naw! Don't shite in ma mooth . . . don't . . . shite in ma mooth . . . shite in ma mooth . . . SHITE IN MA MOOTH!

Boab saw it all now. While he was mechanically relieving

himself upstairs by skillessly poking Evelyn in the missionary position, his parents were trying to cram the three-piece suite up each other's arses. The very thought of them have a sexuality had repulsed him; now it shamed him in a different way. There was one aspect, however, where it was like father, like son. He knew he could not trust himself to see his mother's shite. It would be too arousing, that succulent, hot sour faeces, all going into his father's mouth. Boab felt his first conscious twinges of an Oedipus complex, at twenty-three years old, and in a metamorphosised state.

Boab sprang from the wall and swarmed around them, flying in and out of their ears.

— Shite . . . that fuckin fly . . . Doreen said. Just then, the phone went. — Ah'll huv tae git it! Boab. Stey thair. It'll be oor Cathy. She'll jist pester us aw night if ah dinnae answer now. Don't go away. She undid the belt, leaving the dildo in Boab's senior's arse. He was at peace, his muscles stretched, but holding the latex rod comfortably and securely. He felt filled, complete, and alive.

Boab junior was exhausted after his efforts and retreated back to the wall. Doreen grabbed the telephone receiver.

— Hiya Cathy. How are you doin, love? . . . Good . . . Dad's fine. How's the wee felly? . . . Aw, the wee lamb! N Jimmy . . . Good. Listen love, wir jist sitting doon tae oor tea. Ah'll phone ye back in aboot half an hour, n will huv a proper blether . . . Right love . . . Bye the now.

Doreen's reactions were quicker than the weary Boab's. She picked up the *Evening News* as she put down the phone and sprang over to the wall. Boab didn't see the threat until the rolled newspaper was hurtling towards him. He took off, but the paper caught him and knocked him back against the wall at great speed. He felt excruciating pain as parts of his external skeletal structure cracked open.

— Got ye, ya swine, Doreen hissed.

Boab tried to regain the power of flight, but it was useless. He dropped onto the carpet, falling down the gap between the wall and the sideboard. His mother crouched down onto her knees, but she couldn't see Boab in the shadows.

— Tae hell wi it, the hoover'll git it later. That fly wis a bigger pest thin young Boab, she smiled, clipping on the belt and pushing the dildo further into Boab senior's arse.

That night, the Coyles were awakened by the sound of groaning. They went tentatively down the stairs and found their son lying battered and bloodied, under the sideboard in the front room, suffering from terrible injuries.

An ambulance was called for, but Boab junior had slipped away. The cause of death was due to massive internal injuries, similar to the type someone would sustain in a bad car crash. All his ribs were broken, as were both his legs and his right arm. His skull had fractured. There was no trail of blood and it was inconceivable that Boab could have crawled home from an accident or a severe kicking in that condition. Everyone was perplexed.

Everyone except Kev, who began drinking heavily. Due to this problem, Kev became estranged from Julie, his girlfriend. He has fallen behind on the mortgage payments on his flat. There are to be further redundancies at the north Edinburgh electronics factory where he works. Worst of all for Kev, he is going through a lean spell in front of goal. He tries to console himself by remembering that all strikers have such barren periods, but he knows that he has lost a yard in pace. His position as captain, and even his place in the Star line-up, can no longer be considered unassailable. Star are not going to be promoted this year due to a bad slump in form and Muirhouse Albion almost contemptuously dismissed them at the quarter-final stage of the Tom Logan Memorial Trophy.

SNOWMAN BUILDING PARTS FOR RICO THE SQUIRREL

The silver squirrel undulated across the yard and scuttled up the bark of the large Californian Redwood tree which overhung the rickety wooden fence. A tearful little boy in sneakers, t-shirt, jeans and baseball-cap watched, helpless in torment as the animal moved away from him.

— We love you Rico! the boy shouted. — Don't go Rico! he screamed in anguish.

The squirrel scrambled deftly up the tree. At the sound of the boy's despairing voice he stopped and looked back. His sad brown eyes glistened as he said, — Sorry Babby, I have to go. Some day you'll understand.

The small creature turned and launched itself along a branch, catching onto another, disappearing into the dense foliage of the woods behind the border of the flimsy fence.

— Mommy! young Bobby Cartwright shouted back towards the house. — It's Rico! He's going, Mommy! Tell him to stay!

Sarah Cartwright appeared on the porch and felt her chest tighten at the sight of her disconsolate son. Tears welled up in her eyes as she strode forward and held the boy to her. In a breathless, sugary voice she said wistfully, — But Rico has to go, honey. Rico's a very special little squirrel. We knew that when he came to us. We knew that Rico would have to go, for it's Rico's mission to spread love all over the world.

— But that means Rico doesn't love us, Mom! If he loved us he'd stay! Bobby screamed, inconsolable.

— Listen Babby, there are other people that need Rico too.

He has to go to them, to help them, to give them the love they need, to make them realise just how much they need each other.

Bobby was not convinced. — Rico doesn't love us, he whimpered.

— No Babby, that's nat it at all, sugar-pie, Sarah Cartwright simpered, — the greatest gift that Rico ever gave to us was making us remember just how much we loved each other. Remember when Daddy got paid off from the plant? We lost our home? Then your little sister, our little Beverley, was run over, killed by that drunk Sheriff? Remember how we all fought and yelled at each other all the time? Sarah Cartwright explained, tears rolling down her cheeks. Her face slowly broke into a smile, like the sun rising triumphantly over dirty grey clouds. — Then Rico came. We thought we'd lost each other, but with Rico's love, we came to realise that the greatest gift we had was our love for each other . . .

— I hate Rico! Bobby snarled, pulling away from his mother and running into the house. He mounted the stairs two at a time.

— Babby, come back . . .

— Rico left us! Bobby shouted miserably, slamming his bedroom door.

— Switch that fuckin telly oaf! Ah've telt yis before! Oot n play! Maggie Robertson snapped at her children, Sean and Sinead. — Watchin fuckin telly aw day! Daft wee cunts! she half-laughed, half-sneered as Tony Anderson's hand slipped under her t-shirt and bra and roughly grappled her breast.

Young Sean switched off the television and looked up at her, a briefly uncomprehending but fearful expression frozen onto his face. Then it relaxed again into dead apathy. Sinead just played with her broken doll.

— Ah said oot! Maggie screamed. — AH'M NO TALKIN TAE MASEL, SEAN, YA DAFT WEE CUNT! The children had become inured to her normal level of scream-

ing. It was only this hacking, throttled noise that drew a response from them.

— Gies a bit ay peace yous two, c'moan, Tony pleaded, rummaging in his chinos' pocket for change. All he could feel was his erection though. — C'MOAN! he shouted in angry exasperation. The children departed.

— C'moan doll, get thum oaf, Tony said with urgency but no passion.

— N yir tellin ays ye wirnae wi hur last night?

Tony shook his head in a gesture which was intended to convey exasperation but only came across as belligerent recalcitrance. — Ah fuckin telt ye! Fir the last fuckin time: ah wis doon the snooker wi Rab n Gibbo!

Maggie held his gaze for a second. — See if you're fuckin lyin . . .

— Ud nivir fuckin lie tae you, doll, you kin read ays like a book, Tony said, sticking his hands up her skirt and sliding down her panties. They were stained with discharge from the combination of a severe UTI and a non-specific sexual disease, but he scarcely noticed. — Ye ken whit's oan ma mind now, eh? Extra fuckin sensory perception n that. A right fuckin Paul Daniels you, eh . . . he gasped, undoing his trousers, allowing his constrained gut and erection to fly freely into space.

Bob Cartwright tapped gingerly on the bedroom door. He felt a sadness lie heavily around his heart as he saw his son Bobby junior lying face down on the bed. He pushed onto a corner of it and said softly, — Hi sport, room for another? Bobby junior grudgingly shuffled along. — Hey pitcher, still sore about Rico? Huh?

— Rico hates us!

Bob senior was somewhat taken aback by his son's vehemence, in spite of the warning from his wife, Sarah. He sat back and thought for a while. He'd kept a brave face on, but if the truth be known, he'd sure miss that little guy too. After taking a sad few moments to consider the depths of his own pain, Bob senior began, — Well, you know, Babby, sometimes it maybe seems like that, but Babby, let me tell you, folks, well, they got a habit of doing all sorts of things for all sorts of reasons, some of which we don't rightly know about.

— If Rico really loved us, he'd have stayed!

— Let me tell you a story, Babby. When I was a kid, prabably nat more then your age, maybe just a lill bit older, there was one guy who was my hero. Thet was Al 'Big Al' Kennedy.

Bobby's face lit up. — The Angels! he screamed.

— Yeah sport, that's it. Al Kennedy, the best goddamn pitcher I've ever seen. Phoo-ee! I remember that World Series when we were up against the Kansas Royals. It was Big Al who came through for us. Those Royals hitters fell one by one. STRIKE ONE!

— STRIKE TWO! Bobby squealed gleefully, mimicking his father.

— STRIKE THREE! Bob senior roared.

— STRIKE FOUR! Bobby yelped, as father and son gave each other the high five.

— I'll give you strike four! C'mon sport, lets give it the seventh-inning stretch!

They sang in a lusty chorus:

> Take me up the ball game
> Take me up to the crowd
> Buy me some peanuts and crackerjacks
> I don't care if I ever get back
> and it's root root root for the Angels
> if they don't win it's a shame
> cause it's one, two, three strikes you're out
> at the old ball game!

Bob senior felt gooey inside. That one always got the kid going. — Thing was, son, he said, his face focusing into grim seriousness, — Big Al went away. Signed up for the Cardinals. I said, if Big Al loved us, he wouldn't have gone. God, I hated Al

Kennedy, and every time I saw him on TV, playing for the Cardinals I used to put this curse on him: Die, Big Al, I'd say, die, you lousy punk! My pop would say: Hey son, take it easy. There was once I got real mad, started screamin at the box about how much I hated Big Al, but the old man just said: Son, that hate's a funny old word, one you wanna be a little careful bout usin.

— A few days later my dad brought me some newspaper cuttins. I got em here. Always kept these cuttins, Bob senior said, putting them down in front of his son. — Don rightly expect you to read all these now, sport, but lemme tell you, they told me a story, a very special story, Babby, one which I've never forgotten. It was about a school-bus crash in St Louis, Mo. One little fella, why, I guess he drew the short straw in the whole goddamn affair. This little tyke was seriously ill, in a coma. Turned out thet this kid rooted for the Cardinals and his hero was none other than Big Al Kennedy. Anyway, when Big Al heard about this kid, he cut short a hunting trip in Nebraska and travelled back down to St Louis to be by the kid's side. Big Al said to this kid: Listen champ, when you get outta here, I'm gonna show you howta pitch, ya know? Bob senior explained. — Then something incredible happened, Bob senior said softly and dramatically.

Bobby's eyes opened wide in anticipation. — Waht Ded? Waht?

— Well, son, Bob senior continued, swallowing hard, his Adam's apple bobbing, — that little kid opened his eyes. And something else happened. Guess what?

— I dunno, Ded, Bobby junior replied.

— Well, I guess I kinda opened my eyes as well. You know what I mean, Babby?

— I guess . . . the young boy said quizzically.

— What I guess I'm tryin to say, son, is just cause Rico had to go don't mean that he ain't thinkin of us, that he don't love us; it's just that maybe there's somebody that needs him a whole laht more then we do just now.

Bobby junior thought about this for a bit. — Will we ever see Rico again, Pop?

— Who knows, son, perhaps we will, Bob senior said wistfully, as he felt a hand touch his shoulder softly and he looked around and met the open, watery eyes of his wife.

— You know Babby, Sarah Cartwright spoke with wavering emotion, — everytime you see somebody with the light of love in their eyes, you'll see Rico, cause there's one thing you can be sure of, honey, if there's love in people's eyes, it was Rico that put it there!

Sarah looked at her husband who smiled broadly and put his arm around her waist.

He'd been at her now for five minutes and his attention was starting to wander. Bri and Ralphie would be down the Anchor now, their names up for the pool. It was prize money night. As he thrusted, he saw the balls shooting from the tip of the cue, ricocheting off the cushion and rattling softly into the pockets. He had to dump his load into her soon.

Tony poked away as hard as he could and he felt himself so close, but yet so far from that relief. He reached across the coffee table which was adjacent to the couch and picked up the burning cigarette. He arched his neck back and took a long puff and thought of images of Madonna on the singles collection video.

It's no even thit Madonna's a bigger fuckin shag thin a loat ay the fanny roond here, bit whit she dis is dress up. Burds roond here ey dress the fuckin same; each day ivray fuckin day. How ur ye supposed tae cowp somethin thit looks the same ivray fuckin day? That's whit fanny like Madonna understand, yuv goat tae dress up fuckin different, pit oan a bit ay a fuckin show . . .

They were together, Madonna and Anthony Anderson, joined in a mutual coupling of shimmering, sensual, passionate lovemaking. Not a million miles away, Maggie Robertson was giving her man, Keanu Reeves, the most exciting time that Hollywood

> *star ever had. He was about to come, and although a long, long
> way from climax herself, she was pleased, she was delighted, that
> she had been able to please her man so . . . that was satisfaction
> enough because that fat hoor could never have turned him on like
> this . . .*
>
> *Then Keanu / Tony saw the face pressed against the window-
> pane, staring in, watching them, watching him; his stiff jaw, his
> dead eyes. As his penis grew limp, those eyes filled with passion,
> for the first time. — SEAN, GIT AWAY FAE THAT
> FUCKIN WINDAE, YA DURTY WEE CUNT!
> YOU'RE FUCKIN DEID BY THE WAY! GUARAN-
> TEED! THAT'S FUCKIN GUARANTEED, SEAN, YA
> DURTY WEE CUNT! Tony ranted as his limp dick spilled
> out of Madonna / Maggie.*
>
> *Springing up, and pulling on his jeans, Tony stormed into the
> stair and headed into the back green in violent pursuit of
> the children.*

— This is terrible, Mr C. switched off the television. They
shouldn't have this on before nine o'clock. C'mon, sport, he
looked at Bobby, — time for bed.

— Aw pop, do I have to?

Yep, you do, sport, Bob senior shrugged, — we could all use
some shut-eye!

— But I wanna watch *The Skatch Femilee Rabirtsin.*

— Listen Babby, Sarah began, *The Skatch Femilee Rabirtsin* is a
horrible programme and your father and I agree that it's not
good for you . . .

— Gee Mom, I like *The Skatch Femilee Rabirtsin* . . .

They were diverted from their discussion by a scraping sound
which came from the window. They looked out and saw a
squirrel on the ledge.

— Rico! they shouted in concert. Sarah opened the window
and the animal scampered in and ran up Bobby junior's arm,
perching on his shoulder. The young boy stroked his friend's
warm fur lightly.

— Rico, you came behk! I noo you'd come behk!

— Hey buddy, Rico laughed, lifting up his paw and giving Bobby junior the high five.

— Rico . . . Sarah simpered, as Bobby senior felt a spasm of emotion rise in his chest.

— I thought to myself, the squirrel said, — there's a lot of good work needs doin, so I'd better get me some help.

He turned his head to the window. The Cartwrights looked outside and could see hundreds, or perhaps even thousands of squirrels, their eyes glowing with love, and ready to spread that love across a cold world.

— I wonder if one of those squirrels will go and help the little Skatch boy n girl on the television, Bobby junior thought out loud.

— I'm sure one of them will, Babby, Sarah simpered.

— Don't hold your fuckin breath on that one honey, Rico the squirrel muttered, but the family failed to hear him, as they were so consumed with joy.

SPORT FOR ALL

See that big skinny gadge wi
the tartan skerf? Big Adam's
aypil hingin ower the toap ay
it? Ah'm jist gaunny huv a wee
word wi the cunt.

Whit d'yis mean leave um?
Ah'm jist spraffin wi the boy,
aboot the game n that, likesay.

                    Hi mate, been tae the rugby?
                    Murrayfield, aye? Scotlin win,
                    aye?

                    Fuckin sound.

Hear that Skanko? Scotlin
fuckin won.

                    Whae wis it thi wir playin,
                    mate?
                    Fiji. FIJI? Who the fuck's
                    that?!

FIJI? Some fuckin islands ya
doss cunt.

Aye?

Aye, well we're jist some
fuckin islands tae these cunts,
think aboot it that wey.

It's right enough though, eh
mate?

Still, wir aw fuckin Scotsmin
the gither, eh mate?

No thit ah ken much aboot
rugby masel. S'a fuckin poof's
game if ye ask me. Dinnae ken
how any cunt kin watch that
fuckin shite. It's true though,
it's aw fuckin queers thit play
that game.

Yir no a poof ur ye, mate?

Whit d'ye mean leave um? Jist
askin the boy if eh's a poof or
no. Simple fuckin question.
Mibbe the cunt is, mibbe eh
isnae.

Whair's it ye come fae, mate?

Marchmont!

Hi Skanko, the boy's fi
Marchmont.

Big hooses up thair mate. Bet
you've goat plenty fuckin
poppy.

Naw? Bit ye stey in a big
hoose bit.

No that fuckin big!

No that fuckin big, eh sais!

You stey in a fuckin castle!

D'ye hear the cunt? No that
fuckin big.

Whit's it ye dae, mate, ye
wurkin?

Aye, fuckin right ya cunt!

Aye . . . bit whit dis that make
ye? Whit's it make ye whin yir
finished?

A fuckin Accountint!

Hear that Skanko! SKANKO!
C'mere the now. C'MERE
THE NOW, YA CUNT!

This cunt's fuckin tellin ays
eh's an Accountint.

Eh? What the fuck you sayin?

Aye, right.

Well, a trainee Accountint.

Trainee Accountint,
Accountint, same fuckin
thing; tons ay fuckin hireys.

Naw.

Naw, the boy isnae a poof.

Ah jist thoat that, mate, ken wi
you bein intae the rugby n
that.

Ye goat a burd, mate?

Eh?

Thoat ye sais ye wirnae a poof.
Ivir hud a ride?

Whit d'ye mean leave the
cunt? Jist askin a simple
question.

Ivir hud a ride, mate?

Either ye huv or ye huvnae.
Jist a fuckin question. Ye
dinnae huv tae git a beamer.

That's awright then.

Jist a question, see.

Jist wi you bein intae rugby, ken.

That's ma burd ower thair.

HI KIRSTY! AWRIGHT DOLL! Be ower in a minute. Jist huvin a wee blether wi ma mate here, likesay.

No bad, eh? Tidy, eh?

Eh! You fancy ma burd, ya dirty cunt?

Eh! You tryin tae say ma burd's a fuckin hound? You tryin tae git fuckin wide?

Naw?

Jist is well fir you, ya cunt.

So ye like rugby, eh? Fitba's ma game. Ah nivir go bit. Barred fae the fuckin groond. Anywey, fitba's fuckin borin shite n aw. Dinnae huv tae go tae the game. Maist ay the action takes place before n eftir the game. Heard ay the Hibs Boys? The CCS? Aye?

Take the swedgin ootay fitba, it's fuckin deid.

Goan gies a song, mate. One
ay they poof songs ye sing in
the rugby clubs before yis aw
shag each other.

Jist a wee fuckin song then,
cunt!

Jist askin the boy tae gies a
fuckin song. Nae hassle likes.

Gies a song, mate. C'Moan!

EH! SHUT UP WI THAT
SHITE! Flower ay fuckin
Scotlin. Shite! Ah hate that
fuckin song: Oh flow-ir-ay-
Scot-lin . . . fuckin pish. Gies
a real song. Sing Distant
Drums.

Whit dae ye mean leave um?
Ah'm jist askin the cunt tae
sing. Distant Drums.

Eh?

Ye dinnae ken Distant fuckin
Drums? No? Listen tae me,
mate, ah'll fuckin sing it.

I HEAR THE SOUND
DUH-DUH-DUH-DUH
DUH-DUH-DUH-DUH
OF DIS-TINT DRUMS

DUH-DUH-DUH-DUH-
DUH-DUH-DUH-DUH

SING YA CUNT!

I hear the sound of distant
drums. It's easy. You're the
cunt wi degrees n that. Ye kin
understand that. I-HEAR-
THE-SOUND-OF-
DISTANT-DRUMS.

That's better, hi, hi, hi.

Skanko! Kirsty! Hear the cunt!
Distant fuckin Drums!

Barry. Right. Mine's a boatil
ay Becks mate. The mate n
aw. The burds ur oan
Diamond Whites. That's
Leanne, Skanko thair's burd
ken?

Cheers, mate.

See Skanko, the cunt's
awright. Sound fuckin mate
ay mines, by the way.

Whit did ye say yir name wis,
mate?

Alistair, right

That's fi Alistair.

Cheers, mate

S'at you away now, mate? Aye?
See ye then.

Distant Drums, eh mate!

What a fuckin nondy cunt!
Hud the daft cunt singin that
auld song.

Distant fuckin Drums, ya
cunt.

Becks then Skanko. Jist cause
ay the the boy gittin yin,
disnae mean tae say you
dinnae need tae. Short airms
n deep poakits this cunt, eh
Leanne?

Cheers! Tae rugby cunts;
fuckin poofs bit here's tae
thum!

THE ACID HOUSE

Something strange was happening over Pilton. Probably not just Pilton, Coco Bryce considered, but as he was in Pilton, the here and now was all that concerned him. He gazed up at the dark sky. It seemed to be breaking up. Part of it had been viciously slashed open, and Coco was disconcerted by what appeared to be ready to spill from its wound. Shards of bright neon-like light luminated in the parting. Coco could make out the ebbs and flows of currents within a translucent pool which seemed to be accumulating behind the darkened membrane of the sky, as if in readiness to burst through the gap, or at least rip the wounded cloud-cover further. However, the light emanating from the wound seemed to have a narrow and self-contained range; it didn't light up the planet below.

Then the rain came: at first a few warning spits, followed by a hollow explosion of thunder in the sky. Coco saw a flash of lightning where his glowing vision had been and although unnerved in a different way, he breathed a sigh of relief that his strange sighting had been superceded by more earthly phenomena. *Ah wis crazy tae drop that second tab ay acid. The visuals ur something else.*

His body, if left to its own devices would tend towards rubber, but Coco had enough resources of the will and enough experience of the drug to remember that fear and panic fed off themselves. The golden rule of 'stay cool' had been mouthed by wasters down the decades for good reason. He took stock of his situation: Coco Bryce, tripping alone in the park at roughly three o'clock in the morning, lightning flashing from a foreboding sky above him.

The possibilities were: at the very least he'd be soaked to the skin, at worst he'd be struck by lightning. He was the only tall thing around for a few hundred yards, standing right in the middle of the park. — Fuck sakes, he said, pulling the lapels of his jacket together. He hunched up and stole quickly down the path that split the massive canine toilet which was West Pilton Park.

Then Coco Bryce let out a small whisper, not a scream, just a murmur, through a soft gasp. He felt his bones vibrate as heat surged through his body and the contents of his stomach fell to displace those of his bowels. Coco had been struck by something from the sky. Had his last vision before he let go of consciousness not been one of the concrete path rising to meet him, he might have thought: lightning.

Who   What   Where   How   WHAT AM I?

Coco Bryce. Brycey fae Pilton. Brycey: one ay the Hibs Boys. Coco Fuckin Bryce, ya radge, he tried to shout, but he had no voice with which to make himself heard. He seemed to be blowing limply in a wind, but he could feel no currents of air nor hear their whistle. The nearest he could approximate to any sensation was that of being a blanket or a banner, floating in a breeze, yet he had still no sense of dimension or shape. Nothing conveyed to his cauterised senses any notion of his extent; it seemed as if he both encompassed the universe and was the size of a pin-head.

After a while he began to see, or sense, textures around him. There were images alright, but there was no sense of where they were coming from, or how they were being processed, no real sense of him having a body, limbs, a head, or eyes. Nonetheless these images were clearly perceived; a blue-black backdrop, illuminated by flickering, sparkling shapeless objects of varying mass, as unidentifiable as he was himself.

Am ah deid? Is this fuckin deid? COCO FUCKIN BRYCE!

The black was becoming more blue; the atmosphere he was moving around in was definitely getting thicker, offering more resistance to his sense of momentum.

Coco Bryce

It was stopping his movement. It was like a jelly, and he realised that he was going to set in it. A brief panic gripped him. It seemed important to keep moving. There was a sense of a journey needing to be completed. He willed himself on and could make out, in the distance, an incandescent centre. He felt a strong sense of elation, and using his willpower, travelled towards this light.

This fuckin gear isnae real. Eftir ah come doon, that's it, that's me fuckin well finished!

✷ ✷ ✷

Rory Weston's hands shook as he put the receiver down. He could hear the screams and shouts coming from the other room. For a moment, no more than a few seconds, Rory wished he wasn't occupying this particular space and time. How had all this happened? He began to trace the sequence of events that led to this, only to be disrupted by another violent shriek from through the wall. — Hang on, Jen, they're on their way, he shouted, running through towards the source of the agonised cacophony.

Rory moved over to the swollen, distressed figure of his girl-friend, Jenny Moore, and crushed her hand in his. The Parker Knoll settee was soaked with her waters.

Outside, the thunder roared on, drowning out Jenny's screams for the neighbours.

Jenny Moore, through her pain, was also thinking about the cumulation of circumstances which led her to be in this con-dition in this Morningside flat. Her friend Emma, also pregnant, though a month less advanced than Jenny, had caught sight of their waddling figures reflected in a shop window in Princes Street. — God sakes, Jen, look at us! You know, I sometimes wish, looking back to that cold winter's evening, that I'd given Iain that blow-job instead, she exclaimed.

They had laughed at this; laughed loudly. Well, Jenny wasn't laughing now.

I'm being torn apart and this bastard sits over me with that stupid fucking expression on his face.

What did it take out of them physically? It was just another fuck for those bastards. We had it all to do, but there they all were telling us how to do it, controlling us — gynaecologists, fathers to be, all men; together in a sickly pragmatic conspiracy . . . the scumbags have already disengaged emotionally from you; you're just the receptacle to carry the precious fruit of their sweaty bollocks into the world, through your fucking blood . . . But you're being hysterical darling . . . it's all those hormones, all over the place, just listen to us, we know best . . .

The bell went. The ambulance had arrived.

Thank god they're here, the men. More bloody men. Ambulance-MEN. Where the fucking hell were the ambulanceWOMEN?

— Easy Jen, there we go . . . Rory said with what was meant to be encouragement.

There WE go? she thought, as another wave of pain, worse this time than anything she had known, tore through her. This time the thunder and lightning of the freakiest freak storm to hit Scotland simply couldn't compete. She was almost blacking out with the pain as they got her on the stretcher, down the stairs and into the van. No sooner did they start up than they realised they wouldn't make the hospital.

— Stop the van! shouted one of the ambulancemen. — It's happening now!

They stopped the van by the side of the deserted Meadows. Only the flashing bolts of lightning; strange, persistently luminous and following awkward, uncharacteristic trajectories, lit up the starkly darkened sky. One of these bolts struck the ambulance parked in that deserted road as Jenny Moore was trying to push the offspring of her and her partner Rory Weston out into the world.

★ ★ ★

AW THIS IS NOWT TAE FUCKIN DAE WI ME

COCO

COCO BRYCE

BRYCEY

COLIN STUART BRYCE

```
        C        T     B R Y  C   E     Y
        O        R                      A
      L        A
        I       U                       F
      N    S T                          U
                                        C
                                        K
                                        I
                                        N

                                        R
                                        A
                                        D
                                        G
How long dae ah go oan fir              E
```

I N STUUUUUAAAAAAARRRTTTT T T T B R
COLINSTUARTBRYCE

Colin Stuart Bryce, or Coco Bryce, the Pilton casual, as he perceived himself to be, although he could not be too sure anymore, floated in the heightless void of gel, toward its white luminous centre. He became aware of something racing toward him at great speed, approaching from that far-off central point he had sensed. While the now thick and solidifying gel had begun to constrain the life-force that was Coco Bryce, this other energy source negotiated it with the

```
Hi-bees here
Hi-bees there
Hi-bees every
```

ease of light travelling through air. He could not see this, only gain a notion of it through some strange, indefinable conglomeration of the senses.

```
fuckin where
na na na na na
na na na na
```

It seemed to sense him too, for it slowed down as it approached him, and after hesitating, shot past him at speed and was gone, vanishing into the indistinct environment around him. However, Coco had a chance to sense what it was, and it was like nothing he'd witnessed before, an elongated blue, glass-like, cylindrical-shaped force, yet in a bizarre way it felt human; just as he, Coco Bryce, still considered himself to be human.

```
we scored one
we scored two
we scored seven
more than you
```

```
Dad's comin back tae us, Colin.
He's better now son. He's
changed, Colin. We'll soon be the
gither again son. Yill see a big
difference, you mark ma words.
Dinnae be frightened son, yir Ma
widnae lit um hurt us again. Ah
widnae lit um back in the hoose
unless he'd changed, son . . .
```

He felt elated as the light grew closer, more powerful, beckoning him. He felt that if he could get to it, everything would be all right. Hopeful, he willed himself on through the rapidly thickening gel. Propulsion, achievable purely through the exercise of will, was becoming increasingly difficult. No idea of where he was, of his shape, size, or his senses in the discrete categories of sight, touch, taste, smell, hearing, these seeming obsolete, yet him somehow able to experience the exploding kaleidoscope of colours beyond the gel that engulfed him; to feel the movement and the resistance to that movement.

```
There is one nasty,
malignant little
creature in this
class, an odious
young fool of a
boy who spreads
```

```
his poisonous
influence to
other, keener
pupils. I am
referring, of
course, to
```

It was growing darker. As soon as that awareness hit him, he noted it was pitch black. Coco felt fear.

> Colin Bryce, the most common and disgusting little man I've ever had the displeasure of teaching in one of my classes. Step forward, Colin Bryce! What have you to say for yourself?

He had slowed down completely now, grinding to a halt. His will no longer served as a driving mechanism. The light was closer though. The Light.

It was upon him, around him, in him. LIGHT LIGHT LIGHT LIGHT LIGHT LIGHT LIGHT LIGHT LIGHT LIGHT LIGHT LIGHT LIGHT

> YILL DAE IS YIR FUCKIN WELL TELT, COLIN, YUH WEE CUNT! AH SAIS TWENTY FUCKIN REGAL! NOW! MOVE IT!

LIGHT LIGHT LIGHT LIGHT LIGHT LIGHT LIGHT LIGHT LIGHT LIGHT LIGHT LIGHT LIGHT LIGHT LIGHT LIGHT

> Yir a tidy cunt,mate. Coco, is it no? Welcome tae the family. Fuckin main man!

LIGHT LIGHT LIGHT LIGHT LIGHT LIGHT LIGHT LIGHT LIGHT LIGHT

> Kirsty, ah really like ye, ken? Ah mean, ah'm no much good it talkin like this, bit ye ken whit ah mean, likesay you n me, ken?

LIGHT LIGHT LIGHT LIGHT LIGHT LIGHT LIGHT LIGHT LIGHT LIGHT LIGHT LIGHT

> Ye shag that burd Coco? Fill hoose? Tony's been up it likes. C'moan Coco, dinnae git stroppy. Only sayin likes! Hey boys, Coco's in luurrve! Hi! hi! hi!

LIGHT LIGHT LIGHT LIGHT LIGHT LIGHT LIGHT LIGHT LIGHT LIGHT LIGHT LIGHT LIGHT LIGHT LIGHT LIGHT LIGHT

> Too much fuckin ridin, too many fuckin collies n no enough fuckin swedgin. That's whit's wrong wi us these days.

LIGHT LIGHT

LIGHT LIGHT LIGHT LIGHT LIGHT LIGHT LIGHT
LIGHT LIGHT LIGHT LIGHT LIGHT LIGHT LIGHT

You're on a slippery slope, Bryce. It's no LIGHT
game, son. I kid you not. The next time I get LIGHT
a hold of you, the key gets thrown away.
You're vermin, son, pure vermin. You think LIGHT
you're a gangster, but you're just a silly LIGHT
wee laddie to me. I've seen them all come
through here. Oh, they aw think they're so LIGHT
hard, so cool. They usually die in the gutter LIGHT
or the lodging house or rot their miserable
lives away in a cell. You've blown it Bryce, LIGHT
totally blown it, you silly little toe-rag. LIGHT
The saddest thing is, you don't even realise
it, do you? LIGHT

LIGHT

LIGHT LIGHT LIGHT LIGHT LIGHT LIGHT LIGHT
LIGHT LIGHT LIGHT LIGHT LIGHT LIGHT LIGHT
LIGHT LIGHT LIGHT LIGHT LIGHT LIGHT LIGHT
LIGHT LIGHT LIGHT LIGHT LIGHT LIGHT LIGHT
LIGHT LIGHT LIGHT LIGHT LIGHT LIGHT LIGHT

The thing is that ah'm a fuckin LIGHT LIGHT
businessman. Right? The demolition LIGHT LIGHT
business. LIGHT LIGHT

LIGHT LIGHT LIGHT LIGHT LIGHT LIGHT LIGHT
LIGHT LIGHT LIGHT LIGHT LIGHT LIGHT LIGHT
LIGHT LIGHT LIGHT LIGHT LIGHT LIGHT LIGHT
LIGHT LIGHT LIGHT LIGHT LIGHT LIGHT LIGHT
LIGHT LIGHT LIGHT LIGHT LIGHT LIGHT LIGHT
LIGHT LIGHT LIGHT LIGHT LIGHT LIGHT LIGHT
LIGHT LIGHT LIGHT LIGHT LIGHT LIGHT LIGHT
LIGHT LIGHT LIGHT LIGHT LIGHT LIGHT LIGHT
LIGHT LIGHT LIGHT LIGHT LIGHT LIGHT LIGHT
LIGHT LIGHT LIGHT LIGHT LIGHT LIGHT LIGHT
LIGHT LIGHT LIGHT LIGHT LIGHT LIGHT LIGHT
LIGHT LIGHT LIGHT LIGHT LIGHT LIGHT LIGHT
LIGHT LIGHT LIGHT DARKER DARKER DARKNESS

*Heaven or hell, wherever this is, ah'm fuckin closin in! Thir's gaunny
be some changes aroond here, ya cunts! Coco Bryce. Pilton. Distin-
guished honours at Millwall (pre-season friendly), Pittodrie, Ibrox and
Anderlecht (UEFA Cup). Coco Bryce, a top boy. A cunt that messes is
a cunt that dies. See if any cunt . . . if any cunt gits . . . if any cunt . . .*

His thoughts trailed out insipidly. Coco was frightened. At
first the fear was an insidious quease, then it became brutally
stark and raw as he felt great forces on him, crushing and pulling
at him. It felt as if he was in the grip of a vice while simultaneously another power tried to tear him from its grasp. These
forces, though, enabled him to define his body for the first time
since this strange journey had begun. He knew he was human,
all too human, too vulnerable to the powers that crushed and
wrenched at him. Coco prayed for a victor in the struggle
between the two great and evenly matched forces. The torture
lasted for a while, then he felt himself being torn from the void.
He had only sensed THE LIGHT before, but now he could
actually see it, burning through his closed eyelids, which he
could not open. And then he realised there were voices:

— It's a beauty!

— A wee laddie for ye, hen, eh's a wee cracker n aw.

— Look, Jen, he's wonderful!

Coco could sense himself being held up; could sense his body,
where his limbs were. He tried to shout: Coco Bryce! Hibs
Boys! What's the fuckin score, ya cunts?

Nothing came from his lungs.

He felt a slap on his back and an explosion of air within him,
as he let out a loud, wrenching scream.

★ ★ ★

Dr Callaghan looked down at the young man in the bed. He had
been comatose, but now that he had emerged into consciousness, he was displaying some strange behavioural patterns. He
couldn't speak, and writhed around in his bed, thrashing his

arms and legs. Eventually he had to be constrained. He screamed and cried.

Cold.
Help.
— Waaahhh! screamed the youth. At the foot of his bed he had a nametag: COLIN BRYCE.

Hot.
Help.
— Waaahhh!

Hungry.
Help.
— Waaahhh!

Need hug.
Help.
— Waaahhh!

Want to pish, shite.
Help.
— Waahhh!

Dr Callaghan felt that, through his screaming, the youth was perhaps trying to communicate; though he couldn't be sure.

* * *

On the ward Jenny held her son. They would call him either Jack or Tom, as they had agreed, because, she considered with a sudden surge of cynicism, that's what people like them tended to do. They were located in an eighties English-speaking strata where culture and accent are homogenous and nationality is a largely irrelevant construct. Middle-class, professional, socially-aware, politically-correct people, she reflected scornfully, tended to use those old proletarian craftsperson names: ideal for the classless society. Her friend Emma had announced her intention to call her child Ben, if it was a boy, so the choice had been narrowed to one of two.

How's my little Jack, Rory said to himself, his index finger touching the baby's doughy hand.

Tom, Jenny thought, cradling her son.

What's the fuckin story here then, ya cunt?

★ ★ ★

Over the following few days the family of Colin Bryce became resigned to the fact that their son seemed to alternate between the vegetative and the rambling lunatic states after the accident. Friends testified that Coco had taken not one, but two tabs of acid, Supermarios to boot, and the press seized onto this. The youth in the hospital became a minor celebrity. The newspapers posed the same rhetorical question:

DID COLIN BRYCE GET HIS BRAINS FRIED BY
LIGHTNING OR LSD?
COLIN BRYCE — A VICTIM OF A FREAK ACCIDENT OR YET
ANOTHER OF OUR YOUNGSTERS DESTROYED BY
THE DRUGS MENACE?

While the press seemed to know for sure, the doctors were baffled as to the nature of the young man's condition, let alone the possible causes of it. However, they could see signs of improvement. There was growing eye contact over the weeks, definite indications of intelligence. They encouraged friends and family to visit the youth, who it was felt would benefit from as much stimulation as possible.

★ ★ ★

The baby was called Tom.

521

*Coco, ya radge cunts! Coco Bryce! Brycie! CCS! Hibs boys smash
all fuckin opposition. Too true.*

Becks then, cunt.

Jenny breastfed her baby.

*Phoah, ya fucker! This'll fuckin dae me. Coco Bryce, who he? Ma
name's Tam, eh Tom!*

The child fed greedily, sucking hard on Jenny's nipple. Rory,
who had taken some holiday time on top of his paternity leave,
observed the scene with interest. — He seems to be enjoying
himself. Look at him, it's almost obscene, Rory laughed, con-
cealing the growing feeling of unease which swept over him. It
was the way the baby looked at him sometimes. It actually
seemed to focus on him and look, well, contemptuous and
aggressive. That was ridiculous. A small baby. His baby.

He reasoned that this was an important issue to share with
some of the other Persons Of The Male Gender at his men's
group. It was, he reasoned, perhaps a natural reaction at the
inevitable exclusion of the male partner from the woman-parent
and child bonding process.

Phoah, ya cunt ye! Some fuckin jugs oan it!

Jenny felt something small and sharp pressing on her
stomach. — Oh look, he's got a stiff little willy! she exclaimed,
holding up the naked baby. — Who's a naughty little boy? she
kissed his plump stomach and made quacking noises.

*Lower, ya big fuckin pump-up-the-knickers! Git yir fuckin gums
roond it!*

— Yes, interesting . . . Rory said uneasily. The child's face;
it looked like a leering, lecherous old man. He'd have to see
about this terrible jealousy, talk it through with other men who
were in touch with their feelings. The thought of having a
genuine hang-up to share with the rest of the group thrilled
him.

That night Rory and Jenny made love for the first time since
she'd come home with the baby. They started gently, warily
testing the tenderness of her sex, then became increasingly passionate. Rory, though, was distracted during his performance by

sounds he thought he heard coming from the cot at the side of the bed. He looked around and shuddered, sure that he could see the outline of the baby, this baby only a couple of weeks old, standing up in the cot watching them!

Ya dirty cunts! Doggy style n aw! Phoah . . .

Rory stopped his strokes.

— What is it Rory? What the fuck is it? Jenny snapped, angry at the interruption as she was chasing her first post-birth climax.

They heard a soft thud from the cot.

— The baby . . . it was standing up, watching us, Rory said weakly.

— Don't be bloody stupid! Jenny hissed. — C'mon Rory, fuck me! Fuck me!

Rory, however, had gone limp, and he spilled out of her. — But . . . it was . . .

— Shut up for fuck's sake! She moved around, angrily pulling the duvet over them. — It's not an it, HE is a HIM. Your own bloody son! She turned away from him.

— Jen, he put his hand on her shoulder, but she shrugged it off, its limp creepiness sickening her.

After that, they decided it was time to put the baby in the room they'd made into a nursery. Jenny found the whole thing pathetic, but if Rory was put off that much, well, so be it.

The following night the baby lay silently awake in its new location. Rory had to concede that he was a good baby, he never seemed to cry. — You never seem to cry, do you, Tom? he asked wistfully as he stood over the child in the cot. Jenny, who'd had a panic attack in the night due to the child's silence, had sent Rory through to check on him.

Ah'm feart ay nae cunt. Whin ah goat cornered by they fuckin cunts at Cessnock whin wi pissed aw ower thum at Ibrox, ah jist goes: Come ahead then, ya fuckin weedjie cunts. Ah'm no exactly gaunny burst oot greetin cause some specky cunt's five minutes late wi ma feed now, um uh? Fuckin tube.

Could handle a fuckin Becks.

* * *

There was still no change in the condition of the youth in the hospital, although Dr Callaghan was now sure that he was using attention-seeking behaviour to meet his basic needs of food, changing and body-temperature regulation. Two of his friends, young men in hooded sweatshirts, came to see him. They were called Andy and Stevie.

— Fuckin shame, man, Andy gasped, — Coco's fucked. Jist lyin thair greetin like a bairn, eh.

Stevie shook his head sadly, — Tell ays that's fuckin Coco Bryce lyin thair, man.

A nurse approached them. She was a pleasant, open-faced, middle-aged woman. — Try to talk to him about some of the things you did together, things he'd be interested in.

Stevie stared at her with open-mouthed bemusement; Andy gave a snigger followed by a mocking shake of his head.

— You know, like discos and pop, that sort of thing, she cheerfully suggested. They looked at each other and shrugged.

Too warm.

— Waah!

— Right, Andy said. — Eh, ye missed yirsel the other day thair, Coco. The semi, ken? Wi wir waitin fir they Aberdeen cunts at Haymarket, eh. Booted fuck ootay the cunts, man, chased thum back doon tae the station, back ontae the train, doon the fuckin tracks, the loat! Polis jist fuckin standin thair n aw, didnae ken what tae fuckin dae, eh no. How good wis it Stevie?

— Fuckin barry, ya cunt. Couple ay boys goat lifted; Gary n Mitzy n that crew.

— Waah!

They looked at their screaming, unresponsive friend and fell into silence for a while. Then Stevie started: — N ye missed yirsel at Rezurrection n aw, Coco. That wis too mad. How radge wir they snowballs, Andy?

— Mental. Ah couldnae dance, bit this cunt wis up aw night.

Ah jist wanted tae spraff tae ivray cunt. Pure gouchin the whole night, man. Some fuckin good Es floatin aroond the now, Coco, ye want tae git it the gither man, n will git sorted and git some clubbin done . . .

— It's nae fuckin use, Stevie moaned, — eh cannae hear us.

— This is fuckin too radge, man, Andy conceded, — cannae handle aw this shite, eh.

Feed.

— Waah! WAAAHHHHH!

— That's no Coco Bryce, Stevie said, — no the Coco Bryce ah ken anywey.

They left as the nurse came in with Coco's food. All he would eat was cold, liquidised soup.

★ ★ ★

Rory reluctantly started back at work. He'd grown worried about Jenny, concerned about how she was coping with the baby. It was obvious to him that she was suffering from some form of post-natal depression. Two bottles of wine had been taken from the fridge. He'd said nothing to her, waiting for her to raise the matter. He'd have to keep his eye on her. The men at the group would support him; he'd have their admiration, not just for being in touch with his own feelings, but also for his unselfish responsiveness to his partner's needs. He remembered the mantra: awareness is seventy percent of the solution.

Jenny had a bad fright on Rory's first day back at work. The baby had been very sick in his cot. There was a strange smell coming from him. It was like . . . alcohol.

We do not carry hatchets, we do not carry chains, We only carry straws to suck our lemonade.

Oh, ya cunt ye . . . ma heid's fuckin nippin wi that vino. Cannae drink as much as ah used tae, no as a sprog . . .

The horrible truth dawned on Jenny: Rory was trying to poison their baby! She found the empty bottles of wine underneath the bed. That sick, warped, spineless fool . . . she would take the child to her mother's. Though perhaps it hadn't been Rory. A couple of workmen had been in, young lads, sanding and staining the woodwork: the doors and skirting boards. Surely they wouldn't have tried to give a new baby alcohol. They wouldn't be that irresponsible . . . she'd get onto the firm. Perhaps even contact the police. It could be Rory though. Whatever, Tom's safety was all that mattered. That inadequate fool could bleat piteously about his sick little problems to the inspid like-minds in his pathetic group. She was leaving.

— Who did it, Tom? Was it bad Daddy? Yes! I bet it was! Bad Daddy's tried to hurt little Tom. Well we're going away, Tom, we're going to my mummy's down in Cheadle.

Eh? What?

— That's near Manchester, isn't it Tom-Tom? It is! Yes, it is! And she'll be so pleased to see little Tom-Tom, won't she? Won't she?! Yes, she will! Will Will Will Will Will! She smothered the baby's doughy cheek with wet kisses.

Git tae fuck, ya daft cunt! Ah cannae go tae fuckin Manchester! Goat tae pit this fuckin sow in the picture. Ah'm no her fuckin bairn. The name's Coco Bryce.

— Look, eh Jenny . . .

She froze as she heard the voice coming from that small mouth which twisted unnaturally to form the words. It was an ugly, shrieking, cackling voice. Her baby, her little Tom; he looked like a malevolent dwarf.

Fuck sakes. Ah've done it now. Stey cool, Coco, dinnae freak this daft hoor oot.

— You spoke! Tom. You spoke . . . Jenny gasped in disbelief.

— Look, said the baby, standing up in his cot, as Jenny swayed unsteadily, — sit doon, eh sit down, he urged. Jenny obeyed in silent shock. — You'd better no say nowt tae nae cunt aboot this, right? the baby said, looking keenly and sharply at its mother for signs of understanding. Jenny just looked bemused. — Eh, I mean, Mother, they would not understand. They would take me away. I would be treated like a freak, cut up oan a laboratory table, tested by aw they specky cunts . . . eh,

the people in white coats. Ah'm a sortay, eh, a sort of phenom-
enon, I've got eh, special intelligence n that. Right?

Coco Bryce was pleased with himself. He thought back to
the videos of *Star Wars* he'd watched avidly as a kid. He had
to act cosmic to keep this gig going. He was doing alright
here. — They'd want tae take ays away . . .

— Never! I'd never let them take my Tom away! Jenny
screamed, the prospect of losing her baby galvanising her into
some sort of sense. — This is incredible! My little Tom! A
special baby! But how, Tom? Why? Why you? Why us?

— Eh, jist the wey it goes. Nae cunt kens, ah mean, it's just
the way I was born, Mother, my destiny n that.

— Oh, Tom! Jenny scooped up the baby in her arms.

— Eh right! the child said with embarrassment. — Eh listen,
Ma, eh, Jenny, one or two wee things. That scran, eh, the food.
It's no good. I want what grown-ups get. No aw that veggie
stuff that yous eat. Meat, Jenny. A bit ay steak, ken?

— Well, Rory and I don't . . .

— Ah'm no giein a fuck aboot you n Rory . . . ah mean, eh,
yous have no right to deny me my free choice.

This was true, Jenny conceded. — Yes, you're right, Tom.
You're obviously intelligent enough to articulate your own
needs. This is amazing! My baby! A genius! How do you know
about things like steak though?

*Oh, ya cunt. Dinnae fuck up here. This is a good fuckin doss yiv
goat.*

— Eh, I picked a lot of it up from the telly. I heard they two
joiner boys that ye hud in daein yir woodwork bletherin. Ah
picked up a lot fae them.

— That's very good, Tom, but you shouldn't talk like those
workmen. Those men are, well, a little common, probably a bit
sexist in their conversation. You should have more positive role
models.

— Eh?

— Try to be like somebody else.

— Like Rory, the baby scoffed.

Jenny had to think about that, — Well, maybe not, but, oh . . . we'll see. God, he's going to be so shocked when he finds out.

— Dinnae tell um, it's oor secret, right.

— I have to tell Rory. He's my partner. He's your father! He has the right to know.

— Mother, eh Jenny, it's jist this ah git a vibe offay that radge. He's jealous ay me. He'd shop ays, git ays taken away.

Jenny had to concede that Rory had been unstable enough in his behaviour towards their child to suggest that he wasn't emotionally equipped to handle this shock. She would go along with this. It would be their secret. Tom would just be a normal little baby with others around, but when they were alone he'd be her special little man. With her guiding his development he would grow up non-sexist and sensitive, but strong and genuinely expressive, rather than an insipid clown who clings to a type of behaviour for limp ideological reasons. He'd be the perfect new man.

★ ★ ★

The youth they called Coco Bryce had learned to speak. At first it was thought that he was repeating words parrot fashion, but he then began to identify himself, other people and objects. He seemed particularly responsive to his mother and his girlfriend, who came to visit regularly. His father never visited.

His girlfriend Kirsty had cut her hair short at the sides. She had long wanted to do this, but Coco had discouraged her. Now he was in no position to. Kirsty chewed on her gum as she looked down at him in the bed. — Awright, Coco? she asked.

— Coco, he pointed at himself. — Caw-lin.

— Aye, Coco Bryce, she said, spitting out the words between chews.

His heid's finally fried. It's that acid, they Supermarios. Ah telt um, bit that's Coco, livin fir the weekends; raves, fitba. The week's jist something tae get through fir him, and he'd been daein too much fuckin

acid tae get through it. Well, ah'm no gaunny hing aboot waitin fir a
vegetable tae git it the gither.

— Skanko n Leanne's suppose tae be gittin engaged, she
said, — that's what ah heard anywey.

This statement, though it elicited no response from Coco,
sparked off an interesting line of thought for Kirsty. If he could
remember nothing, he might not remember the status of their
relationship. He might not remember what a pain in the arse he
could be when it came to talking about their future.

Toilet.

— Number twos! NUMBER TWOS! the youth screamed.

A nurse appeared with a bedpan.

After he had shat, Kirsty sat on the edge of her boyfriend's
bed and bent over him. — Skanko n Leanne. Engaged, she
repeated.

He pushed his mouth towards her breasts and began sucking
and biting at them through her t-shirt and bra. — Mmmmm . . .
mmmm . . .

— Get the fuck offay ays! she shouted, pushing him away. —
No here! No now!

The sharpness in her voice made him wail. — WAAHH!!

Kirsty shook her head scornfully, spat out her gum, and left.
If, though, as the doctors were suggesting, he was a blank piece
of paper, Kirsty had realised that she could colour him in as she
liked. She'd keep him away from his mates when he got out.
He'd be a different Coco. She'd change him.

★ ★ ★

All Jenny's material on post-natal care hadn't quite prepared her
for the type of relationship she and her baby were developing.

— Listen Jenny, ah want ye tae take ays tae the fitba oan
Setirday. Hibs–Herts at Easter Road. Right?

— Not until you stop talking like a workman and speak
properly, she said. The content of his conversation and the tone
of his voice concerned her.

— Yes, sorry. I thought I'd like to see some sport.

— Em, I don't know much about the football, Tom. I like to see you express yourself and develop interests, but football . . . it's one of those terribly macho things, and I don't think I want you getting into it . . .

— Aw aye, I mean, so I can grow up like that wanker! Eh, my father? C'mon Mum, wise up! He's a fuckin toss!

— Tom! That's enough! Jenny said, but she couldn't help smiling. The kid was definitely onto something here.

Jenny agreed to take the child onto the East Terracing at Easter Road. He made her stand over by a heavily policed barrier which divided the rival sets of fans. She noted that Tom seemed to spend more time watching the youths in the crowd than the football. They were moved away by startled police who remonstrated with Jenny on her irresponsible behaviour. She had to admit the grim truth; great freak of nature and genius he may be, but her baby was a yob.

Over the weeks, though, Coco Bryce grew happier in the new body. He would have it all. Let them think that the old body in the hospital was the real Coco Bryce. He was fine here; there were opportunities. At first he thought that he missed shagging and drinking, but he found that his sex drive was very low and that alcohol made his baby body too sick. Even his favourite food was no longer palatable; he now preferred lighter, runny, easily digested stuff. Most of all, he felt so tired all the time. All he wanted to do was sleep. When he was awake, he was learning so much. His new knowledge seemed to be forcing out much of his old memories.

★ ★ ★

An extensive programme of reminiscence and recall therapy had failed the youth in the hospital. Educational psychologists had decided that rather than try to get him to remember anything, he would learn everything from scratch. This programme paid instant dividends and the young man was soon allowed home. Visiting the surroundings he had seen in photographs gave him a sense of who he was, even if it was a learned rather than a recalled concept. To his mother's shock, he even wanted to visit his father in prison. Kirsty came round a lot. They were, after all, as good as engaged, she had told him. He couldn't remember, he remembered nothing. He had to learn how to make love all over again. Kirsty was pleased with him. He seemed eager to learn. Coco had never been one for foreplay before. Now, under her instruction, he discovered his tongue and fingers, becoming a skilful and responsive lover. They soon became formally engaged and moved into a flat together.

The papers took an occasional interest in Coco Bryce's recovery. The young man renounced drugs, so the Regional Council thought that it would be good publicity to offer him a job. They employed him as a messenger, though the youth, continuing and rapidly progressing with his studies, wanted to get into clerical work. His friends thought that Coco had gone a bit soft since the accident, but most put it down to his engagement. He had stopped running with the casuals. That was Kirsty's idea; it could get him into bother and they had their future to think of. Coco's ma thought this was great. Kirsty had been a good influence.

One evening, around eighteen months later, the young man known as Colin Bryce was travelling on a bus with his wife Kirsty. They had been visiting her mother and were now heading back to their flat in Dalry. A young woman and her chubby infant sat in front of them. The child had turned around and was facing Colin and Kirsty. It seemed fascinated by them both. Kirsty jokingly played with the toddler, pressing his nose.

— Tom, the baby's mother laughed, — stop disturbing people. Sit round straight.

— No, he's awright, Kirsty smiled. She looked at Coco, trying to gauge his reaction to the child. She wanted one. Soon.

The infant seemed mesmerised by Coco. His doughy hand reached out and played over the youth's face, tracing its contours. Kirsty stifled a laugh as her husband pulled his head back and looked self-conscious.

— Tom! The baby's mother laughed in mock exasperation, — You little pest. C'mon, it's our stop.

— KOKORBIGH! KOKORBIGH! the child squealed as she scooped him up and carried him away. He pointed back at the youth, tearfully wailing as they left the bus, — KOKORBIGH!

— That's not Kokirbigh, she explained, referring to the dream demon that persistently plagued her son Tom, — that's just a young man.

Kirsty talked about babies for the rest of the journey, engrossed in the subject, never noticing the fear and confusion on her husband's face.

A Smart Cunt

A NOVELLA

For Kevin Williamson,
rebel with several causes

CONTENTS

1

PARK PATROL

I'd been living and working in the park for a month now, which was too radge. The digs were adequate and free. The wages were pretty shite but the poackle was good, if ye got a chance in the golf starter's box, which I generally did a couple of times a week. If I could get another month out of it before the cunts in the mobile tippled tae ma scam, I'd have a splendid bankroll the gither for London.

Inverleith was an okay park, dead central like. I couldn't have crashed in a park on the ootside of the city, that would've been a drag. I'd be better off at the auld man's place. The bothy I slept in was spacious and comfortable. It already had a Baby Belling, for my cooking, and an electric-bar fire, so all I needed to conceal was my mattress, which I crushed behind the boiler, the sleeping-bag and my black-and-white portable telly, which I could keep in the locker provided. I had a spare set of keys cut, so that after the mobile patrol picked up the set at the end of the shift, I could go for a pint then return and let myself in.

There were more than adequate toilet and shower facilities in the pavilion, which contained the footballers' changing-rooms as well as my bothy. So my outgoings were purely drink and drugs which, although substantial enough, with a bit of dealing, insurance and credit-card fraud, could be met fairly comfortably while allowing me to save. How good was that?

And yet it wisnae such a good life. There was the small problem of actually having to be on the job.

The great killer for the parkie (or Seasonal Park Officer as we were somewhat pompously entitled) was boredom. Humans tend tae adjust tae their environment and subsequently, in the parks, you become so inactive that even thinking of doing anything feels threatening. This goes for the essential duties of the job, which only take up about half an hour of the eight-hour shift, as well as any extras. I'd rather sit all day reading biographies (I read nothing else) and occasionally have a wank than go and clean out the changing-room, which would be just as dirty within a few hours as the next set of footballers came in. Even the prospect of a short trip to the cupboard a few feet away to switch on the thermostat becomes fraught with tension and loathing. It seemed easier, when my mind was set in this way, to tell six filthy teams of footballers that the showers were broken, or playing up, than to just go over and switch the cunts on. It was also a way of testing out how the Park Patrol hierarchy reacted tae such occurrences. The lessons learned could always be used in the future.

The players, for their part, reacted fairly predictably:

— NAE FUCKIN SHOWERS! MOAN TAE FUCK! FIR FUCK SAKES!

— YE PEY YIR FUCKIN DOUGH FIR THE FACILITIES . . .

— WE SHOULD GIT A REFUND! YE NEED SHOWERS FIR FUCK'S SAKE!

I find myself surrounded by seventy-odd sweaty players and nippy, rid-faced officials. At that point, yes, I wished I'd got ma arse intae gear and turned the showers oan. My strategy on such occasions is tae come out fighting and act even more disgusted with the shower problem than they are. Steal those clothes of righteous indignation.

— Listen, mate, I said, shaking ma heid angrily, — ah fuckin telt the cunts the other week that the immersion was dodgy. Ah'm fuckin well fed up tellin thum. That fuckin immersion. Sometimes it works fine, other times ye git fuck all ootay it.

— Aye, it was working fine the other week whin that other boy wis oan . . .

— That's the fuckin thing; jist cause it works two or three

times oan the trot, they cunts think they dinnae huv tae bother gittin thir erses doon here tae huv a look at it! Ah telt the cunts fae the council tae send the engineer doon. Complete fuckin overhaul, that's what's needed. Ye need reliable showers in this type ay weather, ah telt the boy. Did they move thir fuckin erses?

— Aye, no these cunts, they widnae bother.

— Aye, bit the thing is, yous boys come doon here eftir the match wantin yir fuckin shower. It's no these cunts thit git the hassle; it's fuckin muggins here, I pouted tersely, thrashing my chest with my finger.

— Hud oan pal, said one of the skippers, — wir no sayin nowt against you.

— Aw naw, naw, naebody's blamin the boy, another player says to the skipper. They all nod in acquiescence, apart from a few cunts on the periphery, who moan away. Then one skipper stands up oan the bench and shouts: — Wi cannae git the showers tae work, lads. Ah know it's a pain, but that's it. The boy's done his best.

A series of loud hisses and curses fills the air.

— Well, that's the way it goes. It's no the boy's fault. He telt the council, another player says supportively.

They grumblingly get dressed; the daft cunts. That's their night fucked. They'll have tae go hame tae shower, rather than hitting the pub straight away to discuss the match and pontificate on the state of fitba, music, television, shagging and the embarrassment of mates in the modern world. The momentum for the night has been lost. The pub they go to, with its shitey beer garden, will experience lower than normal takings. Tough shit, in these recession-hit times. Girlfriends and wives will be met with sour expressions by partners who feel deprived of their night out with the boys. The men will sullenly head for the bathroom shower feeling despondent and cheated: a win which cannot be savoured, or a defeat which cannot be consoled and massaged by lager. Councillors and recreation officials will be harassed by the squeaky, rid-faced, menopausal, bloated, sexually inadequate turds who run the beautiful game at all levels in Scotland.

All this misery because the parkie can't be bothered clicking on a switch. That's real fuckin power for you. Take that, ya cunts! How crazy am I.

As the last of the players files out, I go intae the boiler-room at the back of my bothy and switch on the immersion. I'll need hot water for ma shower before I go oot the night. I do some push-ups and squat thrusts before settling down to another chapter in the book I'm reading: a biography of Peter Sutcliffe.

All I read are biographies; I don't know why, it's not as if I particularly enjoy them. I just cannae seem tae get intae anything else. Jim Morrison, Brian Wilson, Gerald Ford, Noele Gordon, Joyce Grenfell, Vera Lynn, Ernest Hemingway, Elvis Presley (two different ones), Dennis Nilsen, Charles Kray (Reg and Ron's brother), Kirk Douglas, Paul Hegarty, Lee Chapman and Barry McGuigan have all been consumed since I started working in the parks. I cannae really say I've enjoyed any of them, with the exception, perhaps, of Kirk Douglas.

Sometimes I wonder whether taking oan this job was a good career-move. I like it because I enjoy my own company and can get a bit ratty after too much social contact. I dislike it because I can't move around and I hate being stuck in the one place. I suppose I could learn to drive, then I could get a job which offered the two important features of solitude and mobility, but a car would tie me down, stop me from taking drugs. And that would never do.

Mr Garland, the parks boss, was a kindly man, liberal enough by parks standards. He understood the condition of the parkie. Garland had been through enough council disciplinaries to suss out the problem. — It's a boring job, he told me on my induction, — and the devil makes work and all that stuff. The thing is, Brian, that so few Park Officers show initiative. The slovenly Park Officer will do the bare minimum, then just slope off, while the more conscientious officer will always find work to do. Believe you me, we know who the bad apples are, and I can tell you this: their days are numbered. So if you make an impression, Brian, we could very well be in a position to offer you a permanent post with the Parks Department.

— Eh, right . . .

— Of course, you've not even started the job yet, he smiled, realising that he was leaping massively ahead of himself, — but while it might not be the most exciting job in the world, many officers make it worse than it need be. You see, Brian, his eyes went large and evangelistic, — there's always work to do in a park. The job needs walking, Brian. The children's swing park has to be kept free from broken glass. The teenagers who congregate behind the pavilion; I've found needles there, Brian, you know . . .

— Terrible, I shake my head.

— They have to be discouraged. There are forms we have to complete on damage and vandalism to Parks property. There is always rubbish to pick up, weeding around the bothy and of course the constant cleaning of changing-rooms. The enterprising Park Officer will always find something to do.

— I think it's better to do a good day's graft; makes the time pass quicker, I lied.

— Precisely. I admit that sometimes, especially if the weather is inclement, boredom can be a problem. Are you a reader, Brian?

— Yes. I'm a fairly avid reader.

— That's good, Brian. A reader is never bored. What sort of stuff do you read?

— Biographies mainly.

— Excellent. Some people stuff their heads with political and social theory: it can only cause resentment and discontent with one's lot, he mused. — Anyway, that's besides the point. I'll concede that this job could be better. The service has been run down. We can't even replace the old mobile vans and intercom equipment. Of course, I blame our political masters on the Recreation Committee. Grants for single-parent black lesbian collectives to put on experimental theatre projects; that sort of stuff they'll always find money for.

— I couldn't agree more, Mister Garland. It's criminal, that sort of misuse of the poll-tax payer's money.

I remember that thoughtful, acknowledging nod Garland gave me. It seemed to say: I see a model Park Officer in the making. What's the cunt like.

I took a quick shower before the mobile came. I was just in time; no sooner had I dried off and got dressed than I heard the Park Patrol van pulling up. The Park Patrol vans, the mobile, are the uniformed cunts. These fuckers are on the same grade as us, only mobile. Technically, they are supposed to check the smaller parks which are unstaffed by a Park Officer. Unofficially, it's a different matter. What they actually do is to police us; we who, I suppose by reverse definition, have to be called the stationary Park Officers. They make sure that we are on the job, at our official work-stations, and not in some pub. They caught one guy, Pete Walls, literally on the job last week at Gilmerton. He was shagging a schoolie in the bothy. They suspended him with pay, pending enquiry. The council really knows how to hurt you; giving you official licence to do what any parkie strives to do unofficially: not be there but get paid for it.

I empty some roaches out the ashtray into a bin-liner as mobile Park Officer Alec Boyle steps out of the car. Boyle has his cap pulled down over his mirror-lens shades. His shirt-sleeves are rolled up, he usually leans out the window of the car when it's at the lights, and he must spend a fortune on chewing-gum. All that's missing is the Brooklyn accent. What sort of shite is going 'hrough that cunt's heid is anybody's guess. A wee guy; a few inch.. too small and brain cells too few even for the polis. How fucked-up is he.

— What's this aboot the fuckehhnn showers? he asks.

— Dinnae mention these cunts tae me, Alec. Ah've been at the fuckers aw day. It's sortay like the pilot light keeps gaun oot, ken? Ah've goat it started now; but the water wisnae hoat enough for the fitba guys, ken? They wir daein thir nut.

— Ah ken that. Jist hud the fuckehhnn Shark oan the radio. Gaun fuckin radge.

The Shark. Divisional Park Superintendant Bert Rutherford. He's on today. That's aw we fuckin well need. — Well, we'll huv tae git the engineer doon.

— He's fuckehhnn been doon but, couldnae find nowt wrong.

—How's it this always hus tae happen when it's me oan shift? I moan in the self-pitying way guys on the job here always do. — Ah think ah'm fuckin jinxed.

Park Officer Boyle nods empathetically at me. Then a reptilian smile twists his features. — Your mate Pete Walls, he's some fuckenhhn cunt, is he no?

I wouldnae really class Wallsy as a mate, just an okay guy I've done a bit of work on the golf with, a bit of poacklin. I suppose that's as good a mate as you can get, on the parks like. That's where the real money's made in the parks; on the golf starter's box. Every cunt wants in on that action.

— Aye, Wallsy wis caught wi his pants doon ah heard, I nodded.

— Stoat the baw, Boyle's face crinkled as he idly polished his shades with a hanky. The daft cunt doesnae suss that he's smearing snotters over the lenses, then he tipples and stops, vaguely self-conscious for a moment.

I spare his embarrassment. — Ah heard that the lassie wis sixteen; it wis his girlfriend. Getting engaged n that like. She just came in wi some sannys and it got a bit oot ay hand.

— Ah heard aw that shite. Disnae matter a fuck. That cunt's oot the door. Fuckehhnn dismissal joab.

I wisnae so sure about that. — Naw, ah'll bet ye a fiver he gets oaf wi it.

I had a feeling about this. The council was a very asexual organisation. If things got a bit steamy they'd bottle out. This was a potential Pandora's box that they might not want to open. Cha McIntosh at the union would find an angle. I thought there

543

was a very good outside chance that Wallsy would get off scot-free. Well worth a fiver.

— Git away, Boyle sneers.

— Naw, come oan. Bet ye a blue one.

— Done, said Boyle. As I shook his greasy paw, he assumed a conspiratorial expression and whispered, although we were in an empty pavilion in the middle of a deserted park, — Watch the fuckehhnn Shark. He's got his beady eye oan ye. Thinks yir a wide-o. He goes tae me: How's that boy at Inverleith? Ah goes: Awright, good lad likes. He said: Seems a bit ay a smart cunt tae me.

I set my face in an expression of contrived sincerity. — Thanks, Alec. Appreciate ye giein ays the nod.

Bullshitting wee cunt. The Shark might be oan ma case, then again, he might no. I didn't fuckin care. These mobile cunts always played games to keep you para and set themselves up in a better light. They were just as bored by the job as us; they needed to generate intrigue to keep the interest levels up.

He departed, screeching his car tyres across the gravel outside the bothy. I went to the local pub and had a voddy and a game of pool with a guy with a nervous tick. After this, I went back, had a wank and read another chapter in Peter Sutcliffe's biography. Boyle came back to pick up his set of keys and my shift was over. I left the park, but doubled-back after Boyle departed, letting myself back intae the pavilion. Before I prepared to set off intae toon, I set up my telly and bed, in case I was too wrecked tae dae it the night. Then I realised that I was off for four days. In the parks you had five days on and two days off, the two days changing each week. My days were running intae each other, so I had a long weekend. This meant that someone else would be here the morn. I locked my stuff back up. It was unlikely that I'd crash here tonight. I usually crashed out in some cunt's gaff at the weekend, or at my auld man's.

I hit the toon feeling that alienated, traumatised way I gener-ally did when I came off a shift, especially from the backshift, which finished at nine. There was that sense of having being shut out of things, that everybody had already started having serious fun. No doubt I had a bit of catching up to do. I went to see if I could get some speed from Veitchy.

2

AFTERNOON TELLY

My auld man sat drinking tea with Norma Culbertson from up
the stairs. He puffed on a cigarette as I was making a sanny: a
piece on Dundee steak.

— Thing is, Norma, it's always places like this they pick oan.
As if the area hasnae goat enough bloody problems as it is.

— Couldnae agree mair, Jeff. It's a bloody disgrace. Let them
build it in Barnton or somewhere like that. Supposed tae be a
council for the ordinary working person, Norma shook her
head bitterly. She looked quite sexy with her hair piled up and
those large hooped earrings.

— What's this? I ask.

The auld man snorts. — Thir planning tae open a centre fir
aw they junkies. Needle exchange n prescriptions n aw that. It's
eywis the same; cater fir aw these bloody misfits, never mind the
tenants that have been peyin their rent every single week regular
as clockwork.

Norma Culbertson nods in agreement.

— Aye, it's a sick scene, right enough, Dad, I smile.

I note that they seem to be getting some kind of petition the
gither; daft cunts. What are they like? I leave the kitchen and
eavesdrop for a bit from behind the door.

— It's no that ah'm hard, Jeff, Norma says, — it's no that at
aw. Ah ken these people have goat tae git help. It's jist thit ah've
goat wee Karen n ah'm oan ma ain. The thought ay aw they
needles lying aroond . . .

— Aye, Norma, it disnae bear thinkin aboot. Well, we will
fight them on the beaches, as they say.

The pompous auld fuck.

— Ye ken though, Jeff, ah really admire ye, bringin up they two laddies oan yir ain. Couldnae huv been easy. Rare laddies thuv turned oot n aw.

— Ach, thir no bad. At least thuv goat mair sense thin tae git involved in any ay this drugs nonsense. Brian's the problem. Ye never ken whair he is, or whair he's gaun. Still, at least he's working now, just a temporary job in the parks like, but at least it's something. Mind you, ah dinnae think he kens what he wants tae dae wi his life, that one. Sometimes ah think he lives on another planet fae the rest ay us. Wait till ye hear the nerve ay this: hudnae seen or heard ay him for weeks, n he comes back wi this lassie. Takes her up the stairs. Then later, he's doonstairs wi her cooking up a big meal. Ah takes him aside and sais: Hi you, c'moan, this isnae a knockin shop ye ken. He gies ays some money for the food. Ah sais: That's no the point, Brian. Ye treat this place wi a bit ay respect. This is him that's supposed tae be heartbroken cause his girlfriend went away tae some college doon in London. Well, he's goat a funny wey ay showin it. Too smart for his ain good that yin. Now Derek, he's a different story . . .

So, it looks as if I'm getting on the auld man's tits. It's true that you never hear anything good about yourself if you listen in like that, but sometimes you're better knowing the way the wind's blowing.

I sit up in my room watching my telly; well, Derek's telly if we're being pedantic about it, which the wee cunt invariably is. I hear my auld boy shouting on me and go to the top of the stairs. — We're eh, jist gaun upstairs tae Norma's. A few things tae sort oot aboot the committee, he says, all furtive and uneasy.

Good show. I light a candle. Then I produce my works and start to cook up some smack. This gear looks okay, there's a bit of a glut on right now. God bless Raymie Airlie; God bless Johnny Swan. I'm no a smack-heid, no really, but a feast usually precedes a famine. Best take advantage.

I look for a belt, but I can only find a useless, elasticated

snake-belt, so I fling it away and use the flex fae Derek's bedside
lamp. I wrap it round my bicep and tap my wrist until a huge
dark vein materialises. Then I stick the needle in, and draw back
some blood before shooting for goal. Barry.

Fuck.

I can't fuckin breathe.

Fuck sake, how bad is this.

I stand up and make a move towards the lavvy, but I don't get
that far. I manage to direct my puke onto an old NME. I lean
against the wall for a bit and get my breath, then I open the
windae, and fling the mess out intae the backsquare.

I lie on the bed. That's better. There's a nice-looking woman
in the soap opera on the telly. Suddenly I see her as a wizened
old witch, but she's no longer on the telly, she's in the room.
Then things change and I'm with a guy called Stuart Meldrum
who, when we were kids, slid off the roof of this factory in
Leith. This was before we moved out here. It was a corrugated-
iron roof, sloping steeply. Stu lost his footing, fell off and started
sliding down it. Thing was, there was a row of double rivets
sticking out and they sort of tore him apart.

Now I'm with him again, and his face is ripped open, with
parts of him spilling out of his bloodied body. He's got a ball, a
yellay ball under his arm. — Fancy a game ay shapes, Bri? he
asks.

That seems awright tae me. Shapes. Against the factory wall.
He moves up dead close to the wall and kicks the ball hard
against it. It ricochets off at a tight angle and starts rolling away,
this yellay ball. I start running eftir it, but it seems to be gathering speed. I'm trying to get a bend on but I can't seem to get any
pace up. All I can see is this ball, bouncing down the road, like
it's wind-assisted, like it's nearly a balloon, but at the same time
everything else is still and quiet. My Ma stands in front of me in
a floral dress, holding the ball. She looks young and beautiful,
like she did when I last saw her, when I was still at the primary.
I'm the same size as her, the same as I am now, but she takes my

hand and leads me up this hilly street, full of suburban, posh hooses and I ask her, — Ma, why did you leave us?

— Because I made a mistake, son. You were a mistake. It was never meant to happen. You, your father, these places where we lived. I love you and Derek, but I needed my own life, son. You were never meant to happen. I never wanted to give birth to a Smart Cunt.

I see Alec Boyle and the Shark, dressed in white suits. They are nodding sagely. Then I realise that I'm staring at the screen and it's all okay, I'm back in the telly's soap opera, not my own.

I start to get really bad cramps after a bit, so I get under the duvet and try to sleep it off. When my old man comes in I tell him I think I've got a flu bug and spend three days in bed, before I'm due back on the park.

3

ASSOCIATES AS OPIATES

I'm never touching smack again. That's a loser's game. Every cunt I've met who said that they can control it is either dead, dying or leading a life no worth living. What a radge I've been. I'm still strung out here in the bothy. A waste ay a weekend. Naw, speed's ma drug, speed and ecky. Fuck smack.

It's going to be a boring backshift. Sutcliffe's book was okay. A good read. The truth is stranger than fiction. Sutcliffe was a very disturbed man. Sutcliffe was an arsehole. How tapped was that cunt. Some things you can never understand, some things don't lend themselves to reason, to rational analysis and explanation. I've started on Mother Teresa's biography, but I can't get into it. I don't really have that much time for her; she seems a bit fuckin loopy tae me. She claims God tells her tae dae the things she does; it's got fuck all tae dae wi her. This is precisely the same argument Sutcliffe uses. That's all jist pure shite; people should take on a bit mair personal responsibility.

This park is depressing. It's like a prison. No it's not. You can leave, go to the warm, inviting pub, but it will mean your cards if the mobile catches you. The parks are about appearance money; you get paid to be here. Not to do, but to be. I sit in a bothy; therefore I'm a bam.

There's a knock on the door. It can't be the patrol; they never knock. I open the bothy and there's Raymie Airlie. He looks at me with a grim smile scored onto his face. — The renegade robots are now long dead, the metal ones rusted, the human ones bled.

My sentiments entirely. Raymie is either a moron or a genius and it doesn't interest me enough to even try to work out which.

— Awright, Raymie? Moan in.

He strides into the bothy. Then he inspects the changing-rooms and showers with a thoroughness that would credit the most vigilant mobile Park Patrol Officer. He returns to the bothy and picks up the Mother Teresa book and arches his eyebrows, before throwing it back on the table.

— Got works? he asks.

— Aye . . . ah mean, naw. No oan ays, likes.

— Fancy a hit?

— Eh, no really, ah mean, ah'm likes workin, eh . . . aye, but just a bit, likes . . .

He cooked up some smack and I took a shot, using his works. I started thinking a lot about swimming, and fish. The extent of freedom they have; two thirds of the planet's surface n that.

The next think I knew, the Shark was standing over me. Raymie had gone.

— Keys, he snapped.

I looked at him through glazed eyes. I felt as if my body was a corridor and the Shark was at the door at the other end of that corridor. What the fuck did he mean? Keys?

Keys.

Keys.

Mother Teresa and the children of Calcutta. Feed the world.

Keys.

Keys open doors; keys lock doors.

Keys.

It sounds good. — Keys.

— Have ye goat thum then? The keys? he asks. — C'moan, son, it's knockin oaf time. You no goat a home tae go tae?

I started to take the keys out of my pocket, not my set, the set I had made, but their set. Have I no got a home to go to?

Mum, where are you?

— This is my home, I tell him.

— You're tapped pal. You been drinking? He moves closer to

see if he can smell anything on my breath. He seems puzzled, but stares deep into my eyes. — You're as high as a bloody kite, son. What are you on? You been on that whacky baccy? What are you on?

I am on planet Earth. We all are. All pathetic Earthling scum. Me, Shark, Mother Teresa, Sutcliffe . . . I hand him the keys.

— Jesus Christ! Ye cannae even speak, can you?

Jesus Christ. Another Earthling. This is planet Earth. The Shark and I; human lifeforms sharing the same planet in this universe. Both humans, members of the dominant species on planet Earth. Humans have set up structures, institutions to govern our lives here on this planet. Churches, nations, corporations, societies, and all that shite. One such structure is the council. Within its sphere, leisure and recreation, of which the Parks Service is part. The human known as the Shark (a humanoid referred to by the name of another species due to his perceived similarity in appearance and behaviour to this species, by members of his own) and myself are engaged in economic activity. We are paid, in our small way, to maintain the structure of human society. Our role is a small one, but an integral part of a mystic and wondrous whole.

— We have a role to play . . .

— Eh? What's that?

— A role to play in the maintenance of human society . . .

— You're tapped, son, fuckin tapped. What are ye oan?

The Shark. An ocean to swim in, a whole ocean. Two thirds of the planet's surface to roam around in. Moreover, he can swim at different levels, so the possibilities are almost endless. Infinite choices in the ocean and this thing has to come onto dry land; has to come onto this small patch of dry land I occupy. I cannot stand being in the vicinity of this creature.

I walk past him, out of this bothy, out of this park.

— Garland's gaunny hear aboot this! he shouts.

Well, neh-neh-neh-neh-neh, cuntybaws.

The thing about the Montparnasse Tower is that it's so tacky, really dirty and shoddy looking. It's a marvellous structure though, but it's in the wrong city, the wrong continent. It's a very new world structure, but because it's in Paris, nobody's impressed. The Louvre, the Opera, the Arc de Triomphe, the Eiffel Tower; people are impressed with all that shite, all those beautiful buildings. Nobody really gies a fuck aboot the Montparnasse Tower. Thing is, you get great views over Paris from the observation floor of the Montparnasse.

We're sitting, the two of us, at the restaurant on the top of the tower. It's an ugly, overpriced restaurant with garish fittings and a poor selection of food. But we're happy there, because it's just the two of us. We've had a little look around the internal observation floor, with its huge glass frames which are marked and grubby. Rubbish, old rotting foods and fag-ends have been dropped behind the radiators underneath the handrail which surrounds the observation floor. The most impressive things on this floor are the pictures of the Montparnasse Tower in various stages of construction, from foundations to completion. Even these fine pictures, though, have been faded by the sun. Soon you'll be able to see nothing in them.

However, I don't care about the dirt and grime, because we're together and it's beautiful. I can't think of the parks. The only reality is the texts and images. I tell her that I wrote a poem about her when I was on duty in the park. She asks me to recite it, but I can't remember it. .

She stands up and tells me she wants to walk down. All those floors. She moves down the steps, out of the restaurant towards the fire escape. — C'mon, she says, moving into the darkness. I look into the darkness, but I can't see her, I can only hear her voice. — C'mon, she shouts.

— I can't, I shout.

— Don't be scared, she says.

But I am. I look back onto the observation floor and it's light. Out here is light and she's trying to lead me into the darkness. I know if I start after her now I'll never be able to catch up with her. It's not normal dark down there, it's not shades of dark; it's ugly, stark, pitch blackness. I turn around, back into the white and yellow light. As well as her voice down there, others are present. Voices which have nothing to do with her but everything to do with me. Voices I can't face; it's too mad.

I get into the lift. The door closes. I press for the ground; forty-two floors below.

It doesn't move. I try to open the door but it seems to be stuck. I feel uneasy. My feet are sticking to the floor; it's like there's bubble-gum on the floor of this lift. Sticky strands of pink gum cling to the soles of my boots. I look down at the lift floor; it starts swelling. It's like the floor covering is bubbling up. My feet sink into it, then my legs seem to go right through it. I fall through the lift floor, slowly, covered in a stretchy, transparent pink film which is all that stands between me and falling to my death in this dark lift-shaft.

It's not snapping though; it's still stretching. I look up and see myself descending slowly from a hole in the floor of the lift. Floor 41   40   39   38

Then I start to speed up as large white-painted letters indicating the marked floors whizz by: 37 36 35 34 33 32 31 30 29 28 27 26 25 24 23 22   21   20   (slowing down again, my bubble still holding, thank fuck.)

19 (Dangling stationary, my cord now just the width of a string, and so tensile.)

(Then more movement, more fast movement.) 18 17 16 15 14 13 12 11 10 9 8 7 6 5 4 3 OHH NOOOO!! 2 1 G B −1 −2 −3 −4 −5 −6 −7 −8 −9 WHAT THE FUCK IS THIS? −10 −11 −12 −13 −14 −15 −16 −17 −18 −19 −20 −21 −22 −23

I'm still sliding down trapped in this bubble-gum film. I'm now at minus −82 −83 −84 −85 −86   −87   −88   and at   −89 my feet gently touch solid ground. It seems as if I've landed in another lift, this one roofless. I put my hand above my head and the tensile gum-like strand snaps under my touch.

My body is covered in this pink film, covered from head to toe. It corrodes my clothes, just dissolves them, but it doesn't react to my skin. It settles on it, like a second layer, hard and protective. I must look like a mannequin. I'm naked but I don't feel vulnerable. I feel strong.

The lift indicator tells me that minus 89 is the bottom. More than two-thirds of this building lies underground. I must be miles, well yards or metres, underneath the earth's surface.

I step out of the lift-shaft. The lift door seems to have gone and I just alight at minus 89. I'm still inside some sort of structure, and although the walls seem to be moving and breathing, it still seems like the huge basement it should be. It's barren and appears deserted. Giant concrete pillars support this weird structure which is man-made and organic at the same time.

A small human-like figure with the head of a reptile shuffles along in a brown overcoat, wheezing, pushing what looks like a shopping trolley full of boxes.

— Excuse me, I shout, — where is this?

— The fuckehhnn boatum flair, this thing shouts, seeming in distress.

— What's through there? I pointed to a sign marked EXIT, a sign that the creature was heading towards.

— Complaints, he smiles at me, his lizard tongue lapping the side of his scaly face. — Some cunts've been fuckehhnn well pittin greenfly in ma central heating. Ah want that sorted oot right now. You doon here fir a woman?

— Eh, naw . . . ah mean, aye, I was thinking of her, where she was, how far up this building.

His cold eyes rest on me. — Ah'll fuck ye the now if ye want. Ah'll fuck ye fir nowt. Ye dinnae need women, he gasps, moving towards me. I back away . . .

BLEEEEEGGGHHHH! — STUPID FUCKIN CUNT!

A horn sounds and a voice roars.

I'm on Ferry Road with the heavy traffic bound for Leith docks whizzing past me. A lorry pulls over and the driver leans out the cab and shakes his fist. — Daft fuckin cunt! Ah nearly fuckin kilt ye! He opens the cab, jumps down and comes towards me. — Ah will fuckin kill ye!

I run along. I don't mind being hit by his lorry, but I don't want to be hit by him. It's the indignity of it all. It's all too personal. There's nothing worse than a violent beating from an unremarkable person. Physical violence with someone is too much like shagging them. Too much id involved.

I feel terrible, but I can't go home. I can't go back to the park. I walk around for a bit, trying to get my head together. I end up at Veitchy's gaff in Stockbridge. Minus 89. Thank fuck I'm out of that place. But now I'm shaking, feeling sick. I can either tough it out or go back to level minus 89.

— Awright, cuntybaws?

— Ha ha ha, the man himself! Veitchy smiles and lets me in. — Ye look like yuv seen a ghost.

— Naw. Ah saw worse: Raymie, a Shark, a woman, a reptile. Nae ghosts, but.

— Ha, ha ha, yir some cunt, Brian, so ye are. Want a beer?

— Naw, any speed?

— Naw.

— Ah'll take a cup ay tea offay ye. Milk, nae sugar. Penman aroond?

That's obviously a sair yin for Veitchy. — Dinnae talk tae ays aboot that cunt. Thinks he kin jist leave shite here in ma gaff. Tellin ye, Bri, ah'll help a mate oot, but he's takin liberties. Liberties the cunt's takin, I kid you not.

I sit down on the sofa and watch the telly, leaving Veitchy slavering on about Penman. Fuck this life; give me another please.

Next day Ian Caldwell tells me that I was up at his flat in Inchmickery Court in Pilton. A tower block. I can't remember. I have to go back to Paris one day, back to the Montparnasse tower. With her. But she's gone. All the women in my life have gone. My own fuckin mother's gone.

The backshift was more eventful than I thought it would be.

4

CONSTRUCTIVE DISCIPLINE

Garland wore a sad expression; he was a man more disappointed and hurt than angry.

— The worse thing, Brian, he told me, is that I took you for an intelligent and decent young man. I thought that you would prove a diligent and conscientious Park Officer.

— Yeah, ah suppose ah messed things up a bit . . .

— Is it drugs, Brian? Is it? he pleaded.

— No, it's more a kind of depression, you know?

The Shark was in attendance. — Depression my arse! He was zonked out of his bloody brains!

— That's enough, Mister Rutherford! Garland snapped. — Let Brian speak for himself.

— It's just that ah've been oan these anti-depressants. Sometimes ah go over the score, forget ah've taken the pills and take a double dosage, ken?

Garland looked thoughtful. — How can a young man who has everything to look forward to possibly be depressed?

How indeed. Working in a temporary job in the parks. Staying in a drab scheme wi his dad, who's just about to alienate every psycho that lives in it with an anti-drugs crusade. No seen his Ma since he was eight years old. Knocked back by his girlfriend. He's got the whole wide world in his hands . . . everybody, join in . . .

— It's exogenous depression, the doctors say. Chemical imbalance. Comes on without warning.

Garland shook his head sympathetically. — You didn't mention this at the interview, this condition.

— Ah know, ah apologise for that. Ah just felt that it would by prejudicial to my employment prospects with the District Council's Recreation Department, Park Patrol Division.

The Shark's bottom jaw twitched. The union boy nodded solemnly. The personnel guy remained impassive. Garland took a deep breath. — You've given us food for thought, Brian. Leaving the job, though, that is a serious breach of discipline. If you'd kindly leave us for a few minutes.

I went outside into the corridor. I stood around for a wee while before Garland summoned me back in.

— We're going to suspend you for the rest of the week, with pay, pending a decision.

— Thank you, I said, and I meant it.

I went drinking with my mate The PATH that night. I checked my account. Whatever happened regarding this disciplinary, I was off to London.

I got back to my auld man's, carrying the portable telly I kept at the park. Deek was crashed out in my bed. What the fuck was he daein in ma bed?

As I went to shake him, I saw him appear at the door. Either there were two Deeks or it wasn't him in ma bed. Both propositions seemed equally plausible in my current frame of mind.

— What's this? I asked the Deek at the door, pointing tae the possible Deek in the bed.

— It's Ronnie. He wis looking fir ye. He's really jellied. Ah took him up here soas the auld man widnae see um. Ye ken how he is about drugs n that.

— Aw right, thanks. That useless cunt Ronnie. Ah'll let the fucker sleep it oaf.

Ronnie lay there for hours. I couldn't move him. When I was ready to go to bed I pulled him onto the floor and threw a blanket over him.

The next morning I packed for London. As I got ready, Ronnie was coming to.

— Heavy day yesterday, Ron? I asked.
— Fucked, he said, pointing to his head.
I was looking forward to London.

5

SPEEDING

I've still got that out of it fae the night before feeling; or is it still the night before or what, but who cares cause Simmy's racked up the balls and ordered up one Guinness and one pint of bitter and auld Harry's saying: Fucking drunken Jock gits and Simmy's hugging the grumpy auld cunt then picking him up and sticking him on the bar and Vi's telling me that I was in some state last night, her sulky, mean doughy face propped up on her white flabby arms and I'm hating Simmy's automatic, arrogant, soap-dodging assumption that I want to play fuckin pool, as if it's just part of the natural order of things . . .

Oh ya cunt ye

Fuck . . . I thought it was all coming back up there; that curry. I don't know whether to spit, swallow or chew and Simmy's split the pack, he's looking at my flushed, sweaty, uncomfortable face and is explaining the concept of:

— Momentum. Momentum big man, that's what it's aw about. MO-MEN-TUM. Wuv goat tae ride that wave, go wi the flow, take it aw as far as it'll go. Momentum. When it's workin fur ye, ye jist cannae ignore it.

Simmy's been talking to Cliff in the flat. Cliff reads *The Independent*. They use words like that; usually in the sports pages.

I send a stripe down the table into the bottom left-hand pocket. A fine effort. The butt of Simmy's cue thumps the lino appreciatively. — Nice wahn, ma man, Simmy says.

— Momentum ma fuckin arse, it's this speed we've been snortin and dabbin at for days now n see when ah stoap this, whin ah finally settle doon and say: beddy boys, it'll be fir days, naw, make that fuckin weeks, naw months, fuckin months.

Simmy goes: — Tell ye whit though, ma man, you n me up fuckin west next week. Straight oan that 207 bus doon the Uxbridge Road. No gettin oaf at Ealing Broadway or stallin at the Bush. Up west. Clubs n wimmin. No compromise. No surrender.

He starts whistling 'Derry's Walls'.

The cunt's broken my concentration and I fuck up on an easy ball into the centre pocket. Too busy trying to get position on the yellow.

It's that cunt who's always shitein it tae go up west, it's him that gets us lumbered in Ealing or the Bush, mashed out of our fuckin brains. That's okay for him; he's a fat, ugly, weedjie, soapdodging orange-bigoted, hun bastard with a small cheesy cock and a face disfigured by Indian ink, scar tissue, burst blood vessels, and he's got that frizzy hair that a lot of huns seem to have which looks like it's been transplanted from somebody's pubes and he also has a gross arse which is prone to faecal leakage. All of which makes his chances of meeting a woman who doesnae look as if she could eat tomatays through a tennis racket highly improbable. How repulsive is he. The problem is, though, that the cunt's a hindrance tae me, in ma quest tae meet somebody reasonable, and he has the flat as boggin as he is with fish and chip wrappers and chinky cartons everywhere, plates piled up all ower the place, n as for his room, well, you'd have to get Rentokil in tae make that fuckin bed. Then there's that cunt Cliff, n his fuckin soacks, that lie in the lobby ootside his room, stinking the whole flat oot. Even they lassies that we've got tae ken fae ower the road, Nazneem, Paula and Angela, they'll no come over for a blow now, so how can I take anybody back there? It was me who got pally with them n all, going up to them wi ma classic chat up line: — I share the same birthday as Ian Curtis, Linda Ronstadt and Trevor Horn, you know Trevor Horn? 'Video Killed The Radio Star'? 'Living In The Plastic Age'? Big pop producer of the eighties, he wis. How could anybody fail with chat-up lines like that? But fail I did, thanks to ma association with that cunt. Now they don't want me coming over to their place because it encourages him to go over and make a nuisance of himself. But I have to go there to get out of our place because the smell of that cat's litter tray is overpowering, swimming with pish and shite. It's no the animal's fault, although the bastard sprays everywhere. Simmy should've hud it done; it rips the wallpaper n curtains n sofa tae bits but he just says that cats are hygienic creatures and they keep the mice doon . . . I'd have been better off at my auld boy's, better off with the fuckin parks who didn't even sack me, at least it was a job . . .

— C'moan big man, yir sleepin . . .

I down two balls. Tonight I'll go over and see Nazneem and tell her that I'm in love with her. No. That would be a lie. I only want to have sex with her. I've had enough of cynical games now that she's gone, gone, gone, gone, and never wrote although the last time I saw her she says hopefully we can carry on where we left off once she's got a few things sorted out and that was months ago now and she's here, here in London, and I suppose that's why I'm here; as if it was possible to casually bump into someone in London, shopping in London, like on Oxford Street, like you can on Prinny. Perhaps I could run into her at a club, the Ministry of Sound or something, but I never shop in London, in CENTRAL LONDON, I never go to clubs, just pubs or late-night drinking clubs full of alcoholics Simmy describes as the salt of the earth, but who are just beaten, broken people with nothing to say, no insights, nothing . . . I'm on the black, auld Harry sniggers maliciously and a Scots guy from Greenford says: — C'moan mate, sort out this orange bastard, and he and Simmy burst into the mundane, tedious double-act of football and religious rivalry that passes for high weedjie wit and we're all supposed to fall around pissing ourselves and be interested and only the black ball stands between me and the humiliation of this fat hun bastard.

He silently lets me pot it.

— Sorry, big man, ma gemme. Ye didnae nominate yir poakit. Auld Harry nods sagely. The ranks are closing even before I start to protest. Simmy's never out of Greenford's Red Lion, I hate it here. They all take the side of the house rules and the avuncular chatty Glaswegian. How sneaky is that cunt.

— Hard lines, big man, nae luck at aw, he smiles extending his hand and shaking mine theatrically.

— Moral victory, the other Scots guy says, — cheated by masonic refereein. That's huns fir ye.

— Right, I say, — ah'm off. I said I'd meet Cliff down the Lady Margaret. I can't conceal my annoyance. Fuck Cliff, it's Nazneem I want to see; this woman who shares the same birthday as Barbara Dickson, Meat Loaf and Alvin Stardust.

— They east-coast punters. A few days oan the bevvy n that's thum fucked. Nae stayin power, Simmy laughs. — See ye back at the flat, big man.

I leave him holding court with the prospective victims of lung cancer, cirrhosis of the liver, alcohol-induced asphyxiation through vomit inhalation, chip-pan fires and domestic stabbings who inhabit the Red Lion at Greenford, Middlesex.

I go back home and try and read for a bit, but my head is buzzing and I can't concentrate, even on Marilyn Monroe's story.

When I go to Nazneem's and put forward the proposition, I get knocked back. — I don't have sex with people like that, she says. — I like you as a friend, that's all. She laughs a little then passes over the joint. Nazneem's room is all fresh, pastel, planty and feminine. I feel like staying here forever.

I suck on the joint. — Okay then, what about swapping gaffs? Ah'll stay here and you can move intae ma room, over the road with Simmy and Cliff.

This second proposition has, if anything, even less appeal tae her than the first.

— No, I don't think that's on, she smiles. Then she looks penetratingly at me and says, — You're not happy in yourself, are you?

It hits me in the centre of my chest. I always thought I was. Maybe not though. — I don't know. Who is?

— I am, she said. — I like my friends, I like my job, like where I stay, like the people I live with.

— No, you need to be in love to be happy. Ah'm not in love, I tell her.

— I don't know if that's true, she says. Then: — You're a bit of a smart

NONONONONONONONONONONONONOOOOOO

My brain involuntarily makes loud echoing, ringing noises in my ear, which drown out her words.

— Sorry, a bit of a what? I ask.

— A smart-alec. You think you know all the answers.

A smart-alec. A posh name for a smart cunt.

We spraff all afternoon and I go to the Ministry of Sound with her and some of her pals. It's a nice night, great vibes, great sounds, good ecky, nice people. We sit around and chill the next day. I pray for a bad road-traffic accident for Simmy. Later on that Sunday night I decide to face the music. I go across.

— Whair you been, big yin? Our company no good enough fir ye? Ye'll git nuthin sniffin aroond that wee wog tart, tell ye that fir nowt.

I got more from her in a few hours than I had from him in two months. Just when you think the gig's totally fucked, someone like Nazneem comes along and you think the world isn't so bad after all. As for Simmy, what was I doing breathing the same rancid air as that prick?

It was time I headed back up the road. On Monday I bought a one-way bus ticket to Edinburgh. On Tuesday I used it. It was near enough Christmas anyway. I'd probably be back after the New Year. Probably.

6

CHRISTMAS WITH BLIND CUNT

Our antipathy towards Blind Cunt had simmered away for as long as I could recall, but it fairly blazed once we broke that shared taboo of its acknowledgement. The taboo had been a fairly powerful one. After all, you are supposed to empathise with, and perhaps give greater social licence to, someone with such a terrible disability. Fate has been cruel to some people; you as a human being are expected to compensate. The arbitrary nature of this disability is striking; the attitude of there but for the grace of God go I prevails. Or should.

This attitude, though, is governed by self-righteousness and fear. Self-righteousness, as the sighted are able to appear superior and benevolent, or even worthier because they make a big thing out of treating people like Blind Cunt in exactly the same manner as they treat everybody else. Fear comes into this too: as well as the primitive fear that we will be struck down by an omnipotent force if we are not good, there's a more sophisticated one. It states that we are contributing towards defining what is acceptable behaviour towards individuals in such circumstances and if a similar fate befalls us, then we should expect to be treated decently.

However, being blind does not make you a good person. You can be just as much of a cunt as any sighted fucker. Sometimes even more of a cunt. Like Blind Cunt.

It was on the fourth pint in Sandy Bell's that the taboo was shattered. We were slagging people we disliked and Roxy eventually drew in a breath and glared at me over the silver frames of his glasses. — And ah'll tell ye one cunt who I fuckin cannot stand: that blind cunt that drinks in the Spider's. Tell ays he's no a fuckin pain!

I spluttered nervously into my beer. A chill briefly descended on me, only to be quickly supplanted by a glorious feeling of liberation. Blind Cunt. — That cunt gits oan ma fuckin tits, I agreed.

The following Thursday night me, Roxy and The PATH were up at Sidney's flat having a blow. It was a fucker of a night; icy roads, gale-force winds which had caused much damage, and occasional snowstorms. A night to stay in; but as it was a Friday, this was simply not possible. After we finished the blow, we braved the elements and struggled up Morrison Street to the pub.

— Fuckin Bertie Auld, The PATH said, as we staggered into the boozer, shaking and tramping the snow from our coats and boots.

— Fuckin brutal, man, Sidney agreed.

Big Ally Moncrief was at the bar, doing the *Evening News* crossword. I started moving towards him, but then I saw Blind Cunt's twisted face poking out from behind the big fucker. I stopped in my tracks as I heard Blind Cunt's high, jagged squeal:

— CORRECKSHIN! HEART OF MIDLOTHIAN FOOTBALL CLUB PLC, AS THEY ARE OFFICIALLY REFERRED TO IN THE REGISTER OF COMPANIES!

Bobby from behind the bar looked at Blind Cunt as if he wanted to burst his mouth. Big Moncrief smiled tolerantly, then noted us. — The boys! What yis fir?

So we were thus sucked into the company of Ally Moncrief and, as Blind Cunt had been enjoying the big bastard's sponsorship, that of the visually challenged vagina himself.

We had to put up with Blind Cunt's pedantic asides for most of the evening. It didn't bother Sidney or The PATH, they were both really stoned, but Roxy and I had worked up a fair steam of hate and loathing for the fucker in Sandy Bell's the other night, and he was quickly reactivating it.

The crunch came when The PATH, Roxy and Big Moncrief

were discussing some seventies revival programme that had recently been televised.

— The classic clip though, Roxy enthused, — was that Roxy Music one from the Whistle Test.

A few nods followed, but I thought: well, Roxy would say that, being a Roxy Music freak.

— CORRECKSHIN! Blind Cunt snaps. — THE OLD GREY WHISTLE TEST TO BE PRECISE, jabbing a pedantic finger in the air.

After this Roxy and I extracted ourselves from the company, making the excuse that we wanted to talk to Keith Falconer, who was sitting down the other end of the bar. We sat blethering to Keith for about an hour. When he made to leave, we talked to a couple of guys we didn't know, rather than go back up beside the others.

After a bit, The PATH waved his hand and shut his eyes as he and Sidney staggered past us, out into the snow. The last bell had gone. Later Big Moncrief, obviously drunk, slipped away, quiet and stoical, into the blizzard. Blind Cunt was left alone at the bar.

— That Blind Cunt, Roxy said, pointing down the bar at him, — ye check oot the size ay his wad there? Tell ays he wisnae fuckin flush.

— Naw.

He looked at me, treachery filling his eyes. — Something tae think aboot but.

We managed to get another beer out of them before we braved the storm. It was horrible, the snow driving into us at force, my face numb and throbbing, my head splitting in no time. It was impossible to see more than a few feet ahead. We could make out one slow, ambling figure holding onto the black railings, however.

— There's Blind Cunt! Roxy shouted.

At that point, a slate dislodged from a tenement roof, crashing down a few feet in front of us. — Fuck sake, Roxy gasped, — that could've taken our fuckin heids oaf! Then he grabbed a hold of me, his eyes charged up in realisation and anticipation. He picked up the slate and hurried down the road. Standing a few feet behind Blind Cunt, he hurled the slate like a frisbee. It flew past his ear, but in the racket the driving snow and gale-force winds made, Blind Cunt heard and, of course, saw, nothing.

— Ah'll gie the cunt CORRECKSHIN! Roxy snarled. He picked up another slate from the snow and ran up behind Blind Cunt. Two-handedly and with great force, he brought it crashing down over his head. Blind Cunt staggered forward and hit the deck. Roxy whipped the wallet out of his coat pocket. I kicked a pile of snow in his face, for no reason other than malice, and we departed in silent haste along the road, bouncing mirthfully up the subway to Fountainbridge as Roxy extracted the notes from Blind Cunt's wallet, throwing the empty purse over the graveyard wall. We got a number 1 bus which struggled up to Tollcross where we went into Tipplers for a late drink.

Blind Cunt did have a fair old wad. — Christmas shoapping dosh, ah bet, Roxy said gleefully. — Try telling ays that's no fuckin sound! Two hundred odd sobs!

— CORRECKSHIN! I snapped. — Two hundred and seventeen pounds and thirty-four pence to be exact.

Roxy was intae a fifty-fifty split, but I was happy with eighty bar, as he had taken all the risks, such as they were.

The next day we were back in the same pub for a lunchtime drink. We were soon joined by Big Moncrief. — Ye hear aboot last night?

— Naw, we said in chorus.

— Ye ken what's his name, the blind boy, likes? The boy we hud a drink up at the bar wi last night?

— Aye, Roxy said, with a fake concern.

— Died last night; brain haemorrhage. The poor bastard died in the snaw at Dalry Road. The council gritters found um last night.

— Fuckin hell! We wir jist wi the boy the other night! Roxy said.

I was too shocked to admire his front.

— Fuckin sin, Big Moncrief snarled, — a harmless cunt n aw. Ye ken what? Some rotten cunt dipped ehs poakits. The perr cunt's lyin in the snaw dyin. Did they phone an ambulance? Did they fuck! Some cunt jist goes, aye, aye, what's this then? Instead ay phonin an ambulance, the cunt's dipped ehs poakits, took ehs wallet. They found it empty in the graveyard.

— That's fuckin terrible, Roxy shook his head. — Ah hope they find the cunt that did it.

— See if ah goat ma fuckin hands oan thum . . . Moncrief growled.

— How bad is that? I said timidly, before changing the subject. — What's everybody fir?

Poor Blind Cunt. No a bad punter n aw. Wish I could mind ay his name but.

7

JELLIES AND COCK SUCKING

You could tell that the boy was suspect when he says, I've got to
see a man about a brown-paper package. You could tell that the
boy thought that I thought he was suspect. You could tell that
he enjoyed the fact that I thought he was suspect. The problem
was that I thought he was suspect not because, as he thought, I
saw him as some big sleazy dealer or all that shite; I thought that
he was suspect because I thought that he was a wanker.

Brown-paper package my Granny's sagging tits. What's he
like.

Ronnie might have thought that the guy was a wanker n aw
had he not, as the song goes, been so busy playing carousel. His
pupils were like pin-pricks despite the heavy, hooded eyelids
which hung loosely over them. The pint of poison which lay
untouched in front of him was losing its chill and fizz, leaving it
looking like the rancid pish it was. It would not be touched now.

I was continuing my successful boycott of Scottish and Newcastle Brewers products, swilling away at my Becks. This boycott, which I tried vainly to pursue over a number of years, was
now abetted by the stagnant mediocrity of the S&N products;
they had stood still in the face of competition.

I wearily raised my hand in acknowledgement as the wanker
departed; no doubt to procure the first ever quart of Edinburgh
hash which came in a brown-paper package. As he said, —
Cheerio boys, Ronnie managed to do something marginal with
his eyes and lips.

—Jellied, Ron? I asked.

In reply, Ronnie rested his head in his hand, elbow propped up on the table, and allowed his lips to faintly crease.

I looked again at the pint before him; the dealers had no real competition from the legal drug sector. I resented more than ever the fact that S&N had managed to fight off that take-over bid from the Australian punters. I remember it being described as a hostile bid. Hostile to who? No me anyway. Surely no other race in the world put up with such crap drugs.

I get Ronnie out into a taxi, mildly resentful that we have missed an hour's worth of the mis-named happy hour, which is neither: a bit like the fuckin moral majority. Its duration was a five-till-eight weekday slot at this pretentious dive where they sold toxic chemicals at prices which were merely exploitative rather than criminal. Looking at the punters fighting for the attention of the barstaff, happiness was the last emotion on display. It should be renamed the desperate hours.

Ronnie flopped back into the taxi, his face slamming hard off a side window. — Stockbridge, mate, I shout to the driver, reasoning that Ronnie was suffering from chemical imbalance and what he needed was some amphetamine to get him back into some kind of equilibrium.

When we get to Veitchy's place Denise and Penman are there. They're all quite high, through snorting coke. Ronnie can go and get fucked. No way would we consider wasting coke on him. He'd have to sleep his way through this gig. Veitchy helps me to put him on the couch, and he just crashes out uncon- scious. Denise puckers his lips, — My my my, Brian's brought us a trophy. Is that what Ronnie is, Brian, our ain wee trophy?

— Yeah, that's it, I say, catching Penman's eye. He chops out a line for me and I go down on it like it was a fanny that pished Becks. Suddenly, everything's better.

— What have we here? Denise has unzipped Ronnie's flies and taken his floppy dick out. It looks pretty repulsive, bouncing around on his thighs like a broken jack-in-the-box.

Veitchy laughs loudly, — Ha ha ha ha ha ha perr Ronnie ha ha ha ha, no real. Denise yir some cunt so ye are ha ha ha ha.

— Now that's a whopper, Denise pouts with a saucy wink, — but it'll be even bigger erect. Let's see if ah kin breathe some life intae poor old Ronnie.

He starts sucking on Ronnie's cock. Veitchy and I check Ron's face for signs of recognition, signs of enjoyment, but it seems dead to me. Veitchy then produces a magic marker and draws glasses and a Hitler moustache on Ronnie's coupon.

— Fuck sakes, I turn to Penman, — there's me lugged that cunt intae a taxi and brought him doon here tae look eftir him. Cannae leave the cunt in the pub like that, ah thought. Ah'll take him tae Veitchy's, he'll be awright thair.

— Yeah, typical ay they cunts, Penman snorts, then he picks a bogey out of his nose. He sees that there's a load of coke stuck to it, so he swallows it. — How ye livin they days anywey? he asks me.

— Shite, I tell him. — It's funny though man, but ah'm gaunny miss the parks this summer, ken? Shouldnae huv burned it doon. Gies me time tae write songs, for the band n that, ken?

A few of us had been thinking of starting a band. That was what I was into; being in a band.

— Well, ah'm pittin ma name doon fir the bins this summer. Intae that? The Cleansing Department, ken?

— Aye, mibbe, I said. It sounds a bit too much like work for me, too many people aroond. No enough time tae think, tae get in touch wi yirself, tae just enjoy the isolation. No like the parks.

Denise is having no luck with Ronnie's cock. It's still as jellied as the rest of him, but Veitchy's got the polaroid out and he's taking snaps of them.

— Ah wee bit ay love talk first, Denise, whisper some ay they sweet nothins intae the cunt's ear, Penman advises.

Denise puckers his lips and says, — Tsk, Penman, ye ken ah keep aw that talk jist for you. Ye think ah'm a slut or something?

Penman smiles, stands up and gestures me to the door. We go through to the bedroom. He stoops down at a chest of drawers;

producing a box which he unlocks. It contains a plastic bag full of pills.

— Eckys? I ask.

— Snowballs, he nods, smiling. — Many kin ye punt fir ays?

— Ah could dae forty nae danger. Thing is, ah've nae dough up front.

— Disnae matter, he says, counting them intae a smaller bag. — Gies it when ye git it. Ah only want ten quid fir one. They'll go fir fifteen easy, eighteen if ye hud them until the week before Rezurrection. Square ays eftir. Veitchy's nervous wi the number ah'm hudin here.

— One question, Penman. How's it ye always stash them at Veitchy's gaff?

— Veitchy's a fuckin radge; he's he only cunt that'll let ays. Ah'm no gaunny keep thum at ma ain place, um ah now?

It sounded logical enough.

A few minutes later, Denise's excited screams follow us into the bedroom. — BRI-IN! PEEHN-MIN!

I return into the front room to find Denise and Veitchy straddling the back of the couch, facing each other. They have their cocks out, both erect. Ronnie is still slumped unconscious, his head resting on the back of the sofa. Denise and Veitchy have their erections poking into his ears.

— The camera, Denise hisses, — take a picture!

— This'll be a fuckin classic ha ha ha, Veitchy babbles.

I pick up the camera and get into position. — Whair's the fuckin button? I ask.

— The toap, Denise squeals excitedly, — press the fuckin black button oan the toap! Mind yir fingers oan the lens, daft radge thit ye are!

I take a couple of shots which come out well. They really capture the personalities of the three punters involved. That's surely what portrait photography is all about.

We pass the snaps around and laugh for a bit, then Denise goes: — Ah need mair coke. Any mair fuckin coke?

Veitchy says, — Naw man, that's it finished, likes.

— Could dae wi a bit mair but, Veitchy, Penman says. Penman and I have taken half an ecky each, but mair coke would be sound.

— Suppose ah could nick doon tae Andy Lawton's in the motor, Veitchy agreed.

That sounded okay. We sorted Veitchy out with some cash and he left us in the flat.

After a while I was getting a bit bored watching the telly. — Any fuckin beer in this doss? I asked.

— Yuv jist taken half an ecky. Ye no gittin a rush oaf that ecky yit?

I was getting fuck all off the ecky. I pretended I was though; it's crucial tae think positive on such occasions. — Aye, it's sound, but it's a bit mellow likes. Stick oan some techno. Git this telly shite oaf; kills the art ay fuckin conversation.

We ploughed our way through Veitchy's record and tape collection. I'd never seen so much shite.

— This is fuckin rubbish. Cunt wants his fuckin jaw tanned fir huvin shite like this. Nae fuckin house stuff at aw man, Penman moaned.

— Some ay this isnae bad, Denise opined.

— Stuck in eighties disco shite that cunt, said Penman bitterly. — That cunt is a fuckin erse. He always hus been an erse, he always fuckin will be an erse.

— C'moan, Penman, I said, — Git oaf the cunt's case. It's his hoaspitality wir enjoyin here.

—Aye, Penman, yir such a fuckin bitch at times, Denise said, kissing his cheek softly, — bit yuv goat yir bad side n aw.

— Well ah'm gaunny git a beer, I said. As I spoke I started rushing. What a fuckin waste, rushing like this here when I could be at a club.

— Dinnae take alcohol wi yir ecky, Denise says. — Ye cannae drink if yuv taken ecstasy, he minces smartly, — cancels oot aw the effects.

— That's a myth, I say.

— Tsk, listen tae yirsel, Brian! Mind the time at The Pure ye sais tae ays: Yir mad tae drink, bevvy n ecky dinnae mix, yill bring yirsel doon, Denise remonstrates.

— Aye, bit that's whin yir tryin tae dance, but. Dehydration n that. If ye jist want tae gouch, it doesnae really matter. Besides, ah've been oan the Becks maist ay the day.

— Ah'm no touchin the bevvy again, no fir ages anywey. Ah'm no takin any ecky either until ah find oot the coke situation. Ye should pick jist one drug n stick tae it. That's the lesson ah've learned. Last week ah wis up the toon pished ootay ma heid. Ah'd hud eight Becks n six Diamond Whites. Some cunt went n gied ays a tab ay acid. Then this radge wis hasslin ays in The Pelican so ah jist turns roond n sais: Dinnae fuckin bother ays man, kick yir fuckin cunt in! Anyway ah goat pure para so ah ends up in the City Cafe. Ken that goth burd, quite a hard-faced lassie?

— Her that used tae hing aboot wi that Moira? I asked.

— Ah think so.

— Moira. You legged that, did ye no? Penman asked.

— Aye, in the lassies' bogs at the Ceilidh House, I told him.

— Anywey, Denise snapped curtly, irritated by our interruptions and digressions, — this burd wis really fag-hagging ays oot, man. Ah goes hame wi her, she says she's goat some blow. Then she starts askin ays aboot ma sexuality, ken, aw that how'd ye like tae come ower tae the other side, aw that vain crap that fag-hags come oot wi man, ken? Ah mean, as if ah've nivir fucked a lassie before! Stupid wee hoor!

— Ye gie hur the message? Penman asked.

— Hud oan, hud oan a minute, I cut in. I hated interrupting Denise in full flight, but something about this tale was disturbing me. I needed something clarified. — Lit's git this straight. Wir talkin aboot that lassie that hings aboot wi Moira n Tricia. Olly, or something doss like that, is it no?

— That's hur! Denise says.

— Hammer n sickle earrings? Oan some sortay Stalinist trip?

— That's the yin awright, Denise says. — So ah'm shagging her like, in the fanny n aw, he says, standing up and doing a theatrical pelvic thrust. — She kept they long black gloves oan, like a silly wee tart, n she's gaun: AW THIS IS GREAT . . . THIS IS MAGIC . . . FUCK ME HARDER n aw that. Then she comes n ah starts thinkin aboot Hutchie fae Chapps, this big fuckin piece ay meat ah've been cruisin fir yonks, n ah comes n aw. Then this daft hoor turns aroond n sais tae ays: Tell ays that wisnae somethin else, she goes, aw cocky like. Like she'd expected me tae throw away the tub ay KY n run doon tae St James's Centre fir a fuckin engagement ring! Well, ah hud tae pit hur in the picture; ah tells her it wisnae even as fuckin good as a bad wank, wi her ah hud tae use ma imagination mair, tae pretend ah wis shaggin something worthwhile. She goes aw fucked up and tells ays tae go. Ah jist sais: Dinnae you fuckin worry, hen, ah'm gaun.

This was a disturbing story. I remember being kb'd by that lassie. I think it was the City Cafe, but it might have been Wilkie House. I saw her a few times at 9Cs, even once at The Pure. As I smiled at Denise the phantom quiver of that woman's rejection slid through me, setting off that internal crumbling dam of self-esteem that our pals can seldom sense. However, I tempered that feeling with the thought of her humiliation at the hands of Denise. I felt a delicious vindication, followed by a vague sense of guilt. This is what being alive's all about, all those fucked-up feelings. You've got to have them; when you stop, watch out.

God, the telly was fuckin boring, and there were only two cans of McEwan's pish in the fridge. I couldn't bring myself to look at that shite. — Whair's fuckin Veitchy? I cursed, to nobody in particular. Chancellor Norman Lamont came on the telly.

— Ah'd like tae kill that cunt, if he wisnae already deid, Denise bitched.

I felt another ecky surge and got up and started dancing on the spot. I couldn't keep it going though; there was no fuckin stimulus. I fancied doing another one and heading up to the Citrus or 9Cs. — That cunt, I said, pointing at Ronnie, who was still slumbering with his flaccid prick hanging out off his keks like some dead surrealist snake, — what's he like: a fuckin liability. Cartin that fuck around, n he jist crashes oot aw ower the place!

In a surge of anger I pulled Ronnie off the couch onto the floor. He inspired a wave of disgust in me, his stupid glasses and moustache. — He's as well oan the flair, gie us a shot ay the couch. He's too fucked tae notice the difference.

The three of us sat on the couch, using Ronnie as a footstool. He was dead to the world. We were still bored, so I got up, brought some flour back from the kitchen and poured it over Ronnie. I gasped at a brief acid-style flashback of Blind Cunt lying in the snow.

— Hi, Penman guffaws, splitting his keks with laughter, — better mind perr Veitchy's cairpit.

— It's only flour, I said, but Denise had gone through to the kitchen and he returned with some eggs and started breaking them over Ronnie's prostrate body.

That was the cue for us to go mental, gripped by a collective hysteria. We went to the kitchen and saw what there was. We then systematically covered Ronnie with every sort of foodstuff, cleaning fluid and powder we could get our hands on.

When we were finished he was covered in a largely grey-white evil sludge, partly coloured in places by orange beans, yellow egg yolks and green washing-up liquid. Penman came back from the kitchen and emptied the contents of a bin-liner over him. I tipped a couple of full ashtrays across him. The sludge rolled off him and seeped into the ugly red carpet. Still Ronnie wouldn't wake up. Denise then shat on his face; a huge, steaming, wet turd. By this time I was fearing for my own health. I was convulsing, with a crippling pain in my side caused by too much laughter, and Penman had almost blacked out after a giggling fit.

We took more pictures. I'd made myself sick, easy considering the mess, and what I'd had to drink, and vomited over Ronnie's unrecognisable face and chest. He looked like a mound of bacterial sludge from a septic tank; a lump of toxic waste; a spillover from a council tip.

We laughed ourselves out and our adrenalin dipped simultaneously as we surveyed the mess.

— Fuck sakes, I said. — What are we like. How mad is this!

— Veitchy's gaunny be well pissed-off at us. His cairpit's fucked, Denise goes.

Penman looked a bit shat up. — Ronnie n aw. Ron's pretty radge. He hud a blade that time in the Burnt Post. Ye dinnae ken what any cunt whae's jellied'll go n dae whin thir cairryin a chib.

This was true. — Let's fuck off, I suggested. — Leave some money fir Veitchy n Ron. They can git cleaned up.

Nobody was putting up too many strong arguments for staying and facing the music. We took off and headed for Tollcross in a taxi. We got very drunk but were still thinking about chancing our arm and trying to get into the Citrus Club, when Veitchy walked into the pub. To our surprise, he took it okay, better than Ronnie apparently.

Veitchy looked really freaked, as in amazed, by the whole thing. — Ah've never seen anybody look like that in ma puff. It wis just fuckin crazy. Ah shat masel when ah came in and pit the light oan. Ah jist pit doon some auld newspapers, aw the wey tae the bathroom. It wis radge whin Ronnie woke up. He just shouted: THE FUCKIN BASTARDS! THE FUCKIN CUNTS! SOME WIDE–O FUCKIN DIES FIR THIS! Then he jist trails through tae the shower, n gits under it, fully-clathed likes, n hoses hisel doon. Then he walks oot soakin wet n goes: Ah'm away hame.

I looked at Denise n Penman. Sometimes mates are the last people ye kin trust.

— Ye git any coke, Denise asks Veitchy.

— Naw, jist these, he says holding out some capsules.

— Eckys? Penman asks. — No wantin eckys. Goat loads ay fuckin ecky ya daft fucker.

— Naw, it's ketamine. Special-Ks like. Ken?

— Ah'm no touchin thaim, Denise shudders.

Penman looks at me. — Ah'm game, he says.

— Might as well, I agree, — jist fir the crack like.

We each down one, except Denise, but within minutes he's begging Veitchy to sort him out as well. I start to feel heavy and tired. We're all talking shite.

The next thing I remember is dancing on my own in the Meadows at five o'clock on a Sunday morning.

8

PARANOIA

I'm thinking about my life and that is always a very, very stupid thing to do. The reason for this is that there are some things that don't bear thinking about, some things that if you try to think of them they'll just fuck you up even mair.

I hear my auld man shouting at me, — BRIAN! UP! C'MOAN! MOVE IT!

— Aye, jist comin. It's pointless arguing. I have to sign on today. Once the auld boy decides I should be up, then he won't stop.

I rise wearily. Derek's in his bed, stretching tae life.

— You no workin the day? I ask him.

— Naw. Day oaf.

Derek's doing well for himself. Planning to sit the Civil Service Executive Officer exam, or perhaps has already sat it. I don't know. The details of the working classes' trivial activities have never held much attraction for a man of leisure.

— Mind ay Ma, Deek? I can't believe I just asked him that.

— Aye, of course ah do.

— You wir jist six when she took off.

— Still mind ay her likes.

— Aw . . . ah mean it's jist been a long time since ye talked aboot it . . . ah suppose ah mean since we talked aboot it, I said.

— Thir isnae that much tae talk aboot, he snorted, — she went, we stayed.

I didn't like that c'est la vie attitude, and wondered if he was trying to conceal something, then I wondered what. I supposed it was just because Deek was a bit thick. He'd probably pass the Civil Service Executive Officer exam though.

Downstairs the auld man had made a plate of toast and some tea. — You were in some bloody state again last night, he says sourly.

Actually, I wasn't in some state. I was a wee bit pished. Roxy, Sidney and I had broken into a chip shop in Corstorphine and stolen a load of confectionery and tobacco. We'd managed to fence a bit to the Rox's brother-in-law, who has an ice-cream van. Then we'd got a bit drunk. I know I wasn't in some state, for if I had been in some state I wouldn't have come home.

— Jist a few pints, I mused.

— If ye want tae make yirsel useful, come roond the scheme wi me n Norma collecting some names for this petition.

Now why didn't I think of that. A sound idea. I'd only be fuckin crucified, that's all. It's bad enough him trying to get me killed with his stupid, pointless activities, he now wants me to pull the fuckin trigger masel.

— Ah'd love tae, Dad, mibbe some other time, yeah? It's just this signing-oan shite the day. Then ah've goat tae go round the Job Centre. How's the campaign going?

— We went tae see that bloody councillor. That's nivir a Labour man. Ah've voted Labour aw ma life, but nivir again, ah'm tellin ye.

I took a hike into the city. It's fuckin miles, but I grudge paying fares. I'm skint. That chippie job paid sweeties, metaphorically as well as literally. I go and sign on. Then I head up to Sidney's gaff for a blow. It's weird how I tend to hang around with different people when in different drug scenes:

Alcohol:	The PATH, Roxy, Sidney, Big Moncrief
Non-opiate illegal drugs: (speed, acid, ecky, etc.)	Veitchy, Denise, Penman

Opiates: Swanney, Raymie, Spud

But whatever scene, there's always Ronnie. That cunt is my
penance for being a . . . for some crime committed in a previous
life.

That afternoon, I meet Penman who's fucked from a scene he
was in over the weekend. His eyes are bleary and red. We do
acid. Monday afternoon and we do a microdot. It's strong stuff n
aw. — You know your problem man? he asks in a way which
disconcerts me.

— Eh, I say, — ah didnae ken ah hud one . . .

— Ye jist illustrated it fir ays, man. Ye jist provided ays wi, as
you might say, a graphic illustration ay what ah meant wi what
you sais thair, ken?

— What dae ye mean? I ask, a bit nippy.

— Dinnae git stroppy, mate. This is mates talkin. Ah'm only
sayin this cause me n you go back a long way. Right?

— Right, I agree, full of unease. I haven't been sleeping and
I'm always para when I haven't been sleeping. It isn't the drugs
that make me para, it's the lack of sleep that makes me para. The
drugs only make it hard for for me tae sleep, so they're only
indirectly responsible. If I could just get something to make me
fuckin sleep . . .

— This 'ah didnae ken ah hud a problem' shite, Penman
scoffs. — Wuv aw goat problems. Every cunt in this bar's goat
problems. He sweeps his arm around the seedy pub. It wasn't
easy to refute that proposition. — Every cunt in the world's goat
problems.

— This isnae the maist representative sample . . . I say, but he
picks up on this and cuts in.

— There ye go again: 'this isnae the maist representative
sample . . .' he mocks me, using a voice that sounds more like
Denise's than ma own. — Ah'm tellin ye mate, yir awright, but
yir too much ay a smart cunt. Point is, everybody laps up a smart
cunt at one time or another. The smart cunt makes a joke, every
fucker's chuffed tae bits. Then the smart cunt gits oan people's

tits. Then the smart cunt gits a burst mooth. That's the way it works.

I sit flabbergasted.

— Now ah'm no saying that you've like, croassed that line. Aw ah'm sayin is that some cunts kin git away wi it mair thin others.

— Whit dae ye mean?

— Take Denise fir instance. Every cunt kens what he's like. So he gits away wi things thit you or me couldnae. One day though, he'll go too far . . .

I was really para now. I'd never had Penman talk tae me like this before. — Any cunt said anything tae ye aboot ays?

— Look mate, aw ah'm sayin is thit yir startin tae gie oaf a vibe, he takes a sip of his coke and puts his arm around ma shoulder.

— Ah dinnae go aboot thinkin ah'm better thin any cunt else, I plead.

— Look mate, dinnae go taking it aw personally. Ah'm jist sayin watch. Right? He shakes his head for a while, then lets it fall into his hands. — Aw look, he gasps in exasperation, — forget whit ah sais, it's jist the acid.

— Naw bit, you look, whit's the score? Whae's been sayin things?

— Forget it.

— Naw come oan, ah want tae ken. What's the fuckin score?

— Ah sais forget it. Ah wis oot ay order, right?

There is a hardness in Penman's eyes, so I feel comfortable deferring to him. — This fuckin acid man . . . I observe.

— Aye, that's right . . . he agrees, but there is a meanness about him, an unsettling edge. I feel like bursting into tears and begging: PLEASE BE NICE TO ME.

Penman had fucked up ma heid. Penman and the acid. When I started to come down I went back tae ma auld man's place and up tae ma room. I lay on the bed taking stock of my life with a cruel, self-loathing brutality. No job, no qualifications except O Grade English and Art, no romantic attachment now that she's away and definitely not coming back, mates who only tolerated me. Prospects pretty fuckin grim all round. Yes, I did have a certain outgoing social vivaciousness but the self-belief that drove me on in face of all overwhelming evidence to the contrary was now evaporating rapidly. Penman wrote my epitaph: A Smart Cunt. Nobody likes a smart cunt; a smart cunt who is also an accessory to murder has got real problems.

It could be the drugs, it could be Blind Cunt, or I could be going mental, but things are not right. When I get on a bus or go into a pub, people stop talking when they see me. On the bus nobody sits beside me. I am the very last person anybody will sit beside. Do I smell? I think I do smell of something. I sniff at my clothes, armpits, crotch. I take a shower. Am I ugly? I look at myself in the mirror for ages. I am ugly. No worse, I'm totally unremarkable. A completely bland face; no character in it. I have to get out of here, so I go to Roxy's.

— This Blind Cunt thing's fuckin ma heid, man, I tell him. — How fucked is it?

— It's drugs that's fuckin you up, he scoffed, — leave them alane and stay cool ya daft cunt.

— Ah might go doon tae London for a bit. This place gies ays the fuckin creeps. There's some tapped people oan the streets, man. Yir walkin hame and any cunt could be cairryin a knife, jellied oot thir box. That could be your life over, jist like that. Some cunt who gets a result fae the AIDS clinic: You tested positive. What have they goat tae lose? They could just grab a car and mow ye doon.

— Bullshit.

— Look at Blind Cunt, though. It happened tae him! We did it tae him! It could happen tae us. It should happen tae us. Justice n that.

I was shaking and my teeth were chattering. There was a raw core of queasy fear in the centre of my body which was spreading toxic shivers through my limbs.

— That's shite. Awright, so it wis mibbe a bit ootay order whit we did tae Blind Cunt, but that brain thing could've happened anytime. That's a time-bomb, that sort ay thing. Disnae make us murderers or nowt like that. The cunt could've goat up one morning and hud a yawn tae hisel and bingo! Goodnight Vienna. Jist cause it happened tae happen by coincidence when ah panelled the cunt means fuck all. Ah read aw aboot this brain haemorrhage shite in the library. It's a shame fir Blind Cunt but it disnae mean tae say that we should fuck oor lives up. Tell ays thit us gittin the nick's gaunny bring Blind Cunt back, cause that's shite!

— Aye bit . . . I started.

— Listen the now, Bri, he interrupted, his head shaking belligerently. — Dinnae shed any tears fir Blind Cunt. Tell ays he wisnae an annoyin fuck. That cunt would've got his eventually, the wey ah see it.

— Blind Cunt might have saw it a wee bit differently, I replied, suddenly realising the ugly irony of what I'd said. The poor bastard. I felt awful. Roxy didn't spare me.

— Blind Cunt saw fuck all, that's how he wis called Blind Cunt, he said, contorting his face in a cruel sneer.

Once again I wanted to leave. I was surrounded by demons and monsters. We're all bad people. There's no hope for the world. I left and walked along the disused railway line and cried my eyes out at the futility of it all.

9

PLASTIC SURGERY

I'm sitting holding my face together in my hands; or that's how it seems. I'm aware of people around me, their outraged gasps indicating that it's bad. I know that. The blood falls through my fingers and hits the wooden pub floor in steady, even drops.

Hobo and I were close mates once, a few years ago now. He didn't like me pulling him around, begging him to get me sorted out.

— Git ootay ma fuckin face, Bri, ah'm warnin ye, man!

I was given plenty of warning. I never took Hobo seriously enough. I always thought he was bit of a poser, him hinging aboot wi they nutters. By keeping that company, though, you can become a nutter yirself. He's far more a man of substance than I thought. Being proved wrong hurts almost as much as my face. My cells, my fucking sick junk-deprived cells hurt the most. I hit the smack heavily this week. Things were getting a bit much; I needed to blot it all out. Everything.

It took one sweeping motion of the glass. One motion and I'm here holding my face together, and Hobo's shouting defensively about junkies fuckin hassling him, and extracting himself from the bar as the collective wrath develops:

— That wis ootay order . . .

— Boy wisnae bothering nae cunt . . .

Hobo slips away. I've no resentment, no thoughts of revenge. No yet anyway; I've bigger fish to fry. I need something to get this fevered ape off my back. Let Hobo think I'm obsessed with him, scheming revenge . . . it's all divine retribution for Blind Cunt, and if so, I've got off lightly. I deserve to suffer . . .

Why did she go.

She goed because of the same reason you got a glass in your face man different manifestations of the same reason namely that you are a

Somebody's dabbing at my face with a hanky. — Better get him to the hospital, that'll need stitching. A woman's voice. I can see out of at least one eye. Not like poor Bli . . . No

A gothic angel of mercy; black hair, black eyes, white face . . . it could be any old hound from the City Cafe . . .

I'm going down the road with her and some others, but I'm only aware of her, my sick body and the stinging air in my face. God, the wounds are fuckin sair now. — You got a weedjie accent? I ask this benign goth-dess.

I saw it on her lapel. The hammer and sickle badge of a Stalinist Goth. The one that kb'd me. The one that fag-hagged Denise oot.

— Ah'm fae Ayrshire, she said.

— What was it Burns said about Ayr: nae toon surpasses for honest men and bonnie lassies . . .

— I'm from Saltcoats, not Ayr.

— Saltcoats . . . the Metro. Good club. Apart fae that though, it's no really got a lot going for it, has it?

— Oh aye? And whair dae you come from then?

— Muirhouse.

— Huh! you're in no position tae talk.

— Listen, at ma auld man's hoose he's got panoramic views across the Forth over tae Fife. There's a golf course across the road, a nice beach a pleasant fifteen minutes' walk away. Additionally, there's a well-stocked library particulary strong on biographies of the famous . . .

More blood spurts out.

— Shh, she says, — you're stretching the wound.

It's getting sore. God, it's sair.

— Good! says the boy at the Infirmary. — That means it's not damaged any nerves. Quite a superficial cut, really. It only needs about eight stitches.

He sewed me up. Eight poxy stitches. I was right first time; Hobo was a namby-pamby blouse. Eight stitches. I laughed nervously, — Eight stitches.

I was brave when they put the stitches in. It looked quite good on my cheek; with any luck it wouldn't fade too much. My bland face needed a bit of character. The scar was a conversation piece. People would think I was a hard man. It's okay for Yul Brynner to say, in *The Magnificent Seven*: It's the guy that gave him the scars you have to worry about, he never drank in the Gunner, the shitein cunt.

The goth woman tells me she is called Olly. — As in Stan and Ollie? I ask.

— Oh, that's very good. Nobody's ever thought of that one before, she said, her tongue dripping sarcasm. — Actually, it's short for Olivia, she explained patiently. — The only famous Olivia is Olivia Newton-John and I hate her. So it's Olly.

I could understand that. It must be bad shite to be a goth and get compared with Ms Neutron-Bomb. — What about Olivia De Havilland? I asked.

— Who?

— She was a film star.

— Before my time, I'm sure.

— Mine as well. It's just that ma auld man had the hots for her. Used to say ma mother was her double.

I saw boredom etched onto her face. Why had she helped me? — Eh, thanks for helping me, I said.

— That bastard Hobo. I hate that crowd. Forrester and aw that bunch. You know that Forrester raped Liz Hamilton? He fuckin raped her! she hissed. Olly hated someone who was the friend of someone who assaulted me.

— Listen, dae ye ken anybody whae can get ays some jellies? I asked.

— Nup! Ah widnae touch them fir anything!

I needed some. — Can I use your phone?

We went back to hers and I lay on the couch, strung out. I tried to phone Ronnie but he'd vanished. His Ma had seen nothing of him for weeks and seemed completely unconcerned as to his whereabouts.

Olly eventually got a hold of a guy called Paul who came along and brought me some valium. I swallowed a few then smoked some blow. He left and Olly and I went to bed. I couldn't shag her though, I felt too sick. I had an erection but the idea of our bodies together was terrifying to me. I waited until she was asleep and I had a wank over her, shooting against her back.

The next day we had a good shag in the morning. It was barry having sex. She had a skinny body and it was therapeutic. It got the system going. In the afternoon we did it from the side, on the couch, so that I could watch the scores coming in on the videoprinter. I was happy.

5.40

PREM Manchester City 1 Nottingham Forest 0

D2 Bolton 3 Gillingham 1

— Oh this is lovely baby . . . really fuckin beautiful . . .

D1 Newcastle 4 Portsmouth 1

SC1 Cowdenbeath 0 Raith Rovers 4

D3 Barnet 2 Colchester 2

SPL Aberdeen 6 (Six)*

— Oh babes . . . I'm coming . . . I'm coming . . . I start to rant.

— Hud oan, hud oan . . . she twists and thrusts.

5.41

SPL Aberdeen 6 (Six) Heart of Midlothian 2

— Ya beauty! Yes! Jesus Christ, ah cannae keep gaun . . .

— OOOOOHHHH BRIAN I'M COMING . . . OH MY GOD!

D2 Oxford United 2 Bristol City 1

PREM Wimbledon 1 Tottenham Hotspur 1

PREM Chelsea 2 Everton 1

— Ah'm gaunny keep going babes, you're gaunny get there
again . . .

— Oh God Brian, keep fucking me . . .

— Easy for Bri, doll, it's all too easy . . .

5.42

SC2 Arbroath 3 Stenhousemuir 0

D2 Southend United 0 York City 0

. . . for Bri, when ah get intae ma stride ah kin fuck all night . . .

SPL Hibernian 3*

. . . ooh ooh OOOHHH OOOHHHH

SPL Hibernian 3 St Johnstone 1

. . . AAGGHHHH!!! OH YA FUCKER!

God, the earth moved. How good was that. Glory glory to
the Hi-bees.

We ate a Chinese takeaway and watched game-shows on the box
that night. It was what I needed. Relaxation.

What I needed.

What did she need?

Olly had looked after me. Kindness was what I needed. What
was in it for her? Perhaps some people are just basically good and
kind. I thought of her and Denise. Of the time she knocked me
back.

— Why did you knock me back that time?

— You were out of your face and totally obnoxious, she
replied. — Just really-so-fuckin-boring . . .

I suppose it was a good enough reason.

She was not so happy when I mentioned Denise's name.

— I hate that sick little bastard. Fucking sick queer. He's been
saying I went with him. Why would I go wi a poof? I'm no

fuckin fag-hag. He's giein his mind a treat, the dirty wee prick. What does he think he's trying to prove by talkin shite like that?

I decided to drop the subject. My face was tight and numb. It was a sore numbness, not a comfortable numbness. It felt like it was made of badly sunburned tissue which had been crudely sellotaped together. It was worth it though. Yes, it definitely had a lot more character now and yes, it would be an interesting conversation piece. There was also the prospect of sympathy. On balance, it was for the best the way things had panned out.

10

YOUNG QUEENS

I've been trying to moderate my drink and drugs intake so I can get some kip in and feel less para. My old mate Donny Armstrong has come up to see my auld man. They've been arguing about politics. As a revolutionary, Donny tends to hunt out the single-issue punters in the community groups, like the auld man, and attempt to convert them to fully-fledged revolutionary politics.

— Some Mars Bar you've got yourself there, man, Donny says.

— You should see the other guy, I say, all cocky. It sounds good. The other guy, Hobo, has a face like a bairn's powdered arse and is about as concerned at the prospect of me looking for him (and I'm not looking too hard) as the continental big guns are at Hearts returning to European action.

The auld man exasperates him, though. Donny has to admit defeat here. Norma pops her head around the door and my father slyly slips away. Donny turns his attention to me, trying to recruit me into the 'party'. — You can't skate over the surface of social reality all your life, he says. This depresses me, it's revolutionary speak for: Ye cannae be a smart cunt aw yir life.

The answer, according to Donny, is to build the revolutionary party. This is done by militant political activity in the workplaces and communities at the point of oppression. I ask him how effective he feels this has been, and whether the collection of students, social workers, journalists and teachers that seem to make up the membership of his party constitutes a fair cross-section of the proletariat.

— Granted man, but it's the downturn, he says, as if that explains it.

— How is it, though, that Militant seem to be able to get ordinary punters while you lot get all those middle-class types?

— Look man, I'm not going to slag Militant, cause there's enough sectarianism on the left, but . . .

He launches into a long and bitter attack on the politics and personalities of Scottish Labour Militant. I'm thinking, what can I do, really do for the emancipation of working people in this country, shat on by the rich, tied into political inaction by servile reliance on a reactionary, moribund and yet still unelectable Labour Party? The answer is a resounding fuck all. Getting up early to sell a couple of papers in a shopping centre is not my idea of the best way to chill out after raving. When people like Penman, Denise, Veitchy and Roxy are ready to join the party, then I'll be ready. The problem is, there's too many, God rest his soul, Blind Cunt types in that sort of thing. I think I'll stick to drugs to get me through the long, dark night of late capitalism.

Donny goes, the both of us totally drained by our arguments. He does look healthy and happier than me though; he has a glow to him. The involvement in the process of political struggle may indeed be quite liberating in itself, irrespective of the results it yields, or rather doesnae yield. I'm still pondering it all an hour later when Ronnie shows up. I haven't seen him since that regrettable incident last weekend.

He touches my stitches lightly, and smiles with a weary compassion. Then he shuts his eyes and wiggles his finger in the air.

— Ron, man, ah'm really sorry about the other night . . . I start, but he puts his finger to his lips and shakes his head slowly. He staggers through the hallway, into the living-room. He's on the couch like an American heat-seeking missile onto a Baghdad orphanage. Nice one, Ronnie.

—Jellied, Ron?

He shakes his head slowly and blows out heavily through tightly-puckered lips. I put on a video and he dozes. I put on a second one and I fall asleep in the middle of it. I feel a tapping on the sole of my foot, and look up to see Ronnie going. He raises his thumb slowly, mumbles something and vanishes into the night.

Deek comes in. — Whair's Dad? he asks.

— No sure. He went oot wi Norma fi upstairs.

Deek rolls his eyes and leaves.

I stagger up to bed.

The next day I've arranged to met Denise in the Beau Brummel.

Denise is in a state of transformation from one queen stereotype into another. I suppose he's no a wee laddie any mair. None of us are. It comes home to me when he walks into the Beau Brummel with a pair of young queens who look exactly like Denise used to look. Denise, on the other hand, looks like a cruel scoutmaster in his flak jacket.

— Drink fir ma friend. A whisky, he snaps at one of the young queens. The wee buftie immediately springs up to the bar. I was going to say something because I don't really like whisky but Denise always loves to decide what will be the appropriate drink for his friends based on his view of how they look and I hate to spoil his sense of theatre. My need to have Denise exhibit that sense of theatre is stronger than my need to exercise freedom of choice in my drug-taking. Therein lies an illustration of the bigger problem.

— I saw your ma the other day, I tell him.

— My Ma! How is she!

— No bad.

— Whair wis this? The scheme?

— Naw, in toon.

— Ah'll huv tae arrange tae meet her in toon fir a cup ay tea. Ah cannae be bothered gaun tae the scheme. Too fuckin depressin. Ah fuckin hate that place.

Denise never really fitted in back there. Too camp; too much of a superiority complex. Most people hated that, but I loved him for it.

One of the bufties makes a terrible error of protocol and puts on Blondie's 'Denis', as in 'Denise Denee'. This upsets the fuck out of Denise.

— WHAE PIT THAT OAN!? WHAE?! he stands up and screams over at the juke box.

One of the young queens apologetically pouts, — Bit Din-e-e-e-esssse, you sais the other night thit is wis yir favourite song, mind the other night, at Chapps?

The other buftie boy looks on in malicious enjoyment at his friend's discomfort.

Denise clenches his fists then lets them fall by his side. — THE WHOLE POINT IS THIT IT'S MA FAVOURITE SONG! AH'M THE ONLY YIN THIT'S ALLOWED TAE PIT OAN THAT FUCKIN SONG! BATTER YIR FUCKIN CUNT IN, SON! He shakes his head angrily, — Dinnae bother ays, jist dinnae fuckin bother ays, son, he dismissively hisses. The disgraced young queen slopes off. Denise turns to me and says, — Young queens, ten a penny, the fuckin wee jessies.

The observation of such protocol is crucial with Denise. Everything has to be done just right. I remember several years ago he gave me a blank cassette tape to record this Fall record. — Remember, he told me, — dinnae write the track list doon oan the index caird. Write it doon oan a separate bit ay paper n ah'll copy it oantae the index caird. Ah've goat a special wey ay daein it. It's only me thit kin dae it.

I cannae really remember whether I genuinely forgot, or whether I did it deliberately to wind him up, but I biroed the track listings doon ontae the cassette card. Later, when I presented the tape tae him, he freaked. It was too mad. — WHIT'S THIS? AH FUCKIN TELT YE! AH FUCKIN TELT YE NO TAE WRITE THUM IN, he hissed. — IT'S SPOILED NOW! THE WHOLE THING'S NAE FUCKIN USE NOW!

He crushed the tape and case under the heel of his boot. — FUCKIN SPOILED EVERYTHING!

How uptight is the cunt?

We have a few drinks. I don't mention Olly to him. His queen patter with the young guys is mildly amusing for a while. Gay punters that hang around Chapps, The Blue Moon and The Duck hate Denise. His stereotypical queen stuff embarrasses most homosexuals. Denise loves to be hated. They detested his high-camp act back in the scheme. It was funny then, funny and brave, but now it starts tae grate and I make my excuses and depart, wondering, as I leave, what he's going to say about me behind my back.

11

LOVE AND SHAGGING

Olly's mate Tina was a friendly, nervy, high-adrenalin lassie who was always on the move; talking, chewing gum, checking out everything and everyone with sharp, hawk-like eyes. At the party at Sidney's, Olly said, in a mock-schoolie way: — She fancies yir mate. Ronnie.

— Fuck off, Tina hissed, either embarrassed or pretending to be. Ronnie was sitting on the floor watching the Christmas tree, mesmerised by it. He'd taken a few jellies. Sidney, somewhat surprisingly, was jellied as well. He explained to me that he'd been getting 'too uptight' about the flat getting trashed and had been giving the party 'negative vibes', so he had taken some jellies to 'mellow out'.

Olly then said to me, — If that sick poof Denise comes up, don't you talk tae him! No while ah'm around anyway!

I found this a bit irritating and offensive. Her feud with Denise had nothing to do with me. — Of course I have to talk to Denise, he's my friend. I practically fuckin grew up wi Denise. And stop aw this homophobic shite: it's a total drag.

She then said something which frosted me over. — No wonder people say you're a smart cunt, she hissed, storming away.

— What . . . who said . . . I moaned at the back of her head as she vanished into the kitchen. I was too mellow to get para; but her words rang around in ma head and the paranoia would eventually come, as sure as night follows day. I'd be sitting tomorrow at my old man's trying to pretend that I wasn't feeling sick and miserable and worthless, and her words would shudder through my system like psychic spears and I'd agonise over their meaning, relentlessly torturing myself. I've a lot to look forward to.

I started talking to Spud Murphy, a mate of Raymie Airlie's. I like listening to Spud and Raymie. They've got a few years on me, they've been there, and they're still around. Survivors. You can't really learn anything from people like that, but their patter's okay. Spud's still lamenting getting ripped off by his best mate ages ago. It was a junk deal, and his mate absconded with the loot. — Best mates, likesay, man, best mates, ken? Then the cat goes n pills a stunt like that. Completely doss, likesay. Ken?

— Aye, ye cannae even trust mates these days, I said, the realisation bringing on my first substantial para attack of the day. I finger my scar. Thank fuck for Hobo; at least I've got a bit of concrete evidence for my paranoia.

— It's jist, likesay, drugs, man. It's horrible, likes, but whenever thir's collies involved friendships go oot the windae, ken?

We spraff on for a bit, then Tina comes over to us, a bit drunk, waving a Diamond White bottle in her hand. — Ah'm gaunny fire intae yir mate, she says, matter-of-factly, before going over and sitting beside Ronnie. The next time I look they're necking, or rather, Tina's eating Ronnie's face.

— Could dae wi somebody firin intae me like that, man, that would dae me barry, likesay, Spud said.

— Naw, ah'm disillusioned wi women. I'm useless in relationships, Spud. I'm a selfish fucker. Thing is, I never, ever pretend tae be anything other than a selfish fucker. Take Olly there, I ventured.

— That wee goth love-cat ye came wi, likesay? he asked.

— She played the saint. Took ays hame eftir ah'd been glessed by that Hobo cunt . . .

— That sounds a good woman, man. Ye want tae hud oan tae her, likes.

— Ah bit listen tae this: one decent act ay kindness and she thinks that gies her the right tae tell me how tae live ma life. It's: nae collies, get a job, go tae college, buy some clathes, dinnae speak tae people ah dinnae like, even if yuv kent them yir whole fuckin life . . . aw that typical burd shite, man. How bad is that?

— That's a bit seriously radge, catboy. No that ah kin really gie much advice, ken? Chicks n me, likes, sortay oil n water, ken? Ah'd love us tae mix mix mix a wee bit better, but somehow the gig jist nivir quite materialises, ken?

Olly came back over to us. She put her arms around me. — I want to go home, she whispered. She thought she was Joan of Arc. — I want to go home and fuck you.

I shuddered in fear at the thought. I'd had far too many drugs over the weekend. I couldn't be bothered shagging. It just seemed so pointless, a total waste of time. We didn't have strong feelings for each other, we were just playing out time waiting for the real thing tae come along. I dinnae like shagging just for the sake of it; I like to make love. That means with somebody I love. There are times, sure, when the bag just needs to be emptied, but no when you're full of drugs. It was like the other day when we were shagging; it was just like two skeletons rattling away the gither. I just thought: why the fuck are we doing this?

The thing that worried me even more than the shagging was staying round at Olly's for any length of time. I disliked her friends. They were hostile and offhand to me, which didn't really bother me, in fact I enjoyed it. What fucked me over though was the way they patronised her. They were all City Cafe types: waitresses, insurance salesmen, local government clerks, bar persons et cetera, who wanted to be musicians, actors, poets, dancers, novelists, painters, playwrights, filmmakers, models and were obsessed with their alternative careers. They played their dull tapes, recited their crap poems, strutted around like peacocks and pontificated with endless dogmatism on the arts that they were excluded from. The thing was, Olly lent herself to this patronisation. Her friends wanted to be like somebody else; she only wanted to be like them. I thought I had low ambition, but she couldn't see what limited horizons she had. When I mentioned this I was dismissed as jealous and bitter.

We got into an argument and I ended up staying the night at Roxy's place. I told him about her friends and he said: — So you should be perfectly at home there, man.

He clocked my tense, hurt expression and said: — Fuck me, tell ays you're no nippy the day. Only joking man. But I knew he wasn't. Or maybe I was just being para. Or maybe not. I was still full of drugs and hadn't slept properly in donks.

Anyway, I gave Olly as wide a berth as I could until I got it together. I tried to chill at ma old man's which was difficult as the house was always full of his campaign mates, or Deek's pals. Deeks pals never seemed to drink or take drugs or go raving. They 'werenae intae that shite'. All they did was nothing, they just sat around and did nothing. Deek had passed his Civil Service Executive Officer exams, but showed no excitement about it, or any interest in a career. I admired his nihilism relating to work, that made sense to me, but he and his pals seemed to have no interest in anything at all. Everything was 'shite' to them: drugs, music, fitba, violence, work, shagging, money, fun. They seemed to be a bunch of completely isolated basket-cases.

Olly harassed me on the phone. She was rambling and expansive when she talked about what her friends had done or were doing, but when she focused on us she always became tense and confrontational. It would end up with her abusing me over the phone, then slamming it down as if she was the aggrieved party.

— Woman problems? my dad would laugh. — Never run for a bus or a woman, son. There's always another one coming around the corner.

A great strategy that one. That's why he's never had his hole in fourteen years since my Ma fucked off. That's why one day they'll probably find him dead through hypothermia at a bus-stop.

After a few days of living on tea, chocolate digestives, McCain's oven chips and Presto's pizzas, I feel strong enough to go into town. I've read David Niven and Maureen Lipman's biographies, both absolutely fucking dreadful. I take them back

to the library and ask the librarian if he can keep the Viv
Nicolson biography back for me. I don't want to take it into
town, as I might end up wrecked and lose it. Besides, I hate
carrying things about. He refuses, saying I'll have to take my
chances. I board a bus and start to feel horny with the vibrations
from the engine. I make a mental list of all the women I'd like to
have sex with. I feel awkward and self-conscious getting off the
bus with an erection. It subsides, however, as I stand at the West
End at a bit of a loss as to what to do next. Shoplifting is a
possibility, and I try to think of what I need, so I can go to the
appropriate store rather than just go somewhere and chory for
chorying's sake.

I see Tina. It's good to see someone by chance in town. —
Tina! Where ye off tae?

— Gaunny git something fir Ronnie. It's his birthday oan
Thursday.

Of course it is. I remember Ron's birthday. I get him fuck all,
not even a card, but I always remember the date. — How's it
gaun wi yous pair? I ask, raising my brows in what I hope is a
light, playful gesture.

— It's awright, she says, chewing briskly and never looking at
me as we walk side by side up Lothian Road, — but he's ey
jellied aw the time. Ah mean, the other week, we goes tae the
pictures. Ah peys tae git us in. *Damage*, that wis the film, likes.
He jist sat there asleep fir the whole film, and ah couldnae git
him awake once it finished. Ah jist fuckin well left um.

— That's wise, I reflected. I liked this lassie, I empathised
with her. I was still feeling a bit strung out, but my load seemed
lighter these last few days. I realised why: no Ronnie. Tina had
taken a considerable burden off my shoulders.

— Another thing, ah took um up tae ma hoose the other day.
He jist crashed oot oan the couch. Never even spoke tae ma Ma
or ma Dad. Jist nodded at thum, then sortay dozed oaf.

— No the wey tae make a favourable impression, I ventured.

— Well, ma Dad never really bothers that much aboot people
talkin, but if he thinks it's drugs, he'll go pure radge. Mibbe next

time you n Olly could come up wi ays, so that they can see that aw ma pals n Ronnie's urnae intae drugs.

It was the first time in my life that I'd ever been asked tae provide a character reference of this sort. While touched, I was a little wary and a bit doubtful of Tina's powers of observation. — Eh, ah'm no sure that ah'm the best person for a home visit. Did Olly no tell ye about how ah met her, how she took ays back that time?

— Aye, but that wisnae your fault. At least you can stey straight sometimes, she said.

We parted and I felt great for a bit. After reflecting why I felt great, I started to feel terrible. It seemed that drug-taking over the years had reduced me to the sum total of the negative and positive strokes I received from people; a big blank canvas others completed. Whenever I tried to find a broader sense of self the term: A SMART CUNT would come back to mind.

Ronnie was face-fucked when we all met up in the Gorgie-Dalry Oyster Bar. What's that cunt like. He was awake, but was lolling his tongue around his mouth and rolling his eyes like he was having some kind of stroke. I was a bit angry at being put in this position. Olly and I had shagged a lot that afternoon and my genitals felt very raw and sticky with our juices. I hadn't been into washing. I always felt disorientated after sex, always wanted to be alone. We'd smoked some hash, and that part was good, but now all these people were around me in this bar.

I said nothing in the bar, nor anything in the taxi up to Clermiston. Tina and Olly blethered away, ignoring me, while Ronnie stared out of the window. I heard him say: — Clermiston, mate, to the driver when we were already halfway there. The driver took no notice; nor did anyone else. Ronnie just kept whispering: — Clermiston, mate, and giggling under his breath. The cunt was getting on my fuckin tits.

— Try to be civil, Olly hissed at me, clocking my sour puss as Tina's ma let us in.

It was embarrassing. Ron just flopped down on the couch and twisted his head, taking in the room with one eye. I sat beside him, Olly sat next to me and Tina curled up at our feet. Her father sat in a chair facing the television and her mother put some drinks and snacks out on the table. She then settled down in another chair and lit a cigarette. The telly was still on and it took all Tina's dad's attention.

— Dig in, he mumbled, — we dinnae stand oan ceremony in this hoose.

I grabbed a somosa and a couple of sausage rolls. The blow I had smoked with Olly after our shagging session had given me the munchies really bad.

Ronnie started to snore, but Tina elbowed him and he shuddered awake. Her old man was very unimpressed. I should have sat back and enjoyed this, but I seemed to be all on edge.

— Backshift, I said stupidly, — that's the problem, eh Ron? The backshift. Yir like the livin dead comin oaf the backshift.

Ronnie looked perplexed; in fact he looked stupid and subnormal.

Tina's father snorted at her, — Ah thoat you sais he wisnae workin?

— He's been daein a wee bit wi me, no through the books or nowt like that, I cut in. — Fittin smoke alarms. Wi aw they tenement fires, everybody wants yin. We've been daein the Sheltered Housing schemes for the council, ken? Long shifts.

Her father nodded in apathetic acknowledgement. Tina, her mother and Olly blethered about the sales and the old man fell asleep. Ronnie was also soon back in the land of the nod. I just sat stuffing my face, bored and hash-greedy. It seemed like the worst evening I'd ever spent. I was elated when we got ready to leave.

After we taxied back to Dalry, Olly wanted to go home and fuck. I wanted to go to Ryrie's and get drunk. We argued and went our separate ways. In the pub I met Roxy and The PATH. The PATH was just on his way out to meet this woman in the Pelican. — Come doon, he suggested.

— Mibbe later, I said. I needed a drink. I needed several. He left us. Roxy and I got a good lash on, without once mentioning Blind Cunt.

After a bit we decided to go to the Pelican. A smarmy English middle-class student-type cunt was on the door and wasn't going to let us in, but fortunately Rab Addison was coming out and let on to us. He gave the wanker a steely look and the poor cunt almost shat himself. Roxy and I walked in like the Duke and Duchess of Westminster.

The place was mobbed out, and we couldn't see The PATH, although we could hear him.

— ROXY! BRI!

Looking in the direction of the sound I could only see this large, fat woman smiling at me. She was absolutely gross, and had a bloated red face, which was nonetheless very kind and pretty looking. The PATH's head poked out from the side of her. I realised that he was sitting on her knee.

— This is Lucia, he said, slurping on a pint.

— Hiya, Lucia, I said.

Lucia turned to The PATH. — Ye want ays tae suck yir mates oaf n aw? she said, in a high excited voice. I couldn't catch The PATH's reply.

Then she put her hand on Roxy's thigh. — What's it they call you?

— Loads ay things, doll, he smiled. She felt him up for a bit through his troosers, his cock n baws. He seemed amused, yet unaroused. I was quite turned on. My head was starting to swim with the thought of the three of us fucking this big cow at the same time. The PATH gave me a lecherous wink.

Lucia then pressed her face close to mine and put a tongue which tasted of sick into my mouth. I sat transfixed as she slurped around inside my mouth. She flicked her tongue in and out for a bit, then pulled slowly away. — See you n yir mate here? she nodded at Roxy, — ah could bring yous oaf in nae time at aw!

— You already have, I told her.

She liked that, letting out pneumatic-drill laughter which cut through the loud buzz of the surrounding conversations. Then her elbows thrashed at The PATH, who had his hands up her skirt from the back, right between those meaty, cellulite thighs.

We drank on. The PATH told a joke about a guy who had an arsehole transplant and we all laughed loudly. I laughed, even though I'd heard it before. Lucia laughed the loudest. She laughed so much she started gagging. She drank back some Guinness from her pint, then threw it up, back into her glass. She looked only momentarily upset, then she slung the mass of blackened vomit back down her gullet in a oner.

— That's ma doll, said The PATH, and they French-kissed languidly.

I was into fours up, no question about it. I nodded to Roxy, — Your place?

— Like fuck, he scoffed. — Tell ays you're no sick, by the way. Ah widnae touch that wi a fuckin bargepole. Nae wey eftir The PATH had been thair.

That was a consideration. I got some more drinks up, and got some speed from a guy called Silver who was alright. I whizzed around the bar, talking shite. I was talking shite anyway, but now I was talking it with more purpose and conviction.

We didn't see The PATH go, but when we came up Anderson's Close we could hear his and Lucia's voices. He was bouncing on top of her like a football on a spacehopper. He's screaming: TAKE THE FUCKIN LOAT YA BITCH! YE COULDNAE TAKE MA FUCKIN COCK! SPLIT YE IN TWO!

She's saying: THIR'S FUCKIN WELL NOWT THAIR! GEEZ IT WELL! IS THAT YOU STARTED HA HA HA.

We walked past them, then stopped to watch for a while. Lucia rolled the PATH over and got on top. Her wobbly flesh hung over him.

— MOVE THEN IF YIR GAUN OAN TOAP! MOVE, YA BASTARD! he roared.

She shook her flesh over him, then looked up at us, — Yis want tae help um oot boys?

— We'd nivir git in the wey ay true love, Lucia, Roxy smiled.

We walked up the close a bit and pished. Our two steaming rivulets joined together and sped towards them, around the PATH's head, neck and shoulders. They kept shagging. Two guys walked nervously past us.

— Depraved wee cunt, The PATH, Roxy shook his head.

— Yeah, real fuckin slag.

I was feeling horny, and I was tempted to go to Olly's. Roxy was into more beer. There was a way to kill two birds with one stone: Olly would probably be at this party a friend of her's was having, a trendy, posey cow named Lynne.

Roxy never let me down at the party; he detests that sort of scene. We installed ourselves in the kitchen and freeloaded as much drink as possible. When Olly arrived she was in the company of some cunts and cold-shouldered me. We'd been shagging during the day, now she treated me like I was a stranger. Yet it somehow made sense. Life was a weird gig.

I woke up on the floor the next morning, to the sound of people cleaning the flat. Roxy lay next to me.

— God, thir's some fuckin foul taste in ma mooth, he said.

— That's ma fault, I shrugged, — ah shouldnae huv given The PATH one up his shitter before ah goat you tae gam ays.

— So that's what happened. Well, that makes sense. There's fuck all memorable aboot gammin you.

Lynne was clearing up; throwing cans and emptying ash-trays into bin-liners, flashing us looks which said: LEAVE IMMEDIATELY.

A merchant-school voice pleads, — C'mon lads, get up and give us a hand with the tidying up.

— Suck ma fuckin cock, ya radge, Roxy snapped. The boy moved away, taking this as a sign that he was on his own with the tidying. — Tell ays that cunt wisnae wide. That's fuckin

Edinburgh, fill ay fuckin English bastards and snobby rugby cunts. Treat ye like a fuckin peasant in yir ain toon. Well, fuck them, lit them clean up oor shite, it's aw the cunt's are fuckin good fir! he boomed.

I got to my feet and found some bottles of beer. We staggered out of the flat, down the stair and into the street, drinking.

— Whair is this? I wondered.

. — Stockbridge, Roxy said, — ah mind gaun through the New Town last night.

— Naw naw. I remembered. It was Lynne's. The South Side. We emerged onto South Clerk Street.

Roxy's mouth opened.

— Aye, Stockbridge, right enough! I said. — What are ye like!

We decided to head for the Captain's Bar, which opened at seven o'clock, about three hours ago. My nerves were starting to fray and I just wanted a few beers inside me to take the edge off things.

I was shaken to the core by a blood-curdling scream: — BRIAN!

Mad Audrey stood propped up against a bus-shelter. She wore a long black imitation-leather trenchcoat with padded shoulders. Two greasy flaps of black hair hung on either side of her white pimply face. Her sharp, vicious features contorted as she slurped from a carton of milk, some of which trickled down her front.

— WHAIR'S THE FUCKIN PATH?!

— Eh, no sure Auds. We left him last night, at the Pelican.

— TELL UM HE'S GITTING FUCKIN STABBED WHEN AH SEE UM! HE WIS WI THAT FUCKIN FAT SLUT! TELL UM HE'S FUCKIN DEID! N HUR N AW! MIND, YOU'D BETTER FUCKIN TELL UM!

— Eh, aye, ah'll mention it tae him, likes, I tell her. We don't stick around. The Captain's Bar had been calling loudly; now it was screaming.

— MIND N TELL UM! she shouted after us. — N TELL

UM TAE COME DOON TAE THE MEADOW BAR AT
SEVEN!

I waved back at her. Roxy said, — When The PATH dies, aw
the repulsive hing-oots in toon should git the gither n build a
monument tae the cunt.

— Aye, wi a vibrating prick they can impale themselves oan.

A few in the Captain's did the trick. I went back to Roxy's
and had a good long kip on his couch. When he woke me I was
fucked. — The PATH phoned, he told me. — He's meeting us
doon the Meadow Bar at seven.

— The Meadow? What did ye say that fir . . . you, ya bastard,
I laughed. This would be a good one.

— Ah telt um tae bring big Lucia along n aw. Audrey versus
Lucia, some fuckin swedge that would be. A dog-fight in the
Meadows. Who needs Hank Jansen? Cannae wait tae see The
PATH's face. Tell ays he'll no be shitein his keks.

I missed out on it, simply because I couldn't move. I got an
account from The PATH though. Audrey was more vicious,
and scored Lucia's face heavily, but eventually the larger woman
used her superior strength and power to subdue Auds and
pound her into the turf. She was lucky it was a square-go
and Audrey wasn't tooled. Apparently, while the swedge was
going on, The PATH was rubbing his crotch discreetly. He went
home with the winner.

12

CAREER OPPORTUNITIES
AND FANNY LICKING

Cliff from London got in touch and told me that Simmy had got put away. Cliff himself had moved into a new flat, over in Hanwell. There was a space for me, he said. My bags were packed and I was back down to the Smoke.

It was a good gaff. I was on the floor in the front room for a couple of weeks, but I picked up a temporary job in the offices of Ealing Council. It involved keying information on planning applications into a VDU. They had put in all this new technology, but needed dogsbodies to key in all the manual records. Myself and four middle-aged women were taken on. The work was not interesting.

A bloke called Graham moved out of the flat and I got his room. He was a bit of an alcoholic and his mattress smelled badly of pish, so I got a new one on the Sunday, and was looking forward to a good night's kip before work on Monday. I'd never been able to kip properly in the front room; too many people coming and going at all hours.

— Wakey, wakey! Cliff shouted to me, poking his head around my door. I'd had no drugs the night before, not even hash. I'd gone to bed early and it was like I had only slept for an hour.

— It's surely no yon time already, surely tae fuck, I whinged.

— Yeah, seven-fifteen. C'mon mate, rise n shine!

I rose, but didn't shine. It was brutally cold as I made my way to the bathroom in my t-shirt and pants. I had to get to work on time. Gleaves, the office manager, was watching me. However, I was going to May and Des's for tea tonight, god bless them, so

I decided to wash my cock, balls and armpits in lukewarm water. It wasn't a comfortable experience. I brushed my teeth, squeezed a couple of spots, pulled on my ripped jeans and my cashmere sweater. I laced up my Doc Martens and stuck on my Oxfam overcoat and my scarf and mittens. No breakfast; it's hi ho hi ho . . .

Work is a fuckin drag. Gleaves thinks I'm demotivated. That's how he describes me. Gleaves recruited me: rather than say I picked a duffer and couldn't pick my nose, he persists in this delusion that inputting into a VDU, stuffing papers in envelopes and photocopying will sort me out. I'd bought a guitar and was jamming with Cliff and Darren in the flat but this job was costing me valuable practice time. However, I need the money for that amp. Stardom is surely just around the corner.

When I get in May says softly to me, — Mister Gleaves wants to see you, love. As soon as you get in, he said.

Fuck me. What now? Is that cunt tapped or what.

Penny has a gleeful expression on her face. That cow has hated me since I was too out of it to fuck her at somebody's leaving party. Women hate these things. If they're going to lose control and go away with someone, they figure they might as well get a good shag out of it. If they go away with someone and the someone can't get it up, well that's a big fuck-up: the worst of all worlds.

Gleavsie, as I call him in a Chinese accent (the Slaint and Gleavsie), is a small, overweight man with glasses and a Russian-style beard. He has a small, stumpy cock, the kind that is practically all cherry, but which is hopefully more formidable when erect. (I stood next to him in the latrine in the staff toilets to check it out.)

— Mister Gleaves, I smile, taking a seat.

— I want to talk about your dress, Brian.

— Which one is that? The yellow chiffon one, or the blue print number, I ask rolling my eyes.

— I'm deadly serious, Gleaves sombrely informs me, sounding like a character in a middle-class soap opera. Big fuckin drama queen. — For God's sake Brian, the arse is hanging out of your trousers.

That was true. My purple pants were clearly visible. My bum was freezing. My cock and balls were shrivelling up. They'd invert to a fanny by the end of the month. Next pay cheque it's Carnaby Street. I shouldn't travel so light.

— Well, at least when I'm famous you can say with justification you knew me when the arse was hanging out of my trousers.

— I'm not sure you understand the gravity of the situation . . .

— Okay okay. It's healthy having this circulation of air. It keeps me ventilated.

— You're either deliberately missing the point or you've lost the sense God gave you. I'm going to have to spell it out for you. At Ealing Borough Council we try to maintain certain standards of dress and behaviour. The local citizen, after all, pays our wages and it entitled to . . .

— I'm a local citizen n aw. I pay my poll tax, I lied.

— Yes, but . . .

— Whose standards are we talking about here? Just who's setting themself up as the big fashion consultant here?

— We're talking about corporate standards! The standards we expect from all employees of this authority.

— Listen, man, ah cannae afford tae buy a tin flute. Ah choose tae dress functionally, tae dress in gear ah feel comfortable in, soas ah kin perform better in ma joab. Ah couldnae hack wearin a tie, man, that's a pure phallic symbol, a compensatory psychological device for men who feel insecure about their sexuality. I cannae get into that sortay arena. I cannae be made to conform to the mass psychological hang-ups of Ealing Borough Council's male employees. What are yis like?

Gleaves shook his head in exasperation. — Brian. Please be quiet for a second. Look. I understand how you feel. I know what you're about. You're an intelligent guy, so don't act the fool. It'll get you nowhere. You've got the potential to get on within this organisation, he tells me, his tone changing to one of encouragement.

That was a statement which would have been humorous had it not been so frightening. — To do what? I asked.

— To get a better job.

— Why? I mean, what for?

— Well, he began in tone of slightly smug self-justification, — the money's not bad when you get to my level. And it's a challenge being involved in the full range of council activities.

He stopped, sensing his growing ridiculousness in my eyes. — Listen, Brian, I know you think you're some kind of big radical and I'm some reactionary, fascist pig. Well I've got news for you: I'm a socialist, I'm a union man. I know you just see me as an establishment figure in a suit, but if the Tories had their way, we'd have kiddies down the mines. I'm every bit as anti-establishment as you, Brian. Yes, I own my own home. Yes, I live in a desirable area. Yes, I'm married with two children, I take two foreign holidays a year and drive an expensive car. But I'm as anti-establishment as you, Brian. I believe in public services, in putting people first. It's more than just a cliché for me. For me, being anti-establishment is not about dressing like a tramp, taking drugs and going to rave-ups or whatever they're called. That's the easy way out. That's what the people that control things want; people opting out, taking the easy route. For me it's about knocking on doors on cold evenings, attending meetings in school halls to get Labour back in and Major and his mob out.

— Yeah . . .

This guy makes the term arsehole redundant.

— Well, I've almost had it with you, Brian. Unless you buck up your ideas, your behaviour and your dress, you are on a disciplinary. Look at you. Worse than a tramp. I've seen better-dressed people in cardboard city.

— Listen. Are you talking to me as employer to employee, or as man to man? Cause if it's employer to employee I consider your behaviour insulting and harassing and I want my union representative in here to witness this victimisation. If you're talking to me man to man, then it's more straightforward. We can go outside and settle it. Ah'm no taking this shite, I said, rising. — If there's nothing else, I'd like to go and get some work done.

I left the shitein cunt red-faced behind his desk. He muttered something about last warnings. How many last warnings can you have? I swaggered back to my work station and plugged away for a bit at the NME crossword. I was entitled tae a brek, for fuck's sake.

At finishing time, May took me home to her and Des's. They were a lovely couple from Chester-Le-Street, Co. Durham, who had sort of adopted me. May would cook up a big scran, lamenting my thinness, while Des and I talked football over cans of Tetley Bitter. He was a great Newcastle United fan and he'd wax on about Jackie Milburn, Bobby Mitchell, Malcolm McDonald, Bobby Moncur and the like.

A normally very relaxed and laid-back couple, they used to fret a great deal over what I took to be their son. — Nae sign o the lad, Des would frown at the clock, — he's never normally as leet as this.

I knew they had four daughters between the ages of sixteen and twenty-two. The girls were always out, taking drugs, going to clubs, shagging guys, the things girls that age with any sense did. One of them went to the Ministry of Sound, which was sound. That was the one I fancied, the sort of New Age lassie, the youngest, I think. I fancied all of them really. However, Des and May didn't seem to bother about them, their chief concern was the welfare of the lad.

— There he is! Des exclaimed, as a noise came from the back door of the kitchen and a grumpy-looking selfish black cat meandered in through the flap. — C'mere lad, owah heah by the fyah! You moost be freezin! Tell us what you've been oop to then? Eeeh, you leetal boogah!

It is a good scoff and I get back to the flat a little bevvied. It's good to have a stomach full of stodgy food again. Best of all,

Monday was cracked. Granted Tuesday was a cunt, but it got better on Wednesday. We all went down the local pub on Wednesday nights, me, Cliff, Darren, Gerard, Avril and Sandra. It was good living in the same flat as lassies; they kept standards high, well, higher than they would have been otherwise. It was a barry flat and everyone got on or got on most of the time. I thought of Simmy languishing in the Scrubs for housebreaking and felt pretty good about it. I tried not to think of her, of Blind Cunt, of my mum, of Scotland. We all did drugs here, but it seemed less desperate, more of a recreational thing rather than a lifestyle. We'd sit in the pub on Wednesday and Thursday nights talking about what clubs, gigs and drugs we'd be into at the weekend.

After getting home from Des and May's, I went straight to my room. I put on a KLF tape and lay back on the bed feeling pretty pleased with myself. I thought of Des and May's daughters, then of Gleaves, and resolved to borrow a pair of strides from Cliff, to keep the tie-wearing penile-challenged toss-bag oaf ma case.

There was a knock on the door and Avril came in. I didn't really know her that well to talk to; she was far more self-contained than Sandra, though pleasant enough.

— Can I talk to you for a bit? she asked.

— Sure, sit down, I smiled. There was a basket-chair in the room. My spirits rose. It was fairly obvious that she nursed a passion for me and wanted to shag me. I should have picked up the vibes before. I expanded my smile and let a bit of soul seep into my watery eyes. This poor lassie's been besotted and I haven't even noticed.

— This is really difficult, she began, — but I just have to say it.

I felt for her. — Listen, Avril, you don't have to say anything.

— Darren . . . Gerald . . . they've told you? I told them not to tell you! I wanted to say this myself!

— No, no, they haven't . . . it's just . . .

— What? It's not you, is it?

This was confusing. — It's not me what?

She took a deep breath. — Listen, I think we're talking at cross-purposes here. This is very hard for me to say.

— Eh, but . . .

— Just listen. I want you to know I'm not accusing you of anything. Please understand that. I've spoken to Darren and Gerald. I've not had a chance to speak to Cliff yet, but I will. This is pretty embarrassing. It's just that some of my underwear's been taken from my drawer. I'm not accusing you, though. I want to talk to everyone. It's just that I don't like the idea of living with a pervert.

— I see, I said; hurt, disappointed but intrigued. — Well, I smiled, I'm certainly a pervert, but not that type.

That got a mild, brief laugh. — I'm only asking.

— Yeah, well it has to be somebody, I suppose. To you, it's as likely tae be me as anybody. I can't see Cliff or Darren, or even Gerard behaving in that sortay way. Well, Gerard would, but he widnae be sneaky aboot it. That's no his style. He'd go intae the pub wi yir knickers aroond his heid.

That thought didn't amuse her. — As I said, I only asked.

— You don't think it's me, do you?

— I don't know what to think, she said sourly.

— Well, that's fuckin' great. My boss thinks I'm a smelly tramp and someone I live with thinks I'm a pervert.

— We don't live together, she frostily corrected me, — we share a house.

— Well, I said, as she got up to leave, — if I see anyone behaving suspiciously, like not taking drugs, paying the rent on time, that sortay thing, I'll let you know.

She left, obviously unable to see the funny side. It made me wonder who was the pervert. I thought it had to be Sandra.

On Thursday I was back at May's for tea again. I stayed late because Lisanne, her youngest but one daughter was in. She was good to talk to and look at. Moreover, she didn't think I was a pervert, although, I suppose, she didn't really know me that well. Des was out, and May insisted on giving me a lift home.

This was unusual, but it was late. I thought nothing of it as I piled into the car. She was chatty, but nervously so, as we drove along the Uxbridge Road. Then she pulled off at a turning and stopped in a carpark at the back of some shops.

— Eh, what's up May? I asked. I thought something must be wrong with the car.

— Do you like Lisanne, then? she asked.

I felt a bit coy. — Eh, aye, she's a really nice lassie.

— Surprised you haven't got yourself a girlfriend.

— Well, ah'm no really intae getting too involved.

— The love em n leave em type are you?

— Well, ah widnae really say that . . .

I was more the love em and they leave me type.

She put her finger in one of the rips on my jeans and started stroking my bare thigh. Her hands were doughy, her fingers like stumps. — Mister Gleaves was right about you. You're going to have to invest in a new pair of jeans.

— Eh, ay, I replied. I was feeling uneasy. Not aroused, far from it, but gripped with a morbid curiosity as to what she was about.

I looked at her face and all I could see were teeth. She started making circles in my flesh with her fingers. — You've got baby-soft skin, haven't you?

There isn't really much you can say to that. I just laughed.

— You think I've got a good body? I'll bet you reckon I'm past it, don't you?

— Naw, naw, ah widnae say that, May.

I thought: by light years.

— Des is on these pills you see. He had a heart-attack a while back. It stops the blood coagulating by keeping it thin. Trouble is, he don't get hard. I love Des, see, but I'm still a young woman, love. I need a little bit of fun, a little bit of harmless fun, don't I? That's not so unreasonable, is it, love?

I looked harshly at her. — Do these seats fold down?

They did.

I went down on her and gave head; flicking my tongue deftly onto her clit, then lolling it around teasingly. I started thinking about Graeme Souness, because he had heart trouble. I wonder if he has a problem getting it up due to the pills? I started to think about his career, focusing on the 1982 World Cup in Spain which I remember watching with my dad. My mum had only been gone three years, and we'd come back from my Auntie Shirley's. She'd looked after us all that time, until Dad felt able to cope. He'd had some sort of breakdown. Never talks about it. Thing was, we had liked it at Shirley's in Moredun, and we didn't really want to go back to Muirhouse, or have 'the family all together' as he described it. As a sweetener, he let us watch all the 1982 World Cup games. A huge wallchart was stuck up in the front room above the fireplace. The tapemarks still show where the four corners were, although it's been painted over at least once to my knowledge. Cheap paint, I suppose. Anyway, the praise that was heaped on Souness then, but I thought that he just posed and preened his way through that tournament. I mean, the two-each draw with the Soviet Union, for fuck sake.

— Ohh, you're a naughty one and no mistake . . . ooh . . . ooh, she hissed excitedly, crushing my face against her cunt. I was going nowhere, struggling to take in air through nostrils which were filled with a pungent scent. There was no taste, only the smell which suggested it.

I have an image of Souness strutting arrogantly like a peacock in the middle of the park, but he's doing nothing with the ball, just holding it, and we need a win as the seconds tick by. Still, that was in the days when people actually gave a toss about the Scottish national football team.

— Give it to me . . . she whispered, — you've got me all juiced up, lovey, now give it to me . . .

I was too soft to go in, but she took it in her mouth for a bit and I firmed up. I got in and she was moaning so loud I got really self-conscious. I jutted out my jaw Souness-style and pumped away. After about half a dozen strokes she came power-fully, kneading my buttocks in her hands. — YOU DORTY

LITTLE BOOGAH! EEH, YOU DORTY LITTLE SHITE!
LOOVLEY . . . she screamed.

The old tongue-job never fails. The only fuckin real use for
the guid Scotch tongue. I thought about her daughter and blew
my muck inside her.

I wondered if I'd get asked back for tea again.

13

MARRIAGE

May carried on as if nothing had happened, except that she gave me an occasional saucy smile and she'd also taken up goosing my arse by the photocopier. I was a bit bemused by the whole thing. How mad was that.

It was the next week after my liaison with May that the invitation came through the door. It read:

TOMMY AND SHEILA DEVENNEY

Invite you to join them at the wedding
of their daughter

Martina

to

Mr Ronald Dickson

on Saturday, 11 March 1994 at 3.00 p.m.
at Drum Brae Parish Church, Drum Brae,
Edinburgh and afterwards at the Capital
Hotel, Fox Covert Road.

I stuck it on my bedside table. It was next month. In one month's time Ronnie would be a married man, although the potential hurdles that stood in the way of that actually happening didn't bear examination.

A couple of days later I got a phone-call from Tina. I was tempted to offer congratulations, but I hedged my bets in case the gig was off. The whole thing wasn't really constructed on a very firm basis.

— Brian?

— Aye.

— It's Tina, ken?

— Tina! Barry! How's tricks? Ah goat the invite. Brilliant! How's Ron? There was a silence from the other end of the line. Then: — Ye mean he's no thair wi you now?

— Eh . . . naw. Ah huvnae heard fae him.

The pause was even longer this time around.

— Tina? I wondered whether she'd hung up.

— Sais he wis gaun doon tae see ye. Tae ask ye tae be best man. Wanted tae ask ye tae yir face, he sais.

— Fuck . . . dinnae worry aboot Ronnie though, Tina. Must've goat waylaid. Probably jist a bit emotional, wi the weddin n that, ken? He'll show.

— He fuckin well better, she snapped.

Three days later I had just got home from work and was eating a bacon sanny and watching the six o'clock news with Darren. We were ranting bitterly everytime someone we hated appeared on the box, which was every other feature. Avril was reading a magazine. She got up to answer the door.

— There's someone here for you, Brian, she said. — A Scots guy . . . he seems a bit out of it.

Ronnie slouched into the room behind her, obviously jellied. I didn't even attempt to ask him where he'd been. I took him upstairs and let him crash on my floor. Then I phoned Tina to tell her he'd shown up. After this I went downstairs and sat on the couch.

— A friend of yours? Avril asked.

— Yeah, it's this mate who's getting married. Wants me tae go best man. I think he's had a tiring journey.

— Look at that slimy cunt Lilley, Darren hissed at the image of this politician on the box, — I'd like to get that fucking arsehole and cut his bollocks off. Then I'd like to stuff them down his throat and sew his mouth up so he has to swallow them . . . fucking child-killing cunt!

— That's terrible, Darren, Avril tutted, — you're no better than he is if you think like that. She looked at me for support.

— No, Darren's perfectly correct. Sick, exploitative vermin ay that sort need tae be destroyed, I said and, recalling Malcom X, added, — by any means possible.

I had been reading the biographies of radical black Americans. X's was an interesting read but Bobby Seale's *Seize The Time* was far more enjoyable, as was Eldridge Cleaver's *Soul On Ice*. My favourite was *Soledad Brother* but I can't remember which of the Jackson brothers, Jonathan or George, actually wrote it. Perhaps it was Michael.

Darren shook a clenched fist at me. — That's the difference between me and those fucking wimpy arsehole socialists, I don't want the Tories out, I want them fucking dead. Just because I've got a bus-pass doesn't mean I'm part of the system. An anarchist with a bus-pass is still a fucking anarchist. All hate to the state!

— You're sick, Darren. Avril shook her head. — Violence achieves nothing.

— It is satisfying when you see a polisman with his heid burst open though, you have to admit it, I ventured.

— No it's not. There's nothing satisfying about it at all, she replied.

— Naw, c'moan Avril. You're no tryin tae tell me that you didnae feel good when you saw the pictures of those slimy dead-souls looking shit-scared in that pile of rubble after the Brighton bomb? Tebbit n that?

I remember that well. When it came on the telly, my old man said, — Aboot time somebody had a go at those fuckers. I remember being full of pride and admiration for him.

— I don't like to see any human being suffer.

— That's all very well as an abstract moral principle, Avril, a coffee-table theoretical construct, but there's no denying the sheer gratuitous pleasure to be derived from seeing members of the ruling class in pain and torment.

— I really hope that you two are winding me up, she said

pityingly, — I really hope so for your sake. If not, you're sick, brutalised people.

— Too right, said Darren, — but at least we're not brutalising anybody else in turn. We don't mug, rape, serial-kill or starve the innocent. We just fantasise about destroying the vermin that have been fucking us over for years. And another thing we don't do, he added snidely, — is steal people's underwear.

Avril told him to fuck off, and left us. It was at that point I strongly began to suspect that Darren was the guilty man, the undergarment thief.

Ronnie didnae really get to know anyone. He slept for two days, and on the odd occasion he joined us was almost comatose. Then it was time for him to return as his ticket had been booked. He took some downers before getting on the bus at Victoria Station. I didn't bother waving at him as the bus pulled away; he had fallen asleep as soon as he'd taken his seat. The only things I remember him saying during the time he was down were: Darren . . . I thought, naturally, that he was talking about Darren in the flat, but I realised he wasn't. — Darren Jackson, followed by an appreciative nod, and, — Best man . . . sound, with a wink and cock of his head. When Ronnie winked, the act involved the opening, rather than the closing, of one eye.

The month dragged. I was looking forward to getting back to Edinburgh but no so much tae the wedding. I got into town the night before the stag and took a taxi tae the auld man's.

When I got in, Norma Culbertson and her wee lassie were there. There was something different about the house.

— Hello, son, my dad said awkwardly, — Eh, sit doon. I suppose I should have told you this before, but eh, well, wi you bein in London n that. You know how things are . . .

— Aye, I replied, totally fuckin clueless as to how things were.

— Has Derek, eh, mentioned anything?

— Naw . . .

— Well, Derek's moved out. He's in a flat now, in Gorgie.

Stewart Terrace. No bad flat as well. Wi him getting that Civil Service promotion, he had to go for it. You know?

— Jeff . . . Norma urged.

— Oh, eh, aye. The thing is, son, Norma and I have decided to get married, he smiled weakly, apologetically.

Norma simpered and exposed an engagement ring for my examination. I felt a dull thud in my chest. Surely this was a wind-up. Norma was a young woman; not bad looking either. Deek once admitted to me he used to wank about her, though that was a while ago. She was too young for Dad; he was old enough to be her father. Mind you, Dino Zoff was still playing European club football at my auld man's age. But that was Dino Zoff. This was real life.

My Ma and him

My Ma this was too young for him anyway my Ma gone for years him getting married again his business, what's it to me?

— Many happy returns, I stammered, — eh, I mean, congratulations . . .

Norma started talking about how she wanted us to be friends and my auld man ranted on about my mother . . .

— I'm saying nothing against her, but she abandoned yous laddies. Abandoned yous and never wanted tae see yis. Surely a real mother would want tae see her sons . . . bit no her, no sae much as a letter . . .

I started to feel a bit sick and thankfully the door went, saving us all further embarrassment. It was Crazy Col Cassidy, an animal from the scheme with a fearsome reputation for violence against the person. — Yir auld man in? he growled.

Well, the chickens have come home to roost now, Daddy. This anti-drugs campaign is about to blow up in your face.

— Col! my dad shouts. — Come in mate, come in! Cassidy pushes past me. My auld man gives him a matey slap on the shoulder. — This is ma laddie, he says, — he's been in London.

Cassidy growls an incomprehensible greeting.

— Col's the secretary of Muirhouse Action on Drugs, he explained.

I might have guessed: the nutters will always take the side of the forces of reaction.

— We ken the dealers in this scheme, son. We're gaunny drive them out. The polis willnae dae it, so we will, my auld man says, seemingly unaware that he's talking in a low Clint Eastwood drawl.

— Good luck with your campaign, Dad, I said. I had no doubt that he, with Cassidy's assistance, would succeed; succeed in making every fucker's life a misery. I made to hit the town.

— Oh, son, remember that wee Karen's got your old room. You'll be down here on the couch now.

Welcome home: evicted from your room in favour of some cretinous brat. I left and bounced up the town. The stag started off good-naturedly enough. Ronnie was jellied, out of his face, when we met up. Things were happy but uneventful until we met Lucia and a couple of her mates who insisted on tagging along with us. She got drunk and had a heavy spraff with Denise about who should get tae suck Ronnie off.

We went on to a few pubs, a couple of silly arguments started and a fight broke out. I swung at Penman who'd been on my case all night. I was held by Big Ally Moncrief while Penman danced away from me gesticulating sharply and breathlessly: — Moan then, moan then . . . ootside . . . think yir a wide-o . . . cunt think's he's a wide-o . . . moan then, ootside . . .

Big Moncrief said that he hated to see mates fight, particularly on such an occasion. Denise said that we should kiss and make up. We didn't, but we did hug and make up. We did an ecky each and clung to each other like limpets to a rock for the rest of the evening. I'd never felt so close to anyone, well, not another man, as I did to Penman that night. It was a lovers-without-the-shagging type scene. Conversely, I've seldom felt so awkward as I did when we met up with Tina's crowd at the Citrus. Olly was there. Former lovers generally find these things a strain; too much ego, no too much id involved. Once you've been with each other in a primal, shagging state, it's hard to talk about the weather.

Olly called herself 'Livvy' now. She had been going through
A Period Of Personal Growth and now seemed enough like her
friends to want to be like someone else, someone they wanted to
be like. She was painting now, she told me. It seemed to me that
what she was actually doing was talking and drinking. She asked
what I was doing. I told her and she said: — Same old Brian, in
a condescending way, as if to make the point that I was a useless
reprobate from a mildly embarrassing past she'd left behind; a
figure of pity.

She then shook her head in contempt, though I was not her
target. — I've tried to tell Tina that she's being stupid. She's too
young and Ronnie . . . well, I don't think I can ever comment
on him because I don't know him. I've never seen him straight;
never had a conversation with him. What the hell does he get
out of being like that?

I thought about it. — Ronnie's just always enjoyed the quiet
life, I told her. She started to say something, then stopped, and
made her excuses and left me. She looked good, the way that
somebody who used to be but is no longer into you can do. I
was glad she'd left though. People who are undergoing Periods
Of Personal Growth are generally pains in the arse. Growth
should be incremental and gradual. I hate these born-again
wankers who try to completely reinvent themselves, and burn
their past. I went over and held Penman in my arms for a long
time. Over his shoulder I cringed as I caught Roxy's malevolent
gaze and I thought of Blind Cunt for the first time in ages.

I could see the stag passing into the next week. I'd be drunk
and stoned the whole time, and it would roll seamlessly into the
wedding. I was wondering whether or not I'd bother going back
to London, my room in that flat, my arrears and my crap job.

The day after the stag, when I had been in the Meadow Bar
with The PATH and Sidney, I ran into Ted Malcolm, a guy from
the parks. He was at me to put my name down for a Seasonal
Park Officer job. — You wir ey well thought ay in the parks,
ken? he told me in the confidential bullshit manner that people
associated with the council used. The culture of civic corrup-

tion and innuendo permeated down from the shit-brains at councillor level to the ranks of the lowest official; Stalinism with a sweetie-wife's face, complete with headsquare.

— Aye, I said noncommitally.

— Garland always liked ye, he nodded.

Yes, in spite of it all, I'd maybe give Garland a bell. London had been starting to feel like Edinburgh had before I'd left it. Gleaves, May, even Darren, Avril, Cliff, Sandra and Gerard; they all constituted a set of expectations which snapped around me like a sprung trap. You can only be free for so long, then the chains start to bind you. The answer is to keep moving.

It was a nightmare getting Ronnie up and ready for the church. A total fuckin nightmare. His ma gave me a hand dressing him. She never seemed to show any concern at his state. — It must've been some night last night, eh? Well, ah suppose ye only git married the once.

I felt like saying, don't count on it, but I held my tongue. We bundled Ronnie into the car then into the church.

— Do you, Ronald Dickson, take Martina Devenney, to be your lawful wedded wife, to have and to hold, to love and to cherish, forsaking all others, so long as you both shall live?

Ron was jellied, but he managed tae gie the minister cunt the nod. It wasn't enough for this fucker though, he looked intently at him, trying tae elicit a more positive reaction. I nudged Ronnie harshly.

— Sound, he managed to mumble. It would have to do. The minister tutted under his breath, but left it.

— Do you, Martina Devenney, take Ronald Dickson to be your lawful wedded husband, to have and to hold, to love and to cherish, forsaking all others so long as you both shall live?

Tina looked a bit reluctant, as if it had at last dawned on her that this was serious shite she was getting intae. Eventually she managed to cough out, — I do.

Anyway, they were duly pronounced catatonic and wife.

We went to the Capital Hotel for the meal and Ronnie fell asleep during my speech. It wasn't a particularly inspired speech, but it scarcely deserved that sort of response.

At the reception I got a stance up at the bar with Raymie Airlie and Spud Murphy, two space cowboys of the highest order.

— Crimson style, bantam prince, Raymie observed, looking round the bar.

— You took the words right out of my mouth, Raymie, I smiled, then turning to Spud, — still skag-free, ma man?

— Eh, yeah . . . until there's free skag, ah'm skag-free, ken, catboy?

— Aye, me n aw. Ah went a wee bit radge the other week thair, but ah dinnae want tae git a habit, ken? Ah mean, how bad is that, right?

— Yeah, habits are nae fun, likesay. Sortay full-time occupation, catboy, ken? Sortay diverts the attention fae what's gaun oan.

— Mind you, it's the jellies that's fuckin every cunt now. Look at Ronnie. His ain fuckin wedding fir fuck's sake . . .

Raymie sighs and sings a chorus of Echo and The Bunnymen's 'The Cutter', then puts his tongue in my ear. I peck him on the cheek and pat his arse. — You're raw sex, Raymie, raw fuckin sex man, I tell him.

The PATH, Big Moncrief and Roxy come over to join us. I do some intros. — Awright boys, yous ken Spud n Raymie, eh?

Looks of suspicious acknowledgment are exchanged. My bevvy and druggy mates never really hit it off.

— Funny thing though, the marriage stakes n that, ken? Good if ye kin work it oot, likesay, Spud ventures, breaking an uneasy silence.

— The only thing that marriage is good for is sex oan tap, Moncrief says, with more than hint of belligerence.

Roxy puts on a Glasgow accent: — But ah like tae go oan the boatum sometimes.

We all laugh at this, except Moncrief. One thing about hard

cunts that I've never understood: why do they all have to be such big sensitive blouses? The Scottish Hardman ladders his tights so he rips open the face of a passer-by. The Scottish Hardman chips a nail, so he head-butts some poor fucker. Some other guy is wearing the same patterned dress as the Scottish Hardman, and gets a glass in his face for his troubles.

We move onto television. — Telly's fuckin shite, says Moncrief, — the only thing worth watchin oan the fuckin telly is they nature programmes. Ken wi that cunt, what's his name, that David Attenborough cunt.

— Aye, agrees Spud, — that cat's got the gig sussed, likesay. That's the kinday job that would be right up ma street, man, ken wi aw they animals, likesay. Freaky that would be, ken?

We spraff on all night, too drunk to dance with the wizened aunties and shaggable cousins. I drop some acid and note that Roxy's taken something. He's drunk, but he's taken something. Spud's given him one of those Supermarios. That's far too much for the Rox. He's an alcohol man. He's shaking his bowed head and babbling, — Ah kilt um! Ah fuckin kilt um, and he's close to tears.

I was struggling with the acid as well. It was not a good idea. These Supermarios; fuck me the whole world could be a hallucination the colours are clashing and reverberating and Tina's face is sick and vampire-like in that dress and Roxy's babbling and there's a polar bear running around on all fours . . .

— Spud, d'ye see the bear, man? I asked.

— It's no a bear, man, it's a sortay bear-dug likesay, sortay half-man half dug but wi a bit ay bear in it, ken?

— Raymie, you saw it, you ken it wis a bear?

— Yes, I personally thought it was a bear.

— Fuck me! Raymie! You've just said something straight, something sensible.

— It's just the acid, he tells me.

Roxy's still shaking his heid; — That perr boy . . . that fuckin blind boy . . . they took his eyes . . . ah took his life . . . fool's fuckin gold . . . ma soul's sick, made sick for fool's fuckin gold . . . tell ays that's no sick . . .

— This acid is mental shit . . . Spud says.

I see Moncrief, sitting beside this plant monster. Moncrief's face is changing colour and shape. I see that he's no a human being. Denise comes over: — Taken any ay they Supermarios?

— Aye . . . too much, man.

He buys one from Spud. Eight quid for this. My skin's been taken off. Eileen Eileen Eileen the Montparnasse Tower I had and lost love cause I was too young too stupid to identify and recognise it as such and it'll never come my way again not ever in a million fuckin years and I'll never make three score years and ten and anyway I don't want to without her what a mess that would be without Eileen who's at college in London I don't know what which one or at least was last year I hope you're happy now happy without your old smart cunt boyfriend who thought he was being entertaining but was just being an exasperating immature selfish prick not exactly a shortage of them never is and you were right to leave him as a decision purely rational . . .

— Whit's up wi Roxy, Denise asks.

— Too much acid. They Supermarios . . .

I grabbed Roxy's face in my hands. — Listen, Roxy, you're having a bad trip. We've got tae git ootay here. There's too many malignant spirits aroond here, Rox.

We were out of our faces, but we had to get out into the air. Olly gave me a disgusted look, but there was a little bit of pity in it. — Don't fuckin pity me, I shouted, but she couldn't hear me, or maybe she could but I got outside with Roxy, my legs rubber. The PATH tried to follow us but I told him it was okay, and he goes back inside to look for a shag.

It was a cold and crisp evening, or maybe it was just the Supermarios.

— AH KILT UM, AH FUCKIN KILT UM! Ah'm gaun tae the polis . . . Roxy was in torment. His face seemed to be folding in on itself . . .

I grabbed his shoulders. — Naw yir no! Think fuckin straight! Git a grip fir fuck's sake! Us gaun doon's no gaunny bring that cunt back, is it?

— Naw . . .

— Then thir's nae sense in it. It was a fuckin accident, right!

— Aye . . . He grows a little calmer.

— An accident, I repeat. — Yuv goat tae keep control ay yir tongue. It's that acid. Jist dinnae fuckin touch it again, it disnae agree wi ye. Stick tae the bevvy. Ye'll be awright whin ye come doon. Ye cannae go spraffin shite like that aroond. Yill git us fuckin jailed man. Thir's nae such thing as truth, Roxy, no wi these cunts. The polis willnae bother a fuck. It's jist another couple ay bodies fir thaim. Makes thaim look better, thaim n aw they slimy politician cunts, whae can say that the polis are winnin the war against crime; how sick is that? Blind Cunt's death wis fuckin tragic, let's no make it even mair tragic by giein they cunts what they want. Wise up! It wis a fuckin accident!

He looks at me with fear in his eyes, as if he's realised for the first time what he's actually been saying: — Fuckin hell, yir right man. What wis ah fuckin thinkin aboot spraffin away like that . . . nae cunt heard ays, did they, Bri? NAE CUNT HEARD AYS, BRI?

— Naw, jist me. No this time. But leave the fuckin acid alane. Right?

— Aye . . . this is mad. Ah took acid before, Bri, yonks ago. It was fuck all like this bit, this is fuckin mad. How fuckin mad is this, Bri?

— It's awright. Will go back tae your place and come down. Any bevvy in the hoose?

— Aye, loads ay cans. Whisky n aw.

It's strong acid, real head-fucking gear, but when we get to Roxy's we start drinking like there's no tomorrow. It's all you can do on acid, just thrash it out your system with alcohol. Pish is a depressant; it bring you down. You start to get control back.

It was imperative that Roxy didn't speak. I hadn't booted snow in Blind Cunt's face that night. I'd booted *him* in the face.

The decisive blow was as likely to have been mine as it was Roxy's. It was wrong; just horrible, stupid, cowardly and reckless. I can't wreck my life for that one stupid mistake in the heat of the moment. No way. I just won't fuckin well do that. The Blind Cunt and the Smart Cunt; a tale of two cunts. Well that's that tale finished, I hope. Finished for good.

14

INTERVIEW

Fuckin hell, it's yon time again. I got a hell of a shock when Garland's signature appeared under the Edinburgh District Council logoed notepaper, inviting me along for an interview.

I had gone back down to London, but after the job at Ealing folded I did the Euro-Rail with Darren and Cliff. Darren and I ended up in Rimini. He's still there, doing barwork, security work, raving and shagging all the time. It was sound, but I had to come back for another wedding, my auld man's this time. They moved out of the scheme, into a Barratt box across the road in Pilton. It would be a slum within five years. The government wanted home-ownership to regenerate the area. It makes no real difference whether you pay rent to the council for a shit-house or mortgage payments to a building society for one. Stop paying the mortgage and you see exactly where the ownership lies. I had planned to head back to Rimini but got a chilly note from Darren saying that he had got into a big heavy lovey-shag scene with this woman and while I was welcome to stay in the gaff for a while . . . blah blah blah. So I moved in with Roxy and put my name down for the parks.

— Hello, Brian, Garland extended his hand and I shook it.

— Mister Garland.

— Let me say, he began, — that the regrettable incident last year, I feel, on mature reflection, was a little out of character with you. I'm assuming that you've overcome all your, eh, depression problems?

— Yes, I feel on top of things now, Mister Garland. Health-wise, that is.

— That's good. You see, Brian, you were a model SPO until that little problem with Bert Rutherford. Now Bert is the salt of the earth, but I'm prepared to admit that he can be a zealot. The patrol needs Bert Rutherfords, otherwise the service would collapse into apathy and disarray. You've been at the coal-face, Brian; you know what a dull job it can be. You realise that the parks tend to attract disaffected groups of youths, who are not there to use it as a place of recreation, but for more sinister purposes . . .

— I believe that to be the case, yes.

— That's why I want you back on the patrol, Brian. I need people this summer who know the ropes. Above all, I like you because you're a reader, Brian. A reader will never be bored. What are you reading these days?

— I've just completed Peter O'Toole's biography. I never realised he was from Leeds.

— Was he indeed?

— Yes.

— Good. So have you started on anything else?

— Yeah, I'm reading Jean-Paul Sartre's biography.

— Good. Biographies are good, Brian. Some seasonals read all those heavy philosophic and political works, books that by their very nature encourage discontent with one's lot, he said sadly. — After all, a beautiful day in a park. Life could be worse, eh!

— That's true, Mister Garland.

I was back on the parks. How weird was that?

15

PISH

I found myself in the City Cafe. I hated the place, but that's how it goes. The main reason I was here was that it was full of fanny and I hadn't had a shag in five months. That is far too long for someone my age; it's far too long for someone of any age. I always ended up here when I was feeling shite and wanting to feel better. That's probably why I hated it.

I'd been in there for about twenty minutes, drinking a coffee, when I felt someone sit beside me. I didn't turn around to see who it was until I heard the words: — No speakin?

It was Tina. I'd heard that she and Ronnie had split up recently.

— Awright, Tina?

— Aye, no bad. Yirsel?

— Sound, eh, sorry tae hear aboot you n Ron, but.

She shrugged and told me: — He goat really borin. It started when he goat that Nintendo system. Ah preferred it when he wis jellied; ye goat mair ootay um then.

I knew that Ronnie had taken to that Nintendo game system like a duck to water. I thought that it was a positive step though, that it would give him an interest other than just being jellied all the time. — Did it no gie him an interest ootside ay drugs?

She looked at me with an ugly bitterness. — What aboot me? Ah should've been an interest! Him sittin thair plugged intae that telly, aw day n night, shakin like a leaf when ah came in fae work in case ah wanted tae watch somethin other thin his silly fuckin games! Me workin aw day, then huvin tae watch him playin games aw night!

— What's he fuckin like? Ah might go roond n see um, Tina. Try to talk some sense intae his heid.

She shook her head knowingly, recognising the impossibility of the task, yet warming to me for offering support. — Come n sit wi us, she suggested, pointing through the back.

— Is Olly thair?

— Aye, but it's cool, likes.

— Any of her friends around?

Tina raised her eyebrows in disdainful acknowledgement.

— Dunno, ah wis thinkin ay gaun doon tae the Pelican tae see Sidney n The PATH.

I had no intention of going to the Pelican, but then I heard a voice coming from Olly's table. It was loud, overbearing, posh and grating: — AND SHE'S A FREELANCE JOURNALIST WHO'S BEEN DOING A FEW BITS AND PIECES FOR *THE LIST*. SHE'S ONLY BEEN SEEING TONY FOR A COUPLE OF MONTHS BUT SHE WAS HAVING INCREDIBLE HASSLES WITH THIS FLAT SHE MOVED INTO, SO THE NATURAL THING SEEMED TO BE . . .

I had every intention of going to the Pelican. Tina did as well. When we got down The PATH was there with this lassie who looked a bit radge; radge in the sense of not being all there. The PATH freely admits that the Government's Community Care policies have been the best thing that ever happened to his sex life. Sidney was chatting with these women who looked disinterested to the point of boredom. — Awright, boys? Nae Roxy the night?

He was there though, holding up the bar, spraffin wi some wee guy.

We just sat around, drinking and blethering. Sidney and Tina seemed to be getting on. By chucking-out time they were feasting on each other's faces. The PATH and his troubled accomplice vanished into the night, while I left with Roxy.

— Ah'm gaunny take ye somewhair, he said. — Secret destination.

We piled into a taxi. It headed down to Leith, but then we

continued, heading out to Portobello. We stopped in Seafield Road and got out: the middle of fuckin naewhair.

— Whair the fuck's this? Eh? I asked.

— Follow me.

I did. We went around the back of Seafield Crematorium and climbed over a wall. It was a long drop down into the darkness on the other side, and I twisted my ankle badly in the fall. I was too drunk to feel much pain, but I'd feel it tomorrow alright, nothing was surer.

— What the fuck's this? I asked as he took me around some of the graves. Some of the headstones were recent. — How's it they bury people here? Ah thoat it wis supposed tae be a crematorium.

— Naw, thir's some plots ay land. Fir faimlies, likes. Recognise this yin?

CRAIG GIFFORD

— Naw . . .

— Look at the date.

BORN 17.5.1964
DIED 21.12.1993

— It's . . . the boy . . . I couldn't bring myself to say it.

— Blind Cunt, said Roxy. — That's the cunt's grave. It's time tae exorcise the cunt's memory at long last . . .

He had his cock out and was pishing. On Bli . . . on Craig's grave.

BELOVED SON OF ALEXANDER AND
JOYCE GIFFORD
WE WILL NEVER FORGET YOU

— CUNT! I shouted. I punched the side of his head.

He grabbed me, but I tore free from his grip and booted and punched him. This was not a good idea. He took off his glasses and fairly wired into me. Every blow I dispensed seemed puny, while every one he hit me with threatened to break me into pieces. My nose burst open, but thankfully the sight of my blood seemed to make him stop.

— Sorry, Bri, he said. — Nae cunt punches me though, Bri, understand. Nae cunt.

I stemmed the blood with one hand while holding him off in acknowledgment with the other. Roxy is a big cunt, but I'd always thought of him as a gentle giant. Huge cunts always seem that way, until one of them panels you. Still, at least I was pished. I realised then a sick and horrible truth: getting a kicking from some cunt is worse than killing some other cunt. The ugly fact of the matter is that this has become a governing principle for too many people. If I'd had a blade on me I would have used it on Roxy. I might have only felt that way for a few seconds, but that's all it would take. What a fuckin thought. How sick a species are we?

Craig Gifford.

If only Roxy knew.

If Roxy knew, I'd be the one who went down. He'd probably be pointing his finger at this dangerous psycho.

— It's no that bad. Sorry, Bri. Ye shouldnae huv punched ays though, Bri. Ma eye's gaunny be oot in the mornin. Ma shin as well, Bri, ye caught ays a beauty thair. Me n you swedgin though bit, Bri, tell ays that's no too mad.

The daft cunt's trying to make me feel better by cataloguing the damage I've inflicted on him. There's no victors in this type of gig; only those who lose the least. Roxy's lost the least, in terms of both physical injury and macho self-esteem. We both know it, but I appreciate him trying to make me feel better.

I leave him, fuck knows how I get out of the cemetery, and head for the auld man's. I throw up down my front on the way. Confused, I go back to the old place in Muirhouse. The hoose was still a void property, it hadn't been let. I tried to kick the door down and I would've, had auld Mrs Sinclair next door not reminded me that my dad had moved.

I staggered off and threw up again. My front was a mess of

sick and blood. A couple of boys came up to me at the shopping centre. — That cunt's ootay his face, one observed.

— Ah ken that cunt. You hing aboot wi that poof, eh mate?

— Eh . . . I tried to articulate a reply but I couldn't. I was aware enough, it just wouldnae come oot.

— If ye hing aboot wi poofs, that makes you a poof, that's the wey ah see it. What dae ye say tae that then, mate?

I look at the guy, and manage to ask, — Any chance ay a gam?

They look at me incredulously for a few seconds, then one says, — Smart cunt!

— That's ma name, boys, I concede. I feel a numb blow and crash to the ground. I take a kicking I can't feel. It seems to last quite a while, and that worries me, because you can usually judge the severity of a kicking by its duration. However, I take it with the passive, sick calm of an alienated worker putting in his shift and when I'm convinced it's over I stagger to my feet. Perhaps it's no too bad; I can walk easily. In fact, it seems to have cleared the mind a bit. Thanks, boys.

I cross the dual-carriageway, leaving posh Muirhoose, and get over to scruffy Pilton. That might no be how people see things now, but that's how it's always been tae me. Muirhoose is the newer hooses. Pilton's for the scruffs. It disnae matter what problems Muirhoose's got now and how much they tart up Pilton. Pilton's Pilton and Muirhoose is Muirhoose, always fuckin well will be. Fuckin scruffy Pilton cunts. These cunts that gave me the kicking were fae Pilton; that's these cunts' mentality. I've probably got fuckin lice jist through being in the vicinity of the dirty Pilton scruffy fuckin cunts.

I find the hoose and I don't know who lets me in.

The next morning I pretend to be asleep until they all leave for some twee little family outing: Dad, Norma and her loud, excitable daughter. I feel fucking shattered. When I try to get up I can barely walk. I'm covered in cuts and bruises and I piss blood, which shits me up. I have a bath and things start to feel a bit better, so I decide to have a sniff around. There's still a lot of stuff in packing cases. They are decorating this tawdry little egg-box of a home. I come across this small leather case which I haven't seen before, and I assume it's Norma's. It's not, however.

The case was full of photographs. Of me and Deek as bairns, of him, of my Ma. Photos I'd never seen before. I looked at her, with him. I tried to imagine I could see the hurt in her, see the discontent, but I couldn't. Not at first. Then I got to some photos which I knew were later ones, cause Deek and me were a bit bigger. In those pictures I could read it; with the benefit of retrospect it was all too easy; her eyes screamed pain and disillusionment. My tears spilled onto the tacky photographs. There was a lot worse in this leather case, however.

I read all the letters, every one. They were all really similar in content, only the dates differed. They ranged from a few months after she left right through to 1989. She'd been writing to him for eight years from Australia. All the letters had the same basic propositions repeated ritually:

I want to get in touch with the boys.

I want to have them over to stay.

Please let them write to me.

I love them, I want my children.

Please write to me, Jeff, please get in touch. I know you're getting my letters.

What happened in 1989, I don't know, but she never wrote back after that.

I copy down the address and phone number in Melbourne onto a piece of scrap paper. This is total shite. This is another load of shite to get through. There's always more, always more of this fuckin shite to get through. It never ends. They say it gets easier to handle the older you get. I hope so. I hope tae fuck.

It takes a while tae get through on the international direct-dialling. I want to talk to my Ma, a long talk, get her side of the story, at his expense as well. A guy answers the phone. I got him out of bed; the time difference; I forgot. He asks me who I am, and I tell him.

The guy was really upset. He sounded okay, I have to say that, the boy sounded okay. He told me that there was an electrical fire in their home. It was bad. My Mum died in it, back in 1989. She managed to get their daughter out, but she died of smoke inhalation. The guy was breaking down on the line.

I put the phone down. As soon as I put it down it started ringing again.

I let it ring.

MARABOU STORK NIGHTMARES

for Trish, Davie, Laura & Sean

Thanks time again. Always first and foremost to Anne, for reasons which you could write all the books in the world about and still not do it the slightest bit of justice.

Then to Kenny McMillan and Paul Reekie for providing me not just with stacks of ideas for this book, but also much of the information I needed to complete it, as well as numerous other East Terracing (now sadly, the East Stand) boys for their specialist info. To Kevin Williamson, Barry Graham and Sandy McNair for casting their beady eyes over the manuscript and providing useful feedback. It goes without saying that the above can't be held responsible for the many defects, only that such crap bits would have been more numerous without their intervention.

To the City of Munich local authority, without whose generous hospitality this book would not have been so quickly completed.

To all at the publishers, especially Robin Robertson and Nicky Eaton, and Lesley Bryce, the best editor in Western Europe. To Jeff Barratt at Heavenly.

To various pals in Edinburgh, Glasgow, London, Manchester, Amsterdam and other places whom I can always rely upon to drag me into clubs or pubs or onto the terraces for mischief whenever an outbreak of sanity threatens. You know who you are; nice one to each and every one of you.

Nods, winks, hugs and best wishes to all the punters and posses I've met up with over the last year at Pure, Yip Yap, Slam, Sativa, Back to Basics, The Ministry, Sabresonic, Desert Storm, The Mazzo, The Roxy, Sunday Social and Rez. Well done to all the DJs for keeping it going.

A very big thanks to my family for not being the one in this book.

Massive respect to all.

Zero Tolerance

The material used in this book is taken from the Zero Tolerance campaign which originated in Edinburgh. Zero Tolerance is the first campaign to use the mass media to challenge male violence against women and children. The campaign believes that there is no acceptable level of violence against women and children.

Scepticism was formed in Edinburgh two hundred years ago by David Hume and Adam Smith. They said: 'Let's take religion to the black man, but we won't really believe it.' It's the cutting edge of trade.

— P.R.

We should condemn more and understand less.

— Major.

Contents

part one

Lost
Empires

1 Another Lost Empire

It.was.me.and.Jamieson.

Just us.

On this journey, this crazy high-speed journey through this strange land in this strange vehicle.

Just me and Sandy Jamieson.

But they were trying to disturb me, trying to wake me; the way they always did. They willnae let this sleeping dog lie. They always interfere. When the cunts start this shite it makes things get aw distorted and I have to try to go deeper.

DEEPER. Things get dis

up – – – –   – We're just going to take
coming   your temperature,
start   Roy. Have you got the
I   bedpan, Nurse Norton?

I lose control when they interfere – – – and   Number Twos now Roy, time for Number Twos.

– Yes, he's looking brighter this morning, isn't he, Nurse Devine? You're brighter this morning, Roy lovey.

Aye right ye are, take your fuckin hand oot ma fuckin erse.

DEEPER

DEEPER – Sandy Jamieson is my best friend down here. A former professional sportsman and an experienced hunter of man-eating beasts, I enlisted Jamieson's aid in a quest I have been engaged in for as long as I can remember. However, as my memory is practically non-existent, this could have been a few days ago or since the beginning of time itself. For some reason, I am driven to eradicate the scavenger-predator bird known as the Marabou Stork. I wish to drive this evil and ugly creature from the African continent. In particular, I have this persistent vision of one large blighter, a hideous and revolting specimen, which I know somehow must perish by my own hand.

As with all other events, I have great difficulty in recalling how Sandy Jamieson and I became friends. I do know that he was of great help to me when I first came here, and that is enough. I do not wish to remember where I was before. I am averse to my past; it is an unsavoury blur which I have no wish to attempt to pull into focus. Here and now, Africa and Sandy, they are my present and my future.

I feel a cool breeze in my face and turn to face my companion. He's in good spirits behind the wheel of our jeep.

— You've been at the wheel far too long, Sandy. I'll take over! I volunteered.

— Wizard! Sandy replied, pulling over by the side of the dusty track.

A large insect settled on my chest. I swatted the blighter. — Yuk! Those insects, Sandy! How positively yucky!

— Absolutely, he laughed, clambering over into the back of the vehicle. — It'll be great to stretch these damn pins! He smiled, extending his long, tanned muscular legs across the back seat.

I slid into the driver's seat and started up the jeep.

All Sandy and myself had in the world were this rotten old jeep, some limited supplies and very little money. The majority of our possessions had recently been expropriated by a cunning but somewhat morally deficient native fellow, whom we'd rather foolishly hired as a guide.

For a while we had planned to engage the services of some young native boys, but the undernourished specimens we had encountered had proved to be unappetising prospects . . . that is, manifestly unfit for the physical demands adventures with Sandy and I would inevitably place upon them. Eventually we secured the services of one shifty urchin who went by the name of Moses. We took this to be a sign of good luck. It proved anything but.

Moses hailed from one of the shanty towns that lined the banks of Lake Torto. While I have to admit that we were not in the position to be able to pay our manservants generously, our behaviour towards Moses scarcely merited the response of this roguish boy: the blighter did a runner with the bulk of our money and supplies.

I find this attitude of 'something for nothing' sadly prevalent amongst the non-white races, but I put the blame fairly and squarely on the shoulders of the white colonialists, who by assuming responsibility for GOD THAT
BLINDING BLOODY   up – – –   – Roy, I'm shining this torch
FUCKING   coming   into your eyes. Pupil dilation
SUN – – – – – – – I'm   seems more evident. Good. Good.

FUCK OFF

— Definitely more of a response that time, Roy. It's probably just a reflex, though. I'll try it again . . . no . . . nothing this time around.

Naw, cause I'm too quick for youse, you'll never find ays in here.

DEEPER
          DEEPER
                    DEEPER – – – – – – – – Sandy is masturbating in the back of the jeep and she is just laughing . . . eh . . . what the fuck's gaun oan here . . . what's *she* dacin here . . . it's just supposed tae be Sandy n me . . . I'm losing control and all I can hear is her laughter and I see her face in the mirror; her face warped and cartoonish as his semen shoots onto her blouse. Her face is like . . . is like I want to . . . I'm feeling jealous. Jealous of Jamieson. What I want is for her not to just sit there laughing, not to sit and encourage him; I want to scream, don't encourage him you fucking slut, but I have to concentrate on the road because I've never driven before . . .

I can't keep my eyes off Sandy Jamieson. There is a sick tribe of demons lurking behind his generous if gormless facade. I am moved to shout, — You're a metaphor, Jamieson. You don't exist outside of me. I can't be angry with nothing, you're just a manifestation of my guilt. You're a projection.

This is ridiculous. Sandy's my friend. My guide. The best friend I've ever had but

But Jamieson now has his penis in her mouth. Its head bubbles her cheek outwards from the inside. It looks horrible, that swelling, that distortion of her face. Sandy's face, though, is even worse; it reddens and inflates, providing a contrast to his dark, shaven head and the whites around his dark green eyes. — I'm real enough, he gasps, — this rod is in your girlfriend's head.

In my mirror, while at the same time trying to keep my eyes on the dusty, winding track that they ridiculously refer to as a road, I see a blade come tearing out of her face. Panic sets in as I realise that the vehicle I'm travelling in is a structure now indivisible from my own body and we're dipping and flipping over, rising upwards in a shuddering rush into a buzzing wall of light. I'm gulping frenziedly at air which is so thick and heavy it feels like water in my lungs. I hear the shrieks of a large, predatory bird soaring past me; so close to my head I can smell the diseased remnants of carrion from it. I regain some sense of control over the vehicle only to find that she's gone and Jamieson is sitting in the front passenger seat with me.

— It was getting a tad crowded back there, he smiles, gesturing behind us to a trio of Japanese men in business suits who are occupying the back seat. They are excitedly snapping with cameras and speaking in a language which I can't make out but which doesn't seem to be Japanese.

This is totally fucked.

Is Sandy the best guide in all of this?

DEEPER
   DEEPER
      DEEPER

Yes.

I'm starting to feel happier. The deeper I get, the further away from *them* I get, the happier I feel. Sandy Jamieson's expression has changed. He is reassuming the persona of a loyal friend and guide rather than that of a sneering adversary. This means I'm back to where they can't get to me: deep in the realms of my own consciousness.

But they keep trying; even from in here I can feel them. Trying to stick another tube up my arse or something similar, something which constitutes a breach of my personal no no can't have this . . . change the subject, keep control.

Control.

Sandy

DEEPER
    DEEPER
        DEEPER --------- Holy
Cow! Sandy exclaimed as an unwanted Marabou Stork flew past the passenger window. I knew that it was our bird, but pursuit was difficult, as I had little control over this vehicle. The bird was impossible to follow in flight, but later on we would endeavour to locate its nest on the ground and destroy the beast. As things stood, however, we were coming down slowly, with a strange hydraulic hiss, towards the surface of this tropical, forested terrain.

— I've absolutely no control here, Sandy, I defeatedly observed, pulling at levers and pushing at buttons, but to little avail. I threw my hands up in exasperation. I wanted to stay up here. It seemed important not to land.

— Any biscuits left, Roy? Sandy asked eagerly.

I looked at the packet on the dashboard. There were only three left which meant that the greedy blighter had scoffed most of them!

— Gosh Sandy, you're a Hungry Horace today, I remarked.

Sandy gave out a high, clear laugh. — Nerves, I suppose. I don't particularly want to land, but at least this place might have some proper tuck.

— I hope so! I said.

The craft descended implacably, coming down over what at first seemed to be a small settlement, but which appeared to be expanding continually beyond our line of vision until we saw it as a giant metropolis. We were hovering down into this old stone colonial building which had no roof; only the jagged remnants of glass around the periphery showing where one had been.

I thought that our craft would never squeeze through the gap and braced myself for collision. However, its dimensions seemed to alter to fit the shape it had to go through, and we touched down in a rather splendid hall with some interesting gothic stonework. This was obviously some sort of public building, its grandeur hinting at more affluent times and its poor state of maintenance indicative of a more sordid and less civic present.

— Do you think we're allowed here, Sandy asked shakily.

— I don't see why not. We're explorers, aren't we, I told him.

As we got out of our car (for this was what the vehicle now seemed to be, a simple family saloon car) we noted the presence of many people, wandering around aimlessly, and taking little notice of us. Some broken glass crunched under my feet. I started to feel more than a wee bitty paranoid, thinking that the natives would perhaps blame us for breaking the roof. While we were innocent, circum- stantial evidence could certainly be weighted against us by an unscrupulous and malevolent set of officials in a corrupt regime, which to a greater or lesser extent meant any regime. I had absolutely no intention of getting back into that vehicle, nor, evidently, had Sandy; engaged as he was in the removal of his backpack which contained half our supplies. I followed his lead and swung my own pack over my shoulders.

— Strange little performance this, I noted, turning to Jamieson, who was surveying the scene with increasing distaste. Two white men walked straight past us, completely ignoring us. I was just starting to entertain the possibility that we were invisible when Sandy roared, — This is preposterous! I am a seasoned explorer and a professional footballer! I demand to be treated in a sporting manner!

— It's okay, Sandy, I smiled, placing a comforting hand on my friend's shoulder.

This outburst was certainly effective in registering our presence, but only at the expense of generating hostility from some of the citizens present. In particular, one band of youthful roughs were sizing us up.

Gosh and golly.

Damn and fucking blast.

— Sandy's the *enfant terrible* of British soccer, I limply endeavoured to explain.   up — — — Okay Roy?

Then I felt something — — — — — — — — — — — — coming

AH FEEL SOMETHING AH FEEL IT BUT YOUSE CUNTS CAN FUCK OFF AND DIE CAUSE YOUSE'LL NO GIT AYS IN HERE YA CUNTS

DEEPER
                         DEEPER
                                                DEEPER — — — — — Let's scarper
Sandy, I nodded, noting that the mood of the mob had turned sour and — — — coming up — — — oh fuck I've lost control again **THESE CUNTS' FAULT, LEAVE AYS ALANE** and now I feel the stabbing beak in my arm, it can only be the Marabou Stork but it's my injection, it's the chemicals, not ones that dull and chill my brain, not ones that make me forget because with these ones I remember.

Oh my God, what dae ah fuckin well remember . . .

Lexo said that it was important that we didnae lose our bottle. Nae cunt was tae shite oot; eftir aw, the fuckin hoor asked fir it. She'd've goat it fae some cunts anywey the wey she fuckin well carried oan and the fuckin fuss she made. Aye, she goat slapped aroond a bit, but we wir fuckin vindicated, British justice n that. She wis jist in the wrong place at the wrong time n anywey, it wis aw Lexo's fault . . .

. . . change the subject . . . I don't want this. I want to keep hunting the Stork. The Stork's the personification of all this badness. If I kill the Stork I'll kill the badness in me. Then I'll be ready to come out of here, to wake up, to take my place in society and all that shite. Ha. They'll get a fuckin shock, when they see this near-corpse, this package of wasting flesh and bone just rise and say: — Awright chavvy! How's tricks?

— Awright son!

AW FUCK! *THIR* HERE. ALWAYS FUCKIN HERE. ALWAYS ASSUMING I WANT THEIR FUCKIN PRE-SENCE. DAE THEY NO HAVE FUCKING VISITING HOURS HERE?

My father. Nice to see you, Dad. Please, continue, while I doze.

— How ye daein? Eh? Well, that's us in another final. Disnae seem two whole years since the, eh accident, but enough ay that. Another final! One-nil. Darren Jackson. Ah didnae go masel mind. Tony wis thair. Ah wis gaunny go, bit ah nivir goat a ticket. Saw it oan the telly. Like ah sais, one-nil. Darren Jackson, barry goal n aw. Tony made up a tape ay the commentary, like ah sais, a tape eh made up. Eh Vet?

— Aye.

— Ye goat the tape then?

— What?

— The tape, Vet. Ah'm askin ye, ye goat the tape?

— Tape . . .

— Whit's wrong, Vet?

— Thir's a Jap ower thair, John.

— It's jist a nurse, Vet, jist a nurse. Probably no even a Jap. Probably a Chinky or somethin. Eh son? Jist a nurse ah'm sayin, son. Eh Roy? Eh that's right son?

FUCK OFF AND DIE YOU DAFT AULD CUNT

— A nurse . . .

— Aye, the wee Chinky nurse. Nice lassie. Eh son? Lookin better the day though, son. Mair colour. Like ah sais, eh Vet, like ah sais, Roy's goat mair colour aboot um.

— They nivir git it. Every other perr bugger gits it, bit they nivir git it.

— Eh?

— AIDS. Ye nivir see Japs wi AIDS. Here wuv goat it. In America thuv goat it. In India thuv goat it. In Africa thuv goat it. Oor Bernard might huv it. No thaim, though. They nivir git it.

— What the fuck ye oan aboot? Chinky nurse . . . nice wee lassie . . .

— Ken how? Ken how they nivir git it?

— Vet, this husnae goat nowt tae dae wi . . .

— Cause they inventit it! They inventit the disease! Soas they could take over the world!

— You fuckin stupit or somethin?! Talkin like that in front ay Roy! Ye dinnae ken what the laddie kin hear, how it effects um! Like ah sais, ye fuckin stupit? Ah'm askin ye! Ye fuckin stupit?

MUMMY DADDY, NICE TO SEE YOU IS IT FUCK DON'T WANT TO SURFACE DON'T WANT TO GET CLOSER TO YOUR UGLY WORLD GOT TO GO DEEPER, DEEPER DOWN, GOT TO HUNT THE STORK, TO GET CONTROL

DEEPER

      DEEPER

            DEEPER————————————

————————————————————————————————Jamieson.

We've somehow given the baying mob the slip and find ourselves on the edge of a run-down shantytown. A huge, festering garbage dump lies alongside a now poisonous lake. Malnourished children play in its squalor. Some of them come over to Sandy and myself, begging without really expecting any results. One little boy, a wild-looking creature with a face as brown as dark chocolate, stares intently at us, never averting his gaze. He is wearing nothing but old, dirty blue shorts and a pair of worn shoes without any socks.

— I say, Roy, what an extraordinary looking creature, Sandy smiled.

— Yes, a funny little thing, I said.

The little boy gave a loud, long laugh and suddenly poured out quite an extended speech. I couldn't understand a bloody word of it.

— Bantu, I suppose, Sandy said sadly. — Sounds all very splendid and lovely, but I can't make head nor tail of it!

We gave them some coins and Sandy produced a small bag of sweets. — If we only had a ball, I could do a bit of coaching, get a scratch game up, he said wistfully.

I looked up at the blinding sun. It had been relentless all day, but soon it would retreat behind the green hills which rose up over the Emerald Forest. This was a beautiful spot. This was . . . my thoughts were distracted by some shouts and the sound of the rattling of tin against the compressed clay track. Jamieson was expertly shielding a Coca-Cola can from the rangy limbs of a group of the local Bantu children. — There you go, you little blighters . . . it's all about possession, he told them.

He was forever the sport.

While Sandy's interest in sports coaching and the development of youth was touching, we had more pressing matters to consider. Our vehicle had been left behind in the civic hall, neither of us caring to travel in anything *quite* so unreliable. — We need transport, Sandy, I told him, — our Stork must be nesting around here somewhere.

Sandy signalled for the kids to disperse. One tyke, our funny little creature, glared at me in a sulky way. I hated to be the spoilsport, but there was business to take care of.

Sandy crisply and clinically volleyed the can into the rubbish-infested lake, then looked at me and shook his head sadly. — This is not going to be quite as straightforward as you think, Roy. The Storks are dangerous and formidable opponents. We're alone and isolated in hostile terrain, without any supplies or equipment, he explained. Then he looked at me with a penetrating stare, — Why is slaying that large Marabou so important to you?

Damn and fucking blast.

This made me stop to consider my motives. Oh yes, I could have gone on about the spirit of the hunt. I could have produced a welter of damning evidence of the carnage that these despicable beasts can perpetrate on other wildlife and game; on how they can upset the entire ecology of a region, how they can spread pestilence and disease through the local villages. Certainly, such reasoning would have struck a chord with both Sandy's sense of adventure and his humanitarian principles.

The problem is it wouldn't have been true. Moreover, Sandy would have known that I was lying.

I cleared my throat, and turned away from the blinding sun. Feeling a shortness of breath, I felt the words about to evaporate in my throat as I prepared to speak them. I always seem to feel something sticking in my throat. I cough, miraculously finding strength, and carry on. — I can't really explain, Sandy; not to my own satisfaction, so certainly not to anyone else's. I just know that

I've met that Stork before, in a previous life perhaps, and I know that it's evil. I know that it's important for me to destroy it.

Sandy stood looking at me for a few seconds, his countenance paralysed with doubt and fear.

— Trust me on this one, mate? I said softly.

His face ignited in a beautiful, expansive smile, and he gave me a powerful hug which I reciprocated. We broke off and gave each other the high-five. — Let's do the blighter! Sandy smiled, a steely glint of determination entering his eye.

Another two small black children from the football game approached us. Their clothes were in tatters. — Homosexual? One young boy asked. — I suck you off for rand.

Sandy looked down at the crusty lipped urchin. — Things may be bad little one, but selling your body to the white man is not the answer. He ruffled the child's hair and the boy departed, skipping across the path back down towards the settlement.

We moved on by foot, carrying our backpacks and heading out of the village towards the other side of the lake. The wind had changed direction and the smell from the rubbish was overpowering in the hazy heat. Ugly bugs of varied sizes swarmed around us, forcing us to beat a hasty retreat along the path. We ran until we couldn't go any further, although I must confess that was the royal 'we', for Sandy, as a professional sportsman, had quite an edge on me in fitness and stamina, and could probably have stuck it out a bit longer.

We set up camp with our provisions, enjoying a feast in a shady glade by the more picturesque side of the lake. We opened our packs to examine their contents.

— Mmmm! Pork pie; homemade of course, said Sandy.

— And what's this . . . golly, it's a cheese! How enormous. Smell it, Sandy, it's enough to make you want to start eating straight away!

— Gosh, I can't wait to get my mouth around that, Sandy smiled, — And that homemade bread! Can't we start?

— No, there are new-laid boiled eggs to begin with, I laughed.

— Gosh, all we're missing is some homemade apple pie and ice-cream, Sandy smiled, as we tucked in to our feast. Then, suddenly inspired, he turned to me and said, — I've got it, Roy!

What we need is sponsorship! Somebody to fund this Stork hunt. I know a chap who'll sort us out with provisions. He runs the Jambola Safari Park, access to which is a few miles' trek on the west side of the lake.

I knew instantly whom Sandy was talking about. — Dawson. Mr Lochart Dawson.

— You know him?

I shrugged non-committally. — I know *of* him. Then again, most people know of Lochart Dawson. He sees to that.

— Yes, he has a flair for self-publicity, does our Lochart, Sandy said, his tone implying an affectionate familiarity. I then recalled that Sandy mentioned that he'd previously been in the employ of Dawson.

Sandy was correct about the self-publicity; you just couldn't keep Dawson out of the news. He was currently planning on expanding his park by taking over an adjacent leisure reserve. Whether in the long term Dawson actually envisaged any animals in what he described as the 'superpark' was more open to conjecture. He had made his money in the development of property, and there were more profitable uses for land in this region than a Safari Park. Nonetheless, Dawson could be useful.

— We'd have a smashing time at old Dawson's, I said eagerly.

— I'll bet he's got enough food to feed an army! Sandy agreed.

Suddenly we were interrupted by a chorus of frenetic squawking. We looked back, and I saw them. Although one or two social groupings could be evidenced, they were largely standing in isolation from each other, in the rubbish by the lakeside. Some squatted on their breasts, others paced slowly at a short distance. One large devil; it must have had a wing span of around eighty and weighed about nine kilos, turned its back to the sun and spread its wings, exposing those spare filamentous black feathers.

The beast's throat patch was reddish; it had scabs of warty dried blood on the base of its large, conical bill; its legs were stained white with dried excrement. It was the large, bulky scavenger-predator known as the Marabou Stork. More importantly, it was our one.

— Look Sandy, once again I felt my words dry in my throat, as I pointed across the lake to the mountain of rubbish and the large bird. The sheer evil power of the creature emanating from its deathly eyes shook us to the marrow.

— Come ahead then, ya fuckin wide-os! It squawked.

I felt sick and faint.

Sandy looked pretty fazed.

— Look Roy, we need more hardware to take on that bastard. Its bill must be razor sharp, containing the venom and poison of rotting carcasses: one scratch could be fatal. Let's see Dawson. His resort was once plagued by these beasts, but he found a way to sort them out.

THESE BEASTS ARE KILLERS. THEY ARE INTERES-
TED ONLY IN MAYHEM. THEY CARE NOTHING FOR
THE GAME . . .

up – – –

back

Eh?   coming

Aw fuck – – – – I'm

– We're away now, son. Yir Ma n me. Like ah sais, that's us away now. CHEERIO SON! CHEERIO ROY! – Cheerio Roy! Cheerio darlin.

Like yir Ma sais, that's us sayin cheerio. See ye the morn though son. Ah'll be in in the morn. CHEERIO ROY!

Aye, aye, aye. He's always so fuckin loud. Ah'm no fuckin deaf, ya cunt! Sometimes ah just feel it would be so much fuckin easier tae just open my eyes and scream: FUCK OFF!

— The min-it choo walked in the joint dih-dih, I could see you were a man of dis-tinc-tyin, a real big spender . . .

What the fuck is this? Ma. She's finally fuckin blown it.

— . . . good loo-kin, so ree-fined . . .

— What ur ye daein Vet? Whit the fuck ye playin at?

— Bit mind they sais John, mind they sais that ah could sing tae um. The doaktirs said. Ken, wi the music hittin a different part ay the brain. That's how wi bring in the tapes, John. Ah jist thoat this wid mean mair tae the laddie, likesay a live performance. Mind eh eywis liked ays singing Big Spender whin eh wis a bairn?

671

—Aye, well music n singin, that's different like. Different sort ay things. That's jist singing you're daein. Ye couldnae really call it music, Vet. Like ah sais, ye couldnae really call it music.

—Bit ah could git Tony tae play the guitar. Make up a tape ay me singin Big Spender, fir the laddie's cassette player, John. Ah could dae that, John.

OH FUCKIN HELL, GOD PRESERVE US . . .

I could tell that my Ma was upset, and they had another blazing argument. I was relieved when they departed. So fuckin relieved. Even now they embarrass me. Even in here. I've nothing to say to them; I don't think anything of them. I never really had, besides I was anxious to get back to Sandy and our pursuit of the Stork. I hear a different voice now though, a sort of fluffy feminine voice, the voice of Nurse Patricia Devine. —That's the visitors away now, Roy.

Her voice is soft, mildly arousing. Maybe I'll get a bit of love interest into my little fantasy, a bit a shagging into things no no no there will be no shagging because that's what caused aw this fuckin soapy bubble in the first place and I'm being turned over in my decaying organic vehicle, and I can feel the touch of Patricia Devine.

Can I feel her touch, or do I just think I can? Did I really hear my parents or was it all my imagination? I know not and care less. All I have is the data I get. I don't care whether it's produced by my senses or my memory or my imagination. Where it comes from is less important than the fact that it *is*. The only reality is the images and texts.

—There's nothing of you, she says to me cheerfully. I can feel the frost in the air. The staff nurse has given Patricia Devine a dirty look for making a negative comment in front of the veg. Me who used to weigh thirteen and a half stone, too. At one time I was heading for Fat Hell, (Fathell, Midlothian, population 8,619) with a fat wife, fat kids and a fat dog. A place where the only thing thin is the paycheque.

Now I can hear that 'Staff' has departed leaving me with the simply Devine Patricia. Patricia is possibly an old hound, but I like to think of her as young and lovely. The concept adds quality to my life. Not a lot of things do at the moment. Only I add the quality. As much or as little as I want. If only they'd just fuckin leave ays tae get on with it. I don't need their quality, their world, that fucked-up place which made me the fucked-up mess I was. Down here in the comforts of my vegetative state, inside my secret world I can fuck who I want, kill who I please, no no no nane ay that no no no I can do the things I wanted to do, the things I tried to do, up there in the real world. No comeback. Anyway, *this* world's real enough to me and I'll stay down here out of the way, where they can't get to me, at least until I work it all out.

It hasn't been so easy recently. Characters and events have been intruding into my mind, psychic gatecrashers breaking in on my private party. Imposing themselves. Like Jamieson, and now this Lochart Dawson. Somehow, though, this has given me a sense of purpose. I know why I'm in here. I'm here to slay the Stork. Why I have to do this I do not know. I know that I need help, however, and I know that Jamieson and Dawson are my only potential allies in this quest.

This is what I have instead of a life.

2 The Scheme

I grew up in what was not so much a family as a genetic disaster. While people always seem under the impression that their household is normal, I, from an early age, almost as soon as I was aware, was embarrassed and ashamed of my family.

I suppose this awareness came from being huddled so close to other households in the ugly rabbit hutch we lived in. It was a systems built, 1960s maisonette block of flats, five storeys high, with long landings which were jokingly referred to as 'streets in the sky' but which had no shops or pubs or churches or post offices on them, nothing in fact, except more rabbit hutches. Being so close to those other families, it became impossible for people, as much as they tried, to keep their lives from each other. In stairs, on balconies, in communal drying areas, through dimpled-glass and wire doors, I sensed that there was a general, shared quality kicking around which we seemed to lack. I suppose it was what people would call normality.

All those dull broadsheet newspaper articles on the scheme where we lived tended to focus on how deprived it was. Maybe it was, but I'd always defined the place as less characterised by poverty than by boredom, although the relationship between the two is pretty evident. For me, though, the sterile boredom outside my house was preferable to the chaos inside it.

My old man was a total basket case; completely away with it. The old girl, if anything, was worse. They'd been engaged for yonks but before they were due to get married, she had a sort of mental breakdown, or rather, had her first mental breakdown. She would have these breakdowns intermittently until it got to the stage it's at now, where it's hard to tell when she's *not* having one. Anyway, while she was in the mental hospital she met an Italian male nurse with whom she ran away to Italy. A few years later she returned with two small children, my half-brothers Tony and Bernard.

The old boy, John, had got himself engaged to another woman. This proved that there were at least two crazy females in Granton in the early sixties. They were due to be married when my Ma, Vet (short for Verity), reappeared in the lounge bar of The Anchor public house. As Dad was to remark often: Ah jist looked acroass n met yir Ma's eyes n the auld magic wis still thair.

That was that. Vet told John she'd got the travelling out of her system, that he was the only man she'd ever loved and could they please get married.

John said aye, or words to that effect, and they tied the knot, him taking on the two Italian bambinos whom Vet later confessed were from different guys. I was born about a year after the wedding, followed about a year later by my sister Kim, and my brother Elgin, who arrived a year later again. Elgin got his name from the Highland town where John reckoned he was conceived.

Yes, we were a far from handsome family. I suppose I got off relatively lightly, though I stress relatively. While my own face and body merely suggested what people in the scheme would, whispering, refer to as 'the Strang look', Kim and Elgin completely screamed it. 'The Strang look' was essentially a concave face starting at a prominent, pointed forehead, swinging in at a sharp angle towards large, dulled eyes and a small, squashed nose, down into thin, twisted lips and springing outwards to the tip of a large, jutting chin. A sort of retarded man-in-the-moon face. My additional crosses to bear: two large protruding ears which came from my otherwise normal-looking mother, invisible under her long, black hair.

My older half-brothers were more fortunate. They took after my mother, and, presumably their Italian fathers. Tony looked a little like a darker, swarthier version of the footballer Graeme Souness, though not so ugly; despite being prone to putting on weight. Bernard was fair, slim and gazelle-like, outrageously camp from an early age.

The rest of us took 'the Strang look' from the old man, who, as I've said, was an A1 basket case. John Strang's large, striking face was dominated by thickly framed glasses with bottom-of-Coke-bottle lenses. These magnified his intense, blazing eyes further. They had the effect of making him look as if he was coming from very far away then suddenly appearing right in your face. It was scary and disconcerting. If you were in possession of a Harrier Jump-jet, you could have chosen either his chin or forehead as a landing pad. He generally wore a large brown fur coat, under which he carried his shotgun when he patrolled the scheme late at night with Winston, his loyal Alsatian. Winston was a horrible dog and I was glad when he died. He was instantly replaced by an even more vicious beast of the same breed, who also rejoiced in the name Winston.

I later had cause to be less than pleased at the first Winston's demise; the second one savaged me badly. I was about eight, and watching a Superboy cartoon on the television. I decided that Winston Two was Krypto the Superdog and I tied a towel to his collar to simulate Krypto's cape. The dog freaked out and turned on me, savaging my leg so badly that I needed skin grafts and walk with a slight limp to this day . . . only now I don't walk at all.

I feel a spasm of hurt at that realisation. Remembering hurts.

— Dinnae tell nae cunt it wis Winston, Dad threatened and pleaded. He was terrified in case they took the dog away. I said it was an unprovoked attack by some of the strays which congregated on the wasteland adjacent to our block. It made the local paper and the Tory council, who hated spending the snobby ratepayers' money on anything to do with our scheme, grudgingly sent an environmental health van over to round up the savage pack-beasts for extermination. I spent four months off the school, which was the best part of it.

As a kid I did the normal things kids in the scheme did: played fitba and Japs and commandos, mucked about on bikes, caught bees, hung around stairs bored, battered smaller/weaker kids, got battered by bigger/stronger kids. At nine years old I was charged by the polis for playing football in the street. We were kicking a ball around in a patch of grass outside the block of flats we lived in. There were no

NO BALL GAMES signs up, but we should have known, even at that age, that as the scheme was a concentration camp for the poor; this like everything else, was prohibited. We were taken up to court where my mate Brian's dad made a brilliant speech and embarrassed the judge into admonishing us. You could see the polis looking like tits.

— A fuckin common criminal at the age ay nine, my Ma used tae moan. — Common criminal.

It's only in retrospect I realise that she was fucked up because the auld man was away at the time. She used to say that he was working, but Tony told us that he was in the jail. Tony was awright. He battered me a few times, but he also battered anybody who messed with me, unless they were his mates. Bernard I hated; he just stayed in the hoose and played with my wee sister Kim aw the time. Bernard was like Kim; Bernard was a girl.

I loved catching bees in the summer. We'd fill auld Squeezy detergent bottles with water and skoosh the bee as it sucked at the nectar on the flower. The trick was to train a couple of jets on the bee at the same time and blast it to fuck, the water weighing down its wings. We'd then scoop the drenched bees into a jar and then dig little prison cells for them in the softer material between the sections of brick at the ramp at the bottom of our block of flats. We used ice-lolly sticks as the doors. We had a concentration camp, a tiny Scottish housing scheme, for bees.

One of my pals, Pete, had a magnifying glass. It was great getting a shot of it. I used to like to burn the bees' wings, making them easier prisoners. Sometimes I burned their faces. The smell was horrible, the smell of burning bee. I wanted the glass. I swapped Pete an Action Man that had no arms for his magnifying glass. I had earlier swapped the Action Man fae Brian for a truck.

I was embarrassed when any of the other kids came roond to the hoose. Most of them seemed to have better hooses than us, it was like we were scruffs. That's how I knew the old man was in the jail, there was only my Ma's wages for doing the school dinners and the cleaning. Thank fuck my Ma did the dinners at a different school than the one I went to.

Then my Dad came back. He got work in security and started daein the hoose up. We got a new fireplace with plastic coals and twirly things inside a plastic funnel which made it look like heat rising. It was really just an electric bar fire but. My Dad was awright at first; I remember he took me to Easter Road for the fitba. He left me and Tony and Bernard and my cousin Alan in my Uncle Jackie's car ootside a pub. They bought us coke and crisps. When they came out they were pished from drinking beer and they got us pies and Bovril and mair crisps at the fitba. I was bored with the fitba, but I liked getting the pies and crisps. The backs of my legs got sair, like when my Ma took us tae Leith Walk tae the shops.

Then I got a bad battering fae my Dad and had to go to the hospital for stitches. He hit the side of my head and I fell over and split it on the edge of the kitchen table. Six stitches above the eye. It was barry having stitches. The auld man didn't understand that it was only clipshers I put in Kim's hair. — It wis jist clipshers, Dad, I pleaded. — Clipshers dinnae sting.

Kim just gret and gret like fuck. She wouldnae stop. It was only clipshers as well. Just clipshers. It's no as if it was bees. They have these pincers at the back, but they dinnae sting. I think Devil's Coach-Horses or Earwigs were their real names.

— Look at hur! Look what yuv fuckin well done tae yir sister ya silly wee cunt! He gestured tae Kim, whose already distorted face twisted further in contrived terror. The auld man thumped me then.

I had to tell everyone at the casualty that I was mucking aboot wi Tony and I fell. I had headaches for a long time eftir that.

I remember once watching my Ma, Vet, scrubbing the tartan nameplate on the door of our maisonette flat. Somebody had added an 'E' to our name. Dad and my Uncle Jackie went around the stair cross-examining terrified neighbours. Dad was always threatening to shoot anybody who complained about us. Other parents therefore always told their kids not to play with us, and all but the craziest ones complied.

If the neighbours were terrified of my Dad and Uncle Jackie, who was really just Dad's mate but we called him 'Uncle', they were also pretty wary of my Ma. Her father or grandfather, I could never remember which one, had been a prisoner-of-war in a Japanese camp and he had gone slightly loopy; a direct result, Vet claimed, of his cruel incarceration. She grew up indoctrinated with tales of Jap atrocities and had once read this book which contended that the orientals would take over the world by the turn of the century. She would scrutinise the eyes of my few friends, proclaiming them unsuitable if they had what she considered to be 'Jap blood'.

I think I was about nine or ten when I first heard the auld man mention South Africa. It seemed that no sooner than he mentioned it, we were there.

— See us, Vet? Meant fir better things. Me wi aw they security joabs. Nae prospects. Like ah sais, meant fir better things. This country's gaun tae the dogs. Aw they strikes; cannae even git yir fuckin bucket emptied. They trade union cunts: hudin the country tae ransom. Sooth Efrikay, that's the place. Like ah sais, Sooth Efrikay. Ah ken thuv goat problems in Sooth Efrikay n aw, but at least thuv no goat this fuckin Labour Governmint. Ah'm gaunny see aboot gittin us ower thair. Oor Gordon wid pit us up, nae danger. Ah'll take us oot thair, Vet. Fuckin well sure'n ah will. Think ah'll no? Ah'm askin ye! Think ah'll no?

— Nae Japs . . .

— Aye, bit git this though, Vet. Thir's nae Japs in Sooth Efrikay. Nane. That's cause it's a white man's country, like ah sais, a white man's country. White is right oot thair, ah kid ye not. Like ah sais: Sooth Efrikay, white is right, Dad sang, all high and animated. His large flat tongue licked at a stamp which he stuck on a letter. It was probably a letter of complaint to somebody. He always wrote letters of complaint.

— Jist as long is thir's nae Japs . . .

— Naw bit this is Sooth Efrikay. Sooth Fuckin Efrikay Vet, if yi'll pardon ma ps n qs.

— Somewhair ah kin git tae dry clathes . . . they Pearsons . . . eywis in the dryin green . . .

— Eh! Ah fuckin telt that cow! Ah fuckin telt hur! Ah sais tae hur, nixt time ah fuckin see your washin in that fuckin dryin green whin ma wife's tryin tae wash, the whole fuckin loat's gaun doon the fuckin shute intae the rubbish! Fuckin ignorant, some people, like ah sais, fuckin ignorant. Bit see in Sooth Efrikay Vet, we'd huv a big hoose like Gordon's. Dry oor clathes in the sun, in a real fuckin gairdin, no in some concrete boax wi holes in it.

Gordon was John's brother who had left to go to South Africa years ago. Possibly John's closeness to 'Uncle' Jackie was due to him seeing Jackie as a brother substitute. Certainly at the drunken parties he frequently hosted, when squads of guys and couples would pack into our egg-box after closing time, he seemed at his happiest telling old stories of himself, Gordon and the Jubilee Gang, as he and his hippy-beating Teddy Boy mates used to call themselves.

— It wid be nice tae huv a real back gairdin . . . I remember Ma saying that. I remember that clearly.

It was decided. Dad's word generally went in our family. We were making plans to go off to South Africa.

I didnae really ken whether or no I wanted to go. It was just eftir that that I lit my first really big fire. I'd always liked fires. Boney nights were the best nights of the year in the scheme, Guy Fawkes because you got fireworks, but Victoria Day n aw. We'd go doon the beach tae get wood or find other boneys in the scheme and raid them. Sometimes, though, we got raided ourselves. You would get cudgels and stanes and try to defend your bonfire against raiders. There was always fights with stanes in the scheme. The first thing I learned tae dae was tae fling a stane. That was what you did as a kid in Muirhoose, you flung stanes; flung them at radges, at windaes, at buses.

It was something to do.

The fire, though, that was something else. It was eftir the boney. I had a lighted torch and I put it doon the rubbish chute. It ignited the rubbish in the big bucket in the budget room at the bottom of the building. Two fire engines came. Ma mate Brian made ays shite masel.

— Ooohhh! You'll get taken away, Roy, he telt me with wide-eyed glee at my fear.

Ah wis shitin it, nearly fuckin greetin n aw that. Brian kept taking the pish, but I'll gie him his due, he never telt nae cunt. The polis came roond every door and asked aw these questions. My Dad said nothing. — Never tell these cunts anything, he used to drum into us. It was the one bit of sense I ever remember him talking. He was really chuffed about the fire as well, because Mrs Pearson from up the stairs had her washing ruined by the smoke. It rose from the budget room to the drying greens above it.

— Serves the cow fuckin well right, like ah sais, the fuckin ignorant boot. Shouldnae be monopolisin the fuckin drying greens whin thir's people wantin tae hing oot a washin! That's what she fuckin well gets!

It dawned on me that the auld man was probably prime suspect in the lighting of the fire. He was chuffed to have a cast-iron alibi; he was playing in his dominoes league match up at the Doocot when it started. He was so chuffed that I wanted to tell him it was me, but I resisted the temptation. The cunt could change moods quickly.

Sometimes me and my pals used to go out of the scheme, but it was usually just doon the beach. Me, Pete, Brian, Deek (Bri's brother) and Dennis, we would think aboot running away and going camping, like in the Enid Blyton books. We usually just got as far as the fuckin beach, before getting fed up and going hame. Occasionally we'd walk to snobby bits like Barnton, Cramond or Blackhall. The polis would always come around and make us go hame, though. People in the big hooses, hooses that were the same size as our block, which sixty families lived in; they would just go away and phone the polis. They must have thought we were gaunny chorie aypils or something. Aw I wanted tae dae was tae watch birds. I got an interest in birds, used to get loads ay books on them fae the library. I got this from my auld man, I suppose. He was really interested in birds as well.

I mind ay askin ma Dad if we would live in a big hoose like the ones in Barnton when we went tae South Africa.

— Bigger than thaim though son, much bigger. Like ah sais, much bigger, he telt ays.

The funny thing is that it was in the period when we were preparing to go to South Africa that I have some of the most vivid memories of John, my Dad. As I've indicated, he was a little bit crazy and we were all frightened of him. He was far too intense about things, and got himself worked up over nothing. I worried about the shotgun he kept under the bed.

Our main point of contact was through television. John would take the TV pages from the *Daily Record* and circle the programmes to watch that evening. He was a keen nature freak, and as I mentioned, particularly interested in ornithology. We both loved the David Attenborough style nature documentaries. He was never so happy as when programmes on exotic birds came on the box and he was very knowledgeable on the subject. John Strang was a man who knew the difference between a Cinnamon Bracken Warbler and, say, the Brown Woodland variety.

— See that! Bullshit! A Luhder's Bush Shrike, the boy sais! That's a Doherty's Bush Shrike! Like ah sais, a Doherty's Bush Shrike! Jist as well ah'm tapin this oan the video!

We were the first family in the district to have all the key consumer goods as they came onto the market: colour television, video recorder and eventually satellite dish. Dad thought that they made us different from the rest of the families in the scheme, a cut above the others. Middle-class, he often said.

All they did was define us as prototype schemies.

I remember the note he sent to the BBC, smug in his knowledge that for all the research capabilities he imagined them having at their disposal, their presenter had got his facts wrong. The reply was initially a great source of pride to him:

Dear Mr Strange,

Thank you for your letter in which you point out the factual error in our programme WINGS OVER THE BUSH which was transmitted last Thursday.

While this particular nature documentary was not made by the BBC, as commissioners of the group of independent film-makers who produced the programme, we accept liability for such inaccuracy in our broadcasts.

While we at the BBC strive for accuracy in every area of our broadcasting activities, errors will inevitably occur from time to time and keen members of the viewing public with specialist knowledge like yourself provide an invaluable service in bringing such inaccuracies to our attention.

The vigilant and informed viewer has a key role to play in ensuring that we at the BBC maintain our high standards of broadcast excellence and adequately fulfill the responsibilities of our charter, namely: to educate, inform and entertain.

Once again, thank you for your correspondence.

Yours sincerely,

Roger Snape
Programme Controller, Nature Documentaries.

The old man showed every fucker that letter. He showed them in the pub, and at his work with Group Six Securities. He freaked out when my Uncle Jackie pointed out to him that they had misspelled his name. He wrote a letter to Roger Snape saying that if he was ever in London, he would kick fuck out of him.

Dear Mr Snap,

Thank you for your letter in which you show yourself to be an ignorant person not spelling my name right. I just want you to know that I do not like people not spelling my name right. It is S-T-R-A-N-G. If I am ever in London I will snap you . . . into small pieces.

Yours faithfully,

John STRANG.

The only things which seemed to give Dad enjoyment were drinking alcohol and listening to records of Winston Churchill's wartime speeches. Pools of tears would well up behind his thick lenses as he was moved by his idol's stirring rhetoric.

But these were the best times. The worst were the boxing lessons he gave us. He had a thing about me being too uncoordinated, especially with my limp, and considered Bernard too effeminate. He bought us cheap, plastic boxing gloves and set up a ring in the living-room, with four confiscated traffic cones defining its perimeters.

Bernard was even less interested in the boxing than I was, but Dad would force us to fight until one or both of us broke down in tears of misery and frustration. The gloves caused a great deal of scratching, scarring and tearing, and it looked as if we'd been slashing rather than punching each other. Bernard was older, bigger, and heavier-handed, but I was more vicious and had quickly sussed out that you could do greater damage with slashing swipes than punches.

— C'moan Roy, Dad would shout. – Punch um, punch um, son . . . Keep that jab gaun Bernard . . . dinnae fuckin slap um like a pansy . . . His coaching advice was always a bit one-sided. Before the fights he used to whisper to me: — You're a Strang son, mind that. He's no. Mind that. Right? Mind, yir fightin fir the Strang name. He might git called a Strang, but eh's no. Eh's a fuckin crappin eyetie bastard son.

On one occasion when I had marked Bernard's eye and swollen his lip, John could scarcely contain himself: — Keep that fuckin jab in ehs eye, Roy! Poke ehs fuckin eye right oot!

I kept jabbing away at that reddening queer face, my body tight with concentration as Bernard's eyes filled with petulant unease.

BANG

      QUEER-FACED CUNT

BANG

      TAKE THAT YA FUCKIN SAPPY BIG
      POOF

BANG

I opened up his eye above the brow with a tearing twist of the glove. I felt a jolt of fear in my chest and I wanted to stop; it was the blood, splashing out onto his face. I was about to drop my hands but when I looked at Dad he snarled at me to fight on: — GO FIR THE KILL, NAE FUCKIN PRISONERS!

I battered into the fearful face of my broken-spirited pansy half-brother. His gloves fell by his sides as I kept swinging wildly, urged on by John's frenzied cries. Bernard turned his back on me and left the room sobbing, running up the stairs and locking himself in the toilet.

— Bernard! Ye'll huv tae learn tae stick up fir yirsel! John smirked, a little worried as Ma would not be pleased when she came back from the shops in Leith and inspected the damage. On that particular occasion, I came off the best, but it wasn't always like that. Sometimes it was me who beat a humiliating retreat, overwhelmed by pain and frustration.

At such times I envied my younger brother Elgin, silently rocking or gently humming, trapped in a world of his own, exempt from this torture. Perhaps Elgin had the right idea; perhaps it was all just psychic defence. At times I envied Elgin's autism. Now I have what he has, his peace and detachment from it all.

As for me and Bernard, those fights made us fear Dad and hate each other.

Bernard was

Ber no I've no time for this.

Now the nurses are back. They're doing something to me.

THIS IS ALWAYS UNPLEASANT

Turn the cabbage, prevent him rotting away . . .

I have to go deeper.

Deeper.

DEEPER

DEEPER

Away from them.

Better.

Now it's time to go

        to

             the

                 hunt – – – – – – – –

There is one lush green national park which is unique. Nowhere else in the world does such a park exist in a major city. Only a few miles separate the centre of the city from this park where game animals and the large carnivores which prey on them exist in the splendour of half a century ago

– – – Easter Road Nairobi got to stop this shite deeper deeper – – – –

The area of the park, around fifty square miles, is small in comparison
to other faunal reserves in this part of the   again –   – just bad news,
world, but the park nevertheless   up   I really made a fool
                                    of myself. Once he
possesses a diversity of   coming   got what he wanted
environments   I'm   he was off, off like a shot
The entrance . . . – – – – – – – aw fuck   into the night, back to his life
                                      and there I was, left alone, again.
                      Left with nothing. I should have known. I should have known.

I'm not deep enough. I can hear her. Nurse Patricia Devine. She's confessing to me, her vegetable priest, he who cannot affirm or condemn. I've found my perfect role.

    — You always think that the next one will be different and I suppose I let my emotions get the better of me, got all carried away and read what I wanted to read between the lines. He was so charming, so wonderful, so understanding but, yes, that was before he got me into bed . . .

Sobbing sounds.

    — . . . Why am I telling you this . . . why not . . . it's not as if you can hear me, it's not as if you'll ever wake up . . . oh God, I'm so sorry I said that . . . I'm just upset, I didn't mean that, I mean some people do wake up . . . they do get better . . . I'm just not myself just now. Roy, you see, I let this one

687

get right into my head as well as into my pants. Letting them into your pants is bad enough, but when they get into your head . . . it's like . . .

No

Don't want this

DEEPER

        DEEPER

                DEEPER – – — Mwaaa! A loud, nasal sound. The sound of an adult Stork threatening a human intruder. I look around and Sandy Jamieson is boldly starting the ugly bird down.

— Net the bastard, Roy! Net the cunt! he shouts.

My psychic quality control is bloody bloody bloody damn well fucked and everything has changed and suddenly I'm standing with a ball at my feet on a football pitch. I slam it into an empty net. A couple of players in the same jerseys grab me in celebration; one of them seems to be Lexo, oh fuck naw, no Lexo, and I try to get free but he willnae let ays go and over the shoulder of his crushing bear hug I see Jamieson looking deflated, his hands resting wearily oan his hips.

3 The Pursuit Of Truth

The old man had always been a nutter, but it seemed to me that he started to lose it really badly when we were preparing to move to South Africa. He probably knew he was a fuckin loser and this was his last throw of the dice to make something of his life. His nervousness was apparent, he was smoking more than ever. He would sit up most of the night, either with my Uncle Jackie or even sometimes with Tony, who was only fourteen but was very mature in certain ways for his age. Anytime we were out and he saw a young lassie, Tony would mutter, — Ah'd shag the fuckin erse oafay that . . .

From an early age Tony hung around with girls fae the scheme. He was always driven by hormones and completely oblivious to any other forces like logic or conscience which might serve as a counterbalance. It was inevitable that he would get some dopey cow up the stick, which he did. Her father came round to the house looking for justice. John instantly freaked out, threatening to blow him away with his shotgun. I remember this incident as I was trying to watch Superboy on the telly. The introduction was in full swing and Superboy and his loyal friend Krypto were flying through the air, dedicated to what the commentator described as 'the pursuit of truth'. I remember looking down at Winston Two, who sat curled up in front of the electric fire. I stared at the soft-breathing beast and thought of how his rib cage could be so easily shattered by simply jumping on it with a pair of heavy boots. I had a pair of heavy boots. It was something to think about. The scar tissue on the wounds Winston Two had given me tingled.

Elgin was sitting on the settee, his expression vacant, lost in a world of his own.

My concentration, divided between fantasising the slaughter of my canine assailant and watching Superboy, was shattered by my father's voice coming from the front door and ricocheting around the concrete blocks of the scheme.

— YOU KEEP YIR FUCKIN HOOR AY A DAUGHTER AWAY FI MA FUCKIN LADDIES OR AH'LL GIT MA FUCKIN SHOTGUN N FUCKIN WELL BLAW YIS AW AWAY!! RIGHT!!

I stealthily sneaked outside to see the guy timidly capitulate, leaving his daughter to face the alternatives of abortion or single parenthood. His conversation with the old man probably convinced him that these were sounder options than marrying into my family.

I crept back into the living-room, leaving my father bellowing at the retreating man, as every net curtain in our block and the one opposite twitched. John Strang was at it again. A bit later he came in, shaking, and Tony followed him sheepishly, tears in his eyes. My Dad looked down at me. I kept my attention on the set but he snapped, — Roy! Doon tae the shoaps fir ays. Forty fuckin Regal!

— How's it ey me that hus tae go? How no Elgin? It was a stupid thing to say. It just came out in my anger at being disturbed from my telly programme.

My Dad shook with rage. He gestured over to my brother who was now rocking on the couch. On sensing that he was being referred to, Elgin let out a steady mmmmmmmm.

— He cannae go! HE CANNAE FUCKIN WELL GO!! Ye fuckin well ken that, ya stupit wee . . . use the brains God gied ye, Roy. Like ah sais, the fuckin brains God gied um, he turned to Vet.

— It's no as if he's a stupid laddie . . . my Ma said to him.

— A dreamer, that's whit the school sais! Like ah sais, a dreamer. Heid stuffed too fill ay they fuckin comics!

I felt a horrendous tremor rumble through me as Dad's eyes burned with inspiration. — Ah'll fling aw they daft comics oot! How wid ye like that! Eh? Ah'm asking ye! How wid ye like that!

— Ah'll go . . . ah'll go . . . I helplessly whined.

— Think ah'll no? Eh? Think ah'll no? Ah'm asking ye! Think ah'll no?

— No ehs comics fir fuck sakes, John, Ma pleaded. — No the laddie's collection ay Marvel comics.

There was self-interest underpinning her concern as my Ma was a big fan of the *Silver Surfer*.

— Well then, git! Dad snorted. — N dinnae think thit yi'll no huv tae improve yir schoolwork, son!

I was putting my coat on in the lobby when Dad came out. — Ah'm jist gaun . . . I said, terrified of those intense, blazing eyes.

He put his hands on my shoulders. My head was bowed. — Look at ays, he said. I looked up, but I couldn't stop my eyes from watering. — Whit's wrong? Look son, ah ken thit ah'm harder oan you thin the rest. It's cause you're the one wi the brains, son. Ah ken that. It's jist thit ye dinnae use these brains. Like ah sais, brains, he tapped his large forehead. — Ah hud brains n ah didnae use thum. Ye dinnae want tae end up like me, he said, looking genuinely tormented with remorse. — Sooth Efrikay, it'll aw be different thair though, eh?

— Aye. N wi'll be able tae go tae a Safari Park, Dad? I asked.

— Ah've telt ye! Ah'm gaunny git a joab as a Park Ranger. Wi'll be practically livin in a Safari Park.

— Barry, I said with genuine enthusiasm. I was still at the age where, despite being embarrassed at their weirdness, I essentially believed in the omnipotence of my parents. I skipped along to the shops.

The old man was right though. I was a dreamer, stuck in my own world for much of the time. I'd have my head buried in the adventures of the *Silver Surver* and the *Fantastic Four* and the likes. This was because I never really fitted in anywhere. I was quiet at school, but had got intae trouble for stabbing a laddie with a compass. They were laughing at me. They called me Dumbo Strang or the Scottish Cup because of my ears. On top of all my other Strang defects, I had to be cursed with those protruding lugs. I was, though, working out a simple formula: if you hurt them, they don't laugh, and I can't stand anybody laughing at me. I had learned that I could take pain. Physical pain I could take. If you can stand pain you're going to give any cunt problems. If you can stand pain and you arenae feart and you're angry. Pain I could stand. Them laughing at me; I couldnae take that.

The teacher and the headmaster expected me to feel guilty for what I had done. They expected me to fear them. I didn't fear them. I lived in a houseful of sociopaths so the disapproving threats of middle-class teachers calling me a warped, evil and nasty little creature didn't bother me, they just lowered my self-esteem further, became a set of terms of reference for me to embrace.

But it wasn't as if I was disruptive at school; I was nothing. I withdrew as much into anonymity as I could. I wanted to be invisible. I wanted nobody to see the misshapen, twisted Dumbo Strang. I just sat at the back of the class and daydreamed.

At home in my bedroom, I rubbed my cock to illustrations of Sue Storm, The Invisible Girl, in my *Fantastic Four* comics. The drawings of Sue being kidnapped and restrained were the biggest turn-ons. Sometimes you got well-defined tits, arse and lips in the drawings.

I wonder now if the pursuit of the Marabou is about anything as fundamental as the pursuit of truth. I'll have to go deeper to find out.

DEEPER
        DEEPER
                    DEEPER ———————— Now I'm back in the hunt, heading deeper, because I feel the heat and see the light. On my face, in my eyes. I feel the warm, dusty sweet air in my lungs and cough and wonder if it registers in my slumbering near-corpse up in the other world.

We had got back into town and Sandy, forever the sport, had traded our photography equipment for an old jeep. — All this has to do is to get us out to Dawson's. He'll see us alright, Sandy smiled.

— But your equipment, Sandy . . . I felt awful, knowing how keen Sandy was on photography. He always said ruefully: the camera never lies.

— Photos won't be much good against the Stork. We need

hardware, and Dawson's the chap to get it for us. The time for photographs is later on!

— I can't wait, I said excitedly. — I can think of lots of things I want to photograph!

We found cheap lodgings in a poor area of the town and spent the evening drinking bottled beer in a spartan hut of a bar.

— Do you have any food? Sandy asked the bartender.

— We have the best homemade steak pie and mashed potatoes in Africa, said the barman, — followed by the most scrumptious apple crumble absolutely drenched in whipped cream!

— Gosh, that's just what we could do with after all that travelling, Sandy said eagerly, and we sat down to a feast.

Despite the bartender's enthusiasm, the food simply wasn't up to scratch. That night I experienced a fevered, alcoholic sleep. The Storks were pursuing me in my dreams. Then it was the group of youths from the large, municipal building. I woke up more than a few times covered in sweat. On one occasion I came to absolutely terrified, after having been followed by something which did not reveal itself, but which I could sense lurking in the shadows. This thing suggested such horror and evil that I dared not trust myself to the mercies of sleep. I left Jamieson slumbering heartily and sat up at an old, marked wooden table, writing up my notebook.

The next morning we set off. The burning, sweltering sun had turned the dark continent into a vast furnace. I was weary and out of sorts. Nothing felt right. My bare legs in my khaki shorts stung with pain every time they came into involuntary contact with the hot body of our jeep. Avoiding such unwanted bonding was impossible when we were shaking in gravelly ascent towards the Alpine Moorlands, our four-wheel-drive vehicle still struggling to negotiate the rough surface and steep inclines.

My discomfort lifted as almost imperceptibly we found ourselves travelling through an environment I can only describe as paradise. My awareness of it started as we passed through a magnificent belt of juniper and podocarpus, and I began rushing on the magical fragrances that filled the air, before we reached the high altitude bamboo forest with its mighty gorges, sylvan glades and fast trout streams.

— Isn't this heavenly! I exclaimed to Sandy.

— I'll say, Roy, Sandy agreed, tearing open a packet of chocolate biscuits. – Munchie wunchies, he smiled.

We drove past a couple of elephant and buffalo herds grazing in a grassland clearing and Sandy even claimed to have spotted a rare black rhino. Ahead was our destination, one of Dawson's lodges, No. 1690, which lay approximately 7,000 feet above sea level in the heart of the forest.

On our way up a particularly challenging incline, Sandy passed over the large joint he had been smoking. After a couple of enthusiastic tokes I was feeling somewhat out of sorts. Generally, when I take drugs of this type I can reserve a small central part of my brain for sobriety. This becomes a lens, through which I can, with concentration, view the world with a certain

clarity – – – but it – – – was all fuckin

falling apart eftir jist one fuckin toke . . .   – Time

this shouldnae be happening   up   for your
                                                                                       injection, Roy
– – – shouldnae be – – – – – – – – – – coming

Simply Devine, Patricia.

Sidney Devine.

I'll be back, Sandy.

— Your girlfriend looked nice. I hadn't seen her before. Still, I suppose I'm quite new on this ward.

What girlfriend? Surely that fat hoor wisnae back. Some mistake surely. She'll be gettin fucked by somebody else long ago and good riddance. And I gave that fuckin boot a ring. Fuckin joke. Git back tae Fathell, Dorie my love.

No don't talk about her that way don't talk like that about Dorie who isnae real nowt's fuckin real

Stay cool

— I think she's a bit shy. Very pretty though. You're a bit of a dark horse, aren't you Roy?

I've not got much to say for myself, Patricia. Plenty to think about though.

— You know Roy, I heard all about you. It came as a shock to me.

— Right Nurse Devine, let's get him changed.

— Oh, Staff, Right.

Caught again Patricia, caught blethering to the veg.
Fuck getting changed.
· Fuck getting shaken aboot like a pea in a whistle . . . this whistle

the whistle

This requires DEPTH.

D
     E
          P
              T
                    H– – – – – – – – – – – – – – – – – –

– – – – – – – – – – – – – – – – – – – –

After circling around on a path on the periphery
of the forest for a while, we eventually pulled
into a yard. The lodge was a strange building,   k   – Still quite
constructed on stilts. The smell of diesel from   c   heavy aren't
our vehicle was overpowering. It smelt like   u   you, Roy?
hospit not hospitals – – – – – – – – – – –   f   Isn't he, Tricia?
                                            – Yes, he certainly

is . . . I feel really bad about us moving him into the corridor like this, Bev.

— I know Tricia, but it's only going to be for a couple of nights, then he'll have his room back. Won't you, Roy?

Ah dinnae gie a fuck where ye pit ays. Stick ays oot wi the rubbish
fir aw ah care, ya cunts.

— I think it's terrible though. Some rich private patient needs the room, so a long-term, coma victim is dumped in the corridor until the wealthy case is ready to go . . .

— The hospital needs the funds these people bring in though, Tricia.

— Well, I'm just glad I'm not on duty when we have to explain to the family what he's doing in the corridor.

Deeper.

Can't I get some shagging interest in this? Conjure up a fleshy hologram of Nurse Patricia Devine and fuck her no no no

Dawson

Dawson, who looks like a criminal seal, eyes alert and open in all that blubber . . .

What does Patricia Devine look like

HAIR

EYES

TEETH

COMPLEXION

TITS

ARSE

MINGE

LEGS

It needs a woman in this not as a real person just for the shag interest just for

DEEPER

  DEEPER

    DEEPER

      DEEPER

        DEEPER

          DEEPER

            DEEPER

            DEEPER

                DEEPER – – – – – Dawson . . . on our arrival at the lodge he had stolen over to me, completely ignoring Sandy, and shaken my hand with a theatrical warmth. He let his eyes hold mine for a few seconds of contrived intimacy and boomed in a deep, affectedly sincere voice, — Roy Strang. I've read so much about you in the papers. A pleasure to meet you.

— You're no slouch in the publicity stakes yourself, Mr Dawson, I commented.

— Lochart, please; call me Lochart, he implored. He grinned idiotically for a few more rather excruciating moments then once again looked penetratingly at me. There was a snidey, manipulative aspect to his eyes which was totally incongruent with the open, garrulous set of his mouth. He reminded me of nothing more than a desperate old queen attempting to score in a singles bar, apparently casual but ever conscious of the remorseless clock. He looked mildly uneasy for a brief second or two, as if he was reading my thoughts, and then cackled, – We'll, I hope that my publicity is a little more, eh, salubrious, than yours. But they say that there's no such thing as bad publicity. That is an adage that I have at least some sympathy with.

This conversation was becoming rather upsetting. — I don't believe that to be the case. Few people would welcome what I've gone through . . .

— All this self-pity, Roy! Very disappointing, he boomed, slapping my back, his hand making a sound like a wet fish hitting a slab. Then he ushered me through to a library, leading to a conservatory at the back of the Lodge. As we moved towards the French windows, he plucked a book from the shelf and handed it to me. — For you, he smiled. I looked at the title:

YOUTH IN ASIA

I stuck it in a plastic bag I had been carrying.

— I see you have the toolkit handy, he smirked. Damn and fucking blast, I felt a little uneasy at this statement. I started to remember something, no, not remember a thought, but an experience, I started to *feel* something unpleasant and was happy when Sandy came through and interrupted this sensation before it could flower into recall.

Sandy had said something about a jeep. Our rusty ancient blighter had buggered up badly on reaching the lodge. As Sandy had suspected, Dawson was pleased to sell us an old one from Jambola Park, at about three times the normal price. — This one, he smiled, and looked at Sandy in a way which caused him to visibly twitch, — is surplus to requirements.

As well as being ripped off with the jeep, we were forced to accompany Dawson on a visit to his favourite spot in the hills, a place he visits regularly for its natural beauty. We had to walk about two and a half miles from Lodge 1690 and it was now overpoweringly, miserably hot; a smudge of sweat on the back of Jamieson's shirt had become a large heart. I made reference to this and Dawson smiled approvingly, lavishly, from his one-man buggy. Sweat trickled down my legs. Sandy looked quite fresh but Dawson, despite the motor cart, was saturated and breathing in a laboured, heavy manner. One of the wheels of his vehicle crushed a snake, mashing the animal into the path. His head poked out the side of the cart and grinned hideously back at us.

— Unfortunately, only one available, he'd smiled widely as he'd twisted his girth into the motorised cart. Starting it up, he had, with snapping jocularity, bade Sandy Jamieson and I to follow him on foot. Dawson's skin was the colour of barbecued tandoori chicken; clashing vividly with a Brylcreemed shock of brown, thinning hair, white and blue eyes, and pearly teeth which seemed permanently hanging out to dry. He also appeared to be covered in a strange, translucent oil.

Dawson stopped the buggy, climbed out and swept a doughy paw around his terrain. Our track wound around the precipice of a spectacular gorge, which swung down towards a fast-flowing river. — Not bad for a lad who left home with the less than princely sum of ten pounds sterling in his pocket, he smugly observed.

I saw a dead rodent by the side of the path. I picked it up by the tail. It had a fat slimy leech attached to it. I dropped it and looked at Sandy. — I came to Africa to study parasites, I told him, glancing back at Dawson. Sandy appeared a little bit uneasy, and gestured at me to keep my voice down.

I remembered Sandy saying that he once worked for Dawson. Gosh and golly.

Our destination was a building which on the outside looked rundown and ramshackle, but internally was very stark, modern and functional, its harshness only dissipated by a number of large, exotic plants in pots. We were greeted by a stout, middle-aged African woman, who made a particular fuss of Lochart Dawson.

— This is great pleshah, Missuh Dossan, she smiled.

— On the contrary, Sadie, the pleasure is always mine in visiting your fine establishment.

His smile made me feel as if I'd eaten or drank something decidedly unpleasant.

— For my guests, he smiled, turning to Sandy and myself. — You see, I own this place, and I use it as a sort of unofficial hospitality suite for potentially special customers. Special being defined as those who can advance the interests of Jambola Park PLC. This facility was specifically constructed on the impetus of the board of Jambola Park PLC, of which I am a member.

Dawson owned seventy-eight per cent of the Jambola Park PLC shares.

At that point Sandy went to light a cigarette but stopped after noting the look of disapproval on Dawson's face. He extended his palms and looked at me in appeal. I shrugged briefly.

I felt the hand of the African woman called Sadie rest on my shoulder. — You are veh tense, she said. — Would you like me find girl massage you neck? Perhaps bit more than you neck?

— Eh . . . if I could just have a glass of water, please.

Dawson curled his lips downwards in disapproval. — Yes, Sadie, the water. For myself and Mr Jamieson as well. I should imagine you two are rather thirsty camels after your exploits.

— I'll say! I nodded appreciatively.

Sadie departed but returned quickly with a tray on which sat three glasses and a pitcher of iced water. Also now in attendance were three young white girls. They looked skinny, malnourished and dirty and their eyes were thickly clouded over.

I sipped at the water which was so cold that it made my teeth hurt.

— So you are, like Mr Jamieson, a hunter?

— Yes, though perhaps not as successful as Sandy . . . I started.

Dawson interrupted me with a nasty smirk. — I would hardly say that Mr Jamieson has been particularly successful on the trophy hunting front. I must say, though, that I've found it persistently difficult to find hunters who look like bagging trophies. What is your specialisation, Roy?

— Sharks mainly, but also scavengers.

Dawson raised an eyebrow and gave a knowing nod. — And you, Mr Jamieson, still hunting the maneaters?

— Eh, yes, said Sandy nervously, — I mean, with only spears to rely on in defence, African villagers are effectively helpless in the face of lion attacks on their settlements . . .

— Yes, smiled Dawson, — in nearly all cases the maneater is an animal well past his prime. He has lost all his youthful agility and is simply not up to the capture of wild game for food.

— Man, though, is easy to procure, Sandy said, the unease of realisation coming into his voice.

— Oh yes, agreed Dawson with a slow, sly nod, — oh yes. Then he looked intently at Sandy and, with his face strangely blank and dead, said in a teasing tone out of synch with his expression: — I'd like to ask you, Mr Jamieson, have you an awareness of the role of ritual?

Sandy, obviously fazed, looked across at me, then back at Lochart Dawson. — As a sportsman, he began, but Dawson raised a Pillsbury Dough-boy hand to silence him.

— A sportsman. How . . . anachronistic. I should not have addressed such a statement to a sportsman. His voice went low and mocking at the term 'sportsman'. — The role of ritual is to make things safe for those who have most to lose by things not being safe. Wouldn't you agree, Roy?

— It's not a concept I've thought about exploring deeply Lochart, though I have to confess it does have a certain prima facie appeal.

Dawson seemed irritated that I was not getting into things with him. — And my proposal that the sportsman is an anachronism? Is that a concept you've had time to explore? His pitch is now challenging.

— I'd probably need to have the proposition defined in a little more detail before I would presume to comment.

— Very well, Dawson smiled, tucking his shirt into his trousers and belching, — I contend that sport, like everything else, has been replaced by business.

Dashed if I didn't find myself arguing in spite of what I'd intended. — Up to a point. Sport though, when it has a cultural locus, becomes a source of identity to people. Lose such sources of identity, and you have an atomised, disjointed society. Sport can move some people in a way that the profit motive can never. Our values have become obscured and warped to the extent that the means for self-actualisation, i.e. money, has become an end in itself. One of the ends is the appreciation of sport. Another might be art. Another might be the precipitation of chaos.

Dawson chuckled pneumatic-drill style, his flesh wobbling steadily as he laughed. — Yes Roy, sport does move the masses, but they only gain any relevance insofar as they are involved in the economic process, insofar as they become consumers. Sport has to be packaged to the masses, leisure has to be sold to them in a way they understand. Yes, in the past people had families, communities. There was a sense of living together. Through this they developed a shared understanding of the world, developed different cultures. Now not all of these cultures are in empathy with the profit system, and therefore they have to be replaced by another, stronger, richer culture, or at least assimilated into it. Families and communities have to be broken up further, have to be taken to where the work is, have to be denied at all costs meaningful interaction with each other. They have to live in, as our American friends call them, subdivisions. They have to be economically and physically subdivided . . .

I smiled and cut in, — And the old culture replaced by advertisers and marketeers telling people what to enjoy. Easy when they have no other ponts of reference, e.g. other people in the same economic and social circumstances. So through the media you have people in different economic and social circumstances telling them what to consume. The key is the increasing of choice through the process of subdivision you alluded to. The increasing experiencing of leisure and sport indirectly, has encouraged a decrease in real participation, which is direct communion. Therefore you have the replacement of one or two really decent experiences with loads and loads of crap things.

— Yes. But what you're doing is merely illustrating my point.

— Or you mine. Perhaps sport has colonised capitalism rather than the other way around. The rampant self-promotion of businessmen in the eighties is an example. They refer to themselves as main players and their vocabulary is a sporting one; whole new ball games, level playing fields, moving goalposts, and all that.

Dawson looked a bit shirty. — Yes Roy, but we have colonised sport and plundered its language . . .

— But perhaps the superiority of that terminology illustrates that sport and the sporting instinct are sovereign and that capitalism is just a branch of sport, a warped, inferior branch of sport, sport with money . . .

— In which case, then, it disproves your contention that the pursuit of profit, the only truth, cannot be self-actualising, if the accumulation of that wealth has sporting elements.

— No, it proves it. Capitalism has had to graft on sporting culture, the culture of games, in order to make the pursuit of money seem a worthwhile endeavour in itself.

— Look, Dawson began, exasperated, — you obviously don't understand the process of debate. Anyway, it's time to water the plants.

He snapped his fingers and began rubbing at his groin through his flannel trousers. The three girls took up position in front of him, squatting over some of the plant pots.

Unzipping his flies and removing a stumpy, semi-erect penis from his trousers and pants, Dawson masturbated himself hard as the girls discharged hot, steamy urine into the soil of the robust plants. He came powerfully, looking like a man going into cardiac seizure, gasping like

like

like somebody else. Just somebody else.

I REMEMBER   up the road tae the Ferry Boat.
                up   A guy had a fit
I REMEMBER   up   a fit at this party
           up   eftir my Uncle Jackie glassed him
Coming back up .   the boy was nearly fucked for good

I REMEMBER the party we had in the lounge bar of the Ferry Boat
public house, a couple of days before we set off for London on our
way to Johannesburg. They booked the top bar. Everyone was
there. We were allowed in; me, Kim, and Gerald with our lemonade,
Tony was allowed beer. It was brilliant.
    Mum serenaded John with 'Big Spender'.

> The minute you walked in the joint,
> I could tell ye were a man of distinction,
> A real big spender.
> Good lookin, so refined,
> Suppose you'd like to know what's goin on in ma mind.
>
> So let me get right to the point do-do,
> I don't pop my cork for every man I see.
> Hey big spender,
> Hey big spender,
> Spend a li-ril time with me.
>   do-do-do-do-do

— Still got the voice, Vet, Uncle Jackie said.

> So would ye like tae have fun, fun, fun,
> How's about a few laughs, laughs, laughs,
> Let me show you a good time,
> I could show you a good time . . .

I sat in the corner with Bernard and Kim, munching on our Coke
and crisps. I was enjoying myself. My Ma was a good singer,
especially with the band backing her, and I was drinking in the

applause she was getting. I felt like royalty. The only ghost at the feast was Elgin. It had been decided that he wasn't coming to South Africa with us.

He had got a place at the GORGIE VENTURE HOSTEL FOR EXCEPTIONAL YOUNG MEN. There, it was explained, he'd be properly looked after by specialist staff. My Gran would visit, so would my Uncle. and Auntie Jackie. (They were called John and Jacqueline respectively, but when they got together, neither had wanted to surrender their accustomed name of Jackie, so they were both known by that title.) One day, Dad had told us, we would send for Elgin. Kim was heartbroken, but I was relieved. To me it was one less embarrassment to have to worry about and I still had plenty.

I remember that night. It was good until Ma spoiled it by getting pished and acting like a slut. Dad punched this guy who'd been chatting her up. Uncle Jackie then glassed the guy's pal, and the polis came and broke up the party. Dad was done for causing a breach of the peace, which resulted in a minor fine for him, while Uncle Jackie got six months for malicious wounding. The guy went into shock following the attack and his heart stopped. He had to be revived by the ambulance crew. They were quite near at hand, coming from the Western General. Now they've shut down the accident and emergency there, so he probably would have died if it had happened today.

— Ah nivir fuckin well touched um! Jackie roared unconvincingly as blood spilled from the man's twitching body and he and Dad were huckled into the station which was right next door to the pub.

I remember walking home with Tony, Bernard, Kim and Ma down Pennywell Road. The night had ended in disaster, our last proper night in Scotland, and it was all Ma's fault. I hate to see women who should have dignity acting like sluts. I hate because it

No way.

Deeper

deeper. In fact I'm further up
get   because I can hear Patricia
can't   Devine telling me that
This is disturbing because I   I have a visitor. I'm so
conscious, I'm almost
awake. I fear waking up.
I fear it more than ever.

Patricia Devine's voice; cloying, but yet with a harshness to it. When we're alone together she tells me all about her life. I want to gather her up and protect her and love her because of all the hurt and disappointment she's suffered. I want to do this to make up for my . . . there's nothing to make up for. It was all Lexo's fault.

I've revised my image of what Patricia looks like. I see her now as slightly older than I first imagined, formerly very attractive but now a little gone to seed. Perhaps a bit over made-up and carrying a couple of extra pounds. She never married that surgeon. She seems a bit like the air hostess I saw on that plane to Johannesburg, the first time I'd flown. Bitter, having failed to marry the pilot. Travelling from one ugly airport building to another, from one systems built airport hotel to another. The glamour of flight my arse. What was she? The airways bike. Even at ten years old, I knew what she was like.

Patricia is similar. After the doctors, it's the male nurses, then perhaps the technicians. She'll be on the porters soon. Downwardly mobile sexually. You're simply Devine though, Patricia. If only I could brush your tears away. No. I know you too well now. I'd just be another source of hurt and betrayal to you. You scream desperation. It's going to take an exceptional piece of luck to arrest your decline, to break this sad cycle.

Why is it that I can only see people in the negative, only recognise them through their pain and their thwarted ambitions?

Because I'm a

— Yes Roy, it's your visitor friend from yesterday. She's back, Patricia says. Yes, we have company. I can tell by Patricia's tone. She has her in-company voice on; sugary, pretend intimate but in reality anything but.

The visitor does not respond. It is a she though. I can smell traces of her perfume. I think I can smell it. Maybe I'm just imagining I can smell it. Whatever, it's oddly familiar. Maybe I fucked her once.

I went through a phase when I fucked loads of women. This was after I discovered that all you had to do was be what they wanted for about twenty minutes. I suppose we're talking about a certain type of woman here. Each time you went through that bullshit act to get closer to them, you got further away from what you wanted to be. At the time it made me feel good about myself because I was younger. This shagging period represented a change in what I was doing before, which was not getting a ride and this was not a good place to be, for all sorts of reasons. Now it seems a very good place to be, but that was then. I doubt if a shag would make me feel good about myself now. I doubt if I'll ever fuck again. It wasnae about sex anyway, no at that time, what it was about was . . . oh fuck all this shite. Stick to the Stork; maybe if I could kill the Stork.

No.

I'll never fuck again.

I hear the nurses leave, their sensible shoes clicking on the floor. I'm alone with my lady friend. I wonder who she is?

— It's funny seeing you here, Roy. It's been a long time.

Who the fuck are you?

— I'm sorry to be the bearer of bad news. It's your old pal Dempsey. Alan Dempsey. He's no longer with us, Roy. I thought you'd like to know that.

WHO ARE YOU?

It's no good. I hear her steps start up and fade. She's leaving.

Dempsey. Ali Dempsey. Demps. Total Niddroid. One of the top boys. One top boy deid, another a cabbage. The Cabbage and Ribs.

The bearer of bad news departs but the sound of her leaving becomes the sound of someone else appearing.

— Yir gaun back tae yir right fuckin room, son. Ah goat they cunts telt. Ah sais, youse cunts git ma fuckin laddie back in that room or ah'll git ma fuckin shotgun right now n yis'll be needin mair fuckin beds thin ivir by the time ah've fuckin finished!

— The laddie disnae need tae hear that, John. It's aw sorted now, son. We goat them aw sorted oot.

— Too fuckin right we did. Eh hen? Telt these cunts the score.

— Yes, well you'll have to leave now, Mr and Mrs Strang. I need to get Roy prepared.

— Aye, wir gaun . . . bit naebody better try n move him ootay this room again . . . right! Cause like ah sais, ah'll be right doon here!

— Nobody's moving Roy, Mr Strang. Now let's just keep our voice down shall we, it might upset him.

Aye, right.

— Aye, well, so long as youse mind what ma man sais!

— Yes Mrs Strang.

— Tro Roy!

— Cheerio son. Mind son, we'll no lit thaim dae nowt tae ye. Like ah sais . . . cheerio Roy!

CHEERIO YA FUCKIN RADGE.

Nurse Beverley Norton is getting me sorted. Patricia must have finished her shift. Talk to me in your soft Coronation Street accent, Nurse Norton. Just like Dorie's . . . naw, no Dorothy's.

— We've got a visit from Dr Park this afternoon, haven't we, Roy loovey? Got to get you all nice and spruced up for Dr Park.

Fire ahead Nurse Norton. Never mind auld Strangy here. Roy Strang. Strangy fi Muirhoose. A vegetable now likes, but still a sound cunt. Still a top boy. Now Dempsey's wormfood though. The rest? Who the fuck kens. Two years ah've been here. Thir probably in Saughton, or worse, in some tenement or Gumley's, Wimpey, or Barratt box with a bird and brat checkin oot B&Q's wares. Sittin in front of the telly. Are they cabbages too? C'mon you cabbage. Not as much as me: a biodegradable piece of useless shit incapable of fulfilling its intended purpose in this life, just as incapable of passing on to the next one.

Thank fuck for a childhood in a large Scottish housing scheme; a wonderful apprenticeship for the boredom that this kind of semi-life entails. Pull the fuckin plug.

Wonder how Demps kicked it?

Thank fuck for Sandy Jamieson. Time
to
go
back
down
under
Bruce — — — — — —

— — — — — — — — — — It's all about good service, old Dawson explains
to us, wiping large remnants of a substantial starter from his face.

Sandy and I eagerly set to work on our hors-d'œuvre although we
both found that we were rather full after them.

— We haven't been *quite* so hungry today, Sandy said.

— I blame this confounded heat, I nodded, — but I could make a
meal of this homemade bread and butter alone!

Our food is served by a strange creature, the likes of which I had
never seen before. It was stunted and furtive, and although its
short-arsedness seemed to suggest a range of possibilities, it was too
dour looking to be a leprechaun, too ugly to be a pixie and too
clumsy to be an elf. Its malevolence seemed far in excess of what one
might expect from any self-respecting imp. Dawson informs us that
it is his faithful manservant, Diddy. Sandy tries to avoid making eye
contact with the dwarf valet as he ladles copious amounts of
vegetables onto Dawson's plate, a contrast, it has to be said, to the far
less liberal helpings he furnishes us with.

— Take Diddy here. He used to run this reserve. Now all he does
is skivvy. I had to dismiss him from a position of executive
authority. He was yesterday's man, incapable of taking us onto the
next phase. Is that not so, Diddy?

Dawson slowly enunciates the phrase *incapable of taking us onto the
next phase.*

— Yes, Mr Dawson, Diddy solemnly replies.

— And how do you feel to be serving my food now, Diddy?

— It's an honour and a privilege to serve Jambola Park PLC in any
way I can, Mr Dawson.

— Thank you, Diddy. Now please leave us. We have matters to
discuss: executive matters.

708

Diddy scuttled out the door.

Dawson reclined in his chair and let out a loud, appreciative belch.

— You see Roy, Diddy may have no class, but he possesses an important quality. Not really important any more in top execs, they can always be rewarded, but crucial in footsoldiers. I'm talking, of course, of loyalty. Good old Diddy; aye ready to serve the empire. Men like him have been rewarded by men like me ever since the British set foot in this godforsaken continent.

— The hun never sets, I smiled, and Dawson raised a lascivious eyebrow in fruity acknowledgement.

— And if I may say so, Diddy has been rewarded handsomely, Sandy ventured.

It was a remark which Dawson largely close to ignore. I kept forgetting that Sandy was once in the employ of 'Fatty' Dawson.

— Wonderful food, Lochart, I smiled.

— Yes, said Sandy, — especially after that simply *horrid* stuff we had in town.

— That *was* beastly, I agreed, — the chap in the bar made so much fuss about it as well. It's so difficult to get good service nowadays. You're lucky to have Diddy.

Dawson rubbed his swollen hands together and let his face take on a serious bearing. — You see Roy, humans have a wretched tendency to pledge devotion to insitutions rather than individuals. This can be problematic for people like myself who require loyalty in service. What happens, of course, is that one simply buys the institution. Of course one is changing this institution at the same time to suit one's business plans and, yes, many people do notice this. Fortunately, tribal loyalties are pretty well-honed and the fools can't help but to subscribe.

— Goodwill is one of the greatest assets an organisation can have, Sandy remarked.

— Tremendously difficult to quantify on the balance sheet though, Dawson smiled, directing his remark at me rather than Sandy. Sandy began rocking in his chair and letting out a low sound. — Mmmmm.

— So what does this mean, Lochart? What sort of a role do you perceive for Sandy and myself? I asked, impatient to discover where Dawson's game was leading us.

As you may know, he smirked, — I'm planning to take over a debt-ridden park which lies adjacent to us. I've made a reasonable offer, but I've been subjected to the predictable, tiresome cries of asset-stripping and child-molesting and so on and so forth. Kicking Lochart Dawson around is something of a thriving industry in these parts. Well, I've news for the loudmouths, I've never run away from anything.

— So where do our interests converge?

— I want the land they have. It's over two hundred square miles. With my smaller park joined to these resources, we could be in business. Big business. I'm offering opportunity, Roy. I'm offering vision. However, there will always be malcontents who choose to resist progress. The neighbouring park, Emerald Forest, is infested by the most vicious and unscrupulous predators/scavengers on this continent. I'm referring, of course, to your old friends . . .

— The Marabou Storks.

— I hear that there is one you're interested in? The leader?

— You hear correctly.

— I want to help you take him out. I'll put all my resources at your disposal.

— Well, we need a couple of pump-action shotguns, some maps . . . explosives . . .

— Anything! Dawson bounded across and shook my hand. — Well, as they say, let's kick ass, or rather, you chaps kick ass. I'm going to disappear for a while. It's, eh, the family; slightly jittery about all this. We also have a hostile media to contend with.

Dawson barked instructions to Diddy to kit us out, and we were off.

4 Leptoptilos Crumeniferus

The Marabou Stork is a predator. The Marabou Stork is also a scavenger. These qualities make it detested and despised by human beings. Humans are into animals whose qualities they covet, and hate ones whose characteristics they vainly like to feel are not at all 'human'. The world we live in is not run by cuddly, strong bears, graceful, sleek cats or loyal, friendly dogs. Marabou Storks run this place, and they are known to be nasty bastards. Yes, even the vulture does not get such a bad local press.

Fatty Dawson was sold on the concept of taking out the leader, creating a vacuum, and watching the birds turn on each other and tear each other apart in disarray. I knew that this would not happen. I knew that these birds were far more sophisticated and organised than Dawson gave them credit for. Dawson was from the west; he didn't understand these creatures. Another leader would swiftly emerge. You couldn't eradicate the Marabous, they were purely a product of their environment, and this scabrous environment totally supported them. The best you could hope for was to perhaps force them into a temporary migration. Nonetheless, I was happy to let both Dawson, and my guide Sandy, believe that the eradication of the leader was an appropriate strategy for ridding the Emerald Forest of the Marabou Stork.

For me it was personal. There was only one Stork I wanted, one of those beasts which had to die. I sipped some cool water from my canteen. My lips had dried in the heat. I removed a tube of Vaseline from my coat pocket to apply to them, just as Sandy emerged naked from the river, where he had been taking a dip to gain respite from the omnipresent heat.

He looked at me tensely, then glanced around at the deserted

711

wilderness. There was nothing and nobody about for miles. He
rolled his eyes   naw   he

– One could think of other uses for that, Roy, he smirked – – – – – – –
– – – – naw   didnae roll
                                  his eyes
                                        Sandy and I
                                              urnae like that it wis
jist mates muckin aboot – – – – DEEPER
                                    DEEPER
                                          DEEPER – – – he quickly got
into his clothes.

Sandy and I were well-kitted out for the task at hand. Tooled up
with rifles, shotguns, explosives and carrying absolute *stacks* of
provisions: jam, English Breakfast Tea, tins of beans, soup,
desserts, all that sort of stuff. Stuff that doesn't go off in this confounded heat.

I did, however, notice some reticence on Sandy's part concerning
what on the surface seemed to be a fairly straightforward task.

— What's your opinion of Johnny Stork, Sandy old man? I asked
him.

— They are evil incarnate, Roy. They have to be stamped out for
the good of the game, Sandy replied, ashen-faced.

— You don't have any concerns about us not being up to the task
do you, Sandy? I enquired.

                                  up – – – – time will tell.
— Time will tell, he said   up
grimly, time will tell. – – – – – – up

What the fuck is this?
  — But I think he's going to come out of it. There's definitely increased signs of brain activity.
I wouldn't be surprised if he could hear us. Take a look at this, Dr Goss . . .
  FUCK OFF!
The cunt wrenches open my eyelids and shines a torch into them.

Its beam shoots right down into my darkened lair and I skip into the shadows to avoid its light. Too quick for these cunts.

— Yes, we're definitely getting some sort of reaction. A very positive sign, says one of the doctors, I forget their names, they all sound the same to me.

— I don't think you're doing enough to help us, Roy. I don't think you're doing enough to get well, says the other. I'll call him Middle-class English Cunt One and the other Middle-class English Cunt Two in order to differentiate them.

— I think we have to increase the stimulus and the number of tests, says Middle-class English Cunt Two.

— Yes Dr Park, says Nurse Beverly Norton.

— Those tapes his family brought in. Keep them going, suggests Middle-class English Cunt One.

So I'm to be subjected to increased harassment, and my energies, which should be concentrated on getting me deeper, deeper into my world, my story, my hunt, now have to be diverted into keeping these fuck-wits out.

— Listen Roy. We're doing our best for you. You have to want to get better, says Middle-class English Cunt One, bending over me. I feel his rancid breath in my nostrils. Oh yes, just you keep that up ya cunt, because if I do come out the first thing ah'm gaunny fuckin well dae is tae rip yir fuckin queer English face apart wi ma chib . . . but fuck, naw man, naw . . . ah'm gettin too fuckin close tae the surface, cause ah feel masel at the top ay the ladders which run up the side ay the deep deep well, half-way down being my lair, further down still the beautiful blue skies of Africa, the world ah just drop into but now I'm right at the fuckin top, right at the top, pushing at the trapdoor and some shards of light are coming through . . .

I *feel* his rancid breath

DOWN

DEEPER

DEEPER — — — — — —

—Funny, I thought that there was something there for a bit . . . must just be my imagination. Anyway, let's move on. Thank you, Nurse.

Exit the bools-in-the-mooth cunts.

—Did you hear that, Roy! Two doctors today! Dr Park *and* Dr Goss. And they're pleased with you. You have to work a little bit harder though, lovey. I'm going to put on the nice tape that your mum and your brother made for you. That brother of yours, Tony, is it? He's a saucy one and no mistake. I think he's interested in some of our younger nurses. Anyway, here you are:

> The minute you walked in the joint,
>
> I could see ye were a man of distinction,
>
> A real big spender . . .

Thank you but no fuckin thank you Bev-ih-leey, chuck. Bring back Patricia Devine. Come back Patsy, Patsy De Cline, all is forgiven . . .

> Suppose you'd like to know what's goin on in ma mind.

DEEPER

        DEEPER

                DEEPER — — — — — — — — — — — —

— — — — — — — — — — Peace.

part two

The City
Of Gold

5 Into The City
Of Gold

Our first home in South Africa was a few rooms in Uncle Gordon's large house in the north-eastern suburbs of Johannesburg. Uncle Gordon was fond of saying that we were as 'far away from Kaffirtown (Soweto) as it was possible to get and still be in Jo'burg'.

Though I was just a kid, my impression of the city was of a drab, bleak modern place. It looked spectacular from the sky as we circled over it on our way to landing at Jan Smuts International Airport, named, John proudly told me, after a South African military man who was a big pal of Winston Churchill's. It was only when we saw it from the ground that I realised it was just another city and that they all looked better from the sky. Close up, downtown Johannesburg just looked like a large Muirhouse-in-the-sun to me. The old mine dumps provided a diminishing backdrop to the ugly skyscrapers, highways and bridges which had long replaced the shanty homes of the first gold pioneers who made the city. I was so disappointed as Ma had told me on the plane that it was called the City of Gold, and I had expected the streets to be literally paved with the stuff and the buildings composed of it.

Gordon's place in Kempton Park was certainly salubrious enough, but all there seemed to be at the end of his driveway was a tree-lined road leading to more houses and grounds. No kids played on the deserted streets, the place was dead. I just stayed in most of the time, or played in the garden, hanging around with Kim. It was okay, though: there were plenty of things to see around the house.

Gordon lived on his own with his black housekeeper, and it seemed bizarre that he should keep on a house of that size. It was probably just to show the world how much of a success he was, financially at any rate. Emotionally, life in the Republic had not been so rewarding for him. There had been a wife, but she had departed long ago, all traces of her obliterated. Nobody talked about her, the subject was taboo. I'd put the shits up Kim by telling her that Gordon had murdered her and buried her body in the grounds. This was plausible, given the way Gordon appeared. Straight away I clocked him as a true Strang: weird as fuck.

On one occasion I took my tormenting of Kim too far, and she freaked really badly, spilling the beans, resulting in me getting a good slapping from my Ma. As she belted me, I remembered Vet saying: — I'm only daein this cause if yir faither finds oot n he does it, ye'll ken aw aboot it. That was true as Kim was my Dad's favourite and teasing her always carried the extreme risk of incurring his wrath. While it was quite a healthy slapping, I took it with a sense of relief, recognising the truth in her words. She was actually doing me a favour and I sensed her heart wasn't in it; but unfortunately she was instinctively quite good at violence. She stopped when my nose started to bleed heavily. Though my ears rang for a few days I didn't even sulk or feel bad about her or Kim after. Everyone seemed lighter, happier. It was a good time.

I knew fuck all about politics at the time, but even I soon sussed that Uncle Gordon was what I suppose I'd now call an unreconstructed pro-apartheid white supremacist. He had come to South Africa about fifteen years previously. His story, which he was fond of telling anyone who'd listen (I heard it literally dozens of times that year) was that he and two of his pals were sitting in the Jubilee Cafe in Granton, thinking about what to do to with their lives. They thought of emigration to Canada, Australia or South Africa. They decided to take one each and Gordon arbitrarily picked SA. They were supposed to report back to the Jubilee in ten years' time, but they never showed up. The cafe had shut down anyway. — We were silly laddies, Gordon remarked, — but it was the best break I ever had.

Even at the time, as an eleven-year-old, I thought that his story was romanticised bullshit.

There was no doubt that Gordon had done well, at least materially, from the system. After taking a few menial but well-paid-compared-to-the-blacks-doing-the-same-thing sort of jobs, he set up a property management agency in Johannesburg. It took off, and he diversified into property development. By the time we arrived, Gordon had this large suburban home, a mansion, really, and a fair-sized timber farm out in the veld of the Eastern Transvaal, on the road to the Kruger National Park. He also had offices in Durban and Cape Town as well as property interests in Sun City.

I think the old man thought that he was just going to walk into a top job in Gordon's business. I can recall Gordon saying to him over breakfast, — Look John, I'll get you fixed up here. Don't worry about that. But I won't have you working with me. I'm a great believer in keeping business and family apart.

I remember this fairly vividly, because it resulted in an argument, and the recurrence of the tense atmosphere I was used to feeling at home and had naively thought that we had left behind in Scotland.

Kim started crying, and I recall putting my arm around her, displaying a tenderness I didn't really feel in order to try and shame my parents into stopping shouting. It proved completely ineffective. I sat with a sad, baleful expression watching the tears roll down my sister's large face. Vet's pus was pinched with tension and John and Gordon both shook visibly. This was the beginning of the end of my father's South African dream.

Dad eventually landed a job as a security guard in a supermarket at a shopping mall in a white working-class district a few miles away. Gordon assured him that it would just be a temporary measure; a first step on the ladder, as he put it. He got Ma a job, typing and filing at a city-centre office in a business run by a friend of his.

I was due to start at the Paul Kruger Memorial School with Kim in a couple of weeks' time. Bernard had enrolled at the Wilheim Kotze High, while Tony had found, again thanks to Gordon, a traineeship as a chef at a hotel in the city.

Before we started school, however, Kim and I were left at Gordon's with Valerie, the large African woman who was his housekeeper. She was very cheerful, always singing us Bantu songs. She had left her family to come and work here, sending the money back out to the place she came from. We quickly built up a relationship with her, as she was warm and friendly and made a fuss of us. This ended abruptly one day; Valerie suddenly acted cold, off-hand and distant, telling us to get out from under her feet. Kim was puzzled and saddened at this change, but I knew that Gordon had spoken to her.

Later on, my uncle, who had taken a particular interest in me, came home and took me aside, ushering me into the large garage which adjoined his house. — I don't want you getting friendly with Valerie. She's a servant. Always remember that; a servant and a Kaffir. She'll never be anything other than that. They seem friendly, they all do, that's the way with them. But never forget, as a race, they are murderers and thieves. It's in their blood.

He showed me a scrapbook he kept of cuttings from newspapers which highlighted what he referred to as 'terrorist atrocities'. I recollect being frightened and fascinated at the same time. I wanted to sit and read the scrapbook from cover to cover but Gordon snapped it shut and looked me in the eye. He placed a hand on my shoulder. His breath smelt sweet and rancid. — You see, Roy. I'm not saying Valerie's like that, she's a good person in many ways. But she needs to be kept in her place. Don't let all that cheerfulness fool you. She's got a chip on her shoulder. They all do. These people are different to you and I, Roy. They are one stage up from the baboons you'll see out in the veld. We had to take this land and show them how to develop it. We made this beautiful country, now they say they want it back. His eyes grew large, — Do you understand me?

— Aye, I nodded doubtfully. I was staring at the black hairs which grew out of his nostrils and wondering when we would get to see the baboons out in the veld.

— Think of it this way, Gordon continued, smugly inspired, — if a nasty, stupid, lazy, bad-smelling person had an old garden shed that was falling to pieces and wasn't being used, then you come along and say, I can make something of this shed. So you take on the responsibility of making the garden shed into something better. You put your heart and your soul into rebuilding it, and over the years, through your sweat and toil, it becomes a grand, beautiful palace.

Then the lazy, stupid person with the dirty-coloured skin which gives off a bad smell comes along and says: — That's my shed! I want it back! What do you say?

— Get lost! I said, eager to impress.

Gordon, a thin, spindly man, with tired, watery eyes, which could suddenly glow with violence, beamed and said: — That's right! You're a true Scotsman, Roy! A real Afrikaaner! He smiled at me. Gordon always seemed to hold you in his gaze a second or two more than felt comfortable. I didn't know what an Afrikaaner was, but it sounded alright; like a true Scotsman.

I started to look at Valerie in a different light. She had had babies in the bush, knowing that she couldn't feed them, because as Gordon had explained, blacks couldn't organise themselves, couldn't do anything right. Even the good ones needed white people to look after them, to provide them with jobs and homes. It was important not to get too friendly with them though, he told me, because they got excited and reverted back to a primitive state. — You remember your dog, Winston, wasn't it?

— Yes, I said. Winston Two was in kennels somewhere. He had to spend six months in quarantine before he could join us. I was not looking forward to his reappearance.

— Remember you got him all excited?

— Yes.

— What happened?

— He bit me.

Of course, Winston did more than just bite me, he practically took my leg off. Even now, three years later, after skin grafts and intensive physio, my limp was still apparent.

Gordon looked at me intensely, – Kaffirs are like that. Get them excited, they're liable to turn around and   up   – You're very
bite you! He snapped jokingly, tickling me with up   bony, Roy, what
                                                              are you? I'll bet
his long fingers – – – – – – – coming   up   you've always been
up – – – – – – – – – – – – – up up up   nice and slim though.
You could do with some meat on these bones, Roy Strang. We're going to have to make sure you eat. That's what we're going to have to do. Yes we are.

Leave ays alane ya fuckin daft cow

DEEPER

       DEEPER

              DEEPER – – – – We're driving back out through the shantytown and heading towards Lake Torto in an attempt to pick up the trail of the Stork.

Sandy was recounting a tale from his lion-hunting days: — I recall one little girl running through the village crying: 'Simba mamma wae!', which means, roughly: 'A lion has one's mother', and sure enough, this beast had seized the child's mother by the thigh and bitten the poor woman through the neck. On hearing our cries, it had dropped its kill and made off into the long grass. I headed after it, making speedy progress through the foliage in time to see the brute entering a thicket on the other side of an open range. Taking a steady aim, I fired, the bullet striking the beast and rolling him over. The blighter rose instantly, however, and unfortunately my shot with the second barrel wasn't so keen; I completely missed him. Crossing the clearing, I heard a growling challenge. Imagining that the brute was severely wounded and would before long succumb to the effect of the bullet I'd dispatched into him, I considered that discretion was the better part of valour and thought it prudent to retrace my steps for about thirty-five yards and simply await developments.

— Crikey, I said, enjoying the scent of eucalyptus in my nostrils, — What happened?

— Well, after a lapse of about an hour I became a tad restless and decided the time was ripe to explore the bush. Of course, I fully expected to find the blighter dead. All was silent, so I cautiously entered the dense undergrowth and began to follow his trail. He had clearly lost a considerable amount of blood and appeared to be limping badly. After a few yards of progress I could discern the tawny form of the lion, crouching completely motionless, head between paws, eyes glinting in the shade and staring steadily at me; but the thing was, the bugger was only about ten blasted yards away!

— Gosh . . .

— Well, I raised the bloody rifle pretty damn sharply, but without giving me time to aim and fire the bloody brute somewhat unsportingly charged at me, roaring savagely. I promptly let him have it, the bullet striking the left side of his head and smashing his shoulder. My third shot knocked him down and I thought; that should be *quantum sufficit*, but I'll be blowed if the bugger wasn't straight up again and coming on as strongly as ever!

— Bloody hell, Sandy, what did you do?

— It wasn't what *I* did, old man. I was rather fortunate that Tanu, a stout-hearted native from the village, had followed me, and the brave chap raised his spear and drove it with all his might into the brute's shoulder. The lion seized my courageous ally, though this gave me time to reload and I took up position and furnished the brute with the contents of my second barrel. Another shot finished him. God, I remember the celebrations in the village. They were overjoyed at the news of the killer lion's demise. They fashioned garments from its hide and amulets from its bones and we indulged in some pretty damn prodigious beer-drinking that evening!

— How was the native chap?

— Tanu . . . dear Tanu . . . unfortunately the poor blighter didn't survive the mauling, Sandy said, tears welling up in his eyes.

I let my hand fall onto his knee and gave it a squeeze.

— A fucking brave chap, Sandy sniffed.

We drove down the dusty road in silence for a while. Then, as we cruised along the track that straddled the west side of Lake Torto, I spotted someone. — Look Sandy! It's that young lad, from the football game.

— Yes, a funny little creature! Sandy smiled.

We stopped the jeep alongside him.

— Lift? I asked. — Ride? You like ride?

He looked suspiciously at us.

— What's Bantu for 'ride', Sandy? I turned to my companion. Sandy seemed different. This heat, it was making me hallucinate . . . his face looked a scaly reptilian green.

— I've dem well forgotten all the bloody fucking shitey cunt radge Bantu I ever cunting well learned! Sandy groaned, punching the jeep's body in exasperation.

I'm losing it. Concentrate.

— Never mind, Sandy, I said, turning back to our ragged young friend. — Ride? Brm! Brm! It's alright! We won't hurt you! Get into the jeep!

For some reason Sandy was rummaging through the medical supplies. A forked tongue darted out his head as he lisped in a strange voice: — Come and share some lemonade with us, young fellow. You must be *absolutely* parched!

The little urchin's face lit up in a delightful smile as he eyed the bottle of lemonade, and I thought that he was going to climb into the jeep.

— C'moan little fellow, we'll have some fun! Sandy said. Then he went, — Ye want a fuckin ride ya wee cunt, ah'll gie ye a fuckin ride awright . . .

No no . . . it wisnae like that, Sandy n me urnae like that . . .

The native boy turned on his heels and ran away. Sandy looked distraught.

— Never mind, Sandy, I smiled, — It's just the way they're brought up.

— Yes Roy, he beamed largely, — and anyway, it's just simply heavenly being on our own.

— Tell me another one of your lion adventures, I requested.

Sandy thought about this for a while, then said, — Oh, no Mr Strang. Methinks it's time for one of your shark hunting tales.

— Hmmm, I considered, — did I ever tell you about the spot of bother I got into with Johnny Shark down in Natal province?

— I don't believe you did.

— Well, I was down in Natal investigating attacks on local divers. Some suspected that one of our old friends the Great White, or at least a Tiger shark, was responsible. For some reason, I had my doubts; the bite marks on the survivors' legs seemed inconsistent. Those doubts were confirmed with a vengeance when I was diving alone near the scene of these attacks. I found myself confronted by *Carcharhinus longimanus*.

— The Oceanic White-tip shark, Sandy gasped.

— You know your sharks, Sandy. Anyway, this brute was circling around me. It must have been in excess of three metres long.

The Oceanic White-tip is very aggressive. This was the shark responsible for the slaughter of survivors of the *Nova Scotia*, when that ship sank off the Natal coast. In a similar scenario to your little encounter with the lion, this bugger came twisting towards me, just as I was about to let fly with the explosive harpoon.

— Oh my God, Sandy said, his eyes widening.

— Before I could react, the beast had fastened onto my leg. I felt no pain, however, and I took my knife and thrust it into the creature's snout. This caused the beast to loosen its grip. I quickly jammed my harpoon gun into his jaws to prevent them from closing again on my leg, then I prised my wounded limb off the monster's bed of teeth. The creature began thrashing around, trying to get the explosive gun from its mouth but, fortunately for me, only managed to detonate the device, blowing its own face to pieces. I still have a little memento from that brute . . . I showed Sandy the scars on my leg.

— Gosh, he said.

We drove on, swapping tales, until night settled around the lake. We could hear the trumpeting noises the flamingos made as we drove along the track, our headlights cutting through the darkness. We were growing very tired. Somewhat fortuitously at that point, our maps indicated that there was a hut nearby and we managed to locate it fairly easily.

With our spirits lifted, we found that we were not too weary to conduct a thorough examination of our new abode. The building was constructed on high stilts and it looked out from deep in the forest down a slope over the still lake. I gleefully anticipated the morning appearance of the rising sun which would shine straight into our hut from above the lavish green hills.

Sandy exclaimed in unbounded delight as he opened cupboard after cupboard. — Towels! Cutlery and crockery! Bedding! And look, in the refrigerator: bottles of pop!

— We could light the stove to heat the room up, I suggested, pointing to the old stove in the middle of the room. It seemed as if the hut, which was really more like a small lodge, hadn't been occupied in ages.

– No, we don't need to, Sandy said, – not the way we're facing. That sun will be simply pouring in before too long! If it gets cold we could always wrap ourselves up in one sleeping up – right up the bag. It was a practice I indulged in with up fuckin erse man. the native boys, in order to up Dirty fuckin cow that she wis, Roy, tellin ye. preserve heat – – – – – – – – coming up Thing is, ah'm no even that bothered if Hannah finds oot.

Ah mean, she kens ah've been playin away fi home, but wi her sister . . . well, ah suppose that's different right enough. It's just that she'd try n stoap ays fi seein the bairns Roy, you dinnae ken how spiteful that cunt is . . . ah fuckin gied her it tight the other day thair, telt a few home truths . . . here, ah bet if ye did wake up you'd have some stories to tell though Roy, eh? Mind you, might no be that bad. Gittin a bed bath fi the nurses everday. Ah'd be up fir that. Thir's a couple in here ah'd fuckin ride in a minute man, ah'm tellin ye . . .

Tony. You're visiting me. Fuck. This is a rare treat

— The thing is, her sister, she's gantin oan it . . .

The Big Ride

Shut up

— . . . bangs like a fuckin shitehoose door in a gale, ah'm tellin ye . . .

SHUT UP

— . . . thir aw the same, though, these daft cunts . . . fill their heids fill ay shite n they cannae wait tae whip thir fuckin keks oaf . . .

SHUT THE FUCK UP YA SICK MISOGYNISTIC WOP CUNT IT'S AFRICA AH WANT TAE THINK ABOOT

DEEPER

DEEPER – – – – – – I'm out of range of that crazy spic clown's rantings, but I can't get deep enough to hunt the Stork. I'm deep enough to remember, though.

I remember.

After Uncle Gordon's lecture, I avoided Valerie. I now looked upon her with a mixture of fear and contempt. I quickly put Kim in the picture about her and we kept out of her way, occasionally playing some mean tricks on her to ingratiate ourselves with Gordon; hiding stuff in different cupboards and that sort of thing, which caused her a great deal of distress. We made up nasty songs with words like 'coon' and 'Kaffir' and 'nigger' in them and sang them lustily around the house. Dad and Gordon would laugh approvingly at us.

I ingratiated myself with Gordon successfully; I ingratiated myself too much. Since coming to South Africa, all I had wanted was to get to see some of the wildlife I had read about in my books. One day Gordon came home and took me out with him for a drive into the bush to show me some animals. I was excited, as we had two sets of binoculars and had packed a large picnic. It was hot and I drank a lot of Coca-Cola. Due to this, and my excitement, I got sore guts and had bad trapped wind. I was rubbing my stomach, it was agony. Gordon pulled over by the side of the road and told me to lie down flat on the back seat. He started rubbing my stomach, feeling me, then working his hand slowly inside my shorts and down over my genitals. I just gave a nervous giggle. Part of me didn't really believe that this was happening. Then I felt a diseased spasm wrench through me and I began to tense up under his touch.

— It's alright, it's all connected up, he smiled, — the stomach, the bladder . . . I know what's wrong here.

Then he opened my trousers and told me that I was a good boy while he started stroking my cock, masturbating himself with his other hand.

His face reddened and his eyes glowed strangely, yet appeared unfocused as he seemed to struggle for breath. Then his body jerked before relaxing and a sharpened concern came into his eyes. He spent a few minutes massaging my stomach again, until I farted and burped a couple of times.

This incident stayed in my mind, but the funny thing was that we had a great day out after that. I filled six pages of my notebook with what we'd seen: a Black and white colobus, a Side-striped jackal, a Clawless otter (in a stream by the forest) a Black-tipped mongoose, a porcupine and an African hare on the mammals front, while in terms of birds it was really fuckin ace: European grey wagtail, African marsh owl, Golden-rumped tinkerbird, Olive thrush, doves of the Pink-breasted and Red-eyed variety, African snipe (which might have been a Jack snipe, I couldn't be one hundred per cent sure) and a Steppe buzzard.

I couldn't wait for my next trip, though this anticipation was tainted with a sense of unease and reservation as Gordon's abuse of me continued. It sometimes took place on drives, but often in the garage when he would come home from work during the day on some flimsy pretext. The funny thing was that it didn't really feel like abuse at the time, it felt mildly funny and amusing watching Gordon making a drooling tit of himself over me. I felt a sense of power, a sense of attractiveness, and a sense of affirmation that I hadn't previously experienced, during those sessions in the garage.

I used that power by extorting gifts from Gordon, my most lavish being an expensive telescope. In order to appear even-handed and avoid drawing suspicion, he had to sort out Tony, Bernard and Kim with costly gifts as well. John and Vet, feeling inadequate and jealous, with their meagre salaries, said that he was spoiling us and that caused a bit more aggro.

I loved South Africa. Even when we moved into our own place, a few miles away from Gordon's in a poorer area, we still had a big house with a back and front garden, and I had my own room. Through blackmail I had built up a huge library of nature books, mainly relating to African wildlife. John and I became big pals at this time. Our mutual interest in the natural world and animals flowered into an obsession. All our free time was spent in natural history museums, the zoo or local game reserves; or, chauffeured by Gordon, just driving out of the suburbs into the veld, trying to see some of the animals we'd identified from the books. The zoo was disappointing; the animals looked plastic and drugged. There was something sad and broken about them. I had to pretend to be enthusiastic as the zoo trips meant a lot to the old man; because the zoo was served by public transport, it was the only place he could take me on his own. He was planning to take driving lessons. Although sightings in the parks and bush were more irregular, they were more exciting.

Often Gordon engineered trips so
that Dad was working and we
could be alone together.
This was my life in the City – – – of

fingah . . . the man

Gold   with the midas touch,

A spider's touch.

SWITCH THAT SHITE OAF

Such a cold finger,

Beckons you . . . to enter his web of sin,

But don't go in . . .

The Garage.

— Time for a bedbath, Roy.

DEEPER

DEEPER – – – – – – Bernard and Kim showed little
interest in wildlife. When Gordon asked Tony if he'd like to come
along, Tony told him, — The birds I'm into are of the two-legged
rather than the winged variety. He was still shagging everything in
sight; usually the women who worked or resided in his hotel.

Gordon took us on the Blue Train to Bloemfontein down in the
Orange Free State. We were going to the zoo there to see the famous
Liger, the beast that was a cross between an African lion and a
Bengali tigress. I felt disappointed, then sad, when I saw this creature
in its enclosure. To me it seemed a misfit, a freak, something that
should never have been, would never have been but for human
intervention. I felt sorry for it. The most enjoyable part of that day
had been the journey. I had the best ice-cream I've ever eaten on the
train down, which was a really luxurious vehicle: ten times better
than any crap British shite. To me, everything in South Africa was
ten times, naw, one hundred times better than anything in fuckin
Scotland.

The most memorable trip, though, was a family outing organised
by Gordon to the Kruger National Park in Eastern Transvaal.
We drove out to Gordon's timber farm, stayed at his lodge for

a few days, then journeyed out towards the park, approaching it from the more rugged north-eastern end, which backed onto the Mozambique border.

At the time the security forces were advising people travelling in the area to take care. We were continually being stopped by uniformed police. Gordon explained that it was all due to terrorist activity. He used the term 'terrorist' freely. The terrorists seemed to get around, on the telly, in Gordon's scrapbooks, in the conversations he had with his friends at the *braais*. When I asked what a terrorist was, his face took on a sharp, intense bearing and he said: — A terrorist is a nasty piece of scum; a jealous, warped, evil, murdering immoral shitbag!

I was still no wiser as to what a terrorist actually was.

The Kruger was brilliant. I saw some lions stalking wildebeest and zebra, but did not see any make a kill. Some cheetahs had got hold of a baby wildebeest but got little from it before two lions chased them away. Kim gret at the baby wildebeest getting wasted, and Vet agreed that it was a shame.

— Si law ay the wild bit, Kim, Dad explained, putting his arm around her, — like ah sais, the law ay the wild.

Gordon gave me a matey wink and raised his eyebrows as if to say that lassies were daft, no like us guys.

It was a great time, really exciting, and the lodge we stayed in was luxurious.

The only thing which disturbed me was seeing a group of ugly birds waddling into a flamingo colony and scattering the beautiful pink creatures across the waters of a small lake. They just fled in sheer panic. I had never seen anything as horrible looking as those predators. They were like bent-over beggar-demons, their large beaks gave them a laughing look totally at odds with their dead eyes. I saw one of them trying to swallow a flamingo's head. It was a sick sight. The severed head of one large bird in the jaws of another.

— That's the Marabou Stork, my Dad sang triumphantly, drinking in the carnage through his binoculars, — like ah sais, the Marabou Stork. Bad bastards thaim, eh, but it's nature like.

That night I had my first Marabou Stork nightmare.

6 Huckled In The City Of Gold

South Africa was a sort of paradise to me. Funnily enough, I felt at home there; it was as if it was the place I was really meant to be, rather than shitey Scotland. When I thought back to Edinburgh I recollected it as a dirty, cold, wet, run-down slum; a city of dull, black tenements and crass, concrete housing schemes which were populated by scruffs, but the town still somehow being run by snobs for snobs.

I was glad when we moved away from Gordon's to our own place, but I missed what I had grown to think of as my refuge. Part of Gordon's house was built on top of an old well, and in the basement of the garage there was access to the well, via a trapdoor. The well had a set of metal rungs going down into it, and although I was told to keep away, I used to climb down there and just hang from the rungs, suspended in semi-darkness. I'd hear Gordon sneaking around above, looking for me to touch me up. The things he wanted to do were getting heavier and I was getting more scared. Gordon said if I told anyone I would get the blame; John, my Dad, would believe him and not me. I instinctively knew that this was true. So whenever I went into the garage I'd hide in the well.

The well wasn't very deep, perhaps about twenty foot at the most. Gordon claimed that it was not a well, but was part of an old access point to mineworkings where the prospectors who built the city dug for their gold. At the time, I took this with a pinch of salt, but given Johannesburg's history, it was possible. The bottom of the well seemed solid and blocked with rubble, though I could never bring myself to go right to the foot of it and stand free of the rungs. I would just sit in my semi-darkened lair, enjoy the peace and fantasise. I was sorry when I had to leave the well, as glad as I was to be getting away from Uncle Gordon.

As I said, I loved South Africa. For Dad, though, the honeymoon never lasted. He was fucked off with his security job. It wasn't quite what he had envisaged. Moreover, the social life was getting to him. He was fed up with the characterless suburban roadhouses or the *braais* in gardens, parks and campsites where South Africans did their serious drinking. He was craving the traditional social vice of the lowland Scot; a good, old-fashioned pub crawl in an urban city-centre environment. Gordon had tried to get him into South African culture. My uncle had become a rugby enthusiast and he took us along to a few games at Ellis Park to try to get us interested. — Poofs game, John would snort, — but ah suppose it's something tae dae. He would leave us and spend most of his time at the stadium bars. I hated rugby even more than football. So did John and nothing less than a good piss-up would suit him.

It was a drinking session in downtown Johannesburg that led to us leaving South Africa and returning to Scotland.

At the time I had just settled into the Paul Kruger Memorial. The kids were pretty thick, seeming to me to be even farther behind than at my old school, which was according to all reports, one of the crappest in Scotland, which also meant Europe. The only drag was having to wear a school uniform. I suppose I didn't mind too much, as I could wear long flannels rather than shorts. I was self-conscious of the scars on my legs.

On my first day at the school I was introduced as a 'new boy from Scotland' and shown the map of South Africa. My first piece of homework was to memorise the provinces and their capitals:

CAPE OF GOOD HOPE   CAPE TOWN
NATAL   PIETERMARITZBURG
ORANGE FREE STATE   BLOEMFONTEIN
TRANSVAAL   PRETORIA

One major difference was that the kids here, though easily as thick, were much more docile and well-behaved. Actually doing schoolwork was acceptable. The teachers were okay; my interest in nature and wildlife was positively encouraged. They were nice to me, my accent mattered less to the teachers in South Africa than it had done to those in my native city. Once I got over this culture shock, I found myself relishing the acquisition of knowledge. Schoolwork became interesting and I lost my urge to escape into the Silver Surfer and my other comic-book fantasies. I couldn't learn enough about things. I had, for the first time, ambition of a sort. Before, when people had asked me what I wanted to be, I would have just shrugged; I might have said a soldier, just because it seemed good fun shooting at people, like just a daft kid's thing. Now I was into being a zoologist. On my eleventh birthday I could see possibilities: good grades here, followed by the same at high school, a university place at Witwatesrand or Pretoria or Rand Afrikaans studying zoology or biology, then some field work, post-grad stuff, and there I'd be. I saw a career path.

The old man's piss-up blew that away. It showed me that I'd been a daft cunt to ever have had those dreams.

I recall the day it started. It was a clear Thursday afternoon and looking north-west you could see the Magaliesberg mountain range which towered over the city. I was out in the garden kicking a ball about with my mate Curtis. I was getting hot but I hadn't changed out of my school uniform. I went to do that, then I was going to Curtis's house for tea. He often came to ours, but I was less embarrassed by Mum and Dad now. They seemed happier and lighter out here, and strangely, their eccentricities were more tolerated as there was quite a mix of different white kids in our neighbourhood, likesay Greek and that, and some whose parents spoke no English. Anyway, I nipped in to get changed and I overheard my Ma and Dad talking.

The old man's restlessness was apparent. He would still circle the television pages for our viewing, only now they were the listings of the *Johannesburg Star*. — Fuckin thirty-six rand a year fir this shite, he moaned bitterly that early evening. The television licence fee had gone up. — It's no that, Vet, he implored my Ma, who had said nothing, — it's no thit ah grudge it. It's jist thit wi dinnae want tae become slaves tae the telly aw the time.

— Switch it oaf well, my Ma said.

— Naw . . . naw . . . that's no the point ah'm tryin tae make, Vet. Yir misunderstandin the point ah'm trying tae make. Like ah sais, it's no the telly thit's wrong; it's jist thit thir's nowt else. Like, ah mean tae say Vet, they fuckin braais, or whatever the fuck thir called, thir awright bit thir no ma cup ay tea, ken? Whit ah'm tryin tae say Vet, is thit ye cannae even git oot fir a fuckin pint, ken whit ah mean? Thir's no like a local; nae fuckin pub fir miles, jist that fuckin daft wee place roond at the Mall. Even Muirhoose hud a fuckin pub! Likesay in the toon though but Vet, thir's tons ay pubs doon in the city. Ah wis thinkin thit ah might just go doon thair the morn eftir work; git a couple ay pints wi Gordon, doon in the city likes. Like ah sais, a couple ay pints.

— Well, go oot fir a pint then, Vet snapped, angry at being distracted from her magazine.

— Mibbee ah'll just dae that well, mibbee jist dae that the morn. Fae work like, ken?

I saw a contented smile point his face as he sat behind the *Star*.

So the next day Dad finished his shift, and instead of coming home, went downtown to meet Gordon in his office, after a visit to the boxing museum at Hanson and Kerk Street. After Gordon finished they went out drinking in bars around his office in the Main Street/Denvers Street area. Gordon had soon had enough, and took a taxi home, imploring John to do the same. By this time, though, the old man had a couple of guys from Liverpool in tow and was into a real night on the pish.

Johannesburg's city centre is a drab, functional business area; totally deserted after six o'clock in the evening. Gordon kept telling John that it wasn't safe to wander the streets after dark, presumably in case he ran into someone like himself. My Dad's brother always talked about how lawless the city centre was at night; he went on and on about the gangs of black workies from rival tribes who lived in the hostels and ran amok in the city centre after dark, mugging and beating up each other and anyone else who crossed their path. All this did was set the old man off in a belligerent, aggressive frame of mind. If any cunt wanted trouble, he'd be game. After Gordon told us that John had said to him: — Whin the Luftwaffe wir bombin London, the big brass telt Churchill tae stey safely indoors instead ay gaun fir a walk in the park. Churchill jist turns roond n goes: Aye, right. Whin ah wis a wee laddie the nurse couldnae stoap ehs fae walkin in the park. Now thit ah'm a growin man, that wee cunt sure as fuck isnae. Ah rest ma case, my father had said smugly.

Anyway, John and the scouse guys staggered up Delvers towards Joubert Park. They had a great night out and drunkenly swapped phone numbers, arranging to do it all over again. John lurched into a cab that was parked outside one of the big hotels.

What happened next was contentious. John's version of the story, which I'm inclined to believe, because for all his faults the old man wasn't a bullshitter, he didn't have the imagination for one thing, was that he fell asleep in a taxi. When he woke up, they were parked in a disused layby in Germiston, with the driver rifling through his pockets. Now Germiston is a busy railway junction district to the south-east of the city which is dominated by the largest gold refinery in the world. We lived on the road out to Kempton Park, which is north of the city centre.

John assaulted the taxi driver with such force and vigour that several of the man's teeth were produced, in a plastic bag, by the prosecution in the courtroom, as a theatrical piece of evidence. The taxi driver claimed that he was trying to get this obnoxious drunk who was giving him the run-around out of his car, when he was violently assaulted. John got sentenced to six months' imprisonment. It seems that he was made an example of by the authorities, anxious to clamp down on violence in downtown Johannesburg.

Vet was well fucked up. I remember her at that time; chain-smoking and drinking cups of tarry coffee with around eight sugars in it. We left our new home in northern Johannesburg and stayed briefly at Gordon's before making plans to return to Scotland. John would follow once he'd served out his sentence. Kim and I were devastated at the prospect of going back. We'd settled. I could see myself right back in the same life, the same school, the same scheme.

I was gloomy in my resignation, only a sick anxiety brought on by the dread of leaving occasionally alleviating my depression. Edinburgh to me represented serfdom. I realised that it was exactly the same situation as Johannesburg; the only difference was that the Kaffirs were white and called schemies or draftpaks. Back in Edinburgh, we would be Kaffirs; condemned to live out our lives in townships like Muirhouse or So-Wester-Hailes-To or Niddrie, self-contained camps with fuck all in them, miles fae the toon. Brought in tae dae the crap jobs that nae other cunt wanted tae dae, then hassled by the polis if we hung around at night in groups. Edinburgh had the same politics as Johannesburg: it had the same politics as any city. Only we were on the other side. I detested the thought of going back to all that shite.

Bernard had hated South Africa from the start and couldn't wait to get home. Tony was ambivalent. He'd been shagging a few birds, but wanted to see his old mates. Being older, though, he had a vibe, a vibe about all the political trouble which we never really knew much about.

Maybe in retrospect I could say that there was a strange mood amongst the whites my folks socialised with. It's just possible, though, that I'm inventing it with the benefit of hindsight. Did everybody really seem a wee bit edgy? Probably. The only real talk I remember was of what people (and I do remember there were some dodgy looking cunts Gordon hung around with) referred to as the selling out of Rhodesia, which was now called Zimbabwe-Rhodesia. That and the constant references to terrorists. Gordon spoke Afrikaans and preferred the Afrikaans papers like *Die Transvaler* and *Die Vaderland* to the *Rand Daily Mail* and the *Johannesburg Star*. He once took us to the Voortrekker Monument which dominates the southern approaches to Pretoria and rabbited on about the great trek. This seemed to affect him in the same way Churchill's wartime speeches did my Dad.

Once Gordon took us to the Museum of The Republick Van Suid-Afrika. It was an interesting place to visit. The information boards in the museum mirrored what I'd read in my school textbooks:

The white citizens of the Union are mostly descendants
of early Dutch and British settlers, with smaller
admixtures of French, German and other West-
European peoples. The White man originally came to
South Africa as a soldier, farmer, trader, missionary and
general pioneer, and owing to his superior education and
his long background of civilisation he was able to
provide the necessary leadership, expertise, technical
skill and finance among races who were for the most part
little removed from barbarism.

South Africa is the only country in the world where a
dominant community has followed a definite policy of
maintaining the purity of its race in the midst of
overwhelming numbers of non-European inhabitants—
in most not still administered as colonies or protectorates
either the non-whites have been exterminated or there
has been some form of assimilation, resulting in a more
or less coloured population. Indeed, far from the
extermination of non-whites, the advent of the European
in South Africa has meant that whole native
communities have been saved from exterminating each
other. It is not generally realised that scarcely a century
ago Chaka, chief of the Zulus, destroyed 300 tribes and
wiped out thousands upon thousands of his fellows.

Gradually, however, the remnants of the tribes which
survived the internecine wars were able to settle down to
a peaceful, rural way of life under the protection and with
the assistance of the white man. In the traditional
homelands, which cover an extent about as large as
England and Wales together, nearly one-half of the
Bantu live and lead a simple pastoral life as their ancestors
did through the centuries before them — happy,
picturesque people living the most carefree existence
imaginable.

Thus we find that here on the southern tip of the
African continent, amidst overwhelming numbers of
non-European inhabitants, a small white population has
made its home and is founding a new nation, with a way
of life and an outlook of its own. It is due to the initiative
of these people, to their knowledge and skill that South
Africa has become the most advanced state on the
African continent, and, as sure as night follows day, they

> will evolve a form of co-existence which will allow every
> race to live its full life and to contribute, in accordance
> with its own abilities, to the welfare of the country.

After the museum we went back to Gordon's where he was having a barbecue with some of his friends. There were always *braais* at Gordon's. Some men were sitting in his lounge, watching the television which showed riot police breaking up a black demonstration. They were cheering on the riot police. One tall, blonde woman who looked like an actress came through and smiled at me. Then she turned to a fat guy with a beard and said, — I see that the Kaffirs are taking a dem good beating.

— They shid ten the ficking gihns en those apes, he snarled, slugging from a bottle of beer and belching. There was such a stupid malevolence on his face that I instinctively felt that, despite what the school, the Government and my family were telling me, that something wasn't quite right. I stopped to listen as the news bulletin changed to the Rhodesian situation.

— Botha's fucking sold out our people in Rhodesia, Gordon fumed.

— Yes, but it's tactical, Gordon, one man smiled, — it's buying us favours in the world community. God knows, we may soon need it.

— You're talking like a flaming red, Johan, the fat guy with the beard snapped, — we should be standing by our own. They let twelve thousand ficking terrist skim walk into kemps with their weapons for this bastard ceasefire. I say it's a gelden opportunity to shoot the ficking lit of them. Just turn the ficking guns on those Zanu so-called Patriotic Front red terrist animals and blow them to pieces just like they do to decent bloody farmers.

Gordon sat with tears welling up in his eyes as he watched the pictures of the Patriotic Front guerrillas march into the camps and lay down their weapons, the condition for the ceasefire and the commencement of the free elections. — I can't believe it. I can't believe that they would do it. P. W. Botha. Maggie Thatcher. Fucking whore! Fucking treacherous fucking stupid communist fucking whore!

It was a good thing that John was in the nick at this point. I remember the last time Gordon had ranted about Thatcher's treachery, John had been standing leaning against the patio doors. He stiffened up and turned around. — Hi! C'moan Gordon, it's no Maggie Thatcher's fault. The best fuckin leader Britain's hud . . . the best peacetime leader. Like ah sais, the best. She pit the fuckin unions in thair place right enough. Jist gittin bad advice, fae they cunts in the civil service n that. That's whit it wid be! Dinnae fuckin slag off some cunt ye ken nowt aboot! Like ah sais, you dinnae ken whit she did fir Britain!

— I know she's sold Rhodesia down the fucking river, Gordon said weakly, obviously a little intimidated.

There was loads of political talk, but I suppose that apart from the odd vibe of discomfort, I thought it was just   up – Just turning this up,
what boring auld cunts spraffed about.   up   Roy.
At that time ah didnae really unders – – – up

> So would ye like tae have fun, fun, fun,
> How's about a few laughs, laughs, laughs,
> I could show you a good time . . .

FUCK OFF AND TURN THAT SHITE OFF . . .

DEEPER
DEEPER
DEEPER – – – – – and although the eggs were cooked to perfection and the toast was crisp and the coffee strong, rich and aromatic, there was something strangely amiss that morning we left the hut.

It was the silence. I couldn't hear the flamingos on the lake. I picked up the binos. Nothing.

— Where are they, Sandy?

— This is absolutely puzzling. I'd like to take a closer look.

— We drove down to the shore of the lake. There was immediate evidence of carnage. I saw pieces of dead birds. Then we heard a rustling and some squawking and noted some vultures still chewing at a flamingo carcass. Sandy raised the rifle and fired a shot at them. One toppled, and the others flapped their wings and waddled away. They moved back quickly, the slain vulture joining the flamingo in providing a feast for the other birds.

— Vultures are only cannabalistic under extreme conditions, Sandy observed. — Those poor blighters must be starving.

At that point I saw a pink, swan-like head and neck which had been severed from a body. — Our flamingo colony has been routed, I declared.

— Yes . . . by the Marabou Stork, Sandy nodded sagely.

– Maybe we should take our clothes   nowt. What the fuck off and go for a little dip, I suggested   suggest   wis ah oan . . . naw naw that wisnae it – – –   fuckin   aboot? – – – coming up – – – – – ah didnae

                                                                    Politics. That's what.

The politics of South Africa. Shite, that's what that was to me. It caught up with us, though, caught up with us all in an even bigger way about a fortnight before we were due to head back to Scotland. I was out with Uncle Gordon at his timber farm in the Eastern Transvaal. When we stopped the jeep, he looked around over that sweeping arrangement of trees. I was a bit nervous. Because we were going away, I worried that he'd want to do more than just touch me and wank himself off. He'd kept this up over the year, although his opportunities, with us in our own place and me at school, were few and far between. This time he didn't even try to touch me. He just ranted. He seemed seriously disturbed.

— This is mine. My farm. I'm a Jubilee boy Roy, a penniless Scotsman from Granton. There I was nothing, another skinny teddy boy. Here, I count. No fucking Kaffir is going to take this away from me!

— They'll no take your place, Uncle Gordon, I said supportively, all the time my mind playing with the delicious image of him lying in the gutter in drapes outside the Jubilee Cafe, clutching a bottle of cheap wine. We went back to his ranch house and had some drinks, then went around to the woods so as I could look at some animals with my binoculars. We spotted a Moustached green tinkerbird and a Whalberg's eagle, both pretty rare in the Transvaal. Gordon's heart wasn't in it though and he soon returned to the ranch house. I was left alone to wander around the edge of the forested plantation and it was while I was stealthily trying to get closer to a shitting Bush duiker that I heard the explosion.

I almost shat myself, and I'm sure it helped the duiker's defecation too, the animal shooting off into the forest. I turned back and saw the blazing jeep. As I said, I knew nothing about politics. Despite frequent reports of guerrilla activity by a militant off-shoot of the ANC in Eastern Transvaal, Gordon refused to take heed. For some reason, he'd climbed into one of the four-wheel-drive Range Rovers outside the ranch, switched on the ignition and was blown into oblivion.

The funny thing was, I wasn't scared. I just thought that the terrorists have got Uncle Gordon. I had no real fear that they would do anything to me. I don't know why; I just didn't. I went back towards the house. The warm humid air was even heavier with the odour of gasoline and burning flesh: the smell of Gordon, barbecuing nicely in the blazing truck. I'd never smelt anything like it. While it's impossible for that much meat *not* to smell I had always imagined that humans would smell like bacon. When I was really wee my Uncle Jackie used to tell me that he ate cheeky wee laddies and that they tasted just like salty pork. I recall though that the smell of Gordon was so sweet I thought that if I hadn't known it was human flesh I would have wanted to taste it; would have enjoyed it. All I could see of Gordon was a charred thin, black arm and hand hanging out of the burning body of the vehicle. The smell changed briefly to that of one I could only describe as burning shite as my Uncle's guts popped and splattered as they incinerated in the flames. I went indoors and sat down and phoned my Ma back in Johannesburg.

— Roy, what is it! Ah'm up tae ma eyes in it! she moaned. Gordon had her preparing food for another *braai*.

— Ma, Uncle Gordon goat blown up. Eh's deid, n ah cannae git hame, like.

She gasped loudly and after a long silence said: — Don't move! Jist stey thair!

I sat and waited. I put on the telly and watched some cartoons. The polis came in a helicopter about twenty minutes later. It was fuckin barry being in the helicopter. They took me way up, and I saw, at close range, a magnificent Long-crested eagle, soaring over the thick forest. We landed with disappointing haste and transferred to a car, which drove me to the station where I was reunited with Vet, Kim, Tony and Bernard. Vet hugged me and Tony ruffled my hair. Kim kissed me, which embarrassed me in front of the polis. They had become good pals: the best cops I'd ever met. Bernard was as jealous as fuck of the attention I got: I felt like a hero.

Everyone said I was brave. It was a good time for me, a good farewell to a place I loved. Even Gordon's death, save the minor inconvenience of not being able to extort more presents, left me unmoved. As far as I was concerned Gordon was a sneaky, big-heided poofy auld cunt and it was good riddance. The only person really hurt was John, when we went to visit him in the prison, and his sadness seemed to be based on the loss of Gordon as he was fifteen years back, a 'skinny fucking teddy boy', rather than a crusty old Boer.

His death was actually of some practical benefit to my father. The authorities took a compassionate view of our circumstances and released him early from prison. He came back to Scotland about a month later than the rest of us. Winston Two, who had only been out of quarantine for a few months due to a blissful bureaucratic mix-up, was now banged up again, awaiting release to Scotland.

7 Escape From The City Of Gold

I remember the drabness of Heathrow, followed by the depressing connecting flight north of the border. We were all fucked anyway after the long journey from Johannesburg, but they had cancelled a couple of planes because of ice on the runway. London was freezing; Scotland would be even worse. It shows how dense and in a world of my own I had been eighteen months before, because I had been almost as excited that we were stopping off in London as I was that we were on our way to Johannesburg. I thought of London as somewhere just as distant and exotic; I had been surprised on the outward journey when we arrived there so quickly. Returning though, I saw London for what it was: the grizzled fag-end of the British Islands.

On our last day, I'd had to say goodbye to my friends at school and to my teachers. It was strange, but I seemed to be popular there; a big cheese, a top boy, numero uno. My best pals were called Pieter and Curtis. I was a bit of a bully to Curtis. Pieter was too. He was quite a wild cunt and was well pissed off that I was going back. It was good to have someone miss you. Most of the other kids were a bit slow and sappy. I would miss Pieter but, as this was the first time I'd discovered that I had a brain, the person I would miss most was Miss Carvello, one of my teachers. She was beautiful, with big, dark eyes. I used to wank about her, my first real wank, like, when you get spunk. She told Vet it was unfortunate that I was leaving South Africa as I had come on leaps and bounds at school and was 'university material'. This unfortunate phrase was to be thrown back at me in all my subsequent under-achievement.

I wanted to stay in South Africa. What I had gained there was a perverse sense of empowerment; an ego even. I knew I was fuckin special, whatever any of them tried to tell me. I knew I wasn't going to be like the rest of them; my old man, my old lady, Bernard, Tony, Kim, the other kids back in the scheme. They were rubbish. They were nothing. I was Roy Strang. Maybe I had to go back, but it was going to be different. I wasnae gaunny take any shite.

Back in Scotland, when John finally came home, we had a family meal to celebrate. Everyone was there, not quite everyone, Winston Two being back in quarantine, and Elgin still at THE GORGIE VENTURE FOR EXCEPTIONAL YOUNG MEN. It was considered too off-putting to have him home at the dinnertable, and I confess that I had been one of the principal advocates of keeping him away. Only Kim, Vet and Bernard argued for his presence, but John, as always, had the last word. — It widnae be fair tae the laddie, disorientate um, like ah sais, disorientate um.

The dinner was excellent. Ma made broth, then spaghetti carbonara with sprouts, broccoli and roast tatties heaped on top soas you could hardly see the pasta or the sauce, followed by sherry trifle. The bottles of Liebfraumilch were heartily drained. I'd never seen a table so loaded with food. We seldom ate around the table as a family, generally balancing plates on our laps as we jostled for position around the telly. This, we were told, was a special occasion.

There was, however, a tense atmosphere in the house at the meal; Tony's face was heavy with sweat as he ploughed into the food, while Kim pushed hers around. Bernard had had a violent argument with John earlier and instead of sitting down had sort of collapsed into the chair, ashen-faced and trembling. He was trying to cut a piece of roast tattie, his breath making high little sounds which could have come from the throat of a dog. Later on Kim was to tell me that Dad had heard from Mum about something Bernard had done with another laddie and had threatened to cut his cock off.

Mum and Dad had obviously argued about it and were both wound up so tightly as they sat at the table that the air around them seemed to gel. I ate nervously and quickly, anxious to excuse myself, feeling that one wrong word or dubious gesture might spark off a massacre.

— These tatties are hoat . . . Kim said inanely.

John glared venomously at her. — Well, thir nae fuckin good cauld! Yir Ma's gone tae a loat ay trouble tae make this meal, Kim! Show some appreciation! Like ah sais, some appreciation!

This was really worrying, as John seldom gave Kim a hard time; she was, after all, his favourite. Kim pouted and lowered her head. She looked as if she was contemplating doing what she often did to get attention and bursting into tears, but had decided against it and was struggling to consider what other action she could take.

Vet got in on the act. She turned to Tony and snapped: — Tony, take yir fuckin time. You n aw, Roy. That food isnae gaunny jump up n run away bichrist.

I had always though of my Ma as young and beautiful. Now she seemed to me to look like a twisted, haggard old witch, staring out at me from behind a smudged mask of eyeliner. I noted the strands of silver in her long black hair.

She and rest of them could fuck off. Ah wis going to be strong. Strong Strang. Ah wis gaunny make sure every cunt kent ma fuckin name.

Ah wis gaun . . .

DEEPER

DEEPER into the Marabou Stork nightmares.

8 Trouble
In The Hills

Old 'Fatty' Dawson looked absolutely beastly when we met up for a rendezvous and progress report at his secret guest lodge in the Jambola. His shifty, slimy eyes were blackened and his tanned flesh hung slack and wobbly on his jaw. He was not a happy man and it was more than obvious that we were the source of his disquiet.

Granted, we had failed to establish where our Stork was nesting. There were very few clues. In all frankness, Sandy and I had been rather treating it as a bit of a holiday and Dawson was not amused. There was no warmth in his greeting. He ushered us to sit down around a corner of his oak boardroom table. Then he left for a minute. Sandy turned to me and whispered: — Fatty Dawson's looking rather wild, he said, a little edge of panic creeping into his voice.

— Well, I'm blowed if I know what he's so steamed up about. It's not as if old Johnny Stork has . . .

At this point Dawson came back into the room and squeezed into a chair beside us. His doughy hands drummed the table, then he let out a sigh. — I'm surrounded by homoerotic prats who can't get it together to hunt those murderous beasts! he snapped contemptuously at us. Sandy looked vaguely guilty. This irritated me, as we had done nothing wrong. I was about to say something when Dawson turned his blotchy face away from us towards his valet, Diddy. — Either that or incompetent malcontents. The short-arsed man-servant mumbled something and shuffled out the room looking at his feet.

I considered that it might make for better sport to wind up Dawson rather than to oppose him outright. We still needed the fat oaf. There was little prospect of locating our Stork without his backing. — Take it easy, Lock, I smiled. — Unwind. Crack open a beer or two . . .

— How the hell can I be expected to relax when it's all caving in around me! he snapped. — This Emerald Forest park is rife with Marabous who only care for destruction, and here, in my own back yard, at the Jambola, the local natives are getting restless . . . SADIE! he screamed. – SADIE!

His black madame, the foreign lady, entered the room. — Yes Missah Dossan?

— What the fuck is happening, Sadie? *You* tell me . . . somebody tell me! It's Lochart Dawson this, Lochart Dawson that . . . oh yes, let's all put the boot into Lochart Dawson! Forget conveniently how Lochart Dawson saved this park from extinction!

Sadie shook her head sadly, — We all knows you our fren Missuh Dossan. We knows dat we don have nuthin till you comes heah an makes us all strong. All our people, dey respecks an loves you Missuh Dossan. Is only some of dem youth who is rebellious in de way dat young boys is. Dem boys will be punish badly for deh sins Missuh Dossan.

Dawson put both his hands behind his head and rubbed his neck. Then he gasped slowly. — I'm not a man who is intolerant by nature Sadie, but I am a great believer in examples being made and punishments fitting crimes and all that sort of stuff. Anything else sends signals to the bad eggs that they've won the battle. Well, my message to them is that they most decidedly have not. Those so-called rebels, when you round them up, see to it that I get to oversee their discipline personally. Baiting Lochart Dawson is becoming something of a thriving industry in these parts. Well, this is one enterprise I won't be encouraging thank you very much. You can tell them that Lochart Dawson has never run away from anything in his life and he doesn't intend to start now.

— Yessuh, Missuh Dossan.

— Of course, he bleated petulantly, — there may come a time when Lochart Dawson may just decide that it's all not worth the hassle and simply walk away. Then where would you all be, eh?

— Oh laud, Missuh Dossan, no go leave us, please no go leave us!
You is speshul pehsun Missuh Dossan. We loves you veh much an
we can no cope without you! Please no go!

Sadie was now at his knees, holding onto his legs. He ruffled her
dark hair. — That's fine, Sadie. Thank you.

The woman rose and departed with tears filling her eyes. She
deserved an Oscar.

— They seem to like you, said Jamieson, sycophantically stagey.

— Yes they do, Sandy. I can honestly say that, on the whole, I am
a much admired and appreciated person. There are a minority,
however, who seem to think that Lochart Dawson's a soft touch, a
figure of fun. Well, when they are brought in as prisoners by my
security forces, we'll see just how much a figure of fun I am after the
questioning procedures.

I raise an eyebrow in Dawson's direction.

— It's a vice of mine, Roy, Dawson explained. — Questioning. I
love to question. It's in my nature. I question everything. I question
why so much is spent on state benefits to the unproductive while
grants for business development for the go-ahead are so low. Indeed,
I question why state benefits exist at all.

I smile at him. — Extremely visionary stuff, Lochart, not at all the
type of questioning based on perpetuating the narrow economic
interests of an already wealthy but spiritually impoverished elite at
the expense of their more financially disadvantaged brethren. Truly
the type of questioning which will help enable mankind as a species
to self-actualise and fulfil its cosmic destiny. There's a real sense of
deep philosophy underpinning it all.

Dawson studied my expression to see if I was mocking him. It
seemed as if he couldn't quite tell, but decided to give me the benefit
of the doubt. — That's it, Roy! You're a true philosopher! He
smiled, flashing pearly teeth and presenting expensive bridgework
for my examination.

— You'll sort out those ungrateful malcontents, Lochart, I said
encouragingly.

— They forget that they asked me to come here, Dawson said. —

749

The same as those people in the Emerald Forest. I did this for them.

— Oh, Emerald Forest invited this takeover bid, did they? I asked, intrigued.

— I can't say any more about it now, Roy. Unfortunately I've not got the same freedom as the hot-heads to go around making all sorts of accusations. Lochart Dawson doesn't have that luxury; I'm bound to be silent by the dictates of company law and my position as a board member of Jambola Park PLC. Now, onto other business. What progress on the Stork problem?

— We've not located the nest yet, as I indicated to you last night on the telephone. It's all not bleak though . . . Sandy, I turned to Jamieson who rose and went to his rucksack and, on producing a large map of the area, spread it over the table.

Putting on a pair of steel-framed spectacles, Sandy began, — This map indicates the principal flamingo colonies in the area, and the patterns of flamingo migration.

— So what? We're talking about Marabous here! Dawson boomed.

— Please let me finish, Sandy retorted with a touch of cocksure assertiveness which filled me with a quick flush of admiration. I watched Dawson grudgingly defer. Sandy continued, — The pattern is emerging of rapid movement of the flamingo colonies from the area around Lake Torto up towards the border.

— We can't afford to lose our flamingos . . . Dawson gasped.

— Yes. But there's more. The only thing that could cause mass desertion of flamingo colonies on that scale is the presence of large numbers of the scavenger-predator we know as the Marabou Stork.

— Yes . . . but . . .

— The Storks have routed every flamingo colony they've come across. The next undisturbed ones are up on the north-eastern banks of Lake Torto. That's where the Marabous are headed next.

Dawson raised an appreciative eyebrow.

— And so, I said with what I thought was a rather dramatic pause, — are we.

— There is, however, Sandy added,
cashing in on his increased   we – – – SUPPOSE YOU'D LIKE TO KNOW
stock with Dawson, – one   thing   WHAT'S GOIN ON IN MA MIND

FUCK OFF!

— Just turning this up for you, Roy. The Doctor says as loud as we can have it.
Patricia's back.

— You certainly have some family, don't you Roy? Ha ha. I was propositioned last night by your brother. Tony.

Don't do it, Patricia.

— He's not my type, though. The married type, if you know what I mean. Good-looking, though. Can't really see much of a resemblance to you . . . oh God, I didn't mean it that way. Still, you seem to do alright. Your girlfriend was in. Doesn't say anything. Still, it must be upsetting for her to see you like this.

Who the fuck is that? Surely not Dorothy. Surely she's found another fat boyfriend, had her first fat kid even. Settled into a Wimpey or Barratt number in Fathell, Midlothian, or even Fathell, Fife. No. It would be Fathell, Manches . . .

NO. IT WASNAE DORIE.

Her that mentioned Dempsey. That's who it'll be. Her. Who the fuck is she?

— At least she stuck by you, Roy. She obviously doesn't believe that you're the bad one they're all making out. That's how I feel too. I can see the good in you, Roy. When I shine the torch into your eyes I know I can sometimes see something and I know it's good.

Aye, aye, Patricia. How the fuck would you ken?

I'm mad about the boy

MAD

DEEPLY MAD

DEEPER – – – – Aw aye, this yin. Ah mind ay ma Ma givin it laldy wi this yin. She sang it to me on my birthday. I was embarrassed, surprise, surprise. The daft party we had in my hoose. The funny thing was that when we came back tae Scotland the council housed us in the same maisonette block, on the fifth floor instead ay the fourth one. This was regarded as a come-down in status for my Ma. The poorest families tended to be at the top floor. The funny thing was, neighbours told us, they had only just re-let our old flat after it had been standing empty for the best part of our eighteen-month African safari.

Dexy and Willie, the two mates from school and scheme; I had just started the secondary; they were there. They were scruffy cunts glad to be let intae some cunt's hoose, even if it wis the Strangs. My mate Pete never came, he made some excuse. Brian was there, though. He'd just come back tae the scheme n aw; tae stey wi his auld man eftir being in Moredun wi his auntie. His Ma had left them and his auld boy had sort ay cracked up. They all looked nervous and furtive as Ma belted it out, half-pished . . .

> Even though there's something of the cad
> About the boy . . .

The new school.

Ma's intervention blew my cool, ruined my plan to be free from embarrassment, to take no shite from any cunt who would try to brand me a freak. By and large, though, things went well. I could, of course, have played up to being Tony Strang's brother, but that would also have identified me with Bernard, and that raging poof was two years above me at school. He was a constant source of shame, but was never tormented as he had no scruples about playing up to being Tony's wee brother. I hadn't wanted any of that shite though. I was into doing what people expected me to do least. At the school, as a Strang, they had expected me to be a basket case, so I was bright. Because I was bright, they expected me to go to university. The drab consensus that I was 'university material' had followed me all the way from Johannesburg. There was no way. No cunt told me what to do.

I arrived at the secondary school heavily suntanned from South

Africa; my ugliness now mildly exotic. There were loads of kids
from the primary and from the scheme who remembered Dumbo
Strang. In particular, there was a fat kid called Tam Mathews.

That poor cunt Mathews. All the time he was watching swotty
Strang from the back of the class, he must have been totally unaware
that I was psyching myself up for that moment. Mathews became
my first victim. I was glad it was him; glad because he was big,
tough, loud and stupid. This time it would be mair than just the
spike on the compass.

He spat on the back of my neck as we were leaving the classroom.
At school we used to kid on we were gobbing on the back of each
other's heids, like blowing out compressed air. This cunt really did it
but. I felt the thick spittle run under my collar, down the back of my
neck.

I could see a flicker of disbelief, then hesitancy in his eyes as I
squared up to him. He said something which brought a few laughs
from the kids who had gathered round to witness Dumbo Strang's
humiliation, but the laughter turned to gasps, to ooohhhss as I
produced a small hunting knife from my pocket, one which I'd
bought from Boston's of Leith Walk, and stabbed Mathews three
delicious times; twice in the chest and once in the arm. I then went to
the next period class.

The teachers and the police got involved, although Mathews, to
be fair, didn't shop me, he just collapsed in the playground and was
taken to the hospital.

I simply spoke nicely to them all. After all, I was now Roy Strang,
a hard-working, intelligent pupil; university material. Thomas
Mathews, the teachers fell over themselves to testify to anyone that
would listen, was not a hard-working, intelligent pupil. He was a
bully and a thug. Yes, the police knew the Mathews family. They
also knew the Strangs, but I was far too convincing in my mummy's
boy role for them to make that association. The consensus was that,
obviously, the Mathews boy must have put the fear of god into poor
Roy Strang for the boy to be so scared he had to carry a knife.
Nobody remembered the compass back in primary. No charges
were brought: Ma and Dad never even found out.

Life at school was easier after that, once that basic principle was established: you didnae fuck aroond with Roy Strang.

Out of school, it wasn't so easy. I remember one Saturday night I was sitting in reading a new *Silver Surfer* I'd got from Bobbie's Bookshop. It was late and I cringed inside as I always did when I heard my auld man ask my auld girl: — Fancy some chips, Vet?

— Wouldnae mind . . . my auld girl said coyly and teasingly, as if he was talking about sex.

— Roy, git ays a fish supper n what is it you're wantin, Vet?

— Ah'll huv fish . . . naw, a white puddin supper . . . naw, a mince pie supper wi two pickled onions. Naw . . . make it haggis, a haggis supper. That's it definitely. A haggis supper. Naw, fish! Fish!

— Christsake . . . two fish suppers before yir Ma changes her mind!

— Aw Dad . . . I moaned. I hated going to the scheme chippy this late at night. The pub next door, The Gunner, would be emptying. It was okay when he was down there, he brought the chips hame. It was horrible for me though, so I hated the nights he stayed in. You were on a fuckin doing fae aw the aulder wide cunts and the junkies who'd try to rob you. Cause nae cunt fucked aboot with him, the auld man never saw this.

I made my way out into the stair and headed down through the darkness of the shopping centre. I saw two boys coming towards me and tensed, but I relaxed as it was only my mates Pete Bowman and Brian Hanlon.

— Pete, Bri.

— Roy.

— Whair yis gaun?

— Hame.

— Whair yis been?

— Commie pool, then up at ma big brar's, Pete said.

— Chum ays doon tae the chippy well, I ventured.

Pete touched his eye and laughed, – Aye, that'll be fuckin right. N ye'd better watch, Roy. Hamilton n some ay the third-year cunts are hinging aboot doon thair.

— Ah'm no bothered, I smiled, shitein it.

— Ye gaun tae Easter Road oan Setirday? Brian asked.

There was no way ah wis gaun tae any fuckin fitba. — Aye, probably, I said.

— Come doon fir ays well, Brian said.

— Aye, right.

— Tro Roy.

— Tro Pete, tro Bri, I said as they departed.

I walked on into the darkness. A drunk shouted at me, but I ignored him and charged doon towards the chippy. The light coming from it was the only sign of life in the centre. As I was getting served, trying to act nonchalant as the raucous drunks and nutters from the pub joined the queue and shouted at each other, I noted with a sinking feeling that Hamilton and his entourage were standing outside the shop.

I waited and by the time I got my stuff, they were away. I breathed a sigh of relief and huddled the hot chips to my chest as I walked through the centre into the cold night. I was just starting to unwind when Hamilton came flying out of a stair door and stood in front of me. There were two other guys with him, and two lassies.

— Hi pal, gies a chip!

— Ah cannae, it's fir ma faither, I said.

Hamilton was sixteen. I was still not yet fourteen. This was a different league to Mathews. The other guys were even older. One guy with long, curly blond hair was about eighteen. — Leave um, Hammy, ehs jist a fuckin bairn . . . he said.

— Git um in the fuckin stair, Hamilton laughed.

His mate, another third-year cunt called Gilchrist was sniggering, — Ken whae this cunt is? Eh chibbed Davie Mathew's brar. Thinks eh's a fuckin wide-o.

They pushed me into the stair. I held onto the chips as tightly as I could. All I could think of was what my auld man would say if I let them get tae the chips.

Hamilton had masses of teeth. Protruding teeth. He reminded me of a piranha fish; so many teeth it can never close its mouth. He gleefully pulled a knife on me. — So ye cairry a blade, eh?

— Nup, I said.

— Heard ye hud yin it the school but, eh. Ye a wide-o, aye?

— Nup, I shrugged, still holding onto the chips.

Hamilton laughed and then did a strange bird-like dance in front of me strutting and twisting his head from side to side.

— Leave um, Hammy, ah'm no fuckin jokin, the older guy said laughing, and wrestling Hamilton playfully away from me. One of the lassies came over to me. She was at our school too. Me, Pete and Bri just called her The Big Ride. I'd wanked aboot her before: I'd wanked aboot her tons ay times if the truth be telt. I remember once we were watching a nature programme in Bri's hoose and there wis these two praying mantises and the lassie praying mantis was eating the laddie praying mantis's heid while they were shaggin. We used to joke that that was what shaggin The Big Ride would be like. Ah remember saying that ah'd never shag The Big Ride unless I could tie her doon first.

— Goat a girlfriend, son? she asked, chewing gum so slowly and deliberately that it made her lovely face seem long and horselike. While this made her look uglier, it strangely and paradoxically made her seem even more sexual.

In spite of my fear I felt a twinge in my groin. — Nup, I said.

— Ivir hud yir hole? Hamilton sneered. Gilchrist laughed.

I said nothing.

— Leave the perr wee cunt, the blond guy laughed. — C'moan, Hammy, lit um go.

Then I saw who the other lassie was, it was Caroline Carson from our year, her; a lassie that was in some of my classes. She was alright. Dead nice likes. I just wanted to die.

The blond guy must have caught my shock of recognition, because he put his arm around her, — This is ma wee girlfriend, eh hen? he said with teasing lecherousness.

She twisted away from him laughing, — Dinnae Doogie . . . She seemed a bit embarrassed that somebody had found her with these cunts. I took her for a nice lassie likes.

At that point Hamilton slapped me across the face. I stood staring at him, still holding the chips. — Gie's a fuckin chip! he snapped. I stood looking at his glaring, violent eyes, feeling the side of my face where his hand made contact throb in a strange harmony with my balls.

Then I saw something change in his eyes. It was a kind of startled, ugly impulse that we shared but which I couldn't define.

It was something we shared. I kept staring at him. I wisnae scared any mair: no ay him. I was scared of my auld man, but no Hamilton. He knew it. All I felt was anger at him, and anger at masel fir being too weak tae oppose the cunt.

— Fuckin wide cunt! he roared, moving towards me with the blade. The blond guy held him and at the same time pushed me away, out the stairdoor, but they all came out after me.

I just held the chips. I knew at any time I could have stopped this nightmare by saying: Tony Strang's ma brar, but I didnae want tae. This was me. This was Roy Strang we were talking aboot.

Roy Strang.

I just held the chips.

— What team dae ye support? Hamilton asked casually, as if nowt hud happened between us, as he put the knife back in his pocket.

— Hibs, I said.

I wisnae really interested in fitba, but Dad and Tony were Hibs fans and so were most of my mates in the scheme, so it seemed a safe bet.

— Hebs! Hebs! he repeated, mimicking my unbroken voice.

He ripped the paper of my wrapper and dug out a few chips. I stood frozen. I tried to speak out but I couldn't say anything. — HMFC ya cunt! he snapped and, grabbing my hair, he hauled my head doon and booted me in the face. I felt my bottom lip rip on my bottom front teeth and the sour taste of my own blood fill my mouth.

I held the chips and lifted my head slowly, shaking with anger and frustration.

— Fuck off Hammy, ya Jambo cunt, the big, blond guy shouted and charged after Hamilton and they had a mock fight as I sneaked off, my lower lip tasting like a large piece of rubber in my mouth.

When I got home my Dad looked at me, then at the torn wrapper, which I had vainly tried to disguise. — They chips. Somebody wis tamperin wi they chips!

I told him that I'd got hungry on the way home and had eaten a few chips. He looked hard at me, — What happened tae yir mooth? My knees felt weak and I didn't have the strength to carry on the unconvincing lie. It would only wind him up further. I kept my eyes on the floor and told him the story. I looked up and caught Kim's wide eyes staring at me, punctuating my misery with the occasional: — Ooooohhhh. Bernard, naewhair tae be seen when they were looking for some cunt tae go for the chips, was fighting hard to stop his mouth twisting into a smile and losing. We were all waiting for my auld man to freak and smack me across the heid, but he just looked sadly at me.

— Ye'll huv tae learn tae fuckin well stick up fir yersel, Roy. Yir a Strang, or supposed tae be, he told me wearily, shaking his head in contempt.

I swore I'd get revenge on that cunt Hamilton, but I never did, the cunt goat sent tae the approved school at Polmont, then just vanished off the scene. Gilchrist, his sidekick, moved to another school in another part ay the toon. That cunt I did meet up wi again. Him and the slags.

That wis later but.

Things at the school were easier though. While the news went aroond that Hamilton had gubbed ays, as he was a third-year cunt and hard, that was no disgrace. Indeed, the fact that I hudnae really shat oot increased my stock. In school and roond the scheme it was basically just me, Dexy, Willie, Bri, Monty and Penman that hung arrond thegither. Nae cunt really bothered us and we never really bothered any cunt.

This lasted for a long time. We had a good laugh thegither. Once we broke intae the school at night, intent on turning the place over. We got intae a class that wis our redgie class, whair ye went first thing in the mornin tae git checked in, and we found our redgie teacher Miss Gray's belt in the toap drawer ay her desk.

Wi started giein each other the belt, really fuckin thrashin each other's hands, much harder than when Lesbo Gray or any ay the other teachers did it. The thing wis, wi wir aw jist pishin oorsels n it seemed tae hurt a loat less. Then Bri had a barry idea. He pulled oot the top drawer n goat that daft cunt Willie tae dae a shite in it. Willie goes n droaps this fuckin steamin crap intae the drawer: then Bri pits it back in the desk. We laugh like fuck fir a bit then Bri goes: — The morn wi come in n noise up that carpet-munchin cunt Gray. She reaches in fir her belt . . .

— Ohhh . . . ya fuckin cunt! Penman laughed.

— Right then, lit's no brek anything . . . make it soas nae cunt kin see thir's been a brek-in. Ah jist want tae go up tae the library but, eh, ah telt them.

Ah poackled a couple ay bird books fae the library: *The Urban British Bird* and *Sherman's Encyclopaedia Of Tropical Birds Vol. 1.*

The next day we noised up Dykey Gray. We just shouted: 'Let's be friends' at some lassies in the class, and kept it up until it became: 'Lesbee Friends.' That sort of thing would have got on Gray's tits if she'd had any: as it was it just pissed her off. She reached into her drawer for the belt. Gray always smashed it oan the table and we were all supposed to shut up and pay attention after this gesture. Gray always said the same thing: The first thing on a Monday morning or the last thing on a Friday afternoon or the middle of the week isn't exactly the best time to try somebody's patience! Always the same bullshit.

— Right! she shouted, opening the drawer and sticking her hand in, — a dreadful, wet morning is not the time to try somebody's . . . She felt for the belt and froze. She pulled the drawer open slightly with her other hand, looked in and then started retching and choking. We were pishing our keks. Bri's face was crimson, his eyes watering. Miss Gray took the drawer out and stuck a bit of A4 paper on top of the shite and her messy hand. She stormed out the room holding the drawer in her free hand. — Bloody animals! Fucking little animals, she sneered, as we let out loud ooooohhhhhsss at her language. Gray then shouted on this snobby lassie called Bridget Hyslop, who Bri had nicknamed Frigid Pissflaps, to open the door and she vanished doon the corridor towards the staff toilets.

Fuckin barry.

Good times for a while, but then came a problem I hud tae deal wi. But I dinnae want tae talk aboot that yet. I want tae go back, back tae what happens wi the Stork. DEEPER likes, cause Sandy and me see, we managed tae get some mair supplies fae Dawson . . . no . . . that's not right, DEEPER

DEEPER

DEEPER – – old 'Fatty' Dawson furnished Sandy and I with bountiful extra supplies of equipment and tuck, as we'd demonstrated to him that the flamingos were being displaced by the Marabous.

— Watch yourselves on that road, Dawson boomed as we left, — there is an abundance of terrorist activity.

Once again we were off in the jeep, and feeling pretty pleased with ourselves. — This is fun, isn't it Sandy?

— Yes, Jamieson said, smiling at me. — And I want you to know Roy, that whatever happens from here on in, I've had the best bloody time of my life.

I blushed with embarrassment and, to deflect this, bade Sandy to tell me another lion adventure.

— Well, there was the occasion when I went into a village completely terrorised by an insatiable maneater. The poor villagers were literally too frightened to leave their tents and food supplies were short, with conditions increasingly insanitary, the rubbish just being thrown outside. One couldn't really blame the villagers, after all, the poor buggers had lost three people in a month to this beast. Anyway, it was about three in the morning and myself and my team were soundly asleep in our billets, when the door was violently burst in and before my chaps knew what had hit them, one of the men, who went by the name of Mojemba, was seized by a large lion who proceeded to drag him out of the hut by the thigh. Anyway, I was in a tetchy mood, awakened by the blasted commotion, so I quickly grabbed my rifle and dispatched a bullet into the region of the brute's heart. I was very lucky, obviously haste rather than accuracy had been my priority at the time.

— Nonsense, Sandy, I told him, — you're a bloody good shot.

— Nice of you to say so Roy, but I was never particularly

renowned for my shooting ability. This one, though, was certainly on target, because the animal instantly dropped Mojemba and bolted into the surrounding bush.

Villagers found the beast's body at the break of dawn; it was some seventy yards from the hut. It was nothing more than a mangy old lioness, driven to maneating by desperation. But the thing about this episode was that poor old Mojemba saw this attack on him as a sign of his own failing, a lack of vigilance on his part.

— But surely that's exactly what it was, I said.

— Yes, but I couldn't simply leave the fellow there, bleeding to death and bleating away at me; sorry Bwana this and sorry Bwana that . . . so I told everyone else to leave us while I personally tended to the poor wretch's wounds. I cleaned his thigh with hot water and syringed the lacerations with disinfectant to prevent blood poisoning setting in.

— Good show.

— Thankfully, in this case the precautions proved effective and within six weeks the boy was able to walk again. Hunting duties proved too arduous for him after such a trauma, so I made the lad my personal manservant . . . he was a damn good one too, Sandy's long forked tongue . . . wisnae forked, it was a normal tongue.

Fuck   up   This isnae working. Okay, okay.
                  up   What was the problem that ah hud tae
Fuck   up   sort oot?
            up   The problem.
Coming up
                  Caroline Carson.

Caroline Carson. She had always acted as if her shite didnae smell, but she never bothered me. I thought she wis a nice lassie. It was about a year later when I was in the second year and was put in one of her classes, English, I think. She must've been minding about the time she was there wi Hamilton n Gilchrist n The Big Ride when they terrorised me. Every cunt fancied her and she must have thought her looks bought her immunity, like she could dae what she wanted. One time in the class, she flicked the back of ma fuckin ear. It wis sair, bit it wis mair the humiliation. I was always sensitive about my ears.

It wis they laughs in the class. Always they fuckin laughs.

Nae cunt laughs at Roy Strang.

I knew where she steyed and I followed her hame eftir school. I ran ahead ay her, cutting through the back of the supermarket and across the back greens and I was waiting for her in her stair. I heard her talking to another lassie for what seemed like ages, but eventually she came into the stair alone. I was straight on her and I had her pinned against the wall of the darkened stair recess with ma Swiss army knife (again purchased from Boston's of Leith Walk) pressed at her throat.

— What ur ye daein? What ur ye daein, Roy? she whimpered, fuckin shitein it. That wis the first time she'd spoke tae ays: the first time the cunt hud said ma name.

I enjoyed the look in her eyes. Enjoyed having the knife at her throat. Enjoyed the power. That was it wi the power, I remembered thinking, you just had to take it. When you took it, you had to hold onto it. That was all there was to it. My cock was stiffening in my pants. Everything seemed to be so bright. There was no sound. I seemed to smell pish, then burning. My mouth, chin, lips, hands, feet: they all seemed to tingle. — You fuckin flicked ma ears! What dae ye say!

— Sorry . . . she bleated softly.

I spoke slowly into her ear as she cringed away from me, too immobilised by fear to try any more ambitious movement. — Roy Strang is ma fucking name. Nae cunt fucks aboot wi me . . . lift up yir skirt, I commanded, pushing the blade tighter against her thin, white throat.

She lifted it.

— Higher!

I put my hand inside her cotton panties and tugged them down onto her thighs. It was the first fanny I'd seen in real life, though I'd seen plenty in wank mags. — A ginger minge. Jist as ah fuckin well thought. Ah'd wanted tae see if ye hud ginger pubes like, ah smiled.

The daft cunt produces a forced, wretched parody of a smile back for me.

— What's fuckin funny? Eh? Think *ah'm* fuckin funny? I spat through clenched teeth, pointing at myself.

— Naw . . . she pleaded.

I stood close to her then moved onto her, and started rubbing up against her till I came, talking like they did in the wankmags, my hot breath on her frozen, terrorised face: — Slut . . . slut . . . dirty fuckin slag . . . you fuckin love it ya dirty wee cunt . . . I felt like Winston Two. My hot wallpaper paste filled my pants. That was it; I'd had my first ride, even if it was only a dry ride. A dry ride was what the aulder laddies in the scheme called it when ye didnae get it up a lassie's fanny, ye jist rubbed up against them.

I stood apart from her saying, — You say anything aboot this ya fuckin ginger-pubed wee cunt n you are fuckin well deid! Right!

She stood rooted to the spot with her hands covering her eyes. — Ah'll no say nowt . . . she gasped with fear, nearly greetin, as I departed. I turned back to look at her pulling her pants up. To think I'd wanked over that. She was just a daft wee lassie: hardly any tits, barely any hips. I was going to get a proper ride soon, and it wid be with a real woman.

That was another problem sorted.

I found schoolwork easy and nobody fucked me about. I'd occasionally skive off to watch Wimbledon or the World Cup if my auld man was on the dayshift. It was great having the hoose tae masel. I remember I got really into Wimbledon that summer: this unseeded big cunt with a powerful serve, I cannae remember his name, he was just blowing away all the top seeds. He got as far as the semi-finals. I remember that snobby auld Dan Maskell cunt referring tae the boy as a 'dangerous floater'. That was me, at the school and the scheme: a dangerous floater. I was too anonymous to be one of the big hard cunts, but I carried an air of menace and I was a risky prospect to fuck aboot with. The hard cunts knew this, and so did I.

Rather than stake my place as a top dog in the school or scheme crews, I avoided them, assembling my own team. I wanted to be the top fuckin brass. The punters I hung around with were misfits. They were either too cool, like Pete, too smart, like Brian, too spaced-out like Penman, or too scruffy and thick like Dexy n Willie to fit in with the other crews.

That summer I was desperate for a ride. I must have been really desperate because I captured this baby-faced cunt called Alan or Alec somebody . . . Moncur, I think, in the laddies' toilet. The guy wore a grey duffel coat in the winter and a school blazer in the summer (this is Craigey wir talkin aboot!) and was always neat and tidy, the kind of cunt who seemed as if his Ma still dressed him.

This Dressed-By-His-Ma-Cunt was quite pally though. He sort ay befriended us for a bit as I think he probably got that much stick at school he was looking for mates who'd protect him. On one occasion he played along at being jocularly mesmerised by me as I pretended to hypnotise him:

— . . . hyp - i - no - tise . . .
. . . hyp - i - no - tise . . .

. . . ye could tell he was shitein it but, his eyes like the windaes oan a computer. What wis oan display looked awright, but there was a lot more stacked behind it, a lot more gaun oan behind they lassie-like eyes. I lifted my leg and let my knee surge intae the cunt's groin with force . . .

. . . now your balls are paralysed . . .

. . . he gave a sick, sharp, animal shriek as he bent double in agony. I led off a cold, smirking chorus as we savoured the pain and trepidation which filled his eyes.

Tony had done that to me. One time in the hoose. But Tony wis awright; he never really battered me much. It was mainly Bernard he battered, and that was barry; seein that fuckin poof get battered.

But the funny thing for me was that I always felt a bit shite eftir I did something like that. It made me feel sad and low. I suppose I just felt sorry for what I'd done. The funny thing was though, that I felt sorry *in general*, never to the *particular person* I'd abused. I just hated them even more. But eftir I did something like that I'd try to make it up by doing a good deed, like giving up my seat oan the bus tae an auld cunt or daein the dishes for my Ma. It was just when I did something like I did to the Dressed-By-His-Ma-Cunt I always felt alive, so in control. So while I felt bad aboot it eftir, it was never enough tae stoap ays daein it *at the time*.

One day ah wis in the laddies' bogs at the school, wi Bri n Penman, whae wir huvin a smoke. Ah never bothered wi fags. We were jist fartin aboot in thair when whae should come in but the Dressed-By-His-Ma-Cunt. I felt a dryness in ma mooth as my eyes feasted oan the Dressed-By-His-Ma-Cunt's worried, rabbit-like expression. My throat seemed to constrict and my lips stuck together soas I had to free them with my wet tongue.

— Captured! I roared, pointing at him, and bundled him at knifepoint into one of the cubicles.

— Strangy! Whit ye daein in thair, ya cunt! Bri shouted.

— Keep fuckin shoatie, Bri . . . keep fuckin shoatie . . . I gasped. I forced the Dressed-By-His-Ma-Cunt to wank me off. — Slowly . . . ah'll fuckin kill ye . . . slowly . . . I commanded as he pulled gently on my cock, his eyes wide in fear. Despite the banging and laughing from the boys ootside, I was aroused enough tae blaw my muck ower the sappy fucker's black blazer.

I put it away quickly, then opened the door.

Penman and Bri fell about laughing as the tearful Dressed-By-His-Ma-Cunt finally emerged whimpering from the cubicle, followed by me with a wicked smile on my coupon.

But while all my pals laughed at this, they looked at me sort of differently for a while, as if I was a poof like Bernard. I blamed the Dressed-By-His-Ma-Cunt, and nursed a violent wrath. If that cunt hud never looked like an insipid, fruity wee lassie he would never have made me make a cunt ay masel like that. I hated poofs. I hated the thought ay what those sick cunts did tae each other, pittin their cocks up each other's dirty arseholes. I would castrate all poofs.

Shortly after this, the Dressed-By-His-Ma-Cunt was talking tae his pals in the playground and he fairly squealed as my elbow made a strong, cracking contact with his face. I never bothered to look back and watch the blood spill heavily from that girl mouth, but Dexy and Bri assured me that it most certainly did.

I hated that cunt.

However, the reaction of my mates had made it even more important that I got my hole properly likes, for the first time. Fortunately, I was soon into a proper shag. At night we used to hang around the school gates with a group of lassies, and would fuck about, feeling them up. There was one who was gamer than the rest, a lassie called Lesley Thomson. She was nothing special to look at, and she was a total scruffbag, but she had barry tits and a good erse. A loat ay the other lassies were really too wee: nae real tits or erse. I would separate her from the group and go across the playing fields to the gates at the other end of the school with her. After a few dry rides, I worked up the confidence to fuck her properly.

I got the budget room key from Tony. It was only the block caretakers and the binmen that were supposed to have them but my auld man had one because he was the sort of unofficial security guy for the building. It was council policy to encourage responsible tenants to get involved in the upkeep of the area. However, Tony kept Dad's key as he used the budget room to take lassies for a cowp. Tony was a fuckin total shag artist. Even though he had a flat in Gorgie, he'd still come doon tae oors and use the budget room tae fuck aw the local slags fi the scheme that he didnae want hassling him at his pad.

I was pretty good pals with Tony at this time, and I'd sometimes go up to see him in his flat. It was barry; he'd give me beer and I got to smoke dope with him. I never really liked it, but I kidded on I did cause it was good of him tae let ays try it. — Dinnae tell Ma or John, he'd laugh.

It was Tony who really telt ays everything aboot lassies. — If thir slags ye jist grab a hud ay the cunts. If it's a decent bird ye stey cool fir a bit and chat them up, then ye grab a hud ay them.

The budget room was the place where the rubbish chute led to a giant aluminium bucket, which dominated the cold bleak room. The block's central electricity meters were also in here. There was a manky auld mattress on the floor, doubtless used by Tony. I wanted to fuck Lesley standing up, though, as I was used to that through the dry rides. I got her up against the wall and started to feel for her crack. To my surprise, the actual hole was a lot further down the slit in the bush than I had thought. The pictures of women's fannies in the wank mags were deceiving. I never liked the ones where the genitals were exposed in too much detail; they were like raw, open wounds, totally at odds with the smiling, inviting faces of the models. I bet they were highlighted with paint or gloss or some shite like that. I had bought my first wank mag from Bobbie's Bookshop: this was the very same occasion on which I bought ma last Marvel comic mag, the *Silver Surfer* likes. The wank mags did have some use; at least ah didnae try tae fuck Lesley up her arsehole. I had grown up thinking that was the norm for sex, because of Tony saying: Ah'd shag the fuckin erse oafay that, every time a lassie walked past him. It took the wank mags tae pit me right oan that one. They did have their uses.

It took a while to get it in. I remember being surprised that it actually did go *up*, as opposed to straight in likes. Her fanny was wet and slimy but a bit tight and I had to bend my knees. After a few thrusts I shot my load inside her as my legs buckled and I fell onto the mattress. It was my first proper ride; my first wet ride. Being honest, it wisnae *that* much better than a dry ride, but at least I'd done it. I felt equals with Tony; both men of the world. I went to school next day with a confident swagger. Aw these cunts who called me Dumbo Strang; sitting in their bedrooms wanking over Sue Storm, The Invisible Girl in the *Fantastic Four*, while there was me, the ugly cunt who was getting his hole. It was funny, I used tae hate the thought of Sue Storm getting shagged by that Mr Fantastic Cunt, that Reed Richards. She could've done better for hersel than that boring cunt, though I suppose he had the power tae alter the shape and dimensions ay any part ay his boady. If he could dae it tae his cock then she'd be in fir a good fuckin time. I suppose they didnae call the cunt Mr Fantastic for nothing. If she had a sair heid though, she could jist vanish.

I'd talk to Tony about getting my hole; bullshitting about the number of shags I'd had and the things I'd done. I think he knew

I was making most of it up, and I knew that he knew, but he let me go on and said nothing as it amused the both of us and passed the time.

Lesley Thomson though; she began to disgust me, she really did. The truth was that she always had. She wore these manky white socks which used to make me feel aroused but soon just made me feel clarty. She had that unmistakeable stale-cake smell of the scheme scruff. I hated the way she just stood there, never moving, always looking vacant and stupid. I fucked her a few times that summer, always vowing that each time was the last time but eventually succumbing to the temptation to shaft her again and hating her and myself for it.

There wis one time when she tried tae take ma airm, this wis durin the day, ootside the gates at the school, likesay ah wis sort ay gaun oot wi her. I had to slap the slag's pus thair n then. I had tae dae a bit crawlin later oan, but, soas I'd git ma hole. — Wir gaun oot thegither, ah explained tae her stupid face, — but just at night likes, right? Durin the day we dae oor ain thing.

The slag *seemed* tae understand.

While I was up to all this in the scheme, I was sticking in at school. The next year I went into hibernation to study for my O Grades. Dad insisted that ah wisnae tae be disturbed and Kim was enlisted to bring my tea up to my room on a tray. Although Tony was in a flat by this time, so there was mair room, Bernard was made to sleep on the couch so I could have the room to myself. It always surprised me that Bernard didn't move into a flat, he was out the house often enough with his queer mates.

John was adamant that no sacrifice was too much during my study time. He was proud that a Strang was sitting six O Grades, and he and my Ma would embarrass the fuck out of me by telling every cunt.

I passed all six. They wanted ays tae stey oan n take highers, but I wanted a job soas I could get some cash thegither n get a place ay ma ain. There was another party at the house to celebrate; mostly the auld man and auld girl's pish-heid mates who staggered back too fucked tae realise what they were celebrating. There was the inevitable sing-song. Dad serenaded Ma wi 'From Russia With Love' and 'Moon River'. She sang 'Nobody Does it Better', tae him.

Nobody does it better,
Makes me feel sad for the rest.
Nobody does it half as good as you do,
Baby you're the best.

Dad glowed coyly, his eyebrows rising marginally over those thick frames in a Bond-like gesture. I felt a bit sick.

I held out and got my ain way, immediately leaving the school to take up a traineeship as a systems analyst at the Scottish Spinsters' Life Assurance Company in George Street. I'd always been into computers, at the school n that likes. Ma and Dad were pished off at first that I wisnae steyin oan but they bursted with pride when they heard that I'd got what people termed a good job with prospects. I'm sure Dad saw it as a vindication of the Strang genes.

— Kent ye hud brains, son, he would continually tell me. — Computers, thing ay the future, he would say knowingly, as if he was privy to some secret information that had evaded the rest of the human race. This statement became an almost obligatory utterance in my family at any reference to me, replacing 'six O Grades' and 'university material'. So that was me set up.

I remember my first day at Scottish Spinsters'. I was impressed to the point of being overawed by the building. It was completely new on the inside, but it had retained its grandiose Georgian facade and opulent reception area with marble pillars, and the original oak-panelled rooms and corridors. This was where the boardroom was situated and where the high-up cunts had their offices. This older part of the building led onto an ugly newly-built structure which housed a series of bland, identical offices decked out in pastel colours and lit with migraine-inducing neon strip-lights.

I shared an office with four others. The door was marked SYSTEMS CONTROL and it bore three names; Jane Hathaway, Derek Holt and Des Frost. Myself and Martine Fenwick, the other trainee, were not considered senior enough to have our names on the door. It was that sort of a place. In the office across the corridor was a guy called Colin Sproul, who was our section head.

If the building impressed me, I never really thought that much of the cunts I worked with. Jane Hathaway was like the supervisor, Senior Systems Control Officer, she was called. She was quite overweight with longish brown hair, and glasses which reminded me of the auld man's. There was haughty malevolence aboot her; she was a sad cunt who seemed to thrive on exercising her power over the men in the office. She'd get you to take something doon tae the photocopying for her (which wisnae really ma joab) and then say: —Thank you, young man, in a patronising, jokey sort of way. But she was quite a snidey cunt because she never overstepped the mark to the extent that you could confront her and tell her to fuck off; she just nipped away under the surface, her asides leaving a bad taste in your mooth though you could never be quite sure why.

I got the vibe that Hathaway had the hots for Martine Fenwick, who was a trainee like me, but, unlike me, had been to the Uni. English literature or something: fuckin waste that, eh. Fenwick was an exceptionally skinny lassie with no tits whatsoever. I sometimes used to glance doon her open blouse when she was demonstrating something on the VDU, just tae see if I could spy a *bit* ay tit. But naw, it was like her bra was just an elasticated vest which housed only a nipple. She was a really nervous lassie. Hathaway and her used to go all girlish when they spoke sometimes, it was like that was their patter; and Fenwick would start giggling nervously and jerk and twitch and have to put her knuckles between her teeth to stop herself laughing like an imbecile. She was a gawky lassie, in no way a shag, yet she had a strange, obscure sexuality and I inexplicably used to wank about her.

Hathaway seemed to give Derek Holt a hard time. Derek was an ordinary guy; married with two kids, liked a pint at lunchtime, good at his job, would never blow his own trumpet. He was intae fitba and was a season ticket holder at Tynecastle. I'd sometimes spraff with him aboot it. I was never really intae fitba then, it was just something tae talk aboot. Hathaway seemed to find this guy deeply offensive, like he was some kind of caveman; she'd look at him with withering distaste and her tone would go harsher when she addressed him. Perhaps it was because he wasn't what she was; English, middle-class and a lesbo. Holt never really seemed to notice her behaviour though, or if he did he didnae bother.

Des Frost was quite a smooth cunt. He fancied himself but was detached and didnae get involved. I could tell that he gave Martine Fenwick the hots in a big way.

Anyway, that was the cunts in my office. I didnae really have much time for any of them, but they never bothered me much, eh.

Even though I wanted to find a flat, life in the hoose had got better. I was bringing in money and was treated like mair ay an equal than a silly wee laddie. Sometimes I'd go up the pub wi Dad and Tony and Uncle Jackie and some of their mates. I felt great at times like that. A lot of the auld cunts crawled up my erse, John Strang's laddie, they called me. Winston Two would sit curled at our feet as we sat with our pints and dominoes.

For as long as I could remember, I had fantasised revenge on that fuckin dug for the savaging he gave my leg as a sprog. The animal learned to keep out my road, but I made sure I was never caught kicking him. Winston Two was revered in my family. Kim used to take him out a lot and she had composed a banal and nauseating mantra which was always sung affectionately when the animal had something in his mouth. It went:

> Winners, Winners, Winalot,
> Winners Winners, what you got?

This moronic rhyme quickly gained cult status in my family and it was repeated endlessly by everyone. Kim obviously took this gift for shite poetry from Bernard, who was particularly keen on her daft composition. I hated the way they all idolised that fuckin dog.

One evening I found myself alone in the house with the beast. The old boy had been dozing by the electric bar fire and was slowly coming around. I had been watching him, the rhythmic flare of his nostrils, the rising of the flap of skin at the top of his nose as he slept. I was imagining his long head as the ball on the penalty spot in the European Cup Final between Hibs and A.C. Milan. At the end of an exciting but goal-less contest, the boys in emerald green were awarded a penalty kick which their new signing, Roy Strang, confidently stepped up to take.

Winston's jaw crackled PHAKOH as I caught the bastard a beauty. — Strang . . . one nil! I said crisply, in a nasal English commentator cunt voice, — end shawly nahow the Chempeons' Cup is on its woy to Aistuh Road! The beast let out an injured yelp then whined pathetically, cowering under the sideboard. — Winners . . . Winners . . . I cooed in breathless affection, eventually enticing the terrorised creature back to my side. — You are going to die, Winners, I said soothingly, — as soon as I find a way to get you away from here: You.are.going.to.die. I stroked the old boy as he panted in servile contentment.

I quite enjoyed my new job. I was a bit in awe of all the snobby cunts there, but some of them were okay and the work was easy. Most of all, I enjoyed the salary. Dumbo Strang, making mair poppy than any of the cheeky schemie peasants who had once tried to torment him. My social life, though, was a bit of a drag. I found it harder to get my hole. I wanted a class bird, no just knee-trembling some schemie in a rubbish room. There was plenty of tackle at the work, but it was mostly snobby fanny, or what *ah* would call snobby fanny, and I felt too shy and self-conscious to talk tae them. So there was no action at all. I had never really fancied the idea of taking drugs, apart from a blow with Tony. Pete, Penman and Bri were always oot ay thair faces on something or other. Although I had the odd pint wi Tony or the auld man, drink did little for me, and I wasnae really intae getting pished. I'd seen alcohol as the drug of too many of the plebs I despised. So I suppose I sort of came to the conclusion that the best possibility for me in having a good crack was with the cashies. I had gone to a few Hibs games as a kid with Tony and my Dad, but always got bored quickly. Fitba seemed a drag to me. I identified it with my own lack of ability; too uncoordinated thanks to my gammy leg, courtesy of Winston Two. However, Dexy and Willie were running with the baby crew, and I started listening to some of their stories with interest.

But all this is nonsense.

Let's get DEEPER.

9 The Praying Mantis

Sandy toked hard on the spliff and inhaled powerfully. We were driving Dawson's shabby jeep out towards the Emerald Forest Park. I was at the wheel. I watched the dark, urban landscape of Jambola Park's dank and dingy parent city come to an end as a lush green hill appeared before us. Two young women came into view, hitching by the side of the road. One had honey-blonde hair, streaked by the sun. She was a little overweight, but very pretty. The other one had dark, cascading hair, lovely almond eyes, and a beautiful twisted pout to her lips. She was gorgeous.

— Stop! Sandy shouted, nodding over at them.

I increased speed. — Slags! Fuckin slags! The last thing we want are fuckin slags in tow tae spoil it fir every cunt, I snarled, surprised at the words that were coming out of my mouth.

What the fuck is this?

— We would've been well in . . . Sandy moaned.

— Plenty of opportunity tae get a ride . . . I mean, plenty of opportunity to enjoy the consort of attractive young ladies after we take care of business, Sandy, I said. For some reason I hated those women. The slags gave me the fucking creeps. Hitching like that. They deserved to get . . .

No.

In here I'm doing all the things I didn't do out there. I'm trying to be better, trying to do the right thing, trying to work it all out.

Sandy is not amused. He's well pissed of at me for not stopping. He starts prattling away, his hurt suddenly taking on a more abstract, conceptual bent: — Justice, he urbanely remarked, — is not a commodity we enjoy to any great extent. Yes, we strive towards it, but it seems to be the miserable lot of our wretched species that it persistently evades us.

I ignored him. We'd just had this conversation. When we first got into the town we had hit a bar where we watched some disturbing televised pictures of children starving to death. It was some famine, or a war, or whatever. I took it that Sandy had been moved by this, because he came out with exactly the same sort of stuff about justice.

— Yes Sandy, I had agreed, — those poor starving children; a rather shabby show all round.

— Actually, I was thinking about the infamous handball incident in the Airdrie v Dunfermline League Cup Semi-Final at Tynecastle in September 1991 where a controversial refereeing decision . . .

That was what he'd said then. Now, he's saying it all again, slavering that same shite in ma fuckin ear. I shook my head. Why did he have to bring this up? I'm losing control, I'm fucking well losing it here. — I think I've heard this story before, Sandy . . . I wasn't taking this from a cunt who wasn't real, just a character I'd created in my own mind, based vaguely on the outline of a footballer. Nothing is real, but everything is. I have only my perception to determine what reality is, and in here that perception is so vivid it makes up for my lost senses.

Sandy sulked and took the wheel after we stopped for a slash and a cup of stewed tea in an outlying village. On the other side of the Green Hill was the Emerald Forest Park. I picked up my copy of *YOUTH IN ASIA*, the book Dawson had given me. A cursory glance at the contents revealed a deeply philosophical work in which the author strove to find paths of self-deliverance.

Though far from a light read, it was just what I was after; I would recommend it to anyone grappling with the practical issues of personal political

action which one is faced with   rise   – Hiya son.
after indulging in philosophical   rise
discourse. At which point do   rise   Whae's that . . . Sandy . . .
we transfer our energies   rise
from analysis to action   rise   – Eh's lookin better the day, though, eh no Vet?
in the pursuit of   rise
change? We   rise   – Aye, eh does.
need to do this to rise

           Father is here. John Strang. Mother seems tae be here n aw. Verity Strang, nee Porteous. I'm starting to remember.

The game.

DEEPER

       DEEPER

            DEEPER – – – – – – – – I feel the sun on my face and see Sandy smiling at me. I feel a wonderous, euphoric warmth towards him; it's as if we've taken some MDMA capsules together and the whole world stops and ends at the positive force of love we feel in and around our bodies. We embrace.

     After a long silence I say, — I'm sorry, Sandy. I lost the place a bit back there.

     — The jeep's rather . . . eh, fucked, basically, he says, changing the subject to spare my embarrassment as we break our hug.

     I stand back from him and my senses are overwhelmed by a montage of images in which I see my fist slamming into the twisted rubbery sick queer face of a poof . . . it's Bernard . . . no . . . it's Gordon, his sweet, pukey breath is now in my ear and my spine trembles . . . what the fuck . . .

     Concentrate: get a fuckin grip.

     Better.

     Better.

I notice that we're no longer in the jeep but lying in our underpants by the side of the lake. I enviously give Jamieson's, muscular, athletic footballer's legs the once over. I've treated him badly during this hunt for the Stork, which definitely seems to have lost its momentum of late.

When Sandy looks up at the sun and exclaims, — It was never a penalty, I now fully understand what he's talking about. I've been trying to stage things too much in this little world of mine, trying to exercise total control over this environment, instead of trusting myself to react to events with dignity and compassion. So what if my two worlds are coming closer together? It may be the way I get closer to the Stork. Rather than cut Sandy off, I decide to go with it.

— I'm tempted to agree Sandy, I tell him.

He points to his bare chest, — I've been vindicated by the cameras. I curse that decision every fucking day of my life, Roy. It destroyed my best ever chance of a medal. It destroyed my place in the record books, my shot at footballing immortality. They had no right to do that to me. He gasped in exasperation. — What gave him the right? No man has the right . . . Tears rolled down Sandy's tanned cheeks.

No man has the right.

Where did I see that?

Where did I see that? I'm a little fazed, so I break into a nervy rant, — Come on Sandy, that type of setback's part and parcel of the game. Anyway, look at Scottish football and its dreary toytown sectarian status quo: pro-Rangers, masonic, bigoted, servile and backward. We're talking Scotland here, for God sakes . . .

SCOTLAND. NO. THIS IS SUPPOSED TO BE AFRICA OR SOMEWHERE OR EVEN INSIDE MY HEAD WHICH IS NOT A COUNTRY, IT HAS NOTHING TO . . .

I look at Jamieson, open-mouthed for a second. Fortunately he is too lost in himself to notice my gaffe. — Sandy, consider forgiveness. Consider human error. He may have just made a mistake.

Sandy thought about this, then turned to me in a state of some shock. — . . . Just a mistake? he said.

— Yes Sandy, human error.

Sandy looked up at me, a light in his eye and a smile on his face, — Yes! Of course! It was just a silly mistake. Only a game of football, twenty-two daft overgrown laddies kicking a baw around. No harm done.

harm do — — coming

up — — Darren Jackson's solitary strike was enough to put No Hibs into another League Cup final where they will face Rain-chirs. . .

— Ah'm gaunny pit this oan fir the laddie, the laddie's no wantin tae hear aboot fitba. Ma says.

— How dae you ken that but, Vet? Ah'm askin ye! How dae you ken whit the laddie wants tae hear?

So would ye like tae have fun, fun, fun,

How's about a few laughs, laughs, laughs,

Let me show you a good time . . .

DEEPER

DEEPER

DEEPER — — — — and now Sandy and I are drinking cocktails in a bar which is in a city which is possibly Nairobi or somewhere in Africa, not beautiful enough to be the Cape and this is all wrong because these two slags we saw on the road are in here and Sandy's being all smarmy and saying: – Can I buy you ladies a drink?

The slags flash predatory smiles at us.

I cut in, – No, you two slags can fuck off. This is just me and Sandy, mates like. We don't want youse cunts spoiling our adventure, spoiling our mission, spoiling our fun! It's just boys! Boys only, boys only, boys only!

I hear myself squealing petulantly at them. I fear that I've made a fool of myself in the bar, but it unsettles the women as they have dropped their disguise and are now giant praying mantises with blonde and auburn wigs, lipstick smeared on those deadly pincher-like insect jaws.

— Look Sandy, see them now, I smile, triumphant and vindicated. — See those fuckin slags as they really are!

Sandy turned away from them and smiled at the white, silver-haired barman, — These so-called ladies will not be joining us after all. He gave him a nod and a wink and the barman picked up a baseball bat from behind the bar.

— You leave. Now you leave, he shouted at the insects. They made some whirring mechanical insect sounds and backtracked awkwardly towards the door. As they exit onto the street they leave the door jammed open. We can see people passing by on the pavement outside. The draught is cooling.

I feel a great admiration for Jamieson and the way he equipped himself in circumstances which were obviously difficult. I consider whether or not to tell him so and then I think, the hell of it, yes I will, when I see something outside, shuffling awkwardly past the pub, in a slow, crippled, waddling walk.

Sandy sees it too. He throws back his drink, — Quick, Roy! It's our fucking Stork!

We storm out into the street and pursue the creature down the road and follow it   up   – Naw Vet, hud oan, this into an alleyway – – but I'm coming   up   is the tape fir the boy . . . up here naw – – naw – – naw – – – – – up

And now he's singing his New Year special:

From Russia with love . . .
I fly to you,
Much wiser since my
Goodbye to you . . .

SOME CUNT SWITCH OAF THAT FUCKIN TAPE

I've travelled the world
To learn I must return
From Russia with love.

I remember when Matt Monro played the Bird's Cage at the Doocot up Ferry Road. Matt's career was on the slide by then, but Ma and Dad really enjoyed that night out. Ever since that Bond movie and that song he'd been Dad's hero and the auld man did a passable imitation of Matt.

I've seen faces, places
and smiled for a moment,
But oh
You haunted me so.
Still my tongue-tied
Young pride
Would not let my love for you show
In case you'd say no.

— This is great though, eh Vet?

— Aye.

— We'd better be makin a move but, thirs the tea tae git n a new David Attenborough series is oan the night. Like ah sais, a new David Attenborough. It's goat the birds in it. The secret life ay the Barn Owl's the first yin. See what yir missin, Roy! Any other news fir the laddie Vet, like ah sais, other news?

— No really, everybody's fine.

— The only other news is that ah nivir voted Tory this time, in the local elections like, as a protest against this fuckin poll tax. Mind you, ah should be protestin against the fuckin Labour council; it's these cunts that keep it sae high. Ah voted SNP, no thit ah believe in Scottish independence. The Scots built the empire n these daft English cunts couldnae run it withoot us. That's ma philosophy anywey. Right Vet, ye fit?

— Aye. Tro, Roy.

— Cheerio, son.

They switch off the tape and leave as the nurses come to attend to me. I am turned over and given an enema by Nurse Patricia Devine. At one time this would have been a fantasy.

10 Bernard Visits

Bernard has come to see me in the hospital. He comes in every few days or weeks or months, I think: time has no meaning in my state. Bernard comes to read his poems to me. At last the sad queen has found a captive audience.

The only interesting thing about Bernard's visits is that he alone actually seems to believe that I can hear him. When the others talk to me their tones are strained, forced; full of self-obsessed pity, confessional and self-justifying. Bernard is the only one who seems completely at ease. We were never so at ease with each other. Why is he being so nice to me?

— Mind South Africa, Roy? Johannesfuckinburg, he spits. — I fuckin hated it there. Mind you, there was bags of talent. Ah hudnae really come oot then but. That was the one waste, these boys of all races . . . but of course, you scored more than me in that department, he giggles, — You mercenary wee closet rent-boy you.

EH? WHAT THE FUCK ARE YOU OAN ABOOT YOU SILLY FUCKIN QUEEN . . .

— Oh aye. Ah kent aw aboot you and Gordon. Poor old Uncle Gordon. Fascist prick.

How the fuck . . .

— Oh, he tried it on with me too. With me first. Disappointed Roy? Oh yes, I'm a queen alright lovey, but a damn sight more choosy than that. I mean, it's a bit like you and Gran, both hetero's, right? Well, I'm assuming, possibly naively in light of your track-record, that you wouldn't go down on her arid old cunt. Right? His voice is teasy, jesting, rather than malicious.

FUCK OFF YOU HIDEOUS QUEER . . .

— No more than I'd take Uncle Gordon into my gob. But you did, didn't you, eh Roy? What else did that sick low-life do to you, Roy?

DID AH FUCK . . . WE DID NOWT . . . IT WIS A WANK, THAT WIS AW . . .

— Sorry Roy. That was out of order. Do you mind ay South Africa though? I still think of it now. It inspired a few poems, that year did. Remember when Gordon took us to Sun City for that weekend?

I remember that. We took a short flight down from the City of Gold to the African Vegas, in the nominally independent homeland of Bophuthatswana. Gambling was, of course, illegal in the Republic. The Sun City jaunt was a little package Gordon put together to get John and Vet down there to do what he always tried to do; make them feel inadequate by showing off his wealth and his many business interests.

I remember it okay. It was a great time. We stayed in the Cascades Hotel, the most expensive and luxurious in Sun City. As the name of the hotel suggests, water was its principal theme. Its liberal use of the stuff produced rich, tropical, landscaped grounds. Kim and I spent ages wandering through this homemade rainforest, with its waterfalls, streams, paths and bridges. We were the only kids there and it was like our own private paradise. We found this little clearing by the lake where we would just go and sit, and pretend that all this was ours and we never had to go home. I was a bit of a cunt, and I'd make Kim burst oot greetin just by saying that we would be going back to Muirhouse. I wish I hudnae joked aboot it. Like me, she loved it in South Africa. But these gardens, they were like the promised land. In fact, the hotel grounds were a microcosm of the whole of Sun City. Vast quantities of water had been used to create this literal oasis in the desert, which had been landscaped imaginatively with flowers, lawns, exotic trees and streams all over the place.

It was a wonderful few days.

—with Tony and I being old enough to go out to the casinos and all that shite with Mum, Dad and Gordon

it was paradise

—the sickening greed and avarice, the front-line of South African exploitation, the playground where the settlers enjoyed the fruits of the wealth they'd ripped off

SHUT UP YOU FUCKIN POOF, IT WISNAE LIKE THAT, IT WAS BRILLIANT

—but even worse than the casinos was the fuckin cabaret. You and Kim were the lucky ones, tucked up back at the hotel. I had to sit in silence as we watched Doreen Staar's show. She was crude and extremely racist. I wrote a poem about that time.

OH GOD, SURPRISE, SURPRISE. HERE WE GO.

He bursts into a lisping rant: — This one's called: Doreen Staar's Other Cancer.

Did you see her on the telly
the other day
good family entertainment
the tabloids say

But when you're backstage
at your new faeces audition
you hear the same old shite
of your own selfish volition

She was never a singer
a comic or a dancer
I can't say I was sad
when I found out she had cancer

Great Britain's earthy northern
comedy queen
takes the rand, understand
from the racist Boer regime

So now her cells are fucked
and that's just tough titty
I remember her act
that I caught back in Sun City

She went on and on about
'them from the trees
with different skull shapes
from the likes of you and me'

Her Neo-Nazi spell
it left me fucking numb
the Boers lapped it up with zeal
so did the British ex-pat scum

But what goes round
comes round they say
so welcome to another dose
of chemotherapy

And for my part
it's time to be upfront
so fuck off and die
you carcinogenic cunt.

— What do you think then, Roy?

He asks as if I can reply. He knows I can hear him. Bernard knows.

Bernard

— Went doon a fuckin storm at the club.

Bernard

I thought it was one of your better efforts.

part three

On
The Trail
Of
The Stork

11 Casuals

I first met Lexo on the train from Glasgow Central to Motherwell. I was sitting with Dexy and Willie, out the road fae the top table and the top boys. This was my first away run with the cashies and I was determined to make an impression.

Dexy and Willie had been running with the boys for a while, rising from the baby crew. At first their stories bored me; they seemed exaggerated and I couldnae take their versions of the events, far less their supposed roles in the proceedings with any real degree ay seriousness. However, I got intrigued enough to check out some of the vibes at the home games where you had a substantial casual visiting support, and this was only really games against Aberdeen, and I became hooked on the adrenalin.

It was when Aberdeen were down with a huge crew that I was first bitten. The sheepshaggers had just signed that Charlie Nicholas cunt fae Arsenal, the soapdodger, and there was a heavy atmosphere. These cunts fancied their chances. I did a bit of mouthing and jostling up Regent Road, but there were too many polis aboot for any real swedgin tae take place.

On the train, on this dull Wednesday night, we were assured that it would be different. Dexy, Willie and myself were eager lieutenants, laughing sycophantically at any jocular top boy who played to the gallery, but remaining stern, impassive and deferential when a psycho held court.

Lexo went around the train giving a pep-talk. — Mind, nae cunt better shite oot. Remember, a cunt that messes is a cunt that dies. We're the hardest crew in Europe. We dinnae fuckin run. Mind. We dinnae fuckin run.

We didnae have tae wait long before meeting up with the

Motherwell casuals. They were upon us at the station and I was shit-scared. I didn't know why; it seemed as if I'd been surrounded by latent and manifest violence all my life. This was different though, a new situation. It's only now I realise that behaviour always has a context and precedents, it's what you do rather than what you are, although we often never recognise that context or understand what these precedents are. I remember thinking; swallow the fear, feel the buzz. That was what Lexo said. Then I saw this thin, spectacularly white guy, almost albino, just charging into the Motherwell boys and scattering them. I steamed in swinging, kicking and biting. This cunt I was hitting was hitting me back but it was like I couldn't feel a thing and I knew that he could because his eyes were filling up with fear and it was the best feeling on earth. Then he was on his arse. The next thing I knew was that I was being pulled off one cunt by some of our boys, and dragged away down the road as polis sirens filled the air. I was snarling like a demented animal, wanting only to get back and waste the cunt on the ground for good.

At the game I was trembling inside with excitement. We all were. We laughed with liberating hysteria at any banal joke or observation made about the swedgin. I don't remember anything about the match, except wee Mickey Weir running up and down the wing, trying vainly to play fitba, surrounded by claret and amber giants and a blind referee. We lost one-nil. Back on the train with a police escort to Glasgow then Edinburgh, the match was never mentioned once. Aw the talk was aboot the swedge.

Lexo came over to us. Dexy, looking sheepish, got up to let him sit beside me. Hovering over the table, he was dismissed as Lexo snapped, — Nose fuckin botherin ye, cunt?

He departed looking like a timid dog. Dexy had not acquitted himself well in the swedge tonight.

— Fuckin wanker, he smiled, then shouted back down the train, — Ghostie! C'mere the now, ya cunt!

The albino-looking guy named Ghostie came and joined us. You would never think to look at him that the cunt was particularly hard, but every fucker knew him as a crazy radge. He was on-form at

Motherwell. He'd been first in, he had given me the confidence. I'd never seen anything so fast, so ruthless and powerful.

— Whit's yir name, pal? he asked.

— Roy. Roy Strang.

— Strang. Got a brar?

— Aye, Tony Strang.

He nodded in vague recognition. – Whair ye fi?

— Muirhoose.

— Schemie, eh? he laughed.

I felt anger rise in me. Whae the fuck did this wide-o think he wis? I tried to control it. I knew who he was. Ghostie. The Ghost. I'd seen him in action; only briefly as I'd been too involved myself, but enough tae ken that ah'd never mess wi the cunt.

— Me n aw, he smiled. Fi Niddrie. Stey in toon now, though. Cannae be bothered wi the fuckin scheme any mair. Ye ken satellite dishes? he asked.

— Aye.

— Whit dae they call the wee boax oan the back ay the satellite dish?

— Eh, dunno likes.

— The council's, he laughed. I was pleased to join in.

That was the start of my cashie activities. The season was in its infancy and I was already known tae the top boys.

I was arrested at Parkhead for breaking a Weedgie's jaw; fortunately I managed to sling my knuckleduster. Our strategy for Glasgow games was to merge with the crowd and just start laying into every cunt to panic them. All it took was organisation and bottle. The organisation was really just about timing, moving at the right time. I stiffened some stupid fucker for the crime of being a total spaz-wit with loads of badges of the Pope and IRA on his scarf, but a couple of polis came straight after me. I ran through the crowd, but one sneaky soapdodging cunt stuck a leg oot and I lost my balance and fell and was huckled.

Ma and Dad were fucked off at the court case.

— Ah'm no wantin you gittin intae bother, Roy. Ye could lose yir joab, son. You're supposed tae be the sensible yin in the faimlay,

Dad mused. He was in a strange position; concerned, but gratified that all those boxing lessons hadn't gone to waste. — Ah kent wi shouldnae huv come back here. We should've steyed in Sooth Efrikay.

— Aw, c'mon, Dad . . .

— Dinnae come oan Dad me. Like ah sais, Sooth Efrikay.

— Like ah sais, he droned on, — ye could lose yir joab. They dinnae grow oan trees nowadays, eh. Specially no in computers. Thing ay the future.

— Aye, right.

— N whit fir, eh? Whit fir? Ah'm askin ye! Fir they fuckin casual bampots. Ah mean, it's no as if thir even interested in the fitba these cunts. Ah see yis aw at Easter Road. It's aw designer labels wi these cunts, like ah sais, fuckin designer labels.

— Shite.

— Aw aye, ye kin shite aw ye want tae, bit ah've read aw aboot it. In the *Evening News*. Fuckin mobile phones, the loat. Ye tryin tae tell ays that's aw rubbish, eh? Ah'm askin ye!

— Aye. It's shite. Pure shite.

I was less scared of the auld man now. He seemed a sadder, weaker figure, broken by his brother's death and the end of the South African dream. He now worked as a store detective in John Menzies.

I was getting on, leading a compartmentalised life. The weekends it was clubs and fitba with the boys, and I had been shagging a few birds. Joining the cashies had been a bonus on that score. Although I was never happy with the wey ah looked, being a cashie I had access to aw the fanny I needed. Sometimes just skankers likes, but a ride's a ride. It was something to do eftir the swedgin; it was better than no gettin a ride. That fucks up a cunt's self-esteem. Too right. At work I was getting on alright, doing well in my day release in computer studies at Napier College. I enjoyed setting up programmes to run policies: it was a challenge and the money was okay. I still resolved to get into a flat in town and away from my family. The thing was that I was spending a lot of dough as well, mostly on clathes. Nearly every penny I had went on new gear.

The rumours about me being a cashie started to circulate at the work. It was a busy time for us and the newspapers were on our case. Big-time soccer violence in Scotland had always been aboot really thick Weedgies who never went to church knocking fuck oot ay each other to establish who had the best brand of Christianity. We were big news because we were different; stylish, into the violence just for itself, and in possession of decent IQs.

I enjoyed the notoriety. It was good seeing all the straight-peg cunts at my work look at me with respect and trepidation. I just kept quiet. Even when that nosey dyke cow of a supervisor Jane Hathaway tried to bait me by reading out incidents from the paper on a Monday, I just kept quiet. Nae cunt had the bottle tae come right out and ask me if I was involved. More than the notoriety, I enjoyed the sense of enigma.

There was plenty of opportunity tae make money wi the cashies, but I was only really interested in the swedgin. There was less risk in that. I sussed out quickly that the polis werenae bothered too much aboot crimes against the person as long as you never bothered posh cunts or shoppers. When you started tryin tae extort dough fae the pubs, clubs n shoaps, that was when the cunts got nippy. There wis nae wey ah wis gaunny dae time.

There was a big do at the Pilton Hilton, the Commodore Hotel; Tony was getting married to this lassie called Hannah. He brought her roond tae the hoose one night and announced it. She looked really nice, even though she was obviously up the stick. She was moving intae Tony's flat. I was surprised, because I was sure I kent her from somewhere.

— Aboot time ye wir settlin doon, John said, raising a glass of whisky. He insisted we all drank some as a toast. — Like ah sais, ye cannae beat the mairriage stakes. Didnae dae me any herm! He winked at my Ma who gave him a cloying smile.

Bernard said something simpering and Kim started tae greet. Ah jist said: — Nice one Tone, slapped the cunt oan the back and forced the rancid whisky doon wi loads ay lemonade.

At the wedding I got a right fuckin shock when I saw who one of the bridesmaids was. She was dressed in a long peach dress, matching one worn by another lassie and these two wee lassies. It was The Big Ride; Hamilton's shag. She was Hannah's sister, which I suppose made The Big Ride my in-law, or something.

I had clocked her in the church and I couldnae stop looking at her at the reception. I was staring at her. We were introduced, the two families. They'd aw been up at oor hoose before but I had been oot, I never really took any notice.

— So you're Roy, she said.

The fuckin boot didnae even recognise me.

I kept staring at her. As the night wore on, I never took my eyes off her. Eventually she came over to me. — Is thir something wrong? she asked, sitting down beside me.

— You dinnae mind ay me, eh no? I smiled.

She looked quizzical and started mentioning names. Most of them meant little to me, just cunts I vaguely knew through the scheme and the school.

— You used tae go oot wi Stuart Hamilton, I told her.

She blushed a little bit. — That was ages ago . . . she simpered.

— Did eh fuck ye, aye? I asked, looking her up and down. Good tits oan it like.

She screwed her face up and frowned at me. Her prettiness collapsed into ugliness. She was fairly heavily built as well, much broader than Hannah. She'd be a fat sow in a few years' time. Some lassies just kept getting bigger; it was like the daft cows didnae ken when tae stoap. — What? she said weakly.

— Ah mind ay you. You n Hammy n that Gilchrist cunt. Ye pilled ays up ootside the chippie in Muirhoose.

I saw her face register vague recognition.

— Aw . . . c'moan . . . that wis ages ago . . .

— Aye. Too right it wis fuckin ages ago. Like tae see yis dae it now. Whair is that cunt Hammy these days? Ah've been keepin ma fuckin eye oot fir that wanker.

— Ah dinnae ken, ah jist hung aboot wi um whin ah wis younger . . . that wis ages ago . . .

— Ye married? I asked.

— Used tae be, she said.

— Aw, ah goes, makin ma voice aw soft, — did yir felly find oot ye wir a slut? Wis that how eh kicked ye intae touch? Hus Tony fucked ye yet? Ah bet eh hus.

Her features seemed to draw in towards the centre of her face. — You're fuckin tapped, son, she hissed. — Fuck off! She stood up and started moving away. I just smiled. Then she came back and said: — We might be married intae the same family, bit ah dinnae want tae talk tae you. Jist stey oot ay ma wey. You're fuckin sick!

— Fuck off, ya fat hoor, I sneered, drinking in her rage as she turned away.

I kept noising her up during the reception. I was having a great time. — Hoor, I whispered in her ear every time I passed her.

One time she cracked up and confronted me, — You're fuckin spoilin ma sister's big day, she whispered in a harsh hiss. – If ye dinnae fuck off, I'll tell Tony!

— Good, I smiled. — Go ahead. It'll save me tellin um that his sister-in-law's a fuckin hingoot . . . Benny! I shouted, as my Uncle Benny, my Ma's brother, came across. The Big Ride departed.

— Ah wisnae crampin yir style thair Roy, wis ah? Benny asked, raising an eyebrow. — Tidy piece.

— Naw, nae danger. Widnae touch it wi yours, Ben. A right boot: really pits it aroond. Fanny like the Mersey Tunnel, I laughed. Benny joined in.

Later on I saw the daft sow starting tae greet. She left wi another lassie just eftir that. I went over to the married couple and enjoyed a dance with the beautiful bride. I then escorted her back to the handsome groom and gave her a peck on the cheek. — You're a lucky man, Tony.

— Ah ken that, Tony smiled.

— Great do this, by the way, Hannah, I said. — Your folks have done us proud.

— Aye, it's just a pity aboot Sylvia.

— Your sister? What's wrong wi her? I asked with fake concern.

— She's away. Wisnae feeling well.

— That's a shame.

I enjoyed that wedding. Dad got pished and punched this radge who was, apparently, trying to preach socialism at him. That was the only real upset. I also found Kim necking with this daft cunt in the corridor. — Dinnae tell naebody, eh no Roy, she said, obviously hoping that I'd broadcast to the world that she had a fuckin boyfriend. Bernard sloped off early, no doubt to indulge in the practice of arse-banditry. I ended up pished with my Uncle Benny and the two Jackies.

Not a bad night. I never saw The Big Ride again, although I asked after her regularly.

The house was too crowded, even wi Tony away. Kim had her own room and I was in a room with Bernard. That was bad patter; sharing a bedroom with a poof. Sometimes he'd move oot for a bit, but he always came back. Fuck knows why. I never figured out why he stayed for so long. I never figured out why *I* stayed for so long.

Bernard was constantly blowing my cool. I fancied myself as a hard cunt and it was fuckin shan to have *that* for a brother. It made me sick to listen to his lisping, camp patter as he read out his poetry. He always recited it to my Ma, who was embarrassed by it, but as a teacher had once described Bernard as 'gifted', she gamely encouraged him. That was years ago, in the primary, and he'd done fuck all since but ponce about. He worked as a barman in a queers' pub in the city centre and sold jewelry on a stall at Ingliston Market.

Posing in the fuckin stair, he'd read his shitey poems tae aw the young fanny who seemed tae fag-hag him:

> The situation that is life
> sustainable, yet renewable
> its elements building blocks
> in a completed construction
> yet which cannot be identified as such
>   in isolation
>
> To persecute me for my sexuality
> is to pander to the slavedeck of false illusion
> when the tapes play mixed messages
> through mediums yet to be discovered

> Avanti! I scream, my Italian blood
> courses through my veins
> not to be denied

Aw this wis weird enough, but we'd sometimes get it after our meal on a Sunday, if the auld man went tae the pub. Ma would cook up things like curry and rice, always with chips or tatties and two veg oan the side ay the plate.

One Sunday I asked Tony and Hannah, rather casually, I thought, about Hannah's sister Sylvia, The Big Ride. To my shock my auld man said: — Ah think Roy's goat a wee thing aboot Hannah's sister. Heard ye mention her before, like ah sais, heard ye ask aboot her before.

— Naw ah nivir, I replied. It wasn't that I was being shy, I just couldn't recall mentioning the sow in front of them.

— Aye ye huv, like ah sais, mentioned hur before, he teased, his jaw stretching downwards like Mr Fantastic's. His smile just got broader and broader and as his teeth were exposed, he started to take on the appearance of the Alien in the films of the same name.

In Muirhoose nae cunt can hear ye scream . . . well, they can hear ye, they just dinnae gie a fuck.

He held that radge expression and I felt my face go red and I got a bigger beamer than I had in the first place.

— What a beamer, Tony laughed.

— Aye, right, I snapped.

Laughter filled the room, Kim's shrill tones effortlessly dominating the rest.

I felt my head pound and my pulse quicken. The smell of the food was vivid and intense. Ah'm fuckin Roy Strang. Ah'm fuckin . . . I took a deep breath and pulled myself together.

— Went beetroot rid, so eh did. Like ah sais, beetroot rid, my auld man laughed, jabbing fork into space.

— You'll be the next yin tae git mairried, Roy, Kim said in her banal, nasal way, — cause it'll no be me, that's fir sure . . .

Her nauseating intervention had the desired effect of getting everyone to focus on her romantic life. I suppose I should have thanked her. I resolved to shut up about The Big Ride. I had been weak and had obviously broken, albeit unintentionally, one of my own key rules: say nowt tae nae cunt aboot anything.

When Tony's bairn came, he seemed tae spend mair time back at oor place than ever. For some reason he started to come oan his ain oan a Sunday fir dinner. I think Hannah went tae her Ma's wi the bairn. I don't think he liked her family but I never worked up the bottle to ask him what he thought of The Big Ride. That was out of the question now. I was sure he'd fucked her, or at least tried to. This was simply because, knowing Tony as I did, I couldn't imagine him *not* trying it on with her. Equally, it was hard to imagine The Big Ride not giein him his hole if he did try it on.

Tony would sit in an armchair, glancing up fae the set as Bernard lisped oot his poems. There was one time he looked up and said derisively, — Poetry, schmoetry, pulling the ring on a tin of export. He was browsing at the highlights of the Dundee United v St. Johnstone match on Scotsport. In the words of the commentator it turned out to be a 'game of few highlights'.

— You understand nowt, son, Bernard simpered.

— Ah understand that your poetry is well short ay piss-poor, Tony smiled.

— So we're the world expert on poetry now, ur we Tony? So tell us all, where did you acquire this expertise? Tony, world expert on everything. Armchair renaissance man. As *au fait* with darts as he is pool, Bernard hissed in a derisive manner as I heard a key turn in the door. John had come back early from the pub.

— Ah ken what's shite and what's no. Your poetry isnae shite, ah'll gie ye that. It needs tae improve a hundred per cent before it can be elavated tae that category.

John had come in and sat down and he started slapping his thighs. — Eh's goat ye thair, Bernard. Ha ha ha. Like ah sais, goat ye thair. Yill nivir beat oor Tony whin it comes tae words, like.

— I refuse tae be drawn intae a war of words with stupid people, Bernard said condescendingly, exiting with a camp flourish. I suspected that he was enjoying this performance and felt a twinge of admiration for him which I quickly stifled, reminding myself that he was a sick, diseased beast.

— Hi! John shouted. — Whae're you fuckin well callin stupid! Ah'm askin ye! TRY GITTIN A PROPER JOAB INSTID AY DAEIN AW THAT POOFY SHITE THIT NAEBODY'S FUCKIN WELL INTERESTIT IN!

The front door slammed loudly.

— John! Tony! Vet moaned. — Ye cannae keep gittin oantae the laddie. Leave um alane. At least ehs poetry's hermless. No like some ah could mention, she looked over at me with a sulky pout.

— What's that supposed tae mean then? I asked.

— You ken. They bloody casuals. Yill end up in the jail. You wi that joab in computers n aw. Thing ay the future.

— That's right, Vet! That's fuckin well right! John snapped. — Fuckin casuals. Jeapordisin a fuckin good joab tae hing aroond wi they radge cunts. Computers n aw, like yir Ma sais, the thing ay the future. You want tae buck up yir ideas, son. Like ah sais, buck up yir ideas.

I looked at him coldly. — Ye ken what ah've been daein at work fir the last six months? Ah set up this programme tae call up files when a man reaches retirement age at sixty-five and a woman at sixty. That was aboot a week's work. Fir the past six months ah've been tryin tae train doss-brained cunts how tae operate this simple procedure, which is like gaun tae the toilet, daein a shite but rememberin tae take yir keks of first n wipe yir erse eftir.

The reverence that people who know fuck all about them have for computers disgusts me. Anyway, for me my work was just a refuge: a place to go where my head couldn't be nipped by my family. By either of my families, I suppose, because the cashies were my family n aw now. I could set anything up; that wis barry, you just got on wi it. I set it up, and some smarmy cunt peyed five times as much took the credit. It didnae bother ays though. What did get oan ma tits wis tryin tae teach the system tae doss-brained cunts.

— Aye, bit it's a still a joab! A well-peyed joab! Dinnae tell ays you're no stuffin money away!

Vet cut in, — C'moan John, that's no fair, the laddie earns ehs keep.

The cunt was on shaky ground here. He was always tapping ays up in the week; cash for fags, drink. — Aye, well right, but that's mair thin kin be said ay some. That bloody Bernard. A fuckin buftie!

— Total fuckin embarrassment, Tony said.

— It's no natural, like ah sais, no fuckin natural, John said. — Yir no tryin tae tell ays that ye think it's natural, tae huv sex wi another man? He looked at us all in turn, stopping at Vet.

What's natural? I shrugged, more to support my mother who looked quite upset, than Bernard, who I didnae give a toss about.

— Jist as well eh nivir came fae me, John said.

Cheeky cunt him, with Elgin still at the GORGIE VENTURE FOR EXCEPTIONAL YOUNG MEN, me in the casuals and Kim, perennially a few years behind in her school work, now working at the baker's. Ally that to our hall-of-mirrors look and he's got a fuckin nerve thinking that he's spawned some sort of master race.

Vet looked coldly at him, — Might as well huv come fae you.

— What's that meant tae mean? Eh? Ah'm asking ye! What's that meant tae mean?

— Your fuckin faithir, that's what that's meant tae mean!

This was a sore point with Dad. His old man had been put away for interfering with young boys. Nae cunt really talked aboot it.

— Whit aboot ma faither . . .

— He went that wey.

— MA FAITHER DIDNAE GO ANY FUCKIN WEY! MA FAITHER WISNAE A WELL MAN! Tony and I had to restrain him as he raised his hands to Ma. I'd forgotten his strength and he took me out with an elbow to the nose. The pain was overpowering and my eyes kept filling with water. In no time he had Tony wrestled to the ground and was holding him by the hair, threatening to put the boot in.

— Dinnae Dad! I shouted, trying to stem the blood, tears and snot that leaked out of my face.

He let Tony go, and pursued Ma into the kitchen. She had

grabbed the kitchen knife and was screaming: — COME OAN THEN YA FUCKIN SHITE! AH'LL FUCKIN KILL YE! I ran upstairs to their room and grabbed his shotgun from under the bed. I thought about going back downstairs and confronting him, bolstered by the weapon, but he was radge enough to try and take it from me, and then somebody would be well fucked. I locked myself in the toilet with the gun, and didn't leave until the screaming had died down.

I heard the noise of the front door slamming. I put the shotgun back. Tony was alone downstairs. — Ma and John's gone up the pub. Aw lovey-dovey again. Ye comin up? He asked, clicking off the telly at the handset.

Was I coming up? No. I was going deeper. Deeper into trouble. Deeper into the Marabou Stork nightmares.

DEEPER
     DEEPER
          DEEPER – – – – into the narrow alley with Jamieson, following the stench of the diseased, decaying carrion on the ugly, waddling bird. The alley is dark, the air is surprisingly cold. Something is moving in the shadows amongst the large, stinking rubbish piles. Something very evil and nasty.

— Expose yourself, you sick, twisted demon! Sandy screams into the darkness. — You think you can destroy the game!

— No fucking chance of that, Johnny Stork! I hiss — Sandy and I are wise to your foul plans. We know that you want to destroy the colour, the noise, the fun and the gaiety associated with . . .

The words stick in my throat as the large predator emerges from the shadows.

Sandy moves forward, but I'm rooted to the spot. I feel   eh   what the fuck is this something cold and wet on the   eh   – I know you felt that, Roy. side of my face and smell perfume eh   My little sleeping beauty . . .

it's her, that crazy sow that's coming for me . . . naw . . .

— I'll bet you felt that, Roy, I'll bet you felt me kiss you then.

Patricia. Thank fuck. What are you playing at ya daft cunt?

— You know what I think, Roy Strang? I think all you need is to feel wanted, to feel loved. Let me in, Roy. Let us all in. You're surrounded by love, Roy. Your family, your friends. Let us in.

FUCK OFF YA DIPPIT CUNT!

DEEPER

DEEPER — — — — — — — — but not too deep. Not back to that fuckin alleyway with the Stork. No yet. But naw, I didnae go up the pub with Tony that night, didnae go tae see my Ma and Dad. I sat in on my own, enjoying the rare feeling of having the hoose tae masel. It gave me time to think.

I had been having some minor hassle at work. That cow Hathaway confronted me aboot my activities with the cashies. I'd been done and fined for my part in what I thought was a minor swedge, but which the papers called a riot. Hathaway called me through into Colin Sproul's office.

Sproul was an intense, tormented looking guy. It had been him who had interviewed me for the job when I'd first started. He always came across as a fair-minded cunt likes. It was blatantly obvious that he had been pushed into staging this daft performance by Hathaway.

— Eh . . . hello, Roy. We just wanted a little word with you, Jane and I.

Hathaway gave me a toothy false photo-flash smile.

I nodded.

— Your work's been excellent, Sproul began, — absolutely first class, he beamed with an almost awestruck smile. He shook his head in mock disbelief, — I still don't know how you managed to incorporate that geographical cross-referencing report into the S.S. 3001 system. That was genius.

I felt my face redden with a simultaneous surge of gratitude and resentment towards Sproul. I was about to say something when I looked at Hathaway's face. She was livid and she couldn't control it.

— Yes, it was rather well done, she said briskly, — but I'm sure that Roy would acknowledge the tremendous support and assistance he had from the rest of the team.

That was bullshit; I'd developed that procedure in complete isolation. I said nowt but.

— Oh quite so, Sproul nodded.

Hathaway's face took on a slyer demeanour. — You see, we want people to be able to get on at Scottish Spinsters', to develop with the organisation. You understand that, don't you, Roy?

— Aye, I said.

Sproul smiled benignly, — You see, we're a very old institution Roy, and still pretty conservative in our own way . . . some would say a little too conservative . . . he turned to Hathaway, looking for some sort of endorsement, but got only a sharp glare of disapproval, — . . . but that's by the way, he nervously coughed. — Your work, though, is excellent, excellent. And while you're outside this building, outside office hours; what you do is your own concern . . . but at the same time . . .

Hathaway smiled grimly, — It's come to our attention that you're a member of a soccer hooligan gang.

— Eh? I said incredulously. Soccer hooligan gang. Stupid fuckin fat dyke.

— We're not accusing you of anything, Roy. It's just that certain rumours have been circulating about you, rumours which could be detrimental to your future career progression, Sproul told me.

— Aye, I sometimes go tae the fitba likes. Ah dinnae get involved in any bother though.

— Roy, said Hathaway, with a sombre tone and expression, — we've seen your name in the papers. You broke a man's jaw, it said.

I gave her a tired look, and shook my head wearily. — I'm sick tae the back teeth of these rumours. Yes, I was at a match in Glasgow with some friends. It can be quite rough through there at the games and these men, obviously drunk, started spitting at us when they heard our Edinburgh accents. We just walked away. One guy though, he followed me and started kicking me. I lashed out in self-defence. Unfortunately, that was the part of the incident witnessed by the police officer. Surprise, surprise, the Strathclyde Police took the word of locals over a man from Edinburgh. I thought, though, that my own employers would be a wee bit more inclined to give me the benefit of the doubt on this issue.

I saw Sproul's eyes light up and his lips stretch into a grin. Hathaway looked dejected. She wanted old thick schemie Roy Strang to hang himself, but naw, I wasnae gaunny gie the cunt the satisfaction.

The following week I got arrested at Middlesbrough at an English second division match. We were just doon for a bit of mischief. There was little happening at Hibs v St. Johnstone; the baby crew could handle the Fair City Firm wankers with ease. We had headed south for a wee break and turned over a pub. I bottled some cunt.

I remember Lexo saying to the barman, — Eight Becks, mate. Then he noticed a squad of scarfers come in from a bus. — Naw, make it Grolsch, eh, he said. He turned to me and winked, — Heavier boatils, eh.

They certainly were.

Thank fuck that one didnae make the Scottish papers.

So things were sorted for a bit. It was going well, I reflected, as I sat alone enjoying the solitude in the house, stroking Winston Two. — I'm not a bad Hibby-Wibby Boysie-Woysie, am I, Winners? No! No! I'm just Roysie-Woysie who does the computey-wuteys, eh? A firework exploded outside; Winston Two whimpered and ran under the sideboard. It was Guy Fawkes' night soon. Winston hated fireworks. It was something tae think aboot. I was still up for wasting that cunt ay a dug and ah wis intae daein it really soon.

That night Ma, Dad and Tony came back pished. Kim came in later, her neck covered in purple love-bites, an even more far-away and vacuous look on her face than normal.

— Ye should've bought him a packet ay crisps, Tony smiled at her.

She self-consciously touched her neck and smiled, — Aw this? Dae ye notice it? Kin ye see it that easy?

Dad looked angry, but said nothing. I watched as his knuckles went white gripping the armchair. When Kim went up to bed, he turned to Vet and said: — You want tae huv a word wi that lassie. Actin like a slag, like ah sais, a fuckin slag . . .

— Dinnae be fuckin silly, John. She's a young lassie bichrist.
Eventually Ma turned in, leaving John, Tony and I in the front
room. John looked at us emotionally, it was as if he was almost ready
to cry. — That's some fuckin woman. Your mother, he pointed at
me, then at Tony, — your mother n aw. A fuckin great woman, the
best yir ivir likely tae find. His voice got higher. — Youse remember
that! Whativir else yis dae, yis eywis treat that fuckin woman wi
respect, like ah sais, respect. Cause that's the best fuckin woman yis
are ivir likely tae see in yir fuckin lives! Your fuckin mother!
— Aye Dad, Ma's sound . . . I said sombrely.
— Like you say John, she's the best, Tony nodded.
Dad stood up and went over to the window. His voice took on a
compulsive, mocking bent as he thumbed over his shoulder at the
outside world. — Ah ken whit they cunts think ay us. Ah ken aw
they cunts. Ken what they are? Ah'll fuckin well tell ye what they
are, he slurred, — Rubbish. Not fuckin quoted. That's these cunts:
not fuckin quoted.

He had always been paranoid about the neighbours and had
started to keep a dossier on the other occupants of our block and the
one behind us. He had recently bought a personal computer from a
mate down The Gunner, and I was press-ganged into showing him
how to set up files on the neighbours. I didn't want to encourage him
in this pointless lunacy, but to refuse cooperation would have caused
a bigger scene. Dad would watch the neighbours' comings and
goings and record their *modus operandii* on his files, some of which
became quite detailed.

I enjoyed having the odd look at them:

15/5 BROWN
Father: Arthur   *Mother: Frances*
Children: Maureen (10 ish) and Stephen (6 ish)

Arthur works for GPO. Seems not too bad. Frances seems a nice woman, clean. The two wee yins are always well-dressed. Arthur sometimes plays darts at The Doocot.

Verdict: Decent people; no real threat to security.

15/6 PEARSON
Father: Alan (no longer living there) Mother: 'Fat Cow' Maggie
Children: Debbie (16) Gillian (14) Donna (11)

That fat stupid cow tries to monopolise wash-room. Dirty cunt who does not wrap rubbish before putting it in chute. Caught her twice. Ignorant person with dirty mouth. Always ready to phone police. Alan Pearson a thief. Sold Jackie useless CDs at The Gunner. Lucky for him he has done runner. Debbie is a cheeky cow with a mouth like the mother's. A real slut, the kind of lassie who will end up in a ditch by the side of the road one day. Have told our Kim to keep away from this whore. The other sister is going the same way. The wee one is nice but should go into care before she turns out like the rest.

Verdict: Scum. Maximum security threat, repeat, maximum security threat.

While Dad's behaviour was obviously unhealthy, he actually seemed better after getting the computer, the effort of keeping up and monitoring the records seemed to dissipate a lot of his destructive energy. On this night, however, he was drunk and wound up. I kept thinking of Ma singing that Bond song, 'Nobody Does it Better'.

Like heaven above me,
The spy who loved me
Is keepin all my secrets safe tonight.

Tony raised his eyebrows at me as Dad started to pace up and down the living-room like a caged beast, muttering curses under his breath. Just as he seemed to be settling down, he sprang to the window and threw it open. He shouted into the night: JOHN STRANG'S MA NAME! FUCK YIS AW, YA CUNTS! ANY BASTARD IN THIS FUCKIN SCHEME'S GOAT ANYTHING TAE SAY TAE ME OR MA FAIMLAY, YIS KIN SAY IT TAE MA FUCKIN FACE!

— Take it easy, Dad, I said. — Yi'll huv the fuckin polis roond, eh.

He shut the window and said to me and Tony: — People in this scheme huv been makin a loat ay allegations aboot this faimlay. Well, ah want tae hear what these allegators have goat tae say for themselves!

— Ah heard they were gettin a bit snappy, Tony mused.

I started sniggering as John looked coldly and uncomprehendingly at him. — Eh? he said.

— The alligators John, Tony said, opening his jaws wide and making exaggerated snapping motions.

There was a tense silence for a couple of seconds, then John's face burst into a smile and we all started laughing, Tony and I with relief as the tension drained away. — Huh, huh, huh, no bad Tony, no bad. It wis the great man hissel that sais thit ye cannae deal wi the maist serious things in the world if ye cannae understand the maist amusing.

Aye, right.

My auld man then stroked the servile Winston Two. — We'll show the cunts, eh boy? The Strangs, he said softly, — we'll show aw these cunts. We'll come shinin through. We eywis fuckin do.

The next day I bought some fireworks which I kept in my desk drawer at work.

Apart from nosiness and the odd bit of useful information it provided (I'd decided that I'd try and get a ride off Debbie Pearson, who was Kim's pal: Tony'd already been there) I had little interest in the auld man's daft obsessions. Anyway, the cashies was my time. The violence was brilliant; different from in the hoose. The excitement, the buzz, the feeling of your body charged up with it all. You could prepare for it with the cashies, get psyched up n that, but you didnae want tae live like that at hame. Ye wanted somewhair whair ye could shut the door n forget it aw.

I liked clubbing, but I preferred a swedge rush to anything. I didnae like drugs. I had a fuckin bad time on acid. We were up this club, this place at The Venue oan a Thursday night. A loat ay the boys were intae it: techno upstairs and garagey hip-hop doonstairs. I hated that kind of music, cause ah wis mair intae indie stuff, but I went along cause the boys were intae it and there was plenty spare fanny floating around. I took a tab ay acid and I sort ay freaked. It was awright at first, but it jist goat stronger and stronger and ah couldnae keep the bad thoughts oot ay ma heid. I wis thinking aboot that poofy cunt Gordon n believing that there were dugs coming and they wir gaunny tear ays apart. Ah kept seein the heid ay that flamingo in the stork's mooth and it wis shouting oan ays tae help it, in a sad, sick voice.

Ali Dempsey, one of the boys in the cashies, came n talked ays doon. — Yuv goat tae remember Strangy, it's aw jis a distortion ay light n sound. That's aw acid is, nae matter how bad it seems. It's jist the distortions ay light and sound n your imagination fires up tae fill in the gaps.

— Thir's shite in ma heid, Demps, I gasped. — My heart must be beatin too fast . . . ah'm gaunny fuckin peg oot here man . . .

— Naw yir no. It's cool. Jist stey cool. It's awright.

Demps kept it gaun fir ays. He talked ays doon. Then he took ays back tae his flat n sat up wi ays. Sound cunt Demps. Anywey, that wis me finished wi drugs.

The boys tried tae git ays tae take an ecky, bit ah wis jist intae Becks, eh. Besides, clubs wir jist a place tae come doon n talk aboot the swedge n mibbe bag oaf wi some fanny as far as ah wis concerned. Ah loved swedgin. It was easy, n aw; once you got beyond your second or third pagger, once you learned to get past your fear and pain and just go with it, just keep going, keep swinging and booting at anything that came your way, and inspect the damage later. I never got hurt badly; a few bruised ribs and a deep cut above the eye once at Pittodrie.

There were much harder cunts in the casuals than me, and guys who were much better swedgers. They knew that, and so did I. What I had though, was the attitude that marked out most of the top boys; it wasn't even bottle. It was not giving a fuck about anything.

As I've said, one of the best aspects of being a casual was the fanny. Most of the boys were good-looking or average looking guys. While I was ugly and knew it, I lost a level of self-consciousness as my status as a swedger increased and I did more shagging than most. I'd wasted a lot of time in my adolescence, after I'd shagged that dog in the budget room, just looking at myself in the mirror, wondering why my head was too big for my body, and why my body was too big for my small, stumpy legs. The answer was staring me in the face over the top of a *Daily Record* at breakfast time most mornings. I was the auld man's double. So I'd wasted a lot of time and now I wanted it more than maist cunts. I had access to half the decent fanny in the toon.

One afternoon, I finished work early and picked up a juicy bone for Winston Two at a butcher's in Leith Walk. I got home before everyone else and the beast cowered as he saw me enter. It was strange to think that I'd taken a mauling from that pathetic old thing.

— Winners . . . I panted, and the beast took this as his cue to relax and wag his tail. He gave me his head to clap and jumped up on his hind legs with his front ones resting on the kitchen worktop. His tail wagged and his tongue lolled as he scented the bone with that juicy meat covering it. — Yes, it's your's boy, isn't it, all for Winners . . . a present for Winners, I told him, as I hammered some six-inch nails through the bone and the meat. I put the bone in my Adidas bag and zipped it up. — Later boy, later, I told him as he sniffed at the bag. He continued sniffing. My boot made contact with his side and he let out a yelp and scuttled off.

Just then Ma came in from work. She did the dinners in an old people's home now. Kim got in shortly after her, with some cakes from the baker's. She said that she was going to take Winston Two oot for a walk before tea. — Winners needs to stretch his legs across the wasteland. Yes he does, yes he does, she said, crouching down and frolicking with the panting beast.

— Ah'll git ye doon the road, Kim, ah've goat some records tae droap oaf roond tae Bri, eh. I held up the Adidas bag.

As we walked I noted that a few strays were wandering over the wasteland. One was a filthy brown dog which howled constantly like a wolf. — Listen tae that, I said distracting Kim.

— It's an awfay shame fir they stray dugs thit thuv no goat good homes like Winston, eh Roy, eh it's a shame? Sometimes ah wish that we could take aw they dugs, just sort ay adopt thum aw, eh Roy?

As she babbled looking over to the strays, I slipped the bone out of the bag. Winston went straight for it.

— What's Winners found? Kim asked.

— Dunno, looks like a bone, eh, I replied.

— C'moan Winston, that's no fair cause you git fed enough n thir's aw they perr starvin dugs . . . you're a lucky boy Winalot . . . Kim bleated as the dug went crazy over the bone. — Winners, Winners, Winalot, Winners, Winners what you . . .

Kim's expression turned to one of horror as Winston yelped and a nail shot out through his top jaw.

The beast stormed off across the wasteland yelping and shaking his head and was instantly pursued by the group of strays.

— WINSTON! WIIIIGGHHHNNNNSTIN! Kim bellowed, but the dog ran around in agony, pursued by the snapping pack, unable to drop the bone.

The strays set upon him, unable to distinguish between his cut, bleeding jaws and the tender meat which hung from them.

They ripped his face apart.

Kim started screaming and kicking at them, and I had to join in and help in case the stupid cow got torn to bits herself. Eventually we managed to drag Winston Two away. That brown bastard that howled was particularly persistent, but I caught the cunt a beauty with a segged-brogue heel stomp to the body and he staggered away whining.

The vet stitched Winston Two's face together, but he had lost one eye, part of his nose and a lot of the skin and flesh on one side of his jaw.

— Poor Winners, Kim said sadly as the wretched, forlorn creature squealed piteously as it recovered from the anaesthetic, — but you're still beautiful to us! Yes you are! Yes you are!

Everyone was in shock at what had happened to the much-loved family pet. — Daein that tae a defenceless animal, my Ma snarled. —What kind ay sick mind does that?

— A Japanese mind, I heard myself smirk softly from behind the newspaper. Thankfully nobody picked it up.

John totally freaked when he found out what had happened to the dog. I knew that the signs were bad, because he listened to me and Kim's account of events in total silence as he stroked the sad, mutilated beast at his feet.

After his tea he went out to the wasteland and killed four of the strays with his bare hands. I followed him downstairs to witness the sight. A group of kids looked on in awe, and one wee lassie started greeting as John, displaying treats, enticed dog after dog to him, then strangled them to death or snapped their necks. He was helped by Uncle Jackie and a mate of their's called Colin Cassidy, who was a nutter. They held the dogs while John's huge hands ripped the life from them. The only one which wouldn't come was that wicked brown cunt, it kept well out the way. I felt somehow pleased that it had escaped but I suppose I felt a bit guilty at the carnage I'd caused. I liked animals. Birds especially, they were a symbol of freedom, flying like a bird n that. But I liked other types as well, though I was less keen on domestic pets than on animals in their wild state. I felt myself almost choke as I observed the broken bodies of the four strays lying in isolation from each other on the wasteland.

— Council cannae control fuckin vermin, ah fuckin well will, Dad said to me. — Tae quote the great man hissel: in war ye dinnae huv tae be nice, ye only huv tae be right. Cassidy nodded sagely, and Uncle Jackie tried to get me to go for a pint with them but I headed back up the hoose, turning to watch their backs receding, Dad in that thick brown coat, as they wandered down tae The Gunner.

12 Kim Visits

Things are getting a bit fuckin heavy in this nut ay mine as the control breaks down and the memories come back. Nae two weys aboot it: it's a fuckin radge scene. I try to hide in my little cubby-hole in the darkened well, beyond Sandy and the horrible Storks, but still out of range of the loathsome reality in that sick world on the other side of the trapdoor above. This refuge of mine is becoming more precarious though. I sense it to be like a little platform, a small ledge, jutting out from the side of the hole. It gets shakier and narrower every time I sit on it. One day it'll crumble and I'll be faced with the stark choice: climb out into the real world or fall back into fantasy land.

I would until recently, have unreservedly chosen the latter, only now, it's not my fantasy world. I now have as little control down there as I did in the real world . . .

— Hiya Raw-oy . . .

The dull, nasal tones tell me that my sister Kim is visiting me. I can expect a monologue concerning some guy; it'll consist of either unrealistic, unbounded optimism, or be a sorry tale of woe, but it'll be delivered in the same sick, bleating voice.

—Ah'm seein this new felly n eh's a wee bit aulder n it's likesay eh's mairried n eh's goat two bairns bit it's likesay eh's gaunny leave hur cause it's likesay eh disnae really love hur any mair n it's like, eh loves me now n wir gaunny git a flat somewhair . . .

Yeah yeah yeah

—. . . wi him huvin the mortgage n the bairns n wi his responsible position in the civil service n aw eh sais

Get a fuckin brain, ya daft sow

—. . . bit ah'm like, still sortay seein Kevin n aw, well no really seein um bit wi met it The Edge n ah wis a bit drunk n a really only went back tae his place tae see this leather jaykit thit eh goat bit

813

one thing sortay jist led tae anothir n ah jist sortay ended up steyin the night, ken wi Kevin likes. . .
it wis jist like ah kinday felt sorry fir um bit ah sais dinnae think thit this is sortay like us gaun back
oot thegither cause it's no, cause ah've goat a new felly now . . . bit the thing is, Roy, ken it's like
ah've sortay missed another period again n ah dinnae ken if ah'm, well, ken, that wey, n if aham
whae's it is ken, Roy? Cause ah've been wi Kevin n the new felly, bit thir wis this other laddie ah met
one night it Buster's n we went back tae his fir a perty so ah'm no really sure . . . bit that's jist sayin
like, that's jist supposin aham . . .

You *undoubtedly* are, you daft cunt. Is it Tony's mutant bastard
you're carrying again, Kim? You fuckin stupid sow. The budget
room, I'll fuckin well bet. Standing up or on Tony's pish–saturated
mattress . . . the smell of rubbish . . . the flies . . .

—. . . the bairn's daein fine though, Roy. Kevin's Ma's goat him the now, jist fir the weekend,
cause as ah sais tae Ma, it's likesay Kevin's Ma n that are entitled tae see the bairn . . .

Kevin. Kevin Scott. Poor fuckin doss cunt Kevin. Mairrays intae
the Strangs. What a total fuckin radge of the highest order.

Clickity click, clickity click . . .

Somebody's coming, Kim. I can sense them. Yes, I can hear those
nursey shoes clacking on the lino.

— Hello . . . sorry, we're going to have to disturb you while we see to Roy.

— Aw that's awright, ah wis jist talkin tae um aboot some things . . .

Kim's fuckin verbal equivalent of the Chinese water torture is
interrupted by Nurse Patsy DeCline, who has come to give me a
good seeing to. Just as well: I'm too tired and too frightened to even
try to hunt the Stork just now. The whole thing is becoming far too
draining. It's too much, all this bullshit, just too much. But I have to
see it through. I'll just sit here on my little ledge, recoup my
strength, work up the bottle, and then it's back to the fray.

13 Marabou Stork Hunting

Damn and fucking well blast this shit . . .

There's something in my throat. I try to scream from the narrow alleyway in the festering slum town but the words seem to be stuck. This confounded throat!

The cornered Stork has a bundle in its mouth. It's not going to go down without a fight. Then it mumbles something as it springs to life and stampedes past us, but Sandy fells it with a powerful sliding tackle. As the beast's thin legs buckle and loose feathers fly, Jamieson springs to his feet and swings around, his palms outstretched, with an innocent expression on his face. The Stork is rising behind him.

— Play to the whistle, Sandy! No foul! I yelled. This is SFA rules and we are wearing the blue shirts.

As Jamieson turned, the Stork, which was well over six-foot tall, jabbed at his shoulder with its massive beak. Sandy screamed in pain and fell backwards. I drew my machete and advanced, but the creature turned and ran; flapping its great wings which spanned the alley, building up speed and managing to take off, rising slowly out of the close and into the main street, where it narrowly cleared a bus, before vanishing over the rooftops.

To our great fortune, the beast had dropped its cargo. Approaching with caution, I picked up and tentatively unwrapped the bundle to reveal a foetus, the size of my hand, bloody and prawn-like. — We have to put this devil–child under the sword, Sandy, I said. I took my machete and thought about who, or what, could have spawned such a thing. It had a large head which twisted inwards from the forehead to squashed features, curving out to a big, flat chin. It looked at me in a pleading kind of way, softly shrieking.

I didn't have the heart to machete it. Instead I put it on the ground and recovered the jeep. Reversing into the alley, I backed over the bundle not once, not twice, but three times. There was a squidging sound and I left the vehicle to examine the flattened package which now oozed a dark liquid.

— Whatever you do Sandy, don't look.

It was not a baby. It was

a fuckin weird bastard   up   — Poor Dempsey, Roy.

coming up — — — — — — — up   You remember Dempsey, don't you?

Even though there's something of the cad

About the boy . . .

DEEPER

      DEEPER

            DEEPER — — — — — — — — — — — — —

— Deeper into shark-infested waters. What the fuck are we doing here? Sandy seems reluctant to put on the scuba gear as we take our boat out along the coastline, determined to enter the Emerald Forest Park by another route. Our efforts to locate the beast's nest on the shores of Lake Torto had proved fruitless. The creature could always spy our approach and move the site of its nest accordingly.

Ghostie had the Evening News *coming round to talk about his life as a casual. He sent a couple of the baby crew out to Thins and Waterstones to shoplift some guerrilla warfare and military strategy books. They came back with a big pile; Che Guevara, Liddle Hart, Moshisma, all that stuff.*

— Goat tae gie the media the right impression, he smiled. — Wind the daft cunts up tae fuck.

He made sure he had the mobile phones ready, out on display. We started using the mobiles just to keep track of where the other crews were heading, but in reality, the thick cunts were so predictable as to reduce the exercise to pure self-indulgence on our part. The sheepshaggers we had a bit of respect for, but the soapdodgers were just as dense as fuck. The hun soapdodgers had even taken tae getting English cunts up to try and give them some sort of organisation. If you had a bunch of Weedgies stranded on a small desert island, they wouldnae be able tae organise a fuckin trip tae the beach.

Fuck.

Fuck . . . where am I here? The sea. The beach. The organisa-
tional skills of the Marabou Stork.

STICK TO THE FUCKIN STORY, ROY, YOU STUPID
CUNT.

— These waters are infected by sharks, Sandy said, still reluctant
to don the scuba equipment and dive. I had anchored on the edge of
the reef and it was a short swim to the shore, but I could smell the fear
from Sandy.

— Infested with sharks is what I think you mean, Sandy, I
corrected, then I began to wonder. — Maybe the term infected also
has relevance.

— I want you to know that I'm a professional sportsman and, as
such, do not use drugs. I certainly don't share needles and I practise
safe sex. I am not HIV. This is so as we know where each other are
coming from, okay?

— As you prefer, Sandy.

— I didn't hunt any lions either Roy, that was just bullshit, he
sneered.

I am losing it badly in here. Losing as much as I did on the outside.
In a strange split second I am back in the alley and the praying mantis
is there, the one with the blonde wig and the lipstick on its insect
jaws and it is holding up a red card. Sandy throws off his strip, close
to tears, and exits the alley, comforted by Diddy, with Dawson
shaking his head in disgust. The mantis is writing his name in a black
notebook, which bears the title: *YOUTH IN ASIA*. Then I feel the
spray in my face and we are back on the ocean.

We struggled into our gear, preparing for our dive into the clear,
light-blue water of the reef. We would make our way to the
shoreline and our alternative point of entry to the Emerald Forest. It
was a risky strategy, as it limited us to the hardware we could carry.

I'm not feeling well here; there's a ringing in my ears and a
strange, sterile smell in my nostrils. The smell of hosp . . . no fuck it,
I'm in control here, I'm in control. Sandy's okay again, he's my
mate, my guide. Me and Sandy, we're hunters. We're the good guys
in this.

Then Sandy said something which tightened my stomach and sphincter muscles and made my pulse race. As we prepared to dive from starboard side he looked at me and smiled, — We're going in at the away end.

14 Winners
And Losers

If my auld boy found out that it was me who fucked over Winston Two, the cunt would have killed me. He was even more protective of the beast in its injured state, and he seldom let it out of his sight. Winston wore one of these cone things around his head; to stop the daft cunt from scratching at his wounds with his paws. In the wild the beast would have died. I was all for nature.

Despite Winston Two's suffering, I was disappointed at the outcome. I wanted Winston Two offed for good. To merely mutilate him as he had done to me was not enough. My initial remorse at what I'd done had quickly evaporated and I had to get him once and for all. What made me decide to go for the cunt was this lassie I was shagging.

Julie Sinclair was her name. She steyed up in Drylaw wi her Ma and her sister. She wisnae a bad ride as I recall, and I used tae fuck her in her bedroom then stick aroond and watch the telly wi her and her Ma. I used to sometimes fantasise, no really seriously, just idly likes, about giving her Ma and her sister one as well. Basically, though, I just liked it up at her hoose because you could watch the box in peace.

I didnae have any strong feelings for Julie, but I respected her. She just wanted fucked and went for it in a big way, but she was always in control, you never got intae her heid. That suited ays though; I wisnae bothered aboot getting into her heid and she wisnae clingy like some slags. Anywey, eftir ah'd fucked her one time she asked me aboot the scars oan ma leg. That was what set me thinking about Winston Two again. I remembered how much I hated that monster, and the fuckin family who revered him. I still had my fireworks.

Shagging Julie always made me think of Cramond Island, cause that was where I'd first got intae her. Cramond Island is a small island less than a mile out in the Forth Estuary. You can walk out to it at certain times, before the incoming tide cuts it off from the mainland. There's fuck all to see over there, just a few old pill-boxes from World War Two, full ay beer cans and used condoms.

It was a common tactic of local guys to take lassies over to the island then wait until the tide came in soas that they'd have to spend the night there. Tony told me all about it. I seldom mucked aroond wi Bri and that crowd now that I was a top boy, but one time Bri and I went oot wi Julie and her mate and got 'stranded' on the island and ended up riding them.

That was where I was headed with Winston Two.

I had fortunately accumulated a great deal of flexi-time at my work; I'd been showing the daft cunts in one of the offices how to operate this new set of mainframe computerised procedures I'd installed. My eyes were stinging from constant exposure to the VDU and an eye-test revealed that I needed glasses. There was no way that ah was gaunny be a specky cunt though. Not only would it have been something else to be self-conscious about, I would have looked the spit of my auld boy.

Fuck that for a game ay sodjirs.

I got contact lenses fitted.

The day I took time off to get the lenses sorted out, I decided to go back hame and get Winston Two. I hadn't told anyone that I was taking the day off, and I made sure that nobody, except Winners, would be home.

We walked through the scheme and crossed over by the golf course, passing the Commodore Hotel and going down the esplanade onto the foreshore. I had a large spade I'd bought from B&Q, its head wrapped up in a carrier bag. I felt a little sad when I looked at the dog with the plastic bucket on his head. It was no life for an animal. I began to think of Winston Two as a puppy, and now as a loyal chum. It might have stopped me had the whistling east wind from the north sea not cut through me, particularly stinging my old scar tissue as it swept down the Forth Estuary.

I had my spade, I had my bucket and here I was at the seaside.

It was still quite early, an autumn morning, and Silverknowes beach and the foreshore were deserted. The tide was going out.

I marched Winston Two over to the island, his paws making indentations in the soft sand. The human footprints and the paw prints would soon be washed away.

We reached the island and I tied the dog up to a rusty hook which conveniently jutted from the side of a concrete pillbox.

The bleak wind whistled around us as I removed Winston's cone and taped an assortment of fireworks to his stitched-up face. I bound them tightly around his head with plastic masking tape then put the cone, attached by a separate collar, back onto the beast. I heard him make those almost-empty-Squeezy-bottle noises dugs make when they're shitein it.

As Winston Two struggled, I saw a small bird land on top of the pillbox. It was a robin, that early symbol of Christianity . . .

. . . I thought for a second or two about the meaning of this, about turning the other cheek and Christian forgiveness and all that sort of shite. But nobody believed in that crap anymair. It was you against the world, every cunt knew that: the Government even said it. The wind seared through my denims, stinging my scar tissue again. No, Winston had to go. In Christian terms this was a just war . . .

. . . I looked at the dog for a bit, just looked at him straight on. He was strange; one eye gleaming from the mess of masking tape and coloured cardboard tubes secured to his face, framed by the plastic cone. The funny thing was, he had now stopped that fetching but futile scrape with his front paws and was now just lying down on his side, panting softly.

He seemed almost contented.

My boot cracked heavily on the schemie fashion-accessory's fur-lined rib cage . . .

JUST WHAIR AH WANTED YE
CHILD-KILLING CUNT THAT YE ARE
ME FUCKIN SCARRED AND CRIPPLED FOR LIFE

DINNAE HURT WINSTON DINNAE TELL
THEM IT WAS WINSTON

FUCK YOU FAITHER
FUCK YOU
DUG SHOULD HAVE BEEN DESTROYED
IS THAT HOW MUCH AH WIS WORTH, HOW MUCH AH
WIS VALUED?

DESTROY
DESTROY

Winners . . . Winners . . .
here boy
here boy

Wots wong bwoy?
Huh bwoy?
Winners my woyal fwend . . .

I lit a couple of fireworks where the blue touchpaper was exposed around his face and, following the instructions for safety, stood well back. Winston Two unfortunately chose to disregard the instructions.

THAT WAS CWUMBSY OF YOU BWOY

There was a small explosion, and a splatter of red blood discoloured the clear plastic cone. The dog struggled but was silent. I was trying to work out what was happening and went closer when a screaming rocket shot a sparky orange trail out from Winston Two's face . . .

. . . it was like Krypto, Superboy's dug . . . the dug had heat vision . . . he should have let me put that cape on him . . .

. . . Winston Two thrashed blindly against the leash . . .

. . . then there was a larger explosion and the dog just toppled over as bits of charred flesh and blood shot out of the cone. I winced and moved out of the wind as I caught the scent of an almost overpowering smell; fainter, though, somehow different from

Gordon's. Worried at the noise, I looked over to the mainland, but the foreshore was empty. On the other side there was a small fishing boat, but it was too far away, over by the Fife coast.

It was like Winston Two had no head at all; just a large, black, charred cinder in a wrap-round piece of melting plastic.

> Who did this tae ye Winston, eh boy?
> Show me boy
> Show me who it was

Winners
Winners

> Who do'ed it?
> Who do'ed dat to Winalot?
> Tell us who it was, boy
> Tell us

Winners Winners
Winalot
Winners Winners
what you got

Winners Winners Winners.

Loser.

> Who do'ed it?

> But you can't tell
> and that is
> just too bad for you
> you silly cunt.

I whistled Roy Rodgers' 'A Four-Legged Friend' as I dragged the corpse of the dog, stinking and smoking at one end, across to the other side of the island, the side invisible from the Edinburgh coast. I pulled the body down onto the wet sand and started digging with my spade. I removed the round metal tag with WINSTON on it, and the address overleaf. What was it that the auld boy said about the dug's namesake: in a war ye dinnae have tae be nice, ye just have tae be right.

I looked at the hole I'd dug and cast my eye over the body, before glancing across at the Fife coast. The tide would be in soon. I almost shat myself as I heard a shuffling noise and looked down to see the body of the beast shaking violently. Without thinking I kicked it into the hole and started shovelling the sand over it. Some of the sand was instantly displaced, but I kept shovelling and the movement subsided and the struggle seemed to cease.

I climbed back to a vantage point and watched the tide come in, lapping up to the edge of the island, covering Winston Two's grave, then I ran over to the foreshore side. I had to move swiftly to avoid being cut off as the water started to cover the uneven shelves of sand around the island.

I slung my spade in the woods by the River Almond, which reached the Forth estuary at the old Cramond village. Then I went for a coffee at the small cafe in the village. An old biddy came in with a yappy wee dug, one of these wee bits of fluff on a string. The animal sniffed at me and I patted it indulgently. — I love dogs, I told the wifie.

I sat for a while, drying my trooser bottoms against the radiators. Then I left and threw Winner's tag in the Almond and headed back up towards the scheme, stopping off at the Commodore for a pint on the way. I walked up to Silverknowes and had another pint in the golf club. Then I took a bus up town and looked aroond the shoaps, getting a no bad top oot ay X-ile, before heading home at teatime.

When I got in, they were all back. I tried to merge in the general air of gloom that filled the house although it was some effort. I kept hearing the auld man's voice: — But eh widnae jist vanish like that . . . the dug couldnae jist vanish oaf the face ay the earth . . .

Yes he could, Father.

Yes he could.

Winston made a mistake. He fucked aboot wi Roy Strang. Nae cunt fucks aboot wi Roy Strang.

Dad's investigations, which took the form of threatening and cross-examining locals, harassing the Drylaw polis, sticking up badly photocopied pictures of Winston (the black smudge he came out as in the copies looked uncannily like him just before he died) in shops and on lampposts, and freaking when kids ripped them down; all this failed to yield fruit.

Winston Two had gone.

Dad swore that he'd never get another dog again, but he was knocked out that Christmas when Kim and I got him a German shepherd puppy. Unlike his previous two Alsatians, this was a bitch.

He called it Maggie.

Maggie was, is,   up   — Another bowel movement, Roy! Doctor
a nice dug. Never   up   Goss is going to be very pleased with you,
did me any – – – coming up   Patricia says. — You're looking so well
                                  these days. As a reward, I'm going to put on some more of your
                                  mum's tape. She's got a good voice.

Please no Patricia, just talk to me, tell me who you've been shagging or what you've been watching on the telly, anything but that fu . . .

Even though there's something of the cad
About the boy . . .

— I wish I had a voice like that.

DEEPER
            DEEPER
                        DEEPER – – – – – – – – – – – – –
– in through the away end. The water, we've been right through the water, but I only feel wet up to my ankles. Crazy.

Jimmy and I scale up to the top of the Green Hill. It's a long, arduous climb, but its summit affords a perfect view of Lake Torto. We get out our binoculars. There is a breathtaking display of pink as we watch the flamingos in the water. You could hear them, that toot-toot trumpeting sound. Like the horns of continental football supporters or fairground cars . . .

Just then Sandy says, never taking his eyes from the scene, — Look Roy, to the left.

There were a group of about a dozen Marabou Storks waddling along the shores of the lake, heading straight towards the flamingo colony.

15 The Flamingo Massacres

The Marabou Stork is one of the major dangers to the Greater and Lesser Flamingo. It walks along the shore, causing flamingo flocks to pack in panic; it then makes a short flight and stabs a selected flamingo in the back. Once disabled, the flamingo is drowned and then torn to pieces and eaten by one or several Marabous in three to four minutes.

The intervention of the Marabous has had a serious effect on colonies of Greater Flamingo by causing mass desertion (one recorded instance of up to 4,500 pairs by seventeen Marabous). Flamingos tolerate and may even repel from one to five Marabous, but six or more, always six or more, cause mass desertion. Nature is so specific in its arithmetic.

When it came to swedgin, we always broke up intae groups ay between six and ten. At the Underground at Ibrox we came upon the beasts. They were colourful, those scarfers. Ridiculous, but colourful, in their red, white and blue attire. Their badges and their buntings; Ulster and aw that wanky shite, needing an excuse, a silly toytown reason to muster up the kind ay force we'd learned tae love fir its ain sake, tae have on tap. They were yesterday's thing. They looked around nervously as we walked in our groups throughout their midst. We had nae colours; we wir here tae dae real business. No for the fitba, the bigotry, the posturing, the pageantry. That was just shite tae us. We wir here oan business.

The air was filled with the loud screeching cries of panic and death. Through binoculars, Sandy and I witnessed the carnage over at the north shore of the lake. Things were happening fast, I was losing track. More than that, I was losing control. I kept remembering something else, kept seeing something else . . .

We scattered them and gave pursuit to a group ay young blue Christmas trees who looked as if they had come fae Fathell, Lanarkshire. These bloated, beery ugly Weedgies ran cowering intae a pub, but there wis nae escape for them. They looked different from us. Even though I'd always regarded myself as fairly hideous, those creatures were beyond the pale. We steamed in and wrecked the boozer. Ghostie had a Weedgie over the pool table and wis trying tae sever his meaty hun heid oaf wi a broken gless.

— *Ah'll take your fuckin face oaf ya fuckin Weedgie cunt! he screamed.*

Dempsey was trying to cram a bar ay soap intae the rat-shagger's face. — *Get a fuckin wash ya smelly soapdodging Weedgie cunt . . . dae yous cunt's nivir fuckin wash . . . slum-dwellin fuckin trash!*

Lexo had taken a couple ay thum oot, one interbred hun's face bursting like a ripe tomatay shot by an air pistol as his chunky fist made contact wi it.

— *Whair's aw the fuckin Glesgay hard men now, eh? Fuckin queers!*

I had opened up one skinny hun's coupon with my sharpened carpet tile knife (Boston's of Leith Walk) and then knocked him over and was booting fuck oot the cunt under the juke-box on the waw. Ah remembered the auld man's records, Churchill's wartime speeches, and recalled him saying that the Germans were either at your feet or at your throat. It was the same with the rat-shaggers. Back doon tae they cunts and they're fuckin swarming all over ye, stand up tae them and they're shouting mammy daddy polis . . . I felt a bit bad about using the blade, no because ah had any reservations about improving hun features through plastic surgery, but because bladework was sneaky, like Weedgie shitin cunt's patter and we were intae toe-to-toe stuff in our crew. The jukie was playing Dire Straits' Romeo and Juliet, so obviously brain-dead mutant hun music . . . ah turned tae the half empty pub, only maist ay them wir shitein it tae leave, wi Norrie and Jacksie oan the door n ah shouted, — *ROY STRANG'S THE FUCKIN NAME! REMEMBER THAT FUCKIN NAME! ROY STRANG! HIBS BOYS YA FUCKIN CUNTS! EUROPE'S NUMERO UNO! FUCKIN RAT-SHAGGIN BASTARDS!*

What the fuck . . . I see a Marabou Stork, not our one, stab a young flamingo, then, after thoroughly sousing its prey underwater, swallow it whole.

Lexo turned tae the bar staff; an auld guy, a fat wifie n a younger guy, who wir just standing thair, shitein it, and went: — *Six fuckin Becks then, cunt! Tae take away.*

*They served him and the wide cunt peyed for it as well. No tae have done
so would have lowered us tae the level ay the soapdodger. We were, after all,
Edinburgh snobs . . . but ah wisnae getting as much ay an adrenalin rush as
ah used tae. We'd been daein too much ay this. Ah picked up a pool cue and
jumped on the bar, thrashing the gantry and its bottles. There's something
aboot the sound ay broken gless . . .*

I was really losing it badly, and I was about to scream: STOP!
JUST FUCKIN STOP ALL THIS when I saw our one, our Stork,
and he saw us. The creature lowered its neck and made a short run,
flapping to take off. It looked awkward and ungainly but continued
its laboured ascent until it gained access to thermals where it rose
rapidly to such a height it became almost invisible.

— Damn you, Johnny Stork, Sandy cursed.

Despite our quarry's getaway, I felt a strange elation in my bones.
This was our beast's turf; the bugger would soon return.

— *LIT'S HIT THE FUCKIN ROAD! Lexo roared, his neck
straining, his face seeming tae be just one big black hole. He dispensed the
Becks as we left the pub in ruins and its terrorised occupants nursing their
wounds. Ghostie turned tae ays as we exited the pub and stole doon the road.*
— *That wis no bad. Just under four minutes, eh, he said, pointing tae his
stopwatch.*

. . . I'm seeing clearly again . . . we noted that quite close to us
another couple of large Storks had insinuated themselves into a pack
of squawking vultures who were devouring the unrecognisable
corpse of an animal. It looked like the body of a woman.

not like the body of a woman

no

no . . . it must have been something else. One of the Storks had a
scrap of meat pirated from it by a large Tawny Eagle . . .

Another Stork stood on the outskirts of the group, running in
frequently to snatch dropped morsels, but its bolder friends were in
there with the vultures, tearing at the carcass with them. One was
even attempting to dominate those other scavengers, with some

success. In fact, the vultures' aggression seemed like posturing. They were scared of the Storks.

— Vultures appear aggressive, but have evolved elaborate threat displays to ward off rivals, Sandy observed, tuning into my thoughts as if by telepathy. — That way they avoid the risk of a fracture of the ulna in combat . . . the ulna of course, being the inner of the two principal wing bones.

A broken bottle shattered behind us as a crowd of huns shouted at us. We turned and steamed in and they ran like fuck.

— Yes Sandy, I nodded, cleaning one of the lenses on my binoculars, because I can't trust my vision, — although the ulna is the larger of the wing bones it tends to fracture more frequently than the radius due to its lesser elasticity. Indeed, if I recall correctly, one survey showed that around twenty per cent in a pack of white-headed vultures had shown evidence of a fractured ulna.

Ah still hud the fuckin pool cue in ma hand; a mingin rat-muncher who had been left behind in his mates' retreat tried to block ma swing as I heard the bone in his arm crack and his shrill squeal fill the foosty Weedgie air . . .

— Yes, smiled Sandy, — it's amazing that they can survive.

— Fortunately, although it's one of the largest flying birds, the vulture has a very small bone weight, approximately seven per cent of its body weight . . .

— . . . thus enabling the creature to live off its reserves until the bones heal . . .

— Look Sandy! I cut in, — Over by the far shore!

Some Storks were circling around a wisp of smoke which came from the other side of the Green Hill.

— It's like they're flying over a settlement . . . Sandy said.

— Yes, but the only settlement there is Fatty Dawson's lodge in the Jambola. Let's check it out!

part four

The Paths Of Self-Deliverance

16 Respect

It's coming back to me. It's all coming back. I wish it wasn't but it is.

I don't suppose any of us stopped being on trial. It was her own fault; she fuckin well asked for it. Her and Lexo's; her the big fuckin teaser and him the fuckin sad pervert whae couldnae git a fuckin ride in a brothel wi a Gold Amex stuck in his keks. If ah hudnae got in wi that crowd, nowt would've happened, ah widnae huv goat involved. Except that she'd still've goat it fae some cunt, the wey she cairried oan. Nowt fuckin surer.

The first time I set eyes on her, I knew the type exactly. The Caroline Carson type; her that was at school wi me. Slags like that have to be taught a lesson, or they'll pish all over you. Fancied herself as the top girl, a big fuckin cock tease. Hung aroond wi the boys but nae cunt could git intae her keks. Lexo n me had talked aboot her, one eftirnoon, over a few Becks, as you tend tae dae. I think we were in The Black Bull, eh.

— A fuckin total ride that wee cow, he said.

— Legged it? I asked.

— Like fuck. Nae cunt's been up that sow, far as ah ken. KB'd every cunt. Tell ye one thing, see if she comes up tae Buster's next week n comes back tae Dempsey's perty, she's gittin her fuckin erse shagged. Even if she is a virgin, her fanny'll no be tight enough once ah've fuckin gied it a few strokes, he laughed.

I laughed along with the cunt.

I was thinking about the time I once went to get her up for a slow dance at Buster's. The music that night was dead loud likes, but I shouted, — Ye want tae dance? at her. She stood up and I followed her ontae the danceflair. The slag just kept walking, right across the flair tae the lassie's bog while ah stood thair like a radge in the middle ay the danceflair, every cunt sniggerin away. This was *me*, Roy Strang. A fuckin top boy we're talking aboot here. I remember that night, cause that was the night ah slashed that cunt Gilchrist.

Ah minded ay that time awright, as ah sat n spraffed wi Lexo. — The boys are entitled tae a line up, ah sais tae him.

She reminded me ay that time at school; aw they fuckin smart cows, aw the fuckin same. Well naebody takes the pish ootay me, nae cunt. I thought of her finally getting it, watching her hurt, watching her bleed, watching her say please.

Say please, you fucking slag, say please to Roy Strang. That's ma fuckin name, n nae cunt takes the pish. Say fuckin please, you bitch whore slut

say fuckin

The hoor must think that I never saw her look at me with Pauline, Ghostie's bird. Thought I never noticed her sniggering at my inverted face, my ears like a taxi wi the fuckin doors open. Of course, it was all behind ma back. Once we came back from South Africa and I'd chibbed that fat cunt Mathews, then taught the Carson slag a lesson, it was always behind ma back. But the point was that they were still at it. I didn't hear or see them, but I knew they were still at it. I just sensed it, felt it. They all had to fuckin learn who I was; aw the cunts. Like that cunt who thought he was hard at school, the cunt Gilchrist fae Pilton. He was the guy whae wis wi Ferguson, n Carson n The Big Ride; that fuckin soft fat slut that time at the chippy. I had just come back fae a trip doon tae Millwall wi some ay the boys. A barry time, we went pure fuckin crazy in London. It wis a brilliant swedge at New Cross: ootside ay the sheepshaggers they were the best opposition we'd ever had. We'd been spraffin aboot it, gettin hyped up remembering it, when I ran intae the Gilchrist cunt on the Mile, mouthin it wi his mates.

He wisnae the worse. He wis naewhere near the worse. But he wis thair, right thair in the pub whair I let him sweat for a little. Then I broke his nose by stickin the heid oan the cunt, and opened up his cheek with my Stanley. (Purchased where I always buy my weapons). It was just ma wey ay saying tae the cunt: My name is Roy Strang: mind that night wi the chips ya cunt?

All I'm looking for is a bit of respect. It's my fuckin entitlement.

Yeah, I fuckin saw her stolen stares when we went oan tae the Red Hot Pepper Club. Making me aware of my short legs, my big heid, my ears, every fuckin defect in my skin. Making me feel like a freak.

— Hi Lexo, if yir up fir gang-banging that wee sow, mind n cut ays in oan the action, I smiled.

— A sow's goat tae realise that if they hing aroond wi top boys, they huv tae dae the biz. Examples must be made, he grinned, his mouth cutting a crescent in that square head.

That wis it. That wis the extent ay our plotting; a daft, half-pished bit ay fantasising in a pub. Ah didnae ken the cunt wis serious: ah didnae ken he'd talked tae Cally n Demps aboot it.

It wisnae as if ah wis intae daein anything. I'd enough problems wi fanny as it wis; I'd made a bit of a cunt of myself at the work, eh. It was that Christmas; it wis pretty strange. There was this lassie called Sheena Harrower who worked at Scottish Spinsters'. She went to Buster's and knew some of the boys. I never ever went to work dos, but I wis spraffin wi this Sheena lassie in the canteen and she sais she was going. I fancied getting into her keks, but another couple of boys, Demps was one, I think this guy Alto was another; they'd been talking aboot tryin tae leg it n aw. For that reason I thought it would be better if I fired intae her at the Scottish Spinsters' do; leave the field clear n that. It seemed too good an opportunity tae miss.

She never showed up. I found oot later that that cunt Demps had met her in a pub the night before and fired in first. So that was me oan ma fuckin tod at a Scottish Spinsters' Christmas perty. It was really weird, seeing aw they straight-pegs oaf thir fuckin tits oan alcohol. Maist ay them wirnae used tae it and they were aw totally ratarsed.

Well, ah just fired back some cans oot ay boredom. It wis Scottish & Newcastle beer which wis shite; ah jist drank Becks normally, but it was there. They had this punch n aw, which wisnae bad. Before long ah wis a wee bit pished. In fact I must have been really pished because I was necking with Martine Fenwick. I don't remember how we got started. It was radge because we never really goat oan n she wis a few years aulder than me, but she wis bevvied n aw.

I had some fuckin root oan ays; I jist wanted tae blaw ma muck in Fenwick, then split from the whole depressing scene. I thought about getting her back tae the office and intae the walk-in storage cupboard where we kept boxes of computer hardware and stationery. There was a table there and I'd be able tae gie her one across it. The problem was that the slag was intae letting me tongue her in public, but when she sussed I was trying to get her away, she knocked me back. My head was pounding like ma baws by this time, and I kept smelling this strong scent of urine. I snarled an insult at Fenwick and hit the bar.

After a couple of drinks, I pocketed this cheap plastic lighter which I spied lying on a table. Then I went for a wee wander through the deserted offices. Rummaging through one of the stockrooms I found some inflammable spirit, for cleaning electrical equipment. It was ideal.

I rejoined the party, which didn't last much longer before fire alarm went off and loads of drunken cunts staggered out into the street. Two fire engines came and doused the blaze, but only after it had gutted several offices. One doss cunt who had goat drunk and passed out was taken tae hoaspital suffering fae smoke inhalation. It served the dippit cunt right as far as ah was concerned. The fire damage was substantial and it led to a memo from the Personnel Director, banning the use of office premises for Christmas perties. For me that was sound, I had nae interest in these cunts' perties.

Shortly after this I was promoted. Jane Hathaway got a better job elsewhere, and, as they put it, 'took' Fenwick with her. Des Frost took over as the supervisor and I got his job. That was me made up to full Systems Analyst. It meant mair dosh, but I was just daein the same job really. It showed me how exploited I'd been in the three years I'd been there as a trainee. We got two new trainees, both young guys, one of whom was involved with the baby crew. There was a better crack in the office.

A few months later it happened.

We were up at Buster's again, and having a good night. Even in

the disco when Lexo nodded ower at her dancin and sais tae ays: —
That cunt's ours the night, I just thought it wis like, wishful thinkin.

She looked so fuckin cool and proud	up – Up a little bit, eh Roy?
the way she danced, her hair aw sort	up FUCK OFF
ay long and flowing, her mouth in	up I've seen faces, places,
that pout that seemed tae spit out	up And smiled for a moment,
contempt for all the world, her	up But oh
lithe body twisting to the music.	up You haunted me so.
She hud that clinging top and	up Still my tongue-tied
short skirt on, the fuckin cock	up Young pride
teaser – – – deserved it up her – –	up Would not let my love for you show
	in case you'd say no.

NO

DEEPER

DEEPER – – – – – Can't get deep enough to get at the Stork – – – –
only her – – – – because we were all pretty out of it . . .
   Aye.
   We were all pretty out of it when we got back to Dempsey's. Lexo
stuck a trip on her, and she was out of her nut. It was a crazy time.
There was one tape deck set up in the front room blastin oot aw
that fuckin techno shite, and in one ay the bedrooms we had the
stuff ah wis intae; the Stone Roses n Happy Mondays n aw the
indie stuff. Lexo nodded over to me and then Ozzy, who moved
across tae her. Ah don't think she really knew what was happening when Ozzy ushered her into the bedroom. By the time he got
her there, Lexo and I were waiting, with Demps, who locked the
door. I remember she was still giggling, until Lexo pushed her
onto the bed. Demps and Ozzy held her down and Lexo put a
knife to her throat.
   The realisation ay what wis happening hit her hard. — Please
don't kill me, she said quietly.
   — Open yir mooth n yir fuckin deid, Lexo said. He pulled up her

skirt. She struggled a bit, saying, — Please don't, please don't, over and over again.

I said to Lexo, — C'moan Lexo, we've put the shits up her enough man . . .

He turned and gave me a look like I'd never seen before, never suspected a human being could have been capable of. — Gaunny pit a wee bit mair up her thin the shits, eh, he sneered. I was scared: scared of Lexo. If I shat out I was dead. That's what I thought. Demps, Ozzy; they were just laughing.

— Think ay this is yir initiation, Ozzy said.

— Aye, yuv no been done yit, Demps smiled. — The boys are entitled tae a line up.

— Top boy's perks, Ozzy laughed, — cannae say fairer thin that, eh.

— Lexo hit her across the face and pressed the knife against her throat. She stopped struggling and turned her head to the side. He began pulling up her clinging lycra top, very slowly and carefully, almost with tenderness. Ozzy and Demps had her arms up as the top was jerked over her head. — Dinnae want any signs ay a struggle, he laughed. He pulled her bra down and scooped her tits out at the same time. All the time, her face was frozen, her eyes dead, except for a steady stream of tears. Then she let out a scream, but the music was so loud anywey that nae cunt would've heard. Lexo hit her on the side of her face, then tightened one of his huge hands around her neck. — Ah'll cut your fuckin tongue oot the next time you make a fuckin sound, he whispered. We all knew he wasn't bluffing. Lexo was possessed.

Fuckin right the cunt wis.

— Git a handful ay they titties boys, no bad, he said evaluating a full breast in the palm of his hand.

— She's a fuckin lovely piece ay meat, Ozzy smiled, cruelly tweaking her nipple between his forefinger and thumb.

— Only the choicest cuts for the top boys, Dempsey smiled.

Lexo had her skirt down, and he gestured to me to get the shoes off her feet, which I did, then he slid off her cotton panties.

— Ivir hud yir fanny licked oot? he asked. She was back in a trance of fear, but she closed her legs as his hand went roughly between them. Lexo lay with his full bulk on top of her. — Ivir been licked oot? he asked, right in her face.

She tried to talk but started to gag. Her eye make-up was running. She looked repulsive already. Nothing like she'd looked in the club. The fear had twisted and distorted her face. It wasn't worth it . . .

Lexo pulled down his jeans and boxer shorts, exposing a large, spotty arse. Ozzy and Demps let go of her arms and grabbed a thigh each, pulling her legs apart. I could hear her alternating between sad pleas and insipid threats.

— . . . dinnae . . . please Lexo . . . Alex . . . dinnae . . . please . . . ah'll tell the polis . . . ah'll get the polis . . . please . . . don't hurt me . . . don't kill me . . .

Lexo opened up her piss-flaps with his thumbs and sniffed at her minge. Raising his head, he twitched his nose and pulled a face like a wine connoisseur. — Thir's gaunny be a whole loat ay shaggin the night!

He slurped greedily at her fanny for a bit, then steadily, incrementally, with great care soas no tae show any signs ay forcing, he pushed his finger into her cunt, gently working it. Ozzy and Dempsey still had hold of her thighs.

She screamed as he forced his cock intae her. Again though, he was slow and deliberate. Lexo knew what he was doing. The expression on her face was . . . I remember seeing a documentary about some animal being eaten from behind while its face seemed to register disbelief, fear, and self-hate at its own impotence. That was what she reminded me of. The wildebeest . . .

Ozzy and Dempsey were scrutinising her face, Ozzy brushed her long, dark hair aside as Lexo thrusted, — Nae sign ay her gittin turned oan yit, Lexo, he smiled.

— Mibbe ah'm needin a wee bitty back-up here, boys, Lexo grunted. — Strikes me thit thir's three holes here n only one ay thum in use.

Ozzy unzipped his jeans and brought out his cock. He pulled her head to him and, using Lexo's knife at her throat, compelled her to open her mouth.

I was standing in the corner shaking, wondering what the fuck ah wis daein here, as Ozzy had her next, then Dempsey, by which time she'd almost blacked out. When Dempsey was on, someone tried to come into the room. They knocked persistently. Ozzy clicked the door open and stuck his head round it. — Fuck off! Private perty! he snapped.

— Wir gaun roond tae Murray's. He's goat decks, ken, a guy called Nezzo said.

— We'll catch yis up, Ozzy said, locking the door.

Dempsey eventually came, — Phoah ya fucker, he grunted, before pulling out.

— Nice n lubricated fir ye Strangy, Ozzy smiled.

— Ah'm fucked if ah'm gaun in thair eftir youse cunts . . . I shuddered, trying to keep it light. There wasn't a condom in sight.

— Nae cunt shites oot, Lexo growled.

I unzipped my flies.

Ozzy pouted disdainfully at her vagina. — Like a fuckin soapy sponge in thair man, ah'm tellin ye.

I lay on her. I couldn't have got hard anyway, but I lay on her and faked it, thrusting rhythmically.

— Ah dinnae think the earth exactly moved for it thair, Strangy, Dempsey laughed, as I gave a weak grunt and levered myself off her.

— Last ay the rid-hoat lovers right enough, Lexo said scornfully.

I thought we had finished, but her ordeal was only beginning. Lexo wanted to take advantage of the fact that everyone had left the party. — Watch her, he commanded, then vanished. He returned from the back green with a length of clothesline which he rigged up, with a noose on the end, to the large parallel beams in the living-room. The room was strewn with empty beer cans and bottles, overflowing ashtrays and empty record sleeves and cassette-tape boxes. Lexo came back into the bedroom and tied her hands crudely but firmly behind her back and marched her through the empty flat to the living-room. He had her stand on a stool, almost on her tiptoes, with the rope round her neck. He stuck a large ball of cottonwool in her mouth and taped over it with masking tape.

— If she faws ower n hangs, we're fucked! This is ma flat! Dempsey said.

— Fuck it, said Lexo. — If it faws n chokes, wi jist take it doon the coast n dump it. He rubbed his hands together, — Let's hit that all-night chemist's n git some KY. Ah'm itchin tae gie it one up the erse. Its fanny's been well-fucked enough. Will git a couple ay beers at the club first, eh. Thirsty fuckin work this!

He moved over to her and stood on his tiptoes and kissed her chin. — You're ours now, ya sow. Then he put on a theatrical American accent, — Don't go away baby, the boys'll be back!

We just left her there. Ozzy drove us up to the West End and Lexo procured the KY from the chemist. We then drove down to our club at Powderhall. It was a snooker club and it had shut ages ago, but we had a key and Ozzy put oan the jukey while Demps set up some Becks. — Cheers, boys!

Her trussed up like that back at the flat. Choking on the gag, struggling to draw breath. Fearful of even trying to move. Not knowing when we'd be back, whether we'd be back. I wanted this drink over quickly. I wanted to save her.

— Tae slags that huv tae fuckin learn lessons! Ozzy proposed a toast.

— Slags, we nodded in unison, clanking our bottles together.

How did she feel bound up like that, the noose around her neck? Our spunk trickling down her bare legs?

I was shiting myself that something had happened to her. Demps was too; it was his flat. Lexo and Ozzy didnae seem tae gie a fuck. Lexo picked up on my anxiety.

— Dinnae go aw fuckin poofy oan ays, Strangy. It's an education fir the sow. Be the makin ay it.

— Ye dinnae ken that though . . . it might fuck her up . . . she might never be able tae go wi a guy again like.

He looked at me with withering scorn. — The only fuckin reason it'll no be able tae dae it again is cause it's hud the best n the rest jist dinnae fuckin measure up.

Lexo wanted to stay for another drink, but we talked him into heading back. He hit his motor and drove across the city towards

Dempsey's gaff. Lexo stopped the car before we were there though.
— Eh . . . I said weakly. What was he doing?

She had died. She had fallen over and died. We'd killed her. I knew it. She would just give up, let herself hang. Why fight it?

I knew she was dead.

— C'moan, Lexo! What's the score! Demps moaned.

Lexo pointed to a group of drunks who were sitting on a park bench in the deserted night street. They were drinking tins of strong lager. — Goat tae say hiya, eh.

— Eh? Moan tae fuck! I gasped.

— Nice tae be nice, Lexo said, exiting from the car. Ozzy started to go as well.

We were in no mood for this, no me and Dempsey anywey, but we got out of the motor eftir them, reasoning that it would be easier to try to cajole the cunts back in. We approached the winos who looked cautiously at us.

There were two guys and a woman. One of the boys was bulky and big with curly silver hair, but surprisingly gentle, furtive eyes. The other one was a guy who I realised was a lot younger than I'd thought. His face was discoloured with the drink and the weather, as well as a lot of scars and scabs. His hair was thick and dark. He had that slightly bewildered look a lot of drunks who've not had quite enough to send them away seem to wear.

I wanted back to her. Maybe she'd got free, maybe some cunt heard her. The polis . . .

— Awright gents, Lexo said and, turning to the woman, smiled, — and ladies n aw.

The woman wisnae that auld either. She was thin and pale and probably in her early thirties. She had short greasy-brown hair, but her clothes looked in quite good condition, and she didn't seem dirty.

They gave us some cagey greetings.

Ozzy looked at the woman, — What's your name, doll?

— Yvonne, she said.

— She's awright that yin, the aulder guy smiled, raising his can at us.

— Bet you're a good ride, eh Yvonne, Ozzy asked, winking at her.

The auld guy wrinkled his eyes and puckered his lips, sucking in air, and smiled at me. — Coorse, he grinned. I liked this auld cunt. I had a desire to protect him from the boys.

— Mibbe git Yvonne here back tae oor wee party, eh Lexo. Git some lesbo stuff set up. Ever fucked another bird, Yvonne? Eh? Ozzy asked.

Yvonne said nothing, she just sat on the bench, between the two guys. The auld guy turned away.

— Leave ur, Ozzy, Demps said.

— See if ye wir tae fuck another lassie bit, Yvonne, jist sayin likes; ah mean ah'm no saying that ye wid or nowt like that, but jist sayin if ye wir, jist supposin, eh: wid ye yaze yir fingers or tongue? Ozzy asked, pushing his index finger into his fist and flicking his tongue in and out of his mouth.

The lassie hunched her shoulders up and stared at the ground.

— Fuck off, Ozzy! C'moan! Lit's go! Demps shouted.

I wanted to see her. I needed to see her. We had to go back.

— Mibbe just git a wee kiss bit, eh Yvonne? Ozzy asked. He bent towards her. She turned away, but he kept turning with her and she finally stopped moving her head and allowed him to kiss her on the mouth. Lexo made whooping noises. The other guy had handed him his Carlsberg Special can, which he was now drinking out of.

— That wisnae sae bad, eh? Ozzy said. — Jist like New Year. Wi aw kiss strangers at New Year, in the street n that, up the Tron. Nice tae be nice . . . what aboot a wee flash ay the tit then, Yvonne? Fir the boys!

— Fuck off, Ozzy! I said.

— Shut up, Strangy, he laughed, — ah'm jist giein Yvonne a bit ay a choice. A wee flash ay the tit or she comes back tae the perty wi us. What's it tae be, Yvonne?

The woman pathetically undid some buttons on her blouse and quickly pulled out a breast before covering it again. Ozzy laughed. Lexo looked away in disgust.

Then Yvonne sprung to her feet. It was only then I realised what had happened. Lexo had punched the youngish guy, his huge fist making a bone-crunching sound as it connected with the boy's head. He stood smiling at the gadge, keeping his arms stiff and punching the air jerkily in front of the guy's head. The boy put his hand to his face; he was shaking with pain and fear in the seat. I wanted the daft cunt to stand up and run, or take a swing at Lexo. I wanted him tae dae something, no just sit thair like a fuckin sheep. The auld guy looked away and closed his eyes.

— Nivir saw that one mate, eh no, Lexo laughed. — Too much bevvy. Makin ye slow. Bet ye could've been a contender at one time n aw, eh?

This stupid cunt keeps his hand in front of his face but actually forces a wretched smile at Lexo. Lexo playfully short-jabs the right hand into his guard; — This one . . . this one . . . he says, then he smacks the boy's face with his other hand, — naw, it's that one . . . he laughs, shaking his left. — That one again . . . his left fist again makes contact with a sickening crunch. Then it's the right one.

I'm watching this and I'm ready to put the boot into this cunt on the park bench for being so fuckin stupid and just taking this undignified punishment; just to put him oot his fucking misery quickly. I want to go. I want to see her. The guy's got his head wrapped up in his hands now. Lexo's lost interest. He's watching Ozzy who's necking with the woman Yvonne. I'm shrugging at the auld jakey guy who's looking frightened. I'm trying to send a vibe out that it's okay, that nae cunt's gaunny bother him.

Lexo goes over to him and pulls out his wallet. He crushes a fiver into the jakey cunt's hand. — A drink fir yir mate the morn, eh. Anaesthetic, he smiles.

— Ah wis a coppersmith tae trade. Rosyth, the auld guy says tae him, taking the money.

— Goat the hands fir it, mate. Strong hands, Lexo smiled.

— The Ministry of Defence. The Civil Service it used tae be, he said.

— Ye ken Benny Porteous? I asked.

— Aye . . . ah ken Benny! The auld guy's eyes lit up.

— That's ma Uncle. He wis a coppersmith at Rosyth.

— Ah worked wi Benny for years! Alec, that's me. Eck Lawson. Mind me tae yir Uncle. What's he daein? Whair's he workin?

— No daein nowt. Jist playing the gee-gees, eh.

— Sounds like um! Mind me tae um! Eck Lawson!

— Nae bother, Eck, I said. I wanted to go.

— Moan youse, Lexo snapped and we got back into the car. — What wir you daein wi that auld hound, ya filty cunt? he laughed at Ozzy.

— Could've taken it back, eh. See how the slag liked a jakey boot lickin her oot, Ozzy smiled.

I could see the possibilities racing round in Lexo's head. — Naw, he said. — Discipline's whit's fuckin needed. Gits a wee bit too complicated, polis n that.

— That wis fuckin daft! *They* could've goat the polis. Panel that wino . . . what the fuck d'ye call that? Demps snarled.

We got in the car. We were going back to her. Please let her be alive.

— They'll no git the fuckin polis, ya daft cunt, Ozzy scoffed.

Lexo turned round, his large smile beaming at us. — That wis a jist a wee bit ay foreplay. Git us aw in the mood fir the slag's erse, eh!

I looked at Demps's tense face where we sat together in the back of the car. His mouth was twisted and I could hear his teeth grind but I couldn't see his eyes for his long fringe. We got back to his flat about an hour after our departure.

I was terrified as we mounted the stairs, shit-scared in case she'd tried to struggle free and hung herself.

I was fuckin shaking. I looked at Demps. He looked away.

Ozzy opened the kitchen door. She was there. For a second she was so still it looked as if she had cowped over. I was about to scream as an overwhelming wave of fear washed over me but she turned her head to us, her eyes pleading and panicked. She was still alive.

We got her down, but instead of taking her back through to the bedroom, Lexo lugged the mattress through and stuck it oan the flair. — Better through here, eh, he smiled, — We'll be able tae watch they cartoons oan that breakfast telly while we gie it the message.

Ah didnae take drugs but Lexo and Ozzy did an ecky and the three ay them took a couple ay lines ay speed each, and we just kept her with us, having her over and over again. I managed one more pretend thrust, but the rest were up her all night. Dempsey and Lexo were up her cunt and arse at the same time, their balls pushed together. — Ah kin feel your cock, Lexo, Demps gasped.

— Aye, ah kin feel yours n aw, Lexo said.

Dempsey had put on a tape of Hibs goals on the video and we watched George McCluskey smash home a beauty against Dunfermline. — A fuckin cracker fi Beastie thair . . . Lexo growled as he blurted his load into her rectum for the umpteenth time that night. When we got bored fucking her in different ways we'd put on a video or some sounds. We watched the film Nightmare on Elm Street Part 2, which Demps had on video.

In the morning, we made her take a couple of showers and steep in the bath, supervising her washing herself thoroughly. She was so compliant, looked so destroyed and wretched, that I felt it would've been better if we'd topped her. She crossed her legs and kept her arms over her chest, like one of the female prisoners in concentration camp films. Her body, which had always looked so good, so lithe, athletic and curvy as she danced in her tight and flimsy clothes, now looked broken and bent, twisted and scrawny.

I realised what we had done, what we had taken. Her beauty was little to do with her looks, the physical attractiveness of her. It was to do with the way she moved, the way she carried herself. It was her confidence, her pride, her vivacity, her lack of fear, her attitude. It was something even more fundamental and less superficial than those things. It was her self, or her sense of it.

We had no right. We didnae realise . . . ah didnae think . . . Get away. Get away from this for a bit. Get
DEEPER

     DEEPER

          DEEPER––––––deeper soas I can see Sandy Jamieson, who is now sitting outside our tent on the forested slope which rises in tiers from the lake.

— Ever thought of what you're going to do when all this is over, Sandy old man?

— I think I'll probably end up doing more of the same. I'd like to stay in the game in some capacity . . . I mean, I can't see me pulling pints in a pub. I'd miss the cameraderie of the whole thing . . . oh, it's more than just sharing the bath with a group of other naked men . . . is anything wrong, Roy?

— I think I'll go for a walk, Sandy, eh, try to find more pieces of wood for the fire, I said. I felt nervous and ill-at-ease, I had to get away from all of this.

— Top hole, Sandy shouted and winked as I edgily departed. What was he on about?

I found myself walking deeper into the dense
woods. I crouched down in a clearing and
tried to gather my thoughts. They
kept taking me back though;
taking me back to my   some other world.
memories of some   to   what other world?
other world – – back – – up   A city. A car going
through a city's empty streets.

Harsh daylight.

We drove her into town and she went home. It took her a few days to report it to the police. We'd been rehearsing our story, which was straightforward. We had some bevvy and drugs and had a party. She was up for a bit of fun, and took a couple of us on. It was only in the morning when we started joking that she was a dirty slag, that she got all bitter and twisted and started all this rape fantasy stuff. We got rid of the video we'd watched and the records we'd listened to that night, so that she would make a cunt of herself if she told the polis what we had oan.

We were taken in for questioning, but we were all veterans of being interrogated by the bizzies. There was no way they were going to get anything out of us, especially with our lawyer in attendance. We had employed Conrad Donaldson Q.C. as our defence. Donaldson was the best criminal lawyer in the toon, and he assured us that they had no case. We just had to keep our nerve. Even when we were formally charged, it didn't worry us too much. The polis were a dawdle, their hearts weren't in it; the worse flak I had was from my family.

— Well, that's it now, ma ain laddie, Dad said. — Sick. A sick person. Like ah sais, a common criminal.

— It was her but, Dad . . . well Lexo wis a wee bit over the top, but it wis her . . . she wanted it . . . I pleaded.

I recall Bernard raising his sick queen eyebrows and pouting distastefully. It was fuck all to do with that pansy. I wanted to obliterate that faggot. Ma rushed to my defence though, — Eh's no that kind ay laddie, John! Eh's no that kind ay laddie!

— Vet! Fuckin shut it! Like ah sais, jist fuckin shut it! Dad snapped, his eyes crimson. He turned to me and I felt the re-emergence of a childlike fear as those huge crazy lamps seemed to be reaching right into me, to be probing around in my soul . . . — Ah'm gaunny ask ye this once, and jist once. Did you touch that wee lassie? Did you hurt that wee lassie?

— Dad . . . it wisnae like that . . . ah nivir touched her . . . a wis jist thair whin she pointed the finger at everybody. It wis a perty . . . everybody wis huvin a good time. This lassie, she wis crazy, high oan drugs n that, she jist wanted tae screw everybody thair. Then in the mornin a couple ay the boys started callin her a slag, now ah ken that wis a bit oot ay order, but she goes aw spiteful n starts takin it oot oan ivray cunt. Ah nivir did nowt . . .

— That's whit it wis! Ma screamed at John. — A slag! A fuckin slag's gaunny ruin ma laddie's life! N you're gaunny jist stand thair n take that slag's word against yir ain flesh n blood!

John let the implications of this sink home. He'd always said that the Strangs had to stick together and Vet had captured the moral high ground. — Ah'm no sayin that, Vet, like ah sais, ah'm no sayin that . . . it's no meant tae be like that, like ah sais, it wisnae meant tae be like that . . .

— Eh's a good laddie, John! Eh's goat a joab in computers . . . thing ay the future. Wi eywis brought um up right! It's jist that rubbish eh's been hingin aroond wi, they idiots fi the fitba . . .

Dad's eyes glared like spotlights and his Adam's apple bobbed like a buoy in stormy seas, — We'll see tae they cunts . . . ah'll git ma fuckin shotgun now . . .

Thank fuck Tony was round with one of his kids, wee Sergio, — Naw John, naw. It'll just cause mair hassle gittin involved now. It's up in the courts. It could prejudice the case.

Dad's face twitched as he slowly grasped this. He hyperventilated a little on the spot and I thought he was going to hit one of us. Then he seemed to settle down. — Prejudice the case . . . that's right, Tony . . . aye. Naebody's gaunny dae nowt. The Strangs'll dae thair fightin in the coort. That's whair aw the fightin's gaunny be done, like ah sais, up the coort.

He squeezed my hand, almost crushing my bones in his fervour. — Ah jist hud tae ask son, ah jist hud tae ken. Ah nivir doubted ye though, son, nivir fir a minute. Ah hud tae ask though, son, tae hear it fae yir ain lips, like ah sais, fae yir ain lips. Ye understand that, son?

I nodded. I didn't really understand. I didn't understand fuck all. I didn't understand why I felt so bad. I hated that slag, I hated every cunt: everyone that fucked me around. It was me against them. Me. Roy Strang.

I didn't understand why whenever I thought of her I wanted to die.

Ah never did nowt.

— Wir gaunny clear yir name! We stick thegither, the Strangs. Wir gaunny win! Roy, Vet, Tony, wir gaunny win!

I remember him shaking a clenched fist in the air.

17 Zero
Tolerance

It was a long time before it got to court, and it seemed longer still. I couldnae work. I took all my annual leave from work, one month, and I just sat at home. Kim was there with me. She had lost her job at the baker's shop; been caught with her fingers in the till. We sat at home and chain-smoked. I'd never smoked before, just cause everyone else in the hoose did. I hated cunts who smoked cigarettes: fag-smoked cunts I called them. It seemed to me that the fags actually smoked them; covered them in filthy, rancid, tarry smoke.

Now here I was.

I'd never felt so low, so drained. All I wanted to do was to sit and watch telly. Kim talked incessantly, always about guys she had been seeing. It got soas I couldn't make out what she was actually saying, couldn't pick out the words, I could only hear this eeehhheeeehhhheeeehhh, this constant nasal monotone in the background; a dull, relentless soundtrack to my depression.

Whenever I went out, just local like, doon tae the shops, I felt that everyone was looking at me and I knew what they'd be saying under their breath: Dumbo Strang interbred mutant fuckup sick psychopathic rapist vermin . . . I stayed in as much as I could.

But I couldn't stay in forever. It was just so oppressive. I tried to keep in touch with the rest of the boys on the blower. Lexo and Ozzy were eywis oot, swedgin, partying, acting like fuck all had happened. Demps had gone to ground as well. When I called him and he heard my voice, he put the phone down. He stopped answering after that; his line was disconnected a little later.

I felt like a fuckin prisoner in this madhouse. Kim was a pain during the day, but my depression had inured me to her bleatings, which were fuck all compared to the crazy circus which went on around me all evening when Ma came back fae her joab at the auld cunts' place and Dad came in from John Menzies. He was usually late, he took all the overtime he could get. Thankfully Bernard had finally moved out to a flat, but Tony was often round.

One time Dad came in particularly buoyant. — Caught one sneaky wee bastard the day Vet, tryin tae steal comics. Broke doon in tears, like ah sais, in tears. That's how it starts Vet, the criminal classes, like ah sais, the criminal classes.

— Perr wee sowel . . .

— Ah sais tae um, yir no such a big man now ur ye, ya crappin, thievin wee bastard! Like ah sais, no such a big man now!

— That's a shay-ay-aymmme . . . Kim whined, — a wee laddie . . .

— Ah, bit that's no the point, Kim. Ah did that fir ehs ain good. Psychology Kim, yuv goat tae understand, psychology. Ye lit thum away wi it, thill nivir learn. Cruel tae be kind, like ah sais, cruel tae be kind. Should ah huv jist lit um away well? What if somebody hud seen n ah hud loast ma joab? Should ah? Ah'm askin ye? Should ah huv jist lit um away?

— Naw . . . bit . . . Kim protested.

— Naw bit nuthin! If ah hud loast ma joab, then what wid've happened? Thank Christ thir's somebody here whae kin hud a joab doon! Like ah sais!

This kind of shite went oan constantly.

The worse thing about the auld man was that he watched the fuckin telly aw night, he never seemed to sleep. When I'd go downstairs, insomniac myself with depression, I'd find him there, gaping at the box. Any noise outside and he'd shoot to the window, checking it out. His files were increasing; he'd opened up new ones on the block of flats two down from us.

I had another look at some of his handiwork.

> *23/8 MANSON*
> *Single Parent: Donna (17)*
> *Child: Sonia (less than six months.)*
>
> *I always feel sorry for young lassies in this position, even if most of them just do it to get a flat from the fuckin stupid communist cunts on the council. This lassie seems good and the bairn is always clean. There is usually a drugs risk in this situation though, with the scumbags who hang around lassies in such a situation.*
>
> *Verdict: Possible drugs threat. Continue surveillance.*

Dad had got involved with a local group called Muirhouse Against Drugs: Brian's old man Jeff was the President; Colin Cassidy was its secretary. I don't think Jeff knew what he was letting himself in for, getting those cunts involved. — Ah've goat detailed files Jeff, like ah sais, detailed files, oan a loat ay cunts in the scheme. Ah'm prepared tae make them available tae the group at any time, my Dad once told him.

The anti-drugs group was now all my Dad spoke about.

— Ah think the thing aboot Muirhoose now is it's goat tae the stage whair the kid gloves huv goat tae come oaf, Jeff. It's nae good jist drivin these cunts oot the scheme; the council jist sticks thum back here again. What we need are five good men wi shotguns, like the yin ah've goat up the stair. Jist go roond n blaw these cunts away, like ah sais, jist blaw them away. That's what ah'd like tae dae, that's what would happen in a sane world.

— Eh . . . aye John, Jeff said nervously, — but it isnae a sane world . . .

— You're tellin me it's no! We've goat ma laddie thair whae's workin in computers n he's treated like a leper in this fuckin scheme because ay some slut. Yuv goat aw they junkies stoatin roond, protected by the polis n featherbedded by the fuckin council! The shotgun solution's the only one, like ah sais, the shotgun solution. N ah'll tell ye this n aw Jeff, see eftir ah'd wasted aw that junky trash, ah'd be right up the council n ah'd blaw they cunts away n aw! Fuckin sure'n ah wid. Cause the junkies n the single parents n that, they're just the symptom ay the disease, like ah sais, jist the symptom. The real source ay it is these cunts up the City Chambers. Not fuckin quoted, these cunts!

I couldn't go out but I couldn't stay in; no wi that shite gaun on.

So one day I ventured out and took a bus up the toon. Walking down Princes Street my attention was caught by a series of black posters with a huge white Z on them. They hung from hoardings along the Gardens side of the road.

The first one had:

> **ZERO TOLERANCE**
> **Z.**
> **NO MAN HAS THE RIGHT.**

I felt as if I had been punched hard in the stomach. I couldnae get air, the blood seeming tae run right oot ay ma heid. I stood in Princes Street, shaking.

— THEY DINNAE KEN! THEY DINNAE KEN THE CIRCUMSTANCES! THEY DINNAE KEN WHAT IT'S LIKE! I found myself shouting, drawing puzzled, furtive looks from shoppers and tourists who moved to avoid me. A group of Japanese visitors looked on for a few seconds, and one actually took my picture: like ah wis some fuckin festival street theatre. — FUCK OFF YA SLANTY-EYED CUNTS! FUCKIN TORTURIN BASTARDS! ah shouted. They turned away and made hastily down the road, no doubt cursing ays in Japanese.

Composing myself, I wandered on. The whole ay Princes Street, on the gardens side like, was decked oot wi these fuckin Z posters. Each slogan ripped through me like a psychic machete, but I was compelled to read them all:

> MALE ABUSE OF POWER IS A CRIME.
> **Z.**
> **THERE IS NO EXCUSE.**

> WHEN SHE SAYS NO SHE MEANS NO.
> **Z.**
> **THERE IS NO EXCUSE.**

There were other ones; photaes ay bairns. Bairns that had been abused, making oot that what we had done wis like what aw they sick cunts that touch up bairns dae . . . like wi Gordon n South Africa n me . . . when ah wanted tae greet n he sais that ah wis dirty n that nae cunt would believe ays

cause wi that cunt Gordon it wisnae like how ah telt it, it wisnae like that at aw, that wis oan the surface, thir wis another part ay ays . . .

NO

I ran over into Rose Street, and hit the first pub I saw. The young barman looked at me warily; he must have recognised me as one of the cashies. I asked for a double whisky. I threw it back in a oner. It made me feel queasy; I just drank Becks like. I looked around the pub. It was covered in posters for the festival. Aw the fuckin shows that these daft cunts went tae. Then I saw it again. The Z poster, two wee lassies playin:

> BY THE TIME THAT THEY ARE FIFTEEN ONE OF
> THEM WILL HAVE BEEN SEXUALLY ABUSED
> **Z.**
> **THERE IS NO EXCUSE.**

I was straight oot ay that pub. I went into another, perspiring heavily, my temples throbbing. I checked out the notices. Nae Z ones. I ordered a whisky and a Becks. I sat down in a corner. The pub was busy; it was dinnertime. I was too much in a world of my own to notice the voices around me.

— Busman's holiday, Roy? I turned around and saw this white-heided, rid-faced cunt in a suit n tie. It was Mr Edwards, my boss, or rather my boss's boss.

— Eh . . . aye . . .

— It's just that I thought that you'd find somewhere more exotic than the office local to drink in on your annual leave, he smirked.

I never even realised that this *was* the office local. The cunts at Scottish Spinsters' were as boring as fuck; I never socialised with the drab, middle-class twats.

— Eh . . . aye . . .

— Sorry, this is Roy . . . em . . . Roy; Roy from Colin Sproul's section, the cunt Edwards sais tae this big shag in a suit wi tons ay make up, n this slimy cunt in a suit wi dark, Brylcreemed hair n a moustache.

We exchanged nods.

— Roy's people are doing a wonderful job in dragging us out of the dark ages, into a new, exciting halcyon era of advanced technology, is that not right, Roy? he said, in that plummy stage drama voice which is a required accessory for the exercise of Edinburgh bourgeois wit.

— Eh . . . aye . . . , I went, as the others laughed.

— So you're one of Colin Sproul's mob in S.C.? The Brylcreemed cunt says, like an accusation. That sharp, posh voice, always sounding like a fuckin accusation. Ah felt like sayin: naw, ah'm Roy Strang, cunt. Roy fuckin Strang. Hibs Boys. Ah felt like smashin ma boatil ay Becks ower the cunt's heid, then rammin it in ehs fuckin smug pus.

Bit ah didnae. Wi these cunts, it's like ah'm jist invisible tae thaim n they are tae me. It all came tae ays wi clarity; these are the cunts we should be hurtin, no the boys wi knock fuck oot ay at the fitba, no the birds wi fuck aboot, no oor ain Ma n Dad, oor ain brothers n sisters, oor ain neighboors, oor ain mates. These cunts. Bit naw; we screw each other's hooses when there's fuck all in them, we terrorise oor ain people. These cunts though: these cunts wi dinnae even fuckin see. Even when they're aw aroond us.

— Eh aye, Systems Control . . . was all I could say.

Systems control.

Why was that all I could say? Why did I need my mates to give me a context? Why couldn't I just turn this place over like I did to that working-class pub in Govan? Why couldn't I terrorise these cunts now, now that I had them in my sights, knowing that they'd shite themselves tae death?

— I've a bit of a beef on with S.C. at the moment. You know that death benefits network system your crowd installed?

— Eh . . .

— Uh, uh Tom, Edwards goes, — Roy's on annual leave. He won't want to hear this.

— You're a programmer, Roy? The shag in the suit asks.

— Eh, aye. Systems Analyst.

— Do you like it there?

— Eh, aye.

I fuckin hated it.

No. I didnae. I didn't feel strong enough about it to hate it. It wis jist a place you went to during the day, because they peyed ye tae. While I was there, I just floated around in a void of indifference.

— Roy was just made up recently from a trainee, weren't you, Roy? Edwards grins.

— Eh, aye, I said, feeling this tightening in my chest. There was a strange ringing in my ears, like when the telly's finished. I gulped my drink down. — Excuse me, I'm in a bit of a hurry, I said, standing up. — Got to meet someone.

— Well, she must be nice, you rushing off like that, laughed Edwards.

The shag in the suit looked at me with an expression
which had a mild, playful overlay of flirtatiousness
but which failed to conceal its underlying   baws – – – I'm doing
contempt. I'm out of there, then down   ma   this for you, Roy.
the road to the bus stop – – – ringing   baws   I know you can feel.
in my ears – – – – – my balls – – – – – ma   Why should you be denied
sexual contact? I know what you're feeling; I was on a course on sexuality and the disabled . . . I
want to make you feel, Roy . . . I know they'd say it's unprofessional but it'll be our little secret. I can
make contact with you, Roy . . . you're getting harder with me touching you like this. Would you like
me to take you into my mouth? Would you like that?

No, please don't Patricia, please don't . . . ah dinnae want
any . . .

— That's what I'm going to do, Roy. I'm going to suck you off . . .

No . . . somebody come and help
somebody come
somebody come
somebody
please
come
oooooooohhhhhhhhhhhhhhhhhhhh

— Mmmm . . . it looks like somebody's come! You can make contact, Roy! You're going to
come out of this!

DEEPER
        DEEPER
                DEEPER
                        DEEPER– – –

I'm still in the woods, alone. I'm startled to see that there's blood all
over me; I'm covered in it. I draw in a breath. I let a few seconds tick
by. I don't feel hurt or injured. It isn't my blood. It's not mine. I
follow its dark trail into the woods, but I hear a noise in the forest,
the crackling noise of something advancing through the undergrowth and I run.

I run through the bush until I stumble upon the track and follow it
towards the shores of the lake. The beautiful lake. I step into its soft,
lukewarm waters, and wash the blood from my body and clothing.

After a while I emerge from the water in the heat and I'm walking back up the trail towards our camp, when I come across Sandy, looking distraught.

— Roy! Are you alright? What in the blazes happened?

— Sandy . . . I don't know . . . I just went into the woods and I felt suddenly weak . . . I crouched down and sort of passed out. I woke up covered in blood, and it was like some animal had attacked me or something . . . I don't remember.

— My God! Let's get back to camp! Sandy wrapped his arm around me and supported me up through the woods.

We came across the bloodied trail again. — Oh shit, I said, for as soon as we looked up we saw the prostrate, naked body of a young native boy. The body lay half-covered in leaves and shrubbery. The eyes had been gouged out and the genitals mutilated.

— Oh my God, I said. I felt a gagging sensation, that strange dryness in my throat again, but I couldn't be sick. It was only when I saw the discarded blue pants in the bushes that I realised it was the little fellow we'd met earlier.

— The work of terrorists, I'll wager, Sandy said sagely. — I wouldn't even presume to blame our friends the Marabou Storks for this. Mind you, the removal of the eyes look like they've been done by the beak of a Stork or perhaps a blunt knife . . . possibly a purchase from Boston's of Leith Walk . . .

What in the name of . . . — Sandy, this whole fuckin thing . . . it's just fucked man, d'ye realise? It's just fucked!

— Yellow carded. Yellow fuckin carded, Sandy moaned.

What is this shite? What's happening to me?
What happened when I got hame fae the   up – – – Ah mind.
fuckin toon after ah'd seen they cunts   up
fae the work – – – – – – – – – – – – – up   Ah mind what
     fuckin happened.

Ah mind what happened awright.

When I got home, it seemed as if there was nobody in. Then I heard voices from upstairs, giggling sounds. When I went for a slash I heard heavy panting from Kim's room. She had somebody in her bedroom; somebody was giving her one. Obviously some cunt fae the scheme.

I made some toast and watched the telly with the volume turned low, but I had to switch it off because one of the lassies in the Aussie soap opera reminded me of *her*.

About twenty minutes later, Kim came down. She looked shocked to see me, like she hudnae heard ays come in. I saw why she was so fuckin bothered, because Tony came straight in after her. He was dressed in a suit and tie, which he was straightening.

— Awright, Roy, he said.

— Tone, I goes.

— Tony came roond for a sandwich, Kim said, in a nervous whine.

Aye, n ah ken whae the fuckin meat wis n aw ya cunt.

— Ah felt really fuckin sick, Tony shook his head glumly. — It's the upholstery oan that new motor: gies ays the boak. Threw up n everything. Hud tae go n lie doon, eh. Then this daft fucker, he nods at Kim, — comes in n starts ticklin ays.

Tony knows how to lie. He's been deceiving his wife with everything for years. He'd stick his cock in anything that moved.

— Ah wis only muckin aboot Tony, jist muckin aboot . . . she says, all clumsy and stagey.

Kim does not know how to lie.

Tony departed after we tentatively arranged to go for a couple of pints and onto the match together next weekend. I couldn't sit there and look at Kim. It was her stupid, large potato head; her fuckin idiocy was just so offensive to me. I went upstairs and when I got to my room I was surprised to find that I wis greetin.

Did anybody else live like us? Did any cunt?

I'd never really gret before; no since I was a really wee bairn. I learned not to as a kid. John and Vet just ignored you, or battered you for it, so there was no emotional currency in it. Now it felt good, therapeutic, just to surrender to all the shite and let it flow out. I wasn't Roy Strang.

I wasn't a top boy. I wasn't even Dumbo Strang either. I didn't know who the fuck I was and it didn't matter.

The only other occasion I ventured outside before the court case was to visit Elgin. I don't know what made me dae this. I had long stopped thinking of Elgin as my brother, that was if I ever had; I always cringed when John or Vet referred to him in that way. To me he was just something that pished, shat and drooled over itself, and asked questions in a secret language that no other cunt had ever learned.

Once again I was as para as fuck on my journey. I could see those cunts, all those fuckin schemie bastards that lived in this shit-pit, all of them staring at me. The word 'casual' on their breath was okay, it meant they knew not to mess, but now it was 'rapist' which was worse than 'Dumbo'.

When I got to the GORGIE VENTURE FOR EXCEP-TIONAL YOUNG MEN I saw a boy or a man; I didn't know which, he could have been any age. He had the largest head I'd ever seen. My own, Kim's, even the auld man's, they just paled into insignificance alongside this. Elgin still drooled incessantly, more than ever. I'd forgotten his face, that expression on it, or perhaps I'd never really looked at him before. That was it; all those years in the same fuckin hoose and I'd never really looked at his face, I mean I'd looked at it, but never really seen what was there. All that was human had been sucked out of that face. He just sat on a chair beating out a monotonous rhythm on his thighs.

I didn't even attempt to talk to him; didn't even try to go through the token patronising crap the so-called experts laughingly refer to as communication, as therapy, as meaningful interaction. It was nothing like that for either myself or Elgin. I just sat looking at him for a while. I don't know where Elgin was but I sat looking at him, thinking of my situation and that wherever he was it didn't seem such a bad place to be.

On the eve of the courtcase, John and Vet were dealt another blow. We learned that Kim was up the stick. I suspected it was Tony's, but practically everyone in the scheme had been up Kim: at least that was how it seemed to me. It wisnae her fault. She was gullible, impressionable. No, that's too kind. She was just totally fuckin thick, as solid in the head as the concrete support pillars in a multi-storey car park. John raged at her. — Whae's is it? Ah'm asking ye, Kim! Like ah sais, whae's is it! Tony, who was normally never away fae the hoose, kept a low profile around this time and Kim kept quiet. Her drama, which she seemed to thrive on, didn't really concern me. I had my own problems.

Our brief, Conrad Donaldson Q.C., was supremely confident. He was the best there was. We'd set up a fund for his payment, jointly managed by Ghostie and Lexo's partner in his second-hand furniture shop in Leith, a psycho named Begbie. There were plenty of publicans and club owners only too willing to contribute to Donaldson's legal fees.

Donaldson was a ruddy-faced man with a slack mouth and large, rubbery lips. — Rape's a funny bugger, he told us in his offices in the New Town. — Somebody gets raped, the first thing they want to do is to obliterate all traces of the assailant. They just wash everything away. Then it generally takes a long time until they've recovered sufficiently from the shock to report it. The police's first response is to interrogate the complainant: that generally puts most of them off. Your girlie though, she seems persistent. I can only assume that she's getting some bad advice. She's on a pretty sticky wicket here. Even if the police refer the case to the Procurator Fiscal, in over thirty per cent of such referrals he simply won't initiate proceedings. Even then, only a quarter of defendants are convicted. Most of them get it reduced to sexual assault and almost half don't get custodial sentences. Statistically speaking, the rapist who goes to jail is a most unfortunate sod. The odds are heavily weighted against that happening.

— Thing is, we never raped naebody, Lexo said, smiling and chewing on some gum.

— Quite, Donaldson replied tritely. It was obvious he didn't believe a word of what we were saying.

He explained that there were no real witnesses for the prosecution, nobody who could actually say they had any real evidence to suggest that she'd been raped or held against her will. — It's a minefield for a girlie. Wouldn't touch it with a bargepole if I were her. I don't know who's put her up to this, some dykey feminist group trying to make the unfortunate wench into a *cause célèbre*, no doubt. Well, she has two chances; slim and none. I contend that she can't win; we can only lose. We can only throw it away. So I'm expecting exemplary behaviour from you chaps. Put yourself in my hands and we'll give her a damn good shafting, he said smugly, his smile crumbling around the edge of his mouth in realisation of a poor choice of metaphor.

I cringed and looked away, but something made me glance at Lexo, who just smirked and said softly, — Again.

Demps rolled his eyes and Ozzy laughed.

— One other factor very much in our favour, Donaldson said, anxious to move on, — is the judge. Judge Hermiston's attitudes are very much influenced by his practising of criminal law in the fifties where the dominant school of criminology was the Freudian model. This essentially does away with the concept of the crime of rape by proving that there are no victims. Female sexuality is deemed by nature to be masochistic, hence rape cannot logistically take place since it directly encounters the argument that all women want it anyway.

— Ah believe that, Lexo opined. — Simple whin ye think aboot it. A boy's goat a cock, a bird's goat a fanny. Thir meant tae be thegither.

— Right, Donaldson snapped, distaste for the first time playing across his thick lips, — I think we understand each other.

For the trial we had to move out of being Lexo, Strangy, Ozzy and Demps, top boys. We were now Alex Setterington, busi-nessman (Lexo had his second-hand furniture shop in Leith), Roy Strang, Analyst with a reputable Edinburgh insurance company, Ian Osmotherly, Sales Manager with a busy nationwide retailer, and Allan Dempsey, who was a student. Demps had enrolled to do a Social Care course at Stevenson College before the court case. It gave a better impression than dole-mole.

So it was her word against the four of us. We were described by

Donaldson as 'a far cry from the picture of rampaging soccer yobbos that my learned friend so unconvincingly tried to paint; in fact decent, articulate, upstanding professional young men with excellent prospects, from good families.'

I caught a glimpse of the auld man nodding in stern approval across the court at that statement.

The worse thing for her case was that numerous guys at the party testified to how flirty and out of her face she was. So did several women; top boys' birds we had primed, or just jealous cows cause every cunt fancied her the most.

We had our own skills, our organisation, our cool. Lexo metamorphosised into a large, gentle giant in court; a choirboy with a baleful, slightly nervous and bewildered expression, polite and deferential to the judge.

Most important of all, we had the top lawyer. Conrad Donaldson Q.C. expertly dictated the whole emphasis of the trial. It became like she was the one on trial; her past, her sexuality, her behaviour. She looked really strange in the court. It was the wey she moved. She walked like the centre ay balance in her body had irreversably shifted. It wis like the movement ay some cunt that had come oot fae under the surgeon's knife and who was recuperating from a chronic and ultimately terminal illness.

Donaldson hammered out and established some key propositions:

She danced with several men at the party.
That was established.

Her stammering, plukey, inexperienced Legal-Aid Cunt tried to say that everyone danced with several men, including us, the accused. Most people there were either eckied or tripping, no me though, I never used drugs. I hated the feeling ay being oot ay control. Bad things can happen when ye get oot ay control. Like at the party. But yeah, everybody danced with each other there. It was that sort of party. You could tell that the senile auld cunt of a judge couldnae git his heid roond that concept though.

— When I attended parties, a lady seldom danced intimately with several men, he said.

She wore provocative clothing. That was established.

It was standard Ms Selfish, Chelsea Girl, X-ile type gear. Every woman at the party was dressed the same.

She had sexual experience. That was established.

So did ninety-nine per cent of the people in the court, and she probably had less than any. But allied to her admissions of two previous boyfriends and the posse of cashies we brought in to say that they had aw been there, Donaldson blew her away. I remember the plukey fuck squeaking that her sexual history, false as it happens, had no relevance.

Donaldson shook his head sadly, — My learned friend must concur that it is established practice to allow this line of questioning, sensitively imposed, on the basis that a complainant's previous sexual experience may be relevant to the issue of consent. This is at the heart of the matter surely, the issue of consent.

Then more cashies were filed in.

Conrad Donaldson's next tactic was to ask about 'rape fantasies'; a standard approach, he told us later. This paid off with a vengeance when one guy who had gone out with her, a guy called Bruce Gerber, did her case a lot of damage when he said that she occasionally talked of such 'rape fantasies'. In fact, this was what probably won it for us. — I suppose she did say that she liked teasing guys, liked the danger in flirting, he testified, — I was upset when she started hanging around those casual guys.

— Upset because you felt that she would act on her rape fantasies with these young men? Donaldson asked.

— I suppose . . . , he shrugged, — . . . I don't really know. I just saw that no good could come of it.

— Something must have given you that impression. The impression 'no good could have come of it'. Donaldson prompted further.

Gerber was a bitter man, and a feart one. He kent no tae fuck aboot wi us. — She just . . . she started acting like a slut! he snapped.

The Legal-Aid Cunt, in trying to repair the damage, just made matters worse.

Donaldson then presented an 'expert' who claimed that gang-rape fantasy was a common female sexual fantasy. He circulated lots of academic literature to back this up, even some which he described as 'feminist'. Then our brief concluded: — Witnesses have stated that this young girl, headstrong, emotionally immature, behaved in a way to suggest that she was flirting with this fantasy.

Her brief intervened, — Even if it is accepted what the defence claim, surely acknowledging one's own fantasies is not the same as acting on them. She said no!

— That's not what the four accused say, Donaldson said assertively. — That's not the inferences we're getting from the witnesses. By hanging around with a gang of young lads, by engaging flirtatiously with them, might she not have given out the wrong signals? Was it not the case that Miss X was indeed acting on her fantasies already?

He let that one hang in the air for a while and I could see the straight cunts on the jury absorbing it like dry sponges immersed in a bath full of water.

She was intoxicated and showed flirtatious affection towards several men. That was established.

Every piece ay fanny present did.

She claimed that she was 'drugged', but Miss X took drugs regularly. That was estabished.

Under questioning she admitted to using marijuana. She claimed she never took chemicals. Donaldson pointed out that this established that she did take illegal drugs. That was the bottom line. I saw this blatantly register with the judge, his mouth puckering.

She voluntarily went into the bedroom with Osmotherly. That was established.

She was out of her face after we slipped her the acid. She'd have gone anywhere with anyone.

The thing was, she showered thoroughly afterwards and we took care not to leave any marks. The medical reports were inconclusive.

Donaldson blew their case out of the water. Carefully establishing these key propositions, he built up a bandwagon of unstoppable momentum, fuelled by his flowery rhetoric and grasp of case law, which bulldozed through their defence. I say defence, because as I sais, it was evident right from the start that she was the one on trial. That was just how the whole thing felt. It was mainly just tae dae with the whole setup, but her lawyer was a poor courtroom performer and that made things worse for her. He failed to gain any empathy with the court and made no inroads in trying to attack our characters.

So Donaldson established that there was little evidence of her having had any forced sex. Ozzy claimed she consented to anal sex with him. — I didn't want to do it, not that way . . . but it was as if she was daring us to see how far we'd go. She was very drunk, and I think she'd taken some . . . stuff. I don't really know that much about drugs, but it was like she'd taken something . . .

Lexo, sorry Alex Setterington, admitted to having full intercourse with her, with her consent. — I don't think consent puts it strongly enough. The term I would use would be insistence, he said, putting on a biscuit-ersed face.

Dempsey did the same and Strang claimed that he attempted to, and she was willing, but he was drunk.

I didn't do as well as the others up there in the dock. I was the most nervous. It just wouldn't come out, then I got into full flow and ranted accusingly, — I didn't want to. I thought the whole thing was just . . . sick. It was horrible. If it had just been me and her together, but it was like she wanted everyone. I could've been anybody. She just laughed at me.

Ozzy endorsed this. — She mocked my performance as well your honour. She was out of her head. The whole thing was pretty degrading for all of us. Some of the boys werenae too bothered.

Some guys think: 'a ride's a ride'. No me. I don't like being mocked for not being able to get it up.

All this time she looked like a zombie. She was obviously sedated. It didn't stop her frequently breaking down. I tried not to look at her. Only Lexo looked at her, he looked at her constantly. His face was sad, his head occasionally nodding softly. It was like he was asking: Why? Why are you doing this to us? He was right into his role as the victim.

Summing up, Conrad Donaldson Q.C. said: — It has been established that Miss X was intoxicated and, as people generally are in such circumstances, was not in full control of her emotions. She was belligerent, aggressive and mocking towards the accused. She was out of control, giving sexual favours when under normal circumstances she would not do so. Some members of the jury may feel that one or more of the accused behaved in a cynical and opportunistic manner when presented with an intoxicated and vulnerable young woman ready to give sexual favours, although at the time, as we have heard from witnesses, she seemed anything but the sad and forlorn figure that sits in court today. But behaving with an opportunistic cynicism and showing what many may consider to be a lack of sexual etiquette and concern for others is a far, far cry from the hideous, pre-meditated crimes of drugging, imprisoning and repeatedly raping someone. The jury must, and surely will, find this to be the case.

They did. We were found not guilty.

When I looked at her, she had the expression she wore when we did her over. She crumpled into the arms of her father.

Lexo winked and blew her a kiss. Her brother stood up and shouted at him and had to be forcibly restrained. — That cunt dies, by the way, Lexo hissed to me under his breath, his face quickly snapping back into its baleful expression.

Outside the court my auld man punched the air to celebrate victory. — Ye kin fuckin well say what ye like aboot British justice bit it's still the best in world! Thir's some countries whair innocent laddies wid be rottin away behind bars! Like ah sais, Vet, behind fuckin bars they wid be in some fuckin countries . . . in a wog country or that.

He then collared the triumphant Donaldson and shook his hand vigorously. — Brilliant! Fuckin brilliant mate, he said, — Tae quote the great man ehsel: nivir in the field ay human conflict huv so many owed so much tae so few.

— Thank you, Donaldson said curtly.

— Listen, wir huvin a wee celebration perty later oan the night, doon at oor place. Doon the scheme, ken? Muirhoose likes. Yir welcome tae come along fir a drink. Nowt fancy, like ah sais, jist a wee drink. Doon Muirhoose, doon near Silverknowes like. Near D-Mains, eh.

— Muirhouse . . . Donaldson repeated slowly, — . . . sorry, I don't think so. I'm very busy at the moment.

— Ah kin imagine, mate, ah kin imagine. Anywey, well done. Ah kent that you kent straight away that oor Roy wis intelligent, hud brains like. Eh's in computers, ken? That's whair the future lies. That's what this country needs. N that wee hairy wis gaunny git um sent tae jail . . .

— Well, thankfully it didn't come to that, Donaldson forced a smile.

— Thanks tae you, mate, like ah sais, thanks tae you. Fuckin magic, if yll pardon ma French like.

I had to get away from him, making a tit of himself, a tit of me. I went to Deacon's with the boys for a celebration drink, or at least Ozzy and Lexo. Dempsey went straight hame.

— Easy fuckin meat, Lexo roared.

— Wi wir a bit oot ay order, bit she fuckin asked fir it. Ah mean, she wis lucky it wis cunts like us thit goat a hud ay her, it might've been a fuckin psycho like that Yorkshire Ripper cunt or something, eh. That's the wey she should be lookin at it, Ozzy said.

— That's right. The slag goat oaf lightly, Lexo smiled.

I couldn't get intae it. I left, citing the party back hame as an excuse. I went for a few drinks on my tod, then got back and found that the do was in full swing. There was loads of alcohol around, and quite a bit of blow. Dad'had got into it through Tony. It was good for him, mellowed the cunt oot a bit. He didnae count it as drugs. — The star ay the show, he said, his arm wrapping round me like a boa-constrictor, — proved innocent though, son! Proved fuckin innocent! British justice! Like ah sais: British justice! He put on Churchill's victory speeches full blast and after a short while, started to sob. Uncle Jackie and Auntie Jackie flanked him. Shaking with emotion, he shouted, raising his glass, — THIS IS STILL THE GREATEST FUCKIN COUNTRY IN THE WORLD!

Most people nodded approvingly, thinking he meant Scotland. I was one of the few present who knew he meant Britain.

18 Running

I had been applying for jobs elsewhere; away fae this fuckin place. It was a lot harder daein this than it sounds. The way I wis feelin, just filling in an application form was a massive undertaking. I was relieved and surprised when I managed to complete one, and even more surprised when I got a start, at a slightly reduced salary, at a building society based in Manchester. I had to go: had to get away. The money didnae matter.

— Bit how, son? How should you be the yin tae run away! It's hur, that slag, that bloody Jezebel they should be pointin the finger at, no a laddie that's goat a good joab n works hard.

— Works hard n plays hard, like ehs faither, said Dad. He was still working at Menzies.

— It's a good joab ah've landed masel doon thair, Ma. Cannae settle here since aw that fuss.

They aw knew the score at the work. I'd spoken to Sproul and he'd let me take two months' leave of absence. It was no good, though. It had to be a fresh start, away from aw the cunts.

— Spread the wings, eh? Bright lights n that? Tony said. He was up with his kids, Marcello and Sergio.

What bright lights the cunt expected fae Manchester wis beyond me.

— Jist tae git away, start again. No intae hingin aboot wi the cashies nae mair either, eh. Too much hassle.

— Well, that's the maist fuckin sensible thing ah've heard ye say in a long time, Roy, like ah sais, the maist sensible, the auld man said.

— Bit Manchester, John . . . Ma bleated. She hated the idea of any of us not being in close proximity to her. Tony lived nearby and was always here. Bernard, though he had a flat in town, was always falling out with the other poofs he shared with and often crashed at Ma n Dad's.

— Aye, this is her that went away tae Italy talkin, Dad said. He'd never really forgiven my Ma for shooting the craw tae Italy all those years ago, but it seemed to bug him more these days than it ever did.

This started the predictable argument. They went on and on, until Dad screamed: — THAT'S ENOUGH, VET! AH'M FUCKIN TELLIN YE!

CANNAE FUCKIN TAKE THIS . . .

DEEPER

DEEPER

DEEPER — — — — — — — So Sandy and I have seen the circling Storks but they're much deeper into the bush than we realised. It seems that it's not Lodge 1690 that they are flying over, but Dawson's hideaway in the jungle. Nonetheless we make for 1690 as Sandy recounts another lion adventure.

— This type of woodland with its sudden dense undergrowth and its open tracks reminds me of the terrain I encountered when I had a particularly nasty brush with Johnny Lion.

— Yes? I urged, sticking a whole chocolate digestive in my mouth. The biscuits were melting in the heat and had to be consumed quickly. Then I munched on a jammy dodger, the jam section tasting oddly like cough mixture, as Sandy told his tale.

— We were returning to our camp after a month's exploration in the bush. Darkness was falling and we were still some way from our destination. The natives were starting to get a little edgy. As leader, I decided to push on ahead of my bearers and pack donkeys, accompanied only by my loyal dog Gladstone.

I had never heard Sandy mention a dog before. This made me feel uncomfortable but I let him continue.

— Well, Gladders started barking and I looked towards the source of his aggression, discerning a vague form moving in the darkness out by the reeds alongside this dry river bed which straddled the path we were following. — Enough boy! I snapped, anticipating that my faithful companion had sniffed out some game. A second or two later I made out the shape again. This was no bloody antelope or some such thing, it was a bugger of a lion and it was running towards me at speed!

— Fucking hell, Sandy! What did you do?

— I had no time to do anything. I felt a powerful impact, like a bloody fast car hitting me, and the next thing I recall was that I was being dragged along the path on my back, my arm and shoulder in the mouth of this beast, my body and legs being pulled along underneath it!

— My God!

— As the bugger trailed along, his forepaws kept trampling on me, causing considerable lacerations to the front of my thighs and ripping my trousers to shreds. While dragging me along, those growling purrs emanated from the beast's throat, as if he was a hungry cat anticipating a meal. Yours truly, of course, being the tasty little morsel he had in mind!

— Gosh! Sounds like a damn tricky one, Sandy.

— I'll say! There seemed no prospect of escape. Then I realised that I had my eight-inch sheath knife, which, using my free arm, I removed from the leather case hanging from my belt. I picked my spot on the beast. When the animal stopped, preparing to drop me, either to change its grip or to begin its feast, I stuck the bugger twice behind the shoulder. He dropped me, but continued to stand above me, growling. Then, with all the force I could muster, I stuck him in the throat. His blood cascaded down on me and I realised that I must have somewhat fortunately hit a large vein or an artery. Well, the bugger sprang back a few yards and I scrambled to my feet and just shouted obscenities at him. After a few seconds the maneater walked slowly away, occasionally turning to growl in my direction.

— Gosh Sandy, that was brave to face down the beast!

— I had no choice, Roy. Valour does not come into it. In such circumstances, one is operating, as you know, purely on a primal instinct. With great difficulty, due to my wounded arm, I climbed a nearby tree. It was as well that I did, for a second lion had got Gladstone and I was forced to watch as he and the one I'd wounded feasted on the poor old boy.

— That must have been heartbreaking, I said. I tried to sound sympathetic but I couldn't help a note of glee creeping into my voice. Somehow I was comforted by the death of Sandy's dog. Africa does something to a man; the heat, the silence as the sun descends behind the mountains, trees or horizon. The silence of an African jungle on a dark night must be experienced to be believed. What this place was doing to *me* was something I'd rather not contemplate.

— I stayed all night in that fucking tree, Sandy carried on with his story. — The natives found me at first light. They took me back to camp and superficially dressed my wounds. It took them a couple of days to get me to hospital. My injuries had gone septic and I had blood poisoning due to the putrescent matter lodged under the claws of the maneater that mauled me. The mauling was nothing to the fever I had . . . blast!

Our jeep swerved dangerously as one of its front wheels hit a rock in the semi-darkness. Sandy quickly regained control and stopped the vehicle for a while to compose himself. In the darkness the deathly silence was broken only by our heavy breathing and the soft noises of a few bats which sipped at the limpid waters of the lake in a series of flying kisses. We decided we would concentrate all our energies on the road. I took the wheel for a bit.

There was a campfire outside Lodge 1690 when we arrived. Dawson was strutting around and I saw two natives seemingly hugging a tree apiece. I realised, on approaching, that Dawson and Diddy had the natives stripped naked with their arms extended around the trees and bound at the wrists.

— Roy! Sandy! You're just in time. Some of our so-called rebel friends here are about to realise what it means to cross Lochart Dawson.

Even from the back and in his naked state, Sandy and I recognised one of the prisoners straight away. — Look Sandy! I said.

— So we meet again, my friend, Sandy smiled, examining the naked figure of Moses, the thief who had stolen all our equipment.

— I should say so! And in circumstances rather more advantageous to us! I sang triumphantly.

Moses looked around at us, his large eyes pleading, — No bwana, he begged.

— You'll thank me for this one day, Dawson smiled widely, licking his lips. He went over to the other native and produced a tube of jelly which he began to spread over the boy's buttocks. I took it that this was in preparation for the strokes of the lash, but I was somewhat surprised to see Dawson withdraw his stiffening penis and apply the jelly to himself. He then pushed a finger deep into the sphincter of the native. — Tight. The way I like it, he said.

Diddy the dwarf valet whispered at Sandy, — Remember I always told you to keep it tight at the back.

Sandy ignored him.

— One requires a certain resistance of course, eh Roy? Dawson turned to me smiling broadly. — After all, it's only through resistance that one can sense one's own power: in the overcoming of that resistance. Power always goes on and on until it finds its limits. C'mon Roy, c'mon Sandy. Drop your trousers and join the queue.

We unbuckled our belts and let our shorts fall. I had a semi but Sandy was already firm no I've got to stop this . . . — DAWSON! I shouted, as he was about to thrust his erection into the native.

He stopped and turned towards me.

— We've no time for these games! Time is of the essence! It's the Marabou Storks! We know where they are.

— This had better be good, Mr Strang, he snapped, scooping his subsiding erection into his shorts. — Diddy, watch those traitors, but don't lay a finger on them until I say so!

He gestured to the Lodge and what   up – – – after my Ma and
happened was – – – – I'm coming back up   Dad had that
                                          fight it carried on.

It carried on, eh.

Ma sat in the chair like a tightly wound spring, her face flushed. She sucked violently on a fag and glared at the box. There was one of these really shitey Scottish television Gaelic programmes on; the kind where they always have some straight cunt who looks like a fuckin muppet singing some daft song in a language naebody understands with mountains and rivers in the background. I looked over at the auld man and I could see the cunt was wary. Tony and I knew that the auld girl would explode in a bit.

She started emitting a soft, long twisting sound which built up into an almighty scream at the image on the television: — FAAAHKIN HOOR! FAAHKIN DIRTY FAAHKIN JAP-SHAGGING TRAITOR! She leaned forward and gobbed at the telly screen. Greasy spittle trickled down over the image of the Gaelic singer Mary Sandeman.

— Whit ye daein, Vet? Like ah sais, whit the fuck ye daein? Jist a wimmin singing the Gaelic likes, that's aw it is, a wimmin singing the fuckin Gaelic! Whit is it? Ah'm askin ye!

— It's that fuckin slag that goat done up like a Jap and sung that Japanese Boy song . . .

— Naw . . . this is this Gaelic lassie . . . yuv goat the wrong wimmin, Vet . . . like ah sais, this is the Gaelic, a Scottish lassie, no a Jap. Dis that look like a fuckin Jap? Ah'm askin ye; does that look like a fuckin Jap? Dad gestured at the screen.

Ma glared at him and pointed derisively at Mary Sandeman. — That's worse than a Jap! A Jap cannae help what it is, bit that, dressin like a fuckin Jap, glorifyin these dirty, torturin wee bastards . . .

— She disnae dress like a fuckin Jap bit, Vet, it's the Scottish lassie thit does the Gaelic programmes . . .

— Naw, Tony said. – Ma's right. She did that 'Japanese Boy' song. Goat done up as a Jap oan Top Ay The Pops, mind ay that?

— Aye . . . ah mind that yin . . . Dad started to sing, and Tony joined in:

> Won't somebody tell me where my love has gone,
> He's a Japanese Boy.
> I woke up this morning and my love had gone,
> He's a Japanese Boy.

Was it something I said or done?
Ohhhh
He's breaking up a happy home . . .

— Shut the fuck up! SHUT YIR FUCKIN MOOTHS, YA
FUCKIN CUNTS! Ma screamed.
— Jist a song bit Vet, jist a song. 'Japanese Boy' likes. John turned
his palms outwards in appeal.
This was radge. This was how these cunts lived.
It was time I got away.
But I couldn't get away. Not in Manchester. Not here in my
head. Here in my head she'd come after me. She kept coming after
me. The nightmares, the Marabou Stork nightmares – – – –

DEEPER

    DEEPER

        DEEPER
        into
          the
            Marabou
            Stork
              nightmares – – –
– – – getting closer to the nest, I told Dawson after we went back into
the conservatory of Lodge 1690.
— The Storks have been flying overhead. It seems that the only
place they could be is at your secret hideaway lodge Lochart.
They've probably taken it over and set up nests there, Sandy
explained.
— My entertainment suite . . . Dawson was dumbstruck . . . — a
nesting location for these monsters . . . Sadie . . . the Jambola
malcontents . . . of course. I see it all now. They've conned Lochart
Dawson. Well, let's show . . .
His spiel was interrupted by the crashing of breaking glass and a

cacophony of frenetic squawking as one, then another, then more large Marabous smashed through the French windows.

We were unarmed; our weapons were in the jeep outside. We instinctively retreated from the vile, shrieking clatter and I was about to run to the main door when it fell inwards with a crash, framing a monster Marabou Stork. I followed Dawson and Sandy down a set of flimsy stairs into a basement but the Storks continued to pursue us and we were cornered.

The basement was a dank, dark room. You could hear the sounds of running water below the rotting floorboards. A group of giant Storks surrounded us, shuffling closer like repulsive old beggars. A scent of charred, burning flesh filled my nostrils. We were helpless, unarmed. The largest of the Marabous came forward.

— Looks like it's sort ay panned oot tae oor advantage, eh boys, the creature observed.

It tore a large piece from a bloodied flamingo carcass with a ripping sound, and swallowed it whole. Another held the severed neck and head of a flamingo in its beak. I started gagging.

Dawson stiffened his back and pulled himself up: — As a businessman who is seeking controlling interest in this enterprise, the leisure park does not need the likes of you, people who care nothing for the . . .

The Stork's black, beady eyes focused on him, — Shut it, ya fat fuck! Whae's this cunt!

Dawson's eyes widened briefly with
fear before petulance replaced it as
the dominant emotion. Shaking   o
nervously, he whispered under   i   u
his breath, – You obviously   v   s
don't understand the   b   l
process of debate . . . – – – – – o   y   – I obviously had great
difficulty in going to the police. They say they've changed their procedures, but I didn't find a
great deal of understanding there. Must be something to do with the training, eh? Let me
quote to you from the advice given to police officers on the interrogation of rape complainants,
as it appeared in the *Police Review*:

It should be borne in mind except in cases of a very small child, the offence of rape is extremely unlikely to have been committed against a woman who does not show signs of extreme violence. If a woman walks into a police station and complains of rape with no signs of violence she must be closely interrogated. Allow her to make a statement to a policewoman and then drive a horse and cart through it. It is always advisable if there is any doubt of the truthfulness of her allegations to call her an outright liar . . . watch out for the girl who is pregnant or late getting home at night; such persons are notorious for alleging rape or indecent assault. Do not give her sympathy. If she is not lying, after the interrogator has upset her by accusing her of it, then at least the truth is verified . . . the good interrogator is very rarely loved by his suspect.

But the whole thing was Lexo . . . he set it up . . . ah never even . . .

— So Roy, I was reluctant to become a suspect. Suspected of lying about being held captive, brutalised, tortured and humiliated. A suspected and a proven liar; proven in a court of law. I still get flashbacks, Roy. Two years later. These flashbacks are nothing to do with the acid you gave me. Some people have them ten years later. It never really ends, Roy. It never really ends.

It wis Lexo that gave ye the acid! Lexo's fault! Alex Setterington. He's done it tae lassies before, he's probably still daein it. You'll no remember, bit ah tried tae stoap it! AH WIS THE CUNT THAT TRIED TAE STOAP THUM! AH SAIS TAE UM! MIND AH SAIS!

DEEPER, PLEASE PLEASE DEEPER

Oh fuck, I can see light coming through those thin membranes that are my eyelids . . . I'm going to fuckin open them and stare her in the face . . . please no no no no no DEEPER . . . I can smell this disinfectant . . . this is the fuckin hoaspital . . .

— I was a fool, Roy. A fool to go through the process. It was worse than the rape itself. The judge. Worse than a joke; a sick joke played on me. The whole thing was a theatre. A theatre to humiliate and brutalise me all over again. What was it Judge Wild said in Cambridge in 1982: 'It's not just a question of saying no . . .

NO

— it's a question of how she says it, how she shows it and makes it clear.

NO

—If she doesn't want it she only has to keep her legs shut and she would not get it without force and there would be marks of force being used. That was another good judge, just like our Justice Hermiston. So it was my own fault, Roy. I didn't say no the proper way . . .

NO

— . . . I should have kept my legs shut, even drugged, even with that knife at my throat, even with two men pulling my legs apart . . .

NO

NO

I can't wake now

DEEPER

DEEPER

DEEPER – – – Now I'm away from you . . . I'm sliding down the well, past my platform, out of that tunnel of darkness into a clear blue sky above the tropical savannah of Africa, the place of my dreams, of my freedom . . . but it's going dark again and I'm back in this room with Dawson and Sandy, cornered by the Storks.

— There must be some arangement we can come to, Dawson pleaded with the dead-eyed beast, — I'm a man of not inconsiderable personal wealth. I have a family!

The large Marabou turned to its friends and squawked loudly. The air was raw with the sound of their hysterical screeches and floating feathers and dust flew, giving off a vile stench and irritating me so that I sneezed – – – – – – – – – – – – – – – – – – Eh fuckin moved, Vet! Like ah sais, the laddie moved! It wis like eh sneezed or somethin! Roy! Kin ye hear ays! Ah'm askin ye son, kin ye hear ays!

— Dinnae shout John, the laddie's ill, the laddie isnae fuckin well!

— Bit eh kin sneeze, Vet! Quick! pit the tape oan, the new tape . . . It's goat ays singin Born Free oan it son. Ma favourite film ay all time. Mind, Roy, ah showed ye the video! Like ah sais, favourite film ay aw time that yin: Baw -rn freee — as free is as the wind blows . . . mind ay that son? Matt Monro sung it! Mind! The film Roy, mind; Joy Adamson n her man, whit wis the cunt's name again?

Joy Adamson's man? Based oan a true story! Elsa, the lioness cub, ken bit thit grew up tae be a big lion! Kin ye hear ays, Roy! Born Free! Mind! Vet! C'moan wi the tape!

   —Ah'm comin, John!

> I'd like to run away from you,
> But if you never found me I would die . . .

   — That's you singing Shirley fuckin Bassey again Vet, no me wi Born Free. Pit me singin Born Free oan!

I'm going to wake up if I don't go fucking deeper . . . DEEPER

   — Bit it's a new Shirley Bassey John, a different Shirley Bassey . . .

   — Aye, bit ah wis talkin tae the laddie aboot Born Free. Eh must mind ay that video. Joy Adamson. Eh watched it enough.

   — Naw, bit ah dinnae agree wi that, John. The laddie grew up hearin me singing like Shirley Bassey so that's whit we should be playin fir um . . .

   — Like ah sais, Born Free . . . n thirs a bit ay me singin Tom Jones oan it n aw . . . Thunderball . . . that wis a James Bond theme tune, like ah sais, Thunderball. Aye. Thunderball.

I'd rather face the Stork than listen tae these cunts . . .
DEEPER
DEEPER

I can't get fuckin deeper . . .

   — Here we go!

> He always runs while the others walk,
> He acts while the other men just talk . . .

   — That's the one, Vet! Me singin Tom Jones . . . likesay Thunderball n that. Like ah sais, Thunderball.

   — Aye . . .

> He looks at the world and he wants it all,
> So he strikes like Thuuuunder-ball . . .

   — One ay ma favourite Bond theme tunes ay aw time, this yin. Some chanter Tom Jones, eh Vet?

   — Aye . . .

FUCK OFF FUCK OFF FUCK OFF FUCK OFF FUCK OFF FUCK OFF

— A great number, like ah sais, a great number.

— Ah dinnae really like that yin but John, ah like Tom Jones's other stuff . . . last night ah went tae sleep in Detroit City.

— Listen but Vet . . .

Any woman he wants he'll get . . .

NO

NO

He'll break any heart without regret,

His days of asking are all gone . . .

His fight goes on and on and on . . .

DEEPER PLEASE DEEPER

— Ah widnae really class masel as a belter bit, Vet. Ah'm mair ay a crooner, ken? Mair yin fir the soulful ballads like.

— Mibbe git ma tape on now though, John.

— Soulful ballads, like ah sais.

— Ma tape, John.

— Aye, soulful ballads.

PLEASE GO

— Change the tapes now, John.

— Eh . . . aye, bit we huv tae be gaun now, Vet. Likesay need tae be makin a move. Cheerio Roy!

Ma's cheap perfume reeks as she bends over to kiss me.

— Cheerio sweetheart.

Thank you and goodbye.

GOODBYE.

19 Miss X's Confessions

I feel my senses returning. This is beyond perception. I know she's in the room before she speaks; observing me, toying with me. I'm at her mercy in the same way she was at ours. How will she exercise her power? Will she show compassion or is she just the same as us? Is she what we made her? I know who you are, Miss X. I know who you are, Kirsty.

Kirsty Chalmers. Miss X.

But I didn't . . . it was Lexo. I didn't mean to hurt you.

IT WISNAE MA FUCKIN FAULT
The wey you carried oan
asked fir it
wi wir aw pished

BLAME THE WOMEN
BLAME THE DRINK
BLAME THE WEATHER

Z.

THERE IS NO EXCUSE

I want to go.

You only live twice
Or so it seems
One life for yourself
And one for your dreams . . .

— Your taste in music is strange, Roy Strang. It's fuckin weird, just like the rest of you.

ITS NO MA FUCKIN TASTE, IT'S THESE CUNTS

You drift through the years
And life seems tame,
Till one dream appears
And love is its name . . .

— The funny thing is Roy, Roy Strang, that I actually fancied you. Honest. Crazy eh? I genuinely thought that you were a bit different. Thought you were a nice-looking felly. I know that you were shy aboot your ears, anybody could see that, but I liked them. He looks like Shane in the Pogues, I used to say. I thought that you were tasty. Different, quiet, not full of yourself like the others. Thoughtful. Deep. Ha ha . . . I thought you were deep. Deep in a fucking coma.

DEEPER

And love is a stranger
Who'll beckon you on . . .

DEEPER

Don't think of the danger,
Or the stranger is gone . . .

DEEPER

— I was scared to talk to you though. You didn't show any interest in me, no like the others. You didn't drool. The only reason I hung around with these morons was to get closer to you. How crazy is that then, eh?

This dream is for you
So pay the price
Make one dream come true
You only live twice . . .

DEEPER

I can't get away, I can't get deeper . . . this is fuckin . . . if ah don't watch out ah'm gaunny wake up, gaunny end up right back in thair fuckin world where ah huv tae face aw this . . . and why is she sayin this aboot me, Dumbo Strang . . . why is she tellin these lies, tryin tae fuck ma heid up . . .

— I've decided to get them all, Roy. Your mate Dempsey was just the first. It was so easy. I just waited until he was coming home from the pub, he'd been there a lot lately, and I drove at him at high speed. He was all over the road. Held on for a couple of days as a cabbage, like yourself. I was sad when he kicked it; it would have been nice to have had you all lying before me like the produce on display at a fruit market; the vegetable stall. Then I could inspect the vegetables at ma whim.

DEEPER

— It would be great if you could hear this Roy, although I suppose that's just wishful thinking on my part. Mind you, Dr Goss did say that you were showing greater signs of awareness than ever before and he is hopeful that you'll come out of this one day. I wouldn't count on that though.

I WANT AWAY

— I'll tell you Roy, if you can hear me, you still won't have gathered how much I hate and detest you. I could never really tell you how much. You probably have no idea how you changed my life, how you could have ruined it, if I'd let you. I'll never be the same again Roy. Sex and men. . . it doesnae work for me anymair. I've found something in it all though, Roy. I've found me. I hate you for what you did to me. I understand that hate. What I'd really love is for you to be able to explain how you hated me so much to do what you did. What happened to you? What was your fucking problem, you sad, sad cabbage, you sick, brutalised, fucked-up bastard? Why did you hate me so much, Roy?

I didnae hate ye . . . I wanted you . . . I wanted us to . . .

THERE IS NO EXCUSE

NO NO NO NO

IT WIS LEXO . . . LEXO . . . IT WIS FUCKIN LEXO THAT
INSTIGATED THE WHOLE THING AH NIVIR EVEN
REALLY TOUCHED YE NOWT TAE FUCKIN DAE WI
ME AH WIS FEART, FEART AY LEXO THE CUNT'S A
FUCKIN KILLER

> Make one dream come true
> You only live twice . . .

DEEPER

      DEEPER

            DEEPER – – – – – – – – – – – – – –
– – and
     it's
          happening now . . . and Dawson's jumping on
the spot and throwing a tantrum about how he doesn't want to die
and because of this we go crashing through the rotten floorboards
and run through a cavernous set of tunnels. — Wait for me, Dawson
wheezes, as we hear the Storks squawking in pursuit.

I run and run until I can see nothing around me or ahead of me.
Then it's like my lungs collapse and I black out. I have a pleasant
image of the two of us, me and Dorie, at a club, dancing together,
really high, I feel the music in me, feel the rushes, the uninhibited
euphoria . . . I awaken and Sandy's kind face pulls into focus in front
of me. Dust kicked up by a swirling wind stings my eyes and my
throat. Sandy's got a shooter. It's a pump-action double-barrelled
shotgun. — We have to go, Roy, he says. I get up easily and I see the
Lodge in the distance. We run towards it.

— Let's get that fucking Stork, Sandy, we're so close, so close to
solving the whole fuckin problem – – – coming up – – – so close to
the surface – – – – – – – — A total breakdown, Roy. I blamed myself. For a whole year I was
no better than you, a fucking walking corpse.

WHAT THE FUCK ARE YOU DOING HERE THIS IS JUST SUPPOSED TAE BE ME AND SANDY

SANDY

Sandy

> Diamonds are forever . . .
> They are all I need to please me,
> They can stimulate and tease me,

Sandy

> They won't leave in the night,
> I've no fear that they might
> > desert me . . .

JAMIESON

> Diamonds are forever . . .
> Hold one up and then caress it,
> Touch it, stroke it and undress it,
> I can see every part,
> Nothing hides in the heart
> > to hurt me . . .

WHAIR THE FUCK UR YE, JAMIESON!

20 Self-Deliverance With A Plastic Bag

I couldn't run away from it in Manchester. The nightmares; oddly enough the Marabou Stork nightmares were the worst. Why should that have been? Who knows. Who the fuck knows. The Marabou Storks. I saw them at the Kruger Park in South Africa, the only place in the Republic where you can view them. When that one killed the flamingo, it was fucking horrible. It made me feel queasy. It was the way it held up the flamingo's head, severed at the neck. The flamingo is not a beautiful bird. It is a stupid, ugly-looking creature which happens to have beautiful plumage. Gaze at the flamingo's face, and what do you see?

You see a beautiful bi
You see
The flamingo's blood, her blood. The blood of her on me.
No. There was no blood.
Only my blood. My blood
when he did that to me in
the city of gol – – – – – – den words he will pour in your ear,
 But his lies can't disguise what you fear,
 For a golden girl knows when he's kissed her,
 It's the kiss of death from mis-tah
 Gold-fing-ah.
 Pretty girl, beware of his heart of gold,
 This heart is cold.

I'M NEARLY FUCKIN AWAKE HERE, I COULD OPEN
MY EYES . . .
    No.
    No way. This is my home. My refuge. Like Manchester.
    Manchester was my refuge. I stayed in my flat in Ancoats,
keeping away from everyone, except to go to my work. I watched
videos and started reading again. Not just books to do with my
work, like information technology and software design; books on
politics n that, and no nature books, no ornithology. Apart from that
it was everything really; loads on Africa, imperialism and apartheid.
I wanted to go back, no as it is now but as I imagined it was or as it
could be. Once those fuckin white cunts had been kicked out. That's
all I did in Manchester, I read, and I kept masel tae masel.
    Then she came along.
    I had seen her at work, even knew her name. She worked in the
Pensions Section. Her name was Dorothy. She always had a smile
for everyone, a smile that just made you smile back. It wisnae a
bland, stupid indiscriminate smile though. It was a real engaging,
searching smile; the smile of someone looking for the good they
know is in everybody and invariably finding it.
    It happened when I was coerced along to an office leaving do.
Coerced along by a bossy, domineering middle-aged cow who liked
to organise every cunt's life. There always seemed to be loads of
them in the type of places I worked in. One of those people who
thinks of themselves and is thought of by others as friendly, but who
is anything but, who is another fuckin control freak. As I was new,
or relatively new by that time, this person insisted that I came along.
I would get to know people better. The last thing I wanted to do was
to get to know any cunt. I don't know why, but I went. It was
probably because I was so depressed I didn't have the willpower to
say no, or to contemplate the excuses I'd have to make on Monday.
Roy Strang. Top boy. Ha ha ha.
    The whole thing was just another load of shite to get through. I
took my Becks and sat making small-talk, trying to be as inconspicu-
ous as possible. People seemed to be comfortable talking to me for
an obligatory couple of minutes, before deciding to find better

company. It was as if I was wearing a baseball cap with flashing lights that spelt: FUCKED UP.

Then Dorothy came over and sat beside me. She smiled and I felt myself smiling back. I felt some tightness in my chest unlock. — It's about time I introduced myself. I've seen you around. I'm Dorothy from Pensions. Oh bloody hell, that makes me sound ancient. It's Dorothy from Warrington really. I hate it when people say what do you do, and people talk about their sodding jobs all the time. What do you do? I eat, sleep, shit, pee, make love, get out of it, go to clubs, that's what I flamin well do. Sorry, I'm rabbiting ere. What's your name?

— Eh, Roy.

Dorothy was pretty. She had a nice face and shortish blonde hair. Pretty enough to be thought of as plump rather than fat. Not from Fathell, Lancashire. She seemed not to be drunk, but somehow euphoric.

— Look Roy, I'm sorry about this, but I'm E'd out of my face. If I'm in a club an there's good sounds on, I don't bother nobody, I just dance. If I'm in this sort of environment though, I just want to talk to everyone. Life's too short to be all quiet n grumpy, init?

Life's too short. Her enthusiasm was infectious. In spite of myself I was enjoying talking to her. — What dae these things dae for ye?

— Ain't you done any E before? I thought you were all big ravers up in Scotland.

— Naw, ah like the indie stuff mair, ken? No really intae dance n that.

I was a freak. Legs too short. Gimpy, thanks tae fuckin Winston Two. Rest in peace you canine cunt. I'd always wanted tae dance, I mean really dance, tae really go for it, but naw. I never bothered, eh.

— This gear's brilliant. I never drink now, can't stand the stuff and I've never had such a good time in my life, she smiled. She was certainly having a better time than me. I'd had just two Becks, the rest of the night I'd been on cokes. I didn't want to get drunk and lose control. I was looking at the others; their morose, belligerent beery faces. They didn't seem to be having a good time either.

But she was.

A lot of the boys in the cashies took Es, a lot of them didnae. I never saw the point. I'd always liked the Becks, and couldnae get intae that fucking music. It was shite, that techno, nae lyrics tae it, that same fuckin drum machine, throbbin away aw the time. I hated dancing. It was like playing fitba. It put me up there on exhibition; my savaged, stumpy legs, my large body and my long, swinging ape airms. Swedgin had always been ma dancing.

I suppose I'd built up an aversion to any kind of drugs because of the wey my Ma and Dad got through the drink and how it made the cunts behave. That didnae seem to matter now though. I took one from her; fifteen quid, a wee capsule.

— R&Bs, she said.

I was talking away to her, but getting fuck all from the E. I was still enjoying myself, though, until I realised that I was really rushing, really riding the crest of a wave. Then I felt myself rise and the music seemed to be inside me. It was like the music was coming from me. I felt dizzy and queasy, but I'd never known such an exhilarating high. I wanted to shite for a bit, but it passed. The swedgin was fuck all compared to this; I felt I had all the power in the world but it was positive. I felt a bond with Dorothy, or Dorie as she liked to be called. Her face looked so clear and fresh and beautiful, her eyes were so alive. Her hair was   a 2 Unlimited number came on the juke-box and I felt the drums thrash through me and the synth slabs lift me out of my seat. It had done fuck all for me before. — Whoaahhh . . . , I gasped.

— You alright? she asked.

— Ah'm sortay startin tae see what aw the fuss is aboot . . .

— Paula, she shouted over at her friend, — Roy ere's just lost his virginity. C'mon, let's get out of here. We need a more memorable setting to do this experience justice.

All I wanted was that music. House, it had to be house. When Dorie told me I would get more of it at a club called the Hacienda, but only far, far, better and blasted through a PA, with brain-frying lights and surrounded by people who felt the same, I was instantly sold.

The club was fuckin awesome. I was lost in the music and the movement. It was an incredible experience, beyond anything I'd known. I could never dance, but all self-consciousness left me as the drug and music put me in touch with an undiscovered part of myself, one that I had always somehow suppressed. The muscles in my body seemed in harmony with each other. My body's internal rhythms were pounding, I could hear them for the first time: they were singing to me. They were singing: You're alright, Roy Strang. You're alright, we're all alright. People, strangers, were coming up to me and hugging me. Birds, nice-looking lassies n that. Guys n aw; some ay them cunts that looked wide and whom I would have just panelled in the past. I just wanted to hug them all, to shake them by the hand. Something special was happening and we were all in this together. I felt closer to these strangers than I did to anyone. Dorie and Paula I loved; I just loved them. I couldn't stop hugging them, like I'd always wanted to hug pals, but it was too sappy, too poofy. I knew that after I came down I'd still love them. Something fundamental happened that night; something opened up in me.

I was the Silver Surfer, I looked into the laser lights and zapped across the universe a few times, surging and cruising with the music. It built up into a crescendo and Dorie, Paula and I, it was like we were the world, us and the people around us. I was one with them and myself and I never wanted to lose it. Even when the music stopped — it was hours later but it felt like minutes — I was still right up.

I was overwhelmed. All the shite Bri had spraffed, him and some of the boys in the cashies who we used to say had gone aw soft wi the ravin, it was all fuckin true and so much more. It was euphoria . . . it was something that everyone should experience before they die if they can truly have said not to have wasted their life on this planet. I saw them all in our offices, the poor sad fools, I saw them in their suburbs, their schemes, their dole queues and their careers, their bookies shops and their yacht clubs . . . it didn't matter a fuck. I saw their limitations, the sheer vacuity of what they had on offer against this alternative. There would, I knew, be risks. Nothing this good came without risk. I couldn't go back though. No way. There was nothing to go back to . . .

. . . like now there's nothing to come up for – – – your eyes only

Can see me in the night.
For your eyes only
I never have to hide.

You can see so much in me,
So much in me that's new
I never felt until I looked at you . . .

Oh fuck, go for it Roy you crapping cunt, go deeper, go forward, go
back to the Stork or stay with this reminiscing because it doesnae
matter, it's the same sad fuckin story, it's always gaunny be the same
sad fuckin story – – – – so go DEEPER

DEEPER

DEEPER – – and
now Sandy's back, and I'm thinking to myself, fuck them, fuck
them all.
— Let's hold on a bit, Sandy, I say.
— What? he replies, a little bewildered.
— I'm thinking, why should we be in a hurry to do battle with
Johnny Stork? Why should we run to the lodge to try and sort this
out? It's between Dawson and the terrorists and the Storks . . . I
mean, what's old Johnny Stork ever done to us? Let's enjoy our
picnic! It's nothing to do with us. We've got jam here, and honey and
butter, and plenty of that *absolutely* wonderful homemade bread.
We . . .
— Cut the bullshit, Roy. It's got everything to do with us, Sandy
snaps, his face harsh.
— Can't we have just a small picnic here first? Can't it be just like
the old times?
— No it can't be, Roy. It can never be like the old times, Sandy
says coldly.
— Never like the old times, I repeat wearily, — . . . never like old
times. I felt beaten. I just couldn't be bothered. — Okay, let's go.
We start up towards the lodge, but Sandy turns to me and says,

—I'm sorry Roy, I've been a little abrupt. I think you've realised what the score is now. I think we can spare the time to stop off for a little picnic before we go. For old time's sake, he grinned.

— Thanks Sandy, I appreciate it. For old time's sake, I smiled. Sandy was alright, no doubt about that.

he was a proper – – – – – Diamond – – – – – s are forever . . .

> Sparkling round my little finger,
> Unlike men the diamonds linger.
> Men are mere mortals who
> Are not worth going to
> Your grave for . . .

No. Give me the old times . . .

It can never be like the old times – – – – never like it was back in Manchester – – – – after the club that night – – – – because outside the streetlights were brilliant. I suppose I was slightly shiting myself about taking E because of the bad freak-out on acid once, but this was different. I felt totally in control. I'd never felt so much in control.

I had got dead sad when the music ended. My eyes were watering and it didn't matter. I wasn't embarrassed about being sappy. I saw what a silly, sad pathetic cowardly cunt I was, ever to be embarrassed about expressing emotion. But I wasn't even hard on myself; it didn't matter.

Back at Dorie's gaff, we drank tea, and I told them about myself; more than I've ever told anyone. I talked of my fears and insecurities, my hang-ups. They talked about theirs. It was supportive, empathetic; it was good. Not in a smarmy, false-intimacy, middle-class counselling way, or in a big, weird, spaced-out, hippy bullshit trip. This was just punters saying how they felt about life. I could talk about anything, almost anything, the rape and my family were taboo, but that was my choice.

It was no problem. Nothing was a problem.

Every weekend after that I was E'd out my face and clubbing. I had more pals in Manchester in a few months than I ever had back home.

The problem was that it was so good that it made everything else seem shite. No, that's not quite right: it showed that everything else *was* shite. Work was shite; just something to get through.

Eventually Dorie and I started sleeping together. We felt good about each other and there was nobody else involved. It had just been a matter of time. I was worried about sex, because I hadn't been with anyone since the incident. When we first shagged, I was E'd up and it made no difference, so we always made love when I was eckied. One day she said: — You don't have to be E'd up to make love to me you know.

We went to bed. I was trembling, scared of exposing myself without the chemicals. We kissed for a bit and I stopped shaking. We played with each other for a long time, and after we had joined, my cock and her fanny just became the one thing, then it seemed to vanish as we took off on a big psychic trip together. It was our souls and our minds that were doing it all; our genitals, our bodies, they were just the launch pads and were soon superfluous as we went around the universe together on our shared trip, moving in and out of each other's heads and finding nothing in them but good things, nothing in them but love. The intensity increased until it became almost unbearable and we exploded together in an orgasmic crash-landing onto the shipwreck of a bed, from a long way out in some form of space. We held each other tightly, drenched in sweat and shaking with emotion.

To my surprise, it was just as good as it was with the ecky.

Dorie told me after that she thought I was beautiful. I was shocked to find out that she wasn't joking. I kept looking at myself in the mirror. — Your ears are big, but beautiful. They got character. They're distinctive. They ain't as big as you think n all, your head's grown since you were a little kid, you know.

We went to the Hacienda every weekend. There was always a party at somebody's gaff after. To come down we usually smoked grass. Skunk if we could get it. I loved just blethering away, but more than that, I loved listening; listening to all the punters, their patter, hearing about their lives, getting up to all sorts of mischief with each other. I'd take a deep suck on a joint and hold on to it until a large ripe tomato of pleasure blew to smithereens behind my face.

Dorie and I got engaged. It was stupid and cavalier, we had only known each other for a few months. It was bizarre, but I just wanted to make a gesture, to show her how I felt.

Life was okay; it was better than okay. I read a lot during the week, and went with Dorie to watch arthouse movies at the Cornerhouse. At the weekend we clubbed and partied. Some Saturdays I went to the football with a couple of mates, Jimmy and Vince. We'd go down to the Moss to watch the City at Maine Road. The football wasn't as good as at Old Trafford, but the feel to it was better, more real. The crack in the pub before and after was great. Manchester was a brilliant place, it was the happiest time of my life.

Then something happened to knock the bottom out of my world and remind me who I was. It was an article in the *Manchester Evening News*, talking about the successful Zero Tolerance campaign in Edinburgh.

TWO OUT OF EVERY FIVE WOMEN WILL BE
SEXUALLY ABUSED OR RAPED.

Z.

THERE IS NO EXCUSE.

I lost it completely.

At the Hacienda that night I embraced Dorie most of the evening and through the morning; held her tightly to me. I held her as if I could force her love into me, drive the shit out of me, out of my mind and body, but what I was doing was infecting her; infecting her with my hurt, my pain, my anxiety. I could feel the sickness and doubt transmit in our embrace while my chin rested on the top of her head and my nostrils filled with the scent of her shampoo and perfume. The vibrations of doubt came back through her, right up through her skull and into my chin and into my head. She snorted with irregular discomfort through her nostrils, making a ragged sound against my neck. I got a duff E that night.

— Don't worry Roy, it don't always happen, Dorie said.

I'd lost it completely. All I could do was try to hide how much I had lost it.

Then I lost Dorie.

I got more and more depressed. I literally couldn't move. I just got more and more and more depressed. The doctor said I was suffering from ME, yuppie flu, that fucking post-viral fatigue or whatever they call it. For the first time, my relationship with Dorie was tested and found wanting. We sat in and ate, just fuckin ate, junk food, while watching videos. I could barely string a sentence together. We put on pounds, stones. She couldn't adjust to living with a depressed fuck-up who couldn't go out. Dorie was a party chick. She just wanted to have a good time . . . maybe I'm being hard on her. She wasn't that frivolous. She probably knew I was holding something back, keeping something from her, not showing her the whole me. Perhaps if I had been straight with her she might have

No.

— I'm just going to put the other side of the tape on now, Roy. Your mother has a great voice.

Thanks, Patricia. You sound different. Clearer. Louder. Closer. Your touch as you pull my head up to plump my pillows. Your perfume. The disinfectant smells of the hospital. The dimensions of this small room. I feel them for the first time. The drip in my arm. The tube in my throat, the one in my cock. It all doesnae matter. I lost Dorie.

> Nobody does it better,
> Makes me feel sad for the rest.
> Nobody does it half as good as you do,
> baby you're the best.

— Are you as good a singer as your mum, Roy?

I lost Dorie . . .

We agreed to split. I moved into a new place in Eccles.

> I wasn't looking,
> But somehow you found me.
> I tried to hide from your love.

> Like heaven above me,
> The spy who loved me
> Is keeping all my secrets safe tonight.

I remember when I left the flat. I tried to talk to her, but the words wouldn't come. Even at that late stage she looked at me as if she wanted to hear words that would have made a difference. I couldn't even think them. My brain felt like it was floating in thick soup and my chest was as tight as a drum. Nothing would come.

— I'm sorry I couldn't help you, Roy. You have to help yourself first though. I'm sorry it didn't work out, she sniffed and couldn't stifle a sob. — I've been through this before and I don't want it again. It's better a clean break . . . I thought you were different, Roy . . .

— See ye, I said, picking up my holdall. I walked out the door and never looked back. I hated the cunt. I fuckin hated

No.

No Dorie fuck Roy Strang silly cunt top boy E head good looking so refined Dumbo Strang

> The way that you hold me,
> Whenever you hold me,
> There's some kind of magic
> inside you . . .

Oh God what have I fuckin well done

Oh my God

I stayed in.

I stayed in at the weekends, watching videos. Then the worse part of it passed. I started going out again, though not so regularly. When I did go out, I avoided the Hacienda and I took loads of Es. I started taking sleeping pills to come down. I fucked as many lassies as I could; there were plenty at the clubs who were up for a shag. I respected them, there was massive respect, but we never kidded that it was anything else other than sex. There was no bullshit. It sometimes gave the illusion of happiness, but I was not happy, not in the same way. It's just that the pain was taken away. You can either use drugs as a validation of the joy of life or you can use them as an escape from its horrors. You have to become sensitive to the point where one shades into the other. I wasn't, and I went through a bad time.

I must have gone through a bad time because I started writing home. I got letters back. They'd all write on the one piece of paper to me. Before it would have embarrassed me, now it was strangely touching. It was crazy, but it made me want to be near them.

Dear Roy,

Hope everything is well down in Manchester and that your not getting too English! Nane o' that by the way Jimmy or your no a proper Scotsman n you'll no be alowed back up here. (Only joking!) New neighbours upstairs are a wee bit too lippy, Tony and I paid them a little visit and taught them the meaning of the word respect. Had a wee crowd back the other night and had a bit of a sing-song. We were minding of the time one New Year when we got you to sing A View To A Kill. Mind that? You liked that Duran Duran when you were younger! No denying it! I sang some Tom Jones and your Ma did her Shirley Bassey. A rare night. Colin Cassidy and me taught the Hopes dunno if you ken them a junky family in the scheme well we taught them a lesson they'll no forget in a hurry. Suffice to say our frends the Hopes are no longer resident in the scheme. Anyway, hears Mum.

All the best, Dad.

Hello Roy son,

Mum here. God, it doesn't seem more than a year now since you moved away. Time flies, right enough. Everyone is well here, and the big news we have is that Kim is getting married and is going to be a mum. We are all very thrilled. I don't know if you know Kevin, he is an awful nice fellow. What about you? Any sign of a girlfriend?

We had spaghetti bolognese the other day (is it still your favourite?) and that made us think of you. I had what your Dad calls my 'usual wee greet' at the thought of you being so far away and I hope you can come home soon so it can be like old times.

All my love son,

Mum. XXXXX

P.S. Here's a few words from the mum-to-be, the future Mrs Scott.

Hiya Roy,

I shewd be calling you Uncle Roy because of the baby which is going to be born in February and will be called Jason if it's a boy and either Scarlet or Dionne if it is a wee girl

and the wedding will be sumtime in December at the Commidore Hotel and I have chosen a nice dres

Kevin seys that he's looking forward to meeting you and having a pint cause he is a nice felly and I will be glad when you two have met but no arguments about the football cause he's a JAMBO and I have started to support Hearts two because they are the best time. No arguments like cause that's what Tony does who's going to rite something here.

Love from Kim Scott (soon to be the formir Kim Strang.)

XXXXXXXXXXXXXXXXXXXXXXXXXXXXXXXXXXXXXXXXXXXX

XXXXXXXXXXXXXXXXXXXXXXXXXXXXXXXXXXXXXXXXXXXX

XXXXXXXXXXXXXXXXXXXXXXXXXXXXXXXXXXXXXXXXXXXX

Hi Roy,

Tony here. We've got the Huns in the semi at Hampden, that's next week. A good night out, so get up for it. Hibees on a good run just now. I'm hoping we don't get any injuries or suspensions and have to play Joe Tortolano — a good Italian but a shite player. See you for the semi!

P.S. Hannah and the kids are okay and send their love.

Tony.

I came home to Edinburgh, a glazed-eyed basket case, back into the now strangely comforting chaos of my family.

I was ostensibly up for the League Cup semi-final, where Hibs were playing Rangers at Hampden. Nobody gave them a chance, but they won. I scarcely noticed. Tony's nails were bitten to the quick in that second half as we stood at the open end of the ground. Kevin, Kim's felly, was with us. He seemed an okay guy, a bit slow and bewildered, but harmless. A typical Jambo in fact. John got stroppy and threatened some guys in front of us with assault for putting up their flag and interrupting his view. At the final whistle he crushed one of them in a victory bear-hug. Tony jumped on me, tearing my neck muscles. I allowed myself to be dragged along and slapped by everyone near me.

There was a party . . . ------
----- Me. and. Sandy. Jamieson.

Just the two of us.

At our party. A picnic. A spread of fresh bread, cheeses, farm eggs and mouth-watering preservatives laid out on a pink gingham cloth. It was just the two of us, the way I'd always wanted it to be. ------

------ It was Dorie and me; at the Lake District . . .

Who have I ever really loved?

I don't need ---------- luuuuuurrrrrrvvvvvvve.
What good would love do me,
Diamonds never lie to me,
For when love's gone
They last onnnnn . . .

DEEPER.

There was a party . . . ------

------ a party after the game at my auld man's. A party at my auld man's. You could have replaced the guests with a series of inflatables that wobble on their bases, with a tape deck built in to spout out clichés:

CHEERY AULD CUNT WITH HALF A LUNG AND GIMPY LEG: — Mustn't grumble . . . aye . . . mustn't grumble

MUMPY-FACED GUINNESS-GUTTED AUNTIE: — Pit oan an awfay loat ay weight since her hysterectomy . . . pit oan an awfay loat ay weight since her hysterectomy . . .

VACANT PARTY-CHICK COUSIN: — Hiyaaah . . . Hiyaaah . . Hiyaaah . . .

BROODING TEEN-PUP COUSIN IN CORNER: — Shite in here . . . pit oan some decent sounds . . .

WHINGEY UNCLE WITH ULCER: — Ah like it bit it disnae like me . . . ah like it bit it disnae like me . . .

I thought that it couldn't get any worse but it did. I hadn't told any of the guys I used tae hing aboot wi that I was coming back up fir the fitba. While everyone else had been on tenterhooks at the game's

903

outcome, my only anxiety at being at Hampden was concern that one of the boys would see me.

Somebody had. The phone went and it was for me. It was Lexo.

— Thoat ye'd be up fir the fitba, he said.

— Aye, barry result, eh.

— Stomped a few hun casuals. Her Majesty's Service. Fuckin wee bairns; shitin cunts. Typical Weedgies; fling a few boatils n cairray a blade bit cannae pagger fir fuck all.

— Keith Wright's heider . . .

— Aye, well they'd better no fuck up against any shite in the final. The winners automatically qualify fir Europe, mind. This is oor chance tae cause real bother, oan the continent. This is one fuckin show thit hus tae be taken oan the road; it'll be a fuckin great crack. Whit did ye no come wi us fir the night?

— Eh, wanted tae see the auld man n that, eh. Nivir see thum aw now thit um doon in Manchester, eh.

— Aye right. Ah need your address doon thair. Git a squad doon fir a wee brek one weekend, eh. See whit fixtures are oan. They tell ays that Bolton's the tidiest local firm, eh. Mibbe pey they cunts a wee surprise visit. Anywey, we're doon the club: oan a loak in. Git yirsel doon.

— Eh, thir's a wee perty oan up here . . .

— C'moan ya schemie cunt, git doon tae the club!

— Eh, aye, right then . . . I went, mainly because it was too depressing watching all those cunts get pished in the hoose with their fuckin alcohol, mainly because that persistent cunt Lexo wid be oan the phone aw night and mornin.

I hit Leith Walk, no knowing where I was going or what I was doing. The town was decked in green and white, songs were spilling out of every bar. It was a Hibbie's fantasy; not a Jambo in sight: they were all skulking indoors contemplating thirty years without a trophy on the shelf. I couldn't get into it though. I realised I should have been at Powderhall and I cut down from the Walk.

The club was heaving with casuals. Some of the teen pups that hung around in the baby crew were obviously now staking top table claims. Their bodies had filled out and their faces had hardened and some were looking at me with a lot less than their customary deference. There had obviously been a few changes. The important thing was to quickly suss out what these had been without getting involved with any radges. I was broken; I'd had enough of all this. I sat at the bar and sucked tensely on a Becks, anxious and nervous in the company of my old mates. Demps still wasn't around.

— Cunt's went a bit ay a straight-peg, eh, Ozzy told me.

Out the corner of my eye I noticed one guy who seemed vaguely familiar. He was blethering to Ghostie. He was a huge bulky bastard with a real mouth and a big swagger. I hadn't seen him with the cashies before but ah sure as fuck kent the cunt fae somewhair. I nearly froze in shock as it dawned on me who it was. His face looked the same but his eyes were different. They didn't flit around softly like they once did. They were now still, intense and focused. I couldnae remember the boy's name: I just kent him as the Dressed-By-His-Ma-Cunt.

I was for the off.

I scored an ecky and went with a couple of fringe cashies who were into clubbing, to this new midweek club at The Venue. I was relieved to be away. It was okay, but I recognised yet another cunt, and this time got an even bigger shock. This boy was well into his dancing. I went up and spoke to him. I don't know who was the most surprised, myself or Bernard. He was really E'd n aw. I found myself, to my surprise, hugging him. Bernard and I had never touched like this before, just exchanged blows in makeshift boxing rings. We farted around on the dancefloor, enjoying the hip-hop beat. I'm mair ay a hardcore than a garagey or hip-hop type ay cunt myself, but this was okay. We talked for a long time and my cashie mates filtered away, so Bernard and I ended up leaving and headed down to Chapps, a gay club near the Playhouse.

— Nivir thoat ah'd see you eckied up, Roy, he said.

— Oan it non-stoap fir the last six months, I told him with a sad smile. Bernard was alright.

Bernard. Aye. He was alright.

— Nivir thought ah'd be in here, though, I smiled, looking around. I didn't like the place. I told Bernard that I thought it was pretty sad and desperate, the way all those queens cruised each other out.

— Naw, it isnae really, he explained, — cause here just about every guy who wants fucked ends up getting fucked. It's much sadder and more desperate up at Buster Brown's or any hetro place, cause the number of guys that want fucked is higher than the number of lassies that want to fuck them. At least here, most people get what they want.

I thought about that for a while. There was no doubting his logic. I had to agree. It was easy. I felt good, I was rushing on the E. — Whoahh man, that ecky . . .

— Well, it agrees wi ye, he laughed.

I looked at him and said, slipping my arm around his neck, — Listen Bernard, you're alright man, ken? You had the whole thing sussed way back. I was a fuckin wanker, I couldnae handle anything, I'm no just talkin aboot you bein a buft . . . eh, bein gay, I jist mean everything . . . aw fuck, Bernard, I'm really sorry, man . . . it's not the E talkin, ah've just fucked things up, Bernard . . .

He shrugged. — We aw fuck things up, Roy.

— Naw, bit see when yuv *really* fucked things up, fucked them up so bad soas that thir's nothing ye kin ever dae tae pit it right; just nothin man, like it's always with ye? Bernard, see when ye dae something bad, dae something terrible, it doesnae make ye a bad person, does it? Ah mean ye can change, right?

— Ah suppose ye can, Roy . . . what's wrong, Roy? What is it? Yir talkin aboot love, eh?

I thought bitterly about that, — Nah, no love, the reverse ay that, I smiled, then I gave him a tight hug. He reciprocated.

— Ah nivir goat tae know ye, Bernard. Ah acted like a cunt tae you . . .

— It worked both ways, he smiled, hugging me again. It felt good.

— But ah've changed, Bernard. I've allowed myself tae feel. That means that ah have tae dae something, like tae sort ay prove tae myself that I've changed. It's like I have tae assume responsibility for ending my pain and making someone else feel better. Even if it involves the greatest sacrifice. Try tae understand . . . ah mean, fuck, ah sound like the auld man giein it big licks wi one ay Churchill's fuckin speeches . . . it sounds like ah'm wafflin here . . .

I just couldnae say

— It's okay Roy, he just kept saying, then he seemed tae go sad. — Listen, Roy, I've got the virus. I tested positive. I'm HIV.

I felt as if the life had been crushed out of my frame. — Bernard . . . naw . . . fuck . . . how . . .

— A couple ay months ago. It's cool, though . . . ah mean it's no cool, but that's the wey it goes eh, he shrugged, then looked at me intensely. — But it's the quality thing in life, Roy. Life's good. Hang onto life. Hang onto it, Roy, he smiled as I started to sob. — C'mon Roy, stoap acting like a big poof! he laughed, comforting me, — it's awright man, it's okay . . .

But it wisnae okay.

But me and Bernard, well, we were okay.

The following Friday I arranged to go to the big Rezurrection gig at Ingliston with him and his posse. It was weird, Bernard and I becoming mates. His poetry was still shite, well, that's maybe no fair, but it was certainly patchy. At least he had grown out of inflicting it on people. I actually volunteered to read them. Some of it was to do with ecky and shagging; those were the best ones. The shagging poems would have disgusted me before; the idea of men doing that with each other, men shagging. Now though, it just seemed like two people in love, like me and Dorie. The queenish rants were still a bit hard to take.

Bernard's posse were an okay crowd; mixed gays and straights with a few fag-hags thrown in. The fag-hags were quite pathetic figures. There was something incomplete about them. I spotted it straight away, it was an obscure quality, but I saw it in myself. We had some problems getting sorted with eckies, and Bernard and his posse were just into doing some speed and acid – Supermario's.

I wasn't up for the acid, — No way, man, I said to Bernard. I was remembering my bad trip.

I was remembering someone else's bad trip.

He gave me an as-you-like shrug.

— It's no that, Bernard, it's just that there's too much shite floatin aroond in ma heid tae dae acid the now, ken?

— Fair enough, he said. — I think you're being wise.

But I wisnae wise. I was talking to a guy in the posse called Art, a big fuckin pill-box this cunt, and I got carried away as he talked of his drug experiences. I fired down a Supermario.

At first it was great; the lights, the sounds. We headed for the heart of the bass and I was happily tripping oot ay ma box. Bernard looked fuckin amazing; I tried not to think of him having that fuckin virus in him, he just looked so good. Party chicks checked him out, well fucked off that he was gay. This shag in the posse called Laura shouted in my ear: — I'm madly in love with your brother. It's a shame he's gay. I still want to have his baby. I just smiled. I was enjoying her patter, even hoping that I might be a proxy fuck for Bernard.

Then I looked at the big sign above the stage:

REZURRECTION

The Z luminated and the slogans came rushing into my head:

NO MAN HAS THE RIGHT

WHEN SHE SAYS NO SHE MEANS NO

THERE IS NO EXCUSE

THERE IS NEVER AN EXCUSE

I felt terrible all of a sudden; just all hot, breathless and shaky. I tried to compose myself, moving through the crowd towards the exit and the chill-out zone. I needed to think. I needed to

A girl smiled at me, and it looked like

It was her

They all looked like her

Then there was a guy. A steward. It was Uncle Gordon. — Ah'm no fucking gaun wi you again, right! Ah'm no gaunny fuckin dae that again! I shouted at him.

— Calm doon mate, eh, a raver shouted at me as the security guy stood bemused.

I ran to the toilets and sat in a trap crying and talking to myself. Some guys came in and talked me down. They found Bernard. I heard somebody mutter, — Cunt cannae handle his drugs.

Hospital Bed LYING IN YOUR HOSPITAL BED IN A COMA STUPID RELATIVES NIPPING YOUR HEAD CAN THEY UNDERSTAND WHERE YOU HIDE AND WHAT YOUR LIFE AMOUNTS TO

Their Africa YOU ARE A DYING MAN AND YOU ASK

The Well FOR NO PITY ONLY UNDER-STANDING **Capital City Service** WHICH WILL NOT HELP YOU OR HER OR **Marabou Storks** SANDY OR BERNARD BUT IT IS STILL AN URGE YOU HAVE, A FUTILE URGE TO MAKE SENSE OF THIS FUCKING CRAZY SHITE YOU'RE INVOLVED IN THIS TROPICAL LAND THIS COLONISED NATION OF YOUR DISEASED MIND

Africa, my Africa . . .

Why no death
why only incompetence
why when you purchase the manual
is it that you still can't do it right
in our flat Dorie, mind the time I fucked up
putting up the shelves
I had the manual and all the right tools then

IT WON'T HURT ROY, YOUR UNCLE
GORDON WOULD NEVER HURT YOU
JUST LIE STILL PERFECTLY STILL NOW
ROY, OR THERE WILL BE BIG TROUBLE
WHEN YOUR DAD HEARS ABOUT THIS
SHUT UP YOU LITTLE BASTARD I'M
WARNING YOU SHUT THE FUCK UP
THAT'S BETTER THAT'S BETTER
THERE THERE THERE

I wanted to die. I thought I would die. It felt like the time. It had felt like the time for a while.

Bernard took me home and I spent a couple of days in bed. Kim indulged me a bit; I told them I had flu. Kim was kind, that was what she was. She was nice Kim, and good and kind. That was Kim; people took advantage, but her and Kevin seemed to love each other, they were obviously happy.

I was upstairs in my old bedroom watching a video of the other semi-final. Dad and Tony had kept on at me to take a look at it. They said there was an astonishing refereeing decision in it. Everyone had been talking about it. I decided to watch it. Dunfermline and Airdrie were competing for the right to get fucked in the final by Hibs. The Pars versus the Diamonds. Airdrie were in easy street, but they didn't win. I didn't wait for it to finish, didn't stop to see the penalty shoot out.

I decided it was time to go.

I had a look at my book again, the one I'd picked up in a radical bookshop in Manchester. It was apparently banned in this country. It was called: *Final Exit: The Practicalities Of Self-Deliverance and Assisted Suicide For The Dying*, by Derek Humphry, published by the Hemlock Society. Their motto was:

GOOD LIFE, GOOD DEATH.

With any luck, I'd achieve half of this. I was dying. I knew it, I felt it. It was beyond transitory depression. I wasn't a psychopath; I was just a fool and a coward. I had opened up my emotions and I couldn't go back into self-denial, into that lower form of existence, but I couldn't go forward until I'd settled my debt. For me it wasn't running away. That was what I'd been doing all my fuckin life, running away from sensitivity, from feelings, from love. Running away because a fuckin schemie, a nobody, shouldnae have these feelings because there's fuckin naewhair for them tae go, naewhair for them tae be expressed and if you open up every cunt will tear you apart. So you shut them out; you build a shell, you hide, or you lash out at them and hurt them. You do this because you think if you're hurting them you can't be hurt. But it's bullshit, because you just hurt even mair until you learn to become an animal and if you can't fuckin well learn that properly you run. Sometimes you can't run though, you can't sidestep and you can't duck and weave, because sometimes it just all travels along with you, inside your fuckin skull. This wasn't about opting out. This was about the only resolution that made sense. Death was the way forward.

I looked up the chapter on 'Self-Deliverance With A Plastic Bag', a chapter I'd referred to many times. As it recommended, I took the paracetamol and applied the plastic bag, pulling it over my head and taping it round my neck.

The bag was clear but it all got foggy.

I was drifting . . .

That was when I saw Jimmy Sandison, the *real* Jimmy Sandison, not Sandy Jamieson . . . who was Sandy Jamieson?

The bag was clear . . .

The bag was clear and I continued watching the telly through it as I drifted into unconsciousness. I could see Jimmy Sandison. Jimmy Sandison, the fitba player. The expression on his face as he gesticulated to the referee made me almost want to tear the bag off. I wanted to help him, I wanted to help all the people who'd ever suffered injustices, even though it was just a fuckin recorded tape of a fitba match I was watching. I'd never seen a man so shocked and outraged at what he felt was a miscarriage of sporting justice.

Never a man.

I once saw a woman who was worse, much worse; I saw her face in court . . . then I saw

DAD PUNCHING ME MA SCREAMING AT ME KIM'S GREETING FACE MY FISTS SPLITTING BERNARD'S MOOTH A MAN TWITCHING ON THE GROUND GORDON WITHDRAWING HIS BLOOD-STAINED COCK FROM A FRIGHTENED YOUNG BOY BENT OVER A WORKBENCH THAT BOY LOOKING AT HIS DISCARDED BLUE SHORTS AN EXPLOSION A HELICOPTER A KNIFE AT A LASSIE'S THROAT A

SCARRED FACE BURSTING OPEN A KNIFE AT A LASSIE'S THROAT THEN

NOTHING

Just a blissful void.

After a long blackout, I woke up lying in a tropical grassland, with Jamieson mopping my sweating brow. We've been companions ever since, sharing an interest in wildlife, particularly ornithology, and a concern for social justice and the environment.

Sandy the Diamond.

Diamonds are forever.

21 Facing
The Stork

Sandy Jamieson and I sat enjoying our picnic. Sandy stroked at the mane of a nosy lion who had ambled over to us. I fed the beast some chicken then rubbed its stomach as it rolled over on its back in appreciation. I remembered the Silver Surfer, walking amongst the animals, saying that they were the gentle ones, it was man who was evil and warlike. The Surfer spoke a lot of sense. I like cats; even big ones. I wish we had had a cat instead of a . . .

— Cats are ruthless creatures, and I've had to hunt a few of them down in my time, once they've turned maneater, Sandy smiled. — What I like about them, though, is that they are almost totally devoid of servility.

— I think it's a good quality, I agreed. I looked at the brilliant sun rising up over the distant mountain peak, felt its luxuriating warmth on my bare face, arms and legs.

We sat for a while before Sandy awkwardly cleared his throat. — Hummph. It seems a pity to ruin the picnic, Roy, but the lodge is only a few hundred yards up the road. I think we should go and find a certain predator-scavenger better known in these parts as the Marabou Stork.

— Yes Sandy, as much as we loathe and detest the evil capitalist Dawson, we did enter into a gentleman's agreement with him; the most binding of agreements between gentlemen; namely to rid the Emerald Forest Park of Marabous.

Sandy smiled quizzically. — Whatever happened to the element of personal crusade that seemed to fuel this pursuit?

I shrugged, — I don't really know, Sandy. It's just that when I woke up this morning, it no longer seemed to be so . . . pressing.

We headed up to the lodge, Sandy keeping his gun pointed. We entered stealthily by the conservatory, into the main library. The large Stork was there. But something was far from right.

— — — —I'm here for you now Roy. I'm here to take you away . . .

Meeting you
With a view to a kill
Face to face in a secret place
Feel the chill . . .

Go away . . . I've got to face up to the Stork . . . please Kirsty. Go away.

Nightfall covers me
But you know the plans I'm making . . .

I sang this once at a perty. New Year. I liked Duran Duran when I was a wee laddie. Hungry Like The Wolf was their best yin but, eh.

I'm falling, I feel myself falling — — — Lexo's in here. He's got in. I'm looking at him. He's with Dawson and Jamieson. Lexo is the Stork. But the Stork still stands facing us. Lexo isnae the Stork . . .

Lexo isnae . . .

Jamieson is pointing the shotgun at me.

Until we dance into the fire
A little kiss is all we need . . .

I feel as if I can't breathe. —
— — — — — — — — — — — — — — I'm pulling this little tube out of your useless cock, Roy. Can you feel it?

Dance into the fire
The fatal sounds of broken dreams . . .

Can ah fuckin feel it?

I'm almost awake. I seem to see everything. It's like my eyelids are now just translucent membrane. I could open my eyes.

I could open my eyes.

I feel a sharp pain in my penis. She has it in her hand. She's squeezing it . . . like Dorie . . . like Patricia . . . but not so gentle . . .

—————— I'm going to cut this off and I'm going to stuff it down your throat and watch you choke to death.

It was LEXO, no me, LEXO

> There's crystal tears
> Full of snowflakes on your body
> First time in years
> To change your skin
> From lover's rosy stain
> A chance to find a phoenix in the flame
> A chance to die
> And then we dance into the fire . . .

— Remember when you put this useless shrivelled thing into my arse, Roy? I can't believe how this thing hurt me so much. Well, not as much as it's going to hurt you . . . remember when you put the mirror at the foot of that mattress to see my face as you forced yourself into my arse . . . remember what you said? Do you? You said you wanted me to look at you, and you wanted to see my face. You wanted me to see Roy Strang. You wanted me to feel what happens to any cunt who fucks about with Roy Strang. Now I want to see you, Roy. I want you to see what you've made me, because you've made me just like you. I hid like a sick, twisted vegetable for days, hid inside my flat, frightened of my own shadow. Sleep was an impossibility without the pills. You raped me once, and with the help of the judge and the courts you raped me again. Then I saw those posters, those Zero Tolerance campaign posters. NO MAN HAS THE RIGHT they said, but they were wrong, Roy.

Naw, they were right, I saw them, they hurt me, but they were right . . .

— They were wrong because you *did* have the right. You all wanted to teach me Roy, to teach me a lesson, that was what you said. You did teach me . . .

Naw.

— You taught me that you had the right by simply taking it. The posters were prescriptive, they were talking about a world as it should be rather than as it is . . .

But there's another world Kirsty, it disnae huv tae be this wey . . . we can change it aw, make it different . . .

— I don't know who fucked you up, what happened to make you the sad, wretched excuse for a human being you are and I don't care. It's not my problem. You're my problem, or rather were. Now I'm your problem. Might is right. You *take* the right. I'm taking the right Roy, taking the right to fuck you off, son.

I can feel the cold steel on my cock . . .

— That silly little tube up your cock Roy, taking all the piss out of you. What was it you said: Nae cunt takes the piss out ay me? The nurses do it every day, Roy. They just drain it from you. It would probably be nicer to just leave you, to let you rot away like you've been doing for the last couple of years, but they tell me you might wake up. We're playing Doctors and Nurses now Roy, so let's get rid of this silly fucking tube . . . which one, Doctor? . . . why both of them, Nurse . . .

I feel the catheter tube pulling sharply out of me. It was fuckin Lexo . . . how is it that ah . . .

DEEPER

DEEPER

DEEPER

My throat is burning on this tube . . . it's the tube in my throat . . . take it oot soas ah kin speak . . .

DEEPER

DEEPER – – –
– Sandy still has
the gun pointed at me. But I hear other voices shouting. Their faces
are just at the periphery of my vision but I know who it is, it's Ozzy
and Dempsey and Lexo and they're shouting that she's had enough.

The slag asked for it . . .

What the fuck is this? Sandy! Dinnae fuckin point that at me!
   Shoot Lexo
   He's the cunt that

DUMBO

DUMBO STRANG

                              The slag asked for it
Her face, like Caroline Carson's
                              she was just a young
                              lassie
cruel slags all the same
                              the slag asked for it
mocking the afflicted
                              just a young lassie but
they fight back
                              The slag asked for it
the dog
            cannae go aroond hating fifty per cent
            ay the population
Gordon
            ah didnae want it, ah didnae want that

who do you fuckin hate Roy Strang you hate schemies Kaffirs poofs

Weedgies Japs snobby cunts jambos scarfers English cunts women
only you don't do you Roy Strang the only cunt you really hate is

Roy Strang.

> cannae go aroond hatin fifty per cent ay
> the population just because some dirty
> auld cunt fucked ye up the erse as a
> bairn, nae use that, eh.

— AH'M RUNNIN THIS FUCKIN GIG! AH SAY WHIN
THE SLAG'S HUD ENOUGH! I'm shouting . . . why am I
getting into this . . . it's fuck all to do with anything . . . — Sandy
. . . shoot Lexo . . . he's the fuckin rapist. He's a fuckin nutter . . .

I see an image in the mirror, the image of the Marabou Stork. It's on
the flamingo . . . tearing into it, ripping it to shreds, but the
flamingo's still alive, I see its dulled eyes . . .

THERE IS NEVER AN EXCUSE.

Her fingers are holding my eyes open and I can see her, she's holding
open one eyelid at a time and her surgical scissors are snipping my
eyelids neatly off, I can feel the cold steel and hear the sharp tearing
sound . . .
   . . . I can feel her knife hacking into my genitals, thrashing into
my chest, digging, trying to find me, but she'll never find me in here
. . . and now I'm soaring upwards trying to get out, to fly across the
fields of Africa, but I'm stuck on the hospital ceiling looking down at
Roy Strang being hacked to pieces by Kirsty . . . hacked by a
serrated knife . . . did you get it at Boston's Kirsty . . . --------
— I'm going to let you feel this, Roy! They say a man can hardly feel
it, hardly feel the removal of his prick . . .
   NO
   NO

I'm suddenly back down in here and I feel the pain and I can't move because of her

— Let you taste it, like I had to . . .

NO

It's my prick . . . the dirty fuckin sow's cut oaf ma cock and she's . . . aw what the fuck, the Silver Surfer never had a cock and the cunt seemed to get by as he soared on his board . . . that's all I ask . . .

— This is going in your mouth, Roy, open wide, come on now . . .

NO

NO

NO

— Do I hear sounds there, Roy . . . I can't hear you . . . what is it you're saying to me, Roy, what are you trying to tell me . . . I know you want this, I know you're asking for it . . . you shouldn't speak with your mouth full . . . you have to learn Roy, you have to be taught . . .

NO

PLEASE

NO

> WHEN SHE SAYS NO SHE MEANS NO.
>
> # Z.
>
> ZERO TOLERANCE

She's looking into my eyes, my lidless eyes and we see each other now. She's beautiful. Thank God. Thank God she's got it back.

What we took. I'm trying to smile. I've got this severed cock in my mouth and I'm trying to smile. I can't breathe and she's showing no mercy.

I understand her.

I understand her hurt, her pain, how it all just has to come out. It just goes round and round, the hurt. It takes an exceptionally strong person to just say: no more. It takes a weak one to just keep it all to themselves, let it tear them apart without hurting anyone else.

I'm not an exceptionally strong person.

Nor is Kirsty.

We're just ordinary and this is shite.

We both understand everything.

The sun is rising behind me and my shadow spills out away from it, out in front of me. My spindly legs, my large overcoat, my massive beak . . . I have no visible ears, I never really had much in the way of ears, it was always my nose, Captain Beaky, they used to call me at the school . . . it wasn't the ears, my memory hasn't been so good, nor has my hearing but I can think more clearly now . . . I have the gait of a comical scarecrow, I shuffle like an old man who has shat his pants. I'm so tired . . . I spread my large, black wings . . .

She's going . . . don't go Kirsty, stay with me for a bit, see this through . . . but no no no I hear her hastily depart. Then I hear another voice, the hysterical screaming of Nurse Patricia Devine. She's watching me smoking my own penis like a limp, wet cigar, staring with horror into my eyes that cannot shut. I'm getting weaker, but I'm here now. I can move my lidless eyes, I can see my cock dangling from my mouth and I can see the scissors sticking out from my neck . . . Patricia runs to get help but she's too late because Jamieson's facing me and he's pointing the gun and I hear it going off and it's all just one big

Z.